THE VALLIAN CYCLE

The Dray Prescot Series

The Delian Cycle:
1. Transit to Scorpio
2. The Suns of Scorpio
3. Warrior of Scorpio
4. Swordships of Scorpio
5. Prince of Scorpio

The Havilfar Cycle:
6. Manhounds of Antares
7. Arena of Antares
8. Fliers of Antares
9. Bladesman of Antares
10. Avenger of Antares
11. Armada of Antares

The Krozair Cycle:
12. The Tides of Kregen
13. Renegade of Kregen
14. Krozair of Kregen

The Vallian cycle:
15. Secret Scorpio
16. Savage Scorpio
17. Captive Scorpio
18. Golden Scorpio

The Jikaida cycle:
19. A Life for Kregen
20. A Sword for Kregen
21. A Fortune for Kregen
22. A Victory for Kregen

The Spikatur cycle:
23. Beasts of Antares
24. Rebel of Antares
25. Legions of Antares
26. Allies of Antares

The Pandahem cycle:
27. Mazes of Scorpio
28. Delia of Vallia
29. Fires of Scorpio
30. Talons of Scorpio
31. Masks of Scorpio
32. Seg the Bowman

The Witch War cycle:
33. Werewolves of Kregen
34. Witches of Kregen
35. Storm over Vallia
36. Omens of Kregen
37. Warlord of Antares

The Lohvian cycle:
38. Scorpio Reborn
39. Scorpio Assassin
40. Scorpio Invasion
41. Scorpio Ablaze
42. Scorpio Drums
43. Scorpio Triumph

The Balintol cycle:
44. Intrigue of Antares
45. Gangs of Antares
46. Demons of Antares
47. Scourge of Antares
48. Challenge of Antares
49. Wrath of Antares
50. Shadows over Kregen

The Phantom cycle:
51. Murder on Kregen
52. Turmoil on Kregen

THE VALLIAN CYCLE

Kenneth Bulmer

writing as
Alan Burt Akers

Published by
Bladud Books

Copyright © 2009, Kenneth Bulmer

Alan Burt Akers has asserted his right under the Copyright,
Designs and Patents Act, 1988, to be identified as the Author
of this work.

First published in 2009 by Bladud Books

Originally published separately by Daw Books, Inc., as:
Secret Scorpio (1977)
Savage Scorpio (1978)
Captive Scorpio (1978)
Golden Scorpio (1978)

This first omnibus edition published in 2009 by
Bladud Books, an imprint of Mushroom Publishing,
Bath, BA1 4EB, United Kingdom

www.bladudbooks.com

ISBN 978-1-84319-799-7

Contents

SECRET SCORPIO

A Note On The Vallian Cycle

Secret Scorpio is the first book of Dray Prescot's adventures in the Vallian Cycle on that marvelous and exotic world of Kregen he has made his home.

Dray Prescot himself is an enigmatic figure. Reared in the inhumanly harsh conditions of Nelson's Navy, he has been transported to Kregen many times through the agency of the Star Lords and of the Savanti nal Aphrasöe, those mortal but superhuman men and women of the Swinging City. There is a discernible pattern underlying all his breathtaking adventures—he is sure of that—but the pattern and its meanings remain veiled and unguessable.

His appearance as described by one who has seen him is of a man of above middle height, with brown hair and level brown eyes, with enormously broad shoulders and powerful physique. There is about him an abrasive honesty and an indomitable courage and he moves like a great hunting cat, quiet and deadly. On the savage and beautiful world of Kregen he has at various times and for various reasons risen to become a Vovedeer and Zorcander of his Clansmen of Segesthes, the Lord of Strombor, Strom of Valka, Prince Majister of Vallia, King of Djanduin and a Krozair of Zy, a plethora of titles to which he confesses with a wryness and an irony I am sure masks much deeper feelings at which we can only guess.

Now he is plunged headlong into fresh adventures beneath the hurtling moons of Kregen, in the streaming mingled lights of Antares, under the Suns of Scorpio.

Alan Burt Akers

One

Black Feathers of the Great Chyyan

A foot scraped in the shadows. Instantly we seven came to a dead halt in the blackness of the alley. Ahead the darkness lowered down as mufflingly as in the alleyway, for massy clouds covered the night sky of Kregen, concealing the glitter of the stars and the radiance of the moons.

My left hand gripped Roybin's shoulder and I could feel the fine tremble as he waited, poised like a wild leem, savage, suspicious, ready to leap out in perfect and deadly silence if that scraping foot heralded a murderous enemy.

In single file we seven stood, half-crouched, stock-still, invisible. The foot scuffed the slimy cobbles again and then the disappearing patter of feet told us that the wayfarer of the night was about his business. Seg's left hand on my shoulder pressed, but in the same instant Roybin moved ahead again. We followed, silently. Behind Seg, Turko the Shield fretted, I knew, that he did not stand at my back, a place he considered his by right. Inch, stooped to bring his great height beneath the evil-smelling brick overhang, prowled after Turko, and our rear was brought up by Young Oby, young and a boy no more, who perforce clasped Inch's belt, and by Balass the Hawk whose dark skin blended perfectly with the shadows.

In single file we stole out from the mouth of the alley, aware of the vanishment of the pressing walls and the feeling of greater space about us. The tiny square lay shrouded about us. Yes, I suppose on reflection, we were a pretty ferocious bunch. I know I would not like to stumble upon such a crew as that on a pitchy night when all manner of deviltries are afoot.

Roybin led. We were experienced enough to know when to follow a man who had knowledge of the terrain. This alley led around the back of the fish market in the town of Autonne, on the island of Veliadrin that had lately been Can-Thirda, and our objective lay across the fish-scaled cobbles of the square.

No one spoke. Here, in the pressing darkness before the first of Kregen's seven moons made an appearance, there was no need for words to know what we were about.

Soundlessly we emerged from the mouth of the alleyway, feeling that cloying pressure of pent-up air give way to the freer sense of the square, small though it might be. Water ran between the cobbles and there would be fish scales and heads and tails aplenty strewn about. A scattered rain could not decide whether to cease altogether or to drench down in the long shafting downpour of a Kregan storm.

We inched ahead and cleared a brick buttress, our right hands trailing along the crumbling mortar. A spark of light jumped into life ahead.

We froze instantly.

The light shone from a small lantern set outside an arched gateway closed by a moldering lenken door. That wooden door blended with the decay and dissolution of this tumbledown section of the fish market. In the crazily leaning brick walls stained with the patina of time, in the powdery and splintered timbering, in the gap-tiled roofs queasily lurching at incongruous angles, the archway and door betrayed nothing unusual.

Yet Roybin had certain information so we were here, prowling like wild leem, and the night ahead of us might soon explode with fury and action.

A long running roll of thunder boomed distantly away to the east in the interior of the island.

On the tail of the rumbling echoes Roybin whispered, "Lookouts."

We had expected a sentry. Peering across the darkened square into the isolated pool of radiance shed by the lantern, we made out the forms of three men. An edged weapon caught the light and glittered. They were quiet over there, probably talking desultorily together, resentful at their watch. But they would keep a lookout. All Roybin had told us convinced me that whoever these people were that we intended to spy on this night, they were ruthless and efficient.

For we knew why we were here, creeping like villains along vile, fish-stinking alleyways in Autonne, a city of the western coast of the island of Veliadrin. Veliadrin, of which I was still High Kov, that large island between Vallia and my own wonderful island of Valka, had once been called Can-Thirda. The name had been changed for certain reasons. The island had at one time, in the long ago, been a kingdom, before the Empire of Vallia had obtained the supreme power over all the islands fringing the coasts of the main island of Vallia. Veliadrin was still split into distinct regions. Over on the west coast the people were mostly fisherfolk, given to wild boasting of the old days, not overly rich or well-endowed, but sturdy and resourceful and also, as we had discovered, too prone to superstition.

Oh, yes, we knew why we were here, stalking the shadows like leems.

Rumors and suspicions, malicious gossip and ugly conjectures had at last come together to make a picture that displeased me greatly. That picture spelled evil days ahead if we did not act at once. There are many and varied religions on Kregen, and some are fine and worthy of the utmost effort in a man or woman. And some there are dark and secretive and baleful in their influence.

From the main island of Vallia a new creed was attempting to make a lodgment in Veliadrin. The west coast, a port, a poor and credulous people—the new creed found fertile ground.

Mind you, I knew who must take the full blame.

We had known for some time there were deep stirrings from Vallia, long ground swells of troubles to come, and the emperor was once more a worried man. Many forces, many ambitious men and women, many fanatics, sought to topple him. I had been told that there were far more potential insurrectionists these days than there had been when I had last spoken to the emperor in any privacy and confidence, before my absence on Earth and my adventurings in the inner sea, the Eye of the World.

Now this new creed threatened close to home.

As I had said to Seg Segutorio back in Valka before we left: "My Freedom Fighters did not clear Valka of the slavers and the aragorn and make of it an island where they might bring up their children in pride and justice and freedom, for some Opaz-forsaken devils to worm their way in and overturn all we have accomplished." And I had slammed a dagger into the sturmwood table beneath a mullioned window overlooking a stupendous view of Valkanium and the bay.

Seg Segutorio, the Kov of Falinur, a Bowman of Loh, and the truest comrade a man could hope to find in two worlds, had replied, "Valka is indeed a paradise, Dray. Falinur, well, I try, and hard it is, by the Veiled Froyvil! The people there do not forget the old times, when their kov went up against the emperor and they followed, exultant, and they cast a deal of blame on me, the new kov, for the old kov's failure."

Delia had told me some of Seg's problems with the recalcitrants in his province, and he seemed to be having a worse time of convincing them that he was their new leader than was Inch in his Black Mountains, a province which had also been involved in that old revolution against the emperor.

Seg had gone on, staring moodily across the sun-lit expanse of the bay: "But as Inch and I are here in Valka, we think prevention in Veliadrin may aid us in our own kovnates."

Thus spake Seg and I warmed to him.

There was no need for fulsome words between us. I understood him—and, by Vox, he understood some of me—for, because he was Seg Segutorio, a black-haired, blue-eyed fey maniac from the wild hills of Erthyrdrin, he had added: "Mind you, my old dom, I can tell you a kovnate goes to rack and ruin if you aren't there to keep an eye on things."

He was right.

At least, he was right if an absentee noble could not find a loyal and trustworthy person to run an estate in the absence of the owner. I, to my shame, own I am probably the greatest absentee landlord of two worlds.

But then blame the Star Lords, blame the Savanti—blame also, if you will, my own accursed facility in picking up titles and the possessions that go with them on Kregen. I already had a plan to deal with these problems, plans you shall hear of in due course, and already I had consciously begun the hazy opening moves to unite all of Paz.

"Veliadrin is not Valka," I had said. "Here in Valka, Tharu and Tom and the Elders run things, with Drak. In my kingdom of Djanduin, Kytun and Ortyg handle affairs perfectly. In Strombor Gloag rules the roost. And as for my clansmen, well, Hap has them so well organized we took over another clan without bloodshed, all through obi."

In his dry way, Seg had said, "You're really a Vovedeer as well as a Zorcander, now."

"Aye." He knows when and how to puncture complacency, does Seg Segutorio. "I've been more than lucky in having found good friends to run affairs whilst I'm away. But Veliadrin is split up, occupied by diffs and apims who don't really get on, for the damned Qua'voils still resent their defeat."

"But the Pachaks you have settled in Veliadrin."

"Ah!" I had said, feeling pleased. "I have great hopes for my Pachaks of Veliadrin." This was true. "And the Pachaks of Zamra have finally freed all the slaves. That is progress."

"But this damned new creed." Seg had run his eye along the true shaft of an arrow, brushed his fingertips lightly over the brilliant blue fletchings. "Chyyanists, is it?"

"Aye. Roybin is a first-class spy and he has received a certain report. A preacher or a priest or some devil of that kind is loose in Autonne. He holds meetings. I think a little firsthand information will prove of value."

"There's nothing like seeing for yourself," said Seg.

So that was why we were here, creeping like a gang of piratical cutthroats through the rain-swept darkness, toward the speck of light over the gateway leading on to what unknown horrors we could only conjecture.

Inch had refused to stay behind, swinging his enormous two-handed ax absently as he told me that if Seg and I were going off for some fun he wasn't going to be left out. Turko the Shield considered the matter closed. Oby was raging for adventure and Balass the Hawk deserved some fun. So they all came.

"As to fun," I had said just before we ventured out into the rain from our secluded inn, a place where the attention we attracted had been mitigated by pretenses and stratagems, "this Chyyanist nonsense is likely to lead to a few smashed skulls. At least, that is what I feel in my bones."

"All reports speak of the creed as evil," said Roybin sagely, nodding his head. "But they are all outside observations. No one really knows."

As I padded forward through a few opening flurries of rain toward the gateway and the moldering lenken door, I wondered just how much we could hope to discover in there. The center of the new religion lay in Valia, or so we believed. It had been brought here by a priest or preacher who sought to rouse the simple fisherfolk hereabouts. As an absentee landlord I had no right to criticize my tenants if they rose up against me in a just cause.

However intolerant and objectionable I may be, I do not think I had given any cause to these people to rise up in justice. Maybe that is just another facet of my supposed megalomania. But the fisherfolk of Autonne made a living and did not starve and were housed. I had ordered the freeing of their slaves. This Opaz-forsaken priest of Chyyan sought to stir up trouble out of willful spite, a sullen resentment, a sense of ill-treatment, and if I could not understand and sympathize with feelings like these then no one else in two worlds could do so. And, too, there were far weightier reasons for Chyyanism, as you shall hear...

Not one of my six comrades appeared to think it strange that Roybin no longer led on, that I had pushed on in the front to take the three guards. I mention this to indicate that my thoughts had allowed me to act without thinking about the action I was taking. A bad habit. A nasty habit. A habit that had brought me into dire trouble in the past and was to pitch me headlong into further horrors, a habit that was just one against which I continually strove.

My guard went to leaning sleep with a tap of a dagger-hilt along his skull.

Turko's lolled unconscious from cunning finger pressures.

Roybin's collapsed with a dagger through his throat.

I looked at my spy. Well, Roybin had dealt with these people before, so he should most likely know. The guards were cloaked heavily, but they wore armor and carried weapons and were not of Autonne. I put my mouth to Roybin's ear.

"The roof?"

He nodded.

That cleared up the protocol over the local man leading.

Roybin, who was called Roybin Ararsnet ti Autonne, had served me before, in various dubious capacities. I do not mince matters where brave men are concerned. Roybin was a spy. I gave him credit for that, for credit was due.

Around the side of the building the rain spattered more strongly against the corroded brick, lashed on by a rising wind. The darkness was not as absolute now, for the clouds were piling away invisibly above and every now and again a sliver of the Maiden with the Many Smiles, who shines forth most bravely in the night sky of Kregen, glimmered through the rack. Inch wore a tightly fitting leather helmet and not a scrap of his yellow hair was visible.

I looked back at him as I set my hands to the climb. In the fragmentary light his incredibly tall frame looked angular and sinister with the immense long-handled Saxon ax swinging handily from his wrist-thong. Yes, it was a great comfort to have Inch of Ng'groga at my side.

Seg's Lohvian longbow was unstrung and the string safely in the dry of his belt pouch along with the spares. We all wore decent Vallian buff tunics and breeches, with rapiers and daggers strapped about us and, therefore, looked like perfectly ordinary Vallian koters, although, of necessity, being marked as apim, for we were all *Homo sapiens*.

The crumbling brickwork afforded good handholds and in no time we were all on the roof. I had no intention of leaving any one of these bonny fighters alone, below, as a lookout.

It behooved others to look out when we wandered along.

Megalomania, maniacal, vicious, I know, I know. But I harbored frightful suspicions concerning this new creed of Chyyan. Nothing must hinder us tonight.

Over the roof where the rain blustered and then fell away, only to return with just that little extra edge in its sting, we crept cautiously. Roybin led us to the skylight. The iron was new, replacing worn-down bronze.

Young Oby pushed forward, taking a slender tool from his pocket. Opaz knew what deviltry he had been practicing in my absences, but the lock snicked open and with a single heave Turko hauled the iron bars up and out. He placed their weight down as though replacing one of Delia's priceless cups of Linkiang porcelain on its saucer.

I looked down. Only darkness, until my eyes picked up a faint glimmer, the merest wraith of an orange glow, and I made out three-quarters of the outline of a door. A well-made and tight fitting door sealing off the lower portions.

One after the other we dropped down onto a loft floor where stinking fishnets tangled beneath our feet, and where no doubt the scales clumsily brushed into the corners might once have graced a coelacanth. The door yielded to the forensic ministrations of Oby. I did not shove it open, as a soldier might, the sword mighty in his fist.

Gently, I eased the door inward. The orange glow brightened. I put an eye to the crack. For a moment the world consisted of orange whorls of fire, and then I saw that the door opened onto a narrow gallery surrounding the central area. Here was where the fishermen hung their nets. A low drone of voices lifted. Lights threw orange reflections upon the far wall and struck in slivers of radiance up through the warped planks of the gallery.

Chances were that we could open the door and sneak out onto the gallery before the people gathered on the floor below might look up and see us. It was the kind of chance that always attracts.

I might have listened to Roybin when he made his first report and

simply ordered out a detachment of guards. We would have surrounded
this odiferous place and swept up all who worshiped here. But then we
would catch men and women who had come here out of mere curiosity.
We would have taken the priest of Chyyan. But it was my guess that he
would say nothing.

So we went about our work nefariously, like criminals.

Like wraiths we seven slid out onto the gallery. Not a board creaked,
not a single item of harness chingled. We were old hands, feral as leems,
deadly as Manhounds.

We each found a crack in the planking and set an eye to observe what
went on below.

My first fears vanished the instant I clapped eye on that scene. Gathered
in a mass at the end of the room a crowd of people were in the act of rising
from a deep genuflection—we had chosen our time well, the chance swiftly
and surely taken—and the priest himself, clad all in black vestments, lifted
his arms high, leading the congregation in the opening bars of a chant. The
chant proved to be a moaning, miserable, oafish thing, and most of the
people did not know it. But the priest raised his voice to lead them. At all
this I glanced with the swift calculating eye of the fighting man, seeking
to weigh possible odds. The words of the chant came so garbled they were
practically impossible to make out. Over it all I glanced up and to the wall
behind the priest. And I let out a soundless puff, and felt vastly relieved.

For, set against that back wall draped in its rich cloths and golden tassels, there stood no pagan silver idol of a leem.

A calmness came over me. Whatever vileness this new creed of Chyyan
might bring, I did not think it could be as vile as that of the cult of Lem
the Silver Leem.

Against the rich cloths of the back alcove lifted a bold image of a
heavy-winged bird, an image as tall as a man, with feathered wings spread to
encompass a full twenty feet. All a rusty black, this bird, save for its scarlet eyes
and scarlet claws and scarlet beak. Four wings the chyyan possesses, like its
distant cousin, the zhyan. The four wings were undersize in this image for the
body size, but the whole effect was at once impressive and ominous.

At once surmises sprang into my brain. Native saddle-birds were
unknown in Vallia and Loh, being, at the time, generally confined to the
hostile territories of Turismond and to Havilfar and islands thereabouts.
The mighty continent of Havilfar, south of the equator, was the home of
zhyan and chyyan. I frowned. This bore a little more investigation. Havilfar boasted as its most powerful nation the Empire of Hamal, and the mad
Empress Thyllis was sworn to destroy the Empire of Vallia. Was this creed
of Chyyan a gambit in that game?

Incense rose, stinking and abominable. The chant ceased. The crowd
stood to listen as the priest spoke. As I listened I watched their faces as

well as I could, and some lapped up the ranting words, but others were more critical. A couple of trident-men near the door came as close as may be to openly jeering. I marked them.

This priest had journeyed to Veliadrin from Vallia, and no doubt Autonne was his marked target town. I tried to size him up, wondering from which city, country or continent, even, he hailed. A full-fleshed man, with the bright staring eyes of the fanatic—or the diseased—he presented an imposing figure. His robes were all of black, relieved by embroidered motifs in golden thread and imitation jewels, motifs mainly of chyyans doing unmentionable things to their victims.

Chyyans have not yet been generally tamed to the saddle. They remain unbroken, wild, flying freely over the wide spaces of Havilfar, a dread and a terror to lesser animals and to man. The white-plumaged zhyan is notorious for the uncertainty of its temper, for all that the bird is valued above ten fluttrells, and yet the zhyan in its power and mastery has been curbed to the rein and the bit and the flying harness.

Not so the chyyan. Its rusty black plumage shares none of the brilliant sheening highlights of the impiter of the hostile territories of Turismond. The chyyan is a bird to steer well clear of when you ride the level wastes of the air, astride a saddle-bird, or piloting a small model voller.

So this priest, who may have come from Hamal to wreak the Empress Thyllis's vengeance upon Vallia, lifted up his voice and harangued the simple fisherfolk of Autonne, which is a town under my care.

"It is not for the distant future when you are dead and gone to the Ice Floes of Sicce! No, my children, I tell you in the sacred name of the Great Chyyan, upon whose black breast is taken every arrow that seeks your heart, I tell you that the Great Chyyan brings hope and comfort, delight and joy, prosperity and wealth to you in this life. Do not wait until you are dead to enjoy yourselves! Listen to my words, for they are words from our leader, he who has been chosen in the divine twinning by the Great Chyyan to lead us into the new darkness of the Black Feathers, in which is there light beyond our meager understanding."

At this guffaws broke from the two trident-men. Not for them the finicky parsing of metaphysics. They heard words that appeared to contradict, and they brayed their derision.

"By the silver flukes of Shalash the Shining!" bellowed one, clapping a bronzed hand onto his thigh. "Your riddles make no sense to a coy, Himet the Mak!"

"Hush!" and "Quiet, impious onker!" broke from those standing near the two trident-men, who I guessed were brothers.

The priest, this Himet the Mak, lifted a hand. I saw his black robes stretch over the hilt of a sword belted to his waist.

"The blasphemers speak their own destruction! The word of the leader

twinned with the Great Chyyan is to be obeyed. The leader is the spirit
of the One made Two, spirit and flesh, spirit made manifest to men. Our
leader and the Great Chyyan are in duo, twins, radiant with the Black
Feathers, leading us to light. And the word of our leader tells us we must
wait for a sign. He will come among us. He will tell us when to lift the
banners of the Black Feathers. Then, my children, then all that you do not
have will be yours. When Makfaril our leader gives the divine word you
will gain all, not when you are dead and rotting in the ground, but here
and now, in this life, soon!"

People were dancing up and down and the two trident-men had fallen
silent. It was mumbo jumbo, but the promise, the passion, the pride of
purpose, these drove home keenly into everyone present.

"Listen to me, my children, to Himet the Mak, who comes to tell you of
the Great Chyyan and of our leader, Makfaril. You must do all the things
necessary and pray for guidance, that in the Black Day you will be spared
and live to enjoy the fruits of luxury handed to us by him of the four wings,
Chyyan of the Black Feathers. In that glorious day will you find resurrection in the here and now. All will be yours. Only believe! Believe and pray
to our leader that he may intercede for you with his divine twin, in spirit
and in flesh, pray for your salvation in the day from the Great Chyyan."

One or two shrill yells broke from the embryonic congregation. Again
and again the priest harped on the desirability of achieving one's heart's
desires in the here and now. He gave only a sketchy metaphysical plan for
life after death, for salvation, for the delights of paradise, of being reborn
higher in the circle of vaol-paol, or for the joys of Valhalla; he hammered
home his message that the Great Chyyan and Makfaril the leader sought
to reward their devotees *now.*

When he reverted to supernatural arguments they were all cant phrases,
rolling rodomontade mixed with elements culled from many minor creeds
of Kregen. I have made a little study of the beliefs of Kregen—vastly
edifying!—and could recognize this curious mixture as an artificial con-
struct, alien, almost thrown together. The priest had skill. I wondered who
had trained him.

And yet, despite his skill, despite the lure of grabbing it all now, the two
trident-men grew restive, so that Himet the Mak was forced to take notice
of them.

From the resplendent cloths draped over the alcove at the back of the
statue of the rusty black chyyan stepped forth armed men. They appeared,
suddenly, between the tall drapes. I eyed them.

First I looked at their faces and the way they stood and held themselves,
next at their weapons and then at their uniforms.

They were all apims, like me, and their faces were all of that low-browed,
brutal cast that does not in any way invariably mean brutality in the

possessor. I rather fancied these men would be hard and merciless and take more than a trifle of joy in sinking their weapons into the guts of any who opposed them. They stood alertly, poised, and I knew that at a signal from Himet they would kill and go on killing until he called a halt.

Their weapons remained scabbarded. They wore rapiers and daggers, but as I looked at the way they were belted up I frowned. It seemed to me the thraxters and the parrying-sticks belted to their waists were their prime weapons.

Their uniforms were black, beneath boiled leather armor, well oiled, and they wore profuse ornamentations of black feathers. Their iron helmets carried tufts of rusty black feathers from chyyans. All in all, they looked a formidable bunch. I judged them to be masichieri mercenaries who had never aspired to the quality of paktuns—for paktuns are in general finicky about questions of honor—and who combined a little thievery and assassination and slaving into their mercenary way of life as the opportunity offered, without reaching the power of the aragorn. There were twenty of them, led by a hikdar.

My instinctive reaction was that I wished I had taken up my Krozair longsword when we'd first ventured on this escapade.

The two trident-men eyed the guards uneasily, and their taunts fell away. They were tough and wiry, but they carried only their fishing tridents and degutting knives in their belts. They wore old buff breeches with frayed and unlaced ends, singlets of a coarse weave, and they were barefoot.

Balass the Hawk at his crack in the boards began to stir himself around, reaching for his sword. I turned my head toward him and he stilled. Of us all, perhaps, Balass was less accustomed to stealth in his fighting, being a hyr-kaidur and master of the ritual combats of the arena.

Silently Oby drew his vicious knife. Seg had already strung his bow, all done simply and silently and with enormous professional skill. Inch's ax glittered in a shaft of the orange light. If there were to be handstrokes, we were ready.

Turko, who could rip a fully armed man to pieces with his bare hands, had grumbled and cursed when I'd told him to leave the great shield. Now Turko the Shield flexed his muscles. Oh, yes, if it came to a fight those twenty hard men down there would be in for a surprise.

But I wanted no fighting.

I wanted to observe, to fathom out just what lay behind this new and evil creed of Chyyanism, and then to withdraw and debate, calmly, what best to do.

With a tiny gesture of my left hand I indicated to Roybin that he should retire, and we would follow, one by one.

No one questioned my right to leave last.

Himet the Mak was shouting again, lifting his voice, and I detected a strained hoarseness there, very surprising to me considering the circumstances and the clear power he had been exercising over these credulous people.

"I speak to you and tell you the great words, the great words given to us from Makfaril, the leader, directly from the Great Chyyan. Yet you seek to mock me, to deny the great words. Do you not desire salvation and wealth and luxury in the here and now?"

His voice sharpened, took on an undisguised note of contempt and anger—and a tinge of fear? My comrades withdrew from the little rickety gallery, but I stayed, listening.

"You two, trident-men, brothers, you have been tainted with the falsehoods put about in the island. You know your island is called Can-thirda. Whatever it was called in the ancient days of the kingdom, ever since your island has been part of Vallia it has been called Can-thirda. Yet now you must call it Veliadrin. Why?"

A certain grumbling rumble from his listeners brought a wolfish smile to his lips.

"Aye! I well tell you why! Because the power-mad incubus, the Prince Majister of Vallia, decrees it! That is why. Some unknown master from no man knows where tells you your fate. He holds your future in his hand. Has he visited you? Have you seen him? No, and you have not seen his bitch of a wife, the Princess Majestrix, either!"

My muscles jumped. I took a breath. But I remained lying still, watching and listening. Yes! Well may you who have followed my story marvel. But I remained still and did not leap down and choke this fellow's throat a trifle to induce him to show proper respect for the most perfect woman in two worlds. And, I confess, I not only marveled at my own iron self-control, I actually relished it, as showing how I had matured and grown wise.

"Some forgotten child they had, spawned from their evil union, this Princess Velia, dead and abandoned in some foreign country debarred from honest men's knowledge. Who knows where she died? Who cares? Why should your island be called after the slut?"

My fists gripped and my muscles trembled as a leem's flanks tremble in the instant before he charges. But, despite all, I remained still.

Through the confusion roaring away in my head I understood that my own private problems, my own petty pride, must not interfere or injure the interests of my people, their lands or the intangible debt I owe all those who look to me. If this is pride, so be it; if it is duty, so be it. To me, a simple sailor and fighting man, it was and remains a mere matter of common decency.

So I battened down the hatches on my anger and made myself listen to what this fellow was saying. After all, there was more than a grain of truth in his rantings...

If, because this priest of Chyyan insulted my Delia and our dead daughter Velia, I acted as I was wont and hurled myself down to choke him a little and bash the skulls of his ugly-faced guards, then I would forfeit the advantage of listening and learning in secret. Whoever had sent him would know that much of their designs were privy no more. I must force myself to swallow all that intolerant choler which makes of me a laughing stock, a fighting man and, sometimes, makes me do the right thing.

"Look around you in your island of Can-thirda! Where are the slaves that once did your bidding, that worked for you and made the days light? Gone, all gone. And why? Because your new High Kov, this high and mighty Prince Majister of Vallia, this Strom of Valka, this Kov of Zamra, decrees that you honest working people shall no longer run slaves. Is this fair? Is this justice? Why should a man do his own hard labor, why should a woman slave in the kitchen when she might buy and thrash a slave to do the work for her? Tell me, brethren in the Great Chyyan, if this is a sample of the usage to which this so-puissant Dray Prescot puts you, then will you lie down beneath it? Will you give the tyrant the full incline? Will you be slave?"

They yelled it back at him.

"No!" And, "No! We will not bow down to Dray Prescot!"

I fumed up there on the gallery. I didn't want the famblys to bow to me. I'd already cut out all this fawning and inclining nonsense in Valka. But, equally, I did not want them buying and selling and flogging slaves either. This is the old conundrum, with an answer, and I brushed it aside as I peered through the crack between the sagging boards.

The mood of the embryo congregation had turned ugly. They were sucked in. They saw a hope before them that not only might they return to the slave-holding of the past but might aspire to a seizure of the goodness of life, now.

Useless for me to condemn them. Had I spent more time in Can-thirda, had I even consulted some of the people about the change of name, had these folk seen me more clearly, instead of hearing about their High Kov only by hearsay, then, perhaps, I might have prevented all this, have nipped in the bud the horrors to come. For I knew well and made no mistake that far more lay behind this artificial religion of Chyyan than ever Himet the Mak would tell these poor famblys.

"If he were here now! If this infamous Dray Prescot, Prince Majister of Vallia, were standing before you, what would you do?"

The answering yells bounced in ugly echoes in that tall net-room below the gallery.

"Chop the cramph!" "Cut the rast down!" "Feather the tape!" And, "Make him slave and run him for the good of us all!"

Things had gone to rack and ruin indeed, in Veliadrin, since I had been away. Seg Segutorio spoke the true word. I swiveled an eye back. Seg's face showed in the crack of the doorway. He looked vexed. Clearly, since we had obtained information, he was wondering why I did not join the rest of the party.

I made a face at him, and he smiled, amazingly, in return, as I looked back at the scene below. The people were waving their fists and many brandished degutting knives and tridents. The leather-clad guards in their black feathers stared watchfully on. Himet the Mak gesticulated for silence. "Not so! It is the express command of the leader, of Makfaril himself, that only in the last resort shall Prescot be slain. Make him slave at your peril also. Deliver him up to me so that I may take him to Makfaril. Yes, my children, leave the fate of the wild leem to me and my guards here, my bonny masichieri, to take him to the leader."

One of the trident-men shouted, his voice shrill and cutting through Himet's words to the listening people. "Dray Prescot has a fearsome reputation as a fight—" No doubt he was going to say as a fighting man: Himet chopped him off with, "A fearsome reputation! Yes. Truly, by the Great Chyyan, a horrendous reputation!" That is true, by Vox.

Howls spurted up, execrations against the name of Dray Prescot and dire promises of what would befall him should he be foolish enough to fall into their hands. Himet bellowed.

"You would do well to heed my words and deliver him up for the judgment of Makfaril! Hearken! The torments Prescot would then suffer are beyond mortal men's comprehension."

They had not missed the neat turning of what reputation I had in Vallia from that of a warrior prince to that of a villain. Oh, yes, I am a villain. But only in certain matters.

There was little more to be gained here. We would have to think on what best to do about this new creed of Chyyanism. We were now acutely aware of the problem and its methods.

I cast a regretful glance at the two brothers, the trident-men who stood near the far door. Although uneasy, they showed no more signs of being cowed by words. But their glances at the guards, the masichieri, spoke eloquently enough. One brother shouted above the hubbub.

"And if the Prince Majister were here, among us now, who would know him?"

"Aye!" bawled his brother, red of face. "Who would know?"

Himet quieted conflicting answering yells. He smiled, a slow evil smirk that informed his listeners of his own importance.

"I have seen his representation. I would know. I would know the evil-hearted cramph among a thousand!"

The way the priest phrased this interested me. But it was time to go. The two brothers were scarcely likely to come to serious harm. The thought occurred to me that perhaps Himet had planted them, shills to give him arguments from which to strike sparks. If so, they were consummate actors.

'To the Great Chyyan with Dray Prescot!"

The chant from below grew in volume. I took no notice. What they wanted to do with me sounded highly unpleasant. What I intended to do with them might be highly unpleasant, at first; afterward they would see clearer. At the very least, this new creed had brought to my attention disquiet in Veliadrin, a disquiet I would see was dealt with fairly and rectified, so that the people of Veliadrin might be as happy as the people of Valka, as was their right.

So, still more confused than I probably realized, still holding down my anger, still blanking out what had been said about Delia and our dead daughter, I took my eye away from the crack in the floorboards and prepared to wriggle soundlessly back to the doorway. Seg had gone and the gap showed only a dark slit.

The boards beneath me creaked. They groaned. A spurt of ancient dust puffed past my face. I froze.

The gallery moved.

They were bellowing on about what they would like to do to Dray Prescot, making a hell of a noise, shrieking the most bloodcurdling threats. The groan of the ancient timber might be lost in all the uproar.

The rotten timbers under me sagged. Even to this day I do not know if the pure welling of savage satisfaction justified or condemned me.

The whole wooden structure shrieked as rusted nails gave way, as wooden pins snapped, as corroded bronze linchpins bent and parted. Rotten wood powdered to dust. A miasmic stench of long-dead fish gusted over me. I was falling.

The yells of hatred for the Prince Majister of Vallia belching up from below, the shrieks of venom for Dray Prescot, changed to a shocked chorus of surprised screams as the wooden gallery collapsed in a weltering smother of dust and chips and flailing timbers upon the mob.

Head over heels, I, that same Dray Prescot, of Earth and of Kregen, pitched down onto the heads of the blood-crazed rabble beneath.

Two

"It is Dray Prescot, the devil himself!"

For an instant I lay flat on my back amid the splintered wreckage of the gallery. A damned infernal chunk of wood jabbed sharply into my back. The people broke away in a circle, yelling, struggling to tear themselves free from the descending debris. The noise and confusion, the spouting dust from the ancient building, the struggles of men and women, I suppose all the furor was rather splendid.

But I had an eye out for the black feathers and leather armor of Himet's masichieri. They'd recover more rapidly from the shock of surprise than the fisherfolk.

I sprang up. I did not draw my weapons.

People were turning to stare back at me. Broken planks slipped beneath our feet and the dust made us cough. Dust and muck festooned my hair and shoulders, and my face, I suppose, knowing my own weaknesses, revealed the struggle between laughter and downright cussing fury possessing me. To be thus chucked down like a loon among a mob yelling for my blood—well, it was funny rather than not.

Himet stood with arms uplifted, his mouth open, glaring as though a demon from Cottmer's caverns had miraculously appeared before him.

Oh, yes, the cramph recognized me.

Whoever his leader was, this Makfaril, that rast would not be pleased with his priest. For, forgetting what he had been enjoining the folk around, Himet pointed a rigid forefinger at me. His wide-eyed stare blanked into stupefaction.

"It is Dray Prescot, the devil himself!"

After the thunder of the gallery smashing into the floor a silent moment expanded. Himet's voice shocked out. The fisherfolk understood the enormity of what the priest of the Great Chyyan had said.

"Dray Prescot!"

They repeated the name. A quick babblement flowed through the crowd. They stared at me. Like a monstrous tidal wave growing and surging landward from the wastes of the sea, like a tsunami running from continent to continent, their hatred burst up and broke. In the next instant they roared upon me in a shrieking mob.

A skip and a jump cleared the wreckage. Somehow, the rapier and dagger leaped into my hands. I beat away a reaching trident. A knife whistled past my ear and thunked into a shattered upright. These people were out for blood. These fisherfolk, wrought upon, forgetting what Himet had warned, were out to lay me flat on the floor, to slay me, to kill me stone cold dead.

"Do not kill him!" screeched Himet the Mak. He might as well have shouted into a Cape Horner.

With a shout of rage Himet turned and violently gesticulated, a savage, unmistakable gesture of command. At once his guards, his bonny masichieri, leaped down into the press, their weapons glittering.

Then began as weird a military dance as you could desire. For I had no wish to be forced to kill these simple duped fisherfolk, yet they sought to slay me. I did not mind if a few of the masichieri were cut down, but the guards were under orders not to slay me. And the fisherfolk would not willingly kill the guards of the priest but, as I quickly saw, the guards would slay the townspeople if necessary. This was a ludicrous three-sided encounter with each of the three sides willing to slay one of the other sides but not the third, and therefore, it must follow, to be slain and not reply. I saw a guard run his thraxter through a burly fisherman who poised to hurl his trident at me. So the preservation of my life for the future evil intentions of Makfaril had already cost the life of one fisherman of Veliadrin, and was like to cost more if I did not act now to stop this blasphemy.

I let out a yell. I bellowed over the hubbub as I had been wont to hail the foretop in a gale.

"Yes! I am Dray Prescot! I am your lawful High Kov. I wish you no harm. I have listened to your grievances and they will be redressed in justice. On this you have my word as a Prince of Vallia!"

I might as well have saved my breath.

The business about listening to them provoked only the shrieked response: "He has been spying on us! Slay the rast! Kill Dray Prescot!"

"No! No!" bawled Himet. "He must be taken before our leader. Makfaril demanded him for his own justice!"

Enough of the congregation in the hall had not been fully persuaded by Himet's exhortations and promises to obey blindly the dictates of the priest of the new creed. They had been roused to a sense of injustice. They had been cruelly treated by their new High Kov, and here he was, alone, ready to be chopped down in the violent way of Kregen and thus prove the justice of their own ends.

There followed a bout of confused struggle, wherein I found myself backed up against the far wall, beating away the crude implements of the fisherfolk and ever and anon striking with more deadly intent at a black-feathered guard. To defend oneself and not to slay the attacker—yes, there is a skill in that. It was not too easy in the press. A bulky lad staggered back with red blood pouring from his cheek where my main gauche, in whipping back to parry a trident, had gashed his flesh. Weapons flashed before my eyes. The guards were having difficulty in breaking through the fishermen to get at me, and when they did they died. The masichieri tumbled the fishermen away and advanced with scowls to an unwelcome task.

They handled their parrying-sticks with a fine free skill. As for their thraxters, the thraxter is a weapon of Havilfar, the straight cut and thrust sword, and these masichieri preferred it to the rapier in work of this nature.

The wall at my back was not altogether a good idea. No one was going to sneak up behind me and chop my knees off, but I could not skip and jump with the freedom I prefer in this kind of bash and batter fighting.

I began to angle around and a trident passed perilously close under my left arm as I leaned away to flick a neat rapier slash that unhitched the belt from a portly fisherman's waist. His breeches started to slide down. He let out a furious yell and tried to degut me with a knife so admirably adapted for the purpose, and the breeches tangled while he staggered, purple-faced, enraged, striking ineffectually at me. I did not laugh. Truth to tell, this whole fracas smacked of the ludicrous and I was in no mood for petty levity.

I leaped away and one masichier tried to be clever and earn his hire. He brought his thraxter around, flat, a blow aimed to stun. I slid the blow and bashed him with the hilt of the rapier. Instantly I had to duck a savage sweep from a parrying-stick from a fellow masichier. I almost ducked into a wickedly instabbing trident.

"By the Black Chunkrah!" I bellowed at them all. "Must I break all your heads to make you see sense?"

They snarled and roared at this, pressing in as I foined them off.

"You are not wanted in Can-thirda!" "Go home, Dray Prescot!" "Go back to your palace and your bitch wife!"

The fellow who said this, leathern-faced, scarred of jaw, abruptly somersaulted backward. My fist in the rapier guard tingled with the force of the blow.

"Kill him! Kill him!"

It was all a flurry of blade and tine and parrying-stick, and I smashed them back, beginning to feel my frustrated fury working on me. Soon the guards would tire of their fruitless attempts to take me alive. Then the fighting would begin.

"Slay the tapo!" screeched a lean and emaciated fisherman, hurling his trident. My rapier angled up and flicked the thing away. But the weapon was a trident, three-tined, and the sharp tines caught in my blade. Like the jaws of a shark the trident wrapped around the slender blade. I did not let go of the hilt, but my rapier was angled up and deflected, uselessly pointing to the cobwebby ceiling and the smoking lamps.

A fat and sweating man wearing more ornate clothes than the others, with a narrow gold chain about his neck and embroidered sleeves, even though silver fish scales caught in folds of the cloth glittered as marks of his trade, cursed with joy and thrust his trident hard for my guts.

I wriggled away at the last moment, striking a guard with the main gauche, wrenching it free in a gout of blood. I swung back to meet the next attack of the fat and wealthy trident-man. His sweating face showed a grimace of fierce joy, of that awful crazed desire to kill. I do not think he would have had me. But he would have come close.

He was not given the chance.

One of the two brothers who had mocked Himet the Mak stepped in and wrapped a burly forearm around the fellow's neck. With a chopped off squeal the crazed man was hauled bodily backward.

There was no time to gasp out thanks, for with a swish my rapier came down into line and extended into a bar of gleaming red-stained steel and the guard who had decided it was time finally to deal with me shrieked and spun away, clasping his neck where the long blade had kissed him above the edge of his leather armor.

"Take him, you fools!" Himet the Mak danced about frenziedly, well back of his guards, yelling orders and curses. His fanatical obsession with the instructions given him by Makfaril did not induce him to step forward and take an active part in the fray. Steel scraped and men yelled and bodies fell.

The pressure at least gave me some chance, for the fishermen maintained their yelling and their desperate attempts to get at me, and the masichieri continued to belt them away and so preserve my miserable hide. The rapier smeared with blood, and with the main gauche a similar reeking blade darting and flashing before me, I hacked and cut and kept them off. The rapier glistened before the eyes of a guard, distracting him, cut back viciously. He fell. As he fell so the dagger in my left fist sliced at a precise angle under the chin of his fellow. He staggered away as the rapier went in, slickly, withdrew, and a third guard spun away, shrieking, coughing out his life blood.

Now the masichieri were finished with this tomfoolery. Now these hired guards were out for blood.

A masichier stepped up, bulky in creaking leather armor, bold and confident, his thraxter held in a practiced grip, the parrying-stick slanting and catching runnels of jagged orange light. He thrust. He began his thrust as I whirled away from thunking a fisherman over the head and kicking another off.

The masichier halted his thrust in mid-action.

His shaggy hair beneath the iron helmet fluttered as his head lolled. Blood and spittle began to dribble foolishly from the corner of his mouth. He slid slowly sideways, upsetting a fisherman and his trident. As the guard toppled slowly to the fish-stinking floor I saw the long Lohvian arrow sprouting from his back, driven clean through his boiled leather armor, driven with exquisite force so that it did its business and no more, for it had not burst on through the man's chest.

I did not look up.

Another arrow punched through the neck of the nearest guard.

Oh, yes, you who have read accounts of my life on Kregen, that marvelous and horrible, beautiful and savage world four hundred light-years from the world of my birth, will understand. For Seg Segutorio, the master Bowman of Loh, had shot over me more than once in the past, had preserved my skin with superb displays of archery.

The guards' yelling changed in tone. The viciousness I had known could not be battened down for much longer broke and brought them surging forward with all the old hateful, expected, demoniac desire to slay.

A fisherman sailed up into the air from the back of the ruck. He went spinning up like a Catherine wheel and he landed plump on the heads of a group of others trying to get in at me and they all collapsed like ninepins. I saw Turko grasp another unfortunate wight and hurl him like a bag of beans. Turko, the famed Khamster, a high Kham, a man who had reached very high levels of achievement within the syples of the Khamorros, disdained edged and pointed weapons. Now he bore through the throng like a snowplow through six-foot high drifts.

Inch's long Saxon-pattern ax removed the head of a masichier. No one who wishes to retain their anatomy entire is advised to stand within the sweep of Inch's great danheim ax. His leather cap was slightly askew, and a long braid of brilliant yellow hair swung wildly as he fought.

That meant trouble.

Balass the Hawk, matched as a swordsman without his usual shield against a thraxter and parrying-stick man, made nothing of the disadvantage. The guard's parrying stick was a klattar model, of balass and steel, and suddenly it slanted where he had no intention of allowing it to go. His thraxter swirled as Balass's own superb Valkan sword slid in. Himet was short another guard.

As for young Oby, his wicked long-knife did nasty things to a guard who thought that he, at least, stood a chance.

The fisherfolk fell back, gasping, dazed.

Himet the Mak ... I whirled, for the moment freed from immediate opposition. The priest was nowhere to be seen. He had fled. Well, that was sensible. It was all of a piece with the man, with the artificial religion he sought to introduce to Veliadrin, and with the warped morals of the situation.

"Himet the Mak!" I bellowed up to Seg, who stood braced in the doorway above the vanished gallery. His bow was spanned, ready, and a stray gleam of light from the lamps struck a glittering spark from the steel arrow-point, most comforting to me, but most disconcerting to the poor wights huddled below, I daresay.

Seg spoke clearly, barely lifting his voice. "He vanished beyond the curtains behind the idol after the first shots."

There was no need for me to ask why Seg had not feathered him. Seg had loosed to clear away the guards pressing in on me. He had taken what he regarded as the prime objective. There is no use arguing with Seg Segutorio on these matters. As well argue with me, for I would have done the same had Seg been down there in that riot instead of me.

As Inch said, "Let us go and chase him, for he has made me break a taboo, and I shall have to perform unsightly things hereafter," Oby ran off with a whoop.

Again, there is no profit in laughing at Inch's taboos, which embroil him in ludicrous situations, at least, not too much laughter, for we could always make Inch stand on his head with the mere scent of squish pie. I hauled a guard toward me by his harness. I used my left hand, for my right held the main gauche as well as the rapier in a somewhat awkward grip. Now had I been a Djang, or a Pachak, I could have done that little trick without trouble.

I glared on the guard who rolled his eyes and flinched away.

"Tell me of Himet the Mak, my friend," I said, quite pleasantly, staring on the fellow. He blanched at this and his wild eyes went wilder still. He considered himself a dead man, that was certain, yet he had only been wounded, a long cut down his cheek. He made no attempt to lick at the blood. "Where has the arch-devil gone? Tell me that and you may live, dom."

Whether he believed me or not I do not know. He opened his mouth, slobbering, and I saw the stump of tongue there and felt the disgust in me. Had Himet done this? Did he employ dumb guards? But some had shouted as they fought.

"Can you write?" demanded Roybin.

A rolling, lolling shake of the head.

That was to be expected. Illiterates, even if through no fault of their own, tended to end up in the lower levels of whatever trade they entered. I had no desire to play dwazn* questions with him. Vallia, Havilfar, the islands, there were far too many bolt holes to go through even if this dumb devil knew. And, if Hamal was the homeland of the masichieri, I might ask all night and not get the right answer.

Balass, cleaning his sword, said, "They use the thraxter and parrying-stick. That is not of Vallia."

"They wear rapiers and daggers," said Roybin, fingering his chin. "Yet they left them in their scabbards and chose thraxters. It adds up. Hamal it must be."

Seg had jumped down to join us and we talked, taking no notice of the fisherfolk. I wanted these people of Veliadrin to see the picture and use their common sense. "Not Hamal, Roybin, surely?" Seg's bow gleamed in the orange light. "Shields there. More likely the Dawn Lands of Havilfar, or over to the west...

"Wherever they come from," I said, "and this Himet the Mak, their target is Veliadrin. Right. Tell me, how far have they infiltrated Vallia to venture out here?"

The question was the obvious one, of course. Why bother over an island

____

* Dwazn: twenty.

off the east coast of Vallia, an island moreover split into different provinces, when the main island remained?

Roybin looked worried. "You mean, my Prince, they have already completed their foul work in Vallia?"

Now that he phrased it like that I realized I didn't mean it ... quite.

Perhaps I was growing paranoid. The word is of this later time and my thoughts then were more earthy. I had thought that Himet the Mak was after me personally. All this business about capturing me and taking me to the leader and torturing me was pedestrian stuff. I had thought, perhaps, the Star Lords might be taking up again their interest in me or, perhaps, the Savanti. But this kind of rowdy fracas was not their style, never had been so far. If they wanted me they could reach down and by means of a gigantic and ghostly representation of a Scorpion they could snatch me up from wherever I happened to be on Kregen and dump me down anywhere else they desired. Aye, and they could send me packing back to Earth four hundred light-years off through space.

The Star Lords and the Savanti between them had caused me great grief in my life, as you know, but I was no longer the same blind, ignorant, gasping puppet I had once been. Yet I was still painfully aware that at the whim of forces I did not understand and the dictates of superhuman men and women I might be flung willy-nilly into fights and adventures, into danger and unwelcome distractions, at any moment of any day.

I would not again struggle against the Star Lords in the same stupid way I had done the time they had summoned me and, because Delia and my friends were in peril, I had refused them. Then they had flung me back to Earth for twenty-one miserable years. No. This was not the handiwork of the Star Lords, who sought to work out a destiny for Kregen I could not comprehend.

The fisherfolk were growing restless. We were, as I have indicated, a right tearaway bunch of fearsome fighting men. But once we had seen off the black-feathered masichieri, why, there we stood, all talking and arguing away together as though the fisher people of Autonne did not exist. What were those good folk to make of that?

They had heard of Dray Prescot, their new High Kov, and they did not like him or his high-handed ways in renaming their island or of freeing their slaves. Fingering their tridents, shuffling their feet, they began to edge toward us.

Their faces hardened with determination ousting shock. They formed a half circle about us with their women safely in the rear. Their feet shuffled with more purpose as they advanced.

The way the orange lights caught on the sharp tines of their tridents and flashed sparks about the lofty room reminded us that perhaps we had not finished here yet.

Seg was saying, "More news would have come out of Vallia about them if the Chyyanists had grown really strong. In Falinur there have been rumors only, with nothing positive. This is the furthest I've gone yet in discovering—"

"They're a secretive bunch," observed Inch, who had come back in after chasing after Oby. Now the tall man was carefully winding his braid of yellow hair and stuffing it up under the leather cap. He looked more than a trifle put out, adding, "Secretive. And they preach revolution."

Casually, unhurriedly, Seg Segutorio turned around. His superb muscles put out their awful power and the bow string drew back. The arrow cast cleanly. The sharp steel point struck fiercely into the floorboards before that advancing semicircle of men determined to slay us out of ignorance and folly and hatred. The blazing blue feathers with which the arrow was fletched quivered as the shaft thrummed in the floor.

Seg turned back and answered Inch. "We'd have known something, you long streak."

It was magnificently done.

Instantly the forward shuffle of those desperate men stopped as though each man had been stricken with paralysis.

I said, "There is no profit, really, in running after Himet. Oby is on a fruitless errand. He will seek us out, all in due course. He will come to us, of that I feel sure."

As though on cue Oby walked back in looking disgruntled. He shook a few raindrops from him and the wind gusted in through the rotting doorway, half sagging from broken hinges.

"He took a flier and went—whoosh—and I can tell you, my Prince, the voller was a good one. Made in Hamal for a damned Hamalese."

If anybody would know about airboats, Oby would.

As Oby spoke I was fretting away about my response to Roybin and my insistence that Himet would seek me out. Were these the responses of a megalomaniac? Did I see conspiracy everywhere, plots to drag me down to destruction in every unusual occurrence?

I just was not sure.

"I believe this Himet the Mak will seek us out again. This is not just a fresh religious creed, which is open and exultant about its origins. If Hamal is involved, and that certainly seems to be so, we all know that Hamal has not been crushed but only halted in her aggressions. So it makes sense to strike at us in this new way. When this Himet returns we will deal with him. And, Roybin, I did not exactly mean what you suggested about Vallia..."

Seg and Inch and Turko!

Oh, yes, I caught their delighted mocking smiles. Each one of my true comrades favored me, each in his own way, with that secret, mocking, almost indulgent smile each one reserves for me. I sometimes think they humor me as they would a little child. Clearly they must have been thinking something along the lines that this so-puissant Dray Prescot, who was Prince of this and Kov of that and Strom of somewhere else, needed a little of the old headlong action to bring his addled senses back.

Since when, it seemed to me their sly and good-humored smiles were saying, since when has the high and mighty and great Dray Prescot not been sure of anything? Ah! If they only knew! If they only knew of the torments of indecision I suffered then—and still do suffer, by Zair!—then they would revise their opinions drastically.

I supposed they thought of me as a rough and ready soldier of fortune who had won through to great wealth and power—as indeed, with their help I had—and so therefore a man fit to be gently mocked. So I thought them. This amiable irony, this cheerful mockery of my comrades is returned by me, and it is never hurtful or cruel between us. Rather, it adds a zest to our comradeship, a spice, for each one of us knows that if he does a foolish thing—as who does not, by Vox!—the others will remind him of it, from time to time, gently.

So, being a cunning old leem-hunter after my own fashion, I pointed at the two brothers in the pressing crowd halted by Seg's single arrow standing in the floor as though held back by a solid wall of granite.

"You two. Step forth."

They stepped out, apprehensively, and other men near them hurriedly drew away to give a clear path as though afraid of contamination or the plague. What the two trident-men thought, or what the people thought lay in store, Opaz alone knew.

"You two. Brothers. Twins. Names?"

They swallowed, alike as twins, alike as twins ought to be and so often are not.

"Please, your honor, I am Tarbil the Brown."

"And, if it pleases your worship, I am Tarbil the Gray."

"It pleases me, Tarbils both," I said. "I saw. And I heard. Why did you attend this meeting tonight?"

Both spoke at once, then Tarbil the Gray yielded to Tarbil the Brown. "Our lives are poor, your honor. We thought there might be a little... fun."

"I would like to know why you did not shout for Chyyan with the rest."

"These people, your honor, would bring back slavery."

"Ah!" I said, understanding. I looked at the mob. "And that sweaty one whom you dragged back. He was your master?"

"Aye, your honor. We were slaves from childhood until the High Kov said all slaves must go free."

He looked at me under his eyebrows, his head ducked, this stalwart, muscled, hardy fisherman. He would go out in his little dory all night with a light, spearing fish. He was whipcord tough. Now he swallowed and shuffled his feet and wet his lips. "And, your honor, you are really him? You really are, your honor, you really are the new High Kov, Dray Prescot?"

"Yes."

I did not add, as I might unthinkingly have done once upon a time: "For my sins."

That was true enough, Zair knew. But they would have misunderstood, believing the words rather than the oblique thought behind them, an altogether too common failing, and a false word could have spread. I was hated enough in Veliadrin as it was.

Both brothers began the full incline until I stopped them, somewhat roughly, with a word, and then bade them stand up like men.

"There is no slavery in any place where the people look to me," I told them, trying not to give the impression of smugness or of righteousness. That never wears with simple folk. "You who once were slave are now free. It is your right. And I would thank you for your help."

I did not, there and then, in view of some of the murderous looks bestowed on the Tarbil brothers, give them a gold piece each, or a ring or any other trifle. That would come later, when I confided the details to Panshi, my Great Chamberlain. He had remained at his post in the palace fortress of Esser Rarioch overlooking the bay and my capital city of Valkanium in Valka. And it would be no trifle. The Tarbil brothers would be useful.

Yes, I own it. Already I was thinking how they would fit into my schemes to free all the slaves of Vallia.

The Tarbils bobbed again and then drew back. They were given plenty of room. I looked questioningly at Roybin.

"They will be safe, my Prince. I believe you have put such a fright into these folk they will be quiet for a space, to the glory of Opaz and the Invisible Twins."

Oby and Balass were busy picking up the scattered weapons dropped by the black-feathered masichieri. They knew my ways. I did not give the Tarbils a rapier or a thraxter. Giving a man a weapon he does not know how to use is no act of friendship, and is a good way of getting him killed. But Roybin, who would stay in his home town of Autonne for a space, would see to the Tarbils before they were brought to Valka for the greater work.

I lifted my voice so all could hear.

"And we have more work to do." I spoke to the fisherfolk of Autonne. "Go to your homes. Ponder on what you have seen. Remember that the spirit of the Invisible Twins made manifest in the heavens above us is a beneficent spirit; but remember also that Opaz will strike down the wrongdoer. Put away from your thoughts this evil creed of Chyyanism. It is a fallacy to dream that each one of us may have exactly what he wants in this life, all at the same time, without effort. You must work, I must work. You will say I am your High Kov, and so I am and may be. The burdens laid on me are different from those laid on you, but they chafe no less harshly. But if any one of you wishes to take that task upon himself he knows the ways, both in law as elsewhere, and I warn you, he will grieve mightily."

Yes, all right. I know that was double-edged. I damned well meant it to be double-edged.

On Kregen land and wealth and titles are for the taking, but only by due process of law after the battle, despite a forest of dead bodies. I was legally the High Kov of Veliadrin. I could give the title to whosoever I wished, obtaining the emperor's agreement. Anyone could fight me for it and, if he won, have the emperor ratify his success if he could. That battle might be harder than the preceding one. A man might marry into lands and wealth and, perhaps, into a title. The system is not the same as those obtaining on this Earth. On Kregen it is far more what a man is and what he does that makes a man, and not what a man is born into.

As for women—the whole gorgeous world of Kregen is their oyster.

The famblys shuffled out, still dazed, and some, as I was very well aware, still resentful. We desperadoes were left in the deserted hall, with the shattered gallery and the stink of ancient fish and the four-winged black idol of the Chyyan.

Turko bent and picked up a parrying-stick. He turned it over in his hands, weighing it, studying it. "A klattar," he said.

I recalled how in Mungul Sidrath Turko had bent and picked up a shield.

Roybin coughed and began to say, "I will arrange for everything to be cleared up here," when Oby let out a strangled screech that snapped us all about to glare at him.

"Dray! My Prince, *look!*"

We all stared where his rigid finger pointed.

The black idol against the rich cloths glowered down somberly upon us, the four wings black and seeming to span the heavens. And the idol's eyes glowed! Twin pits of emerald fire, they shone down with an eerie, baleful flame of malefic evil.

Three

Burning eyes of a pagan idol

Glowing with baleful fires, the eyes of the idol poured out a malevolent radiance. Twin pits of flame beside the arrogantly beaked nose, the eyes smoked greenly with a sense of contained horror most unnerving.

Impossible to say which one of us moved first.

As one we rushed toward the idol in its alcove.

What we shouted, what we said, I do not know. I think each one of us wanted to get a grip on the bird-idol and rip away the masked face to discover just what trickery was at work. The emerald fire blossomed into a fierce blaze of green fire. Then it vanished. As we reached the statue only cold lusterless glass eyeballs gazed dispassionately down on us.

"Sink me!" I burst out. "Here's a task for Khe-Hi and old Evold!"

We prowled around the idol, glaring at it, hitting it experimentally with our sword hilts. It sounded hard almost everywhere save for the center of the back, where it gonged with a hollow note. Those tearaways of mine would have pried the back open there and then, but I halted them.

"Let the wizards deal with this. There is bound to be trickery here, protection against opening."

They grumbled, but they saw the sense of what I said. We all knew a little of the powers of the Wizards of Loh, although no man not a wizard could comprehend them fully, I judged, and it seemed likely it might need a wizard to open the idol without disaster. Inch, hefting his ax, was maundering on about an idol of deepest Murn-Chem that had opened to let loose a flood of poisonous insects. Oby, eager to display learning, could cap that with the story of Rosala and the Eye of Imladrion. Seg and Inch stood back and Inch lowered his ax. I fancied a blow in the right place would open the idol of the chyyan easily enough, but we might not welcome what emerged.

Only later, thinking back, do I realize that the horrific appearance of those eyes suddenly glowing with sentient light, gleaming emerald pits of fire glowering down upon us, had not scared us witless as, doubtless, had been intended.

We'd simply yelled and charged straight for the idol.

I fancied that was behavior the manipulator of the idol was unaccustomed to.

Truth to tell, this whole affair of the Great Chyyan was a most serious business, but levity kept intruding. I'd fallen head over heels into a secret meeting. A horrific light had flashed from the glass eyeballs of an idol, and we'd simply gone for the thing baldheaded instead of shrieking and running off. When one gets into low company, one's habits tend to lower also. Like Oby having to be told to take his damned great long-knife out of the idol's eyesockets.

"If there are demons and poisonous insects or what not in there, Young Oby, you'll let the things out if you pry its eyeballs out, will you not?"

He jumped down agilely, saying with some resentment, "I've always wanted to prod out the fabulous gems from the eyesockets of a pagan idol."

So, sharpish, I said, "Then you can help the wizards when they dismember this thing, you imp of Sicce."

Whereat he scowled and fingered his knife and then, when Balass whispered to him, perked up. Balass had hinted that the fabulous gems might accrue to a light-fingered young scamp, when the wizards were otherwise occupied...

As you will readily perceive, after a little exercise and for all their forebodings, my comrades did not take the new creed of the Great Chyyan with overmuch seriousness. I hardly think it necessary to remark that in that they made a grave mistake.

There would be much to do, I considered, to stamp out Chyyanism. I would stamp it out, for it posed a threat to Vallia, my adopted country. Had the creed been genuine I would not have interfered. Religions originate and take root and flourish when there is a need for them. Changes of religion occur when the times cry out for new vessels for old wine. But this Chyyanism was artificial, a hodgepodge, a deliberate throwing together of ideas culled from the deepest recesses of the wish-fulfillment sections of the human mind. Chyyanism had been created as a weapon, for a far deeper purpose than merely to stir up credulous men and women resentful that their slaves had been taken from them.

In all this I tried to remember that my own origins were those of the rebel. I detested authority imposed by brute force without concern for evil results. Despite my friends in whom I joy, I am a loner. I have resisted authority all my life, often enough to my sorrow. Now that I had certain responsibilities I could see the other side, but, even so, I knew that Chyyanism merely used resentment against authority as a weapon, that the glib promises of luxury and paradise now were hollow, false and could only lead to ruination for all.

"Very good, Roybin, then you will see to this. Before I leave for Valka you must have a settlement. We owe you much."

"My thanks, my Prince."

So we left Roybin to summon his own people to clear up the mess and we took ourselves off to our secluded inn. The innkeeper was Roybin's cousin, and he asked no questions of these strangers recommended to him. But we all knew the word that the High Kov of Veliadrin was in Autonne would be all over the town by morning. It was high time to pack our traps and leave.

We had discovered certain things about Chyyanism and our agents would continue to burrow and pry and we would discover more. We had the great black idol. And I still felt convinced that this Makfaril, the leader of the Chyyanists, was aware of my interest and would take steps to counter the threat.

All this would make life interesting, as though life on Kregen can ever be anything other than fascinating!

We had flown here in small, inconspicuous fliers. Even so, airboats are rare enough in the backcountry of any nation of this continental grouping of Paz, with the natural exceptions of those countries where vollers are manufactured. So folk would still look up from their work on their nets or in the long tended rows of their fields when the shadow of an airboat skipped over them.

Seg would be leaving for his province of Falinur and Inch would be leaving for his province of the Black Mountains, both in Vallia. They would be flying west and north; I would be flying east.

We made our partings brief, with a compact to meet up again shortly.

The twin suns were just lifting above the eastern horizon as our fliers took off, the last shouted Remberees ringing in the limpid dawn air. Well, Seg and Inch are the finest company a man can wish for, and at every parting I sorrowed, but all the same, acknowledging that I am a loner, I could look ahead with some fascination to the future.

The journey to Valka proved uneventful, although we spotted a flier which contrarily kept pace with us for a time and then vanished behind clouds. Oby, who was piloting, looked at me enquiringly. But I shook my head.

"The fellow may be something to do with the Chyyanists, and he may not. Our task is to get home and have the wizards inspect the idol."

Oby's face expressed a certain disappointment.

"Don't fret! By Vox! Makfaril and Himet and their crowd will cause us enough strife to keep you well occupied, you bloodthirsty leem."

Only a little mollified, Oby drove us on through the morning as the mingled lights of Antares fell about us, streaming in jade and crimson across the voller and the fleeting countryside below.

By Zair! But it was good to be alive and on Kregen!

Turko kept twitching his new parrying stick about and Balass sat out of the slipstream methodically polishing up his sword blade with an oily rag.

A few seasons ago I would have gone blindly off charging after that elusive flier and thereby dropping myself headlong into fresh adventure or, most likely, failing to find him in the scattered clouds, so my present conduct gave some small indication of maturing. I wanted to chase the fellow. But the mystery of the idol fascinated me more.

So we bore on steadily through the levels, homeward-bound for Valkanium, the capital city of Valka, and the high fortress therein of Esser Rarioch.

Since my return from Earth and the adventures in the Eye of the World I had a deal to do in catching up with events on Kregen. Things had changed. The sparkling vista of the Bay and the city opened up as we flew down in a beeline for the high landing platform of the castle. I did not sigh. The sound of a sigh in that bright scene would have been out of place. Just as I felt out of place. My son Drak, Prince of Vallia, appeared to be running Valka very nicely, thank you.

He was called the young strom, and I had heard men refer to me, unaffectedly, as the old strom. This was an eventuality I had not entertained, for despite what might happen on Kregen I had always thought of Valka as my home.

Oh, yes, I had other homes on Kregen, there was Strombor and Djanduin and the wide plains of Segesthes where my clansmen roamed. There was even Paline Valley in hostile Hamal. But Valka... Well, as Oby brought the airboat around in a sweeping line for the landing platform and touched down with that perfect sweetness of touch of the master flyer, I choked back that ridiculous sigh and hopped over the voller's coaming with a riotous bellow for the guards and attendants.

For a space it was all yelling and Lahals and rejoicings, and then Delia appeared and everyone fell respectfully back, and we touched hands. I looked into her eyes and, as always, saw there the amused wonder at these carryings on, the deep love between us and also that damned mocking smile which told me, clearly enough, that she had a word or two to say to me when we were alone.

Balass, I noticed as we turned to go into the palace, was engaged in a very close conversation with a superb black girl, a maiden of Xuntal, and so I rejoiced for him.

As for Oby...

"Yes, Dray, he has to run very fast to keep ahead of all the girls who have matters to discuss with him!"

Delia smiled as she spoke, so I knew the matter was not serious.

For Oby had ducked down beneath the voller, crept around the other side, and the last I saw of him that day was a fleeting glimpse of his breech-clout as he vanished down a back stairs. Hot on his heels ran half a dozen rosy-limbed girls, all yelling after him, waving their arms like a bunch of love-crazed nymphs. Well, they were, in a way. I found my craggy lips twisting into a smile.

"It seems Oby has made himself at home in Esser Rarioch."

"Very much. Which," added my Delia tartly, "is more than can be said for Esser Rarioch's strom."

But she smiled as she spoke. One day I would have to tell her about Earth and all the rest of that story, which she, dear girl, would find almost impossible to believe. How could any intelligent person believe in a world that had only one sun, only one moon, possessed only *Homo sapiens* as intelligent people to live on this fantastic world, did not have flying saddle-birds or any other of the everyday marvels of Kregen?

It would take a lot of belief to believe a story like that.

The only consolation I had was simply that there is no woman more perfect than Delia on two worlds. She, at least, would listen in her grave, lightly ironic way, half laughing and yet deadly serious, and would give me the benefit of her love. She, at least, would not condemn me out of hand as a madman, makib, fit only for the ice-chains of Hegenor.

So, together, we went into the palace where everyone seemed pleased to see me back, and where we were soon served up a capital meal in a small private room. Melow the Supple, the ferocious Manhound who had dedicated her life to the care of Delia, as her two children cared for my first twins, prowled in, splitting her frightful muzzle in a grin of welcome.

We drank tea and ate miscils and other light pastries, and munched on fruits of all kinds, with the ever-present dish of palines to hand.

"And this new creed is then a serious menace?"

"Most serious, I judge. To tell simple folk that they can have all they want, here and now, for the asking, is ruinous folly. By Zair! Had I all I wanted, here and now—" And then I paused. I had so much. Was I then so greedy?

Delia had told me the news of our children. Each was about his or her business in the greater world of Kregen. I had seen my three sons in action, and in them I could feel content mingled with apprehension. Drak, as the eldest, handled my affairs for me. Zeg was now a famous Krozair in the inner sea, the King of Zandikar. Jaidur had remained in the inner sea to finalize his acceptance into the Krozairs of Zy. I value my membership of that order among the highest of the good things that have happened to me on Kregen. I had ideas to put the mystic disciplines and teachings of the Krozairs to a wider use. So the lads were accounted for. Our daughter Velia was dead, but we had another new daughter, Velia, and she I looked upon with a dread joy, for the stories about lightning are not true.

As for the other two girls, Delia simply told me that Lela, Drak's twin, was busy with the Sisters of the Rose. And Dayra, Jaidur's twin, should— and then Delia corrected herself, and said was—also concerned with the Sisters of the Rose.

"But they are making arrangements to visit Valkanium to see their father. They have to call at Vondium first."

I nodded, thinking. So with Delia and the children I had all I wanted. Why should I then cry out that I did not have all I wanted? Perhaps the thought of the perils and problems besetting Kregen prompted the remark. All I knew then was that I felt a gnawing sense of anticlimax, and a restless desire to be up and doing once again.

"As soon as the idol is here the Sans can probe and pry." I munched palines, tasting the flavor, forcing myself to feel a content foreign to me. "To promise anyone instant success in the here and now rings false."

"But there is more to it than that?"

"Yes, my heart." Trust Delia to see through my mumblings. "The idea of this creed could be a new attack from Hamal." I outlined some of my suspicions. "I shall have to go back there at some point. The devils still sell us inferior fliers, so I believe."

"Oh, they do not fail so much as they used to do. But the silver boxes go black and fail much earlier. And they charge us greatly inflated costs. And—"

"If nothing else turns up, then I'll go back to Hamal and this time rip the secrets from the very throats of the Nine Faceless Ones themselves."

Delia did not say in an arch way: "You mean that too!" For she knew I meant it. But I caught her expression, and at once felt deflated, an idiot, a veritable onker. To talk about going away again so soon after so long an absence was thoughtless cruelty. I reached over and touched her arm.

"Let us open up the idol and see what we find. Then we can talk with more sense."

She took the words as an apology. And then she said, "This time, I think I shall come with you."

So I laughed and we drank more tea, and Panshi, the Great Chamberlain, came in to tell us that the black pagan idol bird had arrived. So up we went through the colonnades and passageways and along the long hall of the images to Evold Scavander's laboratory. The black idol squatted against the wall opposite the windows, and dominated the room with an aura of evil. The thing looked just as impressive and malignant there as it had in the makeshift temple of the fisherman's net-room.

Old Evold sniffed and hitched up his robes and fussed around his princess, bellowing for Ornol to find chairs and refreshments. Delia sat calmly, smoothing her trailing skirts, accepting the services with that delicacy that marks her as a true princess born.

Turko walked in with his loose limber prowl and settled down quietly and watchfully by the door. I noticed the parrying-stick thrust through his belt, the jags turned out, and I fancied he'd have Balass foining away at him with a rudis in short order.

Evold Scavander, given the honorary title *San*—which means sage or master or dominie—was the wisest of the wise men of Valka. His wizardry extended into different spheres from those of the famed Wizards of Loh, who are, I must confess, real sorcerers. If they are not genuine, then they are the most consummate confidence tricksters of two worlds. Much remained to be learned of the Wizards of Loh. I was engaged in a long-drawn-out struggle with the master-wizard, Phu-si-Yantong, a man who was more evil than could be understood by mortal men, and yet who was not a cardboard villain without features that made him both darker and, contrariwise, human. Yantong had not bothered me in the inner sea. I surmised he knew I was back in Valka and therefore I must expect a visitation from him, a ghostly apparition that would spy on me.

The Wizard of Loh, Khe-Hi-Bjanching, whom I had brought out of danger to a position of importance in Esser Rarioch, had been erecting defenses against Yantong. I knew these defenses must be put to the test. I did not look forward to that time.

Evold, spluttering and blowing, prowled around the idol, peering up at it, tapping, feeling, prodding.

Once he would have started in to prize the back off without a second thought. But for all their arguments and quarrels, Evold and Bjanching had come to a kind of understanding. I felt only a little surprise when Evold burst out: "Now where by Vox is Khe-Hi? He's never here when he's wanted, and always underfoot when he's not." So that salved some of Evold's *amour propre*.

By my orders there were few people in the laboratory. The tables were loaded with the paraphernalia of Evold's studies. Here we had broken some of the secrets of the silver boxes that powered airboats. Here we had sought to uncover the secrets of past ages, and to make experiments for the future well-being of Valka. But my concern now was for what might happen when the idol was opened.

When Khe-Hi-Bjanching came in I saw that look that flashed like two flung stuxes between the two wizards. Like two flying spears their looks clashed and crossed. But much had changed in Valka since I had been away, and I knew I would find much had changed as I took up once again the threads of life on Kregen, so I watched with a small sly inward approval as the two wizards prepared to cooperate. Young Khe-Hi and Old Evold, wasn't that becoming the story of my homecoming?

"You have touched nothing, San?"

"Nothing, San."

Their exquisite politeness one to the other tickled me. I remembered them yelling at each other and hurling scathing remarks about aptitudes and abilities. Now the two wizards walked together all around the black chyyan and cocked their heads back to stare up at the malignant eyes and drew long thoughtful expressions. In short, they behaved as professional men consulted on a case of intricacy behave.

Finally, Khe-Hi said, "The idol is certainly sealed by sorcery. I know that."

We all understood. A wizard of Loh who deals all his life in sorcery knows when sorcery is being used, or, at least, knows most of the time.

"You say the eyeballs flamed emerald, my prince?"

"Aye."

"Yet they are plain glass with a yellowish tinge." Khe-Hi gestured and Ornol, Evold's assistant, brought across a ladder which was propped against the statue. Khe-Hi, hitching up his pure white robe cinctured by the crimson cord, mounted and peered closely at the eyes. I wondered what would happen if they blazed their incredible malignant green into his face.

Many men of the continent of Loh have red hair. Not all. Loh is a land of mystery and terror and remained locked away from exploration after the collapse of its famous empire. Khe-Hi's red hair shone darkly against the black of the statue. He peered this way and that. Then he descended and stood looking thoughtfully upon the back of the idol where a single light tap gonged a hollow note.

"There are preparations I must make," he said at last, coming to a decision. "San, I would value your help." Evold nodded without speaking.

"Will this take time?" I spoke calmly.

"Three burs only, my Prince."

A bur is forty Earthly minutes. There would be time for more tea and a slap-up meal in two hours. I nodded. "Then I leave the idol in your care." Then, because of reasons that remained too obscure to be articulated, I added: "And Oby has settled a lien on the eyeballs with his long-knife."

There was a laugh at this. Delia rose. We went out together and Turko followed. Like my return home, this first investigation of the idol had been an anticlimax.

Four

Eggs of evil

There was so much for me still to learn about what had chanced on Kregen during my absence that every spare moment was occupied in Delia's dredging her memory to retail the choicest bits of information. We had recourse to the records of Valka, of course, kept by the stylors in Esser Rarioch. How all this fresh torrent of facts and conjectures would influence my life had to be weighed and judged. I think it best if I simply fill in what it is needful to know about any given situation as it arises in this narrative.

For instance, I was fascinated by the scraps of knowledge gleaned from distant Hyrklana, where Queen Fahia, poor soul, was having trouble finding fresh fodder for the Jikhorkdun. Likewise, I was mightily impressed by the progress made in raising and equipping three full regiments of Pachaks mounted on flutduins from the Pachaks of Zamra. But these and many and many another affair of state had nothing, as I saw it, to do with my present concern with the Chyyanists. I mention these two to give examples. Also, I handled some pressing affairs of business that my son Drak would have taken care of had he not been in Zamra dealing with the construction of a new seawall, jetty and pharos for the new town of Veli-asmot put in hand to provide another secure harbor for the great galleons on which rested our trade.

So, as I ate vosk pie and momolams, I listened to Jiktar Larghos Glendile recently returned from Vondium, the capital of the Empire of Vallia, telling me of the latest decrees of the Presidio. The Presidio ran the country, although the emperor, as well as holding titular power, controlled enough real power to maintain the balances so necessary for government. It was all a matter of balancing one power group against another, of taking advice and of making laws that would maintain.

"But the racters, my Prince! They have shrunk in numbers but have increased their powers through carefully placed men in the right positions."

The racters, the most powerful party in Vallia, who wore the black and white, held their wealth and positions through high commerce, through land, through slaving, through mining. There were other parties, notably the panvals, who stood against the racters. But all, as I well knew, had their own candidates to take the emperor's place.

"They maneuver the emperor so that he will stand alone. Then they can reduce him."

"Do you know who it is whispered will take his place?"

"No, my Prince. That information is held close."

This Jiktar Larghos Glendile presented an imposing picture as he reported. He was a Pachak. Now Pachaks, being blessed by nature or by gene manipulation with two left arms, are among the most renowned of Kregen's fighting men. Also, they have a hand on their long whiplike tail. Loyal were Pachaks, and first-class mercenaries. I had built up centers of Pachak habitation in both Valka and Zamra that were based on a full life. That is, the towns occupied by the Pachaks were proper towns, with all the facilities of towns. They were not mere military barracks for mercenaries.

Larghos Glendile was a Jiktar, a rank I suppose most nearly equated with that of colonel. His uniform of the brave old scarlet glowed. He wore two bobs, the medals given by my Elders of Valka. His tough face, with the harsh yet human features of a man who has had wide experience, betrayed his desire to do well not just as a hired fighting man, which he no longer was, but as a full-fledged citizen of Zamra. Zamra, the larger island to the north of Valka, of which I am kov, was to prove of surprising worth in the seasons to come.

The necessity of thus building up a powerful fighting force was one I loathed. Yet the necessity remained. There are many foes in Kregen who will cheerfully sail up over the ocean rim, or drop down out of the skies, and seek to take whatever portable property is lying around not chained down. My duty as a prince was to protect my people. And, equally, when I called on them for help, their duty was to help me protect them. But of course it is not as simple as that.

Jiktar Glendile of Zamra went on to tell me more of what was transpiring in Vondium, and I listened and ate my fruit and quaffed tea and finished with a handful of palines.

The clepsydra indicated half a bur to go.

Delia came in looking radiant. I rose. Glendile straightened to ramrod attention.

Delia looked at me accusingly.

"And have you kept the Jiktar standing all the time?"

I gaped.

Neither Glendile nor I had noticed. We were warriors.

So the moment passed and Jiktar Glendile finished up his report sitting down, drinking, his booted feet stuck out, his rapier cocked up and his tail curled decorously around the chair legs. That tailhand could whip a long blade up between his legs and have a foeman's tripes out in a twinkling.

When the Pachak had gone I said to Delia, in more of a groan than I intended, "There is so much to learn! By Zair! Things have moved on Kregen since I have been away!"*

She laughed and tinkled a fingernail against the clepsydra.

I stood up.

"Then let us go and see how the Sans have got on with that damned black idol."

So as I stood up and spoke I saw Delia, half turned in the doorway, looking back at me, and the breath caught in my throat.

Often and often I have tried to find expression to convey some sense of the beauty of my Delia. How impossible a task! As she stood there, half laughing at me, the sheer ivory-white gown relieved only by a small brooch of brilliant scarlet scarrons, her brown hair with those shimmering tints of chestnut striking through and making a wonder and a halo around her head—yes, I felt my flinty old heart thump and the blood pulse through my veins. By Zair! Was there ever a girl like Delia, my Delia of Delphond, my Delia of the Blue Mountains?

Sweetly she looked at me, mocking, knowing very well what thoughts were prancing through my mind.

I scowled. What chance of that! The scowl died and I realized I was smiling, grinning away like a loon.

---

* Although a fresh supply of cassettes from Dray Prescot has come into my possession, for which we should thank all the gods of Kregen, I am convinced there are some cassettes missing. *Krozair of Kregen* finished with Dray Prescott and Delia reunited in the Eye of the World. They must have rescued Didi, the daughter of Gafard and Velia, from the Grodnims. Textual evidence lends support to the idea that the rescue was hairy in the extreme. But the present volume, Secret Scorpio, begins with Prescot and his friends on Veliadrin seeking out the secrets of the Chyyanists. How much is missing we cannot tell. *A.B.A.*

"There will be plenty of time, my love," said Delia, the Princess Majestrix of Vallia, "for you to catch up."

If I do not give my reply to that I fancy each of you, in his or her own way, will furbish up the retort suitable. The effect of all this was that we were smiling foolishly away as we walked through the hall of the images toward the laboratory. These images, of ivory and bronze and precious stones, commemorate the Stroms of Valka. I still had not made up my mind if I relished their presence forever lowering down on me, the latest Strom, or if I resented them as reminding me of past glories and past shames.

We had just passed the bust of Strom Natival, I recall, around whom legends clustered, when we heard the explosion. For a single shocked instant I thought gunpowder had been touched by a spark. But gunpowder was not used here. All my old training in a wooden ship of the line, with felt slippers and flash curtains and water buckets and hoses forever at the ready, reared up in me. With a curse I leaped forward and the billowing mass of black smoke choked around the far corner and boiled swiftly forward. The black smoke engulfed me. I swung about, reaching for Delia, waiting for the blast to take us. It was all a screaming nightmare with the concussion still ringing in my ears.

The smoke roiled and eddied. I blundered into Strom Pagan's bust—I knew it was his by the size of the vinous nose—and it went over with a smash. Delia clung to me, saying nothing. Our eyes and noses ran with the stink. This was not ordinary smoke. There was about it a charnel tang, a foul-tasting vileness on our tongues, rasping our throats.

No further blast came.

The smoke thinned. I gasped for air. We waved our hands about, wafting the smoke away.

Delia's ivory dress was spattered with black dots, like mold on cheese. My eyelids felt redly granular, itching. I spat.

"By the foul intestines of Makki-Grodno!" I bellowed. "The infernal idol!"

I pushed Delia away.

"Go back, Delia!"

I started to run for the laboratory.

My Delia ran at my side.

"Go back! Who knows what has happened?"

"I intend to find out. Why don't you go back?"

I saved my breath.

As I ran on I was cursing away at myself for being such a fool as to bring the damned idol into the palace. What a blind idiot! Had I never heard of Troy, and the White Horse? What sorcerous mischief had I unloosed in Esser Rarioch?

A figure blundered into me and I grasped old Evold by the arms and shook him.

"Tell me, Evold!"

"My Prince—" He babbled on, shaking. "The eyes lit up again, just as you said!" He coughed and choked and spluttered and I let him go as he swiped at his streaming eyes. "San Khe-Hi, he was almost prepared as he had promised, and then it was as though the lightning struck. The idol shrieked! There was smoke and flame and a blue-green fire and—"

He had no need to say more.

From the wrecked door of the laboratory Khe-Hi-Bjanching stumbled, beating wildly at the darting black forms surrounding him. They dived from the air, swirling their ebony wings, and their shrill chittering filled the hall with the rustling whispers of the tomb.

Chyyans! Scores of tiny chyyans, with a wing spread of no more than two feet, swooped and darted and struck and clawed. I saw their baleful red eyes, the raking dart of their scarlet talons. Their beaks gaped wide. Khe-Hi stumbled and fell. I leaped forward, ripping the rapier and main gauche free. I stood over him, straddle-legged, and at once my blades swirled and swished to cut down the fluttering horrors.

They appeared almost like bats, vampire bats, lunging in to sink their fangs into my neck and suck me dry.

But each black chyyan had four wings, four wings clad in rusty black feathers. They swooped and darted and struck, and I felt the sting on forehead and arms as they clustered thickly about me and sank their talons into my flesh.

"Wizard!" I bellowed, slashing about me wildly. "Cast a spell or something! Drive them off!"

"I have spelled them already," came the gasping wheeze from the wizard. He tried to crawl out from between my knees and a tiny chyyan slashed at him, so that he cried out and scuttled back.

"Well, for the sweet sake of Mother Diocaster! Spell them again!"

I heard a furious yell from along the hall and between slashing and ducking turned. Turko was there, laying about him with his parrying-stick. And my Delia, slim and glorious in her slashed ivory gown, my Delia sliced and cut with the long slender jeweled dagger in whose use she is so superbly skilled.

"San!" I bellowed. "You must run for it!"

I shoved the dagger into my mouth, ricking my lips back in the old way so my teeth could grip the blade. I reached down with my left hand and hauled Khe-Hi out by the scruff of the neck. My right hand seemed of its own volition to be flickering the rapier about, chunking great swatches of black feathers away, slicing and cutting, never thrusting, for in a game like this that was the sure way to die.

I gave Khe-Hi a good rousing kick up the backside and sent him scuttling and staggering down the long hall.

Then I reached my Delia and with three blades we wove that old deadly net of steel. She flashed me a single smile. We went to work, then, in real earnest.

Jiktar Larghos Glendile appeared, raging, roaring into the fight with a rapier and two daggers, and with a blade gripped in his tailhand. He was worth two men in that kind of fight. Others of my people showed up, and soon we could actually count the numbers of chyyans remaining.

I bellowed.

"Save some! Do not slay them all!"

Then ensued a riotous chasing rout as the fluttering birds sought to escape from the palace, and my people, whooping as though on a rampage, chased them through the corridors and up and down the stairs, seeking to cast nets and sacks and whatever came to hand over them. In the end we caught three of them, penned in sacks, and the stout material bulged and strained. Turko hit a bulge with the parrying-stick and the bird in the sack quieted down.

Once again what had begun as a drama, as tragedy, ended in farce.

"Khe-Hi!" I said, and at my tone he stiffened up, looking woebegone in his ruined finery, but nonetheless still retaining his dignity as a Wizard of Loh. "*Well?*"

We went back to the laboratory and Khe-Hi pointed out what was left of the idol.

Bits and pieces of black stone were scattered about the chamber. The windows were blown out. The tables were overturned. The place was a shambles.

"Khe-Hi!" squeaked San Evold. "You've ruined my chamber!"

"Not me, old man. Rather this Makfaril of whom the prince speaks."

"I'll do more than speak about him," I said, very nastily. "You said you had spelled them."

"So I did, my Prince." Here Khe-Hi pulled himself together and became again a famous Wizard of Loh. "Had I not done so we would have been beset by full-size chyyans."

Turko whistled. Jiktar Larghos Glendile nicked his tail-hand about.

I said, "So you did well, wizard. Did you seek to open the idol before I arrived?"

"No. No, my Prince! The eyes lit up again as you described when my preparations were almost complete. I understand what happened. A wizard was controlling the idol and saw what I intended. He released the hidden sealing spells and there was a sound as of thunder and a blue-green light as of leprous lightning."

That was as good a way as any to describe an explosion to those who did not know of gunpowder.

"The spell I had set reduced whatever was in the idol in stature and power. So the eggs—"

"Eggs?"

"The idol was packed with chyyan eggs that would hatch into full-sized chyyans instantly, bypassing normal growth. It is a trick some wizards employ. My counter-art reduced the size of the chyyans."

"Lucky for us," said Glendile. He had four weapons to clean, and was hard at work even as we stood talking.

"And the light was blue-green?"

"Yes."

That did not square with a gunpowder explosion.

"Damned sorcery," I said. "I don't hold with it. Another wizard?"

"A most potent practitioner of the arts."

I looked at Khe-Hi-Bjanching. We all knew of whom we thought.

It was left to Delia to say, in a calm, even voice, "Do you think, San, it was this infamous Phu-si-Yantong?"

Khe-Hi scowled. "I do not know. By Hlo-Hli, my Princess, I do not know!"

This was a poser. I was prepared to credit Yantong with any evil you care to imagine. Once a fellow has run into evil of that nature he tends to see his opponent as more black than a night of Notor Zan, until, with wisdom, comes the understanding that character shades into gray and purple and bilious green. All the same, Phu-si-Yantong!

"I have told you of the Wizard of Loh, Que-si-Rening, kept by the Empress Thyllis in Hamal. Do you think it could have been him? After all," I added, trying to appear casual and making a dismal mess of it, "after all, everything about the Chyyanists points to another ploy from Hamal."

"I swear by the Seven Arcades, my Prince! I cannot tell. The sorcery was sealed by great power. It is possible among high adepts to conceal ego-traces, to hide the personality patterns. I can do this to an extent. There are few wizards, I venture to think, who would discover what I did if I did not wish them to, but of course there could be a few who would have the power."

This was mighty humble pie for Khe-Hi, I saw.

I nodded, not satisfied, but unable to do anything about that dissatisfaction for the moment.

A clatter of dislodged stones and debris from one of Evold's smashed tables turned our attention to Balass, who straightened up lifting a dusty round object from the jumble. He blew on it and dust flew.

"Now what is this?" he said, turning, walking across with the round plate balanced on his upturned palms.

I was aware of Khe-Hi at my side, of the way a tremor shook through him. I shot a swift searching glance at him. The wizard's face looked

strained, a deep furrow dinting down between his eyebrows. He sucked
in his breath.

"Whatever it is, Balass," I sang out cheerily, "our potent wizard knows!"

"Aye, my Prince! By Hlo-Hli. I know!"

"Well, then, tell us."

He took the plate from Balass, by which I judged the thing exerted no
immediately dangerous evil influence. He turned it over. We all craned to
look. The plate was fashioned from bronze, as thick as two fingers, as wide
around as an Och's shield. Inset around the edge were cabalistic signs; these
Khe-Hi ignored and I judged them decoration. Nine sigils surrounded a
blank center. That center either had once had or had space left for five further signs. Each of the nine signs was different and I recognized none.

"Well?"

"This was secreted in the compartment in the back of the idol."

"Well," exclaimed Balass. "Anyone knows that!"

"Go on, Khe-Hi," I said. Balass shut his jaws with a snap.

"The wizard controlling the idol is able to observe at a distance without
the necessity of forcing a representation of himself to the needful point
and looking through his own immaterial eyes. This saves psychic energy."

Delia was looking carefully at the disk and its nine emblazoned signs,
and Turko lifted it from Khe-Hi's hands so the princess might view it more
easily.

I said, "You mean when the eyes light up with that baleful green fire this
damned wizard is spying out of them?"

"Yes, my Prince. I also think this is a sign for the priest, in this case
Himet the Mak, to open the back in safety."

"But the confounded thing blew up when the eyes lit up!"

"Yes. Because the wizard observed what was happening and knew that
in the next few murs I would have reduced his sorceries and rendered the
chyyan eggs harmless."

"Hmm," I said. "And these signs? Nine of them?"

Nine is perhaps the most magical number on Kregen. There was a fan-
ciful touch about this round plate and the nine symbols that reminded
me, vaguely, of the Krozairs of Zy and their sign, the hubless spoked wheel
within the circle.

"Each sign, I think, is a location. Probably where a temple of the Great
Chyyan is situated. When the sign lights up, it must be a signal to meet there."

Every symbol lay flat and dull and lifeless.

"The first thing," I said with enough acerbity in my voice to make them
understand the seriousness of all this and my inflexible determination to
rise above the farcical element that had been dogging us lately, "the very
first thing is to read the symbols. We must find out where these damned
temples are."

Evold peered at the plate. "They mean nothing to me at the moment. But mayhap I have books. San Drozhimo the Lame may have somewhat to say on these signs. And there is the *Hyr-Derengil-Notash*. Also I have hopes of the hyr-lif of Monumentor ti Unismot."

There were one or two small smiles in the group. We all knew old Evold and the lore he culled from his musty books. All the same, he did come up with answers to problems. No one could deny that.

Khe-Hi sniffed. "This is wizard's work, San. The *Hyr-Derengil-Notash* was compiled by a great wizard two thousand five hundred seasons ago. I know it well. If whoever is controlling the idol used it, you may find what we seek. I doubt it."

San Evold did not look disgruntled. He was used to this kind of deprecation from Khe-Hi.

The *Hyr-Derengil-Notash*—the title means, very roughly, the high palace of pleasure and wisdom—is used by philosophers and in its pages they can find whatever they seek. It is read as the heart commands. If, and I did not savor the thought, if Phu-si-Yantong was the wizard controlling the idol, I did not think he would have recourse to that hyr-lif. Only very important books on Kregen are called lifs, and only the most highly important of all receive the appellation of hyr-lif.

The signs meant nothing to me. One looked like a mess of worms. Another like a ship of no recognizable type, with a fork of lightning joined to the mainmast. Another seemed merely a formal angular maze. Delia looked up at me, and at the look in her eyes I jumped.

"I think," said Delia slowly, her face more flushed than usual, "I think I know where is the place one of these signs refers to."

Five

The Stromni of Valka explains

The plate, with its outer ring of nine symbols and its inner ring of five empty places surrounding the blank center, was very heavy, being fashioned of bronze. The idea, undoubtedly, was to make it difficult to steal. Khe-Hi-Bjanching told us that this kind of plate with symbols, used by the wizards as a means of conveying information, was called a signomant, employing signomancy to give instructions that could not be misunderstood by those who had the key.

I refused to allow Delia to speak until we had all left the laboratory,

Turko and Balass taking turns to carry the signomant, and until we had all settled down in an airy upper chamber after we had washed the muck of the explosion from ourselves. A light white wine was served, for the suns were almost gone, and the birds flitted about the grim stone face of the castle. Wearing a delicious cool laypom-yellow gown, Delia sat in her comfortable chair, gazing upon us in some delight, her cheeks still rosy and her eyes bright with the secret revelations she was about to tell us.

No one was fool enough to mumble some sycophantic nonsense about not being at all surprised that the Princess Majestrix should understand the signs. We all sensed that only some local knowledge had given the clue to Delia. This proved true as she spoke.

"I am called Delia of Delphond," she began. "My estate of Delphond is very dear to me and I have studied all that I can find about it."

Now I am aware that I have said very little about Vallia. One reason is that its puissant empire tended to stifle coherent thought in me. Also, much of my adventuring on Kregen has taken place in countries outside Vallia. But, all the same, as I go on I must tell you of important facts. In the long ago the main island of Vallia and the surrounding islands were all separate, petty kingdoms and kovnates—and some not so petty—and it was only after long-drawn-out and bloody wars that finally the empire drew together with its capital at Vondium.

Delphond is situated on the southern coast of Vallia, not too far to the west of Vondium, and it had been a kingdom in its own right, small and tight and sweet. When the empire-builders advanced from Vondium, the kingdom of Delphond retained an individual identity for much longer than anyone might have expected. There was much trouble with the far southwest, and Rahartdrin resisted stubbornly. Also the northeast maintained a hostility to Vondium that persisted for centuries. So it was that when at last Delphond was incorporated into the empire the final capitulation was swift, with little damage done to the ancient monuments of the past. The old history twined with passion and intrigue—just as these times of which I tell you now hummed with plot and counterplot—and Delphond, when at last she entered the empire, was given over to the empress and her descendants, alternating the generations with other estates of Vallia.

Now Delia pointed to one of the nine symbols ringing the bronze plate.

"The Temple of Delia," she said, and looked up at me like a small girl embarrassed at picking the largest fruit in the bowl.

I laughed.

Now I understood the meaning of the flush in her cheeks, the brightness of her eyes. She may be a princess, a Princess Majestrix, but my Delia is a woman with a mature and yet girlish heart that derides pomp and circumstance, that makes mock of titles, that understands that if Opaz has seen fit to burden her then she must brace up and shoulder those burdens.

Old Evold nodded with quick understanding.

"You are right, my Princess!" That, of course, was a silly thing for anyone to say to some common princess, for whenever can a common princess be accused of being wrong? But Delia is no ordinary princess and we were all friends here, eager to seek out the devil's work threatening our people.

"See," said Delia, her slender fingers busy tracing the lines of the sign. "Here are the pillars, and this is unmistakable." Two dots surrounded by twin circles and with a V-shape joining them had been linked with the architrave. "This has always been taken to be the sign of Delia in her manifestation as Mother Goddess. It is scarcely known outside Delphond. When Delphond lost her kings and became a province of Vallia the religion of the time sought to stamp out all-knowledge and memory of the Mother Goddess."

"That was before we were blessed with the knowledge of Opaz," said Evold. He pulled his nose, blinking. "That would have been in the time of Father Tolki the Almighty."

"Yes." Delia knew all about this. "The fearsome warriors in their bronzen mail trampled down all Vallia, bringing with them their own belief in Father Tolki. They were hard days. The old records show that Delphond escaped lightly, for we are cut off there, a backwater, out of the stream of events."

"But a mighty pleasant backwater!" I said, incensed. "I am particularly fond of Delphond, and I have read of how the mailed hosts of Father Tolki ravaged the land. But they did institute the first Empire of Vallia."

"Which broke up, as empires do. There were many religions and many new peoples and kingdoms and empires before the Light of Opaz guided..." And then Delia hesitated, and stopped. How could she go on to say that her family had taken the ragbag of Vallia and shaken it into an empire, that her family had taken the power thrust upon them by Opaz—or by greed and cupidity and sheer downright cunning and skill and ruthlessness?

"It is a story not unknown in Havilfar," said Turko. "The ancient mysteries of the Mother Goddess, and then the newer, harsher, military religions of men. We Khamorros have fought against oppression for all our history."

"We rejoice in the Invisible Twins," said Delia seriously. "For in them made manifest through Opaz we see the fusion of male and female, of mother goddess and warrior god, and all the other aspects of godhood." She looked around and added not so much tartly as with finality, "As it should be."

How this brought home to me the ancientness of Kregen! Civilizations had risen and fallen, cities built and vanished, kingdoms waxed and waned. And, far back into the past, the Sunset Peoples had lorded it over a young Kregen with the freshness of dawn. Now all that was left of them were the

Savanti, locked away somewhere in their Swinging City of Aphrasöe. One day I would return to Aphrasöe, and with a purpose. But that day could not be now, for there were too many other pressing problems in Vallia to occupy me.

Old, is Kregen, and yet the world is populated now by new vigorous peoples thrusting out to conquer fresh territory, waves of migrations passing across the continents and casting up new kingdoms and republics, new confederations, hurling down the old into ruination. The famed Empire of Walfarg, generally called the Empire of Loh, had fallen into a pile of dusty refuse, and now Loh slumbered, her Bowmen mercenaries in the other continents, her wizards scattered and serving other monarchs.

One day the dark continent of Loh would be opened up again and hosts would march. Perhaps a host of Vallia would penetrate that land of secret walled gardens and veiled women, hear the silver trumpets screaming, bring the Light of Opaz to the deepest darknesses.

But first we had our own stables to clean.

"But which," I asked Delia, "which temple is it?"

"Oh," she said with quick confidence. "It must be the chief temple. Much of it still stands, garlanded with vines and ivy, overgrown, moldy. But the sacrificial pools are still there, with water still in them. The last time I was there—you were gone off, Dray—the golden roofs still stood. Although, of course, the gold was gone long since and only the tiles remained."

"Just the place for a secret rendezvous for a congregation of the Great Chyyan."

"Oh, Dray! I hope not! My poor people!"

"Yes." I was grim about it. "There is no guessing when meetings have been held, or even if any have been held so far. But one thing is sure. This devil Makfaril intends to use Delphond as a base for his Chyyanists. For all we know they are already strongly entrenched there."

"I am not so sure." Delia looked troubled. "My Delphondi are a lazy lot, as you know, slow to anger. They prefer the easy life, sitting in the sun, yarning, eating, singing. It would take a very clever and cunning man to rouse them against their wills."

"Makfaril is clever and cunning. Make no mistake about that."

"Then we must go there at once."

"Agreed. But we go carefully."

Delia's troubled look persisted. She shook her head.

"What a business this is! I love Delphond. I am the princess—it is an imperial province—and I am sure the people love me. Yet I must go creeping back like a spy!"

"Exactly!"

Then I paused, trying to think. "On the other hand, if you went as the princess, in all pomp, acting as you usually act—and I know the people love you—that would show them your care for their welfare persists. I feel convinced only a few may have gone over to this damned creed. You will have to work from the outside, bedazzle them, show them that Opaz is still the religion of their fathers and mothers. Yes," I said, brisking up, seeing a cheerful glow on my mental horizons. "Yes, that's it. You are the Princess of Delphond. The people will welcome you as they always do. But, as for me..."

"Yes?"

"I am not as well known there. Oh, a few of the nobles would know me. But I shall go in my own way, and creep about and ask questions, and prod and pry. I'm looking forward to it. Between us, my love, we'll have these damned Chyyanists in the open where we can get a shot at them!"

She stuck her bottom lip out at me.

"I can put on a disguise!"

I shook my head. "As soon seek to disguise a shonage in a bowl of squishes."

"Inch!" we both said then, and laughed, for all the thing might be serious. But life was for living and Inch was, well, Inch of Ng'groga was Inch, Kov of the Black Mountains.

"We'll have messages sent to Inch and to Seg, apprising them of what is afoot. I know Seg was more perturbed than he said. I think Falinur smolders. Her people are still resentful over the lost coup of that dratted kov of theirs. Seg has a handful with Falinur."

Khe-Hi indicated the other eight signs. "Where are these places? The answers must be sought, my Prince, but I will hazard a guess. We may not know what the five blank spaces are for, but is it not possible that the single central blank space is reserved for the sign for Vondium?"

Old Evold cackled. "A puffed-up Wizard of Loh you may be, San Khe-Hi. But in this you speak sense."

It did make sense. If Makfaril intended to destroy Vallia he would have to strike at the capital. The central space meant Vondium, I was convinced. Also, I fancied that the existence of a sign indicated that a center of Chyyanism had been set up there. A blank indicated the Black Feathers had not yet opened up shop at whatever place they next intended. So we have a breathing space.

"We leave first thing in the morning," I said. "Panshi can organize everything tonight."

There would be a lot to do before we could leave. Didi would have to be left in good care. A message would have to go to Drak warning him. The Elders of Valka, with Tharu still in control and with Tom as his right-hand man, would carry on as they always did when their strom vanished. But this time their Stromni, the Princess Majestrix, would be absent also... More and more I could see that Drak was taking over here, and much though I resented it, the circumstances of my life made it inevitable and cruelly precluded me from taking any steps to halt the process of takeover. Drak was my eldest son, and he was fully entitled to look out for his inheritance.

With preparations made for an early start on the morrow we turned in. Just before she went to sleep, Delia turned over, smiling at me, her hair a torrent of bronze-gold upon the pillows. "When we get to Delphond they'll expect me to behave like a princess. But, my grizzly graint of a husband, be very sure I shall make a journey to the Temple of Delia to find out just what deviltry you've been up to."

Six

At the Temple of Delia in Delphond

I, Dray Prescot, Lord of Strombor and Krozair of Zy, hitched up the ragged brown cloak over my left shoulder and took a firmer grip on the tatty cloth bundle that held my worldly possessions.

Leaning over the bulwark of the flier, Delia handed me the bamboo stick.

"You look a mighty savage ruffian, my love. Try not to scowl so, and cast your eyes down. To act a poor wayfarer is not going to be easy for you."

"Maybe not, my heart. But I've done it before and, by Vox, I'll do it again."

Parting with Delia is always so cruel an experience that I wondered, every time I parted from her voluntarily, why I was such a fool. To hell with Vallia! What did it matter if an evil creed overturned everything? What mattered beside life and love that meant everything with my Delia? But then I would return always to the harsh understanding that I was driven, a man doomed—perhaps by the Star Lords, perhaps by the Savanti, perhaps by Zena Iztar. For all of them I could feel anger, and yet, for Zena Iztar, who had materially helped me in ways beyond belief, I had to feel an affection that transcended my feelings for either Savanti or Star Lords. I might resist them; in fact I had worked cautiously on ways of circumventing their commands, and had succeeded and failed, yet would continue to struggle against them as I could.

But Kregen itself, the world of people, the beauty and grandeur and horror, this drove me. This made me both less and more of a man. So I could stand in the dust of a Delphondian lane with the green of orchards about and say goodbye to Delia and put a brave enough face on it.

"And do not be late for our rendezvous," she said. So we called up the last Remberees and the flier lifted off. I waved as the voller rose and swung and swooped away into the bright morning air beneath the streaming mingled light of the Suns of Scorpio.

I was alone.

Well, that was what I wanted.

This was a decision I had made.

I tucked the bamboo stick into my belt over the old scarlet breechclout, draped a fold of the tattered brown cloak about it and with a final look around started the trudge to the Temple of Delia, about a dwabur off along the coast.

Very soon I found I could take an interest in all I saw, for the world of Kregen is always marvelous. My hand touched the bamboo stick. It was not real bamboo, of course, but it held the same deep orange glow and was ridged at intervals. Just such sticks are carried by the poor folk when they venture out from their own villages at least, just such a stick to outward appearances.

My hair was uncombed and tousled up, and my face bore the marks of grime, although this was fresh dirt newly rubbed on. I was barefoot. Well, I am still more accustomed to going barefoot than to wearing shoes or boots. So I strode on out of the orchards and over the brow of a hill and across springy turf with seabirds wheeling and calling overhead, on along the edge of the cliffs with the wind in my face.

Far out to sea a galleon of Vallia bore on, the spume breaking from her bows, her canvas all stiff and curved, a stately and gorgeous sight in the light of the suns.

And, as always, the smell of the sea wafted in to brace me up and bring the memories flooding in. By Zair! But all this wonderful display of nature—a naive but a feeling thought—deserved to be savored.

Soon I passed a small group of cottages, set in the lee of a low hill. Gray smoke wafted. I did not stop and skirted around past the fences where the bosks nosed up, squealing. The people here would be like all Delphondi, easygoing and lazy, or so I then considered, but I felt disinclined for any company since I had voluntarily debarred myself from the only company for which I care.

The Temple of Delia was set in a wide dell, a kind of lush ravine, through the center of which a narrow and rapid river helter-skeltered to the sea. No one lived hereabouts any longer. The grass and moss-covered outlines of ancient buildings, reduced to mere low mounds, told of the busy activity here when the Goddess Delia was worshiped in the land.

Now I proceeded cautiously. If this Makfaril called his freshly garnered congregations to worship here they must travel a fair way. There were towns within riding distance. Many of the richer sort might own an old airboat or two. The poor people would walk, or ride their draft animals. I kept into the side of a grassy bank and moved steadily forward until the first of the standing columns came into view. The green and emerald suns struck conflicting shadows from the flutings and ornamentation. Beyond the row of pillars a gray slate roof lifted, much worn and, as I judged, repaired within the memory of man.

The quietness seemed very peaceful, with the droning of insects to deepen the hush, but I fancied that quietness to be deceptive. Slowly I inched forward, trying to peer into the blue shadows that lay in cool swathes beyond the pillars.

Nothing moved. The suns beat down and the mellow heat lifted from the warm earth and the insects droned and the air and sky breathed a sweet stillness.

I scouted the ancient temple thoroughly. Nothing human lived within those moldering walls. The place had been surprisingly large, the shattered walls and columns and fallen roofs lushly overgrown, giving clear indication of a rich and thriving community centered around the temple. When this place had hummed with life and worship and the continual processions, on Earth the men of Sumer were considering how best to fashion bricks into the form of ziggurats to reproduce the mountains they had deserted. Well, the ziggurats of Kregen are notorious, as you shall hear, and I was doing no good mooching about here. It occurred to me that the nine sigils of the signomant might not mean nine temples for the worship of the Great Chyyan.

The thought did not depress me. That had been a guess. There would be many wrong guesses before this business was over. Far more likely was our first assumption that the signs indicated places of rendezvous. This temple stood near the coast so it could be the place where ships landed, gliding into the pebbly cove where the small river tumbled headlong into the sea, disgorging money, weapons, priests, to further the cause of the Black Feathers in Vallia. That made sense.

There had been no sign among the nine that we could make tally with the town of Autonne in Veliadrin.

Ignoring the cluster of cottages I had passed, the nearest village lay two dwaburs off. I fancied I would walk there and quaffing good Delphondian ale and eating cheese and bread and pickles, I would ask cunning questions. The villagers would most likely know if torches had been seen in the ruins, if the weird sounds of chanting had been borne on the night air.

No thought that Delia had been wrong in her identification could be entertained. Of course, she could have been deceived by some fancied resemblance of the sign to the ancient symbol for the Mother Goddess aspect of Delia, but I did not think this. What I had been half-consciously looking for I found in the same instant that I heard voices drawing near, voices engaged in the age-old complaint of the soldier performing guard duties when he would rather be off in an ale-house.

Even as I bent and from the broken angle of moldering masonry retrieved the scrap of black feather, I heard the voices.

I held the feather in my fingers, a tip of the rusty black plumage of a chyyan, the feather proved everything. If the mission on which I was engaged resembled some eerie detective story, then this was a clue of the first water.

The voices complained on and I shrank back into the shadows and listened. I put the feather down onto the moist green ferns struggling from the cracked masonry and blew it gently so that it drifted down out of sight. I marked the spot in my mind.

"That Shorten is a right bastard." The voice rolled, rich and fruity, lubricated through the years by many a flagon of medium red. "As a hikdar he'd be a great zorcadrome attendant."

The second voice, sharper, more intense, carried on the bitter complaints.

"We've been nobbled for picket duty three times in a row. By the Black feathers! I've a mind to appeal to Himet the Mak himself."

"Do that, old son, and he'll just refer you back to Shorten. That's how they run things."

I waited silently until the group came into sight. Four lumbering quoffa carts, bundled high and with canvas lashings protecting and concealing all, followed eight masichieri marching two abreast. Right in front and about to enter the ruins, the complaining two marched well ahead.

They were unmistakable. Fruity-voice, glowing of nose, broken-veined of cheeks, with bright protuberant eyes, marched with a rolling swagger that churned his swag belly inside his leather armor. They wore plain black tunics, with the well-oiled leather and the parrying-sticks and the thraxters. The second masichier, smaller, weasel-like, kept in step with his bulkier comrade; and both of them grumped and groused to amuse Vikatu, the Old Sweat, Vikatu the Dodger, that archetypal old soldier, that paragon of all the military vices, that legendary figure of myth and romance loved and sworn by with great vehemence by all the swods in the ranks.

"Get down behind that busted wall, Naghan," squeaked the smaller. "As soon as we're outta sight of Deldar Righat I'm gonna take a good long swig."

"Me too, and it won't be from my water bottle, either."

The moment the two scouts were out of sight of the main body and the deldar in charge they ducked behind a broken wall, driving up a green lizard who sprang away, a flash of green light under the suns. They hauled out squat bottles. Dopa. Well, dopa is a drink wise men steer clear of. But a man generates a thirst marching in armor and girt with weapons.

"By Vikatu the Thirsty!" said Naghan, wiping his mouth. "That feels better, Little Orlon."

"Aye!"

I studied them from my concealment.

They were masichieri, among the lowest form of mercenary, yet they spoke like soldiers, like swods in the ranks. Perhaps the Great Chyyan could enroll people into his new religion and change them, turn an honest soldier into a thieving masichier?

I could believe that, which meant the new creed, through the leader Makfaril, could change other men and women, turn honest men into rogues. How far into the society of Vallia had the disease spread?

No arrogance in these thoughts of mine touched me then—or now. There were many religions on Kregen and some of the smaller were remarkable, seeking to do good, perhaps remaining small purely because their high ideals were too difficult for mortal sinful souls. But the simple basics of Chyyanism were plain. They were revealed as Naghan, sweating, stowing away his dopa bottle, spoke:

"When the Great Chyyan gives the word and it's the Black Day—ah!— then I'm gonna take what is my due from those high and mighty lord muckamucks in Vondium!"

"Too right!" Little Orlon spat vindictively. "I've my eye on a shop run by a fat Relt. I'll wring his scrawny neck and twist his beak until he stares over his shoulder blades! I'll have his shop, and the Great Chyyan will bless me."

If there was a more basic approach than that—excluding a purely sexual lure—then much of history would be falsified.

The quoffa carts lumbered on and the creak of their wooden axles and the grinding groan of their wheels drove the lizards away. The deldar— deldar Righat—bellowed his orders and the column broke up and helped guide the carts into the shade of a half-standing wall. There were the two scouts, the eight men of the main body, and the four drivers.

I fancied I'd test them.

So, hitching up the ragged blanket, I stepped out into the suns-shine and walked, a little slowly, a little unsurely, across to the group.

Hunching my shoulders I put on that old imbecilic look and prepared to act out my part as a wandering laborer.

"And what have we here?" said the deldar in that knowing, gloating kind of voice that immediately spells trouble.

"If it please your honor," I said, getting a splendid wheeze into my voice, "I'm Nath the Gnat and I'm just passing through."

"And why should you be passing through here?" The deldar drew his sword to show me how important he was. He gestured. "Grab him! Hold him fast and let me look at the rast."

I allowed them to seize my arms. They held me and the deldar eyed me up and down, slapping his sword flat-handed, the steel smacking against his palm.

"A foul-looking specimen! Speak up! What are you doing here?"

"I'm just going through," I squeaked, shaking my shoulders. If these men were ordinary soldiers they'd laugh and offer to share a cup of wine and a handful of palines with me. But I thought I recognized these masichieri. They were of the cruel persuasion. If they could not have a little fun with a broken-down old fellow, well, by Krun! what was the world coming to?

"Through? Through where to?"

"To Dinel," I said, naming the next village where I'd thought to eat bread and cheese and quaff ale and ask questions. "There may be work for me there."

"There's work for you here, my lad!" said the deldar, and the soldiers laughed dutifully. I called them soldiers, for they aped military ways, but I had to remember they were mercenaries of the lowest sort, masichieri.

They did not beat me up there and then. But I was kept very busy unloading the carts along with the four drivers, who were slaves. They were all apims. We carried bales and bundles into the main roofed section of the still-standing temple. I managed to get a glimpse of the contents of one box when it was dropped awkwardly from a cart and the lid sprang open. A mass of rusty black feathers within told me what I wanted to know.

We worked for a few burs until everything had been carried in and arranged to the deldar's satisfaction.

More than once I staggered under the weight of a bale that I could have thrown one-handed. These men were convinced I was a simpleton, and they were pleased that they had found a pair of extra hands to help. They offered me no dopa as they drank; to have refused would have looked odd, so I was spared the expected fight breaking out before I was ready.

"All out!" shouted the deldar.

We went out into the declining rays of the suns and I expected that, if there was to be a fight, it would begin fairly soon. I said, "I left my sack in there, your honor," and turned to go back.

The slaves were drinking water and fighting over a crust of bread and a scrap of cheese. The masichieri were lighting a fire and preparing to cook a meal. I went back inside and no one offered to stop me.

The knife over my right hip slid into my hand like an eel. I slashed open the bales, pulling the contents out. Yes. Black robes and cloaks fashioned from feathers, with fierce beaked headdresses in which the priests could dress to look like chyyans. The chests contained food and drink of a refined kind, reserved, not for the use of the guards. There was a little money, gold pieces of Pandahem among the golden talens of Vallia, and these I left strictly alone. There were weapons also. I left them.

Everything pointed to this collection being the paraphernalia for a gathering of Chyyanists.

An iron-bound chest was heavily locked. I did not attempt to open it, guessing it to contain the altar vessels and the more valuable impedimenta to be used in the rites of the Great Chyyan.

While a certain amount of spying is great fun and serves to thump the blood along the veins, I felt I had accomplished enough. I have no truck with those imbeciles who consider all spies as rogues—many are, of course—and during my wartime experiences on Earth I had seen some incredible disasters through the disdain in which spies were held. But enough was enough.

A quick glance outside showed me the masichieri around their fire, the shadows lying long in their twinned bars from the columns, the quoffas munching quietly, the slaves tied to the tailgates and trying to rest. Now was the time for me to walk briskly over to Dinel, find a mount and try to reach the nearest sizable town, Arkadon, where I might find a garrison in time to make it worthwhile to return here. Arkadon is a pleasant place, one of Delia's nicest towns, but the garrison troops would be like most Delphondi, as I then thought, a lazy and inefficient lot. But we ought to be back here before dawn and in time to sweep up this little lot and the worshipers and the priests. I wanted to get my hands on Himet the Mak and find out what he was really up to. He most probably would not talk, but I had grown suddenly weary of spying. Enough was enough. We would at least lop off this branch of the Chyyanists.

A flicker of movement in the tail of my eye caused me to spring abruptly and silently to one side.

I glared into the shadows. An indistinct figure stood impassively staring at me. I could not make out the features, merely a vague blur with deep pits for eyesockets. Clad all in a long robe, dark in the shadows, the figure remained motionless.

I knew.

Phu-si-Yantong!

Yes, this had happened before and I knew it would happen again. As I spied on the Chyyanists so the wizard of Loh spied on me.

Somewhere in the forbidding world of Kregen Phu-si-Yantong had placed himself in lupu, in a trancelike state, and his incorporeal body had visited me, spying on me. I felt the chill in the air, the shiver as of millions of tiny needles pricking into my skin. As I started forward the appearance vanished. There could be no mistake. The blurred figure did not move. It simply winked out of existence.

This ghostly apparition filled me with a fury that was purely ridiculous, for there was nothing I could do about it.

Cursing the damned wizard and all his misdeeds, I took up my sack and my bamboo stick and prowled to the far opening, peered out, saw the coast was clear and so stalked out into the dying light of evening as the twin Suns of Scorpio sank toward the horizon.

There was no direct proof that Yantong was mixed up with the Chyyanists, although circumstantial evidence pointed to that eventuality. If he was, then I knew I was in for the fiercest struggle I had faced so far on Kregen.

In my ugly mood I positively relished the confrontation.

Poor fool, I, Dray Prescot, Prince of Onkers!

Seven

Koter Rafik Avandil, lion-man

The suns sank finally as I rode from the little hamlet of Dinel.

In the last of the light drenching the western horizon with shards of blood and washes of viridian I rode, cursing that the farmers of Dinel had no better mount to offer than this stubby four-legged hirvel, kicking him in the ribs to make him go faster. As I cantered on through the rich farmlands under the night sky, I reflected that even if the farmerfolk of Dinel had no fine zorcas or fancy sleeths to offer me, their work demanding the use of krahniks and calsanys and the occasional quoffa and unggar, at least this hirvel, whose name was Whitefoot, made some claim to be a quality saddle animal. He belonged to the chief man of the hamlet and was superior to a preysany. I could have done worse. So I kicked my heels in and away we went.

She of the Veils, Kregen's fourth moon, rose to shed a fuzzy pink light, golden and glorious. I was in no mood to enjoy the wonder of the night sky of Kregen, even when two of the smaller moons went hurtling past close above. I had to reach the garrison at Arkadon, the marketplace for the surrounding area, rouse them out, select the best-mounted—for I doubted if they'd have any airboats—and then ride like the wind back to the Temple of Delia.

If everything went as ordered we'd catch the worshipers of the Black Feathers. I wondered what they did for a statue here. If Himet the Mak was the priest, as seemed probable, then one of his statues was unavailable.

An elongated black speck darted up against the golden disk of She of the Veils. The swirls of limpid color over the larger moons, evidences of some atmosphere there, confused sight for a moment. Then the golden gleam pulsed clear and I saw the hard black shape of an airboat lifting. It flicked past the limb of the moon and vanished among the stars.

I frowned.

I craned my head back to look along the way I had come. Roads in Vallia are usually atrocious, by reason of the superb canal system, but all country districts must have their roads for the quoffa and krahnik carts. Dust hung glittering in the light of the moon, raised by my hirvel's hooves. I could see no pursuit. Airboats taking off, at night, close to me, always make me reach a hand down to the hilt of my sword.

I nudged Whitefoot along and we trended down past the edge of a corn-field with the somber mass of a wood on the far side. I'd have to get off and walk to rest Whitefoot in a moment or two, for the hirvel, although look-ing nothing like a horse, with his round head and cup-shaped ears and twitching snout, has a performance not unlike a good quality waler.

Dark figures showed at the edge of the wood.

Instantly I slowed the hirvel down. He had been pushed hard and now, at the time when I wished to walk him, he was faced with the imminent prospect of hard running.

The figures were mounted on zorcas. There was no mistaking those glo-rious close-coupled animals with their fire and spirit and energy. So even if Whitefoot had been fresh and in tip-top condition, the zorcas would have overtaken him as a cheetah overtakes a deer.

"By Zair!" I said to myself. "Phu-si-Yantong, a week's wages against a sucked orange!"

I kept on. There are tricks and stratagems in encounters like this.

We met as the dusty roadway curved up at the end of the cornfield to give way to a field of gregarians. I came over the slight ridge past a tum-bledown fence and the zorcamen spurred out to stop me, very fierce, the moonlight glistening on their blades.

They wore the black and leather, and there were black feathers in their helmets. They were Rapas. The vulturine-headed diffs leered on me, com-pletely confident. Mercenaries, like those apim mercenaries at the Temple of Delia, these Rapas with their predatory beaked faces were masichieri, without a doubt. I was absolutely convinced that they had been sent against me by Phu-si-Yantong after his apparition had spied on me. Now this puzzled me, before I reasoned that the Rapas would almost certainly have orders to take me alive.

I knew from an overheard conversation that the wizard with his mania-cal and ludicrous ambitions wished to rule all Vallia through me acting as his puppet. Well, he might try. The effect of this was that I knew he had given orders that I was not to be assassinated, not to be slain.

I spurred forward, yelling, whirling the bamboo stick about my head.

A good rousing charge might carry me through, and I might knock one or two over and leave perhaps three to deal with.

They opened out, very prettily. The light grew as the Maiden with the Many Smiles rose over the horizon. Now there was no escape in the shadows.

The first blows struck down, the thraxters held so the flat of the blades smashed in at me. The bamboo stick could parry that kind of blow without being cut through, or not, given the nature of that stick.

I stuck the end of the bamboo into a beak, heard the Rapa shrill his agony. I swirled around, chunked the stick into the guts of a second, ducked as the swish of a blade passed close over my bare head. The hirvel nudged up into the forequarters of a zorca and the rider swung back, for a moment off balance. Before he could recover my left hand gripped his arm and pulled and he came out of the saddle in a gyrating heap of black feathers and black cloak. He fell under the hooves.

From nowhere a parrying-stick slashed at my shoulder. The jolt numbed my left arm. I kicked Whitefoot and he blundered ahead. Swords and parrying-sticks laced about me and I knew I'd have to unlimber the stick when a magnificent bellow roared out over our heads.

"Hold, you cramphs! Take on a man with a sword, you moldy villains!"

A glimpse I caught, a fragmentary glimpse of a man riding a zorca charging into the midst of the Rapas. He wore metal armor and a metal helmet, all burnished bright as gold in the radiance of the moons. He swung a thick straight sword, a clanxer of Vallia, and he cut the first Rapa down in a smother of blood.

The Rapa nearest me let go of Whitefoot's bridle and swung his mount away. He babbled something about: "You are not supposed—" And the clanxer curved down and went chunk into the leather armor over his shoulder. The man—he was a numim with golden fur under the armor and a bright golden mane—bellowed, "I'm not supposed to beat off foot-pads, is that it, you tapo! I'll have your tripes, every last one!"

I slashed the bamboo, and a Rapa collapsed over his zorca.

The numim, his lion-face snarling and his whiskers bristling, smashed his sword down onto the leather helmet of another Rapa. The vulturine-headed diffs had had enough. They reined away and set spurs to their mounts and galloped off. Two rode as though drunk, just managing to cling to their seats and rolling in their saddles.

The numim glared after them, golden, glorious, swearing that, by Vox! they were a poxy lot of scum.

"I must thank you," I began, in the proper form.

He flicked blood drops from his sword.

"Think nothing of it, my man! A wayfarer is entitled to the protection of a koter of Vallia."

He used the word *koter* in its meaning of gentleman, rather than of mister.

He reached out and grasped the reins of a zorca from which a dead Rapa hung tangled in the stirrups.

"Llahal and Lahal," I said in one of the prescribed forms for making pappattu, the first Llahal with that strong Welsh double-L sound, used in greeting strangers, the second with the softer single L, used for greeting friends. "I am Nath the Gnat." I said this promptly, almost without thought. My cover as a poor old wandering laborer seemed valuable enough to maintain for the moment.

"Llahal and Lahal. I am Koter Rafik Avandil." He appended no further information, but I did not mistake his deliberate use of the title. For a poor laborer koter was a gentlemanly rank that should impress.

Moving slowly yet with sureness I dismounted from Whitefoot. The hirvel had served as well as he was able, not unlike a nightmare version of a llama, with that tall round neck and shaggy body. I took up the reins of the only other zorca left by the Rapas. Koter Rafik looked on. If he wished to claim both animals as his own he would have a fight on his hands. But he offered no comment.

Numims are loud and boisterous, with their golden fur and golden manes and fierce bristly mustaches. Lion-folk are numims, and the lion-maidens are glorious under the rays of the suns. They are also extraordinarily seductive under the moons, or so I am told.

I mounted up with a sack and my bamboo stick. I took up the reins. "I am for Arkadon, Koter Avandil. I am in a hurry. I give you my thanks again for your assistance." He was not to know that I'd been in no real danger. If the Rapa masichieri had turned nasty and attempted to use the edges of their swords I'd have been forced to unlimber the bamboo stick and settle their business. But he had come charging in like a knight errant and so deserved his due of praise and thanks. "I ride fast, Koter, so will bid you Remberee. May Opaz the All-Glorious have you in his keeping."

"Eh?" he said, a little put out. Then, with a real numim bellow, "Oh, yes! By Vox! I don't hold with religion! A man's right arm and his sword, they are the gods of Vallia."

He wore a rapier and a dagger, I noticed, but the clanxer, the cutlass-like weapon of Vallia that is so often derided, had proved a good choice against the thraxters of the Rapas.

I set spurs to the zorca and took off. He followed, keeping pace, but made no attempt to engage in conversation which was, in any event, not too easy as we galloped along the dusty road.

There was an odd, eerie sensation about that wild nighttime ride across Vallia under the moons of Kregen. Only the sounds of the zorcas' hooves and the wind in our ears and the thumping feel of our onward passage kept us in touch with reality. With some thankfulness I saw the sharp-cut outlines of the fortress of Arkadon rising up against the star glitter, and soon made out the circuit of the walls and a few scattered lights from tower and window within.

We made enough hullabaloo at the arched gate to arouse the sleepy sentry. My Delia's Delphond is a quiet, lazy place, but any town near the coast must needs stand a watch. This is one of the ways of Kregen that can never be forgotten, if you wish to keep your head on your shoulders or your wrists and ankles free of chains. The slavers and the aragorn prowl many lands and seek to snatch away slaves where they can. Even here, in civilized Vallia, in sweet Delphond, the slavers sought to carry on their foul trade.

The response was quick enough to surprise me.

A yell and a curse from the ramparts, and then: "What's all the noise! Quiet down, you great villains, you'll wake the town!"

We managed to convince the sentry and the ob-deldar guard-commander he called that we were not slavers or bandits, those drikingers of the wild places unknown in Delphond. The ob-deldar was surprisingly suspicious. My few experiences of Delphond had led me to believe the easygoing people would have welcomed a pack of rascally kataki slavers with a proffered flask of ale.

Rafik Avandil bellowed out in his numim way, quite out of patience.

"Open the gates, you onker! Jump to it! *Bratch!* Or I'll have your deldar rank torn off and burned!"

Bratch is not as ugly a word as the terrible *Grak!* shouted at slaves to make them work until they drop, but it is still a powerful word of command, implying move, jump or you know what will happen! The ob-deldar jumped.

The gates swung open, well-oiled and uncreaking, admitting us to the cobbled street.

"I need a bath and a meal and a bed," bellowed Rafik. "I'll stand the same for you, old man, and you will."

This was munificence.

"I thank you, Koter Avandil. But I think it best for me to finish what I must do. Perhaps—"

"Aye! That will serve admirably." He waved a violent hand at the guards sulkily trailing their spears back to the guardroom under the archway. "These southerners are a puny lot! By Vox! I'd smarten 'em up!" These sentiments appeared to put him in a better humor, for he finished in a roar: "We'll meet on the morrow at an inn that has some pretence to fashion. I'll see you at Larghos's Running Sleeth."

"Until tomorrow, Koter Avandil, at the Running Sleeth."

He cantered off and he began to sing, one of those rollicking numim songs that always bring back memories of Rees and Chido and wild days rioting as a Bladesman in Ruathytu. I took myself off to rout out men and mounts and weapons for the rest of my night's work.

I had to reveal my identity to the town governor before I got any sense out of him, sleepy-eyed in his night attire, tousled of hair, roused from bed. He held the title of Rango and was your usual plump, easygoing, smiling, lazy Delphondian. But I impressed on him, this Rango Insur na Arkadon, the importance and the urgency of the night's business, and soon thereafter I rode out on a fresh zorca at the head of all the zorcamen he could spare, a miserable thirty of them, all sleepy-eyed and cursing away and rolling about in their saddles trying to ride off the fumes of the evening's wine.

She of the Veils vanished beyond the horizon and the Maiden with the Many Smiles would follow and then the suns would rise and a new day would dawn over Kregen. By that time we reached the Temple of Delia. Harshly I ordered the party to dismount and giving them no time to rest their aching backsides gave instructions in a cutting voice to their hikdar and the deldars to spread out and surround the central roofed area, which gleamed in the first chinks of morning light, ominously silent.

Birds were chirping merrily away in the trees, and the dew sparkled everywhere, fresh and sweet. The air tasted like the best Jholaix. But, I, Dray Prescot, took no comfort from all that beauty.

We crept in, and I held a rapier borrowed from Rango Insur, and we stole between the pillars ready to leap upon the congregation engaged in their blasphemous rites to the Black Feathers of the Great Chyyan.

I knew, I supposed, when I heard the birds singing.

We burst in, and the place was empty. We scoured all the tumbled ruins, peering and prying, prodding with our swords. Nothing. Not a single thing gave any evidence of a soul having been there for a thousand years.

"It seems, Prince, we have had a wasted ride."

The hikdar spoke a little sourly. His head was still ringing, I judged, from the party of the previous evening.

"The birds have flown, hikdar. I'll grant you that. But as to a wasted ride, I think you'll eat a better breakfast this morning than you would otherwise have done."

He made a face, but bellowed out, "Too right, Prince!"

It was so, of course.

There was nothing here. I had failed in this night's business. Then I walked quietly around to that crumbled corner of masonry and bent among the dew-bright ferns. The hikdar stared at me curiously, hands on the hilts of his weapons, his booted feet thrust wide. I straightened up. In my hand I held the scrap of rusty black feather.

"Not altogether wasted for me, hikdar, either."

Then we mounted up and I shook the reins and turned my zorca's head for Arkadon and the Running Sleeth and this Rafik.

Eight

A disrobing at the Running Sleeth

Sleep would have to take its turn. I'd been up all night haring about Delphond. If I bothered to ask myself why I should care tuppence about this Koter Rafik Avandil, I suppose, then, I would have answered that the fellow had conceived he was saving my life. And a lone koter against a rascally gang of Rapa masichieri demanded a high brand of courage. So I banished the idea of sleep and rode up to the inn run by Larghos, the inn with the revolting name of the Running Sleeth.

One positive thought I had. I would question Rafik about the airboat that had taken off just before the Rapas attacked. It seemed perfectly clear to me that Phu-si-Yantong had observed me in his trancelike state of lupu and had then whistled up his gang of bully boys to take me. The airboat had dropped them to lie in wait. Rafik might have seen something useful.

All the same, although I kept my usual careful lookout as I rode, I remained firmly convinced that the wizard's orders that I was not to be killed remained in force. His ludicrous desire to rule, physically and in person, vast expanses of Kregen and to set up puppets to carry out his orders told most eloquently that he must be mad. Mad in that special sense, of course, a kind of madness which afflicts people in certain ways. He was clever, brilliantly clever, and fiendishly ruthless, as I knew. He was an opponent to reckon with. Apart from anything else, his sorcerous skills gave him an advantage almost impossible to conceive of on this Earth. I must look to my own defenses within the mystic realms, that was for sure, and get Khe-Hi-Bjanching to earn his keep, although that was hardly fair. Khe-Hi had done wonders. His own powers had grown over the years. He would, if he lived, prove a most potent ally to me and adversary to Phu-si-Yantong.

Thus thinking, I dismounted from the zorca and tied him to the hitching rail. Pulling my tattered brown cloak around my shoulders and with a touch of the fingertips to the bamboo stick, I went into the Running Sleeth.

The brightly painted wooden sign over the lintel had been carved in the round and showed a sleeth running, the reptile's powerful back legs fully extended, its silly front claws curled, its dinosaur-head thrust out, the forked tongue—a strip formed of brass wires—twitching out most realistically. The craze among the young bloods of Hyrklana and Hamal for owning and racing sleeths had not yet extended to Vallia, I had thought. In this I was clearly wrong. The reptilian sleeth can run reasonably fast, not as fast as a zorca, but it is a damned uncomfortable ride, waddling along on those two massive hind legs, with its tail stuck out aft to balance itself.

So the name told me the kind of inn this would be.

The place had been tarted up. Smoky old beams had been painted over. Garish pictures filled every corner. Instead of quaffing ale from jacks or flagons, the customers were drinking parclear or sazz from thin glass goblets. The smells of cooking told me that the over-refined food served here would be all fashionable rubbish, not fit to last half a bur in a man's stomach. Still, it takes all kinds to make a world.

Small round tables on spindly legs, elegant chairs with needlepoint covers, flowers in pots of chunky ceramic—well, flowers are a boon to tired eyes—all gave the impression that this Larghos who owned the place must be a man of taste, well able to satisfy his provincial clientele that they were being entertained in the best fashion of the capital.

Mind you, there is nothing wrong with sazz or parclear or elegant chairs and furnishings. It is when these appurtenances to gracious living are pushed blatantly forward as an end in themselves, catering for empty-headed gadflies, that the ordinary man must recoil. I say must. Some do not see things in this light, and as I went in and sat down in a chair with my back to a wall facing the door—an instinctive action, this, done without thought—I was prepared to let any man enjoy whatsoever he wished within reason. So I scanned the people there and then prepared to ignore them. Farmers, stockholders, breeders, they were unlikely to be found here. Here in the Running Sleeth would be found those men's sons, eating up the family wealth. One or two soldiers of the garrison who fancied themselves men of culture, an artist and poet or two, if they had little talent but large incomes, light ladies and fashionable damsels, the would-be cultured layer of provincial life would come here to ape the ways they imagined to go on in Vondium.

And then, well, I admit it fully and freely, I could not find it in my heart to blame Larghos, the owner and landlord. After all, into this place of conscious refinement and culture stumbles an unshaven common fellow, a wandering laborer, with a raggedy old brown blanket cast over his shoulders and a mop of untamed hair, and puts his odiferous sack on the beautiful embroidered tablecloth and sticks his naked feet out over the charming rugs woven in imitation of Walfarg Weave. Well!

Larghos, slender, oily, charming, with wavy hair, trotted over and his face showed such outraged fury that I almost laughed. I couldn't see what was setting him going.

"Out, fellow! What do you think you're at! Schtump!"

"I only wanted—" I began, beginning to understand.

"You'll have a broomstick over your head! Schtump!"

I made a solemn promise to myself. I would not allow myself to become angry. No. No, this Larghos was right. I had no business bringing my old blanket cloak and my sack into this temple to culture and gracious living.

I sighed. "Is Koter Rafik Avandil here? I am supposed to meet him."

"He is gone out! Paid his bill and gone. Now you go!" Then he lifted his voice and shouted squeakily, "Nath! Cochu! Come running and throw this fellow out, and his verminous sack with him!"

I stood up.

"Thank you for your hospitality, dom, I'm going."

I hefted the sack and put out my hand for the bamboo stick which I'd placed on the table.

Now there are some men who cannot let well alone. Larghos stepped back, his face red, breathing heavily, scandalized at my intrusion into his establishment that had such a good name, but prepared to let me go without further ado. Not so the idler at the adjoining table who had watched all with a bright, birdlike gaze.

He was young, full-fleshed, bright of eye and erect of carriage, and yet about him there were plain to see the old familiar hateful signs of corrupt authority.

"Let Nath and Cochu give him a beating before you let him go, Larghos. The rast deserves a lesson, forcing his filthy self in here among decent people."

Before I could stop myself, I'd said, "I'm not filthy, dom."

He levered himself up from the chair. He wore foppish clothes, not of decent Vallian buff, but of a mixture of bright colors among which the black and white predominated. His rapier was overlong and the hilt was ornately set with jewels. Whoever he was, he was not a citizen of Arkadon.

Larghos began to wring his hands.

"Please, jen, my men will throw him out without fuss—"

"Silence, cramph!" This young lord—for Larghos called him *jen*, which is the Vallian form of addressing a lord—pushed himself up from the table. I saw by the glasses and bottles on the table that he had been drinking wine this early in the morning. So he had that problem as well.

His full-fleshed face flushed with blood. A vein beat in his forehead. His two companions at the table with him rocked back in their elegant chairs, thrusting out their boots, and egged him on with comments that suggested a little workout would do him good and a thrashing would do me good.

Larghos was wringing his hands. I could guess in his mind's eye he saw spindly-legged chairs and tables smashing into costly ruin all over his inn.

There would be no profit in my telling this young bully that I was the Prince Majister of Vallia, for he was a racter and would joy in having the excuse to get his rapier between my ribs, claiming afterward that this filthy tramp could not possibly have been the Prince Majister. How was a loyal jen supposed to know that?

Nath and Cochu appeared, beefy apims in blue-striped aprons, bare-armed. Larghos started to say something and the young lord waved him down. "I shall deal with the cramph myself. I do not care for his manners. You, rast!" he shouted at me. "I shall teach you manners!"

With that, confident in his own limber strength against this bent-over fellow in his brown blanket cloak, he took a couple of dancing steps forward and struck out, with more power than skill. I slid the blow and stepped away from the table calmly. The bamboo stick was in my right hand, held by the end, the thick, ridged end.

The young coxcomb went mad with fury. He shook with rage. "Do you see that!" he yelled. "The calsany! He threatens me with his stick! A filthy tapo daring to lift a stick against me, against the Trylon of Tremi! I'll prick a little blood from his mangy hide!" With that he ripped out his rapier and flung himself into a fighting crouch.

I sighed again, this time with real regret.

He lunged for me. I used the old bamboo stick to parry him off. I judged him to be reasonably skilled with the rapier, well able to take care of himself in an inn fracas, swishing and swashing; as to his caliber against real opposition, I was still unsure.

When he couldn't quite get his rapier to cut me up, as he expected to do just as he expected the twin suns to rise each day, he grew even more angry. His face was blotched. His eyes glared. His lips twisted with rage and frustration.

His cronies at the table, laughing and hawking, did not help him with their crude advice and mocking injunctions to spit the old fellow and have done.

Here in my Delia's Delphond, I knew, a murder would merit the strictest investigation. Delphond was civilized.

He blundered toward me and caught his foot in one of the elegant chairs and sprawled forward. His left hand raked up instinctively. He caught the bamboo stick. His face went mean.

"I've got you now, you cramph!"

He tried to wrench the stick aside and so slice me down the face, as a nice preliminary to what he intended to do to my carcass.

He twisted the bamboo, hauling back.

He was an onker, right enough. He twisted the bamboo. I felt the click and the sweet sliding of oiled metal. He staggered back clasping the hollow bamboo. All the people watching gasped, as this foolish young trylon fell back, pulling the bamboo free of the blade.

In my right fist I held the ridged wooden hilt. Two feet of oiled steel blade glimmered in the lights from the windows. That blade had been forged by Naghan the Gnat in the armory of Esser Rarioch. I had designed it with Naghan, and we had laughed as we'd mounted its slender length into the bamboo hilt, covering the murderous brand with the rest of the hollow bamboo. I keep calling this wood bamboo; it is not real bamboo. It is of a deep orange luster, ridged, and grows in the marshes. Kregans call it pipewood, for it is often used for tubing work in plumbing and the like.

The blade glistened. The Trylon of Tremi stared and his face assumed a caricature of enraged fury, black with passion.

"You murderous rast! Now I'll spit you clean through your filthy guts!"

And he set to, swirling his blade, thrusting and slashing like one demented.

His companions stumbled up from the table, their chairs going over with a smash. They ripped their own weapons free.

One came in from one side, the second from the other.

If I was in for a little exercise then I'd make it reasonably entertaining.

As I fought, foining off the two from the sides and beginning an amusing disrobing of the trylon, I reflected that this Rafik Avandil possessed a rare sense of humor. He had arranged to meet me here in this pseudo-cultural Running Sleeth knowing damn well what would follow. So I felt a double amusement as I cut the laces of the trylon's fancy tunic and so stripped his clothes from him, garment by garment. When his two cronies pressed too close one was sent staggering and yelling away with a slit ear and the other with a punctured right forearm. The good old over and under stop-thrust worked beautifully.

This idiot trylon's overlong rapier most often pointed at the ceiling or the floor, or angled toward one of the garish pictures along the walls, more often than it aimed at my guts. I played him long enough to cut away his clothes down to his breechclout—bright pink, would you believe?—and then I had had enough.

Disgust filled me.

This kind of petty mindless brawl leaves a foul taste in a man's mouth. This kind of bestiality is for the morons of the world, for the morons of two worlds.

Once they had seen how they thought the fight would now go, the rest of the patrons began to laugh. In their stupid heartless way they laughed at the Trylon of Tremi. He, poor fool, gagged on his own spit. His face was now whey-colored, gray and green, his eyes staring, his mouth slobbering. His beautiful pink breechclout with the embroidered chavonths and zhantils looked pathetic. It had blue lace edging. I stripped a little away and then he jumped at the wrong moment and the blade nicked his flesh in a tender spot.

He screamed.

So, wishing to have done, I snaked his blade away and stepped in. I took him by the throat with my left hand. I choked him only a little.

"The next time you seek to bully and thrash a defenseless old man, think, rast. Think, you brainless cramph, and remember this day."

Then I turned him around and gave him a hard toe up the backside and so kicked him staggering across the floor.

His cronies stood back, furious but cowed, unwilling to reopen the fray.

Blood had been drawn from both of them, splattering their finery and the black and white favors, but they had come out of this less injured than their lord. His hurts did not show on his skin. His hurts would not mend as fast as the scratches they had suffered.

The contrast between the conduct of this spoiled lordly brat and that of Rafik toward an old man was to me at the time most edifying. I felt an amusement toward Rafik, engendered as much by his trick as by the circumstances of his supposed rescue.

Larghos was visibly recovering his composure, seeing that no real damage had been done to his establishment. He began to flutter about. So I wiped my blade tip on the corner of my old brown cloak, picked up my sack, cast a last look upon the assembled gaping patrons—remembering to bend over as I did so—and bid them all a pleasant Remberee.

Then I stepped out of the Running Sleeth into the clean air and luminous suns-shine of Kregen.

Nine

Nath the Gnat misses the Princess Majestrix

Delphond is not as well served by the intricate canal system of Vallia as it might be, especially as it is an imperial province, descending in the imperial female line. This has served in the past as a distinct advantage and goes some way to explaining the surprising remoteness of much of the province, situated as it is relatively close to the capital. This fact, too, I suppose, does explain, as Delia maintains, why so many tides of conquest in the troubled history of Vallia have passed Delphond by with little destruction.

The zorca ambled along the dusty road, kicking the thick white powder into a floating trail, and I jogged along, sunk in thought, yet still keeping that old sailor-man's weather eye open. The oiled steel blade was snicked back into its bamboo scabbard and now looked like any wandering laborer's stick.

Making no attempt to discover the whereabouts of Rafik, I had simply ridden out of Arkadon. I could feel the muzziness clouding my head a trifle and a light-heaviness about my limbs; but, if necessary, I could go on swashing and fighting and drinking for another night or two without sleep yet. It is a knack. The rendezvous with Delia drew me on. The moment I reached Deliasmot where a canal trunk system terminated I would transfer to a narrow boat and be rapidly hauled all the way in first-class comfort.

If Rafik was headed this way we would meet. I fancied I'd not seen the last of that golden numim with the sense of humor.

The white road wound between cornfields, with orchards all green and shining beyond, rising and falling over the gentle countryside. The road remained deserted until a cloud of dust heralded a considerable party of country folk taking their produce into Arkadon. I was surprised. The quoffa carts trundled along. Men thwacked on krahniks loaded with bales and baskets. The calsanys trotted along in their strings of patient bearing. Women and children perched on the carts or walked together in the inter-vals. The men marched, I could swear, almost in the form of a guard, with a scouting party ahead riding preysanys, superior forms of calsanys, and carrying not only their sticks but spears and long-knives.

They gave me highly suspicious looks. But I was alone, and so we exchanged Llahals and parted, and I spat dust until free of their trail.

Logic told me that I did, indeed, look highly suspicious.

Here I was, a raggedy old laborer with a tattered brown blanket cloak, bareheaded and barefoot, riding a well-groomed and, if not first water, then reasonably high-quality zorca. Yes. Logic told me the country peo-ple might well have thought it their business to stop me and question me. There would be a reward for the return of the zorca to its owner. They were not to know the Rapa masichieri lay with his blood spilling out into the Kregan dirt.

But they had not stopped me. If anything, they had displayed so extreme a caution that it could be construed as fear.

And this, in Sweet Delphond, Delphond the Blessed, the Garden of Vallia!

The other interesting fact I had observed was simply that these country folk appeared to have shed their fat and lazy indifference. The men—abruptly, it seemed to me—presented an altogether new and different aspect. They had held their spears and long-knives with the firm determi-nation of men intending to fight if they had to. This was remarkably unlike the usual attitudes I had encountered in Delphond.

Ahead along the road the lath and plaster walls of a country inn came in sight, the red tile roofs shallowly peaked, the twisted chimneys lifting in welcome. No smoke rose from the chimneys. A window pane caught the red light of Zim and flashed. I perked up. Here was where I would repair the deficiencies missing breakfast was causing my stomach.

I rode up, feeling cheerful, and the damned place was empty, deserted, with windows smashed and doors hanging loose and weeds choking the neat fenced gardens. I cursed. Just my luck to encounter a wayside inn that was derelict.

"By Vox!" I said, aloud, thoroughly miffed. "By the disgusting bloated swag belly of Makki-Grodno! My throat is like the Ocher Limits."

A voice spoke from the corner of the inn and I was off the zorca and under the eaves before the last words were uttered.

'Temper, temper!" said this light voice. "If you would accept a Llahal and a drink of wine from a stranger, they are here for the asking."

Cautiously, the hilt of bamboo in my right hand and the rest of the stick in my left, ready for emergencies, I peered around the corner. A man sat there on a pile of old sacks holding out a leather wine bottle. The spout was formed of balass, black and shining, stoppered with silver-wound ivory.

"Wine, dom," said this young fellow, smiling.

"It is too early for wine," I said, somewhat surlily. "But Llahal, I thank you and I will take a sip."

I took the bottle. It was deliciously cool. I moistened my mouth—a light white Yellow Unction; so this fellow had a few silver coins to rattle in his pouch—and then took two measured swallows. I looked hard at this purveyor of wine. Young, in that way the Kregans, with their better than two-hundred-year life span look young, he had a peaked, cheerful face, with merry eyes and a droll mouth. He was dressed in a simple open-necked buff tunic and decent breeches. His boots were not black, being of a tan color, well-splashed with the white dust of the road. He had a scrip and a staff, and at his belt hung a strong lesten-hide satchel.

I handed the wine bottle back. "My thanks, dom."

"Oh, I am Covell. Men call me Covell of the Golden Tongue."

"I have heard of you," I said, pleased. "All Vondium rings with praises for your latest—'Time Lost is Time Gained Hereafter,' I believe. A fine poem."

He laughed easily and drank wine himself, moderately.

This Covell was by way of being a poet. I saw that he favored the unconventional life, in order to gain the experiences he distilled into his verses. Some of the older and sterner critics of Vallia condemned his work as trifling, but they were a trifle ossified, or so his supporters said.

"What brings you here? Is Vondium too hot for you again?"

"You know me then? Yes, a tavern brawl and an onker with a knife in his guts; he did not die. But the guards thought to lay me by the heels and question me, and I do not fancy mewing up. So I took to my travels again."

"Who does? I am Nath the Gnat and—"

"And," he said easily, laughing, standing up, "and you are no laborer or farmworker, not even a cattleman. Whoever you are, Gnat is not the appellation for you, dom."

I remembered to bend over at that, whereat he laughed again.

"I have my hirvel tethered in the shade. Should we ride together? I heard uncommon evil stories of Blessed Delphond in these latter days."

I fired up at this. If my Delia did not know what was going on in her estates, then it behooved me to find out.

"Right willingly, Covell. But I am a laborer. That is true."

I meant I labored for a living, not that I was a laborer who dug ditches or built walls. I fancied this Covell of the Golden Tongue understood.

"There are fields of labor that demand other skills than brawny shoulders." He picked up his satchel. "I labor with words, and damned intractable beasts they can be, as well as singing with golden wonder. Why I do so is beyond my limited understanding."

He mounted up on his hirvel. The animal was a fine beast, superior to Whitefoot, whom I had slapped on the rump and sent off, knowing he would find his own way back to his owner. Covell eyed the zorca.

"You are well mounted for a laboring man, Nath the Gnat."

"The zorca came to me by way of a bequest from a dead man."

He laughed again at this and shook his reins; together we rode gently along the dusty white road. He carried a long-knife like Oby's and, as far as I could see, no other weapon on his person, although a short blade mounted on a shaft some six feet in length was stuck down into a boot on his stirrup. His scrip and staff were slung onto the hindquarters of the hirvel, and rode a trifle awkwardly.

So we rode along talking. It is not my intention to regale you with all we spoke of, but you may be very sure I soaked up all the information he gave, and as it bears on this my narrative I will tell you, all in due time.

Covell mentioned the concern felt in Vondium over the continual unrest in the northeast of Vallia. Up there the folk were of altogether a more down-to-earth character, blunt, hardheaded, out for red gold and self-determination.

Using some little skill I introduced a query about black feathers into our talk.

He replied as an educated man interested in literature would reply, quoting *The Black Feathers of Ulbereth the Dark Reiver*, giving a stanza or two of that old epic fashioned from the legends of olden time. But that is another story.

I judged that he did not dissemble and had not encountered the Black Feathers of the Great Chyyan. But I would not completely trust anyone in this thing.

So, later, I mentioned the craze for flying fluttrells in Vondium, and suggested that flying a chyyan might be interesting. Whereat he said: "I have flown a fluttrell owned by a comrade, Nath ti Havring—and an experience it was, too!—but I am told by those who know about these things that chyyans are unridable. Surely, Nath the Gnat, it is zhyans you mean?"

"Perhaps it is," I said. "They are all foreign, out of Hamal. Give me a zorca."

"Aye. But one day these great soldiers of ours will go up against Hamal, and we poets will be forced to sing their praises. I prefer to tune my songs to sweeter themes."

"Amen to that."

I pressed him to recite a line or two of his own, and nothing loath, for he loved an audience, he declaimed his "Ode to Dawning," in which the red sun Zim and the green sun Genodras are apostrophized as mere balls of colored fire, without sentience, marvels of nature, bringing light to all men over the whole of Kregen. He added, when he had finished, that translating Zim to Far and Genodras to Havil ruined the feel of the piece. "I have a large contempt for religiosity in pious hypocrites. Opaz is well enough, I suppose, given as a sop. But a man's heart is his true religion."

I made no direct answer. Rafik trusted in a right arm and a sword, and Covell in a man's heart. What, then, did I trust in? Anything at all apart from my Delia and the Krozairs of Zy?

When I had first returned to Kregen after that hideous expanse of twenty-one years on Earth I had fancied Kregen had not changed. The more I learned the more I discovered that this marvelous world had changed, was changing and was like to change even faster as the days wore on.

When Covell spoke of the emperor he simply laughed and made witty jokes. He did say that the taverns reeked with plots, and then contemptuously dismissed them as wine-soaked dreams. "Trouble is coming to Vallia, Nath the Gnat, and all men can see that plain. There is the northeast. There are the racters. There are other parties and plots. I want none of them! By Vox! I am a poet and as a poet will I live and die a happy man. All else is illusion."

"You do not share the fear of the locals to travel alone?"

"Do you?"

"Ah, well, I was not fully aware of the situation, being a simple wandering laborer. If there is no work here by reason of the troubles—"

"There are no troubles in Delphond, at least not yet. That is why I chose to travel here. But the lonely traveler is not as safe as he once was and isolated houses, like the inn where we met, are no longer little fortresses of peace. The damned aragorn prowl all the land—aye, and the racters aid and abet them. That is where their money comes from."

"You do not like the racters?"

"I dislike all political parties. I am an individual."

"The people take precautions against drikinger."

"Yes, but Delphond is not an easy province for bandits."

"So it is the slavers they fear?"

"If the emperor and the Presidio do not act soon no one will be safe. Vallia is like to be torn asunder."

Deliasmot was its usual charming, smiling self, a typically beautiful, easygoing, life-loving Delphondian town. Yet even here the new edginess was apparent, the more anxious demeanor, the stricter controls at the gates. Here Covell of the Golden Tongue and I parted, for he was contracted to give a recitation of his poetry, a declamation he called it, and I was for the canal and for pressing on to Drakanium where I would meet Delia.

We made our Remberees and I expressed my disappointment at missing his declamation, for he was truly a golden voice, and then I hurried to the canal to make travel arrangements. The zorca ensured a ticket in a narrow boat. I found a quiet seat where I might watch the passing banks, sliding along all green and golden under the suns, and I dozed and took my meals with the best of them and kept to myself, tolerated here in Delphond, and so came at last gliding with the canalfolk all hauling lustily away under the stone vaulted archways of Drakanium's watergate.

As a city, Drakanium was simply a larger edition of a Delphondian town, clean, neat, sparkling, bowered in vegetation, filled with the prosperous bustle of a contented folk—at least it had been. The city was just as clean and neat and the flowers bloomed magnificently and the fountains played. But the people hurried about their tasks with worried looks. A regiment of totrixmen were exercising on the parade ground and I judged by their antics they were newly formed. The Jiktar was near to apoplexy as he bellowed orders, and the awkward six-legged totrixes tangled up and squealed and the lances all slanted at odd angles. But they flew nice banners and flags.

I had agreed to meet Delia at the best inn, instead of her villa here, to keep my cover. A hostler took in my message, giving me a sharp look as he went in through the lenken door under the glowing tiles, where the moon-blooms clustered thickly. Bees droned and the shadows lay across the stone-flagged court. I sat down on a bench and a serving wench brought out a flagon of best Delphondian ale. I quaffed it gratefully.

To these people I was a mere wanderer, a tramp, and if the Princess Majestrix wished to speak with me she would, and that was her business, and if she did not, then I would be told and seen off the premises. They are civilized in Delphond.

The hostler came back. He wore a frown.

"I gave your message to the landlord, dom. He says to tell you the Princess Majestrix is not here."

"When is she expected? Maybe I am early."

"Oh, she's been here. You were expected." He did not add that he couldn't for the life of him understand why a great and glorious princess should worry her beautiful head over a dingy tramp. He went on, almost casually, imparting his news: "She has had to return posthaste to Vondium."

I stood up.

"Did she say why?"

He took a step back. His coarse sacking apron rustled as he switched his arms out. "No. She did not say. Just that she had to go to Vondium on a matter of extreme urgency. A courier came in an airboat. From the emperor, it was said. The princess went with him and her suite with her." He rolled his eyes with the memory of a great dread removed. "She had a ghastly creature with her, a most bloodthirsty monster, all claws and fangs and hair, but they all went in the airboat to Vondium."

That monster was Melow the Supple, and I felt relief.

Relief that Delia was safe. But what could have caused her to dash back to Vondium? What disaster had struck now?

Ten

Of an independent girl of Vallia

The airboat flew swiftly toward Vondium.

Once I had received Delia's message I had wasted no time. A quick trip to our villa in Drakanium, a change of clothes, with a flustered majordomo and flunkies running in circles, a hamper of food and drink, weapons, money, and I was away in one of the small fliers we kept at the villa, as we tried to keep a voller or two at all our places.

I did not think my cover had been broken, but then, I didn't give a damn if it had. What had happened in Vondium to drag Delia away? Was the emperor dead? But everyone would have known—no. No, perhaps not. It paid very often to keep news of the deaths of kings and emperors secret for as long as possible.

The voller was a fleet craft, for its stabling at the villa envisaged its emergency use, and we made a good thirteen and a half to fourteen dbs.[*]

At this headlong speed I would reach Vondium in a couple of hours. So, composing myself as best I could, I sat down and raided the hamper. Of the details of that meal I remain vague, save that I ate and drank and looked continually ahead for the fantastic sight of Vondium, the capital city of the Empire of Vallia, to rear over the distant horizon.

Once again I was entering Vondium at breakneck speed and with a single definite goal in mind. I flashed over the broad expanse of pastureland and agricultural activity surrounding the city. The waters of She of the Fecundity, the Great River of Vallia, sparkled ahead. There were the Hills,

---

[*] dbs. Dwaburs per bur. A dwabur is five miles. A bur is forty minutes.

spread out and bowered in greenery, with the flash and gleam of white villas and red roofs. There were the sky-spanning aqueducts. There the grim gray walls and the higher battlements in gleaming yellow and sapphire, the flagstaffs, the conical tower roofs, the long, incredibly thin extensions of archways beneath the suns. Other fliers circled in landing and ascending patterns. The broad swaths of the major canals and ornate boulevards crisscrossed the city, creating islands of stone or brick, the timber and stucco island given over to parks and preserves, islands covered with barracks and factories, islands for sport, islands for all the devoted pursuits that obsessed the citizens of Vondium.

Of it all I fastened my eager gaze on the enormous Palace of the Emperors.

Over wide colonnaded streets parallel to the canals we flew, this speedy little voller and I, seeing below the broad wharfside avenues thronged with busy people. Over a cluster of temples, built to foreign tolerated gods, over an arm of a canal leading directly to the Great River where shipbuilders worked on the skeletons of galleons of Vallia, bare and ribby in the light. On, and now I slanted down, aiming for the palace. The majestically architectured kyro before the main façade showed its usual hectic activity and few people bothered to look up at a single small airboat.

Chafferings in the marketplaces would not be interrupted for so small an event. But what events were taking place within the glowing walls of the Palace of the Emperors?

The instant I touched down on the landing platform above the small garden of the palace wing reserved for the Prince Majister, I leaped out. Delia's old apartments had been enlarged and improved and when we stayed in the capital we stayed in our own private wing of the palace. I raced inside, seeing servitors running. Delia and I kept no slaves; there were many thousands of slaves in Vondium, aye, and many in the great palace of the Emperors.

Normally we kept only a skeleton staff in our wing of the palace for, to be honest, we spent little time there. Now the place hummed with activity and very soon I had made my way, followed by various flunkies who conceived it their duty to run with me, just in case I might drop something, or require a service—Zair knows why servants will fuss so—through to our inner and truly private apartments. The Jiktar of the guard detail, a Pachak called Laka Pa-Re, bellowed his men to attention.

"The princess?" I asked, not stopping.

"In her apartments and all well, my prince, may Opaz shine the light of his countenance upon her." Then he added, quite outside the usual military formula: "By Papachak the All Powerful, my Prince, it is good to see you!"

"And to see you also, Laka Pa-Re."

His men bashed open the balass door smothered with the gold zhantils with diamond eyes, and I went hurrying through. Laka stood back, still remaining at attention, his tailhand upthrust with that wicked steel blade glistening. He had retained his Pachak name for he was a mercenary, a paktun—the silver mortil-head on its silken cord looped over the shoulder of his armor proved that—and perhaps a greater contrast could not be imagined than between his loyal service as a paktun and the thieving deviltry of those masichieri I had been stumbling over lately.

The tall balass doors closed and I looked down the carpeted corridor with the golden lamps and the ivory ornaments, the great Pandahem jars filled with flowers, the silver mirrors, and the doors at the far end opened and a trim figure clad in hunting leathers stepped through. At her heels a prowling, incredibly ferocious Manhound trotted, tail lashing, fanged jaws opened, saying in that growly, spitting, menacing way of jiklos: "... Deserves to be spanked, the hussy."

They saw me.

Delia simply flew at me, wrapping her arms about me, kissing me, laughing and sobbing, saying breathlessly, "I know, my heart! I know what you will say! But this cannot wait!"

I held her close, feeling her heart beating against mine, holding her, the dizzying scent of her in my nostrils, twining around me, making me wonder why I ever was fool enough to leave her. I forced myself to regain my senses. I took her by the shoulders and held her off, looking at her, at her face, her eyes, her mouth, her hair. "Delia! What cannot wait?"

"I am forbidden to tell you."

I felt outrage.

"Who can forbid the Princess Majestrix of Vallia? Your father—?"

"No." She looked gorgeously lovely, yet filled with a distress I could not hope to understand then.

"All I can say is that I love you, that I must go, that—by Vox!" she cried, which made me realize how serious a matter this really was. "By all that I hold dear I will tell you as much as I may—and more, I dare say, if you hold me so and look at me like that."

My ugly old face must have been a sight, by Zair!

"Well?"

She spoke more calmly. "I must hurry. You know I am of the Sisters of the Rose..."

"Yes." I began to have an inkling now.

"I dare not tell you, even though you mean all there is in the world to me. But, but, dear heart, you are a man."

"And you are a woman and, to pile the cliché upon the banal, I give thanks every day to Zair that it is so."

"Do not laugh at me, my darling! This is women's business. The Sisters of the Rose, we hold our secrets... well!" She flared up as her thoughts sought utterance. "Do I question you too closely about your precious Krozairs of Zy?"

I felt only a small shock.

"No, my love, you do not. For you know I am under vows."

"And may not a woman, even if she is your wife, also be under vows?"

Instantly I felt the biggest boor in two worlds. I felt an onker, a calsany. What right had I to pry into exactly those areas of my Delia's life that were, through other forces, denied her enquiry in mine?

I drew her to me and kissed her. The kiss was long and passionate and if she was in a hurry to be about this mysterious business of the Sisters of the Rose she was in no hurry to end the kiss.

At last I stepped back and released her.

"You have everything for the journey? Melow will go with you? Weapons, clothes, money, food, the fastest voller?"

"Yes, yes, my heart!" She laughed. "Do not take on so!"

"When you go venturing out into Kregen, my love, you must take all the protection you may."

"That is true. But the Sisters of the Rose take care of their own. We do a great deal of good, in a quiet way. We have opened two new hospitals for sick slaves in the past year. And when there is a war... well, you know."

Yes. I did know. The Sisters were invaluable. There were other feminine orders, of course, notably the Sisters of Samphron and the Order of Little Mothers and the like. Delia often abbreviated in the Kregen way, calling the Sisters of the Rose the SoR, as I abbreviated the Krozairs of Zy to Krzy. This was important, truly important.

So I contented myself with making sure she had everything I could think of—save myself—upon her journey. Melow would go, and a female Manhound, a jiklo, can rip up a wersting or a neemu and the chances of a strigicaw are not all that bright.

Melow the Supple jagged her fangs and said in her hissing voice, "Do not fret, Dray Prescot. The princess is a canny girl and knows her way about. I can but wish you had eased two more sets of twins into the world for me."

"Hush, Melow!" said Delia.

The Manhounds of Kregen are indeed a fearsome sight. Artificially bred to run on all fours like hunting cats, ferocious of aspect, deadly in killing skills, superbly muscled, they can strike terror into the stoutest heart. Yet this Melow the Supple, for whom I have a great fondness, savage and vicious as she was, was a kindhearted mother of twins. She was dressed in bright clothes, for she loved brilliance in dress, with neatly groomed hair and wearing sandals over those gut-ripping claws. I put out my hand and touched her cheek.

"Take care of her, Melow."

She grimaced and hissed, as much as to say what an onker I was and I ought to know better than even to mention so obvious a thing.

Then I said another stupid thing.

"Thelda?" I said to Delia.

Well Thelda, Seg's wife, had been companion to Delia in some fraught moments in our lives, and she always meant well, and she always said that she was Delia's best friend. I knew Thelda belonged to the Order of Sisters of Patience—I invariably found a high amusement at that particular trifle of appositeness—so I couldn't be surprised when Delia very calmly said, "This is a matter for the SoR, my love. Now you have delayed me long enough. Come on, Melow."

She kissed me again and I let her go reluctantly, saying, "But you haven't said when you'll be back."

"When you see me." Then she relented, and said, "I'll be as quick as I can, I promise."

I saw her to the voller. And it was no joke; she'd selected our fastest four-place craft. I saw the way she solemnly observed the fantamyrrh as she stepped aboard.

I stood back. The guards and the retainers stood in a ring, all looking up.

The voller sprang away, with Melow looking over the side like some frightful gargoyle, and rose up into the limpid air with the streaming mingled lights from the Suns of Scorpio lighting up her side and blazing like a beacon.

"Remberee, my love!"

"Remberee, my heart!"

And the flier spun up and away and soared over the glittering rooftops of Vondium.

Damned independent in their ways are the girls of Kregen.

But, then, that is just as it ought to be.

Eleven

We sing the songs of Kregen

"All praise to Papachak of the Tail!" said Laka Pa-Re, and he thumped his empty flagon back onto the stained sturmwood table with a crash. All around the low-ceiled room of the tavern men were drinking and shouting, a few were brawling, some were trying to play Jikalla and being continually interrupted. The clatter of dice sounded from the corner and on the opposite side a Pachak was tail-wrestling a comrade amid spilling wine bottles and toppling ale flagons.

This was the famous tavern The Savage Woflo, an example of the warped Kregan humor that either amuses or infuriates, for the woflo is a wee creature of extremely timid nature, overfond of cheese.

Among the tables ran remarkably pretty girls of various races carrying wide wooden trays stacked with foaming jugs or exotically shaped bottles. These serving wenches were, unfortunately, slaves. They were clad in transparent draperies, with tawdry bangles and beads, with colored feathers, all designed to enhance their natural beauties. Well, I suppose that in some cases they did. But generally cunning old Urnu the Flagon, landlord of The Savage Woflo, had an eye for female beauty and his wenches—I dislike the commonly used word *shif* for these serving girls for it indicates a contempt I do not feel—were every one carefully chosen at the auctions and paid for above the standard price.

Normally I avoided places like this and when in Vondium and in need of a quiet drink I would go down to Bargom's Rose of Valka by the Great Northern Cut. Bargom, a Valkan, did not employ slaves and aroused some bemused envy that he managed so well without their unwilling aid.

Now the Pachak paktun, Laka Pa-Re, yelling for more ale, handled these slave girls with a courtesy I fancied was not assumed for my benefit. This tavern, the famous Savage Woflo, was much patronized by the guardsmen. No female customers were allowed. Such a thing was still possible in Vondium. This was a male preserve and, I suppose, on Earth would have been choking with smoke as well as the fumes of alcohol.

"By Mother Zinzu the Blessed!" I said, lowering my flagon. "I needed that!"

Saying that little aphorism cheered me up, although Laka had never heard of Mother Zinzu the Blessed, the patron saint of the drinking classes of Sanurkazz.

"You do me great honor, my Prince, in drinking with—" he said, until I shushed him.

I wore simple buff tunic and breeches and swung a rapier, as we all did here, where brawls and good-humored swishings of blades were common occurrences. I wished to look inconspicuous. Laka also wore plain buff, out of uniform.

"If you must call me anything, let it not be prince," I said. "Rather, merely call me Nath and have done."

"Aye, my Pri— Nath!" he bellowed, and used that cunning tailhand to whip a fresh flagon from a passing girl's tray. She squeaked and laughed— all simulated, for that was how the customers liked to think these girls behaved—and ran on with slender flashing legs to fetch more ale. There were Fristle fifis, and sylvies, and shishis here, as well as other races of beautiful girls. There were no Rapa girls or Och maidens, but then there were few of their menfolk in the tavern either.

A parcel of Chuliks sat glowering at a table, steadily drinking. When the singing began the Chuliks would depart to find a place where a fighting man might drink without having to sing. That is the way of Chuliks.

I had come here because—and then to admit the true reason would be to betray more, perhaps, than I cared to. I knew that I would hear gossip here that might be overlooked in the echoing corridors of the palace. Also, I felt sure that one of the emperor's agents would be here listening. What he would report might not tally with what he heard.

For the emperor's position had been steadily eroded.

Covell of the Golden Tongue had said the tavern plots were all moonshine. Maybe they were. But I felt the need for a drink and a song in masculine company.

Most great nobles of Vallia kept up their villas in Vondium even if they only visited them once or twice a year, and their guards patronized establishments like this, so there were many varieties of uniform and colors among the civilian dress. The Vallian Air Service was notable by its absence. Also, Laka was one of the few high-ranking officers present. I noticed three other Jiktars and quite a few hikdars, but the majority of the drinking, gambling, shouting men were deldars and swods.

When I had quizzed the Pachak paktun as to why he had said he was pleased to see me, he had answered evasively, even defensively, but now he was thawing out and eventually he said: "It's like this, my Pri— Nath. I drew guard duty on the Prince Majister's wing of the palace. I do not grumble at that. But I see things. I hear things. There are men among the guards—aye! Men I have known! Men who speak behind their hands. They have been bought by gold."

"Who is doing the buying? And to what end?"

He took a swig and wiped his mouth. "For one, the Racter Party. Oh, yes, they have a hand in everything in Vallia. But why should Naghan Nadler, who has been a paktun for twenty seasons and will make ob-deldar soon, take gold?"

"Why?"

"Why, because they want to buy his sword! And others like him. There are plots against the emperor. Everyone knows that. A little gold spread around now will buy loyalty when the plots hatch. That is my opinion."

"And you have reported this?"

He opened and shut his lower left hand, and his right hand gripped and tugged at the pakmort around his neck on its silken cord. "I wanted to speak to you."

I was not sure if he had done right. But this was no time to suggest he might better have taken another course. What struck me, forcibly and with a chill of foreboding, was the frightening thought that whichever of the parties—or perhaps all of them—that were bribing guards to fight for them had reached the swods. A simple swod may well be a terrible fighting man, but it is the captains and generals who carry the say when bribery is in the wind. I felt pretty confident that Laka had not been approached because all men knew once a Pachak had given his nikobi to serve an employer his loyalty remained steadfast. But a swod in the ranks, being given gold, told to obey orders that would not come from his employer, this typified the destruction of values, the end of one way of life and, if a new began, a system barely nameable as life.

So, as you can see, I was in a highly wrought state.

Hadn't I suborned guardsmen before, to fight for me against their employer, and, by Vox, wouldn't I do so again? But at the least, no mere petty ambition had driven me, to topple a throne for the sake of the power.

So we drank and talked and I watched the clientele, seeing the many different patterns of banded sleeves, each set of colors denoting a man belonging to a noble house. Even among these soldiers and guardsmen the white and black favors were flaunted openly, along with the white and green of the panvals and other color combinations. A Pachak hikdar, squat, leather-faced, roaring his good humor and slopping ale, plunked himself down on the bench opposite Laka and bellowed a greeting.

When the confusion died down Laka introduced him as Nidar De-Fra, an old mercenary comrade newly arrived in Vondium with his master. This Nidar wore banded sleeves, for he was in uniform, the banded colors of unequal widths of blue and green and yellow, with two thin vertical stripes of white. It must not be taken that these color-banded sleeves of Vallia are like the tartans of the Scottish clans; but with their color-coding, once a man saw a combination of shapes and colors he would know it again and know the owner. This Pachak, Nidar De-Fra, had given his nikobi and his sword to Kwasim Barkwa, the Vad of Urn Stackwamor. He was in the capital because his master wished it. Anyway, as all men knew, the emperor was due to return from his journey around the far southwest. Here the Pachak laughed and said that the southwest was a joke and all men knew the future of Vallia lay with the northeast.

There is good comradeship among the Pachak mercenaries, and their intricate system of nikobi can sort out the rights and wrongs of employment and the puzzles of when a man may in honor fight a comrade under employment. Now these two talked of old days. I looked for a moment at Nidar. He did not wear the pakmort, but he was wholly convinced that northeast Vallia must demand self-determination and break away from the empire. This astounded me. I clamped my ugly old mouth shut and listened.

When Nadar's term of service with Kwasim Barkwa ended he might take employment with a noble of the south, and then he would be as vociferous that the empire should stay in one piece. A mercenary may not have to believe in his master's cause to fight for him, but the Pachaks are deadly serious when they hire out as paktuns, and give their loyalty.

A couple of brilliant Fristle fifis came out with streaming silks and started to dance; they were soon chased off and then the swods began to sing.

So, as you may imagine, I let all my problems slide away for a space and gave myself up to hoggish relaxation. There are many finer things in two worlds than sitting in a tavern singing with swods, and this is so. But all the same, when you are singing and roaring out the old songs, the world takes on a marvelously brighter hue.

My Delia had gone off and left me at home. The idea intrigued me. I felt no indignation. She was as entitled as I was to her own life. Our shared life was so intense and passionate that nothing could interfere. I was dragged away by a great ghostly representation of a Scorpion, blue and shining, whirling me away to some other part of Kregen to fight for the Star Lords, or hurling me back to Earth in despair. Delia had gone because her vows, vows like mine to the Krozairs of Zy, impelled her. I had discarded at once any notion of following her secretly. That would shame us both. Anyway, with Melow along, she should come to no harm. And she could handle weapons with the best of men. I knew that.

So I, Dray Prescot, left at home with the dishes, sang with swods in a tavern.

We sang the *Lay of Fanli the Fristle and Her Regiment of Admirers* and the *Lay of Faerly the Ponsho Farmer's Daughter* and *Tyr Korgan and the Mermaid*. The Jikalla players stopped pushing their counters around the board and the dice fell silent in the cups. We roared out *King Naghan, his Fall and Rise,* and *Eregoin's Promise*.

Then these hard-living, hoarse-voiced, hairy fighting men drew on a sudden maudlin melancholy, and led by a fellow with a thin reedy voice we warbled out *The Fall of the Suns*. This is a menacing song, for its cadences and images invite mournfulness. It tells of the last days when the twin suns fall from the sky and drench the world of Kregen in fire and blood, in water and death. I am not overfond of it, for all the deeper truths it expresses in its roundabout way.

So when a flushed fellow, bulging his tunic and wildly slopping his ale, leaped to his feet and started bellowing out the first lines of *Sogandar the Upright and the Sylvie*, I, for one, joined in with a full-throated roar. And the rafters shook as the swods came to those famous lines that always crease them up, and great gusts of laughter swept across the room as we sang out: "No idea at all, at all, no idea at all."

Yes.

We kept that refrain going until we were all well-nigh bursting. The serving girls scurried in with more flagons and great was the relishment thereof. We quieted down as the tall thin fellow with the reedy voice favored us with a solo, choosing parts of the song cycle composed from fragments of *The Canticles of the Rose City* concerning the doings of the part-man, part-god Drak. Naturally my thoughts winged to what my Delia was doing now, how she was faring, and I offered up a fervent prayer that she would be kept safe.

We did not sing *The Bowmen of Loh*, for almost all the Crimson Bowmen were away with the emperor.

It seemed to me my course was reasonably clear. I would have to discharge all those mercenaries who had become untrustworthy by reason of accepting bribes. I would seek to discover who had paid them; I would make no attempt to match the bribes, gold for gold. If a man takes gold from another when in employment his trust is forfeited. I had experience of that when I'd been a renegade and contracted to Gafard the Sea Zhantil, the King's Striker.

The decision about reporting to the emperor what I had so far discovered about the Chyyanists would have to be taken. There was, in truth, pitifully little to report. A minor religion would appear to offer little danger to the emperor, beset as he was by combinations of powerful nobles. While everyone in Vallia regarded as a foregone conclusion that the conflict with Hamal must reopen at some time in the future, for the present the uneasy state of truce between the two empires offered some hope of continuing peace. The emperor would brush aside any suggestions I might make along those lines, and his Presidio, torn as it was by internecine strife, would greedily pursue the path of individual power.

By Zair! The worst thing of all was how lost, how at sea, empty and forlorn I felt without my Delia. When I'd been dragged away from her before I had struggled always to return to her. I had cursed and raved at the forces keeping us apart. But know well, this was a topsy-turvy situation and one I just did not relish at all, at all, as Sogandar the Upright might say.

The swods were just beginning *The Maid with the Single Veil* and the serving wenches were giggling and laughing as is their wont when that song is sung, when a fellow at the adjoining table, leaning across, began to make directly offensive remarks. He was getting at me. There is no mistaking the idiot who intends to pick a quarrel.

I felt a hot resentment. I'd come out for a quiet evening bellowing out the old songs and this rast wanted to stir up trouble and spoil it all. I determined, mean and vicious, that I'd spoil his fun, that I'd not react, that he could cuss until he was blue in the face and I'd give him no satisfaction. I'd ruin his enjoyment and he could jibe and mock and insult all he liked.

I said to Laka and Nidar, "I'll play the cramph along. Take no notice."

Laka knew me and so laughed, falling in with the ploy. Nidar favored me with an old-fashioned look, but said nothing.

The fellow who got his kicks from being unpleasant wore too much gold lace about his buff. His face was lean and marked by a scar, and his mustaches had been clipped. I noticed the emblem he wore at his throat, a little gold strigicaw and swords, swung on a golden chain.

He did not speak directly to me but insulted me through his cronies, in the way of these fellows.

"He perhaps thinks we are woflos who come here. His senses probably do not even understand that small thing."

Nidar leaned across fiercely and said under his breath to me: "Let me blatter the fellow, Nath."

"Tsleetha-tsleethi," I said, which is to say, "softly-softly." Nidar's offer to bash the fellow in for me amused me. Normally quick to avenge an insult, on this night I wanted to bash this insulting fellow with more subtle weapons than a set of knuckles or a rapier in his guts.

He persevered. His cronies tried to help his game. They called him Rumil the Point. I turned my back on them and bellowed for more ale. The song had changed and so we could all sing *The Worm-eaten Swordship Gull-i-mo* which is a Vallian sailor's song, for a few swordships are employed in sheltered waters. That song is known in many anchorages in Kregen, and I'd sung it as a render up in the Hoboling Islands.

A hand touched me on the shoulder. I turned. I stopped singing.

Rumil the Point stood up, leaning over me, his lean face black with his sense of insult, because I took no notice of him whatsoever.

"Rast!" he shouted, thumping my shoulder, speaking thickly, either drunk or pretending to be drunk. "You do not insult me and stand on your own stinking feet!"

I shook his hand off and started to turn back to the two Pachaks, determined to play my part out to the end. By Zair! But he was in a paddy! He just couldn't believe that I didn't consider him important enough to worry over. He felt at a loss, puzzled, reduced in dignity, his pride shredded.

"Then I'll settle you, you zigging cramph!"

I saw Laka's face go hard and I heard the scrape of steel and so knew I had miscalculated.

With a motion I trusted would be quick and fluid enough I slid aside and turned back.

This Rumil the Point stood glaring at me. His eyes protruded. The tip of his tongue stuck out, and his face was contorted back, ricked, stamped with an awful terror.

Around his neck clamped a buff clad arm, and the paw-hand gleamed with golden fur.

"Lahal, Nath the Gnat," said Rafik Avandil. "I see I may be of service to you once more."

Twelve

A message via the Sisters of the Rose

If I thought that because Delia and I were parted and I was alone in Vondium life would be flat and insipid, I was only partly wrong. Of course, life lacks its deep brilliance and color when Delia is away and I turn to fripperies, but sometimes the trifles turn into matters of more profound importance. The time when I made myself King of Djanduin serves as an example. So life helter-skeltered along in Vondium as I sought to think out the best way of facing the various dangers that threatened.

Rafik Avandil, quite enchanted at his opportunity to rescue me for the second time, as he thought, had spent the rest of the evening with us. Laka kept up my disguise as Nath the Gnat, and for this I was grateful. We saw a deal of each other in the days that followed and eventually I was persuaded to move into the inn at which Rafik stayed. I told Turko the Shield, Balass the Hawk, Naghan the Gnat and whoever else absolutely needed to know. Turko and the others grumbled about having to stay in our wing of the palace while I was off roistering in inns, but I explained that I was on to a lead. They were to call me Nath the Gnat. Here Naghan pulled a face, and I chided him, saying, "A great name, Naghan! And one I am proud to borrow."

"Just let me have it back, Dray. I shall be Naghan the Arm, I think, if we two chance to meet, in remembrance of that hyr-kaidur."

"Aye," I said. "So far I have had no word of a single Black Feather in all of Vondium, and this is strange."

"Maybe not so strange," offered Khe-Hi-Bjanching, putting a finger in his book to mark the place. "The signomant held only an empty space for Vondium, remember."

"I still think that the true reading. By Vox! If only we knew where they would strike next!"

"Agents are out, asking questions. Vallia is being scoured."

"And," said Naghan with the old armorer's shrewdness strong on him, "that is costing a deal of money."

"If the Opaz-forsaken Chyyanists win, we'll have no money, you may be sure. And we, along with our people, will hang by our heels."

"They'll have to catch us first," said Turko ominously.

This wing of her father's palace had been furnished under the supervision of Delia, and I relished that. Even so, I was not enamored of the great palace of Vondium. Delia's vision had created apartments of great beauty, but still the chill of the imperial presence came through. Rafik's inn offered a change, at the very least. I just hoped Bargom at the Rose of Valka did not hear I had stayed at some other hostelry than his own. But, then, a few words and he would understand.

The capital city hummed with news. The emperor was returning in state and bringing with him as an honored guest to the Empire of Vallia none other than the famous Queen of Lome. Everyone was agog to see this fabled woman. The reports of her beauty and wealth had spread over this part of the world, dazzling men with impossible dreams. Everyone gave a curse and said how fortunate the emperor was, and how they'd like to be in his shoes. And some of them, saying that, would laugh and add words to the effect that his shoes would be fine and dandy—*for now.*

One item of encouragement, and of alarm too, we had in those days. Balass received a report that among a group of his countrymen from Xuntal, traders and merchants down in the wharfside area of the city, a man had been heard to speak of the Black Feathers when he'd been drunk.

I said, "Then it is up to you, Balass. You are Xuntalese. You can mingle. May the Curved Sword of Xurrhuk guard you."

"Amen to that, my Prince. By my hopes of entering Xanachang! My people are a fearsome people if they think they are spied upon."

"It's of little comfort to tell you that almost any people resent spying. But look at it in a different light. You go to root out evil. Make no mistake, Xurrhuk of the Curved Sword finds no favor in the hearts of the Chyyanists."

Balass's firmly muscled body glistened black and silver in the light of the suns streaming in through the high windows, for we met and talked in this small enclosed arena set up within our part of the palace. The silver-sanded floor slid and shushed to the quick scrape of feet as we foined and parried with wooden swords. Turko, I knew, had put in a good many burs of practice with his new parrying-stick, and he handled the klattar now with a sureness that pleased me. Mind you, I'd be the last to suggest it was but a small step to go on to handling a weapon very much like a parrying-stick with one blade and with sharp edges. Its name would be a sword. And Turko, the High Kham, would have none of them.

Oby came in, throwing off his tunic, getting ready to have a bout with anyone willing to stand against the liquid cunning of his long-knife. He left the lenken door partly open and Naghan, about to shout out about people being born in bars, stopped. A flunky sailed in through the door. He wore the fancy and immodestly ridiculous court dress for servitors, for we were forced to accept the services of other servants than our own from Valka. He was not a slave. His red and silver and yellow clothes billowed about him as he flew through the air.

I turned to make sure Turko really stood by me. If he had not been I'd have sworn he was the fellow outside thus casually hurling importunate servitors about.

But it was no man.

Through the pushed-open door strode a strappingly handsome girl. Her face was only lightly stained with a flush of blood under the tanned skin from her little exercise. She was clad in tights, with a body-hugging tan tunic strapped about with a lesten-hide belt from which swung rapier and dagger, buckled up in a way which showed she was ready to draw in a twinkling. Her weapons swung in that cunning way I had seen an infinitely more glorious girl scabbard her own rapier and dagger.

So, forewarned by the weaponry and the demeanor of this girl, I knew from whom she came.

She wore her light brown hair cut short. Her face held that open, frank look of the girl who knows she is a girl and is prepared to treat men as men because that is their misfortune. I liked the look of her. Over her heart an embroidered red rose, twined about with gold threads, resembled very much the little red and gold brooch, fashioned in the shape of a rose, Delia had given me in return for the brooch like a hubless spoked wheel I had given her.

"Llahal and Lahal, Prince Majister," said this girl, marching straight up to me with a swing of the hips and a lithe and limber step. "You are well met. Here, my Prince." And she hauled a letter from the small script at her waist.

The letter was written on yellow paper and carried a faint and fragrant perfume to my nostrils. The writing, firm and rounded and yet girlish, in that beautiful running Kregish script, is very dear to me.

My comrades stood back. The girl touched the rose embroidered upon her breast. "I have a letter for the Princess Katri. But yours, my Prince, I was instructed to deliver first." She laughed, a clear tinkling sound. "And the letter for the emperor the last of the three."

So I, being intoxicated on emotion, laughed too. "I cannot wait, for no reply is expected." She turned to leave, her legs in the tights very long and lovely. "But there is one lie I shall no longer believe."

With the letter burning my hands I said, "Will you not stop to take refreshment? And what is this lie?"

She halted at the door and smiled back. "I thank you, my Prince, but I must hurry. As to the lie, all women say the Prince Majister of Vallia never laughs."

And she went out, swinging, jaunty, laughing, the rapier and dagger swinging at her sides. She was a woman, like my Delia, all woman.

I banished her from my mind and opened the letter. I know the words by heart, but many of them are private so I will simply say that Delia said all was well, she was in good health, Melow sent her love, the task was proving more difficult than she'd expected and she was like to be away longer than she had hoped. There was more, but that is for Delia and me. She finished by saying that the letter to Aunt Katri requested the emperor's sister to go to Valka to see after Didi, and that the letters were being entrusted to Jikmer Sosie ti Drakanium.

The word jikmer had been crossed through, but Delia had been in a hurry and so I could read it beneath the quickly scrawled scribble. Jikmer. That would be the Sisters of the Rose equivalent to Jiktar. Hmm.

These girls had their chukmers, their jikmers, their hikmers and their delmers too, without doubt. The notion charmed me. It all added up, without the shadow of a doubt, to a powerful and secret organization of women who, from my knowledge of Delia, were dedicated to philanthropic and chivalrous ends. What the mysticism might be I, of course, could not know.

I think it was the delivery of this letter with its evidence of an efficient organization of women devoted to purposes with which, from the little I knew of them, I could sympathize, that made me finally put into practice a scheme I had been harboring for some long time. As the scheme developed—and I worked on it with some intensity—I will tell you as it impinges on my story. For now, I would have to wait for the first fruits until Seg and Inch were available.

Also, I must make it clear that I am concentrating here very much on the Chyyanists. A great deal happened in Vondium during this time. Instead of being an idle layabout, I found myself hard at work. As the Prince Majister in the capital with the emperor absent I had many official functions to perform. I performed them. Most were very little of a laugh. I sat in the courts for a time and handed down judgments. I canceled work on a new slave bagnio, letting the slave masters see my scathing contempt, and set the laborers and masons into constructing a building to plans I laid out for them. They couldn't really understand what the building was for. A visit to anywhere in Kregen where men and women flew saddle-birds through the air would have told them. It was accommodation for a thousand flyers. One day, and alarmingly soon, I fancied, Vallia would have need of them.

So life was not all dressing up inconspicuously and sliding off as Nath the Gnat. Often one or another of my boon companions would accompany me, but we made a compact that we kept apart. Turko, as usual, grumbled. But he saw the sense of it. My cover, if it was to be kept, would not be served by my suddenly appearing with friends. In a tavern, Turko could sit drinking quietly and keep an eye on me. We all chuckled over the episode of Rafik rescuing me.

That was a strange time. Here I was in Vondium, the capital of the puissant Empire of Vallia, and my Delia not with me. By Zair! I had fought and struggled to reach this place, and had been dragged here in chains, and never had I thought I'd live here without Delia. It was unnerving.

I had all preparations made for the society I formed. There are many secret societies on Kregen. This seems to be a part and parcel of the makeup of all cultures. In the most simple terms, I wanted to instill some of the superb qualities in the teachings of the Krozairs of Zy into Valka and Vallia. But I had no intention of limiting the new order to the island of Vallia. If I could bring Pandahem in and Zenicce and the Hoboling Islands, perhaps even Seg's Erthyrdrin, that would be even better. I would find men I could trust, men of good heart, of good character yet lusty rogues withal, men who could see evil and stare back at it unflinchingly and do what they might to root out evil and plant the good. Of course, these terms are all relative. Good to one man is a mere matter of decency to another; evil to one man is normal human behavior to another. But there are basics on which men of goodwill may agree. The women had found them, it seemed. Of the various secret societies of Vallia none had asked me to join up. I had felt vast relief at this, for I had taken a firm vow to join none, assuming that the others would regard me as an enemy or, at the best, cold toward them. As the Prince Majister I had to remain aloof, if I could.

So do not think I organized the new order out of pique. If they don't want me to join I'll start my own club—no. That was not the case. This I believe. I had heard of no order in Vallia that sought to do what I sought...

As a starting point the Black Feathers of the Great Chyyan would serve.

Balass reported back that the drunk—muttering darkly that when the Black Day dawned the Black Feathers would tear down the koters of Vallia and take all their goods—was a newly arrived trader, due to return to Xuntal. Balass looked worried. Perhaps Xuntal was already infected? I said, "I think not. If it is Hamal behind this, then their quarrel is with Vallia. If it is Phu-Si-Yantong, then—"

"Then," said Balass, very grimly, "it is very possible."

I could not argue. Yantong sought his maniacal ambition's culmination in the domination of all Paz. The man was mad. Anyone who wanted to take on trying to rule these wayward folk must be mad. I'd had a bellyful, I knew, of just a very few of them.

"The ship he traveled in," I said,

Balass nodded. "I will ask."

Again I said nothing to indicate that Balass should have already asked. He was a hyr-kaidur, used to the arena; spying would have to be taught him.

So my days passed, gathering scraps of information, working at being Prince Majister, organizing the new order. Among the many pantheons of Kregen there is a plethora of minor godlings and spirits. One minor spirit of deviltry had, with assistance from others of his ilk, plagued me in Djanduin. I had allowed the miasmic presence of Khokkak the Meddler to influence me out of boredom and screaming helpless frustration to make myself King of Djanduin. Although, as I say, I do not think Sly the Ambitious or Gleen the Envious had a hand, there were undoubted traces of Hoko the Amusingly

Malicious and Yurncra the Mischievous. These devils plague a man. There was no time during that period in Vondium without Delia for them to gain a lodgment in my thick old vosk skull. I was just too busy.

One very good reason for my adopting the disguise of Nath the Gnat was to escape unpleasantness from those who sought to oust me. There were more than just the racters. Although Rafik Avandil had said, "You have come up in the world, dom, since first we met," and I had replied casually that I'd come into money, he provided me with a useful cloak. As Nath the Gnat I could wander freely in the city and mingle with all kinds of people in the taverns. By doing this I know I escaped many an unwanted brawl or duel. And I was learning.

So the day dawned in Opaz-brilliance when the emperor would return to Vondium. He would arrive in his imposing procession of narrow boats, drawn along the canals and through the water gate into the city. On that day I had to dress myself up and be the Prince Majister, and go down to the canal to welcome him.

Among a glittering group of high nobles and koters, all of whom—or nearly all—hated my guts, I stood, glittering in the suns-shine, watching as the haulers guided the emperor's narrow state boat into the jetty. When all was ready and the trumpets pealed and the guard snapped to attention, he stepped ashore onto the crimson carpet. There was, as usual, a little undignified shoving to get forward—and to hell with protocol! I hung back, my left hand on my rapier hilt, watching.

How the men with the white and black favors fawned about him! Yet each one would sooner see him floating facedown in the canal. The factions vied to be seen in his company. I waited as they advanced down the jetty toward the zorca chariot that would carry him through the streets so the people might see him there as well as along the canals. I saw the woman at his side. This was the fabled Queen of Lome. Banners flew, birds screeched up from the water, zorcas and totrixes scraped their hooves, officers barked orders, the crack and smash of sword and rapier as the drills were gone through, the tramp of marching feet—and over all the high shrilling yells of the crowd, welcoming their emperor back to his capital. Yes, this was a day to remember!

He saw me, standing alone, isolated, shunned by the nobles. Oh, yes, there were many nobles loyal to him, but these had gone pushing down with the rest to show that their loyalty, at any rate, was not feigned.

Standing there in all my foppish finery, for I had dressed up with the explicit intention of demonstrating my feelings for this kind of occasion, I refused to budge. Let the old devil walk past me and offer his hand, and then I would welcome him. He and I had had our moments.

Slave girls sprinkled flower petals before the feet of the emperor and this Queen of Lome. She walked with a swaying, gliding gait and she was heavily veiled, whereat a groan of dismay went up from all the assembly. I looked at her. I'd find out about her, that was for sure.

So the emperor, the most powerful man in this part of Kregen, walked past on the crimson carpets. He was between me and the queen. He turned his head. He looked just the same, big and tough with that powerful head, that merciless and demanding expression. He stared at me.

"Lahal, Dray Prescot. And where is my daughter?"

"She is not here, Emperor."

He frowned. He didn't like me calling him emperor. "I have heard stories concerning your misdeeds. Attend me tonight. I shall demand a strict accounting from you, by Vox!"

Thirteen

I displease the Emperor of Vallia

The interview with Delia's father was short and sharp.

"Where is my daughter?"

"She has gone about her own affairs for a space."

"That will be the Sisters of the Rose. She's worse than her mother. I shall have this monstrosity you are building torn down. It means nothing and wastes resources and slaves. The new bagnios will be built."

"More slaves!" I shouted at him.

"Aye, son-in-law! You have served me well in the past, I own that. I don't damned well like you, at least not much, and—"

"And you can believe that sentiment returned!"

"Do you forget I am emperor?"

He sat up in his lenken chair with the gold and scarlet cushions, and the gold cup shook and spilled his wine. It was his purple wine of Wenhartdrin. We were alone in that chamber where I had bargained before, where we could speak our minds—well, as much as we'd ever reveal them to each other.

"No. I don't forget. I saw the disgusting display by these damned racter nobles. You know the plots against you? You are aware of the troubles in the northeast? Do you know your own daughter's Delphond is growing surly and suspicious because of your stinking slavers, your foul aragorn?"

"I have to rule as best I can. By Vox, it is not an easy thing to rule an empire."

"I know. You'll have need of proper stabling for the flyers we must have to meet the Hamalian aerial cavalry. Yet you build more slave barracks. Your agents steal away slaves—"

"Not mine! The business is in the hands of Companies of Friends—"

"In which you have darned high stakes!"

"And if I have, do I not have enormous expenses?"

I breathed in hard. Like the scorpion said, it is in a being's nature to be himself. Vallia had always been like this since he could remember, so why should he change it now because some wild clansman roared in to marry his daughter and shout around impossible ideas?

To get away from the explosion I saw was imminent, I said, "And this queen, this Queen of Lome, this Queen Lush?"

He fired up at this.

"The queen's name is Queen Lushfymi! I will not have her called Queen Lush. It is an insult and I'll have the head off the next cramph who calls her that! She is a remarkable woman."

So wrought up was I that I did not look at him, and so must have missed the first signs.

"Since we knocked the damned Hamalese out of Pandahem," I went on, ignoring his outburst, "it makes good sense to improve our relations with all the nations of Pandahem. I have been away—"

"Indeed, son-in-law, you have been away! And no man knows where." I looked at him and he leaned forward, resting his elbow on the carved arm of the chair. "Mayhap you have been in Hamal again, only this time hatching up plots against me?"

I gaped at him.

Then: "You stupid onker!" I brayed it out, brayed it out to this powerful man, the emperor. "I've told you and told you, you are Delia's father and therefore sacrosanct. I'd as soon skewer a Todalpheme as touch you!"

He reared up, opening his mouth, bellowing at me. He did not offer to strike the golden gong. He could deal with this himself.

"You call me onker!"

"Yes, well, if you deserve it by reason of your stupid remarks, you will get it from me."

He lifted a lace kerchief and wiped his mouth. His hand was shaking. "You had best leave Vondium, leave at once. And, Dray Prescot, do not attempt to return until I send for you."

I glared at him. "I'll go and willingly. If you wake up one morning with a knife in your back or your head looking over your shoulders, don't blame me. I have warned you." He tried to interrupt, but I went on, and I confess I shouted louder as I said: "And if my Delia is in Vondium and I wish to return here I'll come back whether you say so or not, by Zim-Zair!"

He lifted his finger, his hand clutching the scrap of laced kerchief. His finger shook, pointing at me.

"Get out! Get out, Dray Prescot, before I have my guards take your head off your shoulders!"

"I'm going, Majister, but remember you tried that once before, and it did not get you far. Remberee, Emperor, Remberee, and I trust you sleep well in your bed o' nights."

With that petty remark I took myself off, not well pleased. I didn't care a fig about being banished from Vondium. The city is marvelous, without doubt, but I'd seen only a tithe of it and had worked and kept to the Savage Woflo and felt miserable. Now I'd find some better mischief.

I dug my heels into the polished marble as I walked down the long corridor. Crimson Bowmen of Loh, standing guard at the tall double-leaved doors each with its freight of gilded ornamentation, took one look at my face and stiffened into ramrod attention, mute, unmoving, and, such was my vicious frame of mind I thought the thought without compunction, trembling in their boots lest I bawl them out.

Into my own apartment I stormed and kicked an over-stuffed chair across the room. That was mere petty foolishness. If the stupid onker couldn't see what was going on! He let the racters fawn on him. Well, he was playing their game in that, I suppose, and appeared to be shutting a very blind eye on the other parties out to topple him from his throne and place the crown upon the head of their own puppets.

I removed my court clothes and selected a length of scarlet cloth of good quality. I wrapped it around my waist and drew the end up between my legs and tucked it in firmly. A broad lesten-hide belt with a dulled silver buckle held the breechclout in place. A rapier and main gauche each swung from its own swordbelt went over that. The Jiktar and the hikdar were a matched pair, given me by Delia, superb weapons. My old sailor knife went into the sheath over my right hip. I fastened a neat quiver of terchicks over my right shoulder, the swatch of throwing knives snuggling flat and out of the way. I filled a purse with golden talens and silver coins of various countries. A small scrip on the other side held a few necessaries. I was feeling mad clean through. The great Krozair longsword I slung down over my back, the cunningly fashioned double-handed handle raking up to just the right height for me to take a quick snatch and draw the whole gleaming blade free in a single action. That is a knack and a damned useful one on Kregen. I swirled a medium-length crimson cape-cloak about my shoulders and fastened off the golden zhantil-head bosses with golden chains. This was a trifle foppish, but it was worn with a reason. Then, still feeling murderous, I hung a djangir on another belt about my waist, the very short, very broad sword of Djanduin holding a special significance. Finally a great Lohvian longbow and a quiver of arrows all fletched with the blazing blue feathers from the crested korf of the Blue Mountains joined my array of weaponry and I could feel a little better.

What a get-onker I am! But resuming this familiar rig did, without doubt, serve to calm me.

Where Delia was I did not know. I could not, in all honesty, make an attempt, a deliberate attempt, to seek her out. But if I went out of Vondium and trusted to Five-handed Eos-Bakchi, that chuckling Vallian spirit of luck and good fortune, might I not find her? No, I did not really think I would, for Eos-Bakchi does not favor grim faces and hard hearts. But I wanted to rid myself of the feel of Vondium, and I wanted the swift rush of air in my face and the sense of the clean onward surge of life upon Kregen to fill me and drive out the black devils clawing at me like the Imps of Sicce.

It was necessary for me, dressed as I liked to be dressed, to remember to pull on a pair of black Vallian boots.

Now, over all, a massive buff Vallian cloak would conceal all, and one of those peculiar Vallian hats, wide brimmed and with two oblong slots in the front brim, could be jammed down on my hair. The feather in the hat was red and white, the colors of Valka.

Just then Turko came in, beaming, able to walk freely through into my apartment for I had given orders. He saw my cloak and hat and his face fell. Although it was quite obvious I was dressed for going out, it should be remembered that despite their preference for buff tunics and breeches, the men of Vallian culture habitually don loose lounging robes of many colors in the evening. They are seldom blue, and somewhere on them will the colors of the house or party favor be displayed.

"I had thought to try a few falls with you, Dray, but—"

"That old fool of an emperor!" I burst out. "By Krun! He's banished me from Vondium."

"And you'll go?"

"Oh, aye, I'll go! I can't wait to get away."

"Then we shall—"

"Oh, no, you won't! Some of you will have to stay here and carry on the work. Just because Delia's father is a fambly doesn't mean we have to desert the onker."

"Well—"

"I'll probably go to see Inch or Seg. We'll think of something. I want to know what Balass uncovers. And keep an eye on the Crimson Bowmen. You know half of them betrayed the emperor last time. Trust Jiktar Laka Pa-Re and his men. Discharge at once anyone who accepts a bribe if it can be proved against him. As for me, I'm off."

"Dray!"

"Remberee, my old Turko. I'll think of your great shield, but I doubt it'll be necessary. When the emperor has had time to cool off I'll reappear and this time I'll make the old idiot understand."

"By the time you've had time to cool off, you mean!"

"By Zair! Well spoken!"

"Well, by Morro the Muscle! You take care, you hear?"

"I hear."

"I'll come to the landing platform with you."

"I shall ride a zorca. It is good for the liver."

So we went out and along the ornate corridors. We passed one of the many entranceways to the apartments of the emperor and I saw a man dressed in black and silver abruptly turn and go swiftly into an adjoining passageway past an ivory statue looted from some forgotten city of Chem, I shouldn't wonder.

I could have sworn he was Naghan Vanki, that featureless man who had so sneered at my pretensions for the hand of the emperor's daughter. There was no sign of him as we reached the passage.

Turko remarked offhandedly, "That fellow took off like a scorched sleeth. What does he hide?"

"Let it rest. The guards must know him or he wouldn't have got this far without a pass or, if he did reach here, he'd do it with his head under his arm and with chains a-dangling."

All the same, I was half a mind to go after Naghan Vanki, if it had been him. He'd been one of the party of the airboat *Lorenztone* when I'd been drugged and dumped into a thorny-ivy bush in the hostile territories.

Then Oby and Tilly and Naghan the Gnat showed up, all pleased to see me and dismayed that I was leaving. But I slowed them down and went to the zorca stables. Mounted up on Twitchnose, a fine strong zorca with a spiral horn of remarkable length jutting from his chestnut forehead, I looked at my friends.

"Remberee," I said. And then: "By Krun! It is all Remberees for me these days."

One or two of the grooms looked up at the oath, for that is an oath of Hamal and Havilfar. But I didn't care. Let the emperor choke on a little more bile when his spies reported.

Turko and the others offered to ride a ways with me, but the Maiden with the Many Smiles was up and the Twins would shortly follow so I declined their offer and told them to have a party instead. Then I turned Twitchnose's head toward the Mustard Gate, which is a strong battlemented tower set in an angle of the northwest walls of Vondium.

Away to the northeast the monstrous pile of mountains known as Drak's Seat glowered up darkly against the stars, lit by the Maiden with the Many Smiles. I rode on, sunk in odious thoughts, and the zorca riders closed in on each side.

My rapier came out in a moonlit blur of steel under the overhanging balconies where the moonblooms drank up the light. A hulking fellow swathed in a dark cloak husked out. "We mean you no harm, Prince. We are your friends."

"What friends ride up so suddenly from the shadows?" He lifted his hands. They were empty. The street led to the Boulevard of Grape Pressers which, bordered by an arm of the Vindelka Cut, would bring me to the gate I sought. They had chosen their spot well. The overhanging balconies, the pressing walls, the narrow slot of star glitter—yes, they had waited here for me, knowing I would pass this way. How? The answer to that came more rapidly than I expected.

One of the fellows on my left side, a canny position, reined up. He doffed his hat. The moon showed me a thin face with bright sharp eyes, a narrow face, a hungry face. The jaws were hard and lean. I knew him.

"Strom Luthien!" I said, surprised.

"Aye, Prince. At your service."

He was a racter. The black and white favors showed dark and bright upon his tunic and cloak and pinned to the hat he had doffed. Now he sidled his zorca closer, disregarding my rapier point like a bar of pink and golden light between us.

"There is much to be said, Prince, between the chief party of Vallia which seeks to save the empire, and the Prince Majister who has been disowned and banished by the emperor."

Those damned secret ways in the walls of palaces? Spies had listened to the emperor and me talking privately. With a sudden gush of relief I felt reborn. This, then, was what the night held.

I fancy he was surprised at my tone, for I have, as you know, a certain unsavory reputation with villains.

"Lead on, Strom Luthien. It is I who am at your service. Let us go and talk, by Vox!"

Fourteen

The racters intrigue with the Prince Majister

The fuzzy pink light from the Maiden with the Many Smiles and the golden glitter from a distant torch bracketed to a wall ran gleaming up my blade as I sheathed the rapier. We rode through the nighted streets of Vondium, this parcel of avowed racters and I. They were all apim. There are many so-called menagerie-men on Kregen, as you know, and you also know that they are men even if they are not carrying their spirits and souls in bodies exactly like those of *Homo sapiens*. To call them menagerie-men is to demean your own sense of your pride in matters of true value. So we rode and if you think I trusted this Strom Luthien then you misread my nature.

Vondium is a large and sprawling city, not occupied by as many inhabitants as the enclave city of Zenicce, perhaps, but large and prosperous and filled with great wealth and luxury.

Up the paved roadway of one of the Hills we rode, the Hill known as the Ban'alar, past dark masses of vegetation and long walls concealing the villas of the rich. The Ban'alar holds a number of the richest houses in Vondium. We halted by a fortified gateway outside a stone wall with bronze spikes where four samphron-oil lamps cast their pleasant mellow gleam upon the guards and the gates and the shimmer weapons. The simple fact of four samphron-oil lamps conveys adequately the wealth of this house.

We were passed through and rode silently along a winding pathway bordered by missals and flowering shrubs. The sweet scent of night-blooming flowers reached me, most soothing. But I kept my senses alert as we dismounted and slaves ran to attend the zorcas. We passed through ornate halls and lushly furnished corridors and so out a glass door into a crystal-walled conservatory. Heat smote me. The walls and ceiling were fashioned of fireglass and the crystal which resists great heat showed the steady beat of furnaces beyond.

The place was crammed with exotic plants, many from the jungles of Chem, and others from Zair knew where upon the face of Kregen.

In a wicker chair stuffed with cushions the Dowager Kovneva Natyzha Famphreon awaited me.

I let her have a half-bow, a small mark to show irony, rather than any mark of respect.

"So you come to see me, Prince Majister."

"The invitation was pressing."

"Strom Luthien had his orders. You would not have been harmed."

I looked at her. She had been carried in her palanquin this morning, joining in the rush to greet the emperor. Now she let go one of her famous barking laughs. Yes, I knew her, this famous old biddy, this Dowager Kovneva of Falkerdrin. She must now be almost a hundred and seventy. Her face contained that nut-brown, cracker-barrel experienced look of iron authority. Her mouth curved down at each corner and deep grooves extended the arc of her rattrap mouth so that all her habitual callous command lay revealed in that dominating face. Her lower lip was upthrust in a perpetual sneer. And as I could see by the way she was dressed all in gauzy silks, that carefully pampered body of hers remained as lushly alluring as ever. She kept her priorities in order, did Natyzha Famphreon.

Standing with his hand on the back of her chair, her son the kov looked at me uncertainly. He was a weak-chinned, spineless nonentity, his every thought and deed ordered by his mother. That was not his fault, but rather the fault of his breeding. He was still the Pallan of the Armory, and through him his mother wielded enormous powers.

Many of the pallans, the high officials, the ministers or secretaries of state, had changed since my absence. But Natyzha Famphreon held onto her power with iron claws.

"You say I would not be harmed. If you wish to talk I will listen for a mur or two."

She didn't like my tone.

"Will you remove your hat, your cloak?"

They could all see the bow stave thrusting up. The hilt of the longsword was hidden by the upstanding jut of the cloak's collar.

It was warm. I said, "I am comfortable. Speak."

"Let us drink a little wine first. I await others who wish to speak with you."

As to drinking wine with these racters, that was another matter. That I had been called in for conversation meant they had a zhantil to saddle, and I fancied the purpose of my presence, alive and without a slit throat, was to make an attempt to seek my alliance. After all, however they had found out about my banishment from Vondium, they knew and therefore counted on that to make me amenable to their proposals. Those proposals must be obvious. So I refused the wine and waited for a space, removed my hat and looked about this luxurious conservatory.

What a wonderful world this planet of Kregen is! What a profusion of life seethes and ferments there! So much there is to know of Kregen, so very much, and so pitifully little have I been able to speak into this micro-phone. But if you who listen to these tapes have some small inkling of the wonders of Kregen, the marvels, the beauties and the horrors, then you will grasp at the wider reality and the sheer vastness of it all. And I never forget that sheer size, although counting for a considerable amount, is by no means that most important criterion of value. Most assuredly so. So the racters, to bring back the thoughts which crowded my mind to the scene I awaited, so these racters might be the largest political party of Val-lia with most of the big guns; they were not, in my view, by any means the best. Not by a chalk.

Presently in came Nath Ulverswan, Kov of the Singing Forests, just the same, tall and lean and with his scarred face vivid in the fireglow. He wore a lounging robe all of deep dark purple, and the black and white favor was pinned to his shoulder. For all the informality of his attire, the rings and the jewels about him, he carried a rapier and main gauche belted up around his narrow waist.

I said, "We have had no real addition to our parties to talk, kovneva."

The old biddy cackled at this, sticking up her lower lip. Nath Ulverswan was notorious for saying so little as to be practically mute. He gave us a surly "Lahal" and sat down and the slave girls brought wine.

The third attendee—one tended to discount the Kovneva's son in these affairs, rather cavalierly, true—turned out to be Nalgre Sultant, Vad of Kavinstok. I was hardly overjoyed to see him, for we had pointedly ignored each other during the times when official business threw us together. He did not forget my harsh treatment of him when the galleon *Ovvend Barynth* had been attacked by shanks. He was not only a dedicated racter; he hated my guts.

Now he stalked in, and I saw the way he postured, using those thin lips and arrogant eyes to put me in my place as a loutish clansman who had had the temerity to burst into civilized Vallia and marry the emperor's daughter. He gave me a nasty look and sat down on the other side of the Kovneva with a mumbled "Lahal."

I cocked an eye at Natyzha Famphreon. "Any more?"

"One only, for this night's work."

The trouble with these Opaz-forsaken racters was that they were evil in ways they could not understand themselves to be evil. They were not committing any consciously criminal acts. If I died, they would joy, but they would not send stikitches after me to assassinate me in a dark alley— at least I did not think so. My death would have to come as a result of an open quarrel, the legality of my demise beyond dispute.

They made their money through the possession of land and all the wealth that brought. They also operated the Companies of Friends, the trading ventures of Vallia. A great deal of their wealth came from slaving and investment in slaving. With the ruthlessness of those in possession, they ensured the continuation of their wealth and with it all their fancy titles and the very real powers they had taken into their hands.

Under torture, each one, I have no doubt, would swear she or he did what they did for the ultimate good of Vallia. They believed this. This kind of conviction made it hard for anyone with differing views to make any kind of coherent sense in their eyes.

Each of these people with me now, discounting the young kov, was a personality: Natyzha Famphreon, Nath Ulverswan, Nalgre Sultant. Each was a strong personality, a real live person with passions and desires and secret hungers and fears they overcame. Of their family lives I knew little. But to them I was a mere wild clansman from the wide Plains of Segesthes, the Lord of Strombor, a man from outside who had dared to wed the Princess Majestrix and to make himself the Prince Majister. That I had won the title before the wedding would no doubt conveniently slip their memories.

The last racter who wished to speak with me arrived. By the tardiness of arrival and by the sweat stains on Trylon Ered Imlien's buff riding clothes I judged my apprehension had come with speed, and these conspirators had been summoned with great urgency. This Ered Imlien, Trylon of Thengelsax, I had seen from time to time and, knowing him to be a racter, had treated him with my usual courtesy tempered with viciousness. I supposed he detested me like all the rest, and I returned the detestation with what I hoped was greater measure.

A short, squat man with a square red face and deeply set eyes of Vallian brown, he moved with a rolling gait and boomed every word and liked to use a riding crop on his slaves just to tone 'em up, as he would say, bellowing. "So he's here, is he!" he bawled, bashing his riding crop against his booted leg. "Well, put it to him, kovneva. Tell the rast what we want."

This vastly amused me.

It did not amuse Natyzha Famphreon, and her lower lip thrust upward like a swifter's beak rising over the apostis of a beamed foe. "We waited for you, Ered. Have the courtesy to bear with us." Cutting irony was lost on Ered Imlien.

"Why wait? Time presses. The bitch queen is gloating this very minute."

"Just so. Now, Prince Majister." And Natyzha Famphreon gestured so that we listened and marked her words. Indeed, she was an old biddy, but she had power and was accustomed to its use. "We know you have been banished from Vondium. How does not matter."

"Oh," says I, very easy, interrupting. "Spies only cost gold."

"Just so." That was a fact of life to her, if not to me, as you know. "The emperor is no longer fit to rule. We run the empire. There is no shilly-shallying about that."

I wanted to argue the point, but reality forbade. The emperor had the final say in many things, and he balanced party against party, but the power of the Racter party so often bent dividends and results in the directions they desired.

So I said, "I may have my disagreements with the old devil; he is sometimes impossible to live with. He hates me." This was not exactly true. "But he does rule the empire. He keeps you racters toeing the line, for one."

They didn't like this. Again, it was only a half-truth.

"He hates you," spat out Nalgre Sultant. "He is not alone in that."

I ignored the man.

"There is no profit in supporting the emperor any longer," said the kovneva.

"He is doomed!" bellowed out Ered Imlien, red of face, grasping his wineglass as though to splinter the delicate globe.

Movement and shadows beyond a glass screen attracted my attention. This place would be like most of the villas and palaces of Kregen, a rabbit warren of secret ways. But I fancied I could find my way out. Now I saw past the end of the glass screen the unmistakable outline of a Chulik's head. Chuliks, powerful warriors trained from birth to the use of weapons, have oily yellow skins and shave their heads to leave a long pigtail. But the characteristic that betrayed this Chulik to me was the upthrusting tusk at the corner of his mouth. I saw this plainly. Chuliks generally command higher hiring fees than other races, Pachaks apart, and are finicky in their choice of employer. Their delicateness does not come, as it does with Pachaks, from honor or sentiment; their choice of employer rests solely on his or her ability to pay.

Now this Chulik lifted his head, talking to a comrade, and the profile showed me the hard tusk lifting from his curled lip.

Two savage tusks, a Chulik has, and he uses them when he fights, as I can testify.

If I had to fight an army of Chuliks here—well, wasn't that half my reason for going with Strom Luthien in the first place?

So I dissembled a trifle and made the conversation more general, and hinted obliquely that, well, perhaps the time had come for me to give up my allegiance to the emperor. I did say at one point, rather sharply, "But if the emperor dies, his daughter and her husband will take the throne and the crown. You have thought of that?"

"If the emperor dies you are out of it, Prescot. If he dies before things are settled the land will run red with blood, for it will mean civil war, without doubt."

"And you would run that risk?"

"It would be no risk for us," said the kovneva, and she chuckled in her crone-like way, her gorgeous body incongruous in the soft swathes of silk. "For we will win whatever the intervening chaos may be."

They believe that, these high and mighty of the world.

Of course, by Makki-Grodno's disgusting diseased left kidney, it is often true.

"Do you expect me to connive at the murder of my father-in-law?"

"If you were a man with blood of Vallia in him, if you had the breeding, then it would be nothing to you."

I did not say, "If that is breeding a fellow is better off without it." But it was a near thing.

The swathing buff cloak could be ripped off in a twinkling. Depending on the danger, it would be the longbow or the longsword. Either would suit me in my frame of mind.

Eventually they offered a deal in which I would have no part of the death of the emperor and in which I would keep all the lands and titles I now held in Vallia with the exception of Prince Majister. They could not know how little I valued that. In return I was not to oppose them, and was to make sure my people did not interfere during the coup. I asked about this, but they were too cagey to give me any details.

Without attempting to imply any false modesty, it seemed to me they were anxious to get me out of the coming conflict because they feared my influence. They must have some apprehension of what I could do. Otherwise the terms would not have been so generous. Whether or not they'd keep their side of the bargain would be in the laps of the gods.

Had I been acting only for myself, for the old impetuous Dray Prescot who thumped before he thought, I'd have roared out some obscene suggestion at them and then gone swinging into action. I felt a keen regret that I could not do this. I needed the exercise. But more than mere gratification of my injured ego hung on this. The fate of Vallia depended to a very great deal on what was decided here in this conservatory. It was in my interest to appear to go along with them, giving them rope, so that I might more surely bring them down into ruin.

So I said, "Let me think about this. There is the Princess Majestrix to be considered."

Ered Imlien burst out with: "Do not worry your head over her, you onker. The Princess Dayra occupies her mind."

Furious, Natyzha Famphreon rose from her wicker chair. "Speak not of things of which you know nothing, you fambly!" She would have gone on. But I took a few steps toward this Ered Imlien and clutched up his buff tunic in my fist and shook his head a little and I glared into his eyes.

"But you had best speak to me, rast! And quickly!"

Fifteen

Of Natyzha Famphreon's chavonths, and her son

"Speak up, cramph!" I loosed my grip a little and some air flowed down with a great whooping gasp into his lungs. His face was a bright purple, like a rotten gregarian. He wheezed. I thought his eyes might roll out of his head. So I shook him again, just to keep him in the right frame of mind.

He choked out: "The Princess Dayra, she is nothing more than a—"

I hit him before he could say whatever he was going to say.

I suppose I was oversensitive about my daughters because I had held my Velia in my arms as she died. I could never forget that—what father could? So I hit him again and said, "Speak carefully, Imlien, speak very carefully."

"I do not know!" he blubbered out, his face already beginning to swell, a trickle of blood down his chin from a split lip. "I hear only that she—"

"Careful!"

"She runs wild! I cannot tell more for I do not know!"

I became aware of the conservatory again, and of the others frozen in postures of horror. The Chuliks had trotted out from behind their glass screen, their weapons ready, and the kovneva waved them down. If they wanted a fight, by Vox! I was in the mood now, right enough, to my shame.

"He speaks the truth, Dray Prescot! No one knows what your daughter Dayra is up to. That is where the Princess Majestrix has gone. More than that no woman knows."

I let Ered Imlien fall to the floor. I glared at the kovneva. "You are not of the Sisters of the Rose?"

She drew that gorgeous body up and her lean crone-like face sharpened. "No."

She made no offer to tell me which order owned her allegiance. I did not ask. She would not have said if she did not wish to.

"It seems," I said, "that if we make a deal I shall have to watch this lump of offal."

"I will answer for him. He is a trylon. Thengelsax is too close to the northeast for his comfort. His estates are raided. He is foolish only in his concern for his estates."

"And his people?"

"They fight for him as is their duty."

The idea that Dayra had something to do with the raids from those hard folk of the northeast crossed my mind. But it seemed too preposterous. And, anyway, was not all the island one? Was not Vallia Vallia? Perhaps there were no raids at all, and this was an invention of this miserable Ered Imlien to his own dark ends. I looked at him. He was drawing himself up and quite automatically reaching out for his riding crop. If he'd attempted to hit me with it I hadn't noticed. But it was broken in half. Had I done that?

"You have shamed me, Prince," he said, and the words gritted out through his teeth.

"Not so, Imlien. Not so. You have shamed yourself."

"One day—"

"Ered! Keep silence!" Natyzha Famphreon glowered on the miserable trylon and Ered Imlien turned away, muttering, but he kept silence as far as I was concerned.

To the kovneva I spoke and I admit with some trepidation. I was astounded at the quality of my voice. It hardly sounded like the bull-headed, vicious, intemperate Dray Prescot I knew.

"And can you tell me nothing more about my daughter?"

She shook her head. I thought, but could not be sure, that a dark gleam of triumph crossed those arrogant features.

"Nothing more is known."

There was nothing more I could find out. Whatever it was that Delia had gone to sort out, I could only hope that she and Melow would be successful and return swiftly to me.

They had to be successful! We had lost one daughter. We could not bear to face the anguish of the loss of another.

I forced myself to calm down. I could trust my Delia. She was supremely competent in these matters. I had a job to do here and that I must do. There was one other matter I wished to discuss before I left here, either walking out with all due civility, battling my way out with the Krozair brand in my fists or carried out feet first.

So I smashed myself out of that fearful frame of mind. One must, as they say on Kregen, accept the needle.

"We have ranked our deldars in this matter of the emperor," I said. "And we agree I shall think on it. Tell me, Natyzha Famphreon, what know you of the Black Feathers?"

Her arrogant old head went up at this. She started to walk between lines of potted plants, twirling the green fronds. We all walked with her, although Ered Imlien kept well clear of me. The onker was swishing his broken half of the riding crop about and trying to bash his boot and hitting his knee, whereat I was minded to laugh.

"The Black Feathers? Ah, you have heard of them?"

I said in a nasty voice, "If I had not heard of them I would scarcely be able to ask you."

She had the self-consciousness to flush up at this, at my suggestion, at my tone. She snapped a twig from a sweet little loomin, and twitched the flower about, not gently.

"The provinces are full of rumors. Nothing certain is known, as nothing is certain about anything in this life."

"The provinces, but Vondium?"

"I gave orders to my crebents of my estates to root out the priests. They did not catch one. Here in Vondium I have heard nothing." Then the sly old besom glanced at me and drew the mauve and white flowers down her cheek. "Perhaps you, Prince Majister, are of the Chyyanists?"

"I have no time for slallyfanting in this, kovneva. I too have attempted to root out the evil and now, I think, it is time for stronger measures. You are aware of the creed preached by the priests of the Great Chyyan?"

She flicked the flower. "I care not. They are not of Opaz and therefore are damned beyond redemption."

Had this old biddy been a commoner she would undoubtedly have formed one of the people in the long chanting processions that wound through Vondium. "Oolie Opaz! Oolie Opaz!" they chanted, up and down, singsong after singsong cadence. "*Oo*-lie *O*-paz! *Oo*-lie *O*-paz!" On and on and on.

"I know they wish to break our heads and take all that is ours," said

Nalgre Sultant. He looked vicious and mean, a very natural expression for him. "Red revolution! Aye! That is what these Chyyanists want."

I did not think these nobles had penetrated as far as we had in discovering details of the Chyyanists. I pondered. It might be advisable to tell them more than they already knew. I detested the racters. They had the power and the money. The Chyyanists wanted to take that money and with it the power, in the here and now. Those ends were admirable, in one sense, if they could be achieved reasonably. But red revolution is not reasonable and I have had a hand in more than one red revolution. Once you start to sweep away the old, the process can get out of hand. If Vallia ran red with blood from any cause, I would sorrow. And I did not believe the designs of Makfaril were simple honest revolution. How, once a little power is put into your hands, the evil and corruption grow!

So I told them what we had discovered. They took these revelations seriously. They would. They were experienced people with much at stake.

"Then the Chyyanists present a present threat." The kovneva had stopped twiddling with her flower. "Once the temple is brought to Vondium and the priests begin to suborn the masses... Slaves too, I hear, are sometimes present in the congregations."

"They aim to enslave the racters," I said with some satisfaction.

"That has been tried before and was ruthlessly put down. Once the temple is erected in Vondium the evil will gain a greater hold. We must watch every entrance and stop these priests. The idol you describe is not an easy thing to move."

"I'll get my men down to the docks," said the kov, the kovneva's son, and we all turned to look at him, shocked, as though a ghost had spoken.

"Yes, my son." The kovneva spoke in a soothing tone. "You do that."

No real surprise could be felt by me that these highly placed nobles should know of the Chyyanists. This kind of information would flow into their bureaus all the time. Now they would take more concern over the Black Feathers. This all added up. It all made sense. But I was banished from Vondium. I said, "I am banished from Vondium. I shall leave now, unless you have any other ideas, and see what I can do in the provinces. I am concerned over the Great Chyyan." I had told them that Hamal could be the basis of the new creed, but they indicated that did not signify. They'd smash Hamal when the time came. Even Nath Ulverswan was almost reconciled to that view. The main threat, as they saw it, was against themselves.

There was no point in my telling them that my chief concern, a concern almost approaching a guilty anguish, was for the poor deluded people who believed this evil creed and imagined they might indulge in all the goodness of Kregen, at once, in the here and now. These noble racters would never comprehend that point of view.

Further talk and a little more bargaining more or less sealed the compact in the view of the racters. If they suspected I merely toyed with them, for I was scrupulous in not giving my word, they did not reveal it. If I was going to have to fight my way out, that, too, did not appear on the surface. The Chuliks had gone, dismissed by a wave of the kovneva's hand. We walked through the farther recesses of the conservatory. It was a remarkable place. Cages had been positioned about in which were kept examples of many kinds of wild animals, so the place was also a miniature zoo.

I said, "We are now talking in circles. I will leave." I gave a hitch to the cloak and brought the hat up ready to clap it on my head. I was ready, also, to whip out longbow or longsword and swirl the cloak back out of the way for action.

On the way in here I'd observed the fantamyrrh as was proper. It occurred to me I might not be in the mood to observe it on the way out.

Intrigue and dark secrets flourished here as the exotic plants flourished in their heated glass houses. The passions and the feral viciousness here were scarcely matched by the savage beasts penned in their cages.

A number of the kovneva's Chail Sheom, her pretty little slave girls in their silks and bangles and silver chains, trailed after her carrying her fan and her perfumes and the gewgaws inseparable from a great lady of high rank. Two hulking fellows carried her chair. I had given these slaves a casual glance and saw their hangdog expressions. They brightened up with smiles and laughs when the kovneva looked at them, which is the way of slaves. It sickened me.

Now, as we stood there with the intrigues between us and the secret passions held down, as we made our plans and no doubt made alternative plans to deal more effectively each with the other, so the realization struck through to me that I, that same Dray Prescot who had so ruthlessly driven the slavers from Valka and had fought them over the fair surface of Kregen, was in reality standing here and plotting with Zair-forsaken slave masters and slave profiteers.

I moved away, gripping the hat, stood by a cage in which a graint shambled upright to grip the bars. The others moved with me and I didn't give a damn if they saw my face and guessed my thoughts. At that moment I'd have cheerfully seen them all consigned to the Ice Floes of Sicce.

A scattering screech and a ripping, tearing, chopped-off scream from the cages we had just passed brought us all around to stare upon a scene of horror.

Two feral beasts leaped from the blood-streaming wreckage of a half-naked slave girl to smash a second away with a splintered skull and to spring on two more. The beasts were chavonths. Past them I saw the two chair men running. Someone had deliberately opened the cage. Someone who hated the Dowager Kovneva Natyzha Famphreon had released these savage killer beasts upon us.

The scene etched itself on my brain. The parallel lines of cages with their heavy iron bars. The maddened beasts within, scenting freshly spilled blood, joined in the savage chorus. The slave girls huddled, naked arms upraised, silks splashed with blood, feathers and fans and jewels spilling across the floor. The chavonths chewed up their victims and turned, their muzzles smeared, to glare with venomous fury upon us.

And the nobles, these racters, screamed and clawed and ran past me screeching their fear, to find their way blocked by a stout iron grille at the end of the row of cages. Whoever had planned this had schemed well. I fancied the chair men were the culprits. They had run free, arguing a pre-knowledge. But they had so arranged affairs that the chavonths penned us in against iron bars. We were the caged, the chavonths the masters now!

Chavonths are known as treacherous beasts. They are six-legged hunting cats, powerful, and their fur is patterned in hexagons of blue, gray and black. Their fangs may not match those of a leem, their speed not equal that of a strigicaw, but they can smash a man's head in, their claws can disembowel a poor naked slave girl.

Nalgre Sultant pushed past me and ran for the end of the alleyway and stood, shaking the iron bars that blocked him off, screaming, screaming. Ered Imlien swung away, his red bloated face green. Nath Ulverswan gripped the arm of Natyzha Famphreon and they stood, crouched with their backs to the bars, glaring with awful horror upon the death that snarled at them.

The chinless nincompoop, Natyzha's son, Kov of Falkerdrin, stepped forward. He drew his rapier and main gauche. I could see the side of his face, see the sweat dripping there, the way his teeth caught his upper lip. His body trembled. But he stepped out before his mother and the twin blades he held caught the fireglass glow and gleamed.

The dowager kovneva husked out a word. "Jikai!" she said.

This would not be a Jikai—well, perhaps a little one—but it would prove to be highly instructive, that was for sure.

I said, "This is not work for a rapier, kov."

His voice panted. "That I know. But it is all the weapon I have, that and my dagger."

I threw off the swathing buff cloak and unfastened the golden zhantil heads and tossed down the gold-laced crimson cape-cloak. Then I drew the Krozair longsword, for the time for bowmanship had passed. Seg might not have agreed, but I knew what I knew about the Krozair brand.

"When they leap, Prince," said this young kov, "do you take the left hand one and I—"

"Give them no time to spring," I said, and took the Krozair longsword's hilt into both my spread fists and so charged forward, swinging the brand up in a deadly arc of steel.

Through all the hubbub I heard the gasps of horror at my back. What I looked like Zair alone knows. I hurtled forward. The chavonths had given me no time to smash forward to save the slaves; all were dead or fled. Everything had happened with shocked speed, a few heartbeats separating the first scream and the instant I sprang.

This was what living on Kregen was all about, this horrific transformation, in an instant, from peaceful living to berserk toy, from graciousness to terror.

This must be done right the first time, and quick, damned quick...

The two chavonths did not leap exactly together and so I was able to position and slash at the first. The gleaming blade of the longsword swept in that vicious chopping circle as my hands and wrists and forearms rolled over, and the muscles of my back ridged and extended and I felt all the old pull and power. The steel sliced through the chavonth's furred hide just above his left forequarter—his left foresixth—and I went with the blow and rolled away and the slashing claws razored past. A single roll brought me up and a single twist turned me and a single leap brought me from the side against the second chavonth. The Krozair brand licked out like a bar of blood. I drove it point first into the lean furry flank. A blue hexagon imploded. The onward rush of the great beast almost snatched the sword from me, but a Krozair knows how to hold onto a sword hilt. I gave a vicious twist and then withdraw, swirling the blade instantly into an overhand chop that crunched down on the chavonth's backbone just abaft his center pair of legs.

The yelling shrieking of the wounded chavonths erupted in the iron-barred area, the stink of freshly spilled blood poured out in a warm effluvium. There was no time to stop. This beast was done for, although he spat and clawed futilely at the air and at his ruined back.

The chinless kov was trying to get in at the first chavonth, trying to dart his slender rapier in past the wicked claws of its remaining legs. I hurled myself forward in a desperate rush and almost, almost I saved him completely.

But a wickedly tipped claw swept in from the side and gashed all down his ribs and he shrieked and fell back and then I was on the chavonth and the terrible Krozair longsword rose and fell, rose and fell, and three blows took the poor chavonth's head clean off.

Natyzha Famphreon had not fainted. Nalgre Sultant, seeing the dead and dying cats, dragged out his rapier and made a great show of coming forward, twirling the blade, ready to face all comers. Nath Ulverswan kept his grip upon the kovneva. Ered Imlien reluctantly walked forward. He was not afraid, that I knew, but he had not considered what had happened as being possible.

I bent to the kov. His chinless face, so unlike the chinless, pop-eyed face of Chido, glared up at me and a grin ricked his lips. His side was badly torn, but he would live. He was in some pain.

"I tried..." He spoke with an effort. "My mother... it was my duty... but... but a rapier..."

"Lie still, kov." His name was Nath, but I could not call him Nath. There are many Naths on Kregen. "Lie still." I looked up at the others, all recovering from the fright, all sorting out the story they would tell. "You zigging cramphs!" I bellowed. "Run and send for a doctor! Run, you nurdling onkers!"

Ered Imlien ran past the corpses of slaves, the dead and dying chavonths, swirling his rapier, to fetch a doctor.

I held this Kov Nath of Falkerdrin, easing him, feeling only a vast pity, a contempt that embraced all his stupid family and the pride that sustained them. I glared at Nalgre Sultant.

"Fetch cloths from the dead slaves, Sultant. We must staunch the wounds. Jump to it, you rast!"

He jumped.

So we waited for the doctor, for I would not allow Kov Nath to be moved. He lapsed into unconsciousness as the doctor arrived, so the acupuncture needles to ease his pain were not necessary and the doctor, a client of the house, could get to work to stop the bleeding and to draw the ragged wounds together and apply his healing paste. Some doctors of Kregen are useless, many are expert; one chooses where one can.

I stood up.

"I am leaving." I picked up my cloak and the cape-cloak. "I will wash elsewhere, wash this place from me. Until I see you again, Natyzha Famphreon, take good care of that son of yours. Maybe we have all misjudged him. Perhaps all Vallia is wrong about him." Then I went out and no one offered to stop me and I did not observe the fantamyrrh.

Sixteen

Kadar the Hammer rides north to Seg Segutorio

Now began a period of my life on Kregen that, even now, looking back, I cannot decide if I should curse horribly over it or simply stand with my fists on my hips and roar with laughter. It was all a great foolishness. I made my way by the dusty roads northwestward. When it rained in a lashing gale of Kregen that drenched everything and everyone the roads turned to a quagmire and it was useless to attempt to flounder on. Then I sought sanctuary. After leaving Natyzha Famphreon's house where we had hatched intrigues against the emperor, I had called again at our villa in Vondium—the Valkan villa owned by Delia and myself—and besides having a long and glorious bath, taking the full Baths of the Nine, I equipped myself a little more lavishly for the journey.

The villa did not see us all that often, for we stayed at the emperor's command in the wing of the palace given over to our use. But everything was ready, as it was bound to be. So I took a strong preysany loaded with supplies, with a harness or two of armor, spare weapons, provisions. Also I packed the old brown blanket cloak and the bamboo stick with the concealed blade. That had served before; it might serve again.

During the ride north to Seg's estates of Falinur I was embroiled only in four small skirmishes and rode for my life only once, preferring that to fighting the stinking pack of drikingers who howled hairily at me from the roadside and hurled stones and spears and would have skewered me through had I not ducked and clapped in spurs.

This kind of flight was a different matter from running from one's foes. These poor devils might be evil in the eyes of honest folk, but all in good time my plans called for the alleviation of the conditions that created bandits, if it could be contrived, rather than for the removal of the drikingers themselves.

The zorca-ride jolted up the old liver, as I had said. I am fond of the canals and the canalfolk of Vallia, but somehow this canter through the heart of Vallia seemed more in keeping. The canal folk are a staunchly independent lot, and the men and women of the cuts do not call themselves koters and koteras as do the gentry of Vallia; they are vens and venas. But as I passed through the green countryside I would stop at bridges over the canals and talk and spend some time, for I was maturing plans and had no wish to rush. After all, I was not hurrying to a rendezvous with Delia.

A strong eastward swing was advisable toward the north of Vindelka for the Ocher Limits thrust a tongue-like protrusion between that province and Seg's Falinur to the north. I made no attempt to revisit either of the Delkas, and decided firmly against a sentimental side trip to the Dragon's Bones.

All through this central portion of the island large lakes are to be found, with the Great River twining through, and the canals boring on with man's ingenuity at work to maintain the levels by lock and lift. So I trotted on and entered the Kovnate of Falinur and at once I saw what Seg meant about the demeanor of his people.

They did not offer hostility, although they did not know who I was, and when I put up at an inn and told them my name was Kadar the Hammer they merely sniffed and took no more than the usual notice of a stranger one expects. But the undercurrents were strong. As a simple smith, for that is what they took me to be, out seeking some gainful employment, I posed only the threat of any itinerant labor to the homegrown product. But a laughing group of koters passed, tyrs and kyrs and even a strom, and these gentry aroused dark hidden looks of anger and envy. Falinur, as Seg had said, was like to erupt in violence at any moment.

These people had backed their late kov against the emperor with the third party and had lost. So why should that still rankle? Perhaps, for I did not bring the precise subject up, perhaps it was not that which was causing their hostility to Seg. Whatever it was, we had to put it aright by fair means. Any other way would be as abhorrent to Seg as to myself. Anyway, with tough independent people as are most Vallians, brutal repression would repercuss with a vengeance.

A shrunken little fellow with one eye and swathed in furs against an imagined cold gave me a portion of the answer. He rode a hirvel and led a long string of calsanys, all loaded down with trinkets that this ob-Eye Enil hawked from village to village. We rode together for a space, and I listened.

"Aye, Kadar the Hammer! You may well ask. We ride through Vinnur's Garden here and the land is rich." His one eye swiveled alarmingly to regard me with cunning. "And where the land is rich, there, by Beng Drangil, men will fight and kill for it."

The Great River which bordered Falinur's eastern flank made a kinked loop to the east here on the border between Falinur and Vindelka. The Ocher Limits ended to the west. In the fertile area of Vinnur's Garden riches could be won by agriculture on the fertile eastern sections by mining on the more barren western. The border between the two kovnates ran to the north of Vinnur's Garden. The people living there had been under the rule of both Vindelka and Falinur at differing times. Now Vindelka demanded their loyalty, and their taxes. But many folk north and south of the border wished that dividing line to be redrawn much farther to the south, cutting off Vinnur's Garden from Vindelka and giving it to Falinur.

It was scarcely necessary for Ob-Eye to say, "But the new kov of Falinur, this Seg Segutorio whose past is a mystery, refuses to countenance any move against Vindelka."

Ob-Eye wandered the central portions of Vallia, and although he confided that he had been born in Ovvend, he could look upon these squabbles with the single eye of the interested observer.

I knew why Seg would not allow his people to go raiding down into Vinnur's Garden, why he made no move to annex the place from the Kov of Vindelka. For this Kov of Vindelka was Vomanus, a good comrade to Seg and me, and we had fought at that immortal battle at the Dragon's Bones.

But I sensed this did not explain all the hostility to Seg and Thelda. As we rode north and left the parochial problem of Valinur's Garden to the rear, still the impression I received was one of implacable hatred to the Kov of Falinur. I own I was put out by this, upset, angry and baffled.

There were slaves still in Falinur, though there were not many. And I gained some more insight. Acting not just because it was my way but from honest conviction, Seg had given orders that from henceforth no slaves would be allowed in his kovnate. He was obeyed surlily and his edict was broken more and more often, for all that his guards rode to stamp out the evil. One consequence of the abolition of slavery, in intention if not yet in fact, was the resurgence of the slavers who preyed where pickings were ripest. This added another strand; it still did not explain it all. So, taking the chunkrah by the horns, I began direct questions about the Black Feathers.

The answers Ob-Bye gave me filled in about another fifty percent of the problem.

Yes, there were temples and priests and traveling churches spreading the great word and, by Beng Drangil, the great day is coming, the Black Day, and in that day will the Great Chyyan reward all his loyal followers! Thus spake Ob-Eye Enil, swearing by Beng Drangil, the patron saint of hawkers.

This was no fantasy. This was stark reality. As I jogged along toward Seg's kovnate capital city of Falanriel, a place which, despite its architecture, I always looked forward to visiting, I realized more and more the hold the Chyyanists had on these people.

On a day when the suns broke through scattered clouds and the joy of living should have burst all worries—and, sadly, did not—we trotted through a ferny dell. With horrid shrieks designed to chill us, the drikingers leaped from the ferns, waving their clanxers and rapiers and spears, roaring at us to surrender or be chopped.

With a curse I ripped out the clanxer scabbarded to Twitchnose. A smith may carry samples of his wares. If it came to it I'd use the longsword on them.

Then I checked. The bandits closed up around us, fierce, hairy men with thickly bearded faces and bright merry eyes, darting the points of their weapons at us. But Ob-Eye pulled out a leather wallet from his loose tunic, opened it, waved a scrap of black feather in the air.

"Peace, brothers!" he squeaked. He was only a little frightened, I saw, and marveled. "We are all Chyyanists together, you and I. Listen to what Makfaril has said through his priests, listen and rejoice, for the day is coming."

And then these fearsome bandits set up a yelling and a hullabaloo and crowded around, laughing, slapping their thighs and bellowing greetings, and every other sentence had to do with the Black Feathers. In no time a fire had been lit and we were sitting around listening and smelling roast-ing vosk haunch. The wine went around. It was good too, plunder from a vintner's caravan. Good humor prevailed, although the leader, a ferocious villain with a spade beard he had threaded with gold wire and with golden earrings that caught the lights of the fire and of the suns, did bellow out, "By Varkwa the Open-Handed! If many more travelers are Chyyanists the pickings will be small!"

"But soon all Vallia will be ours for the looting!" bellowed his lieutenant, and the gang set up a racket of laughter and promises of what they would do on the Black Day. Chief among these was the heartfelt desire to go into Falanriel and sack the place and take all. And what they would do to the kovneva, the high and mighty, stuck-up, prideful and ignorant Kovneva Thelda, would have set the Ice Floes of Sicce alight.

I chewed on succulent vosk and kept my face down. Listening would help more than a stupid sword-swinging affray. Was this another piece of the puzzle? Was poor Thelda, who always meant well, overdoing her part as a kovneva? She loved the title and took immense pride in her status. Yet once in the long ago she had been forced to spy and scheme for the racters. Now my good comrade Seg had her in his keeping. I made a little vow that not only would I speak to Thelda as a friend, I'd stick a length of steel blade into any of these drikinger cramphs who tried to harm a hair of her head. But, all the same, she could be a terribly tiresome woman, and goodheart-edly never be aware of it.

There could now be no doubt that the Chyyanist creed had caught on like a prairie fire here in Falinur. An attempt had been made to spread the word in Veliadrin. Delphond had been under attack—I was sure Delia was right and there was the black feather to prove it—even though we did not know how far the Chyyanists had reached there. I fancied that Inch in the Black Mountains and Korf Aighos in the Blue Mountains would be facing the same challenge.

If I allowed myself to be swayed by the megalomania I have been accused of, I could see a clear pattern. But Natyzha Famphreon and the other racters knew of the Black Feathers, and their provinces had been infiltrated also. Makfaril, whoever he was, surely intended to sound the call for the Black Day at the same time all over Vallia. With a little knowl-edge I have of human nature, with a little knowledge of running affairs of state, and with the knowledge borne in on me by the demeanor of bandits around the campfire, I knew with a dark foreboding that Makfaril might not be able to hold his followers to his timetable. The explosion might erupt at any moment, triggered by any silly stupid event. The day of the Black Feathers could strike tomorrow...

That ride up through the heart of Valka was all a great foolishness. Bits of it recur to me now. I had hoped the long ride would soothe me and calm me down, but the more I saw and heard the more fraught and tense I became. And the burden of my fear, a true and deeply abiding fear, must be shown by the first words I spoke to Seg after the joyful Lahals.

"And the news from Delia, Seg? Where is her letter?"

He shook his head. "No letter from Delia has arrived here, Dray. There are packages for you forwarded on, flown in from Vondium and Valka, and coming from—well, you know the names."

I did. There would be estate information from Strombor and chunkrah counts from Hap Loder and the Clansmen. There would be news from Kytun and Ortyg in Djanduin. But I hungered to hear from Delia, for now I knew she struggled against some unknown evil that threatened our daughter Dayra.

I asked after Thelda, and Seg spread his hands and said she had been visiting in Vondium and was momentarily expected.

The impression Seg gave was that he wanted to take up his great long-bow and go ask the emperor to repeat the words that had banished me. I fancied the emperor would find life exceedingly uncomfortable thereafter if he did repeat them.

"Well, by Vox! how long does he think to keep you banished, the old onker?"

"Only from Vondium. And the Black Feathers have not sprouted there as yet."

"Come and wet that dusty throat of yours and let us see what we may contrive."

We went down from the battlemented gateway and so across the outer yard and through the inner walls and up through narrow winding stairways of stone into Seg's private chambers in the Fletcher's Tower. Once it had been the Jade Tower, but Seg had changed all that. This castle fortress of his, frowning down over the city of Falanriel, had been built to withstand a protracted siege. Seg kept the place amply stocked. He had a small guard of Bowmen of Loh, backed up by a regiment of Pachaks with a few other diffs in their different specialities. He was no fool, was Seg Segutorio, over these matters, with the wild fey ways and shrewd practicality of his mountain people.

All the same, as we sat and drank in the quiet ease of his rooms, I had to say, "It does look as though we are the high and mighty of the land now, and grind down the poor."

"To the Ice Floes with that, my old dom!" Seg looked annoyed. "I was a miserable starveling, a mercenary, a slave. I know. If a man works in my province of Falinur he is assured of a living and of comfort."

"Slaves?"

Seg made a face and drank his wine. "These devils are sly and secret and run slaves no matter what I do to stop 'em."

"Vinnur's Garden—"

He did not let me go on. "My nobility here, all owing their fine estates to me, all prate on and on about marching into Vinnur's Garden and taking it for Falinur. But Vomanus—"

"He is seldom at home. He is almost as much of an absentee landlord as I am."

"Well, I have put in my stint here. And it looks as though I'd have done better to have stayed in Vondium, or visited Erthyrdrin again, for all the good I have done here."

When I told him, during the course of our long talk through the evening and most of the night, about Natyzha Famphreon and the chavonths, he grimaced and said, "I'd rather not hear what she did to her slaves. They'd all be punished to make sure the guilty got it in the neck, to the devil with the innocent."

"Aye."

"And they actually expected you to fight your father-in-law?"

"Not exactly fight him. But certainly not assist him."

"Remember the Dragon's Bones?"

"Now there was a bonny little fracas."

"Bonny little fracas! Dray, Dray! That was High Jikai!"

"I wouldn't have said so, but it was squeaky, all the same."

"Those days when you and Delia and Thelda and I marched across the hostile territories! Ah, but they'll never come again."

I was not at all sure of that. Kregen is a world of ups and downs. So we talked on through the night, amicably drinking, and our thoughts were as often of the stirring past adventures as of the terrors of the future and the problems we faced.

Two days later Thelda arrived back in Falanriel, flushed, bright-eyed, bouncing, filled with glowing stories of her time in Vondium. She had been desolated that her great friend Delia had not been there. Of all her sprightly babble we took the due meed of attention. "And the dear queen! Queen Lushfymi! What a charming woman she is, and so regal. I own she has quite won me over. And yet the ignorant fools call her Queen Lush. It really is a disgrace."

Seg asked a casual question about the Queen of Lome and Thelda fired up instantly. "Beautiful, oh, yes! She is radiant. And so cultured. She is rich too. Lome is not the largest country in Pandahem, but her wealth is dazzling. The presents she brought, the length of the procession—the animals and the people and the displays—you should have seen it all, my dear. You would have enjoyed it."

"I'm sure," said Seg, looking at me with a straight face.

Seg and Thelda loved each other; that was true, and gave me great joy. When couples split apart friends are hurt also. I felt as confident as of anything that Seg and Thelda knew each other well enough by now. As for their children, the eldest son, named Dray for some odd quirk of desire on Seg's part, was off adventuring. The twins were at school. No—here Thelda pursed her lips up most comically—Silda, the girl, was with the Sisters of the Rose.

I sat up.

"But you are a Sister of Patience, Thelda."

"It's none of your business, my dearest Dray, for you are a man. But, yes, I am. And Silda hankered so after the SoR I had to let her go. I own it mystifies me."

In his droll way, Seg said, "Delia was mystified too."

So, of course, that explained it. It also made me think again about what I both might and ought to do.

A very great deal of our conversations concerned Queen Lushfymi, the Queen of Lome. Lome is the country situated in the northwest of Pandahem where the long east-west central chain of mountains sweeps up northwestward and, extending out to sea, forms the straggling line of the Hoboling Islands. Lome is rich although not overlarge, occupying the space east of the mountains to the border with Iyam. East of Iyam lies Menaham, occupied by the Bloody Menahem. Then comes Tomboram where I harbored most guilty memories of Tilda and Pando. And, in the jutting northeast corner of Pandahem is situated Jholaix. One smacks ones lips at the thought of Jholaix.

So after the Vallians had kicked the Hamalese out of Pandahem after the Battle of Jholaix, it seemed the emperor was attempting to make friends with at least one nation of Pandahem, for that whole island had been in a state of near-conflict with Vallia for many seasons. I welcomed this move. It was statesmanship at the level I sought. I devoutly wished Vallia and Pandahem to come together in comradeship, at first against Hamal and then, and much more importantly, to stand together with other countries of Paz against the raids of the shanks from the other continental grouping on the other side of Kregen.

What with talking about Queen Lushfymi and arranging a party for the castellan's eldest son who was about to go off to be a mercenary, disdaining service under his father, Thelda was kept busy. Seg and I rode and hunted and talked and drank. But for his generally subdued air, Seg was in good spirits, considering the circumstances. He got through a prodigious amount of work. But for the malignant animosity in which these confounded idiots of Falinur held him, he would have been a perfect kov. As for Thelda, she was quite wrapped up in her own doings and seemed unaware of the atmosphere. Seg had even refused to go up to Vondium to greet the emperor on his return, as Inch had likewise not gone, because of his concern.

How I felt the old guilty stab that, when I asked him, he would always manage to get away to aid me!

And more importantly, how he would race across half a world to rescue me from a sticky corner, as you will know.

Only two sword-swinging occasions of note occurred during that stay in Seg's castle of Falanriel, the castle some men called the Falnagur. I will speak of one only, seeing that the other bore on threads of intrigue outside my present concerns, but intrigues that were to plague me woefully in later days, as you shall hear.

The messenger staggered through the main gate, his zorca dead a dwabur down the track, his blood bedabbling his hacked armor. The story was soon told, and familiar. As we mounted up and set spurs to our mounts and galloped headlong out through the frowning gateway of the Falnagur, I found I harbored deep agonies of indecision. Could I cut down some poor wight of a ponsho farmer, a chunkrah herder, a vosk breeder, because they had been willfully misled by the devil Makfaril and his creed of Chyyanism? We rode through the night with the moons casting down their fuzzy pink and golden lights, our shadows blobs of purple darkness, the sound of the hooves and the clattering of armor clear warning to all who would listen.

Seg had placed a number of people he thought loyal and hardworking in positions of trust, trying wherever possible to choose native Falinurese. But as a result these folk were regarded as the minor nobility, which they were, and hated accordingly by the rest. In a steading a mere three and a half dwaburs off along a tributary of the Great River, Tarek Nalgre Lithisfer was besieged and near to exhaustion. We rode. A tarek is of the minor baronage, a gift within the giving of a kov. Seg had told me of Tarek Nalgre, saying he valued him. Now the Black Feathers had risen openly against him, burning barns and dreadfully killing women and children, and I knew that a bamboo stick might not be enough, that the edge of steel might horrendously have to be employed.

In any event, we were able to ride and scatter the besieging people. Mixed with my remorse I found a little comfort in the fact that the hard core of the besiegers was formed of a body of drikingers, three or four bands joined together to effect the mischief. We fought them. Seg's Bowmen shot their terrible shafts. His Pachaks twirled their tailhands and the blades glittered under the moons. Yes, we fought these bandits, for the country folk mostly ran when we galloped up.

But I did not enjoy the work. I mention it to illustrate just how far the malcontents had aroused the countryside and in allying themselves with the Black Feathers acquired a kind of respectability in the eyes of the ordinary folk. It is often thus. Bandits, knaves, villains, all take on the jargon of a new and zealous creed, an idealistic revolutionary appeal, and use what is honest and subvert it to their own dark ends.

Had Chyyanism been an honest religion, had Seg and his baronage been ruthless tyrants, then the situation would have been entirely different. Although it seemed I fought for the haves against the have-nots, the truth was far from that.

We trailed home with one or two wounded, having made sure Tarek Nalgre was safe. The steading had not burned. Seg left a guard there. But our resentment against the Chyyanists had been inflamed. The immediate cause of this outbreak had been Tarek Nalgre's order that a certain slave girl was to be released immediately. The girl's owner, malignant, had appealed to the local leaders of the Chyyanists, and the burnings and killings had followed. No, I was in an ugly mood as we rode back to Seg's castle, the Falnagur, and doffed our armor and rubbed our bruises and counted the cost.

"This Tarek," I said to Seg later, as we tried to relax after a capital meal, quashing all guilt thoughts. "He seems a quality fighter and man."

"Aye. He is a bonny fighting man, and honest and loyal."

"The very man for the order."

Seg looked pleased at this, for he took his position within the order with great seriousness. I spoke to match his mood.

"We must begin with seasoned men. Once we are established and have a base and the beginnings of a tradition—how the Krozairs are fortunate in that!—we can enroll likely young lads and give them the full benefit of proper training."

"And will you find one of your Krozair brothers willing to travel all this way, to teach what he may regard as breaking his vows?"

I had thought of that. "There is no betrayal in teaching young men to be upright and honest and to respect their own strength. There is altogether too much banging and bashing around on Kregen by the strong against the weak. I speak in general terms. I think we are both too cynical and beyond the naive area of simple chivalry. Sometimes a man must be a bit of a villain to survive. But if more people thought more and struck less, then the demands of villainy would die out."

Looking back and seeing myself as I was then, I can smile a little indulgently at my foolish self. Even then I was dreadfully young in the ways of Kregen, for all my vaunted experience—at least, vaunted by others, not by me, who knows far too much about Dray Prescot for comfort.

Came the day when I told Seg and Thelda I must wish them Remberee. I shook my head when they asked if I would visit Inch.

"I think not. His letters say that his Black Mountain Men have little sympathy with the Chyyanists. And as for the Blue Mountain Boys, there was a most distressing occurrence with a Chyyanist priest. Something to do with burned tail feathers, I believe. Most injurious to pride and stern ends."

Seg managed a smile at this. He did not burst out with a complaint that he only wished his Falinurese were of the same caliber as Inch's Black Mountain Men. For that I respected him. He was entitled to the complaint; fate alone had decided this.

"Well, Dray my dear," said Thelda in her managing way, "then it will be Delphond, I suppose. Or," and here she cocked her head on one side in a calculating way, organizing things for me, "or you could go to Strombor. I need some of their beautiful—"

"Thelda!" said Seg, half laughing. So whatever it was Thelda wanted from Strombor we did not find out.

"I shall," I said, "go to Vondium."

"But!" said Seg.

"But," said Thelda, "you are banished! The emperor has published an edict of proscription. The dear queen told me so herself. You will be taken up if you go back to Vondium."

"Maybe. And again, maybe not. But I am not prepared to let the emperor stand any longer between what I must do and my own frail desires. By Vox! I am tired of shilly-shallying around."

"So it is Vondium then, my old dom."

"Aye! And if the emperor or any of his men try to stand in my way it will not be me who will be sorry!"

Seventeen

What chanced during the bath of Katrin Rashumin

Well. From those stupid boastful words you will see exactly how I had been rattled. If only I knew what Delia was up to! If only I was sure that Dayra was safe! To Vondium I would go and try to sort matters out.

And if any chanting, hypocritical, venomous Chyyanist priest got in my way with his damned Black Feathers he had better look out sharpish.

And so, with yet another vainglorious boast in a most un-Dray Prescot-like fashion, I took one of Seg's fliers back to Vondium.

I'd be either Nath the Gnat or Kadar the Hammer as opportunity offered. On Kregen one has to handle names carefully, for names are vital. I own to a delight in handling names, and yet I do not forget that however important names are, and however much it behooves a man who wishes to keep his head on his shoulders to remember names and get them right, it is the reality behind the names that matters, the personality and inner being that counts.

The twinkle and shimmer of Vondium rose before us and the flier swooped down. Seg's pilot helped me unload my zorca and the pack prey-sany, and I stood to wish him Remberee. Then I mounted up and, wearing my old brown blanket cloak and with the bamboo stick across the saddle, started to jog gently along the dusty road toward the city whose topmost towers were just in sight.

If I had been put out of countenance by the changes in Vallia after my absence of twenty-one years on Earth followed by the seasons at the Eye of the World, I could only be dismayed by the changes in Vondium during this my latest absence.

The first thing I saw was a wayside shrine to one of the old minor religions of Vallia, tolerated and even given some small affection by the masses who hewed to Opaz. The shrine's old statue had been removed and the niche with its symbols and little flickering lamp was bedecked with black feathers, and the crude statue of a black chyyan replaced the old. I reined up, staring.

An old toothless crone at the roadside cackled.

"Come the day, good sir, come the day."

I said nothing, but shook Twitchnose's reins and cantered on.

By Zair! Did the emperor—did the nobles—do nothing about this?

There was no difficulty in getting into Vondium. The place bustled with life. People scurried everywhere. The guards at the gate barely gave me a glance. They were Rapas, and usually relished a little idle amusement in hazing travelers they considered suitable game for sport. Now I rode through and found myself in a beehive of rumor and speculation and gossip. The brilliant colors, the jostling lines of calsanys, the palanquins, the tall flickering wheels of the zorca chariots racing fleetly along the wider boulevards, the long steady streaming of narrow boats along the Cuts, the shouts and yells of vendors, all the heady brilliant hurly-burly of a great city broke about me as I guided Twitchnose and the led preysany toward the smith's quarter and the tavern called the Iron Anvil. The area was known to me only vaguely—this was not Ruathytu—but after a few directions I arrived and, by showing the edge of a golden talen, secured a room in the hostelry above the tavern. From here I would have to work.

It would not be proper for me to reveal all the steps that led in the end to a plain lenken door, brass-studded, in a flat gray stone wall on the Hill of Tred'efir. The hunt began at a hospital for slaves, led by way of a school for the children of poor mothers, through a number of other establishments, to this calm white-stuccoed house in its bower of greenery. The guards would only let me through into an outer courtyard, and there I had to kick my heels. The guards were all girls, young and limber and rosy in their health and strength. They were clad as the messenger from Delia, Sosie ti Drakanium, had been clad, and they handled their rapiers with the professional ease of those who understand pointed and edged weapons. There were also girls wearing cool floating robes of many colors, who came to a pierced stone screen to peer at me and laugh quietly amongst themselves.

Presently a lady whom I can only call the Mother Superior came out, although that is nowise her rank or calling.

"Kadar the Smith?"

"Kadar the Hammer, and it please you, lady."

She nodded, studying me. Her smooth face within the framing crimson cap and veil reposed in calm confidence. In her I could trust, as far as a man may trust a woman. I told her what I wanted. She did not laugh, but the corners of her eyes betrayed extra wrinkles and her soft mouth turned up, just a little.

"You must know that is impossible."

"I wish only to speak with the chief of the Sisters. That is all. If you wish I can be blindfolded, in a darkened room. But I must speak with her." I had no need to put any false emotion into my words. "This is very important to me."

"Is it important to the SoR?"

"I do not know. I think so."

"You are honest. But the thing is impossible. Now go, and go in peace, Kadar the Smith."

"Kadar the Hammer. Very well, I will go. But I will not give up."

But she turned away and made a sign and lo! four sharply curved reflex bows held in young supple hands—and four exceedingly sharp steel arrow heads—pointed at my midriff. I took the hint. After all, had some wandering gypsy-like woman approached me and asked to see the Grand Archbold of the Krozairs of Zy I might have reacted in the same way. So I went.

Now I would have to play my penultimate card. I had not wished to do so, for although Katrin Rashumin had been a good friend to Delia and had benefited from our advice over her island kovnate of Rahartdrin, I had not seen her lately, for obvious reasons, and had no way of knowing her present feelings. But, as they say in Hamal, one must come to the fluttrell's vane.

A single inquiry elicited the information that the Kovneva of Rahartdrin was in Vondium.

I took myself off to her villa, a most gorgeous place and splendidly eloquent of her position, for her fortunes had vastly improved after Delia and I had sorted out her island estates for her. We had had to discharge a crooked Crebent and put a stop to certain nefarious practices. Katrin had been grateful then. I think she always remembered a certain flight in an airboat with me, and remembered it with regret. But she had remained loyal to Delia, or so I hoped.

The porter regarded me with disfavor.

"Go away, rast! We have our own smith, young Bargom the Anvil! He will make mincemeat of you!"

The porter was a Fristle, and his cat-face bristled up with his whiskers bright and stiff. I sighed.

At this time I had noticed that the Vallians, as a general rule, did not favor diffs. There were very few diffs among the wealthy and the nobility. They employed diffs as servants and guards and had no scruple about enslaving them.

The villa's wall ran alongside the road for a space and then shot off at a right angle through woods. Further upslope lay the abandoned villa of Kov Mangar the Apostate. I slipped along between the trees and soon found a place where I might climb over. The way was not difficult and I saw no one, walking rapidly but without obvious signs of haste through a large market garden filled with lettuce and gregarians and squishes. I even picked a handful of palines as I went.

The kitchen gateway showed ahead and just as I was casually about to enter, a Brokelsh guard and a girl, a young Brokelsh slave girl from the kitchens, came out, laughing and talking together. The guard, a big fellow, all bristly hair and bully-boy manner, swelled his chest under the armor. His hand fell to the clanxer at his waist. He wanted to show off for the girl.

"What are you doing here, onker?"

I, Dray Prescot, took a chance. It was a risk. I said, "By the Black Feathers, dom! I am glad to see you. Where away are the confounded stables?"

At this he relaxed at once. I felt my relief at the easy outcome of the confrontation more than tempered by the vast feeling of unease. Chyyanism was here, in a great noble's villa. Well and truly had the Temple of the Great Chyyan reached Vondium. So much for the protestations of vigilance given me by the racters!

So with a direction to the stables I wandered off, saying my thanks and moaning over the hardness of life. Presently, by taking a smart right turn, I managed to find a smaller doorway near the stables. Actual ingress to the Villa's interior could only be achieved by my sending a Fristle guard to sleep standing up, but I did lower him gently to the ground. Then I walked swiftly inside, not looking around, and began to nose my way toward Katrin's apartments. I did not wish to cause too much mayhem, but a little was inevitable.

Had she been anywhere else but Vondium there would have been no problem. The trouble with secret societies is that they are secret. At the least I knew Katrin Rashumin to belong to the Sisters of the Rose. Or so I had gathered from the way Delia had spoken on occasion.

A big burly Womox, his fierce upthrusting horns wound with golden wire, bellowed at me, and I had to skip and jump and put him to sleep horizontally. His harness fitted me, more or less. It hung about my waist, but the shoulders snugged well enough.

So it was as a guard in the employ of Kovneva Katrin I went a-visiting. The colors of Rahartdrin are yellow and green with a double red stripe slashed diagonally across them. Katrin also had a fondness for the lotus flower, so this was emblazoned on the breast and back of the brown shifts of her servitors and was picked out in embroidery on the guard's tunics. So I marched along and took no notice of anyone and no one took any notice of me, which is perfectly normal in these gigantic households of many slaves and many guards, not all of whom are apim.

I was stopped by two Pachaks at an inner door. You know about Pachaks. There was no talking my way past these two fine fellows and I would not slay them, for Pachaks are dear to me, so I had to feint with one, knock the second down and deal instantly with his comrade. This I did. Then I pushed through, taking the ivory wand one of the Pachaks had gripped in his upper left hand as his sign of office and tour of duty at the kovneva's private apartments.

I was allowed past a number of girl slaves and somewhat effeminate man slaves until, at the last, I reached places that, by the perfume, the sounds of running water and the warmth and languorous feel in the air, told me plainly enough that no man, and certainly not some hired mercenary, not even a paktun, more likely a thieving masichier, would ever be allowed.

So, saying simply, "If you do not let me in to see the kovneva she will have you girls flogged jikaider," I walked past the befuddled maids. They shrieked out as I dragged the purple curtains apart. Scents of steam and soap and unguents arose. Katrin was taking a small and private bath, not one of the Baths of the Nine, and a gorgeous black girl from Xuntal dropped the sponge in her terror as I barged in.

I knew I had perhaps ten or so murs before the guards came arunning, and they would seek to kill. I made no mistake about that, no mistake at all.

Katrin turned lazily, the soapy water running over one gleaming shoulder, and she looked at my legs and the bottom half of the uniform and the war harness and she said in her caressing voice: "You realize you are a dead man?"

And I answered, "Only if you give the word, Katrin."

And she looked up, shocked, the blood rushing into her face, the water swirling in soapy whirls about her body.

"Dray!"

"Aye! And don't shout all over the villa or—"

"Yes, I know!" She stood up, completely uncaring of her shining soapy nakedness and said in her sharp woman-managing voice to the Xuntalese maiden, "Xiri! My wrap!"

With the lotus-flowered wrap about her she walked swiftly to the door and said to someone outside, "No one enters on pain of death! Tell the Pachak Jiktar! Hurry! No one, mind!"

Then she kicked Xiri out and slammed the door herself, drawing the heavy purple drapes.

She turned to me, and the lotus-flowered wrap half dropped from a shoulder. It was not coquetry. I know she had tried once, and she knew what Delia meant.

"Thank you, Katrin. I have no time. The emperor—"

"I do not know if he will kill you if he finds you in Vondium, my silly woflo. But I would not take bets on it."

"I must know where Delia is."

"Ah!"

I wasn't sure. Did she know?

Her dark hair, gathered into a protecting net, broke in a cascade as she ripped the cap off. Her face had softened over the years, but still she could act as haughtily as any fabled Queen of Pain. Her lips, a trifle thin, smiled up as she tossed her hair loose and began to rub her body with a yellow and green towel. The two slashed stripes of scarlet looked like threads of blood.

"I have an appointment with Master Hork in two glasses. He is a master Jikaidast and I hope to learn much of the game."

"I'm playing no game."

"You cannot see Delia, has she not told you?"

"Only that she has gone away, and an onker knows that." I eyed this Katrin Rashumin evenly, knowing what I knew about her. "I am in a desperate hurry. I must speak with the chief lady of the Sisters of the Rose. She will help me, I am sure she will."

"The chief lady," Katrin said, laughing, and there was a deal of mockery in that laughter. "I do not think there is a single man who knows her name or title."

"Well? Blindfold me, then, a darkened room. Katrin!"

"You remind me, my dear Dray, of Tyr Korgan and the mermaid. You Valkans are famous for your songs."

"In the end you know what the song says occurred between Tyr Korgan and the mermaid. I must meet the Lady Superior—I do not know her rank or name or title. Katrin! Listen, my daughter Dayra, there is some trouble and—"

"Trouble!" About to go on with a quick and passionate outburst, Katrin held her tongue. The effort brought a flush again to stain her cheeks, made her grip the green and yellow towel. When she had recovered, she said,

"Let me do what I can, Dray, out of our friendship. But I will promise nothing."

"A message for Kadar the Hammer at the Iron Anvil will reach me. But for the sweet sake of Zair, hurry!"

"It would be more appropriate to swear by a goddess, do you not think?"

Katrin had probably never left Vallia. Certainly she had never visited the inner sea where the power of Zair was very real. So I said, "In the blessed name of the Invisible Twins made manifest in Opaz, neither man nor woman. Katrin, hurry!"

"And my Jikaida?"

So I knew she had learned from Delia. Her Jikaida, I knew, along with the Jikaidast, this Master Hork who was famous in Vondium for his command of the Chuktar's right-flank attack, could be forgotten. We had been old allies, against her will; now I thought with sincerity she would do what she could.

"I will have you smuggled out of the villa. Talk does no one any good, these days in Vondium. The queen..." And here Katrin revealed the differences between herself and Thelda. "The queen is a dear creature and has her damned spies everywhere."

My own calmness amazed me. This calm was like those brazen flat calms which often precede a violent rashoon of the Eye of the World. But I managed to say, "This Queen Lushfymi. Is the alliance progressing? Does the emperor find her congenial?"

"Oh, most, most congenial. Queen Lush is all woman, and I know." She lifted and redraped the wrap. "I will see you safely out. Xiri can be trusted, as can the Jiktar of my guard."

"I can only thank you, Katrin, and ask you to make all haste."

"The SoR are not inexperienced in intrigues!" She spoke as sharply as she had during the entire interview. Then: "Xiri!"

So I was seen out. Just how I was going to make myself wait for Katrin's message eluded me. I have waited for happenings in my life. On every occasion the wait has been unpleasant, it seems to me. Secret are the ways of Kregen under the Suns of Scorpio, secret and deadly. Plots and intrigues flourished in Vondium. So much of the world is open and bright, filled with the clamor of sword and spear, the bright blaring of the war trumpets, the quick onward rush of mailed chivalry and the high conflict of flyers in the air, and so much is dark and hidden in sorcerous ways, phantasms conjured from the hideous vaults of time, wizardly powers breathing a miasma of fear across the bright suns-light: there are also the darkly secret machinations of ambitious men and women to topple thrones and seize powers and take all unto themselves. Well may Kregen be called Secret Kregen.

Outside I walked almost blindly. I had just passed over a cut on a little brick bridge with pretty little caryatids entwined with loomins enhancing the loveliness of the setting—in my stupor I noticed this by reason of the abrupt chaos that broke beyond. One of the long chanting processions passed down the parallel Boulevard of Gregarians. They were clad in bright clothes, garlanded with flowers, carrying the images and the flags, with flowers and music everywhere and the chant, the omnipresent chant, going on and on and on. "Oolie Opaz, Oolie Opaz, Oolie Opaz." Over and over again.

The people near the center of the procession abruptly scattered. People were falling and struggling on the road. The chanting wavered and died and then picked up again only to falter and fade away. I saw clubs upraised. I saw the distorted faces of men and women who, bare-armed, brandishing bamboo sticks and balass rods, were smiting the worshipers of Opaz, driving the procession into a shrieking, formless mob.

And more I saw. I saw the black-feathered hats. I saw the lifted staffs entwined with black feathers. I saw the hateful symbols of an evil creed flaunted openly, chastising the worshipers of Opaz, the manifestation of the Invisible Twins.

All roiled into a screaming confusion. The bamboo stick in my hand might be put to some use here. So I ran off the little brick bridge and across the Boulevard of Gregarians and plunged into the shouting ranks of the Black Feathers.

Most of the worshipers of Opaz were fleeing, or scrabbling about on the ground with bleeding heads and broken limbs. I delivered a few tasty thwacks with the bamboo, letting all my frustrations boil over, dealing out buffets that stretched the followers of the Great Chyyan senseless alongside their victims.

Someone set up a yelling about the guards, and the mobiles galloped up on their totrixes. Everyone was running, and the long official staves were beating down on heads and shoulders. People scattered. Screams shattered the bright air. I ran. I had no wish to be hauled up before a supercilious magistrate or some petty noble and my identity revealed. I ran and as I ran so I struck three shrew blows that crunched in on black-feathered hats.

The blue coolness of an alley served to conceal me, but I ran on and took no notice of any who sought to stop me. At last I reached the Tunnel of Delight and passed through onto the brilliant Kyro of Jaidur Omnipotent with the hard-edged double shadows of the Forlaini Hills Aqueduct lying across the broad smooth paving stones. I slowed down and walked. People paid me no heed. Everyone was about private business. Riots were more common now than anyone could remember since the third party sought to topple the emperor. I forced myself not to tremble. What could the emperor be about? What was the old fool doing? Didn't he know how this evil creed of Chyyanism had taken so strong a grip upon his citizens of Vondium that a religious procession, one of the most sacred rites of Opaz, could be set upon, attacked, beaten and scattered? Were the racters all blind or fools?

Why was the canker of Chyyanism being allowed to eat out the heart of Vondium the Proud?

Eighteen

The Sisters of the Rose are kind to me

The chief lady of the Sisters of the Rose, whose rank and title and name would never be revealed to me if the Sisters had their way, condescended to see me. The message reached the Iron Anvil as I sat, not drinking, sharpening up my old knife, sitting alone in a dark corner of the inn. The smiths talked about their trade and of bad times for business and of the latest consignment of copper to arrive down the Great River and of the price of tin. The serving girl, a little Fristle fifi, whispered that strangers wished to speak with me, so I rose and went outside, the bamboo held ready. Cloaked figures riding zorcas awaited me. I mounted the animal they provided and with only the single word "Rose!" uttered between us, followed where they led.

While it would not be proper for me to reveal all the circumstances of the meeting, I can say that through it all I had no sense of being ridiculous, of acting the fool. Here was I, a fearsome fighting warrior, renowned swordsman, savage clansman, told to strip off, to wrap a piece of white cloth about my loins, to stand meekly in a room with two samphron-oil lamps shining up, leaving the end of the room partitioned by a pierced ivory screen in absolute darkness.

From the screen the soft rustle of feminine garments told me that the chief lady did not wear hunting leathers or the grim panoply of war, as many of the Sisters did. And this was fit and proper. The Sisters of the Rose, after all, is a female order, and girls do not have to ape the ways of men. Although when they do, by Zair, they often are very good indeed.

"You wished to speak with me, Kadar the Hammer. Your request was put most forcefully; a very strong case was made out for you. Why do you plead to see me?"

I said, "I think, lady, you know my name."

"Kadar the Hammer." A light tinkle of laughter. "Is that your question? You had forgotten your name?"

"I can never forget. I do not know yours. In that, you have the advantage, lady."

The laughter stilled. Then: "I know you. I can tell you nothing."

I flared up. "This is not good enough! I must know where my Delia is. Is she safe? Is Dayra safe? Just that, just that to put my heart at rest."

If this powerful and secret woman decided to obey the emperor's orders and handed me over to him, there would be a few broken skulls. That I knew. But that was a trifle.

"A man's heart, aye! Now there is a wonderfully elastic object."

"I did not come to bandy words. Tell me, for the sweet sake of Opaz."

"Your Dayra has been... is causing..." A hesitation and then, in a sharper tone: "Your Dayra is proving a true daughter of a wayward father."

"And if I am wayward, that I do not quarrel with. But you have educated Dayra! I have been away and I own my fault in that. But Dayra—"

"Do not blame the SoR for all! We teach chastity and humility and pride. We teach a girl that she is a girl, and in this world a girl must be as good as a man. Not better. As good. We are all people in the sight of Opaz, the manifestation of the Invisible Twins. Dayra could not exist without a man and a woman."

"And I am that man!" I bellowed, despite my promise to myself to behave. "And I ask about the woman!"

An indrawn breath. Would I be hurled out? Would a steel-tipped shaft drive through? Would—exotic thought—a bevy of half-naked damsels seek to destroy me by women's wiles?

Then: "I shall tell you, Kadar the Hammer, that the woman of whom you speak is alive and well and reasonably happy. She goes with her eldest daughter in search of her wayward daughter. When they are successful they will return."

So that explained why Lela, as well as Dayra, had not visited their father in Vondium. "Suppose they are not successful?"

"That may well be. The task is difficult. But Opaz is all wise. If that should be her will then so be it." Naturally Opaz, being the twinned life-force, could be either male or female. "If so, your lady and her elder daughter will return."

"And is that all you will tell me?"

"There is nothing more to tell. You are supremely fortunate even to have spoken with me, Kadar the Hammer. The emperor is looking for a smith to sharpen up the edge of his headsman's ax."

That was as clear a warning as you could desire, or not, considering.

The rustle of clothes told me she was leaving. There were a thousand questions buzzing in my stupid head, but I could speak none of them. I was led out by competent girls who carried their bows nocked and their rapiers naked in their hands. Of what use or value my knowledge that I could have fought and beaten them all? Would that bring my Delia any closer? Of course not.

Only half reconciled to what I considered a fobbing off I dressed and, once more clad in the old brown blanket cloak and with my bamboo stick in my horny fist, I was seen off into the moons-shot darkness.

I have said nothing of the rites surrounding this interview or of the room itself. Or of what I observed. Quite so.

One thing I believed with all my heart: my Delia was safe. And Lela and Dayra—whatever that little minx had been up to—were safe, also.

So, and not as easily as I may make it sound, I could go back to the more congenial task of mayhem and murder and smashing up these Opaz-for-saken rasts of the Great Chyyan.

The last thought I allowed myself about the Sisters of the Rose was the reflection that a fellow had to brace himself up and keep a brave face on it when these scheming women put on that kind of show. Many a man would have been half dead with fright at all the mumbo jumbo, and his knees would have knocked together when he stood in the dread presence of the chief lady of the SoR.

Before I went back to see Natyzha Famphreon and try to shake some sense out of the dealings—or apparent lack of them—of the racters, I'd have to nip back to the Iron Anvil. I had no real desire to investigate her warren of a villa with only a bamboo stick, despite the concealed sword, although if it came to the fluttrell's vane I would do so.

"By Odifor!" spat a Fristle who balanced an enormous load on his head. He staggered against the doorway of a house whose overhanging balcony dripped vines and moonblooms. I was scarcely aware of bumping him. "Look where you're going, you apim rast!"

I turned my head away and walked on. There were far more important demands at work this night in Vondium than a stupid affray with a Fristle. His cat-face looked fierce and his whiskers shone in the light of torches. I supposed then that I might some day learn to rub along with Fristles.

Walking thus in a heightened frame of mind, to put my frame of mind in a certain light, I realized that all Vallia could go hang to the Black Feathers just as long as Delia and the girls were safe. But then I reconsidered. That was only a half-truth. It is often easy for the outcast—and I had been chucked out of Vondium—to look at himself in the role of poor Pakkad. No one of Kregen could say with certainty if Pakkad had been a real person of if he was a figure from myth. He had been cruelly treated by the arch devil, Mitronoton, the Destroyer of Cities, the Leveler of Ways, and nowadays, although seldom referred to, Pakkad stood for the image of the pariah and the unwanted. As for Mitronoton, the Bane of the ib, the Reducer of Towers, he was a devil of horror that no sane man would approach.

The Fristle snarled some obscenity or other and hitched his bundle straight; a string snapped and the bundle burst, and a glittering shower of trinkets and trashy bangles and rings cascaded to the cobbles. An uproar began at once as, from nowhere and at this time of night with the moons shining above, a torrent of children burst out and fell upon the gewgaws.

Young girls and boys were scrabbling along the cobbles, snatching up the rolling bangles and rings, stuffing little ornamental figures into their breechclouts. I realized in my half-blind wanderings I had blundered into a net of poor alleys off one of the jewelry souks. The hullabaloo was rather splendid. The Fristle was frantically attempting to preserve his wares, yelling threats and trying to bash kids away and being tripped up and—it was all over in a twinkling—standing up and shrieking his anger and casting about upon the empty cobbles.

He found one trashy little figure of Kyr Nath made from cast brass and he flung it down so hard it bounced and hit a laughing fellow in the eye. That started more trouble. I ambled off, deliberately not going fast.

Of such trifles are the destiny of empires made.

The last I heard of that incident—as I thought, as I thought—was a fat apim with an apron yelling: "The Fristle stole this stuff! Thief! Thief!"

The Fristle let out a yell and raced off. The apims followed all a-yelling and a-screeching and the whole pack vanished into a side alley, even more odiferous than this one. So, going on, I came out at last into the silversmiths' wharf running alongside a canal that gleamed limpid and pinkly golden in the night. I saw the Fristle running across an arcaded bridge. He saw me too, for the moons-light picked me out brightly. Only a handful of other people were walking near. He knew me. He vanished into the shadows. I dismissed him—thieves would have to be treated as rulers usually treated the devotees of Diproo the Nimble-Fingered—and walked on to the Iron Anvil in the smiths' quarter.

My surprise was complete when I found the Wizard of Loh Khe-Hi-Bjanching waiting for me in my room. As I came in he started up; the steel in my fist winked at his throat and then I recognized him. I drew back.

"Dangerous to do that, San."

He laughed a nervous laugh and felt his throat.

"All right, Turk." As he spoke the curtains over the window shook and Turko the Shield climbed in. He was followed by Balass the Hawk. Then Oby wriggled in, most fierce, slapping his long-knife into his sheath.

Well!

It turned out that Khe-Hi wished to obtain a piece of my skin, a hair and a piece of toenail. I do not give these things lightly, for although it is all stupid superstition, there is no doubting the power of the Wizards of Loh.

"Phu-si-Yantong has been searching for you, Prince," said this wizard who had followed me. "I need to create a new and somewhat different... ah... arrangement to hold him off. He has let you slip out of his range of observation. But he has been in lupu and spying a very great deal lately. I think"—and here Khe-Hi chuckled in a very down-to-earth and unwizardly way—"I really think the old devil is worried."

"Amen to that."

I had noticed that Khe-Hi did not mention that he was creating a spell or an enchantment. They were for the lesser sorcerers.

So needing the simple artifices of that trade, he had come to find me. And the others would not let him go alone. I asked, "And how did you know where I was and my name?"

"We had a flier letter from Seg, from Falinur, and—"

"And from now on I'm staying where I belong," said Turko the Shield truculently. "By Morro the Muscle! At your side with my shield lifted."

"That will not be very practical in Vondium."

"Well, my long-knife will arouse no comment," said Oby.

We all told him coarsely that his long-knife would not arouse comment anywhere—except Khe-Hi, who was above that kind of nonsense, of course—whereat he grew most enraged and lively and started swinging his arms about.

Balass the Hawk butted in with: "I know most about the Black Feathers so I am the one to go with the Prince."

While they wouldn't have started in on each other with the weapons each knew so well how to use, they waxed exceedingly warm. I said, "No one goes with me. This is a lone task. Balass, what of the Black Feathers?"

His story confirmed what I had seen. Someone had brought a temple into Vondium. Wandering priests had gathered. The city was like an overripe shonage, ready to burst and spray every which way.

"By the brass sword and glass eye of Beng Thrax!" I used the old arena oath talking to Balass, the hyr-kaidur. "When will your spies find this Opaz-forsaken temple! By Kaidun! Time grows perilously short."

"We have men out everywhere. The racters also search."

A thought occurred to me and I turned to Khe-Hi. "If Phu-si-Yantong has missed me and is searching, will not your visit here put him on my trail once again?"

"No, my Prince. I can cover myself and those with me. He cannot find you through us."

"That is some comfort. But if he really is this Makfaril, and there is no proof, what chance is there he will come to Vondium himself?"

Khe-Hi pursed up his lips. "Very little. He can work his mischief through his agents."

"Quite so. Well, be off with you then, the pack of you."

They wanted to contest this, but I would have none of it. So they climbed out through the window, agile as monkeys, even Khe-Hi, who had done a little climbing with me on Ogra-gemush.

Working swiftly, I donned my familiar scarlet breechclout and strapped and buckled my weapons about me. This time, to be on the safe side, I shrugged on a close-fitting coat of mail, a mail shirt presented to me by Delia, one of those superb harnesses of mesh mail manufactured in the Dawn Lands around the Shrouded Sea in Havilfar. The value of that single piece of armor would leave a rich man breathless. I swirled the big buff cloak over all as usual, but this time hung the Krozair longsword scabbarded at my left side. I picked up the faithful old bamboo and went to place it safely in a cupboard when those confounded Fristles arrived to ruin that particular scheme.

The Fristle thief, no doubt calling on Diproo the Nimble-Fingered, had rustled up some of his friends. The door burst in with a smash and they catapulted into the room. For the tiniest fraction of time I thought they were my comrades, come back this time to insist on going with me. Then I saw the fierce snarling cat-faces, the up-pricked ears, the lean jaws and the furry hides. Spitting their fury, they charged straight for me.

They carried long-knives and wharf-rat knives, and two had stout staves tipped with bronze. The bamboo switched up and deflected the first stave, bounced off the skull of its owner, lined up and prodded deeply into a furry midriff. Two Fristles staggered out of the fight. But the others, three or four, bore in. A flung knife whistled past my head as I moved and smashed into the horn window. A stave swirled down at me and I ducked and stepped back, making no attempt to strike with the bamboo. I was annoyed. I was quite unsure whether to bash them over the head with the bamboo or to whip out rapier or djangir and settle their hash.

So stepping back, I trod on a forgotten gregarian and skidded. I skidded across the floor, flailing my arms to remain upright. I lost my balance and staggered back.

With shrieks of feline glee the Fristles flung themselves on me. They had no compunction. The thief had lost his night's swag and he wanted to take his revenge out on my hide.

I rolled, ready to spring up and bash them all properly, when a great booming numim voice roared joyfully: "Now, by Vox! What a pretty pickle!"

And in rage Rafik Avandil waded in, his clanxer deftly cleaving down a Fristle skull and slicing back to chop another. The other Fristles screamed now, screams far different from those shocks of savage fury of a moment ago.

"If I make a habit of this, Nath the Gnat, blame only yourself!"

And the golden numim, Rafik Avandil, joyfully dispatched the next Fristle and kicked the last headlong out the door and down the blackwood stairs.

Nineteen

In the Cavern of Abominations

The way I extricated myself from the possible little embarrassment of this golden numim's discovering all my arsenal of weaponry buckled up about me, when I was a mere wandering laborer, amused me at the time. Afterward, well, as they say, no man or woman born of Opaz knows all the secrets of Imrien. I gave an almighty yawn and covered my mouth, palm out, and said, "I crave your pardon, Koter Avandil. I am for bed. I have had a plaguey day. How did you find me here?"

If he thought I shot the last question out a little sharply, he gave no sign.

"I heard the commotion and ran up, hoping for a little exercise. It seems I was in time, once again."

"And much am I beholden to you, Koter Avandil. What are you going to do with the Fristles?"

"The landlord will take care of them. Come with me. You cannot stay here now."

This was an eventuality I did not relish. I reached up and touched the bowstave. He nodded, half smiling, his whiskers fierce.

"Yes. I see you have bought yourself a bow with the money you acquired, to go along with your zorca. You should be careful how you spend your cash. Buying things you cannot use is a dangerous pastime."

"Yes," I said with a fine free meekness, adding, "koter."

He laughed again, that great booming numim laugh. "I warrant the fellow whose throat you slit for the money wishes he was here to spend it instead of rotting in a ditch."

"If you think that, why bother your head over me?"

"You ask questions, Nath the Gnat, more than is seemly."

"I crave your pardon. But the landlord will throw these cramphs out and I can sleep." I kept forgetting, the more he pestered me, to add the required *koter* into the conversation.

He saw I meant it when I again refused his invitation, so at last he left. I pondered. One more day, would that make so much difference? I could go up and see Natyzha Famphreon later, after sleep. Yes, that would be the answer. I somehow or other did not relish the thought of slipping out the window and finding Rafik Avandil smiling and waiting below for me.

Had I not sent my comrades away they would have created a diversion. Those Opaz-forsaken Fristles. But for them I'd have been halfway to Natyzha Famphreon's villa by now. So, cussing away in my stupid fashion, I stripped off the gear and slept.

The sleep was needed and I awoke refreshed before dawn with that old sailor's knack of setting alarm bells ringing in my skull, echoes of Beng Kishi's Bells. I ordered up a huge breakfast which I demolished in short order.

The fate of empires hangs on tiny threads.

But for the Fristles I would have been long gone to the racters; but for the state of the haggard old crone who served the breakfast I would have left at once. Now there is disease on Kregen, as seems to be inseparable from man and his nature and the state of the universe in which we live. The ordinary ailments are treated matter-of-factly, and the needle-man of Kregen are skilled at relieving pain, even during surgery, with their cunning twirling needles. I have not so far mentioned the disease which strikes horror into the heart of a Kregan. It is seldom mentioned in polite conversation, just as once on this Earth cancer was not a subject for decent conversation. Kregans can confidently look forward to two hundred years or so of life. Right up until their very last years they do not change much, do not appear to alter. This disease—I will tell you its name just the once— this chivrel prematurely ages its victims. Oh, the men and women stricken down live on. They tend to die around their two hundredth year or before, rather than living that extra golden autumn, but their appearance and their strengths are those of ancients of days. This, as you will readily perceive, explains the appearance of old crones and decrepit men in my narrative of life on Kregen.

The serving woman was old, suffering from that disgusting disease. How it was caught, how transmitted, no one knew. No cure was known. Whenever I think back to my days on Kregen as I fought for what I believed was worth fighting for and recall the conversations and the oaths spoken, always I change that particular curse into a different English equivalent— leprous is an example. People were not afraid to live with the sufferers. Body contact, breathing the same air, none of these things caused the disease.

So instead of flinging my cloak around me and rushing out, I stayed and helped her stack the tray and lifted it so that she might open the door. I was in the act of closing the door after her, ready to don my equipment, when the ghostly form of Khe-Hi-Bjanching materialized across the chamber. He stared at me, peering, as though his trance state of lupu was not perfect. Then his misty body solidified. It seemed the wizard stood in the chamber with me.

Never had I seen the lupal projection of Phu-si-Yantong spying on me as clearly as I saw Khe-Hi. He held out a paper. Like an onker I stretched out my hand to take it. My fingers passed through the yellow paper. I cursed. Khe-Hi pointed. So, a fambly to the end, I looked down and read what he had written.

Famphreon's villa is under observation by the emperor's spies.

As I finished reading, the lupal projection of my Wizard of Loh thinned and wisped and vanished. I stepped back. By Krun! Was I to be foiled by a pack of miserable imperial spies?

I debated.

A hot gratitude to my friends for their work made me realize that they, having discovered the information and sending it as fast as they could via wizardly sorcery, would feel poorly rewarded if I simply barged up there anyway. Mind you, they'd half expect that kind of oafish barbarian behavior from Dray Prescot. But intrigue breeds intrigue, plot conjures forth counterplot.

No, by the Black Chunkrah! I said to myself. I'd play this one very coolly indeed, like a warrior prince rather than a naked, hairy, howling barbarian.

And then the door opened and I swirled about ready to use whatever weapons might be necessary. Rafik Avandil started back.

"Nath! You look—"

"Koter," I said, and I let the barbaric instincts leach from my muscles. Zair knows what he thought then.

A civilized man can display the quickest of reactions when, here on this Earth, he is aware, with his civilized sense, of an automobile hurtling down on him on swishing rubber tires. Then he will jump. With my Clansmen on the Great Plains of Segesthes and venturing among the southern forests I had learned to jump when a leem attacked. Rafik Avandil slid his half-drawn clanxer back into its sheath. He had not touched his rapier. He carried both swords in a fine raffish way, slung low on his left hip.

He said he had come to see if I was all right.

I said, "You show great concern for a common laboring man."

"I am at a loose end. You appear to bring me opportunities for a little light exercise. Let us go out and find an open-air tavern and sit and drink sazz and watch the girls."

I, Dray Prescot, replied, "With a will, koter."

Mind you, at the first opportunity, crossing a wide avenue where the zorca chariots rolled glittering in the dawn lights and the people were already about their hurrying scurry of another day, I lost him. I skidded down a narrow alley on the far side and watched him go running along the avenue, in a right paddy. Numims, as I knew from my friend Rees, have generous hearts. Well, some of them.

So I spent the day prodding and prying. It became clear that, dressed as I was in an old brown blanket cloak, I could penetrate places closed to anyone not of the laboring classes. In Vallia the social structures were organized differently from the way they operated in Hamal with the guls and clums there. So, all in the fullness of time, I picked up the black feather and rolled it in my fingers, looked at the fat apim with the sweaty jowls and small vosk-like eyes and said, "Tonight, dom. I shall be there, to the greater glory of the Great Chyyan."

That had been in a dopa den. I gulped the fresh air as I went outside, for all it was blowing from the fish wharf nearby. The search had not taken me overlong. I pondered.

If I chanced my arm and visited Natyzha Famphreon and the emperor's spies took me up, that would place the old devil in a pickle. Would he take my head off this time? Or would he think of his daughter? The racters with their schemes would have to wait. The Black Feathers posed the greater threat.

The impression of the great city as a gigantic wen about to suppurate and burst and release all the evil oppressed me. Black feathers were to be seen, worn in the fashion of the colored favors of Vallia. My ugly old face drew down into grim lines. Intemperate and headlong as I am, I forced myself to ignore this tawdry panoply of evil and wait until the night's meeting.

I thought of Delia. In all honor I had rejected the notion of having Khe-Hi go into lupu and seek her out. That would negate the understanding between us, if not question her self-sufficiency as a woman. The chief Lady of the SoR had said Delia was safe. I believed that, and suffered and hungered for her, and so compensated my own evil by my intentions to deal harshly with the priests of the Great Chyyan.

The chanting of "Oolie Opaz" heralded yet another procession, flower-bedecked, carrying the golden images, wending along a boulevard. People moved respectfully out of the way. According to the season the words of the hypnotic chant are slightly varied, and among all the Oolie Opazes are to be heard the Oolie Ravox and the Oolie Ra-drak. Oolie, Oolie, they sing, gyrating, swaying, flower-bedecked, letting their inmost spirits lift and rise and soar and conjoin with the spirit of Opaz. Well, I walked discreetly along in the rear, gripping the bamboo staff, and ready for—aye, more than ready, longing for!—a dastardly attack from the fanatical adherents of the Black Feathers. Then a few skulls would be tapped and the claret flow.

A crowd of people in ordinary rough clothes burst from a side avenue. They belched out onto the boulevard. The black feathers flew. I started forward and out of that screaming mob a single face jumped. The face of a man leading them on, waving his arms, berserk with rage, screaming, urging his followers to smash and destroy.

Himet the Mak!

"Right, you cramph!" I shouted. "I'll get you!"

Foolish, stupid me, Dray Prescot, Krozair of Zy, Lord of Strombor, shouting across a street brawl, promising a villain what I would do to him! How low I had sunk!

Before I could bash my way through the struggling, frenzied mob the guards arrived, the mobiles on their lunging clumsy totrixes, laying about them with the long official staves. I ducked a blow. Himet was running. I saw him cast a vicious glance of baffled rage at the guards. He dived into an alley between a tavern and a private house of some wealthy koter. I followed. Men and women ran with me. The black feathers pinned to their clothes incensed me as they riffled as the people ran.

One priest of the Great Chyyan would be a prize worth taking.

The fleeing mass broke across an adjoining square. Fragments of the main body ran into side turnings. I stuck with a gang of men who intrigued me. Although dressed as ordinary laborers they carried themselves with the air of soldiers. They kept together. Some tavern or inn at which they stayed would offer a place to spy on them. These must be masichieri, common mercenaries of low character, employed by the priests of the Great Chyyan. All the masichieri encountered in Autonne had been accounted for and it was highly unlikely any of these would recognize me. A coin does not often bear a true likeness and they would not have been court portraits. Himet was the man to recognize me, and as we passed through barred suns-light and shadow, I kept a wary eye on him.

This was a chance and I would seize it. Soon the outlines of a half-ruined tower appeared ahead, standing alone in an abandoned plot of ground between two canals. Little as I knew of Vondium, I knew of the ruined temple of a minor religion devoted to the worship of Hjemur-Gebir. So the Chyyanists were up to their old game of taking over small or discredited religious shrines. The masichieri passed in a bunch across a wooden bridge over the canal and headed for the tower. Gray stone showed the livid blotches of algae, and vines and creepers hung down, patterned with blazing Kregan flowers. All pursuit had vanished. As an orderly group we entered the fane. No one challenged me. There were many bands of masichieri here, and many were strangers.

A huge stone caked with detritus and bat droppings lifted as powerful muscles hauled the iron-linked chains. Two by two we dropped down into the black hole thus revealed and crept carefully down the slimed steps. Luminescent fungus grew. Water dripped dolorously. Down and down we went, spiraling around a gigantic well in the solid earth. Echoes bounced eerily. The flare of torches lit in ruddy hues the sheen of water below and the slimed path. Along the path we passed, two by two, and no man spoke.

However poor quality these mercenaries might be, they were well drilled. No one spoke a word until we all passed through an ancient doorway with rotting posts decorated by lichens and bulging fungi. A new world opened beyond, for in the deepest recesses of the crypts of this deserted fane had been built a soldier's barracks. The bunks, the arms racks, the cooking and toilet facilities were all of the best. The instant everyone was in, and there were about sixty or seventy men, bedlam broke loose.

Everyone was talking and shouting at once, laughing at what they had done, knocking a poor old woman over, kicking a young worshiper of Opaz in the guts when he was down. They complained bitterly of the untimely arrival of the guard. They had not expected that.

Himet the Mak stood up and they quieted down. He regarded them from the far end of the chamber from a dais of stained stone.

"Rest and eat, my bonny masichieri. Then we will sally forth again and break a few more heads of these Opaz-loving cramphs!"

"Aye!" they roared it back at him. I kept my head down.

Four or five other priests, evidently of the same importance as Himet, harangued the masichieri. Then we all sat down to tables loaded with ample if coarse fare. So I ate. Very few Kregans turn down the offer of a square meal, particularly if it is free.

Among the bunks and along the walls between the arms racks, stands held uniforms, black leather and bronze harness, with black leather helmets, all adorned with the black feathers. There were also shields here, as well as parrying-sticks, oval shields with the black representation of a chyyan painted against the thin bronze coverings to the linden boards.

As I ate, my head down and spooning the food up like a wild beast, I kept one hand against my brow. My eyes seldom left the figure of Himet the Mak, dressed now in flowing black robes embroidered with the golden chyyans. He laughed a great deal and was most lively. Yes, I said to myself, by Vox, you cramph, you may laugh now!

The chances were I would have to grab him by the scruff of the neck and drag him out. I'd given no thought to means of egress. So much for the cool calculations of a warrior prince! In this I had acted in my natural barbaric manner, red and wrathful, recking nothing of consequences.

After the food the masichieri spent the time in the usual ways of swods waiting for duty. They drank sparingly, although more than I would have allowed my men in like circumstances. They played Jikalla and gambled with knucklebones and dice and some pulled out Jikaida boards with games in progress. This proved they had been here some time. Presently I was able to lounge off, with a few coarse remarks, and follow where the priests led down a narrow corridor, smoking with cheap mineral oil lamps, to a moldering door at the far end. Here guards waited, men in uniform. I waited also, until an appropriate moment, and then the guards went to sleep standing up. I propped them against the architrave and eased the door open, went through like a leem and shut it silently.

Beyond the door the corridor continued, ominous, quiet, with the flat tang of oil lamps burning from brass hung bowls.

Creeping along, I listened at the closed doors lining the passage.

Not a sound disturbed the silence. The corridor opened out into a vast shadowy area, lit by vagrant shafts of light falling from a ceiling hazy and distant, festooned with creepers and hanging vines. Lamps and torches shone about the walls. A circle of mighty stone columns upheld the cavern roof. Above that roof the people of Vondium went about their business all unknowing of the chasm beneath their feet, or of the squat and hideous idol crouching on its black obsidian plinth at the center.

The image was of a toad-thing, enormous, crouched, malignant. But its eye sockets gaped emptily, the jewels they had once held long since gouged away. The stone was cracked and flaked away and one of the front clawed arms was snapped off and lying in a scatter of detritus. This, then, was the pseudo-god Hjemur. No wonder honest folk had abandoned his worship!

There was no sign of the priests. If this was to be the place of the temple—and I doubted that—a labyrinth of warrens would stretch out ahead. I went forward cautiously, moving from shadow to shadow.

Spiderwebbed niches along the ebon walls held crumbled statues, tentacles and tusks and obscene conjurations cracked and broken and tumbled away. The blight of powerful superstition had gripped an enslaved people and here lay all that remained of that once-mighty devilry. I passed the profane rotting idols and my fists gripped the bamboo and I prowled, I think, as a leem prowls seeking prey among the chunkrah herds.

Shadows ahead, dark forms, moving in the dim lighting from guttering torch and wavering lamp, halted me, motionless, scarcely breathing, ripe for abrupt massacre.

A small party of masichieri in black armor, led by a deldar, passed uneasily. They gripped their weapons and their eyes roved. They spoke in low whispers, oppressed by the evil of this ancient and profane shrine.

“Come the Black Day, dom, and I’ll never go down a cellar again!”

“Come the Black Day and I’ll be drunk for a sennight.”

“Come the Black Day and I’ll take my pay and be off to Menaham before Armipand can jump!”

Yes, they were uneasy here, these rough tough sadistic mercenaries. They talked of guard duty, of dopa and women and were gone, walking carefully through the torch-lit shadows.

I let them go. They were masichieri, mercenaries for hire; I needed to get the scrawny throat of their paymaster between my fists.

A sudden outcry ahead made me halt again. The sound of scuffles, blows, the grunted cursing of men in action, left me unmoved. Then a woman’s scream rang shockingly through that cavern of abominations. I could hold back no longer. Fool that I was, I ran and hurled myself through the crimson and ocher shadows, whipped out the sword from the bamboo and raced on, and found nothing. No sign of men or women struggling met my gaze as I searched. Had I heard some phantasmal echo of infinite evil from ancient times? Did the foul deeds perpetrated here linger on?

The torchlights near the toad-thing had revealed dark streaks running down the obsidian slab. The marks of dark blood looked recent; there might be a thousand seasons between now and the time the sacrifice screamed and shrieked until the jagged glass knife slashed his or her throat.

Prowling on around this vast cavern I saw hideous things, abominations, things that were never meant to exist in the sweet sunshine of Zim and Genodras. A strange sliding clicking drew my instant attention to a jagged wall where the naked rock gleamed with the green of lichen. Shadows flittered like bats.

Pressed close against a slimy pillar forming one of a rectangle enclosing a small side chapel—and the very word "chapel" brings a blasphemy upon the evil of that place—I saw a rope ladder swinging down from the darkness above. At its foot a man stood, grasping the end, shaking it. The wooden rungs clicked against protrusions in the stone.

He turned slightly and I saw him.

His powerful numim frame was clad in brilliant armor, gilded iron corselet and greaves. His helmet glistened. He held his clanxer in his right hand as his left hand released the ladder. He swung about, big and burly and fighting grim. I felt only the smallest surprise.

About to step forward and say, "And what brings you here, Rafik Avandil?" I saw the slinking shadows at his back, stealing up from the dimness between torches. I saw the black and silver and the quick glitter of weapons, and so I cried, "Your back, Rafik! Beware!"

He swung about like the great lion-man he was, and the first leaping shadow slashed and clanged a great gong note from Rafik's helmet. A gigantic buffet sent the man sprawling back. His comrades recoiled. They gathered themselves. Without thought, I flung myself forward to stand back to back with Rafik Avandil. A noose clung about my leg and I tripped headlong.

A figure bent over me. Hands gripped my throat. A harsh, husky voice said, "Not another word, dom!"

I could not speak. I levered up and other hands bore down on me. I was lifted like a log of lumber. A crazy vision of Rafik running fleetly along past blasphemous statues—he vanished with a wink of bright armor quenched by the shadows—the sound of men breathing hoarsely by me, a sudden exclamation.

The keen edge of a knife hovered under my chin. I could just see it. It was a thick, heavy long-knife, and it would slice through my windpipe as a butcher cuts up chops.

"Hold!" The men carrying me upended me and slammed me on my feet so my neck snapped my head forward and stars flew. I dragged the right-hand man around and smashed him into the left-hand one and a very hard, very sharp point came from nowhere and rested against my throat.

"Stand still, Prince! By Vox! You'll have us all killed!"

I stared owlishly.

In the erratic illumination I saw Naghan Vanki standing before me look-ing charged with rage, emotion almost making his features unrecognizable. Always before he had been smooth and bland and unremarkable.

"The cramph got away, jen," said one of his men, coming up. They all wore the black and silver, hard and supple leather, with steel bands and bracers. Vanki kept the point of his rapier at my throat. His men hung onto my arms.

"Keep silence, Prince. May I tell you something? You are a dead man unless—"

"I thought you served the racters, Vanki. Don't you know they are leagued with me now?" It was a ploy.

He started and then his face assumed that blank, indifferent look. This was the man I suspected had drugged me and thrown me into a thorny-ivy bush to perish miserably in the hostile territories. I had the desire to know, if I was to die now.

I asked him.

"You may be a prince now, the Prince Majister; then you were a savage clansman with ideas beyond his station. No one wanted you to marry the Princess Majestrix."

"In that you lie, Vanki. The Princess Majestrix wished it with all her heart."

"Aye! That is why when the other wanted to slit your throat there and then I counseled moderation. You owe your life to me, Prince."

"Alone, in the hostile territories, on foot, with the Klackadrin to cross?"

"You are here, alive, now."

"And for how much longer? How much is the cramph Makfaril paying you." I stopped suddenly. Then I gasped more than I liked as I spoke: "You, Naghan Vanki, are Makfaril!"

Without any change of expression, he said, "You are a prince, yet you are a clansman still, aye, and an onker!"

"Someone comes!" said one of his men, hissing from the shadows. In a bunch we melted into the darkness beyond the pillared chapel. Black and silver clothes, black and white for the racters, black feathers for the Chyya-nists. I felt then that if Naghan Vanki, who on his own admission had connived at my death, was not Makfaril, then he was very high in the hier-archy and in all probability knew who the leader of the Chyyanists was.

It was pointless for me to call out. The masichieri would be less merci-ful than Naghan Vanki. They'd have slit my throat and gleed in the doing of it, back there in the hostile territories.

Without binding me in iron chains or stout lesten-hide ropes a man can only hold me for so long. There will come a time when he may be taken. I gave no thought to the silent ferocity of these hired men of Vanki's. They kept a perfect stillness. Perhaps Rafik Avandil had brought men with him down the rope ladder. So, taking my chance, I slipped the rapier point and dealt each of the wights holding my arms a most gruesome mischief with my knees, then ran fleetly into the darkness of the Cavern of Abominations.

In the maze of tumbled stonework and fallen rock, the pillared chapels and the half-ruined warren of rooms beyond, there was little chance Naghan Vanki and his men or the masichieri would find me. But, equally and frustratingly, I had as little chance of finding Himet the Mak or one of the other priests of the Black Feathers.

A sensible idea would be to get out of the place and rouse a strong body of loyal soldiers, from Natyzha, from the emperor, from my own Valkans, and return here with fire and sword. That would be the sensible course.

In matters of this nature I am woefully lacking in sense. I no longer had the faithful old bamboo sword-stick. The rasts had not taken my sailor knife, and I drew this now and held it ready as I padded through the semi-darkness. The shafting light from above probably came from a higher cavern whose floor was fitted with fireglass crystal. How far above that lay the surface I did not know, for we had descended that slimy spiral stairway to a considerable depth. However far into the bowels of Kregen we were, I had no mind to return to the surface without a priest of the Great Chyyan to prod along before me.

The grotesquely carved pillar around which I edged screened off what lay beyond. Tumbled walls and toppled arcades, all built within the cavern, surrounded me. I rounded the corner...

The masichieri were surprised and sprang out under the flaring torches. There was only one thing I could do: I charged headlong for them. I bellowed "Hai!" and raced in with the knife held point up and thrusting for them.

I saw the slinger. I saw him unwind. I skidded on a fallen rock and tried to duck and then... The stone must have struck me fair and square between the eyes. I dropped headfirst into the deep dark cloak of Notor Zan.

Twenty

Makfaril's sacrifice

Someone was saying from a great distance: "The yetch is the Prince Majister of Vallia? It is difficult to believe." The words boomed and went up and down as though echoing in a gigantic sea shell. "What did he want creeping about down here?"

And the coarse answer: "By the Black Feathers! Whatever it was he will never find it now. Makfaril has ordained his death."

I opened my eyes. Well, cells are cells. This one cut from the rock boasted a barred window through which torchlight streamed, so I crawled across with all Beng Kishi's tinkers hammering out their bells in my skull, and listened as best I could.

"Come the Black Day and all the princes and Princesses will dangle-o!"

"Aye, dom. And then you'n me'll be princes."

They sounded apim. Masichieri. Hired killers. My head resonated and nausea clutched me. But escape must be attempted at once. Strike while the iron is hot. I tried to stand up and my legs buckled and I slumped back again. The guards talked on outside.

"Course, most of us will grab what loot we can and hightail it back home. Vallia is rich. By Havil! The plunder!"

So the cramph was from Havilfar somewhere, Hamal probably.

"Yes. You're right. But I'm going to sit in the throne for once, aye, and if any princes or kovs is about I'll use 'em for a footstool before we cut 'em up."

A hawk and a spit and: "Once they get this meeting over the priests can go and spread the word. I'm tired of waiting. The quicker they learn the day and go home and tell their people the better. Then, dom, then our swords will drink blood and our pockets will be filled!"

"Aye, may Armipand rot 'em all!"

My legs wavered. I leaned against the wall and shoved upright. I panted. I did not touch my forehead. The blow from the stone must have left a ghastly mess up there and if the blood had dried I did not wish to disturb it. Only my thick old vosk-skull of a head and the dip in the Pool of Baptism in far Aphrasöe had saved me. I stilled the trembling in my limbs. Talk about David and Goliath. That flung stone had nearly done for me. But I felt my strength coming back. I dragged deep lungfuls of air. I forced myself to stand free of the wall and pace about, grunting, working my muscles back to life.

"...Beautiful piece. A waste to sacrifice her first."

I stopped and listened again.

"One of 'em got away. But the man's safely mewed up."

"Bitch women. Why can't they attend to women's affairs and leave men's to men?"

Thank God, I said to myself, Delia and Dayra and Lela were safe dwaburs away from here. Although nothing had ever been said about where they were going or where they were adventuring, I had somehow assumed it was in the north midlands of Vallia.

Well, this was getting me nowhere. While there was no way of telling just how professional these two masichieri were, they were mercenaries, and therefore I must give them the benefit of hard professional competence. If

I made a single mistake they'd not wait for Makfaril to implement his ordinance on my death, whatever gruesome affair that was to be.

A trampling of iron-shod sandals in the corridor was followed by jocular remarks from the two guards to others of their ilk who passed, giving me a little time.

"What a beauty! Treat her gently!"

"Ah! Makfaril's girls will see to her!"

"What I wouldn't give..."

I waited until the guards passed. Apart from the old scarlet breechclout I was naked. Simplicity, that was the only way. Simpleness in plans can defeat the most cunning of experienced professionals.

I leaned against the door and spoke through the iron bars. "Tell Makfaril I have vital information for him. *Bratch!*"

When Makfaril came I'd fling everything into one wild lunge and so finish the cramph.

But these two were incompetent professionals. One looked through the bars, saying, "How do we know you speak sooth?"

"Fetch Makfaril and you will soon see."

So, poor fools, they swung the door open to make sure of me. They were armed. I was naked. It made little difference.

I stood up and slid the thraxter from its scabbard. I took the other one's short compound reflex bow and his quiver of arrows and slung them over my shoulder. A knife, too, would be useful... The two masichieri slumbered on the floor. I shut the door on them and shot the bars and bolts.

A short corridor lit by a single torch led onto a wider cellblock. Probably the sacrifices had been kept here in the old days. At the corner I halted as a screech of metal sounded. Cautiously, ready to fight or run—I was annoyed and did not wish to waste my strength on masichieri when Makfaril was here—I peered around the corner.

The scene was arresting in its action and before I could sort it all out in the tricky light it was all over.

A guard screamed and spun away from a door. I saw a girl drive a long thick poniard into his neck, saw her as a fleeting black-clad sprite, her long limbs splendid as she sprang to the door. The sheening black leather stood out against her white skin. Her mass of brown hair obscured her face, but she was not Delia. She was not Delia. The door opened to her quick fingers and a man staggered out, looking ghastly, with blood dried upon his face and his dark hair draggling with caked blood and his left arm all broken and dangling awry. Quickly the girl dragged him along, taking no notice of his broken arm. She moved with feline grace, like a hunting cat—all the old images sprang into my mind. Like a tiger-girl she dragged the shambling man along and together they vanished around the corner.

I loped along the corridor and looked after them. The next set of cells lay dusty and deserted and of the panther-girl and the man she had rescued remained only a double line of footprints in the dust.

I wished her well. But I had my own zhantil to saddle.

Up. I must go up. Without doubt these cells for the sacrifices would be low down in this pestiferous place. So I hunted stairs and upward-sloping corridors, and only four guards died on the borrowed thraxter. The straight cut-and-thrust sword of Havilfar is keenly adapted to this work.

At the end of a long corridor which by its width and height indicated I must be leaving the deeper warrens, the figure of a girl moved across from one side passage to another. For a single instant I thought she was the girl who had rescued the bloodied, broken man. But this girl's black clothes riffled with black feathers, and she carried a wide silver bowl steaming with fragrant water. She vanished and I padded on. That splendid girl who had used her poniard so ruthlessly, she reminded me of Sosie ti Drakanium, Delia's messenger. Her gleaming tanned white skin and her long lissom legs—yes, well, there had been a sight more skin than black leather on view. All the same, had I not disposed of the two guards at my cell door, of whom she could have had no knowledge, her rescue would have gone awry.

Still, she could not know that.

As I prowled on, very much like a leem among ponsho pens, the absence of people made me realize that the time was much later than I had thought. The palaces of Kregen—and there is an evocative phrase for you!—of which I had knowledge all contained runnels of secret passages and concealed doors. This ancient temple of abominations followed that pattern. I was perfectly confident I could find my way out to the surface and probably emerge through some hidden opening an ulm away from the ruined tower of Hjemur-Gebir, but I wanted to leave dragging a rascally priest of the Great Chyyan with me.

The deserted stone corridors, the decayed barrenness of it all as I wound my way back to the giant cavern of the idol of the toad-thing, convinced me the first meeting was already being held. The other meetings for later on, one of which I had arranged to visit, now meant nothing. This meeting, here, was the vital one. For Makfaril would tell his assembled priests the date of the Day of the Black Feathers. The priests would return to their congregations all over Vallia. They would scatter like a loathsome pestilence all over Vallia and prepare their followers and, come the Black Day, they would strike!

In the end the long ululations of a moaning, whining chant, a succession of weird cadences echoing through the dusty and deserted chambers, led me to the scene. I cautiously came out upon a high ledge of rock, drowned in shadow, and so could look out and down into the torchlit bowl of the cavern with the grotesquely evil idol crouching at the center on its ominous plinth. The black obsidian altar from which the long rusted streaks of dried blood cut corrosive swathes was covered by a wide-spread cloak of black feathers. The cloak was formed into the likeness of the four wings of a chyyan, covering the altar and what lay upon it.

When I had looked down from the balcony that had collapsed in Autonne upon a gathering of the Black Feathers I had had an inkling of what might follow. And here was the reality! This gathering was far removed from that first one. Here the long ranks of the black-feathered priests droned out their chant in perfect rhythms. Tall candle flames flickered among the torchlights, casting gleams that winked back from weapons and armor. The black arms lifted in ritual observances. A knot of high priests upon a fallen block of stone to one side led the chanting. I gazed at the scene, ignoring everything save the gigantic form of a chyyan, chained with silver chains, fluttering its four wings above the toad idol.

A real chyyan. Its rusty black feathers showed the true horror of the situation, as it clashed its wings and hissed viciously, its scarlet beak open and its scarlet claws striking wildly at the air.

The horror lay in this: how could any sane man regard this feral killer of the skies as a god? What difference lay between the living and breathing chyyan and the decayed stone idol of the toad-thing?

Half-naked girls partially clad in scraps of black feathers gyrated wildly. They swirled black-feathered fans. The stink of incense rose dizzyingly. The priests chanted, a long rigmarole of praises to the Great Chyyan and how he was immortally twinned in spirit with Makfaril. Staring down from the shadows of the ledge into the wild torchlights with the naked sprites dancing and the wafting coils of smoke and the chanting lines of priests, I felt the nausea well in me.

The chyyan clashed his wings and tried to drag his head away from the chain around his neck. The chain ran down to a small windlass plugged to the stone floor. The chyyan was captive—aye!—captive to the odious desires of Makfaril.

Captive the killer bird might be, but all the virulence of his nature showed itself in the venomous hissings and the violence of his movements. His scarlet beak gaped ready to rip and rend, his scarlet eyes gleamed like freshly spilled blood. The thunder of his wings and the hissings from the devilish beak clashed and blended with the sonorous chanting from the black-feathered ranks.

The masichieri stood around the walls, standing well clear of the blasphemous rotting statues in their niches, watchful, on guard. What they guarded against, deep here in the vile depths below Vondium, I did not know. The place must have borne some resemblance to the dire evil of Cottmer's Caverns. I saw the guards, their black leather, their metal, the black feathers adorning them. I saw their thraxters and the oval shields they bore, their bows.

When the chanting ceased a high priest stepped up onto the pedestal below the statue. He raised his arms. Above his head the chyyan hissed and spat and struck fiercely downward, his scarlet beak flashing above the priest's head.

Himet the Mak and the knot of other high priests stood in a solid block of blackness at the side. The high priest began a shrill chanting harangue, promising everything, promising all Vallia would be turned over to pillage and plunder, promising that Makfaril would make of them all new men and women.

"Behold, the Black Day dawns! Behold, Makfaril the beloved of the Great Chyyan will reveal to us the day chosen! On your knees, prostrate yourselves, perform the full incline for our leader, twinned spirit with the Great Chyyan! Makfaril! *Makfaril!*"

In a sighing rustling of feathers the whole congregation prostrated itself. Each man performed the full incline. I stared, fascinated. Power was being exercised here, power I understood, power I had fought against time and again.

The gargoyle head of the toad-thing moved. It lifted. The stone jaws gaped, wide and wider. The head lifted and the jaws gaped and a shaft of golden illumination sprang from the opening. A figure stood framed against that radiance, a tall strong figure silhouetted against the glow.

"Rise up, my people, and give thanks to the Great Chyyan!"

The voice boomed and rolled about the cavernous chamber in eerie echoes.

The figure stepped down from the blasphemous mouth of the toad. Clad all in black feathers, imitating a chyyan, the figure of Makfaril stood limned in the golden light.

"Sink me!" I whispered, and slid the bow into my hands. "By Zim-Zair! I'll feather you, you rast, aye, and with a shaft fletched with your own damned black feathers!"

The short compound reflex bow, a construction of laminates of wood and horn with a sinew backing, did not contain the supremely long powerful strike of a longbow, but it would serve. I took up an arrow and nocked it. I'd shoot the rast clean through his black heart. If it was Naghan Vanki then the treachery of the hostile territories would be avenged, although that was now the least of my concerns.

I lifted the bow.

Then I paused. There might be something to learn when the rast addressed these black priests of his.

He spoke, gesturing widely, almost laughing, so commanding a figure and so completely in his power were these poor duped fools.

"The Black Day dawns!" he bellowed in a roar. "Behold, the Day of the Black Feathers is at hand!"

The congregation, prostrate, let fly a long wailing cry of delight.

"Long and long have we waited. And to seal our compact, to prove to the Great Chyyan our love and devotion, we offer a sacrifice. We give a life into the Great Chyyan's keeping, earnest of our intention! We shall strike! Red will flow the blood! And all, my people, will be ours!"

At a signal priests stepped forward, prominent among them Himet the Mak. They ripped away the black feathered cloak in the guise of four chyyan wings. They tore it away from the sacrifice spread-eagled upon that blasphemous obsidian slab.

I stared.

White and voluptuous and naked, thonged by wrists and ankles and yet still glaring up with blazing defiance, my Delia lay spread for the sacrifice.

Redness, roaring, madness, blackness! They were winching down the chain, drawing the violently thrashing chyyan down by the neck. Its scarlet beak slashed the air above the altar, above the slab of sacrifice. Its scarlet eyes saw that superb white sacrifice spread out for it, and now it no longer fought the chain. Hungrily it darted its beaked head down to rip and tear and gorge upon that lovely flesh.

The bow spat.

The arrow winged true. The shaft gouged deeply into one scarlet eye and the chyyan screeched and thrashed and clashed its wings. Makfaril darted sideways with a ferocious leap and the second arrow splintered against the toad-thing where he had stood.

As he leaped, the black chyyan cloak spun away from him. The black feathers floated free. And Makfaril stood revealed clad all in glittering armor, with thraxter and rapier and parrying-stick, a glorious golden numim, powerful, ferocious, bellowing savage commands.

"By Vox, Rafik!" I said, and leaped.

Headlong I leaped from the high ledge and crashed down onto the heads of the priests. They scattered and I felt bones crunch and break. There was no time for me to be winded. I was up and running and the sword in my hand cut left and cut right and there were dead men in a blood-soaked swath behind me and I scarcely heeded them. Only one thing I saw. Like a maniac I raged through the press and reached the slab of black obsidian.

The screams and shouts roared in the cavern. Arrows splintered about me. I cut down two priests, saw Himet running away, shrieking, scrambled onto the plinth.

Four slashes, four sure quick cuts, and Delia was free.

The blood must be paining her cruelly, but she forced herself to stand beside me. Masichieri were running. If we were to die here then we would die. How we died would matter only to us. I did not forget my daughter Velia in those mad manic moments of blood. Death could touch me. I knew that.

"My heart!"

"They said you were safe!"

"So I was, until Melow was wounded."

I cut down the first of the masichieri. If I was exalted, if I was drunk on the red rage and the red blood of battle, then I admit it. I fought. My scarlet breechclout felt wet and sticky with blood and my body gleamed a single crimson flame of blood. But so far none of the blood was mine. Delia had a dagger, snatched from the severed hand of a mercenary. Then she had a thraxter. We fought off the dais and back past the toad-thing. An arrow nicked my left shoulder. I stumbled back and hacked a priest across the face, drove the point past the guard of a masichieri, past his oval shield, deeply into his neck.

Delia slashed a fellow off my back and I withdrew and whirled back again and chopped the man trying to chop Delia.

Like two blood-splashed phantasms, we hacked and hewed our way toward the back of the statue.

We could not go on. There were just too many of them.

The blood stood out in livid patches across Delia's skin.

Black feathers swirled about me. Black chyyans painted on shields closed up and bore in.

A golden gleam glinted at the back of the masichieri. A great numim voice bellowed: "Do not kill him!"

As soon call off hunting dogs from the carcass of a kill when the hot madness is on them.

I slashed and beat away the lunging points, slid the slashing blows. Delia was a brilliant form of red and white, of tanned skin and spilled blood. I snarled deeply and charged headlong at the clustering shields. No coherent thought was left to me now. Only the desire to slay Makfaril and thus avenge our deaths...

Somewhere through the madness beating in my skull I heard Delia yell. "Dray! Keep your fool head down!"

Through all the red roaring madness on me, through the thunder of blood in my head, the beat of blood about my body, the roar of warring multitudes in my brain, I heard my Delia. I dropped flat and squirmed about, and Delia was at my side, gasping and laughing, and a masichieri tumbled down on top of us with a long shaft feathered through him.

Screams burst out from horror-stricken throats.

From the walls, from the niches where the rotting idols slumbered, the Crimson Bowmen of Loh methodically swept the whole cavern with the arrow storm. That sleeting hail punctured skull and leather armor, struck through mail vest and oval shield alike. Among the Crimson Bowmen were the lithe and lissome forms of girls, all clad in trim rose-red tunics, slender and quick, shooting with a deftness to equal the men's.

"The Sisters did not forget me, then, after all!"

I looked for Seg as we shielded beneath a barrier of dead bodies, but I did not see him. This was the emperor's work. The Crimson Bowmen of Loh, and the Sisters of the Rose.

The shrieks died down to moaning whimpers and soon a dread silence hung over that cavern of death. Slowly Delia and I stood up. I swirled a black feathered cape about her glowing blood-spattered loveliness, and so we waited as Naghan Vanki walked slowly through the heaps of slain. The Bowmen had killed with that sleeting storm of clothyard shafts and not a priest or masichieri remained alive.

"So you were not Makfaril, Vanki," I said.

His expressionless features, white and contained, did not reveal a single iota of himself as he said, "Had I been, you would surely be dead, Prince."

Then, with cool insolence, he turned and bowed deeply to Delia. "Princess Majestrix," he said in that flat and chilling voice. "The emperor my master will be overjoyed that you live."

Delia is, after all, a princess, and knows how to conduct herself. She held out her hand. I saw the bloodstains.

"Thank you, Naghan. You have proved yourself a loyal servant to my father today. And to me."

"Always, my Princess, to you."

So that solved that problem.

Even then I still could not make up my mind how I regarded all those gallant men of Vallia who adored their princess and would gladly die for her—aye!—as so many did die and joy in the giving of their lives for that of my Delia.

"And Makfaril?" I said in my surly, oafish clansman's way.

"He ran back through the idol of Hjemur," said Vanki. Then, waspishly, he added, "I had thought you would stop him, Prince."

The cool effrontery of the man had no power to enrage me now. I felt amused. He served the emperor. He was the emperor's spy and, as I more than half-suspected then, the emperor's spy-master. Now girls crowded up and quickly more seemly clothes were found for the Princess Delia.

We walked toward the exit, past the droves of dead bodies. I saw the Jiktar in command. He looked a little at a loss, for once Naghan Vanki's use for him was finished, Vanki lost all interest in him. I said, "Jiktar! Gather up all the arrows! Send search parties to comb out all the runnels. Have the dead disposed of and if you find any living, question them. Check all the cells." Then, because I was the Prince Majister and these things are expected of simpletons in that position, I added: "And, Jiktar, you and your men are to be congratulated. You shot as I expect Bowmen of Loh to shoot. There are barrels to be broached tonight."

I did not mention the great word 'Jikai.' This had not been a Jikai. Rather, mention of barrels brought vividly to mind what the shooting had been truly like. Fish...

Naghan Vanki and an advance party of his men had climbed down the rope ladder. Makfaril—Rafik Avandil—had discovered the ladder, but I had prevented his immediate arrest. Vanki was cutting about that. "And this villain Rafik has been close to you, Prince. He led us to you. Why he wished to have you under so close an observation we do not yet know. But, when he is found, we shall question him."

Naghan Vanki, the emperor's spy-master, might not know. But I knew. When my wizard Khe-Hi set up his sorcerous interference, preventing the monstrously egomaniacal wizard Phu-Si-Yantong from spying on me, that villain had sent his tool to seek me out and report my whereabouts and continue the spying on my movements. Yantong wished to rule all Vallia through me. Well, his plans to bring about the destruction of Vallian life and open this land to his greedy authority had fallen into ruins this day.

"And you suspected Avandil all along?"

"Since he came here from Hamal pretending to be a loyal cheerful Vallian koter. The emperor's agents never sleep. We dogged his footsteps, except when interfered with. That he was Makfaril was a surprise."

"And the emperor knew of this?"

A look of such cold hardness passed over Vanki's corpse-white face as to make his resemblance to the imagined devils of Cottmer's Caverns vivid and repulsive. "The emperor, may he live forever, knows we serve him as best we may. He has other problems weighing on his mind." Then Vanki looked at me with all the chilling presence of a dedicated, clever man who understands not only his own power but also his own limitations. "The racters... you must realize, Prince, how much more powerful they are now? Had you been seen visiting them you would have been taken up."

"But, Naghan," said Delia, smiling, holding my arm. "Not now, I think?"

"There is a night to be lived through yet, my princess."

I pointed to four Bowmen who marched in step. They carried a burden between them by arms and legs and the golden wink of glittering armor scintillated among the heaps of slain.

"You will not question Makfaril now, Vanki."

We looked down on the body of the numim Rafik Avandil, Makfaril, tool of Phu-si-Yantong. From his throat above the golden rim of the corselet protruded the hilt of a long slender dagger. I pulled it out and the blood welled. The jewels clustered on the hilt were red, and they formed the outline of a rose.

"It is mine," said Delia. "But how—"

"What is more to the point, my love, is how you came here?"

We walked a little away from Vanki and his black-and-silver-clad men.

The chamber of death bustled as the Bowmen did as I had commanded. Delia looked at me, her head on one side.

"Again, my heart? I will tell you all that I may in honor reveal. Melow was wounded and I saw her safely to our Delphondian villa here in Vondium. I went about the business that took me away—just for now let me keep that close, for I will tell you, I promise, when I am able—and I remember nothing from the moment I was drugged in some damned inn until they whipped that black covering off me and I saw—" She shivered and I put my arm about her. "It was wicked and scarlet! Hissing! I thought then that—"

"Yes, well," I said, an onker to the end. "You know what thought did."

When I asked about Dayra and Lela as we made our way through the maze of chambers and past the barracks and so up the circular slimy stair and out into the fresh air of Vondium, she told me they were well and as far as she knew dwaburs away and busy about business for the Sisters. She had left them with instructions to come and see their father as soon as they were able. Her smile was sweet, yet I saw the weariness in her. Her experiences had been horrific. Mine had been compounded of her horror, lumped together with my own and hurled full in my face, as a leem springs, near-shattering me when I saw the black-feathered cloak whipped away to reveal the naked body of my Delia spread for sacrifice.

The devilish hand of Yantong was in this, surely. The sacrifice of the Princess Majestrix would have been used in ways I could not comprehend. Chyyanism was finished. All the priests who would have carried the word for the day of uprising were dead. Makfaril was dead. The Day of the Black Feathers would never dawn in Vallia.

The simple people who had been hoodwinked would wait and they would grow restless. If they rose the insurrection would be in uncoordinated attacks, sporadic, local, able to be dealt with. Then the people would tire and lose faith and in the end they would curse the Great Chyyan and his twinned spirit, Makfaril.

"It is sad that people like the Racter party have triumphed," I said later, as we went through into our private apartments in our Valkan villa on its hill in Vondium. "But better, I think, than had the Great Chyyan triumphed."

"The racters are blind in their evil, as we know. Most are corrupted by their own wealth and power. But Makfaril was not Phu-si-Yantong then, after all. And my heart, Naghan Vanki, who is a monstrously clever man, said this numim kept close watch on you."

"Aye! Too close, I think." The callousness of Rafik Avandil seemed to me symptomatic of much that is evil about Kregen. Phu-si-Yantong had spied on me in Delia's temple, knowing my own wizard could foil his lupal projections. So he had sent those poor doomed Rapa masichieri and Avandil, his tool, had slain them and appeared to save me, just to gain my confidence. I recalled what one of the Rapas had cried out in horror. And Rumil the Point—had he too been an instrument of Yantong's? I thought the Fristles heaven-sent to aid Avandil's schemes. So, smiling at Delia, I walked into our private room. "But the numim is dead, and with him for a time the schemes of Yantong."

"The racters have grown stronger, I think. But my father? They will seek to use him even more ruthlessly now."

"They believe they have a compact with me. That can be used to your father's advantage."

"But he has banished you from Vondium."

I looked up out of the window. She of the Veils cast down her golden light, tinged with a pink fuzziness. The Maiden with the Many Smiles stole gently over the fantastic silhouette of Vondium, bathing rooftops and spires with a second roseate wash of fire. All the stars of Kregen glowed in their brilliant constellations. I turned back to the sumptuously furnished room. Truly, life on Kregen is a hurly-burly of ups and downs. But who would have it any other way?

"Your father has been emperor for a long time. Now he has this Queen Lush of Lome to worry him, along with the new factions seeking to destroy him. I shall have to make him see sense."

"And if he will not? You called him an onker. He will not forget. He is my father, and he is a terrible man in his wrath, a true emperor."

"Perhaps onker was too harsh for your father. Not for an emperor." I yawned. "I care not for tonight... Now I am for the Baths of the Nine. Then I shall eat a stupendous meal. And then I shall sleep the rest of the night away."

"That, my love," said Delia, Delia of Delphond, Delia of the Blue Mountains, "is what *you* think."

SAVAGE SCORPIO

Dray Prescot

Savage Scorpio chronicles the headlong adventures of Dray Prescot on the marvelous and mystical, beautiful and terrible world of Kregen, beneath the Suns of Scorpio, four hundred light years from Earth.

Dray Prescot himself is an enigmatic figure. Reared in the inhumanly harsh conditions of Nelson's Navy, he has been transported to Kregen many times through the agencies of the Star Lords and also of the Savanti nal Aphrasöe, mortal but superhuman men and women of the Swinging City. There is a discernible pattern underlying all his breathtaking adventures, he is sure of that; but the pattern and its meanings remain veiled and unguessable.

His appearance as described by one who has seen him is of a man above middle height, with brown hair and level brown eyes, brooding and dominating, with enormously broad shoulders and powerful physique. There is about him an abrasive honesty and an indomitable courage and he moves like a savage hunting cat, quiet and deadly. On the dangerous and exotic world of Kregen he has at various times and for various reasons become a Vovedeer and Zorcander of his wild Clansmen of Segesthes, the Lord of Strombor, Strom of Valka, Prince Majister of Vallia, King of Djanduin—and a member of the Order of Krozairs of Zy, a plethora of titles to which he confesses with a wryness and an irony I am sure masks much deeper feelings at which we can only guess.

Now Dray Prescot is plunged headlong into fresh adventures beneath the hurtling Moons of Kregen, in the streaming mingled lights of Antares, under the Suns of Scorpio.

Alan Burt Akers

One

The Brotherhood Rides Out

Shrill laughter broke excitedly over the Fair of Arial. The deep hum of many voices bartering, chaffering, driving hard bargains mingled with the roars and snarls from the wild-beast cages, the yells of barkers fronting their gaudily striped stalls, the tinkling of bells, the braying of calsanys. The exotic smells of a myriad different foods being cooked and served, the pervasive aromas of wines, the pungent fumes of dopa, coiled above the sweating happy throngs among the stalls and booths in the broad open space cresting Arial's Mound. A living breathing tapestry of noise and movement and color proclaimed the holiday atmosphere of the Fair.

The two half-naked ragamuffins, scratched by briars and panting from a long run, who ran fleetly from the forest into the outskirts of the throngs where hundreds of people haggled and drank and sweated and enjoyed themselves, attracted no attention.

The boys were shouting. Above the din only a few grizzled zorcahandlers near them heard much, and these men, anxious about selling to a credulous fop a zorca whose single spiral horn had cracked and been expertly pinned and varnished over, shooed the boys away impatiently.

Quickly the boys ran on and tried to attract the attention of others; but everyone was too intent about the business of the pleasures of the Day, too self-engrossed to pay any heed to two dirty ragged lads, acting up a mischief. A group of men who by their equipment and rugged looks were tazll mercenaries, men at the moment without employment, gawped and joked before a brilliant tent where feather-clad maidens swayed and danced, clinking silver bells, flashing white teeth, kohled eyes very inviting as their puce-faced barker waved his arms and shouted hoarsely, jingling silver coins, wheedling the tazll mercenaries to enter and enjoy the dancing. The mercenaries sent the boys off with fleas in their ears.

Along the rows of stalls where all the varied produce of the Czarin Sea was displayed for sale the boys rushed, grabbing tunics, pulling decorated sleeves, shouting, and being cuffed and pushed away. Through the packed throngs and the noise moved vendors carrying heaped trays of delicacies, steaming mouth-wateringly. Cutpurses were active and a man must lief keep his eyes open and a hand closed over his purse. A few late Elders, solemn and grave with the importance of the coming ceremony, moved toward the central dais. Priests of many cults and religions walked sedately in the blended gorgeous suns shine of Antares, moving in spaces that opened magically for them and closed as magically after they had passed by. Mostly they were priests of Opaz. There was not one priest of the Great Chyyan, for the last apostle of the Black Feathers had been hanged, very high and very thoroughly from the tallest tree on the island of Nikzm, two of the months of the Maiden with the Many Smiles ago.

The Fair of Arial on the island of Nikzm in the Czarin Sea was, in this guise, only a recent institution. Previously it had been the marketplace for the pirates who thronged the busy sea-lanes. From the island of Zamra just over the horizon to the north through the islands fringing Vallia to the west, from past the twin islands of Arlton and Meltzer to the south and Vetal to the east, the people sailed for this seasonal event. Now most of the renders had been destroyed, the pirates rendered harmless. Now the hullabaloo of commerce and pleasure gave joy and holidays to the good folk of the Czarin Sea.

Even from south of Arlton and Meltzer, from Veliadrin and from Valka, the people would sail in a grotesque variety of ships and unseaworthy boats to the Fair of Arial.

Then, when this fair was over for the season, the folk who followed the Fairs would pack up and travel to the next venue, hoping for richer pickings, perhaps, for more adventure, for a fresh zest and spice to life. For not all of Kregen, that mysterious and ominous planet four hundred light years from Earth is grim and cruel; among the beauty and the splendor there is room and more for fun and frolic and the enjoyment of living.

The two boys, bare of foot, scratched of legs and arms, red of face, continually tried to attract attention and were as continually rejected. A fat woman in a red skirt and black bodice, all wobbling chins and bust and stomach, dropped a wicker basket of loloo's eggs, well packed with straw and moss. Her hands flew up in horror as the two boys caught at her red skirt, shrieking in her ear, dragging her forcibly to make her listen.

The straw and moss proved woefully insufficient. Loloo's eggs rolled and cracked and splashed under the feet of the crowds. The woman threw her apron over her head, concealing her glistening face, and although her face was thus hidden and her screams lost in the merry uproar, by her lurching movements it was clear the boys had caused her the utmost terror. She staggered away. The corner tent pole into which she blundered supported an awning giving welcome shade from the twin suns. The awning collapsed. It billowed inward upon rows of men, dedicated drinkers all assiduously practicing their craft, quaffing good Vallian ale from glazed ceramic jugs.

Through all the bedlam of the Fair, belching out like an erupting volcano, the furious uproar from the devotees of Beng Dikkane, the patron saint of all the ale drinkers of Paz, bellowed and burst with the impassioned fervor of men interrupted at their worship. Flushed-faced men fought the tangles of cloth. Billows and humps of the gaudy material disgorged men raging with fury. Ale jugs flew, cascading their foaming contents over the drinkers, over passersby, over the trampled grass indiscriminately, in a wanton paroxysm of involuntary libations. The two boys, who made no attempt to run away and who—amazingly—did not laugh, would be chastised now for a certainty.

Seg nudged me.

"Brassud, my old dom! Here comes the Chief Elder." Seg shot me a wary glance from those fey blue eyes of his, his strong tanned face beneath the mop of dark hair very merry as he prepared to mock me in his usual way. "Where are your wits wandering? This is the islanders' great moment, and here you are, gawping into the air like a loon."

"I was watching those two lads, Seg. They've disappeared in the confusion—but they're in for a bit of stick, I fancy. Anyone who gets between an ale-drinker's ale and his stomach has only himself to blame."

"I'll allow that," said Inch, standing up so that his full seven feet of height gave him some advantage in peering over the heads of the jostling thousands. "They're having themselves a good time down there. The tent's right over now and there are ale barrels a-rolling every which way."

The confusion really was rather splendid. But my attention had to be directed to the portly, stiff, embarrassed form of doughty old Dolan Pyvorr. The Chief Elder, caparisoned in a blaze of finery, glistening and glittering in the mingled rays of the twin suns, advanced ponderously upon the steps leading up to the dais. He carried his Balass Rod with great ceremony. The Rod was all of two feet in length, banded by nine silver rings, and topped by a silver hirvel head, all fashioned superbly in Vandayha, the city of silversmiths in Valka.

Seg and Inch and the others of my friends and comrades upon the dais stood up to welcome the Chief Elder of Nikzm. I, too, stood up, for the protocol of princes means less than nothing beside the simple virtues of good manners.

A little scuffle of shoe leather at my rear took my attention. Turko the Shield used always to stand solidly at my back, in peace as in war. Now I heard his voice, low, saying: "By Morro the Muscle, Tarek, tread with care—"

And Tarek Dredd Pyvorr's answering voice, low, passionate: "You think I seek to harm the prince, Turko the Shield? Are you mad? Have you lost your senses? I, who owe everything to him? He meets my father, and he has asked that I stand with him at that time."

I took no notice. Turko might be overly officious about caring for my person—that is a great comfort on Kregen, believe me.

A little more shuffling and arrangements went on, and Balass the Hawk and Oby would have to shift along, I guessed. I killed my smile. Yes, we were a real bunch of tearaways, right villains all, comrades in arms, and here we were, dressed up like popinjays and standing on an overly-ornately decorated dais beneath a pavilion of cloth of silver, the focus of attention and—as they say—the cynosure of all eyes, waiting for the great moment, a great inaugural moment, in the Fair of Arial.

Among that group on the dais were others of my friends, some of whom you have met before in my narrative, others who, comrades in arms, have not yet found a personal mention. We were here expressly at the invitation of the Elders and People of Nikzm to take part in the ceremony about to begin. That was the official explanation for our presence. The true reason we were here was to meet in privacy, away from the prying eyes and ears of the capital—from which, anyway, I was banished—and all other teeming cities, to take further steps in the formation of the new Brotherhood.

Dredd Pyvorr stood a half-pace to the rear and to my left. He was garbed resplendently, as we all were, out of honor to the Elders and People of this tiny island of Nikzm. Now as his father climbed the steps to the dais, Dredd Pyvorr whispered his thanks anew to me.

"You have made me a Tarek, my prince. My father has been raised to become an Elder of our island, and to be Chief Elder—"

"I did not make him Chief Elder, Dredd. That he achieved himself, elected by his peers, out of his honesty and courage."

The Pyvorrs were hard-working, simple folk, the salt of the Earth—or of Kregen—and once the pirates had been cleared away and their markets closed to make way for the Fair of Arial, the island needed to be handled afresh. Situated just south of the island of Zamra, of which I am kov, Nikzm needed a council of Elders. Also, because he had fought well for us, and because he pleased me in his forthrightness and gallantry, Dredd Pyvorr had been made a Tarek, a rank of the minor nobility and within the gifting of a kov. Seg had made his Tareks in his kovnate of Falinur, and Inch his in his kovnate of the Black Mountains, both in Vallia.

"My loyalty to you is unshakable, my prince. And my gratitude eternal." In some mouths these words would have raised my hackles, made me think, created suspicion. They did nothing of the kind when spoken by Dredd Pyvorr.

His father climbed up the last few steps, puffing, broad and scarlet, and he bowed. He knew enough of my ways not to go into the incline or the full incline. I bowed in return and held out my hand.

"Well met, Elder Pyvorr. The Fair is a great success." We could hear ourselves speak, up here on the dais, with the bumblebee murmuring of the crowds around us. The fun over at the upset ale tent continued, and I fancied two small ragged forms would be, eel-like, squirming to avoid capture and chastisement.

"Lahal, my prince! Lahal and Lahal! Indeed—!" and here Pyvorr turned himself ponderously around to survey the magnitude of the Fair with the noise and color and jollity. "Indeed this is an auspicious day."

I did not know why the invitation to attend this Fair had been sent me in the form it had. But Seg and Inch and the others seemed to know, and had prevailed upon me to attend. Anyway, I wanted to know how the island was prospering, now that it no longer had piracy to depend on for a living. The economy ran well, and the crops grew and the fishermen reported bumper catches, and copper had been discovered in the rolling hills that centered the tiny island. A tiny breeze licked in and flicked lazily at the banners and guidons, at the standards and flags. My old scarlet and yellow flag flew up there, and the red and white of Valka, and the red and yellow of Vallia, and the blue and yellow of Zamra. And, surrounded by panoply, we stood like peacocks in our glittering clothes.

Pyvorr gestured to his Council of Elders, all standing gravely to one side, waiting for the proceedings to open. The few guards needed to keep the more importunate of the crowds away from the railed off space at the foot of the dais had no trouble. They were Pachaks, and they were every one a picked man, and they were the first bodyguard of the Brotherhood, not as yet fully inducted into the secrets of the Order; but devoted and loyal and soon to become acolytes. They were not mercenaries, having homes and steadings on Zamra.

The Council Elders all lifted their right hands.

Pyvorr turned heavily back to face me and lifted his own right hand. He glanced across at the rank of nine Womox trumpeters. Their horns were gilded and garlanded with roses above the fierce bull-like faces. Their tabards shone with silver thread. They lifted the long straight silver trumpets.

Each massive chest expanded with air sucked into powerful lungs. The trumpets caught the streaming mingled lights of the suns and glittered with silver starpoints.

The trumpeters pealed their fanfare. High and ringing, shrill, imperative, demanding, the silver notes pierced above the hubbub.

Silence did not fall at once. Rather, gradually and with ebbing and flowing disturbances, the uproar slowly faded. People ceased what they were doing—bargaining, buying, selling, eating, drinking, skylarking, testing their strength, having their fortunes told—and drifted out from the booths and tents into the open spaces and alleyways where they might see and hear what went on upon the high dais. The noise persisted as the people settled down in the suns shine for the ceremony.

Two dirty, raggedy figures darted out from the mass, pushing and shoving to make their way through to the front where the Pachaks stood on guard with the steel winking in their tail hands, upflung past their shoulders.

The boys shouted; but their shouts were lost in the bellows of outraged anger from some of the crowd. Others in the crowd began to shout, but in a different key, and to push and shove away, trying to escape the pressing throngs.

The boys burst out into the little cleared space at the foot of the dais. The Pachaks, veterans all, eyed them cautiously.

Amid the confusion of shout and counter shout some words jumped up from those in the crowd trying to push away.

"...all riding sleeths!" and "...leaving us defenseless, open to massacre or enslavement!"

And, coinciding with the two boys' impassioned shrieks as they darted past the Pachaks and halfway up the steps, a word that grew and rolled about the Fairground and drew into itself much of the dark evil that festers on Kregen—

"Katakis! *Katakis!*"

"Slavers! *Slavers!*"

Somehow, my sword was in my fist.

Not all slavers are Katakis, that tailed race of devils, but almost all Katakis are slavers—given half a chance.

I swung about to face that band of brothers there on the high dais. Resplendent nincompoops we looked, decked out in all our finery. But each man wore a sword—except Turko—and each man was a comrade in arms, a bonny fighter, a veteran.

"Brothers!" I bellowed. I lifted the sword in a deliberately theatrical gesture, the long slender rapier blade glittering high. "This is work for the Order! For this we are created." I yelled at Turko direct. "Turko—fetch me up those two lads—and treat them gently. Oby—the zorcas. Seg, Inch, Balass—"

But my friends were already running, leaping down the steps four at a time, pouring out to belt across the flattened grass to the zorca lines. And Young Oby raced ahead of them all.

Turko appeared with a squirming tattered figure under each arm.

"And keep silent until the prince speaks to you, you Imps of Sicce!"

They slammed onto their feet, and Turko held a scruff of the neck in each ferociously powerful fist. I bent down.

"You have done well," I said. I spoke evenly but firmly, well knowing the kind of impression I could make if I was clumsy. "Where away are these Opaz-forsaken Katakis? You will lead us?"

"Yes, koter—"

Turko shook them.

Koter is the equivalent of gentleman, mister, and it was clear these two ragamuffins had encountered koters as the highest form of life. Not that I put store by ranks and titles, as you know, except as artifices to get things done.

"Address the prince as prince, famblys!"

"Yes, prince—"

As useful to ask these two if they could ride a zorca as ask them if they had a pocket full of golden talens.

"You take one, Turko. I'll take this rascal."

Seizing up my lad, who had a shock of brown hair that was probably more alive than many a languid noble of the court, I leaped off down the steps. Turko followed. Tom Tomor ti Vulheim reined past on his zorca, kicking dust as he slewed around and so pushed back the crowd. Vangar ti Valkanium did the same on the other side. Dredd Pyvorr appeared leading a zorca and Turko would have given her to me; but I waved him on and caught at the reins Oby flung at me. Up went my urchin across the saddle, my left boot went into the stirrup, and with a flick of my hand I was seated. My lad squirmed around, for the zorca may be the most beautiful of mounts, with four tall spindly legs, a marvel of grace and stamina; but the zorca is remarkably close-coupled and there is barely room for two.

"Your name, lad?"

"Tim, if it please you, ko— prince."

"Right, Tim. Which way?"

He pointed.

The wide expanse of Arial's Mound covered with the booths and stalls and wild-beast pens and stabling lines, with the now more than a little ludicrous high dais at the center, was rapidly clearing of people. They were running off in all directions. Some, at least, must be heading straight for the viciously-waiting arms of the Kataki slavers.

Tim pointed to the east, a direction that paralleled the coast, distant some two ulms.

Dredd Pyvorr reined across, his face furious, highly colored, intense.

"Briar's Cove, lad? Am I right?"

"Yes, prince, you are right!" sang out the lad with Turko.

"Fambly!" said Turko, incensed. "Only the prince is the prince."

"For the Order!" I bellowed. As of its own volition, it seemed, my rapier had appeared in a twinkling at the first mention of the Katakis, and had scabbarded itself when the lads had run up, so now, once more, the glittering blade snapped out. I waved it high and pointed forward. *"Ride!"*

As a group we rode out, past the last scattering fugitives, screaming and wailing, out along the narrow track that led through this neck of the forest, to curve down to Briar's Cove.

It appeared to me the Katakis, with the Fair as cover, had struck inland to take the chief town of Nikzm by surprise. Once they had possession of that, they could sweep up the people as they arrived. Long memories of pirate raids, of slavers and aragorn snatching away whole families, dictated that only those villages that needs must, say by reason of the fishing, would be built on the coast. In this, this section of the Outer Oceans resembled the Inner Sea, the Eye of the World of Kregen.

As we rode furiously along, a fresh thought rose to torment me. The Katakis are a race strong and powerful, with a tail that, equipped with bladed steel, makes of them formidable opponents. They are also low-browed, dark, with thick black hair, oiled and curled, with gape-jawed mouths fanged with snaggly teeth, and generally of an evil, pestiferous nature. But we had met and bested them before. The thought that occasioned me some agony was simply this; no force of Kataki slavers would raid here, in the very shadow of the puissant empire of Vallia, for all the empire's internal problems, unless they raided in strength. They must be a strong and determined band.

And we were few.

I led my men into a battle that could easily end with us all dead or enslaved.

Yet no one had thought to count the cost. No one had thought to reck the consequences. Katakis had had the nerve to land on one of my islands to raid and enslave; therefore my band of brothers followed me into headlong action.

Through the coldness of these thoughts the warmth flowed that we were a band of brothers, we fought together as comrades in arms. This would be the first real test of the Order, for every man who rode with me had been invited to become a member, and had joyfully accepted. He had accepted the strictures laid on him, the demands that membership of the Order would entail. The simple, pure-minded and naive chivalry of the first rules of the Order may make me smile now; but they remain as true as ever, despite all that has happened since. We were idealistic, believing that too much violence on Kregen was being used by the wrong people, that we should do what we could to redress the balance. And these Opaz-forsaken Kataki slavers had turned up, right on our doorstep, to present us with our first challenge, our first test.

Certainly, as we thundered along the forest trail, kicking dust and twigs, a bright and colorful company, I did not count the discomfiture of the Black Feathers of the Great Chyyan. That evil creed had been bested in Vallia, for the time being, and the beating of it had not been at the hands of the Order as an Order. If I am a credulous man, that is understandable, seeing the marvels I have witnessed in my life. But I detected a fundamental and powerful current of fate in this meeting between slavers and the Brotherhood.

Ahead the track twisted around a giant lenk, the oak-like tree growing to an enormous girth and shedding a deep and somber shadow upon the trail. We roared around the angle and beyond a sharp declivity the trees ended and a long greensward opened up. I reined in, my hand upflung, my zorca skidding and sliding.

Slowly, I cantered out into the open.

The others followed.

We stared.

The ground was littered with color, with steel, with bodies and with blood.

Slowly, we walked our zorcas through the shambles, the animals restive, not liking the stink of fresh-spilled blood, but obedient and going on, well-trained to the stark realities of war.

"So here are your Katakis, Tim."

Tim was being sick.

The ground was littered with bodies and with blood—Kataki bodies and Kataki blood.

I dismounted. As I looked up I saw for the first time that Young Oby had snatched up the scarlet flag with the great yellow cross upon it, my flag, the battle flag that fighting men call Old Superb. It shone in the mingled suns-light.

"These devils have been killed handsomely," observed Seg. He bent over a corpse, kicking the limp tail away so that the bladed steel strapped to the tip clinked against a fallen helmet. He picked up a bow. Oh, it was not a great Lohvian long bow; being of a compound reflex construction; but in Seg Segutorio's hands any bow is a deadly weapon par excellence. He smiled up at me. "I feel only half naked now."

The Katakis had fought hard. They lay in windrows at the end, piled high. Their wounds were all in front. But they were all dead, methodically butchered.

"Who could have done this?" said Dredd Pyvorr. He looked pinched of face. "Katakis are notorious—Chuliks?"

Chuliks and Pachaks command the highest fees as mercenaries, for different reasons. Our small guard of Pachaks remained mounted, instinctively carrying out soldier's work, scouting ahead, sniffing out the devils who had slain devils.

The body of one Kataki intrigued me. He was a big fellow, although Katakis are as a rule not overly tall. His helmet had fallen off. His face reminded me of that of Rukker. The arrow had punched through his bronze-studded scaled corselet.

At my side, Seg whistled.

"A goodly shaft..."

He bent to pull it out.

I said: "You'll find it will come hard. As a wager, I'll venture there are six or seven barbs a side. That's no Lohvian shaft, Seg."

"But it is as long—what bow is there that—oh!"

"Yes," I said. And I nodded and felt the anger in me, and the despair, the sorrow, and the vengeful fury.

"I have never met an archer who can best a Bowman of Loh," said Seg Segutorio, speaking softly. "But you have told me of these devils, and it seems we are to meet them, now."

"They must be devils indeed to destroy these Katakis, who are devils spawned from Cottmer's Caverns," said Dredd Pyvorr, feelingly.

"From around the curve of the world," I said. "From whence no man knows. They sail in their swift, magical ships, raiding, destroying, looting, burning. They are diffs unlike any in the whole of Paz. They are not men like us. They are the Shanks, the Shants, the Shtarkins, Leem Lovers, vile, to be destroyed, vermin—and yet, and yet, I know they are courageous to sail their ships all those untold dwaburs across the open seas. They are not men like us; but they are men."

"And they'll slay us all as soon as look," said Inch, sourly.

Dredd Pyvorr gripped onto the hilt of his rapier. His pinched mouth shook; then he had control of himself.

"I know of whom you speak, prince. We call them Shkanes—they have many names, all vile. Fish-Heads—yes, their horror goes before them."

I turned to young Tim, who had recovered and was now busily plundering the dead bodies, a most sensible occupation.

"You said they rode sleeths, Tim."

"So they did, prince." Tim looked up, his hands full of rings and chains and brooches, with a wicked-looking dagger stuck into his breechclout. I winced. He could do himself a permanent and most unfortunate injury if he were injudicious.

"There are no sleeths here, you imp of Sicce!" roared Balass the Hawk. He was prowling about looking for a sword more to his liking than a rapier, and hoping vainly to come across a shield. "Sleeths are stupid reptiles, at best, but they'd stick to their dead masters."

"That means, brothers, that the Shanks have ridden off on the Katakis' sleeths."

Oby ran off.

The sleeth is a saddle dinosaur, variously scaled and marked, which runs on two legs, the fore claws stunted and in a way pathetically stupid, and with the long thick tail outstretched to the rear to provide balance. They are an uncomfortable ride and I have nothing to do with them. I am a Zorca and a Vove man. I ride a Nikvove when I cannot saddle a Vove, and I like the superb joats of my Djangs, and I have some time for a few other of the riding mounts of Kregen. But sleeths—no, I do not fancy them.

From just over the brow of the slope Oby screeched and waved his arms, so we trotted over there. He pointed down.

The unmistakable tracks of sleeth claws showed in a muddy patch where water trickled past the grasses. The tracks pointed downslope and to the farther side of the greensward where the forest closed in again. The forest did not, at that moment, look in the least inviting.

"Find yourselves battle weapons more suitable than rapiers," I shouted. "Then we ride to deal with the Fish-Heads."

No one passed a comment on our riding to deal with men who had already dealt with the Katakis for us. For all their horrific reputation, the Katakis were small beer beside the Shanks, the Fish-Heads, from over the curve of the world.

Our Pachaks trotted in from their scouting duty and dismounted to search for weapons. The choices were plentiful. If the Shanks had taken any weapons from the shambles of the battlefield it made little impression on the numbers remaining. I selected a good stout cut and thruster, a version of the Havilfarese thraxter or the Vallian clanxer, and buckled it on scabbarded to its own belt. Its owner no longer possessed a face, besides now losing his sword.

Because I had steeled myself to go through with the ceremony at the Fair of Arial, a function whose purpose appeared to be known to all my friends and not to myself, I had donned the bright foppish clothes and had forced myself to ignore them, to grow accustomed to them. Now, and, I confess, with some relief and also somewhat pettishly, I stripped off the belts and ripped away the gaudy silks and sensils, threw down the brocaded pelisse and the feathered mazilla—the thing had been irritating and itching at me all day—and so stood forth clad only in the old scarlet breechclout.

In a battle a man needs protection from the blow he does not see. With resignation, then, I found pieces of armor that would fit and so donned a semblance of a breast and back, finding a reasonable fit over a padded vest. The scaled armor was flexible enough, the bronze studs barbaric against the black. Also, I took up a bow and four quivers, filling them from other, half-emptied quivers. As for the helmets of the Katakis, these are small and round and completely without embellishment, save for what may be painted on or engraved. The Pachaks are the same about their helmets. No fighting man who uses a bladed tail wants gaudy ornaments in his helmet to interfere with the lean lethal sweep of that deadly tail.

Finding one that fit I strapped it up. At the least, it might save my old vosk-skull from a terminal crack.

Inch appeared in high delight, tempered only by the fact that the axe he had found was not a true danheim axe, being double-bitted and short in the haft; but, as he said, it would serve to lop a few Fish-Heads' heads, it would serve...

There were no shields, for, as you know, the fighting men of this part of Kregen regarded the shield as a coward's accoutrement, a stupidity that Balass and I had been doing something to rectify. So Balass had to content himself with a good cut and thruster, and a powerful main-gauche built to mammoth proportions. As for Turko, the Khamster who could rip a warrior apart with his bare hands, the Khamorro who disdained all edged and pointed weapons, he still had his balass and steel parrying stick, a decadence of belief shocking and yet reassuring to me, for he, too, Turko the Shield, could not carry his great shield into battle at my back.

Oby took up Old Superb, and with the old battle flag floating above us, we rode from that scene of destruction and plunged into the gloomy defiles of the forest.

Turning in my saddle I saw the two lads, Tim and his friend, still hard at work. I sighed. Children learn the facts of life hard on Kregen—a phenomenon not unfamiliar to children on this Earth—but the facts they learn on Kregen are altogether more harsh and lurid. Turned in my saddle I noticed the tall whipcord tough body of the tazll mercenary who had been the only one to ride with us when we'd galloped from the Fair. He was a diff, a Khibil, with the hard, sharp, fox-like face of that people, with bristling whiskers and proud dark eyes. He had not dismounted to collect weapons. He carried a long lance, a rapier and main gauche and a cut and thruster. I had not failed to notice the silver mortil-head looped on its silver silken cord at his throat. He was a Paktun, a famed mercenary. He was not of the Order, not one of the Brotherhood, and so I had been wrong when I had so enthusiastically enjoined on us all as a band of brothers that we rode about the Order's business. But, all the same, he looked competent and tough and a useful man to have in such a fight as we would soon encounter.

Just ahead of him rode half a dozen of the minor nobility created by Seg and Inch, Tareks all, young men devoted to their lords and to the ideals of the Order.

Foleanor Arc, the young Strom of Meltzer, rode next ahead, brilliant, laughing, his guitar slung to his saddle bow and, I knew, causing him great anguish that he could not strum the strings and then give us a rousing song to help us on our way. With him rode Kenli ti Valkanium, straight and lean and grim.

They followed Nath Dangorn, called Totrix, who rode a zorca and would have preferred an ugly, six-legged totrix as a mount, and with him Nev ti Drakanium, who owed his loyalty to the Lady of Delphond.

Oh, yes, we were a goodly company, for there were others who rode with us along the forest trails in the somber shadows of the trees, with only the occasional chink of sunlight falling through, burning red when the ruby sun Zim shone down and lambent green when the emerald sun Genodras caught shafts of viridian light through the tracery of leaves. But we were few, pitifully few. Inch and Seg had counted at least a hundred and seventy-five Kataki corpses.

Truly, I had never before been of two minds over the numbers of dead Katakis there might be scattered about. Well, by Zair, to be honest, perhaps only when Rukker had been involved.

The way ahead showed a streaming mass of golden light as the commingled shafts from the suns drenched the end of the trail in radiance. We rode out from the forest onto a broad sweep of greensward. Small white flowers grew in clumps among the green. The little breeze tufted the grasses. Away before us the trail, which was in truth only a narrow beaten way where the grass struggled to cling to life, trended through a copse and then rose to skirt a hillside and so round the bend and, presumably, descend to Briar's Cove. The sound of the sea reached us in long murmured susurrations. Birds wheeled above, but their wheelings soon ceased as they set course for the shambles in our rear. At this sign we all knew the Shanks could not be far off.

I held up my right hand and made chopping motions left and right. The column formed out and we rode abreast. The flowers and the grasses and the breeze, the high blue sky and, over all, the streaming mingled radiance of Zim and Genodras, created an unforgettable picture. We rode on.

The long swelling sound of the sea reached us from the right and on our left the small hill was crowned by a ruin from the olden time. White columns leaned, splotched with lichen. The corner of an architrave hung perilously over nothing. Insects murmured among the tall grasses and flowers bowering the ruin. We rode on.

The greenness of the grass was a greenness that held nothing of menace, lush and bright and soothing. Clumps of red flowers grew here and there, mingled with the white star-like blooms. Blue flowers, perfumed, delicate, drifted above tall stems in the little breeze. A few clouds, white against the blue, drifted in counterpoint to the blue flowers starring the grasses.

Truly, there are times and places on Kregen that are heartbreakingly beautiful. But we grim men, panoplied for war, rode on.

The Shanks rode out from the copse fronting us, a dense column that debouched like a dark river in flood, formed a thickly ranked line that extended to flank us left and right, and sat, waiting, their weapons all a-glitter in the light of the Suns of Scorpio.

We had no trumpeter.

There was no need to sound the charge.

If men exist who prey on other men, looting and destroying and killing, then the victims must either perish or resist. To perish is not always easy, if nonresistance is part of a creed. To resist is sometimes the easier course, even if it does, in the end, lead to total destruction. Then, perhaps, it were better not to have resisted at all.

Who could say that these Fish-Heads did not have the right to sail over the curve of the world from their own lands, and burn and loot and destroy our lands?

These questions are imponderables, particularly when you are pounding along at full gallop, the sword in your fist, the suns light of Scorpio beating on your helmet, feeling the jolting lunge of your zorca, seeing the onrushing blur of Fish-Faces, the glitter of hostile weapons, readying yourself for the scarlet moment of impact.

The Brotherhood hit the thick ranks of Shanks and burst through in a welter of flashing blades and spurting blood, of screaming sleeths and zorcas, of men going down and of Fish-Heads being ridden into the turf.

It was all a blur of action. The sword thrust and cut, parried, leaped, slicked with the greasy green ichor of the Shanks, a live brand in my hand.

We were surrounded. The Shanks closed in. Seg's arrows cut them down as fast as he could draw the string and let fly. Inch's axe slashed with metronomic regularity, cutting swathes through the fishy bodies. Icy eyes glared at us, the abominable stink of fishy bodies clammied in with a foul miasma. We fought. Balass showed all the skill of the hyr kaidur, fighting with professional skill tempered now with the berserk rage of the warrior. Oby, using men's weapons, hewed and hacked and drove down his opponents. The clangor of sword against sword beat across that pleasant grassy sward. Blood dropped upon the flowers, the red blood of Paz and the green ichor of the Fish-Heads.

The Shanks wore bronzen armor, fashioned into fish scales. They possessed man-like bodies, but their heads were the heads of fish. Many varieties of fish, there were, I suppose. But we slew those we could and did not stop to reck the differences. In their fishy eyes no doubt we looked alike, although a Pachak and a Khibil do not look much alike, and diffs differ from apims like me. And apims differ, too, as Inch's seven foot of height marks him out from Oby's lithe youth.

The crowds of stinking Fish-Heads pressed in. Our zorcas reared as we fought, struggling to find space. We were hard pressed. Swords cut and slashed. Over and over again a man would be saved in the last moment by a comrade's blade. Our brands ran thick with green ichor. Soon our arms would tire. We were all fighting men, warriors of Kregen, men who were inured to hardship and suffering and the clangor of war.

But humanity is frail. Muscles and blood, sinews and breath, can only sustain a man for so long. Then strength will fail and breath come hard. Then muscles will fail to bring the sword up in time, to deliver the terminal blow. And there were many Fish-Heads, over twice as many as in the Brotherhood.

We fought magnificently.

But we were pressed in and back. The Pachaks found a weak link in the circle and we smashed our way through. I lifted in the stirrups and waved the dripping sword.

"To the trees!" I yelled. I took the responsibility. I ordered the retreat. I, it was, who took my men away from that death trap.

We galloped hard for the trees and we passed the little ruin atop its hill. There were fewer of us who thus retreated than there had been who so valiantly charged.

At the tree line we reformed. Our zorcas were tiring. We were all panting. Most of us were wounded. Blood shone red upon our armor. And, over all, the sticky green ichor clung, stinking, foul, like a vomit to revolt us all and remind us of the inevitable end.

The dark mass of the Shanks with those evil glittering points of light from point and edge of weapons waited at the far end of the greensward slope. Banners fluttered above them, a multi-colored display that meant much to them and nothing save as targets for destruction to us. I looked at the Brotherhood, panting but determined still. We were few.

"We will chew them up piecemeal and spit them out as one spits out gregarian pips," I shouted. "We hit the left flank and break clean through and retire. Understood?"

"Aye, prince. Understood." The cries came bluffly, strong, confident despite wounds and tiredness. I shook my zorca's reins and led out.

We hit them like a rapier lunge, chopping off the left flank. We lost men, yes, we lost good men; but we trampled down and slew more of them than they of us.

The Shanks—the Shkanes as Pyvorr called them—handled their tridents with superb efficiency. The wicked barbs would degut a man as neatly as a fishmonger deguts a cod. But the wicked tridents had their disadvantages. Seg deflected one with the bowstave in his left hand, his sword blurred down and sliced away an icy Fish-Face, and Inch, the barbs of a trident caught in his saddle, slashed his axe in a merciless horizontal sweep that sprayed bits of fish everywhere.

We reformed back upslope and turned, and hit them again.

Four, five, six times we regrouped and charged.

At each charge we were less. The zorca, as we all believed then, was not the animal for the solid shoulder-to-shoulder, knee-to-knee charge, bodyweight and mass of metal counting more than fleetness and agility. Times change—but that is for later.

Seven times we raced fleetly over the slope, angling the direction of our lunge, trying to chew and chop at the mass of Fish-Heads as a man hews and cuts at a stubborn log of wood to shape it to his satisfaction. The fight was of great intensity during the action; the compass might be small but of individual prowess the battle was of epic proportions.

The arrow storm I had expected to greet us from the Shanks' asymmetrical bows stormed only once. We lost men; but I shouted and lifted my sword and beat away the glancing shafts, and others bent their heads into the sleet. We charged through that ordeal, losing men—the Pachaks suffered here—and so came to hand strokes, again. After that the arrows fell sparingly and I guessed the Shanks were running low.

If ever the relative merits of the reptilian two-legged sleeth and the close-coupled four-legged zorca could be proved, then this battle matched them and proved decisively the zorca as the master. Pirouetting, dancing nimbly sideways, circling, the zorcas outran and outmaneuvered the clumsy sleeths. This gave us one tremendous advantage. We could drive in, deliver our blows and spin away before the sleeth riders could form front to receive our onslaught.

The grasses stained red and green with dropped blood. Men and Fish-Heads lay upon the stained grass, some howling, some screeching, most dead.

Eight times we roared in, and on the eighth time we were fractionally slow through tiredness and so were nearly surrounded and trapped. We fought free. Sword against serrated sword and trident, we hewed and savaged our way through the pressing ranks, rode with bent heads for the tree line past the white columns of the ancient ruin. We were nearly exhausted. All were wounded. We gasped for breath. Our superb zorcas were near the end.

I rode a few paces before the brothers of the Order—with the Pachaks and the Khibil there in the line with us—and I lifted in the stirrups. I surveyed my men from under the helmet rim.

"If any man wishes to withdraw through the forest, he is free to do so. I shall not think any the worse of him for that. If any one of you wishes to go, then go now, and may Opaz guide your footsteps."

There were gaps in the ranks, and the gaps closed up.

No man moved back.

The zorcas shifted on their polished hooves. Oby held the scarlet and yellow banner high.

I let out my breath.

"Then let us all go forward, together, as a band of brothers."

"They fight hard, by Erthyr the Bow," said Seg. He shook his bow at the dark ranks of Shanks, speckled with the cruel glitter from their weapons. "But we'll have 'em!"

"We'll take a few with us to the Ice Floes of Sicce," said Inch. "By Ngrangi, this old axe will lop a few fishy heads."

"By Xurrhuk of the Curved Sword," spat out Balass the Hawk. "We can lick them yet."

"Aye!" sang out Oby. He used an oath of the Jikhorkdun, in remembrance of other days. "You speak sooth, Balass, by the glass eye and brass sword of Beng Thrax!"

Other oaths rose as men swore on their honor. These men would fight to death, however nonsensical that might be. And yet—and yet? Could I detect a wavering among some of those with us? A very slight, an almost imperceptible, reluctance? Some of the shouts and cries carried overtones of hysteria. Some of these men might waver. They could see quite plainly that this affair could end only in their deaths. Where was the sense in that? Yet these men were brothers, of the Order—yet the Order was new, unfledged, with no long-rooted traditions to inspire and uplift and enable men to act beyond their own resources. Could I blame them?

"The island of Nikzm is small," I shouted. "Since we dispersed the pirates there has been no fighting. There is no garrison to speak of. All that lies between these Fish-Heads and the defenseless people—is us—the Order." I did not wave my sword. I sat hard and upright and glared upon these, my men, the brothers of the Order I hoped would achieve so much. "But that is not the whole reason why we fight on. Yes, it is the ultimate reason for our being. For the people of Nikzm represent all the peoples of Paz. All the continents and islands here. But we fight for our own honor. We fight in our own eyes, we are our own judges. It is to us, and us alone, that this Jikai belongs. And in honor we must redeem our pledges so freely given."

The line, so shrunken now, quivered. Zorcas began to sidle. The men were dispirited, despite their words. In only moments one man might break, and with his desertion the whole line could crumble. Was this how my own vaunting ambitions were to end? On a tiny island, destroyed by stinking Fish-Heads? Was my own pride so vainglorious that I would condemn to death this fine company of men, young and proud in their strength, laughing and merry, send them remorselessly to destruction? For myself? For my overweening pride and ambition?

In that dark moment, I, too, I, Dray Prescot, of Earth and of Kregen, came very close to despair.

A voice, an anonymous voice, rose from the ranks.

"Let us ride from hence and gather reinforcements. Let us save ourselves so that we may fight another day."

I looked.

I confess it, I looked to mark the man.

It was Dredd Pyvorr, Tarek, created by me, given honor and rank, his father uplifted, an Elder, the Chief Elder of this island we fought to save.

"If this is your will—" I started to say, not thinking, not even savage, but resigned. I, Dray Prescot, the Lord of Strombor, Krozair of Zy, resigned to running from my foes!

Another voice bellowed, hard and fierce.

"They charge! See, the Shanks attack!"

I swung about, lowering, hating, filled with anger and remorse and fury and shame.

The Fish-Heads bore down on us, a long dark breaking wave of beasts and mounts, tipped with steel, riding knee to knee, hard and savage and utterly without mercy, riding to crush us and smash us into utter destruction.

"Now are we doomed!" The shriek rose and shattered in despair.

The line began to break.

Two

Kroveres of Iztar

As that dark and glittering onrushing mass bore down on us I cursed my own stupidity and pig-headed vanity and folly. I, Dray Prescot, had led these men to their deaths. The horrid clicking and scratching of many sleeth claws reached us with hypnotic intensity. The tridents glittered red in the light of the Suns of Scorpio—glittered red with our blood.

The line at my back moved and snaked, restively. The zorcas were tired. The men were exhausted. Fool! Onker! I should have retreated at the first, sought what assistance there was in Nikzm; small though it was, it would have made the difference. All the mercenaries at the Fair, the stout country-folk, the fishermen—with what weapons we could have gathered up for them, we would have fought—and I realized even as I thus castigated myself that no simple countryman, no fisherman, was going to meet and best in battle these supremely warlike Shanks. The Shanks lived for battle. It was a creed with them, some divine right given to them by their own dark and fishy gods, driving them on, egging them on to plunder and conquest and eternal battle.

The truth was the Brotherhood had achieved against the Shanks what few groups of men of Paz had ever achieved before. And the cost was high, the payment dear, the final reckoning written in blood and spelling death.

"Brotherhood of Paz!" I bellowed, turning in the saddle, glaring back at the shuffling line. "Those of you who will, go! Flee! Save yourselves. Raise the island, carry word to Zamra, rouse the garrisons. And those that will—follow me!"

Lumpily turning in the saddle and ready to clap in heels—no man who is a rider uses spurs to a zorca—I hesitated, and turned back. My face must have borne that old intolerant, savage, devil's look. I bellowed.

"Seg! Inch! Balass! Turko! Oby!" I shouted, loud, intemperately, viciously. "Tom! Vangar! Nath! Kenli! Naghan! You do not ride with me. Your duty lies in other places closer to your hearts! I order you to ride and seek succor! *Ride!*"

They left it to Seg to speak for them all.

Seg Segutorio lifted his bow. He smiled that raffish, fey grin of his, his blue eyes very bright and merry in that tanned face beneath the shock of black hair.

"Oh, aye, my old dom. We'll ride. We'll obey your damned high-handed orders. Only it happens that the quickest way for us to ride to do your bidding—*prince*—is to ride straight ahead. Straight ahead!"

"And if any lumpen Fish-Face happens to get in the way, let him look out," Inch finished.

"Famblys!" I shouted, feeling the gush of warmth, the anger, the pride at their folly, the agony and the shame. "Idiots! Onkers! It is my duty and mine alone—it falls to me—"

"Sometimes you take too much on your shoulders," said Turko. His magnificent muscles bulged. I blinked. In Turko's left hand a green-dripping sword caught the lights of the twin suns. "Turko? A sword?"

He laughed. "They broke my parrying stick. This serves in its stead. Had I my great shield, now, then—"

The clicking scrape of the advancing sleeths bore down on us.

The line shifted and yet, and yet they would not ride off. For a space the tension hung. Now I knew that they must ride. I had been wrong, criminally wrong, in thus dragging these men to their deaths. In my own folly and pride I thought I had been doing the right, the noble, thing. But nobility can be bought at too high a price. It was folly to have these men slain to no purpose now. If we all died here—as we would, as we would!—how would that help this tiny island of Nikzm, let alone the mighty empire of Vallia?

No thoughts of my Delia must be allowed to enter my stubborn old vosk-skull of a head. None.

"Go!" I bellowed. "Save yourselves!"

A few men shook out their reins, they would not look at me. But I did not blame them as they began to turn their zorcas' heads, ready to ride back through the dark defiles of the forest.

So this was how all my brave dreams for a great Brotherhood had foundered! The Order was finished. It had never even begun.

I turned back to face the oncoming mass of Shkanes, and I wished I could have had my old Krozair longsword with me, and I kicked in my heels and the zorca lunged forward for the last time.

Headlong I belted for the black and silver glittering mass of Fish-Heads.

A shrill and shocked shrieking began—began to my rear.

I did not look back. The zorca flew fleetly over the grass where the blue and red and white flowers starred the green, where drops of red blood stained across the flowers. The shouting at my back increased and voices mingled in shocked disbelief. I looked up to my left, toward the white ruins.

I stared, disbelieving.

A light glowed among the white tumbled columns.

A golden yellow light, lambent, blazing, growing in color and luminosity, swelling. And at the heart of that refulgent radiance the figure of a woman astride a zorca. A woman wearing golden armor, astride a white zorca whose single spiral horn blazed with golden light. I stared and the mount beneath me ran loose. I stared at the apparition. She wore golden armor and carried a great banner which flowed freely outspread in a breeze no one else could feel, an unearthly breeze from a land beyond the senses of normal men.

"Zena Iztar!" I screamed it out, shaken, dazed, wondering. *"Zena Iztar!"*

This was the supernatural woman who had visited me on Earth when I had been banished there for twenty-one miserable years. Then she had used the fashionable name of Madam Ivanovna. She had appeared to me before, using supernatural means, and I believed she had helped me. She was not, as far as I then knew, aligned either with the Savanti or with the Star Lords. I gaped and the zorca eased up, and slowed down. Zena Iztar lifted the great banner so that all could see the device coruscating upon the crimson surface.

Outlined in white upon the glowing crimson banner the deep royal blue of her cogwheel device forced itself upon my own senses, yet I had never grasped the significance of that emblem. Always before Zena Iztar had appeared to me alone, with those around us frozen in a timeless sleep. Yet now—now from the shouts and excited and shocked exclamations that broke from the brothers of the Order, she could be seen by us all.

Her voice reached us. Golden, ringing, full-bodied, her voice floated above all the sounds of coming battle, over the shouts and yells of the men, over the clicking scraping advance of the sleeths and the hissing malevolence of the Fish-Heads, over the mingled jingling of war harness.

"Men of Paz! Brothers of the Order! Comrades in blood! Those you call Fish-Heads must be shown the error of their ways. The Order demands sacrifice, loyalty, utter devotion, unswerving purpose, obedience." She lifted the banner in her left hand and golden coruscating sparks shot from her armor. In her right hand a sword—a sword! A sword like unto a Savanti sword—lifted high and pointed. The brand pointed at the Shanks. "Death is a small price to pay for honor! Brothers of the Order! Your duty in honor is to be true to yourselves and to Paz and to the Order."

The light began to fade.

I shook my head. There was much she had said with which I would not, could not, agree. But a great deal summed up something of what I struggled for.

But, in the name of Zair! How did she know the Order existed at all?

But, then, she was no mortal woman. She understood many secrets I longed to know, could see into the hearts of men, must surely comprehend the doings of Kregen and attempt to mold them to her own ends.

The Shanks pressed nearer. They were confident now. They had withstood all we could throw at them. They had suffered and had lost a goodly number from their ranks. But they could see how we had suffered. They shrilled their hideous screeching war cries and they came on, fishy, stinking, scaly, repulsive, deadly.

They had not seen the golden glowing apparition of Zena Iztar.

Her chiming voice rang out for one last time before the vision disappeared.

"Fight for what you believe to be true, Men of Paz. And, remember, never speak to anyone not of the Order of my presence, for I am sacrosanct. This is a stricture laid on you as members of the Order—and a privilege. Follow Dray Prescot. *Jikai!*"

The first man to move was Dredd Pyvorr.

With a high lifting shriek he set his zorca in a straight dead run at the oncoming Shanks.

We saw him galloping madly into the thickest of them. We saw his sword swirling and smiting left and right, saw him engulfed as a stone is engulfed in a pool. In the same instant we were all once more in motion, roaring down, headlong belting down into the repulsively stinking mass of Fish-Heads.

Dredd Pyvorr had shouted as he charged for the last time.

Over and over he had shouted as he roared to his death.

"For the Brotherhood of Iztar! For the Order! For Dray Prescot! Iztar! Iztar!"

I felt the coldness running through me.

There were manipulations here, superhuman twistings of normal human men to supernatural ends.

Then we hit.

The red roaring madness of battle descended on us. I am contemptuous of that notorious red curtain that falls before the fighting man's eyes—so it is said—but it is a thing that transcends humanity and must be used and manipulated in its turn so far as a man may. We fought. We fought.

I think, now, as I thought then, that Zena Iztar brought some of her magical powers to our assistance. Nothing else, in all sanity, serves to explain what happened.

The few of us, the few Brothers of the Order of Iztar, smashed and beat and routed the confident might of the Shanks from around the curve of the world. We destroyed them. The survivors ran. The sleeths poured blood as the Shkanes poured blood. Green ichor fuming onto the grass, smoking under the suns.

We pursued them.

Down the long slope and through the copse and so down the last curve of the trail into Briar's Cove we pursued them, slaying all the way.

Memories are scarlet and monstrous and do not pass.

Our arms did not tire. We were possessed of superhuman strength. Tireless, we smote and slew and drove them down to the beach where we slew them in the water as they tried to reach their ships. Those ships with their clumsy square upperworks and the sleek fishlike lines below water, with the tall banded aerodynamic sails, pushed off with the last few remnants. The black and amber sails slid up the tall masts, curving to the breeze. The ships pulled away, sliding easily through the water, and we stood on the beach and shook our fists at the Shanks, and cursed them, and jeered them, and felt, perhaps, as no men of Paz had ever felt before.

We did not attempt to sail the ships in which the Katakis had landed after the Shkanes. I knew that no ship of Paz, not even the superb race-built galleons of Vallia, could catch a Shank ship.

Some of the very best galleons built in Valka might almost match a Shank vessel, and we were working all the time on improvements; but these Kataki vessels were mere small editions of argenters, broad and squat and with a pitiful sail plan. They were broad-beamed and capacious and designed to hold slaves.

We stood and jeered and fumed until the last Shank vessel vanished from sight, and then we turned back to the dolorous business of clearing up after the battle.

There was much talk, and much to talk about; but one single topic dominated every conversation.

Zena Iztar.

Dredd Pyvorr had been the first to drive into battle at her instigation. He, it was soon apparent, was the original martyr of the Order. His name would live enshrined.

Traditions were built in this fashion.

And, too, I detected a difference about these men. Some inner strength had been vouchsafed them. They were not the same men who had agreed to join the Order. They had been refined, refined in the crucible of agony and battle, and now they gleamed with a luster of spirit I found mightily reassuring—and also worrying in that nagging anxious way I have when events pour past without due design and thought spent upon them.

As with my membership of the Order of Krozairs of Zy upon the Eye of the World, I will not speak of much of our discipline. Much had been taken from the Krozairs, for their Orders are justly famed, and workmanlike, martial and mystic, devoted to Zair, and designed to sustain morale and spirit in the deepest of adversities. So I will content myself with a few remarks only. In the old days of Valka, when that island of which I am Strom was its own kingdom, they had their own knights, men of high-caliber, renowned, given the honor prefix of Ver to their names. This, we chose to resurrect, and members of the Order of Iztar were called, among ourselves, Ver Seg and Ver Inch, and so on.

Ver Seg Segutorio was the High Archbold.

This I welcomed and refused to take on any particular position for myself, preferring to be a plain member, a simple Ver of the Order.

We called ourselves Kroveres.[*]

Kroveres.

The name rang and reverberated, as the name Krozair rings and reverberates.

We were the Kroveres of Iztar.

Also, and at the time much to my displeasure, another name was also used, and I asked questions and was told. Was told.

Seg said to me: "We are the Order of Kroveres of Iztar, Dray. Now we must build. This little Island has witnessed a miracle."

"Surely," I said as we rode lumpily for the Mound of Arial. "And you still haven't given me any idea why we came here in the first place—except to check up on progress."

He laughed.

"Why, you may as well know now. I think Elder Pyvorr will be mourning his son—" All the laughter fled. "It was a great deed, Dredd Pyvorr's. We shall remember him in the Kroveres."

"Yes, that is so. And?"

"And, my old dom, you were asked here to be given the new name of the island as a gifting. You are the Kov of Zamra. Zamra is just over the horizon to the north, and this little island is called Nikzm—"

"I know!" Nik as a prefix means half and as a suffix means small. In the names of lands and islands, however, the prefix often carries the meaning of small, for Zamra was by many times more than twice the size of Small Zamra, Nikzamra, Nikzm.

"The Elders and people of the island have decided and issued the necessary patents and the bokkertu has been concluded to call the island Drayzm. Drayzm. So, my old dom, we are also the Kroveres of Drayzm."

So, as you can well imagine, I was not overly pleased.

I passed it off; but Seg gave me a hard look, and said a word or two

____

* Kroveres. Prescot spells this out. He pronounces it in the same way as Krozair, but does not spell it Krovair. *A.B.A.*

about thick-headed, vosk-skulled ingrates, and how Delia was muchly pleased—

"Did Delia know about this, then?"

"Oh, aye. You don't think we'd go behind your back without consulting Delia, do you? You've told me how they made you Strom of Valka—well! This is no new title—and I know how you feel about them, as I do. They are useful in this world."

"That is sooth, by Vox!"

And Inch leaned forward to say, waspishly: "And if the Kov of Falinur lost that one, he'd not give a damn, hey?"

"Too right!" snapped back Seg. He had had great trouble in his kovnate of Falinur. "Except—except Thelda would—"

"Aye," I said. "Thelda likes mightily to be a kovneva. And so she should. She deserves it."

Inch laughed and chick-chicked his zorca and we rode on. But I began to think how best to relieve Seg of Falinur and find him a kovnate where he was not regarded with hatred, through no fault of his own but because of the ingrained animosity of the people to anyone who deprived them of slaves.

Then, of course, the problem would arise that the new kov would almost certainly approve of slavery, as did most ordinary men and women of Vallia. Slavery, Delia and I had sworn, was going to be rooted out of Vallia. I looked beyond that, as did Delia, I know now, until it was finally uprooted from all of Paz.

As we rode back this kind of talk naturally led on to the problems of Vallia, the huge island Empire. Delia's father, the emperor, had once more gained a breathing space with the destruction of the Chyyanists; but there were always fresh factions seeking to drag him down and install the puppet of their own choice as emperor.

"Mind you, Dray," said Seg, reflectively as we cantered gently into a defile ready to begin the last ascent to Arial's Mound in the last of the suns shine. "The nobles loyal to the emperor remain loyal, or most of them. He couldn't rule without them."

"But the opposition parties still continue, also," pointed out Inch. "They keep changing alliance and pattern; but they are still against the emperor, the whole family." Here he looked at me.

I nodded somberly. Vallia is an enormous patchwork of many different sized estates, run by nobles—by kovs and vads and trylons and Stroms and all the others—and there are many parties and factions, not all of whom seek to destroy the emperor. At this time the main party was the Racter Party, and the second the Panval Party. The Fegters were growing in strength and there was always the North East of Vallia, an area traditionally troublesome. But when Inch mentioned the family of the emperor, he was thinking of Delia and me and our family.

"And, to cap it all," said Seg, "there's this Queen Lush. Thelda is still captivated by the woman. I fancy this queen has her eyeballs firmly set on the emperor. You'll have to have a say there, Dray."

"Sink me!" I burst out. "If the old devil wants to get married again I won't stop him." I added, nastily: "Give him something else to think about."

"Well, my old dom, you're still banished from Vondium."

I grumped in the saddle, and we rode on. By Zair! But I was anxious to see Delia again and find out about our erring daughter Dayra. And even Lela still had not put in an appearance. I'd not seen them for years and years. It was just not good enough. So I was not in the happiest of moods as the final rites were gone through, the Kroveres of Iztar dispersed to their homes, the island was renamed Drayzm, and, at last, at blessedly last, we could take off for Valka and home—and Delia.

Three

Of Processions and Mercenary Guards

The airboat swung in a wide graceful arc over the glittering sea and the dancing wavelets of the Bay of Valkanium threw back splintered shards of ruby and emerald, merging into a deepening golden-speckled radiance as the Suns of Scorpio sank beyond the bulk of the Heart Heights of Central Valka. The sight was gorgeous and nostalgic and always, invariably, awakes in me vast and moving memories. I slanted the boat down toward the high palace and fortress of Esser Rarioch, and joyed that I was coming home.

There was much work to be done. With a premonition I tried unsuccessfully to shake off, I faced a future in which the harsh clangor of strife, the wicked scrape of assassins' steel and the devious and vicious intrigues around an emperor's court held no lure for me whatsoever, and to the Ice Floes of Sicce with the headlong adventure of it all. But I would face danger and the most deadly peril, as I knew, as I knew, and as you shall hear.

The world of Kregen, four hundred light years from Earth, is indeed a beautiful world. It is also a horrific world. It is real. And yet I was more and more convinced that the beauty and horror cloaked far deeper truths. If the Star Lords, who had brought me here from Earth many and many a time, alone were responsible, as I had once thought, with the Savanti attempting to combat them, then how could I either resist or support so powerful a group of—a group of what? Were they men? Were they superhuman beings, divine in origin, godlike in power? I did not know. The

Savanti, the superhuman but mortal men of the Swinging City of Aphrasöe seemed, at least to me, to have more easily understood aims. The Savanti wanted to make of Kregen a better and more civilized world, and they supported apims to do that work for them. Apims, that is, people like Homo sapiens, formed a goodly proportion of the various peoples I had so far met on Kregen. But whose word was it? Did it belong to diff or apim? Or neither? I did not know.

These wider problems of Kregen stayed with me as the flier landed on that high upflung landing platform and we stepped down to be greeted by my High Chamberlain, old Panshi. He looked grave. He bowed formally, his wand of office held just so in the prescribed position of welcome and warning.

"My prince! Messengers from Vondium came for the princess; they left sealed packets and have departed these three days."

Well, Delia was off with her Sisters of the Rose, hunting up information on our wayward daughter Dayra. I trusted she was being assisted by our eldest daughter Lela.

"Thank you, Panshi." We walked swiftly in the last of the suns sets glow toward the outer chambers. "I will see the packets. First I will see the princesses—Velia and Didi."

As I stood by the cots and looked at the two tiny forms, cherubic, sleeping, tiny fists closed, puckered mouths breathing gently, I sighed. What future lay in store for them, on this harsh and hostile planet of Kregen? Delia and I had been blessed by our daughter Velia, when our first daughter Velia had been so cruelly slain. But she had given us little Didi, the daughter of Velia, my Lady of the Stars, and of Gafard, the king's Striker, Sea Zhantil, renegade and man. I sighed again and bent and kissed them and so left them to the capable hands of the nurses and of Aunt Katri, who shooed me away with a fine air of hustle. As the emperor's sister, she spent more of her time with the emperor's daughter and her children than she did in the capital of Vallia, Vondium the Proud.

Panshi handed me the packets as I sipped the first light wine of the evening.

Heavily sealed, they bore the stamps of Lord Farris of Vomansoir, Chuktar in the Vallian Air Service, a great man, utterly loyal to the emperor, who looked upon Delia as a daughter.

With a brutal tug I broke the fastenings and took out the letter.

It was circumlocutory, filled with respect and devotion; but its message was more brutal than the gesture I had used to unseal it.

Briefly, the emperor was gravely ill. No one could fathom out the nature of his illness. There were new doctors who promised much but could find no cure. The presence of the Princess Majestrix was requested.

Turko walked in and saw my face.

"Aye, Turko. Bad news. The emperor is like to die."

"Delia—" said Turko, on a breath. His magnificently muscled body and his handsome face reassured me. He understood.

"He may be an old devil. But he is Delia's father. He once ordered his guards to take off my head, instantly, but—"

Turko half laughed. "Aye! Seg has told us often enough. He has said your surprise when you saw him will last the rest of his life." Sharply, he added: "When do we leave? Now?"

"Aye."

"Remember, you are banished, by the emperor's strict decree."

"To the Ice Floes of Sicce with the old devil's decrees. Delia will have other messages, so she will know. She will go. And there is danger in a capital city of an empire when the emperor dies. We will pack up and leave at once."

Panshi was summoned and ran instantly to do my bidding. I felt that grim chill of premonition again. There were many forces conspiring to drag down the emperor, Delia's father. I was an old sea-leem, a render, a paktun, a buccaneer prince, the king of a fabled far-off land—I admit it freely. I wanted to be in at the death—if there was to be a death. I must add, not for myself alone. Delia must be supported. The emperor's grandchildren must be apportioned their rights. I knew my Delia would think only of her father's health and life; and I being that same Dray Prescot who is more of a rogue than he appears, thought also of what might follow the death of the emperor.

One thing appeared to me certain at the time. I did not then want to be the Emperor of Vallia. I was sincere in that. But what was to happen would be in the hands of the various doctors, the wizards and the gods of Kregen, each acting his part, each with his own rapier to sharpen—or, in the case of the doctors, with his own needle to sharpen—and, as always, I took as my guiding light through the maze of conflicting loyalties and treacheries the single dominant fact of my life. The well-being of Delia alone mattered. For her I would throw over kingships, kovnates, princedoms. They mean little, anyway, apart from the obvious comforts and the powers to alleviate suffering. Even, I would cast aside all I worked for with the Kroveres of Iztar. Even—and I shudder to confess this, for it is a horrendous crime— even I would disavow the Krozairs of Zy for the sake of my Delia, my Delia of Delphond, my Delia of the Blue Mountains.

Banishment from Vondium still hung over me like a cloud. It seemed sensible to land first at my own Valkan villa at the crest of one of the reserved hills of the capital, and equip myself suitably for admission to the palace. So I donned decent Vallian buff, with tall black boots, and slung a rapier and main gauche at my sides. I clapped on one of those peculiar Vallian wide-brimmed hats, with the two oblong slots cut in the front brim.

The raffish curling feather was red and white, the colors of Valka. Also, I wore a red and yellow favor on my left shoulder, to tell any inquisitive rast who wanted to know that my sympathies lay with the emperor. For Vallia's colors are red and yellow, as are mine, except that the Vallian cross of yellow on the red flag is a saltire. So dressed, and carrying a heavy pouch filled with tied leather bags of gold talens, I took a zorca-ride up to the palace.

Turko, Balass, Oby and Naghan the Gnat refused any orders from me to remain in the villa. They said they'd go with me, even if they had to hang about outside the palace, and go they would and that was that.

"If Tilly was here, she'd go as well," said Oby, stoutly.

The little Fristle fifi, Tilly, was away with Delia.

I nodded. "Very well. But we don't want any swordplay."

"We do not want it," said Balass, evilly. "But we may get it, by the carbuncle on Beng Thrax's posterior."

At the time I knew little of Vondium. It is a great and wonderful city, split by many wide boulevards and by the canals that are the glory of Vallia. I knew more of Ruathytu, the capital of the Empire of Hamal, arch-enemy to Vallia. I knew the way to and from the palace from various points within the city—from the villas we possessed, from Young Bargom's inn, from some of the gates, from the prison of the angels. We rode out sedately, taking the broadest ways, determined not to get into trouble.

We came to an intersection, where a wide avenue passed over a canal— it was the Samphron Cut—by one of the myriad bridges of Vondium. This bridge, of ancient and weathered stone, had been decorated with sculpted heads of zhantil and mortil. The fierce old faces had worn away until now they looked merely pathetic, savage fangs blunted and broken, mighty jaws crumbling and lean. Across the intersection passed a long procession, chanting. Many and many a time have I seen these processions, garlanded, brilliant with colors, bright with banners, carrying the sacred images proudly aloft, sprinkling the holy dew-drops, winding in long sinuous trails through the streets and avenues of Vondium. They changed as they walked, the long rolling mesmeric singsong of "Oolie Opaz, Oolie Opaz, Oolie Opaz."

Usually the emphasis falls on the first syllable of each word, so that the long chant goes on and on and on: "*OO*-lie *OH*-paz, *OO*-lie *OH*-paz, *OO*-lie *OH*-paz." Up and down, up and down, a hypnotic singsong chant in time with the shuffle of many feet.

But now all the emphasis, although apparently the same, rolled into a melancholy dirge. Effigies of the emperor were being carried along, heavily draped in black. The yellow and red of Vallia was fringed with heavy black tassels. Many tall poles were entwined with symbolic leaves and flowers, and topped with gilded and silvered skulls. These people, devout, devoted to Opaz, mourned the emperor already. The signs of passionate intercession broke spontaneously from the long columns, men and women flinging themselves into ecstasies of supplication, impassioned bursts of oratory and prayer to preserve the life of the emperor. But the dominant impression remained of a funeral procession, of the pious regrets and observances for a departed monarch.

"By Vox!" I said. "The old devil isn't dead yet!"

We rode on toward the palace and the traffic flow thickened with many riders and palankeens and chairs, with the zorca-chariots flickering their tall spindly wheels, varnish and paint and gilding catching the light of the suns. At the time the palace in Vondium always caught at my throat by its sheer size, its grandeur—as always I reflected that this beauty and glory and power would have been flung aside as nothing by Delia when she would have fled by night with me, a penniless outcast.

Up to the various guard details we rode and, at first, a chingle of the golden talens and the swift transference of a bag procured our passage. These guards did not know me—as I did not know them. They were mainly apims; but a few diffs of the kinds most favored in Vondium stood their duty.

Further into the warren of courts the going became tougher.

Here were stationed the first details of the emperor's personal body-guard, the Crimson Bowmen of Loh.

"No way through here, koter," observed a matoc, a non-commissioned rank, anxious to be promoted to Deldar and put his foot on the first rung of the long ladder of advancement.

The gold worked with him.

At the next court, where flower sellers waited in long lines, their flowers all blue—a color not favored in Vallia—the guard detail was commanded by a dwa-Deldar. He looked at me. The gold did not move him. We dismounted.

I said to my friends: "Wait here and do not cause mischief."

"But—"

"Wait!"

I took the Deldar aside confidentially. I showed him the gold. He started to shake his head in the shadow of the marble column and I put a dagger into the small of his back, twisted it so he could feel the point, and said gently: "It's the gold or the steel, dom. The alternatives are open to you, the choice yours alone."

He made the sensible man's choice.

When we went back I said to Turko and the others: "Do you go back to the main square. I shall not return this way." I spoke forcefully. "If you do not leave now you will be taken up."

Such was the evil nature of my face that they went, albeit grumbling.

Past the next courtyard I found myself in a portion of the palace I knew slightly, and so could duck through a small door and enter the more somber shadows of the inner precincts unobserved. There would be more guards yet I did not think I would have skewered the Deldar; but it was no certainty.

Mind you, I did not recollect the Crimson Bowmen being stationed so far out of the main bulk of the palace before. They usually stood duty inside the palace.

Inside, as I strode along and mingled with the many people hurrying to and fro, a common occurrence in these huge households so that I was for the moment not noticed, I spotted a distinct change. The guards stationed at doors leading to the various inner areas were Chuliks. I felt surprise. Chuliks do have two arms and two legs, two eyes, one nose and one mouth; but they are diffs of so savage and ferocious a nature that many diffs, let alone apims, hesitate to call them men. They habitually shave their heads save for a long pigtail, their skins are oily yellow, they have two three-inch long tusks thrusting up from the corners of their mouths, which are cruel rattraps. They are trained from birth as mercenary fighters, and can use many weapons with great skill. They will remain loyal when paid, and sometimes afterwards, if the prospects seem good.

A few nasty ideas began to circulate around my thick old head. The emperor, despite one nasty experience and a recent scotching of another, still reposed trust in his Crimson Bowmen. Why, then, should he replace them with most expensive mercenaries who were generally disliked?

Perhaps I should have used more guile getting in to see my father-in-law, and instead of taking the direct, golden-paved route, have broken in through one of the many secret passageways.

Persevering, on I went, noticing the air of tension and gloom about the place, but ignoring that in my determination to get through. Long and overly-ornate corridors, mirror-faced, tiled with scenes of the chase and the hunt, led me on ways I knew. This was now the main corridor that led from the outer courts of the palace to the first of the succession of anterooms opening onto the emperor's private apartments. The thickness of the scurrying crowds thinned. Soon, as I approached a tall balass door guarded by two Chuliks, I stood almost alone.

They regarded me as though I had crawled from under a stone.

"You had best begone from here, calsany," said one. He wore a most fancy uniform of red and black, lavishly garlanded with golden cords, with black belts studded with bronze. At his sides he carried scabbarded a rapier and main gauche and in his right hand a three-grained staff. The tassels were red and black, the colors of the emperor's slave masters.

"Will gold unlock that door, dom?" I spoke up cheerily, most friendly. My hands hung limply at my sides. "I know it well, having passed through many times. The Chemzite Stairway lies beyond, and this door is seldom closed—"

The left-hand Chulik stopped my prattling.

"These are not normal times, rast. The emperor is dying. No one passes here save those with authority. *Schtump!*"

Schtump is a most abusive way of saying clear off, and in normal circumstances could never have been used by a Chulik mercenary to a koter of Vallia within the palace. But times they were a changing-oh.

"Since," I told these two yellow-skinned, pigtailed mercenaries, "you will not take gold—take this."

Oh, yes, it was foolish, vainglorious. Even as I twisted the left-hand one's three-grained staff free and clouted his companion over the ear with it, and brought it back to drive the bronze butt hard into ridged gut muscle, I was ruefully thinking that I was becoming overly talkative in these latter days. But, by Zair, that would change!

I gave each one a thoughtful little tap alongside the helmet rim, just to make sure, and leaving them slumbering pushed the balass doors inward. I heard a gasp and twisted at once, fast, to see only the long golden furred legs and delightful tail of a Fristle fifi disappearing past a pilaster along the wall. Friezes of strigicaws and shonages ran along the cove here, and the door slammed sharply. I made no attempt to follow. Instead, I pushed on through and ran up the weirdly deserted Chemzite Stairway. In normal times the balass doors were thrown back and the Stairway thronged with courtiers and supplicants and advocates and nobles, all going about their business with the emperor's personal staff.

Now all those highly-placed nobles with access to the emperor were confined to a few of the great halls. I passed along through narrower stairways, walking the marble of a balcony, and looked down at them as I went. From all over the Empire of Vallia the lords and ladies had come to Vondium to be in at the death. Each one had personal reasons of avarice or ambition or fear. As I walked along quietly, looking down at the assemblage of waiting nobility, my lips wrinkled up. A fine crew they were! Not a one, I daresay, spared a thought in sympathy for Delia, their Princess Majestrix. Not a one thought for an instant that it was a girl's father who lay dying.

But, then, that was not entirely true, for nobles like Farris would care. Many of them I recognized. Some of them I have already introduced to you in these tapes, and many more there were of that crew waiting to step onto the stage and strut their little part, before shuffling off, and, by Vox, a lot of them horizontal, too...

But, adhering to my plan, I will tell you of these high and mighty nobles of Vallia as and when they came into contact with me. And, too, I did not forget that I had vowed to myself to be the new Dray Prescot, the quiet, conciliatory peace-loving man who would talk first. If the emperor died then the streets of the capital might flow with blood. Everyone knew that factions waited for the moment to strike. And, as is the way with desperate men banded together waiting for a single event to strike, each party believed itself to be the most powerful, or the most advantageously placed, or having the most moral force. A detached observer could see only tragedy ahead.

But, of course, there were few—if any—detached observers, for everyone had a zhantil to saddle. And I, Dray Prescot, I was not detached. Oh, I tried to be. I told myself I wanted none of it. But I knew if some hulking lout brandishing a sword and flaunting colors and feathers tried to steal what belonged to Delia, or what should rightfully belong to our children, then all my fine detachment would vanish and the old Dray Prescot, of the devil's face and intemperate manner and vicious determination, would jump in, sword swinging, as he had done long and long in the old days...

As was inevitable I was at last stopped by four Chulik guards before an ivory door banded in gold and emeralds. They wore the red and black and carried the three-grained staffs. They were less polite than the last. True to my desire to be the rational easy-going man I ought to be, I attempted to talk.

The polearm slashed toward me with deadly intent. They'd knock me senseless and hustle me down to the dungeons. The three-grained staff, very convoluted, very ornate, the black and red tassels swinging, the bright curved edges glittering with much honing against the solid olive of the metal head, struck for my skull.

I slid the blow, took the polearm, twisted it free and held it parallel with the ground. I pushed. The Chulik tumbled against the gold and emerald and ivory door. He went: "Whoof!" That was as much from surprise as from having the air knocked from his lungs.

His companions set on at once, so I had to twist the staffs free and, partially regretfully, tap their skulls. As the last slumped down I heard a hard, brittle voice say: "If you do not drop that staff this instant you are a dead man."

Without turning I knew what stood behind me. I dropped the staff. Without seeing the flight of an arrow it is damned difficult—nigh impossible—to judge which way to jump, which direction to use. Slowly, I turned around.

Yes—four Bowmen and an officer stood there, their bows fully drawn, and the lamplight glittered from the sharp steel heads. The odds were against me. I might have dodged, given the mystic disciplines of the Krozairs of Zy, had the occasion warranted. But I persevered in my peaceful overtures—here, in the palace of my father-in-law, for all that I was banished, here!

As it was, I said to the officer at the head of the four Crimson Bowmen: "I do not know you. It is clear you do not know me. I have pressing business—" I got no further.

"Take him to the cells," said this officer, in his brittle voice. "Question him—Naghan the Pinch will know what to do. You know your orders."

The officer in his trim Crimson was a Hikdar, a waso-Hikdar, and the pallid hardness of his face and blankness of the stare in his blue eyes would give any nefarious culprit wandering the palace a severe case of the frights. I looked at him. I thought I knew this type—always a dangerous assumption—and I stared past him at the four Bowmen.

One, I recognized.

I said: "Lahal, Neg Negutorio. Why do you stand in the ranks? You were an ord-Deldar the last time we met. I would have thought you a shiv-Hikdar by now—"

That was as far as the officer was going to allow me to prattle on. My attempt at distraction would not fool him. Furiously, he bellowed out: "Seize him up! I'll have you all jikaidered, by Hlo-Hli! *Bratch!*"[*]

This was a threat no swod was fool enough to ignore.

Three of the Bowmen, taking their bows and arrows into their left hands, reached out with their right hands.

Neg Negutorio gaped at me.

"Dray Prescot!" he said. And: "The Prince Majister!"

The Hikdar took a step back. The hands of the three Bowmen fell away.

Neg shook his head. "Prince. Times have changed. There are many new faces in the Guard. Dag Dagutorio, our Chuktar, has been sent home, and replaced by Rog Rogutorio." He wet his lips. "As for me—I was degraded—it was a trumped-up charge—and now I must obey orders I care not overmuch for—"

"Silence, cramph!" shouted the Hikdar. He stared at me with venom in his face and a twitch about his jaws. "If this is truly Dray Prescot, the Prince Majister of Vallia, then is he forsworn! He is banished from Vondium! Seize him! Chain him! Send word to Kov Layco we have taken up a rare prize. Bratch!"

For a second a paralysis gripped the Crimson Bowmen. Then the four Chuliks groaned, more or less together, and opened their eyes. Like the fierce fighting men they were they came to their feet, grasping their ripped-free rapiers, and the points glittered, centered on my chest. These diffs would have no hesitation in killing me if that proved more convenient than attempting to restrain me.

---

[*] Bratch: "Move!" "Jump!" Get about your duty or you know what will happen, and the punishment will be sore indeed. Not quite so vicious a word of command as the terrible "Grak!" shouted with killing intent at slaves; but still a hard word. A.B.A.

"The Prince Majister is banished from Vondium and sets foot within the city at his own peril!" howled the Hikdar. "Seize him! If he resists—slay him!"

The Chuliks stepped forward. My hand gripped the rapier hilt. In the next second blood would splash luridly across the golden and emerald and ivory door—

"Hold!" rang a clear, perfect voice. A voice I knew. A voice that means everything in two worlds. "Hold! The Princess Majestrix commands! Touch the Prince Majister at your peril!"

Four

Ashti Melekhi, the Vadnicha of Venga

"The emperor my father has revoked the edict of banishment that should never have been passed on the Prince Majister! Get about your duties."

So, together, side by side, we walked along through the ivory and gold and emerald doorway. We left four Chuliks with blank, yellow faces, and three Crimson Bowmen disgruntled, and a waso-Hikdar raging with icy, baffled fury—and one Bowman with a single enormous grin plastered all over the inside of his martially stiff and unmoving features.

Delia!

She held my arm. I was dizzyingly conscious of the limber suppleness of her as she walked at my side. She wore a long dress of deep purple, unrelieved by any ornament save two brooches, one fashioned into the likeness of a rose and all of rubies and gold. The other was the hubless spoked wheel of precious gems I had given her, the emblem of the Krozairs of Zy.

"My heart—my father—he is ill, so very ill. He is dying, I am sure of it. The doctor—" Here she gripped the scrap of lace between her fingers.

"I will see the doctor. We should fetch Nath the Needle—"

"It is no use. Doctor Charboi is most highly respected, and his associates. But they will not let Nath the Needle see my father."

"I think they will," I said.

Nath the Needle had doctored me, and he had taken care of Delia. If the emperor's new doctors did not want Nath about them, that was a matter of concern to me. In the ante room beyond, Seg and Thelda hurried toward us with Katrin Rashumin, the Kovneva of Rahartdrin. She was now wholeheartedly devoted to Delia. With them, Nath the Needle looked just the same, if a trifle absent-minded rather than bewildered in this strange, claustrophobic atmosphere of the imperial palace where we waited for an emperor to die. And, too, here came Tilly, the gorgeous golden-furred Fristle fifi. Now I knew it was she I had seen running off to fetch Delia.

"And has the emperor really pardoned me?"

"Not yet. I said that, for it needed to be said. But he will."

I smiled at Tilly and she laughed, and sobered at once.

"You remind me once again of the Jikhorkdun in Huringa."

"And the silver chains are all melted down—master."

That little minx Tilly knows how to infuriate me, and how I detest being called master by her.

As for Thelda, Seg's wife, she could not do enough for Delia. She had been in Vondium, and Seg had called there after the meeting of the Brotherhood, arriving well before me. Thelda fussed and organized and sorted out all the tangles, she would have everybody running, and was properly reverential when she came within three doors' distance of the sick room. I do Thelda an injustice. She had made Seg a fine wife, and she was a good and loving mother to her children, and yet, and yet, still, I could not stop myself from remarking on the silver heart in blue flowers, from time to time, jocularly, and then feeling the biggest villain in two worlds. Poor Thelda!

"And Nath the Needle is most hurt, dear Dray," said Thelda. A magnif-icently-shaped woman, Thelda always looked incipiently plump, and yet was not. A disturbing trick to play on a man.

"Nath attempted to treat the emperor," said Seg. "He was rebuffed by this Doctor Charboi. He has an enormous reputation and is newly come from Loh. He is not," Seg added, "a Wizard of Loh. But he acts with all the high-handedness of one of those— those—"

"Yes," I said. Ordinary men perforce spoke carefully when they men-tioned any Wizard of Loh.

"Aunt Katri was so upset," said Delia. "She frets in Esser Rarioch, I am sure. Everything seems so—so *odd*."

I could feel the unease within the palace as in all Vondium. Things had changed in Vallia, imperceptibly, and little attention had been paid when, for instance, the old Pallans died or retired and new Pallans—secretaries or ministers of state—had replaced them. Dag Dagutorio had left suddenly for Loh, and Rog Rogutorio had taken his place as Chuktar of the Crim-son Bowmen. The emperor's chief adviser in these latter days was a kov I did not then know, one Layco Jhansi, the Kov of Vennar. His was a name I was to come to know passing well—to my sorrow, I may add—but at the time he was regarded as the savior of Vallia, the man who would hold the empire together, the emperor's Right Hand.

Automatically I thought of Gafard, the Sea-Zhantil, the King's Striker, who had died so far away from Vallia, loving still the memory of our daughter Velia, and I would sigh, and—then—wonder if this Kov Layco could give half the loyalty and allegiance past blindness that Gafard had given his mad genius King Genod.

We passed on and the presence of the Princess Majestrix opened all doors. Yet I gained the distinct and unsettling impression that our little group formed, as it were, a conspiracy, here in the palace. Once the difficulty of my banishment had been cleared up it should have been plain sailing. But it seemed to me, incredibly, as though we hatched a plot. And all we wanted to do was have a doctor we trusted give a second opinion on the condition of the emperor.

Slaves scuttled about their eternal tasks, always an affront. The Archer Guard of Valka which I had instituted had been sent, so I was told the moment I mentioned their absence, to Evir, the most northerly province of Vallia, to help quell a disturbance there. I felt as we walked on that I would welcome the presence of my Archers of Valka right there and then, above that of the mercenary Chuliks, for all their worth and valor as fighting men, and above the Crimson Bowmen, who were fresh strangers to me.

The mood of the palace baffled me. I sensed the heavy oppression, and yet I felt the heady intoxication of terror could not be adequately explained away merely by the emperor's impending death. The factions would fight. There would be slaughter and murder. There would be burnings and looting. But, all the same, the intense, indrawn, coiled-spring of horror I sensed in the very air of the palace contained so much more of menace that, quite instinctively, my hand rested on my rapier hilt as we walked—rested not in an affected, courtly way of fashion, but in the hard professional grip of the bladesman ready to draw in a twinkling.

Doctor Nath the Needle looked exactly as when I had first met him, when I'd been recovering from the infection from the shorgortz and the intemperate orders of the man who was now my father-in-law, the man who was now dying and whom Nath had been forbidden to attend. Dried up, wispy, wearing his old dark-brown clothes, his tawny yellow hair roughly combed, he looked just the same, and he held the same old velvet-lined sturmwood case of acupuncture needles under his arm.

"I am happy to see you, prince," he said, most formally.

"And I you, doctor," I answered gravely. "I do not know what this nonsense is about your being refused an audience of the emperor; but we'll go in and see him now."

Nath nodded and then, because, as was proper, the Princess Majestrix walked first, and Thelda and Katrin walked a half-step to her rear, and Seg was trying to catch a bundle of wool about to fall from Thelda's bag, Nath and I walked at the rear.

Nath began to talk as these savants do, increasingly oblivious of his surroundings, absorbed by his own thoughts.

"The shorgortz poison—you remember that, I am sure, my prince—is proving of fascinating interest. The Blue Mountain Boys captured a specimen in a pit and, knowing my interest, for I sent messages and gold to Korf Aighos, they extracted the poison and forwarded me a sample. It is indeed remarkable. Incredible, if a doctor may ever use that word. I have conducted experiments, see—" Here he halted and began pulling papers from the pockets in the flaps of his old brown coat. I swear dust flew. He bashed the papers about—they were ordinary paper and not the superb paper made by the Savanti—and crumpled them up and dropped some. I helped him collect up these vital medical discoveries.

"I shall look at your work with great pleasure, doctor; but later. Now I want you to see the emperor and tell me just what is the matter with him and what must be done to cure him."

Nath the Needle favored me with a look, jolted back to the reason for his presence here. He made a singularly apt remark about Charboi; but he was perfectly willing to try again. He sneezed a couple of times, stuffing the papers away.

If I thought the obstacles to Nath the Needle seeing the emperor had all been overcome, then I was an onker indeed.

We debouched beneath overhanging arches lavishly decorated with exquisite mosaics depicting—oh, the pictures were filled with the fire and passion of Vallia's turbulent past. Across the wide marble-floored space where cool fountains sparkled in the perfumed air, where fruit trees bloomed and delicately colored birds flitted from branch to branch, the long white wall barring off the emperor's quarters as approached from this direction showed a solid crimson and black band along its foot.

The guards stood shoulder to shoulder, a Crimson Bowman and a Chulik, alternating. Pacing toward us came two Jiktars, high officers, one a Bowman of Loh, the other a Chulik.

Delia proved herself a princess in her handling of them.

Haughtily, yet with just the right amount of friendliness stopping this side of condescension, she avowed the Prince Majister was now free to walk in Vondium, that she intended to see her father, and her suite would go with her. The guards stood back. We walked through. Although I did not smile, my fist no longer rested on the rapier hilt. A little thing—but revealing...

There was no mistaking the abrupt dispatch of a Bowman runner, a lithe young man fresh from Loh, learning his trade.

The light chilled. Heavy doors swung inwards. I knew just where we were, now, and had studied the plans of the palace drawn up many seasons ago when this wing had been built. At last, past a bevy of waiting nurses and minor doctors, we entered the sick room.

The place struck me with a chill repulsion. Delia visited her father constantly, had been drawn away by Tilly's startling news. He lay in the wide bed, on his back, the covers drawn to his chin and pettishly pulled half down one side. His wasted face spider-webbed with etched lines, the cheeks sunken in. I saw the hand he extended to his daughter and was shocked at its skeletal aspect. He had always been a firmly fleshed man.

His flesh was wasting away. His condition really was serious, and Delia's concern struck me, suddenly, with an anguish for her I detested and found biting and acid and altogether hateful. My Delia! Well, everyone must go through the agonies of seeing loved ones die. Because Delia and I had bathed in the Sacred Pool of the River Zelph in far Aphrasöe, the city of the Savanti, the Swinging City, we were assured of a thousand years of life and the rapid recovery from wounds and illness. The wounds I had taken in the Jikai of the Brotherhood of Iztar against the Shanks were already healed. And yet, I had held my daughter Velia in my arms as she died. What agonies mortality tortures us with.

Nath the Needle moved carefully forward in his best professional manner and shooed us from the bed. He took immediate command of the four nurses, pale women, nervous, worried, and at his directions one of them turned back the coverlets and the others lifted the emperor's shrunken body and opened the fancy silk shirt over his sunken chest. I went with Seg to stand over in the bay window where a flick-flick plant looked as though it needed a heaping handful of fat flies. The six flunkeys, armed, who stood along the far walls, blankly regarding the proceedings, could be ignored. The emperor, apart from certain follies, lived a spartan life.

I said to Seg: "D'you know what's happened to Queen Lush? I thought for sure she'd be sobbing at the bedside."

"She had to return to Lome. Some pressing affair of state. The emperor saw her off—Thelda says he was in full health then."

"We haven't seen the last of her. She has designs on the emperor. This dire news will bring her scurrying back."

"Aye. It's bad, Dray."

"Yes. How stands Falinur?"

He knew what I meant. The old recklessness of his face sobered, for the men of Erthyrdrin, Seg's homeland, are fey and wild and also highly practical. "I have worked hard there, trying to make the kovnate into the kind of paradise you have in Valka. There are always cramphs against whatever I try to do. Their malignancy lingers on. They remember. I wouldn't take a sheaf of arrows on their loyalty."

I made no comment on this bleak if expected news. "And Inch? I fancy the Black Mountains will stand with us."

"The Blue Mountain Boys have resolved their ancient quarrels with the Black Mountain Men. That is more Inch's doing than Korf Aighos's—he is one man I wouldn't trust with my bow—but he is loyal to Delia. Between them they have made those mountains and the zorca plains into a stronghold."

"There are other nobles willing to stand up and be numbered. As for Delphond—" I sighed. I thought, then, that Delia's pretty little province of Delphond, a charming, lazy, contented place, now that the Chyyanists had gone, could never raise even a pastang of real fighting men. There had been changes in Delphond the last time I had been through, as you know; but the old carefree, easy-going ways persisted—and I would not change them.

"Lord Farris will bring in Vomansoir."

"Yes. And, if it comes to the fluttrell's vane, we can strike across quickly and so pinch out—" I stopped. Delia and Thelda with Katrin came over to us and the conversation became general, still concerned, low-voiced. I glanced at the doctor. Nath the Needle looked grave. He peered into the emperor's mouth, pulled down his lower eyelids, felt and prodded him, tut-tutting to himself. No acupuncture needles had been used by Doctor Charboi, and Nath had not opened his sturmwood case, so I gathered the sick man was in no pain.

Very carefully, using a piece of verss, that finest of snow-white linen, Nath wiped the emperor's mouth. He folded the cloth delicately and placed it into his lesten-hide satchel. Sight of the piece of pure verss reminded me vividly of the Kroveres—for verss represented the purity for which the old vers of Valka had been famed.

Nath glanced up and met my gaze. He nodded and indicated he was ready to leave, which surprised me, and the door burst open with a crash onto the somber sick room and a group of violently angry men and women entered.

As I stared at them, at their red faces and their gesticulating, ring-laden hands, the sumptuousness of their dress, their jewels and lace, all the habitual airs of wealth and command and authority, I felt repulsion. I felt revulsion. Their vicious unthinking demands on everyone about them they could master, these I had witnessed many times, on Earth as on Kregen, and despaired of, and resisted, and, I own the matching of violence with violence to be a sin, there, in that sick room of a palace where an emperor lay dying, I was particularly revolted by their violence. I am a peaceful sort of fellow, liking the quiet life, and yet I have, to my shame, been forced many and many a time to match violence with violence. The Kroveres of Iztar were one response. I own, I have never made a secret of it, I own the matching of violence with violence to be a sin, and yet I hoped for so much from the Kroveres in milder civilized ways.

But—these people. You will meet them all as my story trundles along. Of them at the moment it is fit you should see just three.

The first was Doctor Charboi. Here on Earth he would have been impeccably dressed, crowned with a distinguished mass of silver hair. He would have worn a neat Harley Street suit, and have commanded the highest prices for nostrums and soothing words from the highest in society. On Kregen, where a person's hair does not ordinarily turn white until past two hundred, Charboi had the red mop of Loh, and he presented the full-fleshed, country-club figure of a man in the prime of life, brisk, efficient, demanding. And violent.

"Out!" he shouted. He was violent. No doubt of it. "Out!"

The second man hulked in the room. Massive, bulky, he towered against the lamplight and it was clear from the set of his mouth and the clamping thrust of his jaws and chin that he spoke seldom. Apim, he was, but built like a Chulik. All the time his powerful figure remained planted at the shoulder of his mistress. He wore the heavy brown tunic called a khiganer, double-breasted, the wide flap caught up over his left side with a long flaring row of bronze buttons, from belt to shoulder, and from point of shoulder to collar. That collar stood stiff and hard and high, encircling his neck. Gold glittered there. He wore buff breeches and tall black Vallian boots, gleaming with polish, spurred. He wore no baldric; but the lockets for a rapier and empty main gauche swung from two jeweled belts. His sleeves were banded after the fashion of Vallia, indicating his allegiance. Brown and green bands, with three small diagonal slashes, marked him for Venga. The sheer ferocity of that lowering face impressed me, the lambent bestiality slumbering in the tiny dark eyes, the cragginess of the jaw. He was a notorious Bladesman.

This was Nath the Iarvin, ruffler, Bladesman, bought body and soul by his mistress.

The third person was a woman.

Thin, she was, hard-edged like a diamond, brittle and bright, with a flame about her that consumed all who were unfortunate enough not to know how to handle her. Her dark hair was caught in a diamond-encrusted net. She wore riding leathers of a sheening green, making her mannish figure even more angular, and long black boots, like a man. On her left shoulder was pinned a golden brooch fashioned into the form of a wersting seizing a korf, the vicious Kregan dog crunching down on the soaring bird. A rapier and dagger were scabbarded at her narrow waist. I fancied she could use them passing well. High, her face, white and scornful, with deep, grey-green eyes, and arched black eyebrows. Red, her mouth, thin and bitter and drawn in at the corners, red and like a wound above her sharp chin. She could have cut ice with her glance.

This, then, was Ashti Melekhi, the Vadnicha of Venga.[*]

She stared at us narrowly, reminding me of the way those carnivorous hunting risslacas stare unwinking at their prey.

"Get out," she said. And her voice, I swear it, hissed as a risslaca hisses

---

[*] Vad is the title of Kregan nobility immediately below Kov. Nich is the suffix denoting the second twin. Nicha is feminine. Vadnicha therefore is the twin sister of the Vad, with certain responsibilities within the same Vadvarate. The Vad's wife is the Vadni. *A.B.A.*

before he pounces. "Schtump! Layco Jhansi, the Kov of Vennar, the emperor's Chief Pallan, has placed me in charge of the sick room and of all the emperor's wants, answerable only to him. I do not care who you are. The Princess Majestrix may stay, because she is the emperor's daughter. The rest of you—out! Schtump!"

I did not speak.

She pointed her riding crop at me. It did not waver.

"You may be the Prince Majister. But you are nothing more than a trumpery clansman, a hairy barbarian. And you dare to bring in another doctor! Have a care lest you go too far."

The crop circled to include Seg and Thelda and Katrin, and then rested, accusingly, on Nath the Needle.

"Let the emperor die in dignity, as befits the end of a great man. You profane his greatness. This doddery buffoon pries and prods—beware lest your heads topple before the suns descend."

I opened my mouth—and then closed it. I speculated on the inner mysteries of philosophy, how the worlds roll through space, how a woman may change a man and the man change an empire, how violence breeds violence, how women are so often nonsensical creatures unfit for their own company, let alone a man's, how I was the new Dray Prescot.

She slashed the crop down. "Now get this rabble cleared out! Go, now. Or I call the palace guard."

Seg was staring at me with that old half-mocking smile on his face. I knew what he expected. Nath stood back from the bed, outraged; but keeping his composure remarkably well. Thelda was already boiling up and Katrin was standing by ready to lay in after. These two ladies were high born, coming from great families, kovnevas both. Delia—Delia looked at me and I managed the smile I can always find for her, and I shook my head, ever so slightly, and so she smiled back at me, uncertain, disturbed, but ready to follow my mood, trusting me. What a wonderful woman is my Delia among all women!

I did not speak. Conscious that I was acting a part, I felt a word would shatter that charade. I could with words have broken this headstrong woman, made her see the errors of her ways, given Doctor Charboi the fright of his life. And no damn guards would have stopped us, either. But I did not. Even now, had I done so, I am not sure it would have changed anything that followed. The details of the tragedy and the heartbreak might have been different; the end results would surely have been the same.

"Are you going?" demanded the bitter, icy voice. This Ashti Melekhi switched her crop around and on the instant would have shouted for the guards.

A weak, breathy voice spoke and for a disoriented moment, so wrapped up were we all in the tension of the situation, we could not understand who was speaking. Then Delia dropped to her knees by the bed, clasping her father's shrunken hand.

"Delia." The emperor gasped with the effort of speaking. "My daughter." He worked his thin lips around each word, as though forcing each one out against enormous forces pent within him. "Aph—" He stopped and swallowed, his Adam's Apple jumping erratically. "Hamal. Todalpheme—"

"No!" shouted Charboi, storming forward. "That is not to be thought of! Do as the vadnicha commands. Go!"

If the rast put his hand on Delia's shoulder to pull her away from the bed I would have forgotten my play-acting and being the new, considerate, understanding, nonviolent Dray Prescot. But he still had the sense not to commit such a flagrant act of lese-majesty. Perhaps, had he taken refuge in his doctor's status, and allowed his temper to lay a hand on Delia, and I had acted as I would surely have done, the world of Kregen would be a different place today. I do not know. I do not really think so. It does not matter. For what was to happen, happened, and that is all that matters, in the whirl of vaol-paol.

"You're not going to stand for this, Dray!" demanded Thelda. Her face betrayed shock and anger, and, also, another emotion. Seg put his arm around her waist and drew her away, and I looked at her, so she went, but not without a squib or two.

The Vadnicha Ashti Melekhi stared with those narrow grey-green eyes after Thelda, and I knew they had sparked before, like a diamond cutting butter—and, suddenly, I knew how much I cared for Thelda, my comrade's wife, despite all. That would not stop me from gently tormenting her, of course, or stop her from fussing and over-pressuring and, in general, of being Thelda.

Seg looked back past me over Thelda's shoulder, and I put out a hand and so stopped Katrin from blowing up. Nath picked up his sturmwood case and walked with measured tread for the door, but he looked mightily offended. So, at last, Delia rose and kissed her father, the dread emperor of a mighty empire, and we walked out sedately, together, side by side.

Still I had said no word.

The brittle voice cut the air after us. "Good riddance to a rabble! Now, Charboi, see if you can undo the damage that doddering incompetent may have done. I am going to find Kov Layco and tell him to make sure these cramphs never have a chance to sneak in to pester the emperor again."

"Yes, my lady," said Charboi, very huffed with himself.

So I took myself off at the side of Delia, and I pondered.

Five

Of a Ruffianly Meeting at The Rose of Valka

"In the old days, my Vovedeer, we'd have slipped six inches of good Zen-iccean steel into the guts of the cramph! By the Black Chunkrah! I am astonished the fellow is walking about with a head on his shoulders!"

And Hap Loder tossed the rest of his wine down and roared for more. The inner private snug of *The Rose of Valka* resounded with heated talk and argument. I knew what must be done. But it must be done the right way.

"Yes, Hap, you fearsome rascal. That is the way of the clansmen who ride the plains of Segesthes. And I know that is what most of my comrades would have done. But unthinking violence will not solve the problems of Vallia now."

"That is right, by all the shattered targes in Mount Hlabro!" quoth Seg, who as a kov of Vallia much bethought himself of his adopted country's welfare. "I'll own I was surprised at first. But that she-leem would have called the guards. Then there would have been a right merry set-to."

Wine went the rounds. Palines and other luscious fruits lay heaped on bronze plates, ready to hand. The people gathered here, and drifting in as the evening wore on, were all my comrades, gathered from many areas of Kregen. After the adventures in the Eye of the World, when I had been saved in the nick of time by these same lusty fighters, we were enjoying one last carouse, although the dismal news of Delia's father laid a gloom across the meeting.

Inch had brought his lady newly arrived from Ng'groga, his home, a charming girl, all of six foot six in height, of a fiery nature and a bold eye, who, I felt with a twinge, would cut Inch down to size. Their taboos still operated, at least to some extent, for they could not be married until—and then so much metaphysical profound casuistry erupted about our thick non-Ng'grogan heads that we could only rock back and hold our sides and laugh. Inch and his taboos...

I liked Inch's lady, Sasha, and she quickly became a part of our roistering group. Of Sasha there is much to speak, later...

My own Wizard of Loh—I say "my own' but that is to pitch it too high, these famous wizards being their own men; but Khe-Hi-Bjanching owed not only his status but his life to me, and he proved trustworthy and loyal. Also, since those early days, he had matured. Now he was a wizard capable of extraordinary feats.

He listened gravely as I told him what the emperor had said and of Doctor Charboi's reaction, and what I felt I ought to do. He frowned. He looked—and I was startled—he looked most confoundedly put out, frightened, even. This moved me to say, half-jesting: "What, Khe-Hi! A Wizard of Loh, scared of anything at all in the world! That is indeed a ponsho-bitten leem." Which is to say, something so extraordinary as to be almost unbelievable.

"By Father Mehzta-Makku!" said Gloag, his bristle hide most carefully groomed, his whole appearance sleek and elegant as befitted my Crebent of the House of Strombor in Zenicce. "I would think three times before I accused a Wizard of Loh of being the cleverest man in all Segesthes—and then I'd hold my tongue."

Khe-Hi-Bjanching wet his lips. "I own I am grown different from other wizards." His voice held a flat deadness I did not like at all. "In the service of our prince I have grown into my powers. I am good. There is no sense in denying it. But I have access to some secrets I would not turn over, as I would not stick my head into a chavonth's jaws."

The racket around us in the snug subsided as they realized some serious talk was going on. They listened, soberly.

"Say on, Khe-Hi. You know, I think, what the emperor asked. You share Charboi's apprehensions?"

"Apprehensions!" Bjanching gripped a fist on the sturmwood table among the wine glasses. "It is more than that. We wizards, well, all men speak of our art. We are adepts. Sorcery is child's play to us. But if you seek out the Todalpheme of Hamal and they tell you—you will be as great a pack of fools as they!"

"But," protested Seg. "The Todalpheme are good, wise savants. They predict the tides. They are sacrosanct. No man dares raise a hand against them. How can the Todalpheme be evil?"

"They are not evil, kov. Of course not. But a secret has fallen into their possession and they do not understand it."

The samphron oil lamps gleamed on their faces. They sat and stood in a circle there in the private snug of *The Rose of Valka* in Vondium. I can see them now, so clearly. My comrades. Men and women who had gone through the fire with me, aye, and were to go through again—and damned soon, too. I am a lonely man, a true loner, as you know; yet I have been blessed with friends such as I believe no other mortal can ever have been blessed with. The charismatic power that clings about me, the yrium, so difficult to define and yet so starkly obvious when the truth is seen, that does not explain it all, not all...

Jaidur, my youngest son, sat very quietly for him, for the overturning of the misconceptions of his world were taking time to work through. My second son, Zeg, Pur Zeg, a noted Krozair of Zy of the Inner Sea, now the King of Zandikar, was away there in the Eye of the World, a great man, Bane of Grodno. My eldest son, Prince Drak, had been sent for. Vomanus of Vindelka, newly arrived from some far-off corner of Kregen, listened intently, and as the half-brother of Delia shared a lively concern over the fate of the emperor, who was not his father.

Yes, we were a ruffianly crew. The others of whom you know were there, and there were new faces, also—Dray, Seg's son, and his twins, Valin and Silda. They listened avidly and spoke little, conduct very becoming. Seg had named his firstborn son Dray when he thought I was dead. This Dray's real name was Seg, of course, as the firstborn, so that he might carry on the Torio. Valin was a good Vallian name, and Silda was the name of Thelda's mother.

We argued on, with the wizard genuinely concerned to deflect us from what increasingly we saw as the only way to aid the emperor. But you who listen to these tapes know far more than my comrades there in the comfortable snug of *The Rose of Valka*. Only I understood with Delia what the Wizard of Loh was hinting at. When the emperor's daughter had fallen from a zorca, he had raised heaven and hell to find a cure. He had been put into contact with the Todalpheme of Hamal through an airboat salesman, for at that time Vallia and Hamal were on more-or-less speaking terms. The information had cost a great deal. The Todalpheme of Hamal, it was rumored, knew also of a fabled land where miracle cures might be effected. Delia had been taken through the various secret channels in a flier and had at last reached Aphrasöe, where the Savanti had been too long in making up their minds whether or not to cure her. So I, that uncouth sailor, Dray Prescot, newly arrived from Earth and out of the thunder of the broadsides as the seventy-fours drifted down into the battlesmoke, had taken it upon myself to cure Delia.

That I had done so, and into the bargain assured her of a thousand years of life, was past history. But the whole business was wrapped about with mystery. During my journeys on Kregen I had asked always for news of Aphrasöe, the Swinging City, and no one had even heard of the place. To me, then, it had been paradise. And I had been thrown out of paradise. But real life had caught up with me and engulfed me, so that, for me, Paradise was Valka and Strombor and Djanduin and the Great Plains of Segesthes. I speak, you understand, of the time in Vondium when the emperor lay dying. Fragrant Azby, the other places, what has happened to me since— ah, well, all that must wait its due turn.

Even when I had at last discovered that the Todalpheme of Hamal had been the ones responsible—or, at least, could put me in touch with the ones responsible—I had been in no case to prosecute further inquiries or do any more about it. Real life has a habit of rolling along everything before its onward surge, ambitions, dreams, nightmares, the daily grind.

The gravity of the burden of our conversation was lost upon no one there. The light from the mellow samphron oil lamps gleamed upon our faces, and reflected without edged menace from scabbarded blades. The menace breathed all about us in the night of Vondium, under the seven moons of Kregen.

Even those two rogues sensed the atmosphere. One drinking happily, the other drinking, but seeming somewhat empty without a wench on his knee; my two favorite rascals, Nath and Zolta, understood what went forward here. And how they reveled in this whole new world outside the inner sea! Any fears I had had that they would be overawed, fail to fit in, become dejected and morose, had evaporated. Nath and Zolta! Fine, fearsome, rascally rogues, my two oar-comrades—and great-hearted Zorg dead and gone and food for chanks in the Eye of the World.

"I know, Dray," said Vomanus, carelessly, popping a paline into his mouth, chewing and swallowing—a barbarous habit, for the paline is a berry of superlative performance on a man's digestion: "I know what the emperor did and said when Delia crippled herself falling off that damned zorca. For a start he had the beast's throat slit. But this Opaz-forsaken airboat salesman was eager to sell, and we poor fools of Vallia eager to buy his rubbish." The old sore spot again... "He gave names and addresses to the emperor, and Delia was sent, all neatly packaged. The fellow was some kind of defrocked Todalpheme acolyte, I believe. Came by his information evilly, I'll warrant. Still, it must have been successful." And Vomanus smiled broadly at my Delia as she regarded him gravely, thinking of those times.

We had told no one of our experiences in Aphrasöe.

"So we do the same," I said. "We take the emperor to this place known to the Todalpheme's contacts. We effect a miracle cure, also."

"Aye!" they shouted, ready to brave a world.

"But," said Seg. "How do we start? You saw how those rasts kept him mewed up."

"Aye. But we can find a key to open the cage."

"I would have thought, Dray Prescot, that the emperor's daughter and the Prince Majister, her husband, could take the emperor to a doctor without such a to-do!"

Thus spake Thelda.

Seg started to say something; but, quickly, Delia broke in gently to say: "We will, Thelda, my dear, we will. And you will aid us, I know."

"Well, of course!" Thelda turned to me, high of color, heaving of bosom, glowing with resolution. "Prince, am I not Delia's best friend?"

Very, very carefully, I said: "Yes, Thelda."

All the old subjection to the racters that had made of Thelda a tool for political designs had gone. Her family, well-born but poverty-stricken through foolish gambling of a rake-hell grandfather, had not been able to give her any assistance in life save that of offering her as a tool for the racters in return for gold. Her marriage to Seg and her friendship with the

Prince and Princess, her own status as a kovneva, and the known wildness of her friends, had protected Thelda from the unwelcome attentions of those who might have sought to employ her again.

"It's high time we did something," growled Inch, very tall and grim in the lamplight.

"Aye!" roared those wolfish fighting men—and those vulpine lady-friends and wives. "Aye! For Delia and for Dray!"

Well, it was all very pretty. But it shod no zorcas, as my clansmen would say.

The door swung open as Young Bargom, the proprietor, hustled in. With him came Prince Varden Wanek and Natema who were staying at a merchant friend's house because one of the children's children had a slight fever. Nath the Needle had hurried round there, and now he came in with Varden and Natema, looking excited.

"What news, Nath?"

"It is as I suspected," he said, swirling his cloak off and sneezing and almost putting his satchel on the table. Someone caught it. He mumbled around and produced a small vial. It held a colorless liquid.

"I refined and clarified the emperor's spittle. There is no doubt. He has been fed solkien concentrate—"

A gasp broke from many gathered there.

Nath nodded, not pretending to lecture. "A most lethal and unpleasant poison. It is secret—and the secret of its discovery even more so. But," he said without false modesty, "I know it. A deadly mixture of the tree Memph, the cactus Trechinolc, a little of the bark Liverspot, one or two other spicy ingredients, all balanced to waste the flesh, to dilute the blood, to destroy most subtly."

Delia swayed. I put out a hand and she grasped it, staring into my face, trying to smile for me and failing.

"Oh—Dray!"

"Tonight," I said. Everyone hung on my words. "Tonight we will go in by certain secret passageways I know of, ways that were inspected with Largan the Rule, the palace architect—"

"Dead and gone these many seasons," said Vomanus.

"I'm sorry to know that. But we may make our way in and we may make our way out bearing the emperor. It is the way I should have taken today, but did not. Thelda! Can you see to the nursing facilities for Doctor Nath the Needle?"

"Of course!" She tossed her head, and then said: "And I do not wish to hear about vilmy flowers, and especially not about fallimy flowers! So there!"

Oby said: "I will see to the fliers."

Turko said: "I'll see to the provisions."

"Right. And, friends all, bring your weapons sharp."

"Aye," they growled. I own, trying to see them critically and not as the dear friends they were, they were a cutthroat bunch and no mistake.

Of course, it had to be Vomanus, careless, bright-eyed, casual, who said: "Mind you, Dray. My half-sister is heir. If the emperor dies you would have a good claim to the throne yourself."

I just looked. The rapscallion had the grace to look away and adopt a less negligent attitude, half-perched on a table. But the thought was there, hanging, ugly, in the air of the snug.

What each one thought I do not know. What I thought I am not sure. "I want nothing of the emperor save what I already have—his daughter. Unless—unless the evil days are too evil." My memories embraced Djanduin and what I had done there.

The door opened on the little silence and Bargom thrust his head in and bellowed: "Prince Drak!"

And here was my son, Drak, Prince of Vallia, most wroth, fuming with rage. He flung his cloak off in a great swirl and hurled it at a chair, snatching up a pot of wine from the table.

"By Vox!" he said. "By all the grey ones of Sicce! They wouldn't let me see grandfather. They threw me out up at the palace, that bitch Melekhi and her scum! And, on the way here, stikitches tried to do for me, assassins tried to skewer me. I tell you, Vondium is become a madhouse!"

Six

We Pay a Duty Call on the Emperor of Vallia

Two closed carriages took the raiding party to the portcullised gate below the Jasmine Tower. The bulk of the Tower wheeled against the stars, blazing in those familiar constellations over Kregen. She of the Veils shed a fuzzy pink and golden light, icing the gables and rooftops, contouring the domes with mysterious shadows, lending a deeper menace to the darkness beneath the craggy walls. The carriages, pulled by four krahniks apiece, rolled to a stop close to the edge of the dried-up moat. Here the old Canal of Contentment, very short, curved about the rear re-entrants of the palace walls. To either hand the long curtain walls vanished into the darkness, battlemented against the sky.

No one spoke a word. Seg and Inch and Turko, Balass, Vomanus, Hap and Oby.

We left the carriages concealed beneath the end arch of a colonnade where moonblooms opened their petals to the drenching moonlight. We crept upon the sentry like leems. We did not kill him, for he was a Rapa, and merely earning his hire. That he was a Rapa guarding the palace in Vondium itself clearly indicated that times had changed. His vulturine face with the fierce warrior eyes either side of his beak stared blankly up at the moon. Soon She of the Veils would be joined by the Twins, and then there would be too much light for nefarious purposes.

So, we respectable citizens of Vallia crept along in the shadows like assassins, spies, drikingers. Sharp left inside the narrow wicket I turned past the buttress and so found a narrow crack in the inner wall, a crack seeming merely the ruin of time, plastered over against the fall of the towers. But the plastering was a mere shell, covering stout wood, and the wood pivoted and revealed a square opening, a foot on a side. I gripped the iron handle, shaped like the handle of a spade, and pulled.

Almost soundlessly, so well wrought was the masonry, the section of stone pivoted about itself. The opening widened into a narrow doorway and onto stairs leading down.

Down we went and with the practiced knack of those accustomed to such things flint and steel lit the lanterns. The stairs leered below us, dark and sinister, running strips of water, darkly stained, brilliant in the lantern glitter.

Down we went.

Niter caked the walls lower down, and greenish slime hung in greasy tendrils. On we went along a jagged corridor where Inch appealed feelingly to Ngrangi, immediately hushing himself and rubbing that tall head of his.

These labyrinthine windings of corridor and tunnel and stair are virtually dictated by any palace architect on Kregen. A whole system of secondary channels exists alongside the proud and ornate halls and chambers. Many of these secret runnels I had had blocked up when first living here; but I had a map of those I knew of remaining in my head. To find the sick room was not difficult; merely tortuous.

I put my eye to the eyehole in the wooden screen and looked out into the room in which the emperor lay dying, in which Vadnicha Ashti Melekhi had screamed invective and had myself and my friends thrown out.

Doctor Charboi was in the act of rising from the bed. A glass shone in his hand. His smooth face looked well satisfied. He spoke to someone out of my angle of vision.

"He will sleep now. Quite safely."

The voice that answered, all cut glass and splinters, all vicious neemu-hiss, said: "Very good, doctor. See that he is not disturbed. Have the guards called at once. The young prince thinks he is very masterful. Kov Layco was most angry."

"I have done my work well, vadnicha."

We knew what devil's work that was.

"I do not deny it. You will be paid."

Charboi gathered up the implements of his trade and went toward the door. He knocked and the door opened. I saw the crimson-clad arm. So the Bowmen kept the door sealed, now, and opened only to those they knew. I did not smile. But I rather fancied Ashti Melekhi would have some hard explaining to do to Kov Layco Jhansi, the emperor's Chief Pallan.

If she chose to remain in the room she would have to take her chances with us. We would have to quiet her before she could cry out and warn the guards. Charboi had only just got away; I think I half regretted that at the time. But, there's no time like the present—I was about to bash open the secret door and spring leem-like upon her, when she appeared. She walked to the outer door, and paused, and looked back.

I waited.

I saw her face. All thin and white and scornful, that face, with its red mouth and arched eyebrows. And she smiled. That smile would have held a Manhound for a space. Bitter, cunning, devilish—and, yet, also, I guessed, a little regretful. I do not wish to paint Ashti Melekhi in colors that are all black. I believe she was an accomplished player on the lute. I know she kept an aviary of exotic birds. But, in the death of an emperor, it is hard to paint lighter tones when the emperor's daughter is your wife.

Then, with a small golden staff slung on a jeweled chain about her neck, she knocked upon the door. The Bowmen opened for her. She said: "Watch the door. Hold it."

"Quidang, my lady!"

No one was going to come into that room through that door this night, unless it was over the dead bodies of the Crimson Bowmen and their new Chulik mercenary partners.

So she went out, all feline grace and thin glitter, hard and brittle and oddly manlike and I wondered when I would see her again.

Gently the secret panel eased open and I stepped into the sick room. The nurse on duty sat looking at the emperor and, I swear, a tear glistered on her pale cheek. The flunkeys were gone. The nurse did not see me, she saw nothing more as the black scarf whipped about her eyes blindfolding her. Turko held her arms, very gently, and we tied her up and laid her comfortably on a thick rug of Zeniccean-made fleecy-ponsho, a gift from Strombor, with a golden cushion for her head. She did not struggle and, no doubt, poor soul, was scared witless.

We lifted up the emperor and placed him carefully in the litter we had brought, using his own bedclothes. He weighed pathetically little for a man who had once been so strong and robust. With a single quick look around the sick room we returned through the opening and I, going last, latched the secret panel shut.

Our return was uneventful. I began to think we had planned so well as to negate all problems. Onker!

We took turn and turn about to carry the litter, for each of my comrades knew my views on manual labor, the status of nobles, and the mumbo jumbo of aristocratic privileges.

We knew the routine of the palace guard. The Crimson Bowmen were professionals and would keep up their hired mercenaries to the same standards. The guard commanders changed the sentries every three burs—two hours by terrestrial reckoning—and we had taken almost the whole of that time. We anticipated leaving just before any trouble from the guard reliefs with their watchwords and their lanterns and their ready weapons.

With soundless speed we filed through the concealing opening, the emperor carried smartly if gently enough, and I reset the plaster-coated wood. At the opening of the gate we paused. Someone swore; but so low the words did not carry.

The two closed carriages were gone.

The pink and golden moonlight, strengthening slowly as the Twins eternally revolving one about the other gradually added their luster, threw odd shadows from the battlements. The damned carriages were not there. Someone had unmistakably purloined them, for they had been left firmly tethered under the colonnade, and the krahniks, useful draught animals, had shown no inclination to break free and trot off.

I caught Seg's arm.

"We walk," I said into his ear.

"The emperor—?"

"Once we clear the palace precincts we become a drunken party with a casualty. There are eight of us. We should not be molested—"

That, onker that I am, was as far as I got.

The devils were clever and they were quick and they very nearly had us.

The deadly glitter of steel in the moonlight... The quick indrawn breath as killers pounced... The scrape of sandals across time-worn stones...

My own rapier jumped into my fist and I swear it was only a fraction of a second faster than my comrades', for we were a right tearaway bunch and, after the first quick shock of the ambush, a certain pitying sorrow for our would-be slayers afflicted me. In that, I suppose, the old haughty pride we all fight down reared more of its ugly head than is strictly desirable. Turko's brand-new parrying stick flashed with smooth-oiled steel and balass, and a lunging rapier skipped and twanged away. Turko put his hand on the fellow and the cramph went sailing up, spread-eagled marvelously against the moons.

"Hai!" said Turko, reflectively, unruffled, taking a sober enjoyment.

Hap's short clansman's axe whirled and bit, withdrew and bit again—fast, fast!

Inch licked out deftly with his great Saxon-pattern axe, and lopped, and reared up, stark against the stars, and so went with the swing, rhythmically, shearing blood and ribs and backbone in a dark welter of spraying offal.

Seg and Vomanus, who had been carrying the litter between them, placed the emperor down as fast as was decently possible. One of the attackers, mere ghost-like figures bundled in dark cloaks, shrieked and shrieked as he held, unbelievingly, onto his insides which were now outside. Silence was of no more consequence.

"Leave a few for me!" bellowed Seg, ripping out his blade, plunging on.

"And me, by Vox! Can't a fellow have any fun!" And Vomanus twinkled his rapier out, very smooth, in that typical careless way of his.

Balass and Oby, in the rear, struggled to get out.

I, Dray Prescot, just stood. I just stood there, my rapier glinting in my fist, and I wanted to laugh. Yes! I wanted to bust a gut laughing. What poor fools these fellows were, to attempt to slay a mean bunch like us. How comical!

So I took no part in that swift and deadly struggle beneath the Moons of Kregen. Balass got in a few whacks with his superb new sword we had built back in Valka. The others stood, weapons ready, crouched, looking about into the shadows.

Young Oby stalked out, mightily upset. His wicked long-knife gleamed sharp and clean.

"Not one," he said. "A right leem's nest. You might at least have saved me one."

The others laughed. Gravely, with broad smiles, they promised Oby first pick next time. They were not speaking altogether idly. So, I stepped out at last.

"Pick up all the gear. We are all reivers, mercenaries. We do not scatter good weapons about. Bundle the offal into the canal. And do not take all night about it. The guards will be here in less than no time."

"Aye, Dray," they said, but softly, already at work. We did not know what further hostile ears might be listening, affixed either side of eyes that had witnessed horror. I thought that no other stikitche who had witnessed what had happened to his comrades—there had been twelve of them— would want to come rushing out upon his death.

We all knew, deeply and with conviction, that this attack must herald some fresh horror, that what all Vondium feared must come to pass and the future lay drenched in blood. This was a prospect that appalled me, careless as I may be in these things. We had to take the emperor to Aphrasöe and there effect a cure and so bring him safely back to his capital and reseat him on his throne, defeat the dark plots of his many enemies, and bring a fresh period of peace and stability to all Vallia.

"Take up the emperor. Quick and sharp. Pull your scarves about your faces." I glared at Inch. "And, tall man, hunch yourself over. We have to win back to the inn."

Silently, feral as leems, we padded away moments before the guards arrived with much heralding of their coming, made our way back to *The Rose of Valka* where the supplies and the fliers were waiting for us.

Among the gear we had stripped from the corpses were twelve fine metal masks. I will have more to say on the subject of metal-work and masks, for the Masks of Kregen form a fascinating, beautiful and horrible story of their own, but for now I will say that these masks were built of fine-quality steel, crafted by a mastersmith. They were all alike; triangular nose, curved lip opening, cunningly slotted to slide above an apim's ears, with brow ridges over the eye orbits chiseled into the semblance of hair.

Mass production is, as you know from Hamal, practiced to some degree on Kregen; but of necessity hand-crafted objects like these must differ in detail, one from the next. They were genuine stikitche masks, most costly; but they did not match the assassins themselves. Each one had worn ordinary clothes, buff, green, amber. I shook my head.

"Although it may seem a foolish thing to say, these do not appear to have been professional stikitches."

They all took my meaning. No assassin is going to parade around with a special badge that lights up and proclaims he is an assassin. But some marks of the trade do sometimes show.

"Look at these," said Oby, his nimble fingers turning over the badges in the lamplight of the snug.

The twelve badges were of a wersting with a korf in its jaws.

"The bitch!"

"Yet they must have followed us to the palace and waited—they cannot report back to her," I said. "This is serious. Ashti Melekhi considers herself powerful enough to assassinate the Prince Majister." No ridiculous thought of self-importance crossed my mind, only the facts as stated. "This must not deflect us from our purpose. The emperor comes first."

"I think," said Hap Loder, judiciously, "that I may return through Vondium. I may have a few words for the lady."

So we all laughed. Clansmen are regarded as the devils of barbarians they truly are in Vondium—was not I a Clansman?

Thelda was all tears and alarms as we bundled the masks and badges into a big black cloak; but Seg hushed her, and young Dray gently took her for a fortifying sip of strong wine. Sasha simply took Inch's fearsome axe and tut-tutted, and taking up a cloth began to polish until the true steel shone. Inch caught my eye and smiled. "The lassies of Ng'groga are trained to support a man, in more ways than the merely amorous."

At this, Tilly bristled up, her fine slanted eyes catching the lights and gleaming, very cat-like.

"You apims think we Fristle girls are trained only for the arts of love, like your sylvies! Well, you are wrong—"

"But, Tilly," said my son Drak, very chivalrous. "All the world knows how the Fristle men care for their womenfolk."

"And we can show our claws, too, Prince Drak!"

I knew that to be true, by Zair!

Melow the Supple, recovered from the wound she had taken in defense of Delia, a story they would not tell me because it concerned the Sisters of the Rose, let rip one of her curdling, snarling chuckles. A ferocious Manhound, once of Faol and now of Valka, she said: "Women know how to look after their brats where I come from."

And her son, Kardo, who never voluntarily leaves the side of Drak, broke out with his own harsh laugh at this. I did not marvel. But I knew a whole lot of people on the Island of Faol who would never believe Manhounds, the fearsome jiklos, savage hunting beasts genetically manufactured from human beings, could ever laugh, let alone share poignant human emotions. As for Shara, Kardo's twin sister, well, she always went loping savagely at my daughter Lela's side, and where they were, Opaz knew.

Delia could tell me nothing of what was happening to our daughters, save they were safe.

The Wizard of Loh, Khe-Hi-Bjanching, pushed forward. We all waited respectfully for him to speak. The snug in *The Rose of Valka*, went suddenly quiet. "You are all going on this expedition. But, my prince, why not have the Melekhi woman arrested? The poisoning will stop then, and—"

Nath the Needle shook his head. "The process is too far gone. Only this miracle can save him." We all knew that Nath was a renowned needleman among his friends; he had no need to advertise. What he said we believed.

"But you are all mad, mad!" cried the Wizard.

"We are surely mad, Khe-Hi," I said. "Of a certainty. But I daresay we will muddle through. I shall go ahead to make the arrangements with the Todalpheme while the expedition is put together. We meet at the Risshamal Keys—you can find at least one of the men who will know the rendezvous."

"So," said my Delia.

"One thing," I told them. "The assassins who attacked Drak must probably have been the same bunch. I think we will all be better off outside Vondium, anyway." My son's fate must be considered involved with mine by Melekhi—which it was not, in truth. He, as the Amak of Vellendur, had his own path to hew. I intended to find a Stromnate for him as soon as may be; but he had run Valka for me with Tom Tomor and the Elders, and done well. As the son of the Princess Majestrix he must know that eventually, given the longevity of Kregans, he stood a better chance than most of becoming Emperor of Vallia himself. I finished somberly: "The emperor must be got to Aphrasöe, and nothing must stop that. Nothing. The fate of all Vallia hangs on that. Until the emperor is returned to the throne, fit and well, anarchy and blood will rule in Vallia."

These tough warriors of Kregen understood that. I could leave the final preparations in good hands. Weapons, food, drink, clothes, supplies, all would be taken care of. As for airboats, well, the gigantic skyships Seg and Inch had stolen from the emperor to rescue me in Zandikar had been returned, not without a sniff and a few cutting remarks from the old devil. So now we would fly in somewhat smaller vollers; but large, well-found craft, all the same, carrying spare silver boxes to uplift and power them in flight.

Of provisions we would take enough to withstand a siege. Of weapons we would take an arsenal, for that is the Kregan way. All in all, as we stood to say our Remberees, we were a most lively company.

Delia made sure I was, myself, accoutred and weaponed correctly. We said our private farewells in a small private room of Bargom's off the black-wood landing, where the samphron oil lamps burned low, and the smell of night-blooming flowers carried heady scents in the lustrous air.

Then the small voller I would use was hauled down from her tether. I kissed Delia and climbed aboard. The stars spread above, the lights glowed from the windows around the small courtyard, built onto the flat roof at the rear of Bargom's *The Rose of Valka*. I observed the fantamyrrh. I waved to the others.

"Remberee," I shouted down. The voller rose. "Remberee."

"Remberee," they called up, dwindling into the shadows below. "Remberee, Dray Prescot, Prince Majister of Vallia..."

If they finished my interminable ridiculous rigmarole of titles I lofted up and far out of earshot long before they finished.

Seven

Hamun ham Farthytu Asks Questions

Speed was vital. There was no time to scout my approaches to the hostile and malignant Empire of Hamal. I had been there before and knew my way around. The voller flashed through the sky of Kregen, heading south, over the sea, on course for Denrette on the east coast of the southern continent of Havilfar.

Hamal's capital city, Ruathytu, lies some sixty dwaburs to the west up the River Havilthytus. This great river empties into the Ocean of Clouds opposite the southern end of the Island of Arnor. The city of Denrette stands at the mouth of the river, and I found it a strange and yet compelling place, filled with the bustle and clamor of fisherfolk, tainted with that dourness so characteristic of Hamalians, yet not without a certain energy that, three hundred miles from the capital, gave it a semblance of the shadow of the real, a reflection of the dark glories of Ruathytu.

Down by the shore, of course, the place stank of fish. But set atop small hills the houses and villas of the wealthier folk bespoke the nature of their affected reflection of the splendors of the capital. The city was large enough to boast an arena; but I steered well clear of the Jikhorkdun. I had had my fill, for the time being, of fighting in the arena away down south in Huringa, the capital of Hyrklana. There happened to be a sennight of games in progress as I arrived. For a single mur I was tugged by nostalgic memories. For a heartbeat I considered going in to join the multitudes to discover how went the fortunes of the Ruby Drang. But I did not. Anyway, quite often here in Hamal the colors and the orders were different from those I had known in Huringa.

Instead, knowing a sick emperor waited, I took myself straight to the Akhram.

The Todalpheme, the wise men of Kregen who measure the tides and keep track of the suns and the moons in their courses, who predict eclipses and who are sacrosanct, would welcome me as any ordinary traveler, anxious to improve his knowledge, of the world and of their lore. Their secrets are open, freely given to those who will join them, and difficult of access to people without that astronomically oriented frame of mind. I carried fine gifts we had put together in Vondium.

The information could be bought, for the emperor had bought the knowledge once before, and where once gold has eased the way gold will find the opening easier of attainment.

Set boldly atop a promontory right out at the eastern escarpment, with a sheer drop to the ocean below, the Akhram presented a massive picture of authority and power and ancient wisdom, its craggy walls one with the rock on which it stood. The dominating pharos would beam out at night, warning the imperial skyships of Hamal and the constant mercantile flying traffic, directing them on their inward courses toward Ruathytu. The Hamalese are not great sailors of the sea. They do not have to be, seeing as they manufacture the vollers which can fly through the empty wastes of the sky.

I walked quickly up the winding path. The river flowed in its deep gorge below, cut through the living rock. Away to the north various channels of the river emptied out and the marshes stretched remote under the suns,

filled with immense flocks of wildfowl. There, also, prowled the aerial pred-
ators, saddle birds gone wild, and, among them, the untamed chyyans.

The air smelled sweet with the sea tang. The blaze of the suns fell about
me, the twin intermingled rays of red and green from the Suns of Scorpio.
Antares, the double star, poured down floods of light. I breathed deeply of
the wine-rich air, swinging the lesten-hide bag containing so much wealth.
The thraxter belted at my waist seemed in that limpid air and in that sybaritic setting to be an anachronism, unnecessary.

Yet—I could never forget I trod the stones of Kregen.

Carts were toiling up the hill, carts loaded with the produce of an empire,
drawn by massive old quoffas with their patient faces and hearth-rug hides,
bringing a pang of remembrance. I gave a shoulder to help heave a cart
from a rut and the Xaffers, diffs so strange and remote they were always
a mystery to apims, thanked me in their fashion, and I strode on, filling
my lungs, my eyes fixed on the grey dominating pile of the Akhram above
with the gilded domes flashing brilliantly.

The carts and the workpeople toiling up served the Todalpheme. For a
single instant I had the horrified thought they were on the same errand
as myself, seeking the whereabouts of the Swinging City. This was a nonsense. The secret was known to very few. The voller salesman who had
sold it to the emperor for Delia's sake must have been an adept in a secret
society of one kind or another if he had been ejected by the Todalpheme.
Secret societies always seem to flourish when men and women think about
their world and their place in the scheme of things. I walked on, trying to
appear inconspicuous.

The knee-length white robe did not materially help in that, for it was
a rustic dress, telling these folk I was a country bumpkin. They wore the
working clothes of Ruathytu, blue or grey or green, where they were not
slaves, and they knew my dress as provincial. Even the thraxter marked me,
for the rapier and main gauche had grown apace as a fashion in Hamal.

The guards carried thraxters and shields, in the fashion of Hamal, and
stuxes, also, the spears of varying kinds for varying work. The Shanks who
raided from over the curve of the world generally steered clear of the coasts
of Havilfar, the southern continent that contains Hamal and Hyrklana—
and Djanduin to the south west. These guards were here to protect the
Akhram not from Hamalese, although they would do that quickly enough
if necessary.

With a polite greeting I was passed through. The Akhram! Well, these
observatories of the Todalpheme are marvelous places, to be sure. When
a world possesses two suns and seven moons the mysterious workings of
heavenly bodies and the conflicting surgings of the tides demand a man's
application to mathematics and accurate observation and a thorough-
going knowledge of his world. These attributes the Todalpheme possess

to a high degree. Once, I had been offered the opportunity of joining the Todalpheme, and had gracefully declined.

Akhram—for usually the chief Todalpheme calls himself just Akhram—lifted up the golden necklace. The gold and rubies glistered back at him in the rays of the suns through the arched windows overlooking the sea. Wide-winged birds pirouetted out there and the noise of the waves reached us, although the beach was not visible. The chamber was airy, light, with a flick-flick plant, and many scented flowers. That superb Kregen tea had been served, and, gratefully, I sipped watching Akhram as he stared at the treasure heaped over the lenken table.

"Fine, fine, Amak," he said. "Princely gifts."

"I respect the Todalpheme too much to weigh the price of gifts." I spoke bluffly, stoutly, cunningly. "It is not the value that matters."

He smiled that remote little smile with which the ascetic will acknowledge the gluttonous follies of the world. A tall, grave, distinguished man, Akhram, almost a hundred and eighty years of age, in the prime of life, with much work still to be accomplished. I will not go into overmuch detail of the transactions in the Akhram of Denrette. They kept me waiting for a space, to cool my heels, then suggested if I sought a cure it would be better to consult doctors, or seek spiritual assistance from any one of the many Bengs and Bengas whose saintly miracles could cure. Akhram himself seemed to size me up, and we talked, and I convinced him that my desire to discover the whereabouts of Aphrasöe was not mercenary. He nodded, and put the necklace back among the piles of treasure.

"We, Amak," he said, "are not the scarlet-roped Todalpheme. You will find them. They know the secret. We can but point you in the right direction."

He called me Amak because I had, naturally, assumed my secret identity of Hamun ham Farthytu, the Amak of Paline Valley. I use the overly dramatic word secret. As Hamun ham Farthytu I was a real person, with a real identity, able to move freely about Hamal, the mighty empire in deadly opposition to my own country of Vallia. But that is what comes of being a spy.

He understood my intense desire for speed, for the person dearly beloved by me—and others, I added significantly—was a most highly placed personage and it would not be too much to say that a deal of Hamal's future depended on the recovery. Thus he said, with a small, deprecating smile: "We have given this information before, for a price. There is a tortuous route to follow; but we have learned ourselves shortcuts. I think—"

"For Hamal, Akhram," I said, most seriously.

"Yes." When he told me I understood why no one I had spoken to hitherto had heard of Todalpheme wearing scarlet ropes about their waists. The old color had come back again to haunt me. I did not smile; but I took up the map Akhram showed me, and with my old sailor skill committed it to memory. Right over to the west, west of the Tarnish Channel of Havilfar, out below the forbidden island of Tambu, the island of Bet-Aqsa. Bet-Aqsa.

There we must go, and at once, to inquire of the scarlet-roped Todalpheme the whereabouts of Aphrasöe.

Listening as Akhram spoke in his quiet voice in the high-vaulted library of the observatory where we had gone to find the map, I had the suspicion he did not truly know how the secret had come into the hands of the Todalpheme of Hamal. As a puissant empire, the strongest power in Havilfar—if, in my arrogance, you excepted Djanduin—it seemed logical for Hamal to come by strange shreds of knowledge, secrets gathered from the four corners of the continent. Maybe some of the Todalpheme down in the Dawn Lands might also know that the Todalpheme of Bet-Aqsa knew of a place where miracle cures might be effected. All that concerned me now was to take my flier as fast as she would fly to the rendezvous up among the Risshamal Keys.

More and more I was determined to avert the consequences of the emperor's death. For the streets of Vallia would run red with blood, the alleys pile with stinking corpses, the crops would burn, the livestock starve, thousands of hapless wights would be branded and herded off to slavery—all these atrocities would happen—might happen, would probably happen—if the Emperor of Vallia died.

Making all due observances as I took my leave, giving them Remberee, I took myself off and walked smartly back down the stony path to the waiting flier.

The Risshamal Keys are merely a number of long, fingerlike extensions of small islands, rocks, cays, shoals and reefs running out in a northeasterly direction from the northeastern corner of Havilfar. I had been shipwrecked there in the old *Ovvend Barynth*. In setting up the rendezvous we knew the certain men who could aid us. As I took off and flew up into the streaming radiance of Antares I wondered who it would be who would guide my friends to the island of the Yuccamots along the Risshamal Keys.

Flying eastward out over the sparkling sea I cleared the coast and then headed north. The Island of Arnor passed away astern. The suns poured their floods of opaz light upon the sea, and I saw a few ships sailing there— not many. A number of vollers passed; but none offered to stop and search me. The simple precaution had been taken of painting out the Vallian recognition signs, and the voller might have come direct from Ruathytu or Paline Valley for all anyone might know. I flew northwards and Bet-Aqsa lay to the southwest. I had always harbored an inkling that Aphrasöe might lie upon some island in the Outer Oceans, and had favored the easterly direction. Maybe—and I hoped most fervently that I was wrong—maybe the Swinging City was situated on the other grouping of islands and continents on the other side of Kregen, around the curve of the world. Kregen runs a longer mileage in the equator than does Earth, for all the fractionally lesser gravity, and there is a damned lot of ground to cover.

The continental grouping in which, so far, all my adventuring had taken place, is called Paz. From the other continents and islands around the curve of the world sailed the fearsome Fish-Heads—call them shanks, shants, shtarkins, shkanes, it makes no difference to their viciousness—to plague and harry us. Every so often their marvelous fleet ships would sail upon an unsuspecting shore and there would follow horror and desolation. I had fought the shanks before the Jikai with the Kroveres on Drayzm, and would fight them again. Always, like any sailor of Paz, one eye was always roving the far horizons to catch the first glimpse of those tall wing-like sails of the shank ships.

And then, as I plunged on through the thin air toward that brave company of friends awaiting me at the Risshamal Keys, I looked up and saw a giant scarlet and golden bird, flying high, circling, watching me with bright black beady eyes.

I swore.

I shook my fist.

By Zair! Not now, not now!

The great hunting bird circled. The raptor was a familiar sight, a hateful sight. This was the Gdoinye, the spy and messenger of the Everoinye, the Star Lords.

Through their malign agency I had been flung about space between worlds like a yo-yo. When I had so intemperately refused to obey their orders I had been chucked back to Earth to rot for twenty-one infernal years. If the Gdoinye was spying on me, all well and good, for I knew the Star Lords kept an eye on me from time to time. But if the Opaz-forsaken bird was warning me that I would be required to perform again for the Star Lords...

I sweated. I clenched my teeth and stopped myself from shouting up insults, as I usually did when the golden and scarlet raptor hove into sight.

If the bird did swoop down and speak to me I would try to be conciliatory, be the new Dray Prescot, refrain from hurling abuse and calling the thing a cramph, a rast, a kleesh. But it swung about up there, glinting magnificently in the opaz radiance, and then calmly flew away.

I let out a great gusty breath of relief.

What a time to be dragged away from Kregen!

Eight

A Brush with Flutsmen

Thinking that, with the appearance of the Gdoinye, the Savanti might have sent their white dove to spy on me, I cast a good look around. I could see no sign of the dove. Well, that meant little, although, to be sure, it made more sense for the Savanti to spy on me now, seeing that my intended destination was their secret island.

The long low straggle of islands of the southern fingering of the Risshamal Keys showed as an extended yellowish grey stain upon the water ahead. The Yuccamots inhabited many of the little islands and gained a precarious living fishing and trading, in communication with the local sailing craft. I had no fear of them, for they were a simple folk and had shown us kindness before. They are, I am glad to say, enormously proud of their broad thick tails, and of their webbed feet.

The Hamalian Air Service was another matter. They maintained a string of stations along the Keys, and it behooved me to avoid those.

What did happen, with the blinding speed of precipitate action upon Kregen, whipped up a nice little froth to send the blood thumping through the veins and open the pores a trifle.

Out of the roseate glow of the red sun Zim shot the dark forms of riders urging on their saddle flyers.

With my fingers up against my eyes I peered into the dazzlement even as I thrust the control levers hard over and up.

They were flutsmen up there.

Flutsmen!

By this time I knew a little of their nefarious ways. Later, I was to learn more. But now, these mercenaries of the skies, flying their fluttrells with sure confident skill, out for plunder and lopped heads, bore down screeching on me. To them, I represented loot, easy pickings, a lone flier in a voller.

If they could take me before I rose and speeded enough to elude them, why, then they'd toss me over the side into the sea, and pilot the voller back to their base. They'd sell her and her contents and get drunk on the proceeds. Then they'd go reiving off for more easy plunder.

Usually, the flutsmen work for hire, bands of professional mercenaries, paktuns of a sort. I'd hardly demean them to the low quality of masichieri, those scoundrels who are more employable bandits than honest mercenaries, but often enough they came close, by Zair. I fancied this band were freelancing, tazll, harrying for themselves. There were about thirty of them, too long odds for me to want to tangle with them, in view of the urgency of the task before me, unless I had to.

The emperor must come first. A fight could wait. There is always opportunity for a fight on Kregen...

The voller lifted. Slowly. Too slowly.

The fluttrells turned their big heads with those large ridiculous vanes into the wind and opened their jaws and lanced down.

I glared up savagely. By Krun! I wanted no fight. But if these haughty, vicious flutsmen wanted to come to handstrokes, then I'd accommodate them. With a juicy Makki-Grodno oath, having to do with the putrescent diseased innards of Makki-Grodno's disgusting liver, I snatched up the great Lohvian longbow. If I couldn't shaft a few of the yetches before they reached me I hadn't been trained by Seg Segutorio, the master bowman of Erthyrdrin!

Down they swooped, their green-feathered harness tight about them, their closely-fitting green-feathered caps with the flaring knotted clumps of ribbon streaming out in the wind of their passage. Flutsmen on the rampage present a brave spectacle. Completely confident of themselves they swooped down, each man ready with crossbow, volstux or long whippy sword.

Before they could start shooting I cast the first shaft.

Clean through the feather-adorned armored body of the leading flutsman the clothyard shaft punched. The brilliant blue feathers of the shaft's notching came from the crested korf of the Blue Mountains of Vallia. Always, Seg would say that the king korfs blue feathers were just that fraction superior to those of a crested korf; but he would affirm that the beautiful bird, the korf of Kregen, provided the best feathers for the shafts cast from a Lohvian longbow. I thought about this as I loosed again.

Before the leading flutsman had time to slide from his high saddle and dangle from the leather straps of his clerketer, the second shaft took his wingmate. The third shaft took the third man in the vee.

Shouts of rage battered down...

"Cramph! You should know better! To slay a flutsman is to die!"

I didn't bother to reply in words but sped another shaft that parted the teeth of a yelling flutsman and did nasty things to the back of his skull. His saddle flyer spun past, spraying bits of the flutsman's bone and gobbets of brain.

Yes, the korf provides the best fletchings. We'd been experimenting in Valka with the rose-colored feathers of the zim-korf. I'd had a few shafts made up and the warmly-glowing red feathers dyed a brilliant blue. Seg, when I'd tried him, had expressed himself as perfectly satisfied with the shafts, and why was I making such a thing out of it. When we washed the dye away, letting the blue color leach out to reveal the brave old red, Seg's face was a picture.

But, as the other flutsmen closed in, I had time to loose twice more—loose the blazing blue feathered shafts in deadly true arcs. Each time the arrow punched cleanly; then I took to my sword.

The Krozair longsword felt good in my fists.

Ah, me! How often I have thought that. But now, with an emperor sick and near to dying, was no time to consider my new image, the quiet, conciliatory, peace-loving Dray Prescot. With the Krozair longsword in my fists, my hands spread in that cunning Krozair grip, I went to work.

Mind you, the first and chief use of the sword at the moment was to ward off the shafts that sliced toward me with the artful two-handed flicking taught in the Krozair disciplines. I battered the bolts away joyfully. I own it. The blood thumped around my veins. The voller shot up now as the speed increased vertically and we went slap bang through the middle of the fluttrell formation. In a clashing smother of flapping wings and raking talons the voller shot up and broke through. For an instant I was slashing and hacking away to my heart's content. Thrusting is a chancy business in these circumstances, for obvious reasons.

The voller clanged as the wooden hull gonged to repeated blows. But she won free. We sprung through the giant saddle birds and up into the suns shine—save for one. One fluttrell rose abruptly directly before me.

There was no chance to swerve the flier. Bird and boat crashed together with an almighty smash.

Staggering, I kept my feet, braced, wrathful, the wicked Krozair brand slanted up and forward. The bird was entangled with the stem of the boat, where the fancy gilding was all scraped away. The stout leather harness did not break. Its wings thrashed. The rider, freeing himself from his clerketer, leaped right nimbly down onto the tiny deck, superbly balanced on supple legs, and came for me directly. His green feathers flaunted in the light.

"Die, onker!" he shouted, and cast his stux.

The spear flew. The Krozair longsword flicked and the spear, ringing like a gong, caromed away into the blue.

Nothing daunted, the flutsman came on, drawing his thraxter. He presented the sword, point first, the Havilfarese cut-and-thruster held in skilled firm grip, and leaped down with a wild panache. Powerful, he was, limber in his strength, supremely at home in the air. The longsword flicked left, halted, surged back, twisting. The thraxter spun up in the air, end over end, sparkling. The sharp steel point of the Krozair brand held without a tremble on the throat of the flutsman, just above the green collar of his lorica.

He glared at me, panting, disbelieving. He was a strong well-built Brokelsh. His bristle body hair bristled even more. A strong, virile race, the Brokelsh, and many people consider them coarse and uncouth. Not apims, of course, the Brokelsh. Had this fellow been wearing a silver or gold trim to the collar of his lorica I might have had a little more exercise in twitching his sword away.

He gaped down at the sword. His expression was one of enormous surprise, as though he awoke from a dream of midnight houris and wine to find himself in this predicament.

His goggle-eyed amazement amused me.

"Why should I not slay you now, dom?"

He shook his massive head and licked his lips. His mannerisms were those of a man, diff or apim, both. "I am a flutsman, apim."

"Aye! A reiving mercenary of the skies who owes no allegiance to any save his own band, despite the hire fees you take. Well, many of your band have gone down to the Ice Floes this day. What say you, Flutsman?"

His blunt chin went up. Uncouth they may be, the Brokelsh, exceedingly hairy with a coarse black body hair; but they are men.

"I am Hakko Bolg ti Bregal, known as Hakko Volrokjid. Perhaps I deserve to die. I do not think so. I have a great hatred for all you Hamalese—and mayhap that will serve."

"In that case, by the disgusting tripes of Makki-Grodno! I shall not slay you. I do not want your blood on my blade."

I said this, you will perceive, to conceal the truth.

He squinted his eyes down, this Hakko Volrokjid. I, too, had had trouble with volroks, those winged flying men of Havilfar. "And this blade," he said. "I have not seen its like before."

"And I've not heard of Bregal."

"A small town, in Ystilbur of the Dawn Lands."

"I have heard of Ystilbur. An ancient land."

"And razed with fire and swords by you rasts. By Barflut the Razor Feathered! I would dearly love to slay you all!"

"Seize your fluttrell, before the onkerish thing strangles himself on his own harness. Get you gone. I am not a Hamalese. And, dom, if you meet me again, remember, and tread small."

He glared for a heartbeat at me, his bristly face working, then he scrambled back and grappled his bird, who would have bit at him had he not clouted it over the head. I spoke big, like that, to conceal deeps I did not want this Brokelsh flutsman, Hakko Volrokjid, to see revealed in me.

He freed the bird and vaulted up into the saddle, doing all this with the practiced ease of your true flutsman. He buckled up the clerketer. His bristly face lowered down on me.

"I shall not forget you, apim. Be very sure of that, by the Golden Feathered Aegis!" He drew up the reins, handled most cunningly in one fist. Then he shouted down words that surprised me, although they should not have. Many a paktun—although he was far too callow to have earned the coveted mortilhead—would not thank a man for giving life. They might feel shame, depression, humiliation, the outrage of their professional ethics, depending on their beliefs. But this young flutsman bellowed down: "I thank you for my life. May the Resplendent Bridzilkelsh have you in his keeping. Rembaree!"

And with a great beating of wings the fluttrell swooped away and this singular flutsman was gone.

I poked my head over the side of the voller.

The flutsmen toiled along after me, all in formation, the wings of their flyers going up and down, up and down. Hakko Volrokjid spun away through the level wastes to join them. Then, all in formation, they swung away and strung out in a beeline for the coast to the west. Hakko flew strongly after them. So, guessing what was afoot—or, rather, in the air—I looked ahead and there were the fliers lifting from the scattering of cays and bearing up for me.

A single look reassured me.

They were not vollers of the Hamalian Air Service.

My friends, waiting at the rendezvous, had witnessed the little aerial affray and were no doubt thirsting to get into the fight.

This was true—deplorably so.

The moment my voller touched gunwales with Seg's impressive craft he yelled across: "One missed, Dray—the blue flash of feathers was not to be mistaken."

"My finger slipped on the string."

"Aye!" he roared, joyously. "You always had slippery fingers."

Inch bellowed across from his flier. "A good long axe, Dray—that's what you need up here in the sky."

Other greetings rose from the other fliers. We formed a little fleet, a tiny armada, there off the coast of a hostile empire. But we wanted nothing of Hamal on this trip.

I landed the little voller across the deck of the large flier Delia had provided for us. She waited for me, alight with joy at my safe return. All my comrades and their families were here, in good spirits, although chafing to have missed that little spat of a fight. So I knew the emperor was not yet dead.

Delia smiled at me, her face pale.

"He still lives. But he is weak, so very weak. We must hurry."

I shouted out the course to Vangar.

"Southwest! Southwest at top speed."

We were on our way to Bet-Aqsa and the men who might tell us where away lay Aphrasöe, the Swinging City of the Savanti.

Nine

In the Akhram of Bet-Aqsa

The encounter between the ranked Pachak swods and the Rapa Deldars had been sanguinary in the extreme. Two Chulik Jiktars, powerful, had been swept away in the bloody rout, and an apim Paktun and a Brokelsh Hikdar were thrown with the others regretfully back into the velvet-lined box.

"Do you yield?" demanded Delia, most fierce.

"Aye," I said. I did not tip my king over in the terrestrial way of chess but I pushed back in the chair and, looking on the ruin of my forces, said: "Aye, I bare the throat."

Jikaida is a game where women can be so damned deceitful it amazes mere mortal men. But I could not help adding: "I notice you are using as your Pallan a female figure. I still do not recognize the representation."

"You are not meant to."

I glanced out through a port. The airboat fled on through the level wastes of air, speeding towards Bet-Aqsa. We had slept and eaten and I had thought to occupy the mind of Delia by Jikaida, that absorbing game that dominates so much of Kregan intellectual thinking, giving opportunities for rigorous mental disciplines. I did not pick up her Pallan, the most powerful piece on the board. But I cast the gorgeous little figure a most baleful glance.

Delia smiled. "She carries the yellow cross on the scarlet field. What more could you ask?"

I grunted. "Only that she play for me, woman!"

At this, Delia laughed, and so I knew much of her fear for her father had been damped by the amazing success we had so far enjoyed in our mission to save his life, and with it the life and well-being of all Vallia.

Most people have a game of Jikaida stuffed away somewhere in a dusty cupboard; most people play from time to time. It demands much more than the game Jikalla. Some folk play so often that the game becomes their life. Gafard, the King's Striker, who was our son-in-law and who was now dead, had once earned a living as a Jikaidast, a man—or woman—who sets up in a suitable place and challenges all comers for wagers. Such Jikaidasts are regarded differently in various countries; usually they are given honor and I, for one, gave them due honor within the craft.

Most people who are halfway serious about Jikaida also own at least one personal set of playing pieces. Although the opposing colors are usually blue and yellow, sometimes black and white—almost never red and green—the individual figures are embellished in wondrous ways. I happened to have been using a mixed set in which diffs and apims filled the functions of representing the various pieces. I admired the fine martial appearance of the little warriors, of whatever race they happened to be. Delia had produced a marvelous set, all of delicately carved ivory and balass and gold, including Pachaks and Djangs. With, of course, her confounded mysterious female figure as her Pallan.

Now, lifting up my own Pallan, a neat little apim with a finely wrought Lohvian longbow and a sword too long for comfort, I laid him away in the balass box.

"Having bared the throat, will you wet it with some wine?"

Our son, Prince Drak, came into the stateroom just then and did the honors, pouring Gremivoh, the vintage favored in the Vallian Air Service.

"It is all going amazingly well," he said. He still experienced difficulty in calling me father, and Jaidur always avoided the embarrassment. "The island will be in sight within a bur or so."

We spoke for a few moments of the trip and the prospects, ground we had covered time after time. Drak expressed himself as most pleased that when we had stopped off in Djanguraj for fresh provisions, nothing would stop Kytun Kholin Dom and Ortyg Fellin Coper and their families from joining us. Then, speaking to Delia although looking at Drak, I said: "Can you tell me why this well set-up, handsome son of ours has not married so far?"

Drak's powerful features lowered on me at this, and Delia shook her head in a quick admonitory way.

"That is my business," said Drak.

"Oh, aye," I said. "But the emperor is your grandfather. We are going to save his life. Rest easy on that. But, one day, it is likely you will be emperor."

His head went up at this. Powerful, Drak, hard and strong, filled with a dark purpose I could only admire at a distance.

"Yes. Consider that well. With a family to sustain you, you will seem an even better choice to the people and the Presidio."

"And you?"

"Me? I want only your well being—as for the emperor—throne, crown, title, wealth—they are all gewgaws. I have enough of that kind of thing already." Here, again thinking of Djanduin of which land I am king, I paused. "At least, if it comes to it, and if your mother agrees, why, then..."

Drak set his glass down carefully. He was worked up, his handsome face, dark and powerful, set in harsh lines of determination that, I suspected, were very like those lines I see in the mirror when I shave.

"I do not anticipate becoming emperor while you or mother live."

He went out then, quickly, and the sturmwood door slammed somewhat too hard.

"I really do not know what to make of that boy," I said.

Delia laughed: "You do realize, my heart, that because of our dip in the Sacred Pool of Baptism, we are younger than he is?"

"Deuced odd that, by Zair!"

She became grave, on a sudden. "They—the Savanti—they would not let me go—you remember—and you—it was a dreadful journey to the pool—" She bit her lip, and said, on a rush: "Suppose they will not let father be cured?"

"I have thought of that. We fly directly to the Pool of Baptism. Once we are there and your father is cured, it will be too late for the Savanti to interfere."

So we agreed on the plan between us. I felt some confidence that with the tearaway bunch of ruffians with us, and with the fine navigation of Vangar—I would help, of course—we ought both to find the River Zelph and the Pool and take care of any opposition along the way. What the Savanti might say I did not much care. I own I felt some concern over what they might do. But they were, as I knew, a civilized people who wanted to make of Kregen a world fit for people to grow into fulfilled lives without the dark fears that plagued them now. The stakes were too high to draw back now out of phantasmal fears of what might be.

We went up on deck into the clean swift rush of wind.

Our friends were peering ahead from every flier. Wersting Rogahan, who could shoot a varter and hit the center of the Chunkrah's eye every time, had been the man they had found to guide them to the Yuccamot island in the Risshamal Keys. He had been shipwrecked with me in the old *Ovvend Barynth*, a rough-tongued rapscallion, an old sea-dog; but he was a man I fancied I understood and could rub along with. He had advanced just one step in rank since I had had him made up to so-Deldar, and was now a ley-Deldar. He still wore that dark strip of chin beard under his jaws, his lean knowing face was just the same with the broken nose and the mahogany tan of a life spent at sea. Up here in a flying craft he had donned a buff shirt where normally he went bare-chested, and the old buff trousers cut off at the knees might have been the same pair he'd worn when we'd shot our varters in competition against the pursuing shanks.

"Land ho!"

The shrill yell skyrocketed up from Oby, perched high. He pointed ahead.

Soon we all saw the low dark outline of coast, with hills beyond, and the cream of surf and the wink of rivers. Bet-Aqsa was a sizeable island, triangular in shape and some one hundred eighty or so dwaburs across at the widest part, smaller than the forbidden island of Tambu to the north.

Kytun Kholin Dom, my fearsome four-armed Djang comrade, bellowed across the wind-rushing gap between fliers: "So that's where those Drig-loving reivers live, is it? Now we know, by Zodjuin of the Silver Stux!

We will pay them a visit and return their gifts to us in fire and the sword!"

Well, knowing my Djangs as I do, and knowing of the raids they suffered from the sea people—not the Shanks—I could not be surprised.

If the inhabitants of Bet-Aqsa as distinct from the Todalpheme of that place made a habit of raiding the western coasts of Havilfar, secure that their home was far enough west to deter anyone reckless enough even to think of sailing that far into the Ocean of Doubt, then they would be in for a nasty shock. The place was secretive enough, Zair knew. Events were changing fast on Kregen, and the world would never be the same again.

Over the horizon to the north and east the forbidden island of Tambu presented no lure. I had met men who claimed to have been there and the stories about the place, not all apocryphal, I feel sure, were calculated to curdle the blood. Gruesome, distasteful, the stories, most of them, as I was to discover. The thought did cross my mind that perhaps the forbidden character of Tambu could be explained away by the unsuspected presence there of the Savanti.

That, we would soon discover.

Over the island we flew, seeing towns and villages of peculiar aspect, and long rolling downlands, forests, marks of cultivation. A few fluttrell patrols winged up after us; but we flew vollers high and fast and left the laboring saddle birds far below. Also, there arose other flyers riding beasts new to us, flying steeds of remarkable appearance, all speckled with ruby and amber feathers, with gappy jaws and long whiplike tails. Still and all, despite their efficient wingspan, long and wide like an albatross's, and despite the gesticulating figures upon their backs, they were outdistanced also.

"Straight to the Western Akhram, Vangar," I told the captain of my Valkan Fleet, admiral, Chuktar, flag-captain and skipper of whatever voller I happened to be flying in all rolled into one efficient, loyal, great-hearted man. He nodded and bent to his map, the self-same map I had drawn out for him from my memory of the one shown me by Akhram of the Todalpheme of Denrette.

Soon at the best speed of our vollers the western coast came in sight, a green-blue glittering expanse of water stretching out beyond the last fingerings of land, a vast mass of empty water stretching out no man knew whither. This was the Ocean of Doubt.

"There!" screeched Oby, pointing, the wind in his hair.

A collection of yellow-green onion domes rose from the edge of an inlet. Ships lay moored and signs of activity from what were clearly dockyards showed that these people kept themselves busy, an impression heightened by the size of the town strung along the water's edge. The low yellow fortress guarding the mouth of the inlet was not lost upon us. These folk trafficked upon the sea, and yet they built defenses. We all thought we knew for whom those stout walls had been built.

The Akhram stood aloof from these mundane pursuits, the cluster of onion domes glistening in the limpid air.

How far we had come! Right to the edge of the known world—over it, for all we had previously known of these foreign parts. Where one might have expected to discover an uncouth half-savage people, it was clear there was wealth down there, industry and commerce—and, for sure, a deal of loot from the coasts of Havilfar, including Djanduin.

I had argued with my friends and overborne them.

Delia said: "But I should go with you! I have been to Aphrasöe before. Therefore—"

"Therefore you will stay here, with the fleet."

She pouted at me, making a mockery of my heavy-handedness. But I would not be swayed. I had brought a fleet and a large body of fighting men, for that is the best way to travel on Kregen when you are in a hurry and will meet foes—and carry a bedridden, dying emperor. The very best way, of course, is alone, like a savage clansman in hunting leathers—and, truly, better even than that, is just the two of you, just the two, alone in the whole wide world of Kregen...

So I would not be swayed now. Nath the Needle said he dare not leave the emperor. The poison wasting away the once stalwart frame was insidious, and any cure that might once have been possible was long since too late, by far. All he could do was administer what antidote he could. Every bur the emperor had to take a teaspoonful of the nauseating mixture Nath prepared, swallowing it down past clenched teeth we had gently to prise open with silver levers. Also, acupuncture needles had to be used, carefully inserted in the right nodes and along the correct lines to ease the increasing pain. I had studied assiduously with Nath the Needle as well as other eminent doctors to discover all I could of the arcane mysteries of the needleman's art. I could insert a needle now and know with sure certainty that it would do the work intended.

Making preparations as the fleet hovered over the Akhram, I gave my last instructions. "I go alone and hope to win through with gold and peaceful talk. If I am not back within three burs then, Seg and Inch, you'd better fly down and see what is keeping me. I trust you will bring a few sturdy fellows with you, and, as well, leave another pack of sky-leems up here to guard our return."

They nodded. They were not joking, even if I tended to treat this whole escapade as just that. They didn't like me jaunting off by myself. Even I had to admit that that was because they cared for my leathery old hide, and not, as I dearly loved to believe, because they fancied I was hogging all the action.

All my experiences on Kregen so far indicated that the Todalpheme were quiet, studious, peace-loving men who wished only to get on with their tasks of tracking the course of the moons and the suns and of predicting the tides. They kept up a force of brown-clad workpeople who were not slave, superintended by the Oblifanters, answerable directly to the Todalpheme. The Oblifanters and their work force were not cloaked by the universal acceptance of the sanctity of the Todalpheme. They might be entrapped, made slave, killed. So they were a rougher bunch. Their methods of work I had seen at the Dam of Days.

The voller spun away and I was lunging for the cluster of greenish-yellow onion domes within the long walls.

While it is not true to say that one Akhram is very much like another, they must all share a deal in common as to the purpose of their architecture. They each possess an observatory and a library and a refectory. As I expected, after a wait, I was shown into a small room where Akhram would see me. Gold, even among the Todalpheme, sometimes eases the way. But the Todalpheme welcome students visiting them, and within the framework of their vital occupations will delight in conversation with visitors, seeing that they are usually cut off from normal human intercourse. As a rule they lead solitary lives, at one with the waves and the winds and the tides. I anticipated only the problem of convincing the Todalpheme of Bet-Aqsa that I was genuinely in need of secret information.

Some thought had been taken as to my dress.

To go with the orange favors of the Djangs would be to excite instant suspicion if not hostility. To go as a Vallian would mean little, except to create wariness almost as much as a Hamalian. Finally I donned a simple short russet-colored tunic, edged with a deep yellow, belted with lesten hide and a great golden buckle—petty ostentation, this last, but designed with a purpose. A rapier and dagger swung at my sides and the old longsword jutted up over my shoulder. I hung a long white cloak around my shoulders, clear of the hilt of the longsword, and fastened off the bronzen zhantil-head clips. The unworldly combination should provoke interest, at the least.

"And are you a prince, dom?" said Akhram, coming into the chamber and sitting down. He was a fat and fleshy man, with pursed lips despite the fat jowliness of his cheeks, and pouchy eyes. I did not like the sound of that "dom" which is common among ordinary folk as a greeting name, and among friends as a mark of affection. For the first time I felt unease, that I had blundered.

"That is not of importance." I put to him the reason for my visit. I opened the lesten-hide bag and showed him the contents. As I did this I watched his eyes. My hackles rose. He was a Todalpheme; I do not deny him that. And, also, I knew there was much and much I did not know about Kregen. But he was like no other Todalpheme, least of all an Akhram, that I had met before.

"Pretty baubles," he said, lifting the golden chains. But his face betrayed far different emotions from his words.

"All yours, Excellency." I used the word deliberately. "The man is very sick. Only the Savanti can cure him."

He looked up quickly, the golden chain swinging from his soft plump ringers. "So you know their name? The brothers grow careless. And you have come far?"

"A goodly way." I pushed the heavy bag nearer. "Tell me where lies Aphrasöe and these are yours and I will leave at once."

No strangeness afflicted me as I considered what I said, what I demanded. The search for information had upheld me for long periods of my life upon Kregen. It was a secret I had hungered for, suffered for, something I had thought meant more to me than anything else in two worlds. Paradise! I had been thrown out of the paradise that was Aphrasöe, the Swinging City. I had asked and asked and always to no avail, and then real life had taken me in and the Swinging City had dimmed. And now, here I was, calmly offering gold to buy the secret. Weird!

So the strangeness of it all did affect me, after all.

"I think, dom," said this Akhram, touching his lips, which shone, moist in the lights through the open windows. "I think the bag of treasure is mine, whether I give you the secret or not."

"How so?"

"We do not impart this to everyone who asks. It is a high trust placed in our hands."

Again, I blundered.

"I do not believe that. You came by the information by chance—"

"Do not presume!" He flared at me, shaking already with an anger he did little to control. This Todalpheme showed a petty emotion. "We have sent our men before. Good men. In vollers that cost a great deal of money in far Havilfar."

By saying "far" Havilfar, he sought to entrap me into some kind of reaction by which he might judge my place of origin.

Stony-faced, I said: "I need the information and I need it in a hurry. I do not quarrel with anything you say of your acquisition or trust of the secret. The man is like to die. You will tell me."

"And if I will not?"

I put my hand on the bag.

He sneered. "We have sent brothers to Aphrasöe and often they do not return. Gold will not buy their lives."

"I do not ask any escort."

Then he said the revealing thing I had sensed and which had caused my blundering, my stiff-necked talk.

"No," he said. "No, we are not as other Todalpheme."

He wore a fine sensil robe of yellow. His thick waist was girded by a scarlet rope. He was, in truth, one of the Scarlet-Roped Todalpheme, men I had sought over the face of Kregen. And now I had found one of that brotherhood and he was proving two-faced, obstinate, greedy, attempting to cheat and defraud me, attempting, also, to browbeat me.

He reached out a hand and touched the bag of treasure.

"I think this is mine, already. I think you had best be gone before worse befalls you."

I said: "Do you consider yourself sacrosanct?"

His astonishment was genuine.

His eyes glittered through abruptly down-drawn lids. Yet he answered obliquely. "You wear swords, dom." He paused. His use of the word dom continued to offend me. I saw quite clearly in it a patronizing sneer; dom is the word between friends for friend, or the kindly word indicating no hostility. Except, of course, when it is used in irony, and then the circumstances are perfectly plain. There are subtleties in the use of words. Here, this Akhram was baiting me. Why? He thought he could take the treasure and kick me out. He had guards, powerful armed men at call.

He put his hands together and continued, heavily. "You wear swords. Only a madman would offer violence to a Todalpheme."

Yes, on occasion I am mad. But I was not as yet mad enough to risk everything on a cheap retort, something like: "I am mad, dom, mad enough to do your business for you if you do not speak up—quick!"

Instead, I said: "What impediment is there to telling me? Surely the gold is not all there is to it?"

He hesitated again at this. I can judge time passably well. The three burs were drifting away through the glass.

"We have been warned by the Savanti. They do not relish strangers visiting them."

This sounded likely. I remembered the vexation with which Maspero, my tutor, had greeted the arrival of the flier carrying Delia. With her had been three yellow-robed, scarlet-roped men—and they had all three been dead.

He leaned forward. "Perhaps, if you told me the name and identity of the sick man...?"

Now it was my turn to pause. Information. The Todalpheme were avaricious for news of all kinds. A mistake now—in all sober truth the fate of Vallia trembled on what I said, hung there, stark and brutal before me.

I said: "It is the Emperor of Vallia."

"Ah." He pushed back in his carved chair and smiled. He glanced at the bag of treasure. "One bag of gold is an insult."

"So that is it. You are greedy."

He flushed. "Take care, rast, lest you regret hasty words."

All I had learned as a good Kregan warred within me with myself. I have a nature. My nature has to be quashed. The Todalpheme are sacrosanct; no sane man will raise a hand against them. But what of tradition, what of the truth of the question when a great empire may run red with blood? Where lay my duty now?

He watched me slyly. He saw the twitch of my hand toward the rapier hilt. He smiled wetly. "The fate of a man who raises a hand against a Todalpheme is awful—awful."

Was my just punishment if I violated the basic tenet of this solemn Kregan belief worthy payment for saving the life of an emperor, of preventing the torrents of blood that would follow? Would my Delia thank me for destroying myself in saving her father?

The decision was mine.

Ten

"In Aphrasöe You Will Find Only Death!"

Everything so far had gone with such amazing ease I should have been warned. Khokkak the Meddler should have been heeded. Trip the Thwarter should have been propitiated. We had spirited the emperor away from his would-be murderers. We had arrested the insidious work of the poison so that he still lived. We had tracked down the clues and found our way here to where the secret would be told. And now we were thwarted by this cunning, greedy, deceitful onker of a man.

He was after the gold, surely, and information, and he did not intend to let me leave alive, I fancied.

What could I say to move him in a spirit of conciliation?

If it was a mere matter of gold...

"If you require gold, then you must know it is yours for the asking. Vallia will pour out her treasures for the life of her emperor."

"Yet you bring one miserable bag."

The answer to that was easy.

"It is but an earnest."

"Ah!" The avariciousness in him was plain now, plain and ugly and degrading. "How soon can you bring more? Much more?"

"As soon as the emperor is well—"

"Not good enough."

"There is no time to be lost. You have my word."

"Words are cheap among the canaille." He used another word; but that is what he meant. I kept my seat. For the moment I had postponed the decision that would destroy me.

"What more do you want of me—treasure—?"

"You could start by showing proper respect and by calling me master, or san, or Akhram."

I nodded. I'd have to force the words out as a constipated man forces himself; but for the sake of Vallia I'd eat humble pie. And, not really for Vallia. For my Delia...

"Listen to me, Akhram. Tell me plain. I can have as much gold as you can imagine brought to you. But it must be clear to you that it is not with me now. Yet the emperor must be treated at once." Then I put a little snap into my words. "If you do not tell me and the emperor dies, you will get nothing."

He put a hand to his mouth at this, pondering the truth.

I gave him no chance to bluster on. I blustered a trifle myself. "Take the gold we have. Save the emperor. Then you will have the reward of a good deed well done, besides the treasure." I leaned a little closer and my hand dropped to the rapier hilt. "You say you are not as other Todalpheme, and I see that to be true. You have threatened to kill me. But I am not as other men of Kregen. A Todalpheme has little respect from me if he does not act as a Todalpheme is expected to act. If the emperor dies, I think you may die, also."

He started up, pushing away from the table, his heavy face red, from shock or indignation or fear, I did not know and didn't damned well care. I had made no conscious decision; I still sought to sway him with words, even if the words were brutal and barbed and vicious.

"I am sacrosanct!"

I ignored him and he sat down, shaking his hands falling from my sight beneath the table edge. "You know of Vallia. I am aware of that. You know that Vallia has beaten the Empire of Hamal. I do not think you would relish a great armada from Vallia wreaking just vengeance on you."

He had regained his composure. "You would not find the swods or the officers who would lay a hand on a Todalpheme!" He sneered the words, getting his courage back, vicious.

So I saw the answer.

I stood up and glared down on him and all the old intemperate evil power must have flooded into my face, for he started back in his chair, unable to rise, all his new-found bravado fled.

"Listen to me, Akhram! If you do not instantly tell me where we may find the Savanti and so save our emperor, then a great armada will come from Vallia. They will not attack the Akhram. They will leave the Todalpheme alone. But they will utterly destroy your island of Bet-Aqsa. All your people will be slain or enslaved—save a few. Save a few who will know why this calamity has fallen on them. They will bear hatred in their hearts for those who caused their destruction. Who do you think will receive that enmity? Whom will they blame for the calamity that will have fallen on them? Who by refusing to help a sick and dying man wrought such terrible retribution upon the heads of an innocent people?"

I glowered down, hard, horrible, hateful. "Think on, Akhram. Your people will refuse to work for you, to support you. They may not kill you; but they will not lift a finger to help you. What will your life be like then? Think on, old man, and be quick about it."

He pointed a trembling finger at me. "You—you devil!"

"Aye! Believe it. And tell me."

"There will be a reckoning... But I will instruct my people. Your emperor must be blindfolded and we will take him—"

About to bellow a vicious: "No! We will take him!" I paused. I had pushed. There would be another way, now, than that of violence, which I abhor.

"The doctor cannot leave his side."

"Our doctors can attend him."

"Then ready your flier and hurry."

The commotion that broke outside the door made my lips rick back. The cunning leem probably had a bell-push hidden beneath his chair. Various combinations of rings gave his instructions. Even an onker could guess what he had rung his minions and his guards for.

"You have boasted and threatened, cramph." His heavy flushed face ran sweat. He descended to insults, also, which is not the way of your true Todalpheme of Kregen. He had waited his time, and now: "Now it is my turn! My people will deal with you utterly. You are alone and although you wear swords I do not think you will stand against my Oblifanters and their swods. Whatever the truth of your story, no one in the whole world will ever see you or hear of you again."

"You make a mistake."

"My mistake was in listening to you. Yetch!" He was suddenly shaking in a paroxysm of fresh rage, bloated, purple, rising to confront me. "You dare to threaten me! Calling yourself a devil! Should the Empire of Vallia lay waste to the whole of Bet-Aqsa and the stupid canaille refuse to bring their offerings to the Akhram and to work for us, why do you think that would concern me? Do you think there are no other places I might go? An Akhram? Sacrosanct?"

"The Ice Floes of Sicce for one."

"Now my people are here—listen to them and the clink of their steel. You are doomed, rast, and I shall spit; but not on your grave, for no mortal man will know where that is."

The door opened. It did not burst in. It opened, all the same, with a pretty smash. The Oblifanters and the guards would tramp in, now, and we'd have a right merry set-to. All my plans had gone wrong—

"Where d'you want these, my king!" bellowed an enormous voice.

Kytun bounced through. In his lower left and right arms he carried two squirming soldiers, almost crushed against his massive ribs. His upper left arm was lifted and his broad hand gripped a writhing Hikdar, his fancy uniform flying, kicking and yelling aloft in the air. In Kytun's right hand a djangir gleamed. The very short very broad sword of Djanduin shone brilliantly, clean steel, without a trace of blood.

Over Kytun's head an Oblifanter sailed up, to land with an almighty crash on the floor between us, so I knew Turko was busy out there. Seg and Inch pushed through, their faces grim.

"Todalpheme!" said Seg. He looked disgusted. "We kept out of sight and sailed in on time. By the Veiled Froyvil, my old dom, this place stinks!"

"If these are Todalpheme, judging by what I saw," put in Inch, "stink is too mild a description."

"Aye," I said. "This man here, this Akhram, will show us where away lies Aphrasöe. He has been told what will happen if he does not."

At the ruination of his plans Akhram shrank. He shook.

"You would not lay a hand on me!" He shrieked, in mortal fear, for the first time in his life, no doubt. "Defilers!"

"Not on you," I said. "Remember. Ponder what I have said."

I was not proud in a loose sense of what I had done. I remembered other Akhrams I had known, and their worth did not excuse my treatment of this worthless example. But he, like the scorpion, only followed his own nature. But, being a man and not a scorpion, and being bound by vows, and being in a high position of trust and privilege, he should have made better attempts to curb his own villainy, and acted his part as an Akhram.

So I leaned, as I used to lean, a little, to my shame.

"And do not think there is a single place in the whole wide world of Kregen where you could scuttle that the arm of Dray Prescot, Prince Majister of Vallia, could not reach out and find you—and, finding, punish!"

Well, it was petty, I'll allow. But the fellow had mizzled me. Delia's father lay dying, and this kleesh had done what he had done, despite my earnest endeavors at conciliation. Ends and means, means and ends, they are all the same according to the wise divines of Opaz, for one creed alone, and so I stand branded as an evil-doer. But, would I not take upon myself all the evil of two worlds for the sake of Delia?

So, after naked, brutal force had been used, and not against the Todalpheme, to overwhelm them in the person of this Akhram, by the threat of violence only, he gave us the directions we coveted. I did not think he lied. Lying would bring upon his head his total destruction. He knew this. If the emperor died because of his treachery in giving us the wrong directions, he knew we would return and great would be our fury.

All the same, as we soared up, the malicious cramph had the last word.

He tilted that heavy face back, and the redness staining his forehead and cheeks glistened in the waning lights of Antares. He shouted up, gloating, crowing, cocksure we were doomed.

"The Savanti will not welcome you! You will never return! If you go you are dead men!"

Then, with a triumphant cackling screech, he shrilled:

"In Aphrasöe you will find only death!"

Eleven

Of Weapons and Colors—and the Scorpion

"In Aphrasöe you will find only death!"

Threats of that kind had little effect on our company—By Krun! they had no effect whatsoever. We were a roughneck, reckless, harebrained bunch, and with the end of our long journey in sight, any tension that might have been expected did not show itself as these tough warriors—old and young—skylarked and joked, treating the whole expedition as a giant escapade put on for their especial benefit. Concern over the life of the emperor had sensibly diminished now we were so close to the Pool of Baptism where he would be cured.

No doubts or thoughts of failure entered anyone's head.

The laggard burs flew past. The large island on which Aphrasöe was situated rose out of the sea before us as the Suns of Scorpio rose, blinding in their opaz radiance, streaming their mingled lights of jade and ruby across the sea and the black mass ahead. What perils awaited us there, in that mysterious island? No sense in anticipating problems; they would find us quickly enough. So, thoughtfully, competently, like the old professional fighting hands we were, we prepared for what the future might bring.

Over the coast we soared. The sea and the land looked like any sea and land ought to look—and yet, and yet this was the island of the Savanti!

Somewhere on this island I had for the very first time been dumped down on Kregen. Floating along the Sacred River Aph in a leaf boat, with only an enormous scorpion for crew. That was long and long ago, by Zair—before I even knew of Zair, or the Krozairs—or Delia.

The powers of the superhuman Savanti were immense, unknown,

frightening. I made up my mind for the umpteenth time that we must fly straight for the Pool, following the course of the River Zelph rather than the Aph, cure the emperor, and then high tail it out of Aphrasöe, if we could. There would be no hanging about, no stopping for Lahals with the Savanti. I would not go swinging in the Swinging City. There was too much at stake—and, anyway, I had found my paradise elsewhere. Well, men grow corn for Zair to reap, as they say. Again and again I went over the plan. Delia knew what it was necessary to do at the Pool itself. All my magnificent fighting men—aye! and their ladies also—knew what must be done.

So we flew through the brightening morning air and the red and the green mingled and fused into that glorious opaline radiance, streaming golden and clean from Antares through the sweet air of Kregen.

The coastline itself trended away and showed no sign that we could see of life or habitation, and we saw not one sail. But, as we flew inland, the ground swarmed with life. I own I felt amazement.

Down there, as we flew over, huge herds of animals in myriad forms of animal life grazed and ran and heaved in a long rolling sea of heaving rumps and wicked upflung horns. We hung over the rails and watched the hunters, leem and graint, chavonth and strigicaw, a whole mad medley of the savage animals of Kregen, all roaming the plains and valleys and jungly defiles below. Just about every kind of animal I had encountered on Kregen passed below, and many more that I saw there for the first time. Kregen is so marvelous a world and so populated with wonders that it is sometimes difficult to remember that this incredible Earth of ours has probably almost as vast a range of different forms. But on Kregen the varieties have been wildly intermingled, and the artful hand of artificial genetic breeding has been at work, and the combinations of animals—and humans—appear much more startling.

Wild animals would from time to time cross the high passes of the craggy mountain ring that surrounds and protects the Swinging City. I had hunted graint with the Savanti, carefully packing them up and sending them back over the mountains unharmed. Now I saw the reality of the enormous profusion of life. It seemed that examples of every kind of animal sported below.

Oby licked his lips. "What a sight!" he stared down, hungrily.

"We shall not starve, that is sure," said Turko. "Seg with his great bow could feed us single handed."

Vegetarianism is known and practiced on Kregen; but if a man is starving and a fat deer passes by—well, a man must live unless he wishes to surrender to the fate high ideals may bring. It is an argument that continues.

"Look!" yelled Oby. And then, as I had taught him, amplifying any sighting report: "Rapas! A whole village of 'em!"

We soared over the Rapa village, and the vulture-headed diffs barely bothered to glance up at our vollers. We passed over other communities of diffs: Chuliks, and Ochs, Brokelsh, Khibils, Fristles, of Blegs and Numims, of Pachaks and Undurkers. As we sailed on over the vastly extensive expanses below we passed many and many a village and town inhabited by one or another of the races of Kregen.

Now this, as you will surmise, puzzled me mightily. I also noticed, and thought I was not mistaken, that the people down there would not look up at us, were frightened to look up, as though the sight of a flying craft in the sky would damn and doom them.

But nothing must stand in our way. Nothing. We flew on.

Mountains rose in a white dazzlement ahead.

I shook my head as Delia glanced at me.

"I think not. They do not wear the same appearance as the mountains ringing the Swinging City."

Vangar spread out the maps. He sucked in his cheeks.

"I would suggest, my prince, that in those mountains yonder rises this fabulous River Zelph."

I felt very conscious that we were a band exploring unknown territory. But I agreed with Vangar. "And we follow that river down. We do not deviate."

Then it was time for those closest, who would be in command, as it were, to come across from their own fliers and to sit with us to a sumptuous meal in Delia's voller. We looked after ourselves, for we had brought the minimum number of servants; of slaves, of course, there was no sign.

When the palines in their silver dishes were being passed around Nath the Needle came in. He looked grave. We quieted our quick talk at once.

"My prince!" he began. "My princess!" My heart sank. "The emperor is sinking. All my art—" He spread his hands in self-disgust at his own lack of skill.

At once, bravely, Delia said: "You have done all you can, Nath. How soon—is it—can you tell?"

Before Nath could answer, I, foolish and loving, burst in with: "Sink me! We'll reach the Pool before your father is any worse. He will be well again and then we'll fly back to Vondium. I'm waiting to see the faces of those rasts who tried to poison him."

"Aye!" said Seg, forcefully. "That Ashti Melekhi will get one almighty shock, as Erthyr the Bow is my witness."

I took comfort from Seg's words. He does not often swear on the name of the Supreme Being of Erthyrdrin.

The others broke in, also, roundly declaring we'd reach the Pool well in time. I warmed to them. Comrades, all! If any power of mortal man or woman could get the Emperor of Vallia to the Pool of Baptism, then, surely, that power flew here with me!

Nath nodded, saying: "I think there will be time..."

I stood up, crushing down a last paline and I looked around the table on my comrades. I felt the silly, choked up feeling that betrays me for a weakling. But I spoke up harshly enough, grating the words out.

Believe me, I did not overlook the fact that the emperor could easily die before we could save him. Then I would have to return to Vallia and take charge. I fancied I would have to do that, although detesting the work. Some men I knew would be amazed that I did not throw the emperor overboard at once and sail back to claim the throne. And, there was no guarantee in this bitter life that any rescue could succeed. Had I not raced to save my daughter Velia? Had I not failed?

So I spoke pungently to the assembled company, knowing they would pass my words on to everyone in the expedition.

"Remember. Nothing must stop us from winning through to the Pool. Once the emperor is cured, we may return. No casualty must deter us. Let no man, beast, god or wizard stand in our way. *Nothing!*"

They roared at this, determined, dedicated, and Nath the Needle, looking at me, nodded as if to say that, well, perhaps his hopes were strong enough, the Emperor would live.

And, as for me—brave bluff words from an inspired leader? Onkerish words from an onker of onkers, a get onker? Reaction to my own dark thoughts? But, all in the fullness of time, I suppose, every man gets his comeuppance. I am not too sure about women, though...

Of only one thing I remained sure. These my comrades would get through to the Pool of Baptism if it was humanly possible. No matter what happened, they'd go on. After the emperor was cured the Savanti might rail—the deed would be done.

With a few final words that reinforced my orders—for, make no mistake, what I told this roaring reckless rout of ruffians to do was an order, hard and incisive—we parted to kit up for the final run in to the Pool.

We must go well-armed and accoutred, for I did not forget the ravening monsters Delia and I had met on the struggle to reach the sacred grove and the rocky overhang and the Pool.

In our stateroom Delia pulled out the long length of brilliant scarlet cloth. Well, now... I made myself smile, and smiling always comes easily for me with my Delia, and I said, lightly: "The scarlet of Strombor and the yellow cross of my Clansmen—yes, my heart, I think it appropriate, for they are the colors of Vallia, also."

"And the orange and grey of your fearsome Djangs."

"Our fearsome Djangs. Of course. And the red and white of Valka. And, for the place grows dearer to me, the yellow and blue of Zamra. I think," I said, twisting up the scarlet around my waist and drawing it through my legs and tucking the end securely in, and then picking up the broad lesten-hide belt with the dull silver buckle. "I rather think we look like popinjays, these latter times."

She laughed; but she, too, understood the importance of colors and badges and signs. In the midst of the dust and hurly burly of a battle, a man needs a flag to rally to. Colors and badges tell you whom to kill and whom not to kill. That is a matter of importance for anyone, and particularly to anyone who wishes to live for very long on Kregen. So my Delia laughed at my words; but her thoughts were with the sick man, her father. I chided her.

"Once he is well again we will fly back to Vallia. There all those who sought to profit by his death will receive the nasty shock Seg and the others promise. There are loyal people in Vallia, still—"

"Oh, yes. But few, I think, very few."

"Once the emperor is seen to be fit and well the waverers will suddenly realize what side they are on. Anyway," I went on with a rush of confidence, "this new Chief Pallan your father has brought forward to such power, this Kov Layco; he will keep things running while we are away. He has shown a misjudgment of character in appointing Ashti Melekhi—but that will be forgiven him, I daresay, if he is as skilled and clever as is said."

"He is clever, no doubt of that. I try to like him."

"Oh?"

"You are so often away, Dray. It is difficult. Once it is all settled you will tell me this dread secret that you feel will—will—I tremble to say it—will come to—"

"Do not say it, my heart. Nothing can destroy our love." I believed it, passionately. "But I do fear to tell you. I feel—I feel the burden I shall impose on you is—" My thoughts were muddled. I had kept putting off and putting off telling Delia of my origins. To her, I was a savage clansman, with a strange underspirit that did not come from the plains of Segesthes. But—Earth! How could I tell her I came from a star in the sky she could barely make out? How could she possibly believe in a world which possessed only one sun? What sense was there in a world with only one moon! And, how could any sensible person of Kregen believe in a world that contained only apims as men and women, where diffs were unknown? My story would be taken as the ravings of a madman. I ploughed on somehow: "You will find it hard to believe me. But I shall tell the truth. I swear it. I swear it by Zair."

"I shall believe—"

Turning for the arms rack I groped around and took up the scabbarded Krozair longsword with the plain strappings that would secure it to my back, the hilt comfortably jutting over my shoulder by the blue-fletched arrow shafts.

I remember, through the maze of impending agony through which I

would have to go in trying to convince Delia and my family that I was not
a raving lunatic, I sought a little tawdry comfort in thinking of ordinary
things. I thought I would have to see about a proper supply of the rose-red
feathers of the Zim korf for my Archers of Valka, and I also remember
thinking I was growing far too accustomed to wearing the longsword
sticking up over my back instead of jutting almost parallel with the ground
at my left side. I was thinking I would like to see my new aerial cavalry of
Valka mounted on flutduins performing against those rascally flutsmen. A
torrent of vague thoughts poured through my mind.

So I turned again to pick up the superb shortsword Hap Loder had
brought me, a present from the Clansmen of Viktrik, the new clan who
had given me obi, a blade built in Zenicce to the very highest standards,
a blade to shame any Genodder of the Eye of the World, and I took the
chunkrah-hide and gold scabbard up into my hand and a red and brown
scorpion, glinting, ran from under the arms rack.

I felt sick.

A scorpion!

Symbol of the forces of the Savanti or the Star Lords, symbol of those
powers that could hurl me about Kregen or banish me back to Earth, contemptuously tossing me about like a puppet, that scorpion stood on its
eight hairy legs, waving its vicious stinging tail at me in admonishing
authority.

Not now! Please Zair! Not now!

But the blue haze dropped upon me, and I felt the coldness, striking
through like the clammy hand of Death himself, and the scorpion grew
and bloated, radiant with the blue fire, and everything spun away in two
worlds, and engulfed in agony I fell into nothingness.

Twelve

Strife Among the Star Lords

This nothingness differed from those other nauseating nothingnesses in
which I had suffered so often before.

Always, so it seemed to me, I had been snatched away by the blue-limned
radiance of the scorpion, caught up, whirled through nothingness, spun
through an achingly cold void, smashed down with a hint of the red fire
of Antares, slapped head over heels, all naked like a newborn infant, sent
toppling helplessly into a new world.

But, this time...

A difference.

I was stark naked, and that I expected.

I was no longer in the voller and that, too, I expected.

I tried to open my eyes and realized they were open. I could see and yet, seeing, see nothing.

The hint of echoes, as of the rushing of a distant torrent far below ground, pent between eon-old walls never opened to sunlight... The whisper of insane voices cackling over the edge of a world, pringling clammily against my skin... I felt the coldness touch me, and ebb, and return. I saw—I saw blue whorls of light gyrating, and, across them and irradiating them with wheels of crimson, red streaks of fire pulsating. The blue was a pale, luminescent blue, and the sharp blue and the crimson struggled for supremacy. And—green! An ominous tinge of green washed across the lower corner of the firmament, clashing with the struggling blue and crimson.

Where had I seen blue and crimson before, recently? My head rang with soundless echoes. I struggled, and did not move.

The sky colors fought and writhed, waxed and waned.

Yellow! Where was the yellow of Zena Iztar?

I bellowed out: "Zena Iztar!" and only a dolorous croak passed my lips, my corded throat bursting with effort, a croak like a frog with hernia.

Blue of that brilliant beckoning luminosity was the color used by both the Savanti and the Star Lords when they sent the Scorpion after me. Yellow had been used triumphantly by Zena Iztar, as I believed, to save me. As for that mysterious woman, who on Earth called herself Madam Ivanovna, I knew nothing—or practically nothing. She came and went at her own whim. Glorious she was, aye, that is true. She showed no fear of the Star Lords or the Savanti; but if she worked for them or against them, or for one or the other, I did not know.

I fell.

As I fell I remembered—remembered Zena Iztar and the Kroveres of Iztar, and the crimson flag and the blue device.

I fell. All naked and bruised, I fell into a thorn-ivy bush and I cursed by the foul anatomy of Makki-Grodno. What was happening I had no idea; all I wanted to do was get back to the voller and Delia and go cure her father.

By an effort of will I had succeeded in erecting a kind of structure of deceits so as partially to mollify the anger of the Star Lords. I had managed to convince them I should stay on Kregen and not be dispatched to Earth. I had also, after some success along the way, like an onker resisted them, willfully, and so been banished to Earth for twenty-one horrendous years.

Resistance might once again cause another banishment.

What Maspero, my tutor in the Swinging City, had told me did make a kind of sense. He had said: "Only by the free exercise of your will can you contrive the journey." That journey had taken me for the first time from Earth—I was literally up a tree at the time, being chased by savages—to sail my leaf boat down the sacred River Aph and after the welcome departure of the scorpion crew to discover a little of what life on Kregen was like and how I would measure up to it—and at last so reach Aphrasöe. Could the Savanti not draw me at will, then? Their monstrous creature in the sacred Pool of Baptism had flung me back to Earth, and it had been the Everoinye, the Star Lords, who had picked me to labor for them about their mysterious purposes on Kregen.

So I exerted my will.

I roared it out, and produced only a croaking sighing like a pair of bellows shot through by musketry. "I will stay on Kregen! I will rejoin my wife in the voller! You have no powers over me, Star Lords! Savanti—I would have worked joyously for you; but you disdained me! Why torture me now? Why?"

And, all the time, I looked for the welcome yellow to gush up among the gyrating colors staining the firmament, and no yellow came.

From the susurrating wash of background noises, from the color-dripping sky, from the mingling scents and perfumes, past the thorn-ivy bush, from everywhere and from nowhere, a voice spoke to me. A voice spoke to me.

"Insolent onker! You are a mere mortal man—do not presume."

I tried to bellow back, and merely wheezed.

I thought. I tried to hurl my thoughts; and the voice crashed down, masterful, dominating.

"I command you now, Dray Prescot. And I demand from you more than you have hitherto given—more than you appear willing to give. But that more I will have." The voice whined suddenly, and became incoherent. Then: "Hearken unto me!"

And, another voice, harsher, deeper: "The man is ours!"

"You do not use him to the full!"

"We use him as we see fit. He is, after all, but a mere mortal man."

"And fit therefore to be driven—"

"He is often stubborn. He is not an easy man—"

"I would drive him! I would—" Again that acrid voice became incoherent. I listened, my mouth dry, my eyes fairly starting from my head, and my backside jabbed thick with the thorn-ivy needles.

This could not be the Savanti, arguing with the Star Lords!

Could it?

The thorn-ivy needles jabbed me cruelly and I rolled away, cursing, feeling harsh rock and stones beneath me, broken twigs, the detritus of a wild animal's lair.

Brittle bones crunched under my hands as I struggled to rise.

"We wish him—" continued the second voice.

The acid voice, the voice that had spoken first and so allowed me a listening post, illuminating with sound the black silent recesses, that voice that kept wavering as though the speaker strove to pierce through the tumult of a tempest, lashed back. "I shall run him now!"

"Not so! He works well—when he does work—"

"Does he know—?"

"Of course not! How could he? He is apim. Apim."

"Then perhaps I shall let him know a little—" The bitter voice trailed. Suddenly I found myself urging the voice to return. He'd tell me what, the rast?

These were not Savanti. I held that conviction with sudden deep resolution. Star Lords. They were the Everoinye.

"He is still too soft. The knowledge might destroy him—"

"I am prepared to take that chance."

I stood up at last and shook my fist at the gory viridian dance of colors against the sky. "You'd take the chance, you kleesh! With my hide! With my sanity!"

Well, that was a mistake.

Like a blind lashing up on a runaway roller, I opened my eyes anew, and stood up, and, lo! I stood on a wide and dusty plain, the thorn-ivy bush at my side, and before me men and women fought among themselves.

I took a breath of sweet Kregan air.

This was more like old times!

A quick glance aloft showed me blue sky—and a whorling diminishing struggle between the blue and the red. And—and! A long beautiful streak of yellow coiled and drifted away into laypom and lemon and so vanished into the clear blue vault of the sky. I let rip a great sob of thankfulness. The yellow, so fragile, creeping in, told me Zena Iztar was at last aware.

I knew I had been brought here—wherever here was—to rescue some wight among that struggling throng, to preserve him or her for the pleasure of the Everoinye. I had served the Star Lords in this fashion before.

Or, so I believed.

I took one step forward.

And blue radiance dropped about me, and I tumbled head over heels, gasping, falling upwards, and so stood with a thump upon a high rampart atop a lofty tower, with a great city spread beneath me. Boulevards and kyros, avenues and temples, spread out beneath the glitter of the suns. And the city burned. Dull wafts of brown smoke rose from the bright buildings. Hordes of crazed people fled in every direction, wildly, not caring where they fled. The smell of blood and fire cloaked the doomed city. From the air echelons of warriors, all steel and bronze and leather, flying their winged saddle-beasts of war, swooped mercilessly down, casting death before them. The beat of the wings sounded the death knell of the city. Fire, destruction, desolation—from that high tower I looked on the casting down of a city.

Where, in all this violence, was I to find the wight I was to rescue? Or, failing to rescue, to find myself packed headlong back to Earth?

Again, I took one foolish step forward, and the light changed.

The crimson beat in, drowning the blue. In crimson flakes of fire I was borne up, whirled headlong about, sent crashing down. I felt the heaving deck of a swordship beneath me and saw the banks of sweating rowers pulling, saw the tangled heap of striped sails about the mainmast, the severed rigging, the varter bolts embedded in the wood of deck and bulwarks, the smashed and splintered scantlings where varter-flung rocks had wreaked their destruction. Up in the bows both below and above the fore-platform where the varter lay scattered in useless shattered timbers and sinews, the frenzied struggle battered on between men who cut and hacked and slipped in blood and shrieked and died, their weapons fouled and glistening in the opaz radiance of Antares. A varter bolt flew past my ear. Fierce bearded men with golden rings in their ears and tall golden-feathered helmets, their eyes alight with the joy of killing, their scale armor glittering, bore down howling on me.

Whom to rescue on the command of the Star Lords? I bent to snatch up a fallen sword—and the crimson light trembled, and faded, and gushed deeply, and was gone and the yellow light limned me, drenching me in golden glory, and I tumbled full length into that damned thorn-ivy bush.

Bellowing aloud that Makki-Grodno's diseased intestines would provide a capital sleeping bag for Star Lord, for Savanti, for whomever sought to drag me away from the voller and Delia, I pulled out of the thorn-ivy bush, stung to blazes.

The struggling mass of people had vanished from the dusty plain. The doomed city no longer existed. The swordship had gone.

I stood alone upon that dusty arid plain, stark naked, prickled by sharp thorn-ivy spines, and I looked about on nothing save dust.

"By Zair!" I roared, shaking my fist at the sky. And then I could not think of anything relevant to say. There was too much pent up within me. I had no real idea of what had been going on. I turned three hundred and sixty degrees and saw nothing save that dusty plain and the thorn-ivy bush.

So I stood, fuming, filled with an enormous baffled rage—and, also fully aware of my ridiculous position.

A voice ghosted in from nowhere, from everywhere, riding the radiance, ringing sweetly from the distant sky, fading.

"Go north, Dray Prescot! North. This is all I could contrive, all I can do..."

The voice of Zena Iztar! Yes, I knew that voice. That mysterious woman who could charm men and animals to a magic sleep, that woman of whom I hoped for much, that woman who seemed to offer sanity in a universe of madness; well, she was trying to help. I felt sure of that. But...

"By Vox, Krun, Djan and Kaidun!" I bellowed. I stamped my foot. "What an infernal waste of time!"

"Fight, Dray Prescot. Go North. Jikai, Ver Dray! There is nothing else..."

The sweet voice faded and was gone and I stood alone under the opaline radiance of the Suns of Scorpio.

Useless to pretend I had not been profoundly shaken by that unearthly experience. Unearthly—Unkregan! I had been a witness to a titanic struggle among superhumans, seeing a tiny corner of the veil of mystery lifted. All was not sweetness and light among the Star Lords, then...

Maybe an old paktun rogue like Dray Prescot could use that information. Yes, I thought, where werstings squabble the gyp gets the bone.

I stuck my old beak of a nose into the north, pulled a last spine from my rump, and set off on my bare feet.

The more I thought about these recent occurrences the more I fancied the Savanti were not involved. They were mere mortal men, superhuman, admitted; but men. They were the tiny remnant of the Sunset People who had once dominated Kregen. Their buildings lay in ruination in many lands. They it was who had constructed the Dam of Days and built the Grand Canal. Now they lived in the Swinging City and sought to train Savapims to work for the betterment of Kregen. No, I did not think the Savanti had been involved in that cosmic struggle.

I plodded on.

The air remained warm, the suns shone, a few birds wheeled about above and you may be sure I favored them with a close scrutiny although their presence comforted me. They would not fly about here if there were no game to hunt. Mind you, I might be the Sunday dinner they had in mind; but I was used to that, and by certain signs near the thorn-ivy bushes I knew small animals lived in this waste that appeared a wilderness but was not to those who knew how to survive. So I trundled on northward, trying to be philosophical.

By Vox! But it was hard. What were my people doing now? How was Delia reacting to my disappearance from the voller? She would shake her head and sigh, and say, no doubt, more or less: "So he's off again." I thought of the gaudy array of weaponry I had been in the act of belting on. By Krun! I could do with some of those edged and pointed weapons now. Particularly, I needed a bow.

The bow I had intended to take had been a good greenwood bow of Erthyrdrin, its manufacture superintended by Seg. Although a kov he would indulge his passion for creating better and better bowstaves, working with his hands. The stave, like any bowstave, looked lumpy and sullen, following the grain of the wood, cunningly built to avoid any weakness. But it looked marvelous in the eyes of a bowman. Bows that look flashy and wonderful do not always work as well as those that follow the grain; they never do. With that bow, six feet six inches, a yard in the pull, I could cast an arrow and fetch up my supper with no trouble.

So, perforce, I stomped along in a foul humor and picked up a sharp stone and carried the thing in my fist and looked about with a fine predatory eye.

The ravening monsters of the air and land that ringed and protected the central mass of mountains would scarcely allow a naked unarmed man to pass. Thought had to be taken.

A black dot on the horizon almost directly on the back track attracted my immediate suspicious attention. I stopped moving at once and crouched beside a thorn-ivy bush. I watched. The black lump came on, growing in size, pirouetting with the heat devils, lumping and parting, coalescing, gradually drawing nearer.

Soon I made out a riding animal carrying two persons.

The beast looked to be some kind of member of the trix family in that it had a blunt wicked head, six legs and a coat of coarse grayish hair. The riders—I whistled. The man was a numim lad, a lion-man, well built, glorious in the numim way with his great golden mane, hardy. The girl was a Fristle fifi, delicate, beautifully formed, charming, her slanted eyes and frolicsome tail eloquent of all that is best about the cat-people. They sat close together on the uncomfortable back of the six-legged animal and they were totally engrossed in each other.

Now numims and Fristles may sometimes get on well together, seeing that they are both of feline stock; and sometimes they spit and snarl and rick back their lips and tear great chunks out of each other. I had an inkling of what was going on here and although I did not smile—I did not forget the indignity and the sheer awful frustration of my predicament—I felt a little lift of my flinty old heart.

It has been my experience on Kregen that a man must make what he can of the situation in which he finds himself. Until I could rejoin Delia and my comrades I must work and fight to stay alive, and take an interest in all that occurred, trying to use events to my own advantage.

So, feeling an intruder, I stood up from the thorn-ivy bush and shouted: "Llahal, dom, domni. Llahal."

The stux whipped up in the lad's hand.

"Llahal, dom. You are apim. I bear you no grudge."

"Nor I, you."

"Shall we make pappattu?"

"Assuredly."

"I am Naghan—" Then, his manners catching up with him, he stuttered and started over. "You have the honor to be in the presence of Fimi Shemi-llifey. I am Naghan Mennelo ti Sakersmot."

"I am Dray Prescot."

"Now that we have made pappattu—" and here he put up his stux, so that he could finish the pappattu, which means, as you know, more than a mere formal introduction. "I would ask you why you wander alone and naked in these perilous parts."

The answer was glib. "My caravan was set upon by drikingers. And you?"

"We elope—" And then he stopped himself, and Fimi, his little Fristle fifi, giggled, and so I attempted to scrape up a smile. So wrapped up were they in their brave and foolhardy solution to their problem they barely heeded my own thin story.

"If you wish, we may continue our journey together." My eyes regarded his water bottle.

He shook his head. "As to the companionship, right gladly I welcome it, even though you have no weapons, for you look a fighting man and the Khirrs prowl hereabouts. But, as to the water... " He shook the bottle. The confounded thing was nearly as dry as my throat.

"As Oxkalin the Blind Spirit chances," I said, resigned.

"Oh, for a long cool drink of parclear!" sighed Fimi.

Naghan chided her. "When we reach Great Aunt Melimni she will welcome us and you may drink all the parclear in Ba-Domek."

Incautiously, always a garrulous onker, I said: "Ba-Domek?"

"Why," says this Naghan ti Sakersmot. "Do not tell me you do not know where you are?"

If the twin suns had fallen from the sky upon my foolish head I do not think I could have been more shattered. Of course I had assumed without thinking that I was still on the island of Aphrasöe. And, instead, I was somewhere else on the surface of Kregen! I felt my face going red and my eyes must have betrayed all the killing passion in me. This Naghan ti Sak-ersmot reined up, smartly, flinching, staring down at me, starting back.

"This is not," I got out in a strangled voice. "This is not the island of Aphrasöe?"

At this both young people shrieked and clapped their hands over their ears. Their young faces expressed extreme horror.

"Do not say that!" screeched Naghan. "Never! We have not heard! As I love Fimi—I shall cut you down!"

"Brace up, lad!" I bellowed. "If you do not tell me where I am or what is going on—for I admit I am lost—how can I know? Tell me of Ba-Domek."

Relief at their reaction to my use of the name Aphrasöe made me weak. I had thought—what a horror that would have been!

"Why," Naghan said, cautiously taking his hands from his ears and the imp had heard me clearly, right enough. "Why, this is Ba-Domek. The city of which you speak is a place forbidden."

Of course. Trust the Savanti to spread a little ghoulish rumor about the Swinging City. I would not press this young couple; but I felt sure they could retail grisly stories about the goings-on in Aphrasöe. So I was still on the island. Zena Iztar had managed to keep me here, at the least. I swallowed down, dry as a bone, for I could not spit.

"So you ride together. In that direction." My arm sliced down toward the north.

"Only for a ways. Then we turn off down the Valley of the Twin Spires. I feel confident of the way," he said, eagerly. "Even though I have ridden it but once before. Always, the way was through the River Feron's lowlands. This is a dangerous route."

"This city of which we do not speak. Where away lies that?"

"Down the other River," he said. That made sense.

Now I had to find where the river began—or where I could join it. I didn't care if it was the Aph or the Zelph.

In answer to my query he looked around the featureless horizon, undecided. He squinted up at the suns. He frowned.

Then: "I think, dom, I think—that away."

He pointed due north.

Thirteen

How Fimi Obtained Her Wedding Portion

For a space then, our ways would lie together.

The six-legged saddle animal, a gnutrix, walked along with that awkward swaying gait of the six-legged, and I tramped on alongside. The two young people made nothing of my nakedness and, partly, I suppose, that was because I was apim and they diff.

Their story was soon told. Miscegenation is not the true word for this kind of marriage across diff-boundaries, where the people in question are closely related. All the same, their own people were not happy; a chance meeting at a fair, the growing realization that a genuine love existed between them, the hostility of their families and, finally, elopement, all added up to this flight across the barren land to the sanctuary of Great Aunt Melimni's house—a fine villa with fountains and arbors,

Naghan confided with pride—situated in the best district of Lowerinsmot. This town, he said with just the hint of doubt, was situated perhaps a little too close to—and here he paused, and ran a hand around his collar. I asked more questions in a general way, and gathered that Naghan knew a fair amount of the geography of this part of Ba-Domek, being a traveling salesman of a sort. I gathered as much from what he did not say as the information he parted with that Aphrasöe did indeed lie at the center of the island surrounded by the ring of sheltering mountains. He confirmed that the island swarmed with animals and birds and diffs. There were few apims. No city of Homo sapiens like me was known. And, of course, of those within the Swinging City itself, nothing would induce Naghan to venture there. He knew what apims were, of course, and regarded me with a lively interest as the representative of a strange and exotic breed.

Always before when I had been summoned by the scorpion and been flung head over heels pell-mell to Kregen I had awakened stark naked, faced with the immediate problem of rescuing someone or other from pressing peril. So, this time, I kept an eye on these two elopers. I did not think I had been dragged from the voller for nothing; equally, I was aware that the circumstances this time were greatly different from anything that had gone before.

"As soon as you reach Lowerinsmot all our troubles will be over." Fimi clung to Naghan, speaking with perfect confidence.

They wore simple tunics of a flaxen color, and Fimi's was trimmed and hemmed with bright embroidery. They had a satchel with dried meats and fruits. Their only weapon, apart from a bronze knife, was the stux, and he handled the spear smartly enough but not, I judged, as a warrior. Traveling salesmen, he said his family were, going from village and town around the countryside. Sometimes there were fights; but few people like to pick a quarrel with a numim.

But for the two suns in the sky—and a fellow gets used to those pretty quickly—and the cat-girl and lion-man riding a shambling six-legged mount at my side, this dusty plain with its willy-willies and its scraps of thorny bushes might have existed on Earth. I might be trudging along on the planet of my birth. But that was dangerous nonsense. I was on Kregen. At any moment deadly danger could spring at us, seeking to rend us into bloody shreds. The wild animals of Kregen would make an Earthly tiger, or elephant, or crocodile turn tail and flee. Those savage beasts of Kregen would look on us all as tasty morsels for dinner. Three appetizers and a couple of mouthfuls, with blood running and white bones splintering. So, as we walked, we kept a sharp lookout.

"I do not fear the strigicaws," said Naghan stoutly. "And we can outrun the graints. As for leems—" He pursed up his lion-mouth, and gripped his stux.

Fimi shivered. "Leems are terrible," she whispered. "But if we meet the Khirrs—"

Looking back as I surveyed our rear and observed the track of our march, I said: "Whatever these Khirrs may be—there are riders following—"

Both Naghan and Fimi let out cries of consternation. The riders behind spurred on fiercely. I could make out the ungainly forms of gnutrixes like the one ambling beside me. The wink of weapons told plainly what was in store.

"Your family, Fimi!" shouted Naghan. "They have tracked us—they will not let you go."

"Ride on." I spoke calmly. So this was the reason I had been dumped down here. Useless to rage. Useless to question the value of these two young people against the value of the emperor of Vallia, The Star Lords kept to their own purposes and to them an emperor might weigh no more than a Fristle fifi. But, was not that a part of my philosophy, also?

Already I had seen the result of similar handiwork. Had not my rescue of two young people at the commands of the Star Lords produced a great genius king, a mad king, who sought to rule all the world he knew?

I gave the gnutrix a slap on its hairy hide and it bounded away. What future lay in store for the child of these two, this Naghan ti Sakersmot and his Fimi, what veiled destiny?

Scattered about on the brown plain at my feet lay stones. Rough, sharp-edged stones. There were four riders. Stooping, I took up four stones of suitable size and shape.

Always a show-off, I suppose, the old onker Dray Prescot.

The riders slackened speed a trifle as they came within range. That fancy showing off was like to cost me dear, for the fourth stone missed its mark. The last rider, seeing his three companions slipping senseless from their saddles, let out a great roar and lowered his head—whereat my rock missed him—and charged, his sword whirling.

Now, the racial weapon of the Fristles is the scimitar. I hopped and skipped and ducked the sweep of the blade. His booted foot slipped at first through my clutching fingers and I had to roll under his beast, taking an infernal banging from the middle pair of hooves, before I could rise wrathfully up on the far side and so grab his leg and hurl him from the saddle.

"You great onker!" I bellowed. "I don't want to hurt you."

He came up on a knee. Quick and vicious, Fristles, particularly in anything touching the honor and well-being of their women folk. Their family would be shamed by Fimi's elopement. He retained his scimitar. The long curved blade glistered finely in the streaming radiance.

"Nulsh!" he screamed. He jumped in, recovered from his fall, scything his blade wildly.

I was not deceived.

At the last second that savage swashing would abruptly turn into a smooth thrusting drive as the scimitar revolved around the center of its artful curve—and the blade would carve me neatly through.

Turko the Khamorro would have relished the situation.

Armed with the Disciplines of unarmed combat instilled by the Krozairs of Zy I was able to feint one way, go the other, and then—very nastily—rake back and so tweak the scimitar from his grip and, instead of running him through or bashing him over the head with his own blade, present the point smartly at his throat.

He lay on his back, hands gripped into the dust, glaring up in murderous fury.

The little exercise was not worth a "Hai Hikai," the unarmed man's equivalent to the swordsman's "Hai Jikai." I had given Duhrra, who had then been called Duhrra the Mighty Mangier, the Hai Hikai after our first encounter, for I recognized in the gigantic wrestler a true man. I had given Duhrra the "Hai Hikai!" not the swordsman's "Hai Jikai."

This is important upon Kregen.

If this Fristle flat on his back wished to make of this little spat a Jikai, he was welcome to try. I told him so. I finished: "But although I do not wish to slay you, and will not do so unless provoked beyond reason, I must warn you that Naghan and Fimi will depart in peace."

Three heavily armed Fristles slumbered in the dust and a fourth glowered up at me, flat on his back. I own it must have made a pretty sight. But I was in a hurry.

"Choose, dom. Let them go—or your life answers for it!"

He believed me. I suppose, looking back, I must have appeared to him a dark malignant demon, broad-shouldered, naked, sweat and dust molding those muscles of mine, ridged, iron-hard, turning me into the semblance of a man of iron. I felt only the need for speed.

In the end, believing me, he took himself off with his three companions. The four rode off on two gnutrixes, and one of them had fewer clothes than when he'd started and all had damned fewer weapons.

So, mounted up, rejoined with the two elopers, accoutred with scimitars and stuxes, we rode on.

Also, we had a filled water bottle and that, you may be sure, I kept under my hand.

"I shall return all these things, the gnutrixes, the weapons, the clothes, to you, Fimi, when we part. After all, they can be regarded as a wedding portion from your family."

Naghan laughed at this. "You are a strange man, Dray Prescot."

"Aye."

When the wind got up and blew devilish stinging sand into our faces we were glad to pull up the sand-scarves, although when I referred to my sand-scarf, calling it a hlamek as we do in South Zairia, my companions tittered and said it was a flamil. The Fristle from whom I had taken this flamil had been violently upset when I removed it from him. But I did not argue. From all I had heard and seen I was beginning to believe I might have stumbled upon another example of the work of the Savanti. All these jumbled animals and people, all living cheek-by-jowl around the outer portions of this large island—surely they must all have been brought here by the Savanti? Brought here to serve the purposes of the superhumans of the Swinging City?

Another explanation did not occur to me. Had it done so I would have seen it only as a further example of the cynicism of the Star Lords.

This island was in a mirrorlike way a representation of the rest of Kregen—or at least of the continental and island grouping of Paz. Diffs lived and worked and raised families here, Katakis prowled on their evil slaving raids, Chuliks maintained their strict Spartan training as mercenaries, along with all the other races who carried out the tasks for which they were best suited. Kings there were, too, so I heard, and wars and harryings and all the old evil ugly patchwork of human ambition and greed, along with the finer things of humanity, like art and love and religion and good works and music.

"Songs?" I said as we jogged along, the sand-storm blown away, the suns shining refulgently from a copper sky and the green of watered land showing on the horizon. "Aye, let us sing."

We took a good swig of the water bottle, for the greenery ahead promised, and started in. We sang *The Pachak with the Four Arms*, which is highly scurrilous, abusing a fine people I greatly admire. Fimi possessed a sweet singing voice, and Naghan roared out lustily and I joined my own bullfrog bellowings. A pang rose up to torture me—aye! The hostile territories... I remembered...

So I launched into *The Bowmen of Loh*, leaving out certain of the stanzas, and found they were not too familiar with that famous and notorious old song. Then we had *King Naghan His Fall and Rise* in honor of the Naghan who rode with us. We were just about halfway through *Golden Fur*, a famous and beautiful song of both Fristles and numims, when the chavonth leaped.

This chavonth was a fine large specimen of his family, a six-legged hunting cat of formidable destructive powers. His hide was all patterned in hexagons of blue, black and grey, and his whiskers bristled and his fangs glinted as he leaped.

Treacherous are chavonths. He had my poor gnutrix. The animal went down squealing, his hide ripped by razor claws.

I rolled and the scimitar came out and I took a wild swipe at the cat as it sprang. At the last minute I managed to get out of the way and the chavonth hit the grass beyond my head. Faster than the cat, so fast I almost overran it, I leaped in and brought the scimitar down in an angled slashing blow. The blade grated into the bones of the chavonth's neck as the bright blood welled. It let out a tremendous screech and wrenched around and the blade snapped clean across.

For a moment we hung together, the six paws with those slashing claws clashing beyond my back as I strained to keep its head away. Fimi had screamed and Naghan's gnutrix had bolted. But all the world was concentrated into that struggle as, locked together, muscle against muscle, the chavonth and I sought to wrest the mastery. The fangs dripped. The red tongue lolled. I thrust back, feeling my muscles strain, feeling the blood thump in my head, feeling all the savagery that had been contained and repressed within me over the past days surging up, bright red, bestial, deadly.

Clamped together, we thrashed across the trampled grass beneath the small bluff where the chavonth had lurked. With every sinew straining, holding him back, my fists gripped around his throat, I pushed his head back and with my leg hooked about his body, hauled him in to me so that his claws could not disembowel. As it was he took a long raking chunk of skin and flesh away, and my blood dripped.

Then, with a last final, bestial effort, a great surging thrusting of bursting muscles, I smashed his head back and the chavonth's neck snapped across where the stupid broken scimitar blade jagged out.

Flinging the corpse from me I stood back. I drew in huge draughts of Kregen's sweet air. I dashed the sweat from my ugly old face. I know I was wearing that frightful devil's mask plastered in blood and sweat across my features.

"By Vox!" I said. "That was close."

"Give thanks to Farilafristle," said Fimi, shaking, her eyes large and horrified. She had stopped screaming and yet, for all her brave words, she turned with a sob of thankfulness from me and the chavonth corpse as Naghan came racing back, flogging his mount unmercifully.

"I give you the Jikai, Dray Prescot." He spoke gravely, dismounting and helping Fimi down.

"As to that," I said. "I must walk again, by Krun."

Gods and goddesses and spirits come in all shapes and sizes on Kregen. Few people bother overmuch which deity is sworn by or appealed to, so long as their own beliefs are not crudely touched. So, collecting the gear I thought necessary and leaving the two corpses, the gnutrix and the chavonth, we set off again through this new tangled wooded country. The rips in my hide would heal; but they smarted sharply.

"Sooner a chavonth than a Khirr," said Naghan. He held his stux at the ready. His flamil rested under his chin. He looked down at me. "Also, apim, it is best to have your flamil handy. Be ready to draw it up over your face instantly if you see a Khirr."

"What? Do they freeze with a look?"

"No—they are no Gengulas of legend. They are real. They spit."

The way became easy after that and we spent five or six nights in comfort, with ample fresh meats and fruit. We were beset on a number of occasions; but fought through. In the process I acquired a knife, a miserable thing; but better than nothing. Gradually Naghan became more nervy. Fimi rubbed the fingers of her left hand over the atra she wore in the form of a bracelet on her right wrist. We were camping in a cave, and she looked about, wondering about a fire. "It is all—so dark and mysterious when the suns sleep and the moons are tardy."

About to make some hard common-sense reply, I hesitated, for Naghan, too, was rubbing his atra. He wore his amulet slung around his neck. I have spoken little of the atras, the amulets and lucky charms, the mystic spell-holders, worn by many people of Kregen. Superstition is as rife there as on Earth, mingled with sorceries and religions, demonic possession and necromancy. The bazaars and souks of cities and towns contained stalls where the magic talismans might be bought, and more money spent brought more protection. Blessings from as many sources of psychic power as possible also helped, and people would go from temple to sorcerer, brazen, bare-faced, to pay for a protective spell and a blessing.

"We are well-protected." Naghan pushed his atra back down inside his tunic. No doubt he believed that had saved him when the chavonth leaped on me, a man without an atra. And then, heartening me, he hefted his stux and added: "Let us rely on ourselves this night, my love. A fire...?"

Naghan, knowing fire would drive away wild animals, would not have asked the question if there were not more behind a mere fire than that.

"What enemy is there," I said, "apart from men, who does not fear fire?"

And, as he opened his mouth, I knew. So, together, we said: "Khirrs!"

This explained Naghan's increasing nervousness. We had a way to go yet before our directions parted. "Humm," I said, just like a frigate captain making time to think before giving his orders, a weak habit, it is true. "Fimi must have food and she will not eat raw meat—?"

Fimi shuddered eloquently, so that was that.

We set the fire as close to the overhang of the cave as we could, and letting the smoke take care of itself in the darkness of the groined stone arch, shielded the little flames by boulders. Soon the Twins would be up and there would be light.

The Twins sailed up as I sucked on the last bone. The space of woodland before us showed indistinctly at first, bathed in the fuzzy pink light, and the glade glimmered ghostly in the moons' light.

A dark round object appeared at the edge of the trees. Another and then three or four more moved among the pink-tinged leaves. I watched, motionless.

Near man-height, rotund, dark, hairy—I could make out little more. They looked to have two thin twinkling legs apiece. They stood for some time, and then they melted back into the forest. I let out my breath.

Naghan crouched at my side. He trembled.

"Khirrs," he said. *"Khirrs!"* His voice quivered. "May Numi-Hyrjiv the Golden Splendor strike them all with their own spit!"

Fourteen

The Fight with the Leem

That night we took turn and turn about to keep watch; but we saw or heard no more sign of the monsters.

In the morning we ate the rest of our last night's meal and drank cold water and prepared to set off.

The land presented a fair prospect of rolling tree-clad hills and tumbling streams and open glades. No distant views were easily obtainable but far ahead I thought I could make out the distant glint of snow-capped peaks. We did not follow any of the tracks and occasional roads that crisscrossed the land, and we avoided the easier paths running beside rivers. In this I took Naghan's advice. We would eventually reach the point at which he would turn off down the Valley of the Twin Spires. He had traversed this way only once before, and then in company with a strong band of well-mounted and well-armed numims, a good guarantee of safe passage most anywhere.

To sustain me during this time I had the comforting knowledge that my Delia was safe. She was surrounded by a group of the toughest warriors in Kregen. She was protected by a wall of steel and bronze, by a band of men and women devoted to her. They would get through to the pool despite my disappearance. No, thank Zair, I had no fears for the safety of Delia.

Ever and anon I cast a glance upwards.

"You look for something, Dray, apart from aerial foes?"

"Aye. Aerial friends."

They smiled a little uncomprehendingly at my words. The Savanti would keep command of the air in their own hands, and that adequately explained the general absence of vollers in Ba-Domek. Truth to tell, there were aerial foes aplenty. We hid from massive coal-black impiters out for a square meal. We bypassed likely looking places where chyyans might nest. Also, we avoided towns and villages, for Naghan advised that they would be unfriendly to us. I did not argue.

Life on Kregen has taught me to be wary of armed strangers, while always being ready to extend the hand of friendship with a cheerful Lla-hal. We pressed on by lonely ways. The Khirrs, too, infested the outskirts of towns. Scurvy, unkempt, hairy, the Khirrs scavenged around the out-skirts of civilization.

Emerging out of a stand of trees and skirting along the edge of the wood so as not to climb over the brow of a hill, we saw below us a road, which, with dusk, we would cross.

A quoffa, huge, shambling, patient, ambled along the road drawing a high four-wheeled cart loaded with local produce. The cart also con-tained four Rapas, taking it easy, their weapons cocked up lazily and their hats tilted over their eyes so that only the wicked vulturine beaks showed beneath the brims. Two other Rapas, big bold fellows, strode alongside the quoffa, arguing away over some topic dear to them.

There are many kinds of Rapas on Kregen, as I have said, and it would be wearisome to detail all the different kinds, by name and color varia-tion and shape of beak and crest, as by nation or belief. These fellows wore bright yellow markings about their black beaks, and their eyes were of a virulent purple. I noticed their pieces of renovated armor, mostly leather but with a piece of bronze and steel here and there. They carried stuxes and swords.

"Hold still," whispered Naghan. Not many races get on with Rapas, so we held within the shadow of the trees to wait until the Rapas and their quoffa cart had passed.

The attack swept in with startling suddenness. The white dust of the road abruptly churned under spindly twinkling feet. The coarse black hair of the Khirrs concealed powerful muscles under that rotund frame. They sprang. They pounced. Instantly the Rapas flung their scarves about their faces, shrieking to their comrades in the cart. I saw—quite distinctly—the quoffa shut his huge luminous eyes.

Naghan gulped and Fimi squealed, instantly silencing herself.

One Rapa was slow. He leaped from the cart, screaming, tearing at his face. The round bulbous bodies of the Khirrs darted in an uncanny gro-tesque fashion across the road. And now I saw they did have arms, and claws, scarlet talons that raked in razors of destruction. But the Rapas fought. Rapas stink in the nostrils of most peoples, diff and apim, but one becomes accustomed to their smell after a time. I had once had a good Rapa comrade, Rapechak, whom I could not believe dead and drowned in the River Magan in distant Migladrin, and my opinion of them was still slowly changing.

Two Rapas were down. The ones from the cart were slashing and cutting blindly. Two had a kind of transparent eye-mask; but raking claws ripped them away. I half-rose.

Naghan seized my arm.

"Suicide," he said. He was a numim, and he shook with the fear consuming him. "It will not be long."

I hesitated—fatally. It was all over.

I saw—quite clearly—the amber glint of liquid globules spurt from a tube in the center of a hairy face of a Khirr. A fleshy spout protruded, ridged, flexible, jutting forward like an obscene brown concertina and shooting its noxious liquid and then withdrawing. The spit struck a Rapa in the face. His scarf flapped. He was down, shrieking, tearing at his eyes.

"Spitballs," said Naghan. He shuddered. "They eat out a man's eyes—ghastly, ghastly."

The streaming mingled lights of Antares shone down refulgently upon that scene of horror. The Khirrs spat their drops of poison with uncanny accuracy. Now they hunkered around the bodies of their victims. Claws opened cavities. Below their round staring eyes, half-concealed by lank hair, the tubes pierced warm flesh and the Khirrs settled down, sucking, to their ghastly meal.

Fimi was sobbing. Naghan held her close. Quietly, we crept away from that diabolical scene.

"Spitballs, they are," said Naghan. He looked fierce and yet cowed. "They spit their poison and no man is safe."

Once again I had witnessed another of the myriad forms of life upon Kregen. Among all the menagerie I had stumbled across, these Khirrs, these Spitballs of Antares, I knew if the cramphs spat their foul poison at me I'd have to skip and duck and swat as, perhaps, never before on Kregen.

Well away, we mounted up and, this time, Naghan and Fimi shared a gnutrix and I rode the other. We cantered off in that awkward swaying gait of the six-legged riding animal, and I pondered. Spitballs of Antares—well, a more perceptive critical mind attuned to euphony—and alliteration—would call them Spitballs of Scorpio. But they were real, vitally alive, scavenging on the outskirts of civilization, vermin in that sense; but, as ever, I saw they but acted out the commands of their natures. They were made to act as they did, and so they acted thus. To condemn them for being themselves was the height of foolishness. They did not appear to have the intelligence that brings thought of consideration and consequences and thus a juster condemnation of evil acts; for to themselves, clearly, they were not evil. It merely behooved any sensible man to give them a wide berth—unless they offended too greatly and insisted on continuing the attack.

So as I rode on with a lion-lad and a cat-girl over the savage surface of Kregen I gave thanks that I was still alive.

We found a grassy hollow later on suitable for a small camp and dismounted and decided to light a fire and cook a meal. Once more, with those shifts of fortune, I was back battling against the perils and heart-stopping dangers of Savage Scorpio.

The two gnutrixes cropped the grass. Naghan and Fimi tended the fire, carefully, and I was just turning back from the edge of the trees with my arms full of branches. I had found a superb paline bush and was feeling pleased. Beyond the two young people and to the side, the long, lean, feline shape of a leem advanced to the grassy lip of the hollow. My mouth went dry.

A leem! The leem is deadly, a feral beast found in one form or another over most of Kregen. Eight-legged, it is furred, feline, vicious, with a wedge-shaped head armed with fangs that can strike through oak. Its paws can smash a man's head in like a pumpkin. Its claws can open rips in chunkrah hide. This was a well-grown specimen, sizeably larger than a leopard, low to the ground, weasel-like, filled with the animate energy of primordial savagery. I could see the beast's dusty ochre hide pulsating along his flanks. His eyes regarded the two elopers with all the bright interest of a gourmet reading a menu.

Among the branches I carried, the palines glimmered yellow. I did not break off a handful of the superb berries and pop them into my mouth, as I longed to do.

The leem's tail moved lazily. He was well aware of his power. That tail carried no tuft; and for that, at the least, I gave thanks to Zair, for I carried no great Krozair longsword, no Savanti sword, only a curved silly little knife called a kutcherer. The kutcherer can best be imagined by thinking of a butcher knife, with a hook jagged a third of the way back from the tip, a wicked tooth of metal jagging up from the thick back. The kutcherer can be deadly against the right opponent. But, with this, I would have to go up against a leem.

Slowly, noiselessly, I placed the branches on the ground. And then, because, I suppose, I am Dray Prescot, my brown hand twitched a fingering of palines free and I did pop them quietly into my mouth. The dryness vanished.

Carefully, quietly, I drew the kutcherer. Always a tricky operation that, by reason of the curved metal tooth; it was done this time soundlessly and quickly. I took a step forward and, even as my foot came soundlessly down, a thought so horrible, so blasphemous, entered my mind that I stopped stick-still, frozen.

Idiot! Always before I had been hurled to some new part of Kregen stark-naked at the behest of the Star Lords to become instantly embroiled in headlong action saving some wight from destruction. The injunction on me was to ensure the safety of the chosen ones until they were safe and I might go about my own pursuits. But, this time? Onker! This time— and I remembered Zena Iztar's words—this time there had been strife among the Star Lords. I had been kept here on the island of Aphrasöe only because Zena Iztar had contrived to thwart the others' plans. But that could only mean the Star Lords had not dispatched me here. I recalled the burning city, the boarded swordship. Surely, then, if this was Zena Iztar's doing I was not brought here to rescue anyone? She had kept me as close as she could contrive to my friends. These two young elopers, they had just happened by, as is the way of Kregen.

I owed them nothing.

The leem flicked his tail and prepared to charge, choosing his time. The two young people busied themselves at the fire, all unknowing. They, themselves, would say of the situation that they were all unknowing of the ghastly fate that leered upon them. But Kregen is full of ghastly fates, and one must do what one can. Was this ghastly fate any different from a thousand others? Yes—for a leem is a leem.

But—why need I embroil myself?

I was Dray Prescot, a stubborn onker; yet I could clearly see the foolishness of rushing down there armed only with an overgrown knife with a hook and trying to slay a damned great leem. Why, a leem could chomp me in half, could knock me over the head and rip that stupid head clean off those broad shoulders. And then where would all my plans for Vallia and Valka, for Djanduin and Strombor be? What would my Delia say? How could I be a helpmeet to her if I was being digested in the guts of a leem?

Yet—at the behest of Delia I had clambered down into a pit, somehow, brought out people I would have left trapped. Delia had explained it to me then. If she could see me now, would she act any differently? I wondered—for my Delia is the most perfect woman in two worlds, and a perfect woman does not ask her man to imperil his life needlessly.

The thoughts rushed through my brain whirling arrow fast, arrow sharp.

Onker! Idiot! Dray Prescot—stupid hulu!

This was no business of mine.

And there was this prickly question of honor...

A fighting man, a warrior, let alone a Krozair Brother—how could such a one leave two helpless youngsters to the claws and fangs of a leem? Was the situation one in which, with honor, I could turn tail? Of course it was! My duty, my life, my honor lay with Delia and the children and all the bright promise of the future for our friends and our countries.

What of the evil plans of all those who would bring down the emperor and bathe Vallia in blood? What of the evil devil, that foresworn Wizard of Loh, Phu-si-Yantong? He had sworn he would dominate the world of

Kregen. With all humility I fancied I might stand in his path and hinder him. Dare I jump down to almost certain death for the sake of an honor that demanded a sacrifice beyond the worth of the prize?

I sweated. I, Dray Prescot, Krozair of Zy, the Lord of Strombor, stood there like a petrified calsany, glaring hideously on the horror that stalked Naghan and Fimi.

No. No! I had fought leems before, and regretted it.

Had I a deadly Krozair brand—but I did not.

Had I a Lohvian longbow—but I did not.

Had I a Savanti sword—but I did not.

Had I any suitable weapon I think I would have gone charging down, roaring out "Hai!" in the old reckless way of Dray Prescot.

But I gripped only a little kutcherer and I did not want to leave this marvelous world of Kregen and all I loved—even for the sakes of a young numim lad and a pretty fristle fifi.

My motives appeared as murky to me as the muddy depths of the crocodile pool of debased Forglinda the Forsaken.

Busy about the camp fire, Fimi began to hum and then sing a few snatches from *The Bowmen of Loh*, variations on that rollicking old song I had taught her. My lips ricked back. By Zair! I am a fool, an onker, a great hulking hairy idiot of a fellow! Even to this day I cannot adequately explain to myself why. I knew I did wrong. Had I not, painfully but with devastating speed, reasoned it all out? Come to the right conclusions? I knew the codes of honor and chivalry were phantasms against reality. Yet reality demanded these phantasm become real. I knew so much, and I knew damn all...

I was wrong, I knew I was wrong, dreadfully wrong, making a hideous mistake as I whipped up the barbed knife and went roaring down into the glade. Bawling, bellowing, kicking up an infernal racket so the leem would turn his attentions to me and away from these two tender morsels by the fire, like a lunatic, I, Dray Prescot, get onker, went charging down...

Barely two heartbeats had elapsed since I had begun this fruitless reasoning.

"Hai!" I screeched. I leaped and cavorted and ran, ran fleetly, waving the knife. "Hai, leem! Hai!"

Oh, yes, a fool, an onker, an idiot—but, then, that is me, Dray Prescot, for you.

If I came out of this little lot alive, I remember the single scorching thought, I would not, most certainly would never, tell all of it to Delia.

By Vox, no!

The leem switched his wicked wedge-shaped head around. He sized up what tasty dish made this noise. He halted his first incipient charge, his tail flicking. I had been in time. Just in the nick of time—but only just.

His tail lashed.

His head went down and his eyes gleamed like coals. Belly low to the ground he advanced on me, putting down those eight claw-armed engines of destruction one after the other, with precision, like a cat. He slunk along, stalking me. The enormous wedge-shaped jaws gaped abruptly and his fangs caught the lights and gleamed, brilliant swords of death.

I ran full at him.

No chance to do any of the clever weaving and shearing I had done with the Krozair longsword in the Jikhorkdun of Huringa. Now only speed, and vital energy, and more speed, could save me. Even then as I charged I was aware of the horror around the fire. Naghan and Fimi sprang apart, shrieking, and for a moment as I ran like a madman they came together again, and clung. Then the gnutrixes at last caught the scent of the leem, for the cunning hunter had crept on them from downwind, and they screamed, rearing at their tethers. For the last blazing instant I saw Naghan hoist Fimi onto a mount, leap up with her and slash the gnutrix across the flanks. In a clashing bounding of six legs and flying tassels, the gnutrix raced away.

Then it was only the leem and me.

I remember little.

By rights I should have been dead. I have had my memory fortified by the dips in the Sacred Pool; but the memories here jog scarlet and ragged, fading and mocking, tormenting and frightful. The first feral leap could be slid, although one dagger-claw gouged a bloody chunk from my left shoulder. I got on his back. Somehow I held on and the kutcherer went in as far as the tooth of metal would allow. And that was not far enough to reach the leem's lesser heart, let alone his main heart. I tried to cut his throat and he whirled his interlocked shoulder blades and I spun catapulting off. I caught an ear in my left fist and held on, burning pain dripping down my arm, and was dragged, and felt claws rake all down my side.

The ground smashed at me and the claws drank my blood. But I was clinging to him like a burr, trying to serve him as I had the chavonth. The strength of a leem overtops lesser wildcats; a leem is no chavonth or strigicaw—a leem is a leem!

Sliding and dangling I was aware I slid in blood dabbling his fur. My blood. My blood, hot and red, mingled with some of his.

Again I tried to slit his throat and felt the blade kiss across fur and windpipe. He bucked and I held on, held on, and the world crashed and whirled about me. With the kutcherer reversed and leaning over that fanged wedge-head I brought the tooth of metal down and dragged back, reeling, gasping, and so pierced into one of his eyes. His roars shattered into the hot air. He swerved. He arched his back bucking, contorting, trying to fling me off. All the time he hissed and screeched and foam flew. The stink of him broke with fetid strength into my nostrils. Fur and sweat and blood all mixed together. Somehow there was strength enough to hold on. Muscles bursting, lungs afire, pain scorching, body hammered and beaten, somehow, somehow I held on.

I sawed the blade across his throat. We rolled. His weight near crushed me. Half suffocated I wrenched violently aside. A claw came from nowhere and razored half an ear away.

His claws scraped again; but I held myself in, clinging, limpet-like, shaking, gripping his fur, grabbing him anywhere, hauling our rolling bodies together, fast locked in a grip of death.

Over and over we rolled. His hisses and spittings shocked frightfully into my ears, through my head, drumming and howling like condemned spirits. But I held on and sawed and slashed and stabbed—stabbing was useless, useless with that tooth of metal halting the clean inward drive of the blade.

His struggles grew ever more vigorous, gaining in power and viciousness despite the loss of an eye as I felt my own strength waning. My left hand, daubed with blood, slipped. I grasped desperately at his stinking fur. The blood oozed through my fingers and I felt the fur slide away as a man slides his fingers down the neck of a chicken. I gasped and heaved back. I was rolling over and over and the leem was high in the air before me, pouncing, leaping, soaring through the air in that long superb leap of the leem.

He landed on his four front paws and that cruel wedge head split wide and the gaping maw opened and closed and the bright fangs crunched around my left arm.

I hardly noticed the pain for the fury that filled me.

If I was to die then I'd be dying a fool!

The kutcherer stabbed forward and up. The point shattered through his remaining eye. His screeches racketed in maniacal howlings. The stink of blood and sweat bathed me in a stench that mingled with his pungent leem smell. I could not feel my left arm. He opened his jaws to screech and I jerked free, and fell, and tried to stand up. The world was going up and down in hideous waves. He swiped at me—one swipe of those paws and my head would burst asunder like a rotten fruit—I ducked and the knife stabbed and hacked. I backed away. Crouched over, panting, drenched in blood, half-crazed, half-ruined, I backed away. He could not see. But he could smell. I could barely stand. I backed, seeking an opening. He followed, blindly. I slashed again, leaping in. I opened his throat. The dark blood pumped out, gushing, shining and viscous, welling in a red stream over his bedabbled ochre fur.

I staggered and fell. I could not move. He lifted his paws, blindly, slashing out. He advanced. Somehow strength fountained from somewhere, with the blood leaching from me, and I slashed again with the hooked knife and his screech sounded as though it echoed up from Cottmer's Caverns.

The ground struck hard under my knees. I tried to stand and could not. My head hung down. I caught a single horrific glimpse of my own left arm—of what had been my left arm. The skin and flesh had been stripped off in his fangs. The pink and white of bone gleamed through, with the blood bubbling; it was a skeletal arm, and the hand hung askew and mangled, broken into an obscene lump. I could feel nothing.

I fell forward from my knees onto my face. The dust stung into my face, smeared and slicked with sweat and blood. The kutcherer, a mere mass of shining blood, dropped into the stained grass. I tried to lift my head. If this was the end then I'd husk out a last Hai Jikai and so take my last voyage down to the Ice Floes of Sicce.

The will forced me up. There was no physical strength in this thing. The will, the driving force of spirit—I was on my knees, my head dangling, feeling blindly about for the knife.

The leem crouched before me. He was not yet dead. It is extraordinarily hard to slay a leem. His hearts pumped blood out through the ragged gaping rents in his hide, from the slashes in his throat. His punctured eyes streamed ichor. His ochre fur sheened with spilled blood. And his cruel mouth dribbled blood that belonged to me.

With that dark effort at which I have long ceased to marvel, I forced myself to stand. My legs shook. My knees quivered. Wavering, reeling, gasping with wide-open mouth for air, laboring, I stood up. I grasped the knife again. I did not recall finding it in the grass and picking it up. The handle was as fouled with blood as the blade. And the metal tooth was gone, snapped off, wrenched away.

And so, more falling than leaping, more toppling helplessly forward than thrusting, I fell onto the leem and drove the knife home into his main heart.

He thrashed. He quivered in the last frenzy before death. His hind legs caught me and knocked me head over heels. I smashed into the dirt and rolled and a bony skeletal object, loosely articulated with a few threads of gristle, wrapped about by a few shreds of flesh and skin, flapped about me as I rolled and I realized that ghastly blood-spraying flailing skeletal thing was my left arm.

The bones of my arm clashed with the bones of my ribs, exposed, showing through the cut and lacerated flesh of my body.

The darkness that was beyond the darkness of Notor Zan flowed over me. I felt—I felt nothing.

I saw the leem. He lay awash in his own blood.

Stupidly, I collapsed onto the dirt.

So I lay there, and my head sank down to the dusty blood-caked grass, and I slept.

Fifteen

Shadow

That I speak to you in these tapes is proof I did not die.

How close to death I drew I do not know. By my immersion in the Sacred Pool of Baptism my body had been endowed with remarkable powers of recuperation and recovery from injury. But my left arm had been stripped away, mangled, practically wrenched from the socket, destroyed. That would not be repaired. It might not kill me; it would never be a sound left arm again.

Someone was shouting at me. The leem fight brought back ghosts.

"By Kaidun! D'you want the glass eye and brass sword of Beng Thrax to do it all for you! Go in, you coys, you hulus. Go in and fight for the Ruby Drang!"

For the Ruby Drang! Aye! I would fight for the Ruby Drang.

And, another voice, leading on the war hosts: "For Vallia! Valka! Valka!"

And, again, yet another voice, shrilling over the war trumpets and the heart-pulsing pounding of ten thousand voves: "Felschraung! Felschraung and Longuelm! Zorcander! Zorcander!"

And, too, the voices bellowing joyfully: "For Djan! For Notor Prescot and for Djanduin!"

The surf-roar of a hundred ghostly voices beat about me, roaring in my head. Visions passed before my eyes. Flames shot up, smoke billowed, the horrendous sounds of combat flowered in my head. Demands were being made upon me. Urgent decisions were called for. There was no time for rest. Rest was a sin.

"For the Kroveres of Iztar!"

I groaned. The weight was too much. I was a mere mortal man and could not support the load. The voices, the demands, the urgency, beat and battered at me, and I moaned and rolled over and so, stupidly, sat up.

The last phantasmal voice roared, proud, defiant, ready to challenge a world: "For Zair! Krozair! Krozair!"

I opened my eyes and winced, shuddering, and so looked about wearily, and remembered.

I had not bled to death.

My left arm pained. The amazement that that was all it did must be pushed aside. A mere string or two of sinew, broken splintered bones, a few scraps of red meat—that was all there was hanging from my shattered shoulder.

What the hell Delia would say I shuddered to think.

My thoughts were not even as clear as that. It is a surmise from later. The disgusting remnants of my arm must be bound up and the gaping cavity in my side staunched, and I ripped away at the tatters of the flaxen tunic to make a sling and pads.

I was, I think, still reasonably coherent at this time. Later the delirium would seize me. If a fever shook me I'd have to fight that, too. I can recall hauling at the gnutrix and clumsily mounting. I had a filled water bottle. What else there was besides a remnant of an arm in a sling and a mangled side I did not know, do not remember. I started off, kicking the animal along, jolting cruelly in that damned six-legged gait.

The corpse of the leem lay there bathed in shining blood, black and green with flies. I left him without a word, without a parting Jikai, left him to rot.

Although the long-term calendar of Kregen is based to a large extent on the precedence of the red or the green sun through the sky, and the forty-year cycle, plus the orbital movement of the planet itself, these give only the broadest outline to calendar measurements. Most immediate date measurements are made by months of one moon or another. For the journey I must now undertake I fancied I'd need a whole sheaf of months, culled from all the seven moons.

What passed along the way remains hazy. Blurred snatches of memory jag through the mists. I think I met a group of little Ochs, who tut-tutted over my arm and gave me potions. Ochs are funny little puff-chopped folk, with six limbs, the center pair used either as hands or feet. I have been helped before by Ochs, as well as being savagely beaten by them when a slave.

They gave me a piece of clear crystal hung on chains from a circlet they cautioned me to wear on my head. Drunkenly I put the thing on and the crystal hung down before my eyes turning the world into a phantasmagoria as though I peered through the bottom of a bottle. I thanked them—I think I did—giving them a proper Remberee, riding on, lolling in the saddle like a man sodden with dopa and too far gone to fight.

The way proved long and tiresome. Go north, Zena Iztar had said, and I had obeyed. Now I crawled along with an altogether more dreadful reason. Now, despite all, I must win through. Forests, tracks, trees, streams, boulders, defiles. I staggered along, reeling in the saddle. Yes, snatches of it come back to haunt me in nightmares, now. I was growing steadily weaker as the dreadful injuries that surely must have killed any normal man fought against the healing properties my body had acquired from the Savanti.

Of all that painful journey only a few incidents stand out at all clearly. Of them, the most vivid, if not the most evil, wrenching in its violence, occurred as the gnutrix lolloped down a slope toward a stream bowered

in trees where I could quench the torturing thirst and soothe my burning
lips. My thirst tormented and drove me insatiably.

By this time I must have been pretty far gone. Only the memory of the
incident remains, like a child's picture torn from a book and mounted in a
frame, isolate, individual, related to nothing else.

Katakis moved about the stream, making a camp, busy in the familiar
tasks of creating a base for the night. To one side the bound slaves, hall-
mark of the Katakis' trade, moaned in their winnowed lines of suffering. I
stared, sick, almost falling off the gnutrix, glaring madly upon these devils
who debarred me from the water. My whole body wracked with cramps,
I burned, yet coldness brushed me with ice crystals. Shuddering, reeling
in the saddle, I had to face the terrible fact that there was no water for me
at this stream, not with the Katakis and their slaving habits in the way.
One look at me, the instant summation I was useless as merchandise, and
they'd whip up a tail-blade and finish me.

Even now, I believe no single thought occurred to me that this might be
a blissful end to all suffering.

Low-browed and with a gap-jawed mouth filled with snaggly teeth is
a Kataki. His thick black hair is oiled and curled in a fashion far different from that of the Eye of the World. His eyes are wide-spaced, narrow
and cold. Evil, vicious and rapacious, Katakis, slavemasters, man-manag-
ers, batteners on human misery. Perhaps the thing that gives a Kataki his
greatest pride is his tail, a long sinuous powerful tail to which is strapped
a sharp steel blade. So, sickly, I stared down on these vile diffs and I could
not summon a single curse.

Jerking the gnutrix away was bewilderingly useless. He scented the
water, parched as was I, obstinately thrusting his blunt head toward the
inviting stream in the darkling light.

He started off and I sawed the reins and he resisted, disregarding the
pain in his mouth for the lure of the water. We picked up speed jolting
down toward the stream.

Had I had the use of two arms; had I been even a little stronger, I would
have held him. But he ran away with me. So I did the only thing I could do,
plunging down to certain death, trying to husk up the last of my voice, to
make a good shouting show of it.

"Khirrs!" I shrilled, and my voice wheezed and cracked. "Khirrs all about
you!"

Croaking though my voice was, the Katakis heard. Instantly, like the
black-hearted reivers they were, they gave thought only to themselves.

The camp boiled with frenzied activity. Pounding down I went, catching a guyline in a gnutrix hoof and pulling the whole lot down, knocking a
cooking fire blazing, scattering pots and pans, bounding along like a scare-
crow. Katakis were forming and each swung a crystal oblong before his face,

so they knew about Khirrs. On lumbered the gnutrix for the stream. Katakis were running to the edge of the camp, their weapons bright, shouting in confusion, ferocious and malignant. The animal reached the stream and plunged in and I sailed over his head into the water. The sweet coolness helped. I lay for a moment, winded, and then tried to crawl, all lopsided like a beetle. The water sloshed about me and I sucked in thirstily. The far bank appeared dwaburs off.

The stream deepened. The current knocked me over and I rolled along banging against the bottom. I am not sure what I felt as what remained of my left arm scraped the gravel; but I expect some more pieces of me fell off.

Somehow the gravel oriented itself under me and I was staggering up out of the stream. But I was still on the same side as the Katakis and their shouts told me that no Khirrs had arrived and the Katakis wanted to know what was going on and to get their hands on the lunatic who had caused the furor. A zorca stood by the bank. He stood impossibly tall on those four spindly powerful legs, close-coupled. His magnificent twisted spiral horn stuck up arrogantly from his forehead. To his saddle were belted sword, bow, saddlebags. I grasped his reins in my one hand and tried to vault onto his back and landed on my belly, dangling across, and he snorted and bucked, so I kneed him, anyhow, and we went galloping off, bashing through the low bushes into the trees.

The next thing I recall, not so luridly, is trotting out into another glade with a rockface and a trickle of water and of falling off and still grasping the reins, of crawling until I could lash the reins around a broken stump and then plunge my head under the water.

I must have slept, for the shrilling of the zorca awoke me and I sat up, sluggishly, that awful dead feeling in my left arm and side reminding me my time was running out. I peered foolishly out into early morning suns shine.

They flitted out from the trees, their spindly legs twinkling, their harsh hairy bodies rotund and hateful in the mingled radiance. I blinked. Spitballs of Antares. Vermin. They crept upon me as I slept, eager to plunge their snouts into my body and drink of my substance and suck me dry. I tried to stand up and fell over. I was as weak as a woflo.

I was ripe game for these Khirrs. They would enjoy spitting at me, weak, feeble, barely able to crawl. With an idiot's fumble I dropped the crystal rectangle before my face, and the world described whorls of distorted circular dizziness. The nausea had to be fought back, pushed away. The bow was useless, for I had but one arm. The sword, a solid, single-edged cut and thruster, somewhat too long for the balance, would have to serve—somehow. My scrabbling fingers fastened on the stirrup. Heaving and grunting I hauled myself up alongside the zorca. He was a fine animal, a fleet runner, strong, well-built. He shivered now and I could smell the sweat of fear.

That broad back of mine would have to be wedged against a support. I could not use the zorca, for the acid spit would burn into his hide. They'd spit their poison at his eyes and if he was done for then so was I. His tether twanged and he twisted and turned; but he remained steady as I pulled myself up, speaking to him, croaking.

"Hold on, my lad, my bonny zorca. Hold on and we'll deal with these cramphs."

I spoke as my father was wont to speak to his horses as he so patiently and skillfully doctored their hurts. The zorca quieted at the sound of my voice. But I lied to him, I lied...

Zorcas are animals of splendid intelligence. He was denied his usual method of dealing with foes. If he swung that magnificent head with the silky mane flying toward them and charged down with the spiral horn lancing to skewer and degut them, he would expose his eyes. And he knew that, he knew...

Holding to his saddle I slid the sword out awkwardly. Peering back owlishly through the crystal at the hideous advancing shapes, seeing their black hairy bodies, the crafty black beady eyes, the goggle effect of the protective rings of horn, the protrusions of the ridged snouts, I lifted the sword. Unsteadily, I slapped the zorca with the hilt and slashed on to cut through the tether. He sprang away. I fell against the tree stump. The fierce effort of turning about and wedging my back against the stump taxed me. I was gasping. But I stood up, shivering, plastered against the stump, and I lifted the sword and faced the shuffling advance of the Spitballs of Antares.

The ridged snouts quivered. They spat. The crystal smeared and blurred and a foul reek stank into the clearing. I felt the deep acid burn of the amber drops on my neck.

Alone, shaking, almost spent, I struggled to stand and face the loathsome menace advancing toward me, these Khirrs, all black and hairy and spitting, Spitballs of Antares, fit food for dogs.

Around their small brilliant eyes each one had a horny ring, a protective circle of bone filmed with a membrane, for all the world like those heavy horn-rimmed spectacles that were once so fashionable on Earth.

The sword wavered. I tried to swash it menacingly and nearly dropped it. I, a Krozair Brother, to drop a sword! The spit hit the crystal square and splashed against the rags tattered about me and bit excruciatingly into the remnants of my arm and side. The reek bit into my throat like acid. That muck must be washed off the naked skin soon, or it would eat and fume away the flesh itself.

I shouted. I bellowed. I croaked. "Stupid rasts! Foul kleeshes! Come on! Come on to your deaths!"

I almost slipped, then, and wedged back against the moldering stump, harsh against my back. The sword glittered as I hefted it. If the Khirrs were puzzled their spit did not blind me, if they were aware of the power of the sword—these things are imponderables. I did not expect to win free; but gradually as they shuffled and spat and did not approach any nearer, I began to think these Khirrs were cowardly at heart. They hesitated. I swung the sword so that it caught the opaline glitter of the suns and shot sharding reflections across the glade.

In all the world of Kregen I could expect no help. I was done for, truly done for, then, as I believed, as the Spitballs of Antares, scavengers, vermin, crept forward again, more cautiously, sending their spurting globs of spitting poison before them. I had to stand on my own two feet. Had to. Had to show them I was not defenseless. I stood. I swung the sword.

Their scarlet claws raked the air before them; vision was almost totally obscured by the streaming mass of amber poison smearing the crystal square. They could see I was weak and trembling and they advanced—cautiously, hesitantly—but with very deadly intent for the last time.

One and one only of the Khirrs ventured within reach of the sword.

Him, I clove down the middle.

A sewer stench burst upward. His insides, all black and vile, glistening, spewed forth. He burst and shrank. The others drew back. Again I shouted, wheezing, taunting them with boastful words and lurid promises of their fate if they tried to molest me further. They drew back. They drew back and skittled away on their spindly legs, and their black hair draggled on their plump frames.

The respite was only momentary. I could barely see for the spit streaming on the crystal square. I had a chance, a bare chance, a last chance to escape from being done for finally.

If I fell over now I was done for. I peered about, dazedly choking, the ruin of a man. The zorca, his silky black coat very splendid in the lights, trotted back to me. He flung his head up, the spiral horn glinting. I took hold of the saddle. I was seated in the saddle. Do not ask me how. The sword, all smeared and foul, dangled beside the scabbard from the sword knot. The stirrups dangled until I thrust my bare toes into them.

I dangled, limp and broken, dangled as a strung collection of bones dangles, jangling. The zorca was superb. He broke into a canter. Then a lunging gallop that took us away from the sullen, cowardly contemptuous ring of Khirrs.

Nowadays I give thanks for that deliverance. Then I merely hunched on the zorca's back and slumped, my head dangling on my breast, and went away without a coherent thought in my skull.

Agony gripped my body. My arm was a mere scarlet branch of fire. And in my skull those famous old bells of Beng Kishi rang and resonated, clanging in time to the thudding to the zorca's hooves.

Sixteen

A Draught to Mother Zinzu the Blessed

That cheerfully rubicund spirit of luck and good fortune, Five-handed Eos-Bakchi of Vallia, must have smiled on me, a mortal sinner. It was all my own fault, my own doing, and there was no one else to blame but myself. No blame could attach to the Krozairs of Zy, for their Disciplines might demand a Krozair Brother hurtle down to the defense of the weak and helpless; but they were chivalrous enough to weigh need against need. They understood when the odds were too great, the cost too high, the game not worth the candle. To throw one's life away selflessly in the name of honor is all very well; but when a higher honor demands a different course the mad act of devoted courage is seen for what it is—vainglorious selfishness.

My Delia, the fate of Vallia, set against an eloping lion-lad, a pretty Fristle fifi—no, never!

Of course, remembering so little of that horrific journey, I can only surmise what happened. No doubt I greatly exaggerated my own importance.

After all, why should the fate of all Vallia hang on me? So what if I had been nearly killed and had my arm just about ripped off? That would affect me and my family—but Vallia? I detest affectation. So I guessed with a somber foreboding that no matter how much I sought to evade the future I did not want and responsibilities that would be thrust upon me, the weight of Vallia would be mine. Only a foolish notion would uphold me. For Valka and Strombor and Djanduin and Azby and my Clansmen—and also to a lesser degree Paline Valley—I not only admit my responsibility and indebtedness, I struggle to prove myself at least half worthy of the trust of my own people.

Some of these thoughts must have collided in my aching head along with the infernal never-ending clanging of the Bells of Beng Kishi as I found a pool and washed myself as thoroughly as I could. The zorca washed, also. Frequently, bouts of emptiness closed in when the enveloping cloak of Notor Zan dropped over me with the silent rush of black wings.

But, in the fullness of time, with the dawning of whatever day it was—for all track of time had flown along with much else in that dreadful journey across the hostile face of Savage Kregen—I found myself riding alongside the river. I seemed to have awoken from a bad dream. I must have found rabbits and edible shoots and roots, and the blessed palines were always there to comfort the ailing. I must have crossed a high pass of the mountains—a vague memory stirred of cold and snow and of hard riding, the frosty breath glittering. But, on this day—which could have been any of the named days out of any moon, any sennight, all with their own different names and attributes—I saw the river and the gorge and heard the titanic uproar of masses of water falling bodily through thin air to crash into the stone basin beneath. Blearily, I peered around.

If I was where I thought I was, where I ought to be, then I'd struck into the River Zelph. I'd avoided many dangers. The last time I'd been here I'd been clad in russet hunting leathers, bearing a Savanti sword, in full health and strength, helping along the beautiful crippled girl who was to become everything that mattered in two worlds.

But all that had been a long time ago.

Delirious, off my head, with a mangled side and a skeletal thing that might have been a bit of arm dangling all green and black, I knew that if I was not where I wanted to be I wouldn't be anywhere else anymore, save the Ice Floes of Sicce.

The sight of spider-beasts dangling from the rocks, the clicking of beetle-beasts as they crowded close, reassured me. Aye! By Zair! These monsters seeking to shred me, to scatter me in pieces, to devour me, these ravening furies reassured me and gave me a fresh confidence.

I was here! The waterfall dropped into the stony basin and bubbled all plum-colored from the sandy amphitheater. As the beasts descended on me I looked for the overhang of crystal rock and the dark entrance to the cave which led to the pool. I staggered and held onto the zorca.

He responded nobly, a proud stallion, full of fire and spirit.

The first spider-beast was dispatched with a straight cutting slash. A beetle-beast was hacked so that he stumbled back, his legs clashing, and fell into the river. Forging on, I led the zorca without holding his reins and he followed because he trusted me and stayed with me. The narrow stony path curved around the last bend and with the thunder of the falls beating up, the mouth of the cave formed a welcoming darkness ahead. The fuzzy pink radiance all about blurred as I remembered.

Yes, the remembrances of that journey are vague and phantasmal, patchy, illuminated by the cutting shafts of recollected horror, misted by things I am thankful to forget.

This path must have led into the amphitheater among the rocks along the narrow way avoiding the majority of the guardian monsters. The route for the candidates and their Savanti tutors lay up from the river. I suppose I must have cut and hacked my way through and swung the sword one-handed, for I arrived; but it is all misty and dim and dream like.

The zorca followed me into the cave and without ado walked daintily over to the far side and beyond a ledge out of sight began to crop gently at fronds that grew there. The wet, fragrant herbs would not hurt him if he ate a few; but I would not allow him too many for the safety of his insides.

Odd thoughts kept spurting through my brain. My arm hung twisted and shredded and horrible, my side bit numbly, the rips and claw-gouges were certain death for anyone without the protection afforded by the balm of the place. The Bells of Beng Kishi clamoring in my head continued and I guessed I had been injured there, also, in the battle with the leem. If I did not drop into the pool and bathe in the milky liquid very very soon I, too, would be dead.

And then—noises, the clatter of disturbed rock, voices, cheerful and excited now the danger of the trail was passed, relieved and yet tensely expectant voices—the noises and the voices echoed from the cave entrance.

So close to victory I was not prepared to be beaten.

There was no time to dive into the water. I sank down painfully behind a screen of rocks and, truthfully, that small respite felt wonderful.

Men and women entered the cave. They did not see either the zorca or myself. They were absorbed in the reasons why they had ventured here through perils that were to them novel and ghastly and out of all the previous experience of their worlds.

Events jerked ahead, I heard and saw in snatches; what I record is far too continuous a narrative. The single searing lump of agony that was me suffered there in hiding among the rocks.

There were eight people—as customary. Four tutors and four aspirants, four fine young people who would one day be Savapims and work for the great plan of improvement for Kregen.

There were two women and two men. They wore the Savanti hunting leathers and carried Savanti swords and they were upstanding, stalwart, brilliant people, picked, chosen, of the elite to be.

One of the tutors was Maspero. Maspero, he who had been my own tutor; from the concealment of the rocks I watched and I longed to reach out the hand of friendship, to hear him greet me, to hear again "Happy Swinging!" But I remained dumb and silent, hidden in my rocks, for I was not the Dray Prescot that Maspero had known. Too much had passed and I had learned more, even, I think, than Maspero could teach.

The four aspirants stripped off their clothes and waded down the stone steps. They remained submerged for the time they could hold their breaths, and when they emerged they were transformed, irradiated, made glorious in the name of the Savanti nal Aphrasöe.

I swallowed down hard. The scene kept flickering and blurring, the stone walls swooping sickeningly. I heard what they said, their awed exclamations, the expression of the realization that they were each possessed of a thousand years of life. They talked animatedly, donning their clothes for the journey back down the River Zelph to the Swinging City.

Listening I picked out the scraps of conversation that held meaning for me and I wished them away. My life was ebbing. The leem had worked cruelly upon me. I have fought leems; this time I had been unlucky as well as stupid. So I listened, hearing some things clearly, and one said: "And they were all dispatched, Harding?"

"Yes," agreed the tutor called Harding, a lean, competent man who looked as hard as his name. "They all profaned the Sacred Pool. Vanti, as is his duty, banished them all back to the places from whence they came."

"Why did they risk so much?" The fair-haired girl had been merely pretty before her immersion. "They say a Wizard of Loh was among their number. Yet the Wizards, you teach us, fear the Savanti—"

"They have cause." Maspero smiled, gesturing. He looked exactly the same as I remembered him, the same dark curly hair, the same air of vivacity, the sense of completeness as a person. "As to why they came, it is always the same story. They hear of a miracle cure. But, this time, they did not even seek our permission." He looked about at the ribboned reflections of the cave, the milky-white liquid shooting shards of colored light against the groined arches. He took a sharp breath. "There is an old story you will be told concerning a man you must know of. A man who—I had an affection for him—a man who failed the tests."

"He would have been a Savapim?" The aspirant questioned, hanging on Maspero's words.

"Yes. But in his nature were darker depths—yet my affection for him remained. He was ejected."

"Vanti...?" said the dark full-faced man with the features of a Roman emperor.

"Yes." Maspero gestured for them to descend from the lip of the Pool and make their way to the exit. The only sound I could hear for a space was my own hoarse breathing and the spurting clicking of their sandals on the rocks. All that I saw jumped and leaped, like a reflection in a racing stream, and the bands of fire about my head, constricting about my body, searing that shattered arm, crushed in, agonizing, choking, deadly. "Yes. Vanti ejected him as was his duty. But he was not with these people who so recently profaned this shrine, as I had expected, knowing him, to be. They were banished. They left their air-boats and all their belongings. We have them now. Safely. Soon, I believe, we shall find out more about them, for this is a serious business, unique. As to where they came from—" He stopped there, and laughed in that old wry manner.

Harding drew his sword in preparation for the return. "Yes. Wherever it was, they are back there now." And he, too, laughed with the others.

"And this man," asked an aspirant. "This man of whom you speak and who failed."

"I often wonder," said Maspero, "far more often than I should, just what has become of him on Kregen."

The remark sounded strange.

"If we fail," said the aspirant with the close-cropped hair and the fighter's face. "If we are ejected..."

They walked toward the cave entrance. I understood that of the aspirants one was Italian, one French, one German, and one, the hard-looking girl with straight dark hair bound with a fillet and a lean muscular body, might not be from Earth or Kregen at all.

The last I heard was Maspero saying, not lightly but with a grave resonance of meaning in his voice: "I do not think you will be called on to face the temptation that destroyed the man—the man for whom I cherish still an affection—the man of whom I speak."

When they had gone I tried to rouse myself to crawl out and drop into the water. I imagined myself crawling. I did not move. I could not move. My muscles locked. Sweat started out on my forehead and along my limbs—all three of them. I strained. If I did not reach the pool... Every last ounce of will power left must be summoned. Sheer muscular power was long since passed. Only by a last enormous effort of will could I drag myself over the harsh stones to the water's edge.

I moved.

Creaking like unoiled leather, my body answered the savage commands I imposed. I moved. Like a half-crushed beetle I crawled out of the rocks. A smear of blood followed in a trail where wounds opened. The whole world of Kregen revolved, inside and outside my skull. If I were to go staggering down to the Black Spider Caves of Gratz I would go down, as ever, clawing and fighting and struggling like a maniac every last inch of the way.

Slowly, laboriously, agonizingly, the water came nearer.

The liquid moved gently with spiraling wisps of vapor rising from the surface, like heating milk. The refulgent blueness of the place pressed down more strongly. I gasped. I do not know what my face looked like; and I am glad I do not know.

The rocky edge scraped under my chest. I leaned over the Sacred Pool of Baptism and I drew a deep shuddery breath and gave thanks I had at last reached its miraculous healing powers.

My friends had reached here and the emperor had been cured. Maspero had said so. The tutors had laughed—why had they laughed? If I have given some semblance of a continuous narrative to my experiences here then that is purely illusory. Everything reached me in chopped-up segments, distracting, dazzling, obscure. My head expanded and contracted with pain. My arm—no, I prefer to forget that, for all the numbing effects of the journey wore off as I trembled on the edge of the pool, trying to find the energy for one last agonized dragging of my body over the stone lip to topple over and into a blessed surcease from agony.

Why did I hesitate? Why did I not make that final effort and plunge to resurrection?

And then—and then! For, of course, I realized almost too late why I hesitated, why those tutors had laughed. My friends had all bathed here with the emperor and they had all been banished, every last one, back to whence they came.

They had been ejected and returned to their homes on Kregen.

If I dropped into the Sacred Pool as I so ardently wished, then I, Dray Prescot, of Kregen and of *Earth*, I would—as I had been once before, so I would inevitably be again—I would be ejected and sent hurtling across the dark spaces between the stars back to Earth where I had been born.

If I achieved the healing and surcease I craved I would be flung headlong back to Earth.

But, if I did not recuperate, if I were not healed, I would die.

To go back to Earth, flung there by the agent of the Savanti, this Vanti whose monstrous bulk moved in the pool, must mean a banishment that might last a thousand years. For in that case the Star Lords would not have banished me and therefore in their distant way might have no further interest in me. So cruelly beset by pain and indecision and torment was I that the thought seemed natural; later I questioned that assumption.

There were two evils, and I must make a decision. The decision was made for me, of course. I dare not allow myself to die. Delia—I would be of no use to Delia if I were dead and wandering like a wraith through the echoing vastnesses of Cottmer's Caverns.

So I must live to fight another day and take my chances of ever returning to Kregen.

Perhaps, I thought, maundering, raging with fever, delirious, out of my head—I remember it all in flashes and spurts and jolting savage impressions of pain and horror and urgency—perhaps it would be better for me just to die, after all, just to let slip rather than live out a thousand years of meaningless life on Earth.

But, as it was in the nature of the scorpion to sting the frog, so it is in my nature to struggle and never give in, however foolish that makes me. There had to be a way around this. I tried to grasp onto my whirling thoughts— confusion, a roaring in my head, a drugged empty feeling as though the evil concoctions of the black lotus-flowers of Hodan-Set wafted through my brain—desperately, near despair, I tried to think and reason this out, trying to act in the puffed-up character of the cunning old leem-hunter so many people credit me with being. I am just an ordinary man—oh, yes, I am blessed or cursed with a thousand years of life and I have seen and done much; but I am no superman.

If I—I remember turning and rolling, slowly, agonizingly, over onto my stomach alongside the stone lip of the pool. First things first. If I—cautiously I plucked at the ghastly bundle that wrapped all that was left of my arm. If I—I did not want to disturb that mess. I may have a strong stomach; I do not think I could have withstood the impact of the horror of my own body that must have been revealed. Slowly, cautiously, I inched out over the water, and let the thing dangle down.

The milky fluid closed around my arm. I felt—well, I wondered if I did feel anything through the bite of agony. Then the warm comforting sensation as of a soft mouth kissing me, a million tiny needles pricking my skin, rather, pricking the shreds of skin and fragments of bone. The rags would all be melted away. I waited, feeling the warm glowing sensation increase and expand. I managed to shift around so my shoulder dipped.

If I ventured any more I would fall in. Then it would be Earth for me...

Weird, to think I thus hung over a drop of four hundred light years...

Presently, in due time, I withdrew my arm.

The arm was whole.

I flexed the muscles. I gripped that iron hand of mine into a fist.

Well!

So I pushed out over the water, gripping the stone lip of the rim with two strong hands, and dipped my head. I dunked my head in and held my breath and all the pains of Kregen flowed and dissolved and washed away as the snows of the Heart Heights of Valka vanish when the full glory of the Suns of Scorpio pours upon them.

When I withdrew, a vast shape moving slowly in the milky waters drew back at the far end of the pool. Vanti...

It was not bravado, not pride, not foolishness, that made me stand up and walk away without dipping my side. I knew enough of the powers of the milky liquid in the pool. My side, which was ripped and torn and poking crushed ribs through in a bloody crust, would heal of itself.

Over at the far side the Guardian grew restless. A vast smooth bulk humped beneath the water. Waves of the liquid flowed outwards in smooth rolling rings to luminous reflections. I walked away, a whole man once again, and I will not attempt to speak of my feelings, for they poured in a hot jumbled tide, irrational, thanksgiving, angry, shamed, glorious. I had sinned grievously and I had been reprieved. Now, there was work to be done.

A voice whispered through the still air.

"Oh, unfortunate is the city—"

"You have no powers over me, Vanti!" I bellowed back. "Return to your hole, hide away from me—for I warned you I would return." Then, I added: "I return in friendship."

The powers of the Guardian of the Pool could hurl me four hundred light years through space back to Earth. Had done so.

I must be an old vosk-skull, for I turned and cupped my hands and splashed the liquid over me, letting it run down over my body and legs.

Yes, an old onker—for as Zair is my witness, I knelt down and took a long swigging drink.

Foolhardy? Of course! But then, that is me, Dray Prescot, Lord of Strombor, Krozair of Zy...

I stood up, tall and straight once more, a fighting man, ready to face what must come on the wild and beautiful, savage and horrendous world of Kregen.

I licked the last moisture from my lips.

"By Mother Zinzu the Blessed," I said, wiping my mouth. "I needed that!"

Seventeen

Gifts from a Savanti nal Aphrasöe

The magnificent black zorca trotted along the path above the waterfall. Proud, high-tempered, a stallion, this zorca was a mount fit for a king. I had formed the impression that he had not been well treated by his Kataki owner. This is no novel thing. Some races on Kregen, as on Earth, care nothing for the suffering of animals, as other races care nothing for the suffering of women and children. For me, the stallion responded nobly, and I think he understood very quickly the difference in attitude between his old master and his new rider.

Mind you, Katakis have no feelings for the suffering of animals, women, children or men. They enslave them all.

Once again back to full health and strength, for my side healed with wonderful alacrity after I had taken the swigging, impudent drink, I jogged along on Shadow. I had decided to call this muscular and elegant steed Shadow because he moved like a ghosting shadow across the land. What lay ahead of me I did not know; but the broad outlines of what I had to do remained clear. What was I going to do. The light-headed exultant feeling persisted.

But, of course, Kregen would always come up with frustrations, and plans gang aft agley under Savage Scorpio.

The way opened out and I stared across a plain of brownish grasses studded by a few wilting trees here and there. My eye was caught by a scrap of white high in the firmament. I stared up, eyes narrowed against the glare, and cursed.

Certainly, surely, the white dove of the Savanti flew down and circled, eyeing my zorca with quick intelligence manifested in every movement, an intelligence far past that of any mortal bird.

So, feeling truculent as well as foolish, I shook my fist at the white dove.

"What d'you want?" I bellowed up. "Sink me! I'm not going to the Swinging City, much as I'd like to. I have work to see to that will not wait."

The Gdoinye, the gold and scarlet raptor of the Star Lords, had spoken to me before, as had the Scorpion—I wondered if the representative of the Savanti would deign to open his beak and speak in human terms using a human voice.

He did not. He swung about and then dipped away, going at right angles to my track.

He flew on, with my watchful gaze on him, swung back with a beautiful lift of white wings, soared high again. Again he circled my head and flew off at right angles. Three times he did this before I understood he wanted me to follow him. I had never observed this conduct in the dove before.

I pondered.

The plain remained bare. No purely human enemies threatened. If the Savanti wanted to take me they had powers to snatch me up no matter where I was—so I thought.

Gently easing Shadow around and jogging along after the bird we followed as he circled and rose and fell, pacing his eager flight to our more sedate progress. That after all these years on Kregen I had phlegmatically turned my back on Aphrasöe struck me not so much as odd as highly practical and a sensible course of action. Opaz knew what might happen in Aphrasöe. And Vallia called.

I knew now where the island of Aphrasöe was situated. When my affairs in the Outer Oceans had been settled, why, then, it might be time to return to the Swinging City. I hoped I might return as a friend.

So I followed the beckoning white dove. In for a zorca in for a vove, as my Clansmen say. Soon a little copse came into view half hidden in a fold in the ground. The dove fluttered and settled on a branch. He cocked his eager head. I halted Shadow and stared.

Around the dove's neck a thin brilliant scarlet ribbon glowed against the white feathers.

I had never seen that before.

The dove fluffed around and then dived off the branch, almost striking the ground where dried leaves were heaped into a pile before zooming up. Three times he dived. So I dismounted, with a quiet affectionate pat to Shadow's neck, and walked across and kicked the dead leaves away.

Well. Looking down I stood for a few moments and did not move.

Neatly wrapped in a length of scarlet cloth lay my own Krozair longsword with the plain strong strappings, the short sword in the lesten hide and golden scabbard given me by the Clansmen of Viktrik, the greenwood longbow of Erthyrdrin made by Seg and a full quiver of clothyard shafts, each fletched with the glowing blue feathers of the crested korf of the Blue Mountains. In its worn old sheath snugged my sailor knife. The lesten hide belt with the dulled silver buckle was drawn up around the bundle. Well, indeed...

These things had been left by me in the stateroom of Delia's voller. There could be one and only one explanation of how they had come to be here pointed out by a dove wearing a scarlet ribbon. So Maspero had known I was in the cave! I remembered his words—he would not wonder what had happened to me on Kregen. He had a dove to send to spy on me. I surmised that perhaps each Savanti tutor operated his own individual dove.

Also there was a filled water bottle and a satchel containing bread and meats, fruit and nuts. Eating, I realized I was hungry; but that formed a tithe of the burden of my thoughts. I had not touched the water bottle I had filled with the milky liquid from the pool. Did Maspero know I had that?

Laid among the weapons and glinting up was a neatly fitting transparent face piece, which I handled with some awe. It was not glass. Now I know it was made of plastic. It strapped about the head and covered the whole face without obstructing vision.

Evidently Maspero had experience of the Spitballs...

After I had eaten I picked up the length of scarlet cloth, and not without a twinge or two, as you may well imagine. It was far finer than humespack, and Delia had been at pains to secure it at some cost. Although silk and sensil are regarded as superior they do have this infuriating tendency to slip. So I wrapped the brave old scarlet around and drew it up between my legs and tucked the end in and cinched it all tight with the broad lesten hide belt. My old knife snugged at my right hip. The quiver went over my shoulder. I hesitated and then, philosophically, slung the Krozair brand there, also. The short sword buckled up scabbarded at my right side. The longbow, unstrung, could slip into the harness at my left side, leaving my hands free, and the case of strings and the satchel could fasten at my belt.

There were no sandals, or shoes or boots.

The spaces for a rapier and a left-hand dagger were left bare.

Just about then a pack of lurfings showed up, lean-flanked, low-bellied, grey-furred scavengers of the plains. Their probing snout-like faces reminded me unpleasantly of the Khirrs.

It was time to mount up and ride.

The Savanti dove had vanished. I took a good look around for the Gdoinye. Evidently, the Star Lords had no interest in me at the moment.

There was no real reason for it; but I said, aloud, looking up and scowling: "By the disgusting diseased tripes of Makki-Grodno, Star Lords! There is a settlement overdue between us!"

That the settlement would come I had no doubt. If I welcomed or dreaded it I did not know. But, in Zair's good time, it would come...

And, now, there was Zena Iztar to add to the reckoning.

Cantering off and feeling extraordinarily wonderful, clad once more in the brave old scarlet, weapons about me, a superb zorca between my knees, I felt the whole of Savage Kregen might take up arms against me and I would win through. Ah, my Delia. Soon, now, I would find my way back to Vallia and Valka.

Maspero, as I was sure it must have been Maspero, had included in the bundle beautiful Savanti leather hunting gloves and arm-guards, and these I donned, with pleasure.

There was, of course, no shield.

Like the Dray Prescot of yore, I rode on, singing lustily through the streaming mingled suns shine of Zim and Genodras.

I sang *The Bowmen of Loh*, and I sang every verse, every last stanza of that rousing song, and I thought of Seg, and I roared. Then, with a different emotion, I yodeled out *The Daisies of Delphond*. I knew the Delphondian Daisy I coveted. Mind you, the Princess Majestrix might not favor being called a Daisy... I decided it was high time I found out.

The journey progressed in grand style. I suppose, looking back, I was drunk on physical fitness. The horror of my experience in crawling like a half-crushed beetle across this savage land had profoundly affected me. By Vox! I'd been as near death and the Black Spider Caves of Gratz as I care to come—although I was to come closer, as you shall hear, and more than once—and so this ride in the brave old scarlet astride a magnificent zorca, well, it turned my head a little.

Shadow carried me surely and safely across the land of Ba-Domek and we avoided habitations and took the back ways and we did not tangle with the Khirrs, save for a little fracas in which three or four of them burst in black slime, and my face mask was smeared, and I washed us all and my longsword most carefully afterwards. For a space the longsword was carried swinging cleanly in the bright air, for I was reluctant to return it to the scabbard Delia had made for me until it was purified, for all I had scrubbed the glittering blade clean with sand and spittle.

Vomanus of Vindelka, with his slapdash ways with weapons, would have to smarten himself up if he tangled with the Spitballs of Antares, that was for sure. Assuming he won free of the hairy black horrors, of course. All along the way expectations of what I would say to all my comrades enlivened my thoughts.

So, on a day with some cloud rolling up to haze over the glory of the suns, I rode out of the last of the foothills beyond the mountains and down through pleasant shallow valleys and along winding river courses and so found myself faced, at last, with the final long haul to the coast. Although I had used Seg's bow I still carried a full quiver; an old paktun always retrieves his shafts when he can.

If I dwell with what must seem a fey fondness on that journey, I think you will understand. I felt reborn. I could taste the glory of Kregen's air and smell the sweetness of the grasses and revel in the warmth of the suns.

On and on we trotted and the plains widened and the sky lifted high above and the clouds rolled and dissipated and I lifted up my head and sang. Silly songs, bawdy songs, stirring war ballads and battle chants, songs of the swods. Vast herds of animals grazed everywhere and the lean forms of the carnivores passed between them, mutually indifferent until the time of hunting. At that time I saw to my weapons and kept a sharp lookout. A massive herd of chunkrah grazed and I gazed at them with the sharp knowing eye of a Clansman, built from wild skirling days on the Great Plains of Segesthes. The chunkrah is perhaps the most superb cattle animal of Paz, deep-chested, horned, fierce, impressive, and his russet coat gleams splendidly. I would not slay one of those magnificent beasts for my supper for that would be wanton waste. Each night I camped and made a fire and slept well away, so that I might espy whoever or whatever sought me by the fireglow.

A sennight later, along with herds of ordel and other cattle, another prairie-darkening herd of chunkrah came in sight, clear proof of the fecundity of the land. Rain fell in due season and the grasses thrived. I skirted the herd, admiring the craggy strength of the chunkrah, giving them no cause to take alarm.

With my old sailorman's knack I had been steering by the suns and the stars and I'd kept on a course that I hoped would be the reciprocal of any vollers out scouting for me toward Aphrasöe. I just accepted with thankfulness the fact—for it is an undeniable fact—that when I am lost and wandering on the face of Savage Kregen my Delia will find ways and means of searching for me. No beautiful idol in a niche, lit by a golden lamp, Delia of Vallia. By Vox, no! She is vibrant and energetic and confoundedly cunning and femininely shrewd. Delia is no stay-at-home dowdy, nor is she a hard and bitter would-be-male chauvinist. She is a woman, and glorious in her womanhood. Also, she casts a too-perceptive eye on me, from time to time, seeing straight through my most artful wiles. So I knew there was a good chance I'd spot an airboat.

Thinking decidedly hot thoughts, I trotted gently over the brow of a hill, a long rolling swaying of the land, and automatically looked for a voller, and all around for potential foes.

A wheeling cloud of Katakis—away in the distance around a scattering of broken rocks beside a broad river Katakis were spurring their zorcas with fiendish cruelty. I stopped at once and pulled Shadow around and rode smartly back over the brow of the hill.

Dismounting and with a pat to Shadow I dropped on all fours and crept up the hill low to the ground and stuck my head out alongside a small chansi bush, its tiny round bottle-green leaves rustling musically in the little breeze. I trusted at the distance that to any sharp eye among the Katakis my shaggy head would look merely like another chansi bush. The wild animals of the plains like the chansi, for it moistens their mouths and chews for a long time, like cham.

The grey rocks out there had fallen in long ago. They lay scattered and broken, weather-beaten. The muddy river humped along and many wildfowl scattered and squawked and commotioned there, a myriad wings against the brightness.

A glint among the rocks took my attention. A careful look, a scrutiny through narrowed eyes—and I let out a sigh of exasperation.

A voller—stuck down among the rocks. She had come down hard. Fastened to a twisted scrap of her prow, upflung, a flag flew bravely—a flag of orange and grey.

Well, it made sense.

Djanduin was the land nearest here to which any of the trespassers at the pool would have been flung. So it would naturally be Kytun and his fellow four-armed tearaways who would reach Ba-Domek first in search of me.

And their voller had crashed, as vollers did on Kregen.

No thought entered my head of rushing down and getting into the fight. Although I will not be pedantic or intractable on the subject, in my view there is no finer fighting man than a Djang, except a Clansman. But—but, again, that must wait. As I stared down I had no concern for the safety of my Djangs man to man with the Katakis.

Katakis are fierce and vicious with their two powerful arms and steel-bladed whiptails. They are excellent if dirty fighters. But Djangs have four arms, and they are better—and dirtier—fighters, when it behooves them to be.

As now, I saw, peering carefully. For there were not above ten Djangs, and the Katakis numbered over a hundred, shrilling around on their zorcas, shooting arrows into the rocks, charging in only to haul around and pull back, taunting the ferocious Djangs to follow them out to be chopped.

On the ring of plain between the Katakis and the rocks lay many bodies. Most were Kataki. There were Djang bodies there, whereat my face grew grim and I ceased from my careless pleasure in once more seeing my Djangs.

I do not forget I am the King of Djanduin.

The simple brainless course would be to mount up and send Shadow flying down there, to burst through the ring, and to join my people in mutual defiance. Then we could fight it out to the end. Oh, yes, there would be joy in that, perhaps some of the tinsel glory that appeals to the boneheads among military men of two worlds, as among berserker warriors. But I was

Dray Prescot, not a stupid thick-headed nincompoop, not a simpleton in these things, even if I am an onker in others. The picture of the leem, stalking the two young elopers, stayed with me. But even the old Dray Prescot, he who had struggled so intemperately in his early days on Kregen, might have thought on before charging down there to the last great fight.

Although I could not tell how long the fight had been going on, by certain signs I judged my Djangs had been cooped up in that rat trap for longer than most men would have survived. The Katakis had set up a camp nearby, and that told much. The actions of the four-armed warriors bespoke tired arms. Unless I did something positive, and soon, my people down there, brave fighting men who looked to me as their king, would be either killed or enslaved.

Wriggling back from the crest I stood up and put a foot in the stirrup.

"Now we work, Shadow," I said. He tossed that superb head, the horn gleaming and sharp. "By the Black Chunkrah! You and me, together. We must do those Katakis a most diabolical mischief."

And I mounted up, foursquare in the saddle, and trotted out.

Eighteen

The King of Djanduin Flies to Vallia

The russet backs of the chunkrah herd heaved and shimmered and rippled in long sinuous lines like a cornfield in the sun. In the sun Zim, I trotted to the rear of the herd and sat looking at them, weighing their configurations and the lay of the land and selecting those specimens who might be trusted to do my work for me. What I purported was neither new or clever; but it would have to serve now.

Maybe it was not new and not clever; but it would be damned tricky to carry through with just one man.

My Clansmen can perform wonders with chunkrahs. They can wheel them about like flying spindrift, they can form them into raging torrents of pounding hooves and tossing horns and fiery eyes, they can split them into neat parcels, and catch and tame one to quietness. In my time as a Clansman I had learned many of these skills; but I was still far more of a simple warrior than a skilled Chunkrah Clanner, although I could get at least a part of this herd moving. Not for me the spiteful bark of a forty-four, and I had no wide-awake to wave, howling. But I shouted, and riding up boldly to the specimens I had selected I nudged them into action, yelling, striking them with the flat of my blade. There are tricks. Soon I had a wedge moving sullenly, the mass beginning to pick up speed. I rode around their rear and flanks, herding them with increasing confidence, and Shadow, although unused to chunkrah work, responded nobly.

Then—if it was Zena Iztar I would try to remember to thank her at a suitable time—a leem prowled over. He was hungry. I had never liked leems. After my ordeal, I liked them even less. But the slinking ochre devil served me for the herd picked him up instantly. Any sensible chunkrah will run when a leem hunts. I have seen chunkrah fight leem, and highly horrible it is, to be sure. A leem will not always win, not by any means. But, with my worrying and the stink of the leem, these chunkrahs chose to be sensible. They ran.

"Hai!" I shouted. "Move along! Hai! Run!"

We roared over the brow of the hill and down the long slope like an avalanche of doom.

I took the larboard side of the pack, for the river was over on the starboard and I knew I'd have to exert every effort to keep the herd running close to the bluffs over the water. Chunkrah are not idiots among animals. So we went smoking down the hill toward the rocks.

The Katakis saw us. They spurred their zorcas about. They do not do honest work, Katakis, and probably had no idea how to halt that wild stampede. A Clansman of Segesthes would have known what to do—after he'd gotten himself and his mount out of the way.

Waving and shouting I drove the larboard flank of the herd in so that the whole enormous mass continued straight on for the rocks. The Katakis hovered, uncertain... Some, with sense, set spurs to their steeds and bolted.

Others tried to hide among the rocks, and four-armed demons of destruction rose, raging.

The chunkrah herd opened to pass each side of the rocks and I let the larboard side spill out, for my work with the russet-clad beauties was done.

"Hai!" I shouted, and stuffed the sword away and ripped out the longbow.

Seg knows how to shoot from the back of a zorca. So do I.

The blue-fletched shafts soared sweetly. Katakis began to drop from their zorcas. One or two tried to shoot back; but their bows were puny things, mere flat staves, not rounded longbows, and the arrows dropped plummeting along the river of russet backs.

So the chunkrahs smashed alongside the rocks and a mess of Katakis was scraped up, trodden down, utterly squashed into the ground. Swerving away from the river the front of the herd broadened; the chunkrah pounded on, dust spurting, horns tossing. I saw a Kataki impaled and flung high, ripped and torn and trailing greasy green and red banners of blood. Another slaver was carried along, the long horn clear through him, wriggling like an insect on a pin. But most were simply trodden down.

The booming stentorian bellowings of the herd clamored away, echoing from the rocks. The hammering thunder of the eight-hooved chunkrahs battered away like the long-running drumming of Balintolian droombooms. Thundering in power and might and sheer irresistible energy, the chunkrah herd hammered the Katakis flat and on and away across the plain.

Cantering up to the rocks I saw a few remaining slaving whiptails being dealt with summarily, and I turned in the saddle and looked back, and, by Krun! I hoped to see the leem. But the beast must have had the sense not to follow. So, gently, I dismounted and sauntered over to the rocks and the crashed flier.

A titanic figure, all blazing blood and energy, bounded up, four arms windmilling. I was seized by the upper right and lower left arms, bear-hugged. The upper left hand clapped me on the back, while the lower right fist gut-punched me in an abandonment of joyous welcome.

I gut-punched back with my fifty percent of his equipment, that, so recently, had been twenty-five percent.

"Kytun! You old devil! Having fun again!"

"King! Notor Prescot!" And thump, thump against my ribs he tattooed. "Dray! What a sight!"

Yes, you see. My Djangs are never surprised when their king turns up to rescue them from a tight spot. It is infuriating, I suppose, the way they just take it for granted that their king will be around in times of trouble; but I am used to it. And, anyway, it gives me a warm delicious feeling, I admit.

The sad truth is I am so often away from Djanduin. But all the sorcery of the Wizards of Loh, all the magical powers of the Savanti, cannot place me in different spots on Kregen at the same time. When a time loop operates, of course, *I have been...*

The others crowded up, the remaining nine. They had lost six of their number in the crash and the fight.

"Katakis!" said Felder Kholin Mindner, dismissively.

"Aye," said Kytun Kholin Dom. "It was a bonny fight. And only ten to one. The whiptails didn't stand a chance."

Mind you, he did not boast. I vouch for that.

Then followed the greetings and the handclasps and the joyous shouted insults, the horseplay. We made a camp and ate, for the voller was well-provisioned. If any Katakis remained alive they dared not show their ugly faces. Katakis, these bladed whiptails, fear very few races—Chuliks, Pachaks who share a racial hostility; perhaps most of all they fear Djangs, when they meet them, which is not often. As for my Clansmen—well, again, that is for another time.

Kytun broke open an amphora of best Jholaix he had been keeping against our meeting. The wine had been a present from me; we eleven drank it down, and right royally it served its purpose.

"And the emperor—?"

"Aye, Dray! The queen, may Mother Diocaster smile forever upon her, went first into the pool, walking at the side of her father down the stairs. And he moved and sat up on the litter—before, by Zodjuin of the Silver Stux, before it dissolved away—and spoke rationally. He was cured, Dray. Perfectly cured. And then, why then—" And here Kytun scratched his head with his upper left hand and his other hands busied themselves in eating and drinking. "Why, there was blueness and coldness in the pool, and we were in Djanguraj and I was shouting for a new voller. It was not Drig's business. We were there, and then we were home. But, as Djan is my witness, it was a mighty strange affair. Mighty strange, by Zodjuin of the Stormclouds."

Afterwards the dead Djangs were prepared for burial, an extempore, battlefield ritual, with due feeling and solemnity. I watched, taking my part, for I was king.

As to my own story, the wonder of their experiences tended to help and, anyway, as I say, my Djangs perfectly accepted that I would turn up to help them out in any little spot of bother if I could manage it. When troubles hit a party of them that they couldn't handle, and I did not turn up, they would swing those four arms of theirs and say, so I was told, that, by Zodjuin, the king could not be everywhere at once.

Talking to Kytun, I could not stop my own overriding concerns from showing.

"You are our king, Dray. But it is Vallia that demands at the moment." He worked his oiled rag over his djangir, setting up the polish. "Of course, they only see you as a prince. One day—"

"Djanduin," I said harshly. "Djanduin means more to me than Vallia. Perhaps Valka—" I had no need to go on. "One day, Kytun, the whole of Paz will be one, united."

He was a good comrade and so he could insult me with a jest; also, I was his king, so he refrained from any comment on so patently absurd a notion.

During the siege among the rocks there had been no time to work on the flier with any consistency; now we went at it to straighten out the link-ages controlling the silver boxes that upheld and powered the voller in flight. After some hot and toiling work, mixed with profanities that encompassed the Pantheon of the Warrior Gods of Djanduin, we had the thing fixed, and the voller was once more operational.

Kytun cocked an eyebrow at me.

"Djanguraj," I told him. "We will take this wonderful zorca, Shadow, with us. There is room. In Djanguraj I shall take a small fast voller for Vondium—"

I got no farther.

"King!" bellowed Kytun. The djangir gleamed brilliantly. "We follow you to chop the cramphs who poisoned the queen's father! By Djondalar of the Twisted Staff! This is our duty—aye, and our pleasure."

I was tempted.

Zair knew, with a rascally gang of ferocious Djangs at my back I could do the business speedily enough. But caution supervened. I explained it patiently.

"Suppose a great crowd of Vallian nobles came barging into Djanduin to punish Djangs? Would you—"

"I would rip their guts out!—Oh..."

"Pride, Kytun, is very foolish at times, as at others it is very necessary in a man. I must go alone. To do otherwise would alienate those who—" I paused, annoyed with myself. I had been about to say, those who did not think things through, and, by Djan! that applies to four-armed Dwadjangs, without a doubt. But I love them, for they are bonny fighters. So I said, firmly: 'The pride of Vallians would be insulted. Anyway, the emperor has probably sorted things out by now.'"

"I trust so, by Zodjuin of the Storm Clouds."

Just whereabouts in their home parts of Kregen Vanti would have dispatched my friends I did not know. That depended on how good a shot he was. He'd dumped me down on the coast of Africa somewhere near where I'd been when the Scorpion first took me up to Kregen. But the emperor, Delia, Drak and Jaidur could all be scattered over the whole of Vallia. They could have been shot cleanly into the throne room of the palace in Vondium. I did not know. As to my other friends—well, they'd been scattered halfway around Kregen, as you shall hear.

Perhaps, looking back, I made a mistake in not there and then deciding to load as many fighting Djangs as possible into airboats and going vengefully back to Vallia to settle affairs finally. But, remember, I was still attempting to be the conciliatory Dray Prescot I fancied I must be to attain my goals on Kregen. So, instead, we flew to Djanguraj, I stayed for the shortest possible time decency would allow, and then, with Shadow, took off for Vallia in a small, fleet craft that should see me safely all the way there.

The journey north along the South Lohvian Sea and across the western section of the Southern Ocean—which lies north of Havilfar—and so skirting close to the Koroles, and away up with a great swing to the west of north around the tip of Pandahem, a place remarkably dear to many men, being called Jholaix, passed uneventfully. Uneventfully, save that twice the scarlet and golden raptor appeared high in the blue, circling, watching, and twice the white dove of the Savanti flew down to take a look at my craft.

I say the white dove—maybe, I wondered, it might be better to say a white dove. The idea that each tutor operated his own individual dove did make sense.

So, at last, the southern coastline of Vallia hove in sight over the horizon. The breakers thundered against the shore, the broad bay of the Great River of Vallia, She of the Fecundity passed below, and away up the shining reaches of the river the enormous fantastical skyline of Vondium came in sight. I slanted down.

There was to be no fooling about with attempts to pass guards this time. No secret passages. From the wardrobe kept up in the Palazzo of the Four Winds in Djanguraj I had selected a suit of decent Vallian bluff, so I was dressed as a Vallian as I brought the voller down to the emperor's own landing platform and leaped out. The patrolling airboats of the Vallian Air Service had been late—I frowned at that—and I started off across the broad paved space toward the porticoed entrance.

Shadow looked at me a little reproachfully from the stall built for him in the aft body of the voller, and I flung him a few words of comfort.

Around me the pinnacles of the higher towers reached for the sky. The wind whispered across the open space where airboats were parked, with men working on them in the shadows of their hangars. Chulik guards ran out toward me, angry, intent, ready to do me a mischief. Up here there were usually the Crimson Bowmen on guard.

"Stand, cramph, for the emperor's guards!" yelled their Deldar, a Chulik of mean aspect, with a golden tip to his portside tusk.

"Out of the way!"

I bundled into them, took the first three-grained staff that came handy, knocked three or four of the fellows over and went on, running, into the shadows under the portico.

Only two arrows splintered against the marble. The Chuliks had compound reflex bows of some power; but any skill I may possess at arrow-dodging was not required.

I knew the way.

Past a few slaves I hurried, along the sumptuous corridors well-lit by tall windows where the brocaded drapes barely stirred in the breeze, ignoring a party of Fristle guards who went stepping past smartly across an intersection. Their uniforms might be considered to indicate they were in the emperor's service; but there was altogether too much green and brown about them, and not enough of the red and yellow.

Various doors were guarded by various guards. If they did not let me through I sent them to sleep without regret. After all, time was wasting.

My calculations told me there would be time for me to reach the penultimate corridor before the guards rallied sufficiently to come in a body to check this madman who had stormed into the palace. The front door, the front aerial door, had been easier than all the other ways. I went on, ignored a group of pretty girls in silks and bangles who shrank away, chattering, angled around the last ornate doorway.

Only four Chuliks stood there. I gave them no chance to speak.

Only one had a chance to shriek out, and then he, too, slumbered. I kicked a silly ornate golden helmet away and bashed the balass and silver door open. Straight ahead of me down a long and brilliantly lit corridor, filled with people waiting, talking, arguing, drinking, lay the folded doors of the emperor's throne room. He was there. I knew that. These people were waiting audience of him. I walked on.

Someone yelled: "Hey, fambly! Wait your turn." I walked on.

A man, he was a kov, a high colored, fleshy man—I knew him—took my arm with anger. I shook him off. I stalked on, and now I was recognized. The whisper ran around the tall room. "The Prince Majister!"

At the folded doors I came at last to the time when the guards would confront me in real earnest. From a narrow side door they boiled out, Chuliks, tusked, blankly fierce, not reasoning, ready instantly to kill to earn their hire. So far I had not drawn a weapon.

A voice lifted from the waiting brilliantly attired throng. "He is the Prince Majister! Treat him well—" The Jiktar at the head of the Chuliks said: "I do not know him. No man enters here without leave of Kov Layco Jhansi. Seize him up!"

I kicked the Jiktar betwixt wind and water, slid the rapid succession of blows, got a sword blade between my elbow and side and wrenched it away from its startled owner, belted a few more, toppling them over. They crashed into their fellows. I was at the doors. The fastenings were immense. I gripped the handles as big as spear blades, dragged the folding doors inward. The oiled panels picked up speed. I had to put my foot into one wight's face to stop his head from being crashed. The massive doors thudded shut.

The bar fell almost of its own accord.

The dinning sound dimmed and faded from outside. The hush fell oddly, menacingly.

Slowly, with the closed doors at my back, I turned around.

The floor of polished marble glimmered in the lights from many samphron oil lamps and from the sparkling rays striking through the wide latticed windows in the curved roof. The distance down to the multiple dais was not great, for this was the third throne room, used for more personal requests. The crimson carpet and the zhantil pelt seatings were familiar, the gold ornaments, the idols, the trophies of battle, the small sacrificial fire and the altar. Beautiful girls waited to bring refreshments when bidden. The room was almost empty.

I started on down the marble floor, my Vallian boots clacking loudly.

The figure in the throne under the ritual canopy sat up. The people standing on the dais, lower down, but not on the floor, went rigid.

"So you return bearing words, son-in-law?"

"Not so, emperor!" I bellowed back. "See—I come empty-handed."

And I held up my hands, palms outwards, as I marched.

A small quick gesture from the emperor halted the reflex action of the bodyguard lining out each side of the throne. These guards, too, were Chuliks. I did not like the look of this at all. I have employed Chuliks as mercenaries, for they are powerful fighters; but the numbers of them, the positions they occupied, argued some calamity had befallen the Crimson Bowmen, or some other deviltry was at work.

"You are banished from Vondium, son-in-law. Tell me why I should not order you cast down to the deepest dungeons?"

"Because you know that will not serve you." I looked about, for the moment ignoring the few men and women in attendance on him, looking for certain faces I hungered to see.

"Where is Delia? Where are Drak and Jaidur?"

"Well may you ask, Dray Prescot. Since I am well again I have seen nothing of—"

I held onto my roaring senses. Didn't the buffoon know what had happened? Probably not. He'd been on the point of death in his imperial bed, and then he'd been dumped down in his palace full of life. Probably he had no memory of what had intervened, or of that moment of lucidity in the Pool.

"You remember your request to your daughter?"

"I have made many requests of her. She usually refuses."

"And damned sensible, too! So you don't remember."

"Enough of this—" he started to say, getting his temper up, which with him was deplorably easy.

"I want to see Delia and the children!" I stopped at the foot of the dais and my left hand rested on the hilt of the Krozair longsword, which I wore angled out almost parallel with the ground, jutting, arrogant, I confess, very boastfully. The rapier hanging from its baldric looked thin and puny in contrast.

"And I would like to see some of these people you tell me are my friends. I was near unto death—and what happened to you and your friends?"

"I was banished—or have you forgotten?"

His dark, heavy face flushed. He was back to full health, all right. Why, the old devil had never felt better in his life.

"This Seg Segutorio, this Inch of the Black Mountains, kovs, both of them, because I gave you the gifting. I have my loyal men about me now." His powerful face showed an intensity of belief. "I have made a winnowing of my enemies. Now I have loyal friends and an impregnable bodyguard of Chuliks—"

I laughed. I, Dray Prescot, laughed. The laugh was filled with scorn, contemptuous.

"Impregnable?"

He swallowed down bile for a space. But he was not beaten by mere words; he was emperor. "I let you live. One word from me and you die."

"And your daughter?"

That nettled him sorely.

It did more than that. I fancied I knew what had happened. No matter where Delia had landed back in Vallia, she had swiftly organized fliers, men and weapons, supplies. Then she had gone haring off back to the forbidden island of Ba-Domek. She had gone to find me. And, no doubt, everyone else of our company she could find had gone with her.

That was an eventuality I had hoped to forestall. But I was too late. So, since the emperor was safe, I had no more business with him.

One more fact remained to be established.

"Of these people you stigmatize by calling them my friends." I named the people I meant, the brave company who had flown with me to Aphrasöe carrying the dying body of this emperor with us. He knew them and of their loyalty to me. "Are there any in Vondium now?"

"No, son-in-law. Not one. Not a single person of those you champion so loudly. I tell you, I have friends, and I know where to look for succor."

He started to shake with anger, working himself up. A further thought occurred to me. I was aware of a small side door opening and of the guards springing to assist the people who entered; but I wanted to ask the emperor one last question before I retired.

"You were nearly dying, emperor. Now you are well. Do you know how that was accomplished?"

"Of course. Need you ask?"

His reply astonished me. He was looking off to the side, to the group of people who had entered and who now came up to the foot of the dais, bowing with the air of those who had power and authority at the emperor's hand.

"Here, Dray Prescot, are those who saved me. Loyal subjects all. To them, I owe my life and Vallia. They should be the lesson you so sorely need."

He gestured, raising them up from their postures of reverence. I looked.

Oh, I looked, like an idiot, like an onker, like the stupid simpleton I am.

These were the people Delia's father put his trust in, these the folk he had given power, and chief among them Doctor Charboi, and hard, bright, cutting, Ashti Melekhi, the Vadnicha of Venga.

Nineteen

"There Stands the Notorious Dray Prescot!"

"Why is this man allowed to wear swords in the presence of the emperor? Disarm him, instantly!"

The vicious words of Ashti Melekhi spattered into the bright radiance of the throne room.

The guard Chulik—he was an ord-Jiktar and therefore very high in the guard, probably the third in command—stepped down from the dais heading for me, and he half-drew his rapier.

"Wait, wait, my dear Ashti!" called the emperor.

I felt nausea at his way of addressing her.

Down in Djanduin my warrior Djangs would feel naked and dishonored to appear in the presence of their king without a ceremonial djangir buckled up to their harness. But this was Vallia, and only on special occasions would the court wear anything other than fancy smallswords for decorative purposes. Vallia was a civilized country.

"This man, Ashti, is the Prince Majister." He relished his power. "There stands the notorious Dray Prescot! He is my son-in-law, I am afraid. I do not care for him overmuch; but he has served me well on occasion. He is a man of swords, a man of blood, a man of violence."

I felt the outrage. "I am not a man of blood!" I bellowed. "I am a man of peace!"

"That is as may be. But you may keep your swords."

The Chulik Jiktar slapped his rapier back. He looked annoyed, as though denied a pleasure. But the emperor knew me better than this yellow-faced, tusked, malevolent Chulik.

The emperor knew I was more malevolent on occasion than any Chulik born—and this, too, was for my sins.

Melekhi stared at me. Charboi had the grace to shuffle away, eyes cast down, and stand nervously some distance off. Ashti Melekhi! A long cool gown of green she wore, with golden motifs, and the strigicaw seizing the korf, her badge, emblazoned upon breast and arm and thigh. She stared challengingly at me and I sensed she had an inkling that I had taken the emperor away, following his gasped instructions, and was not yet prepared to take up that particular challenge. The emperor believed she and Charboi had cured him. To challenge me now, openly, would raise awkward questions, and she wanted to choose her time and place for the confrontation.

I said: "Twelve friends of yours paid me a call. I hope they spoke well of me."

She started, and controlled herself, her thin cheeks pinching in. I noticed she wore a small sword that was, in reality, a strong and cunning dagger, emblazoned with gems.

"Oh," she says, very sure of herself. "No doubt you will meet some more of my—friends—very soon."

"I welcome it. Let them come swiftly. The canals are cooling in the hot weather."

The emperor made a sign and a beautiful girl ran across to give him a drink of parclear. He drank, thirstily. "I don't know what foolery this is; but anyone knows the canals of Vallia are deadly to those not of the canalfolk. Now, Dray Prescot, say what you have to say and go."

"The banishment upon me is lifted?"

Melekhi gasped at this; but the emperor, after another insolent drink, and having his mouth wiped by a Fristle fifi, nodded. "Yes. But if you err again, son-in-law—"

"Only time will tell that. For there are things you must know. And you will not relish the telling of them."

"And will the word onker come into it?"

"Only if an onker listens, instead of an emperor."

His face swelled up again, and he thundered out: "You try my patience sorely! Have a care. You had best go while your head is still on your shoulders."

Considering it redundant once more to point out what that order had come to in the past, I nodded stiffly to him. I faced Ashti Melekhi. I did not smile, as is my wont, and I kept my face as naturally molded into its ugly old lineaments as I could. All the same, something showed, for her eyes narrowed and the tip of a red tongue flicked her lips.

Nath the Iarvin started at this, and stilled. All the time his bulky form towered at Ashti Melekhi's shoulder, silent, unspeaking, his small dark eyes watchful. He still wore the brown leather tunic and buff breeches, with the wide, black, silver-studded belt girt up around his gut. The lockets for his rapier swung empty; but he carried a twin to the dagger worn by Melekhi. The sheer ferocity of that lowering face impressed me once again. This man had been bought body and soul by Melekhi, he would fight and kill and die for her and joy in the doing of it.

I walked out with my shoulders held braced, my boots clacking on the polished marble floor. At the door where Womoxes hoisted up the bar and swung it away, folding the panels open, I turned back. The emperor sat forward on his throne, watching, and the others remained still in the postures I had left them.

"I give you Remberee, emperor. We shall meet again—"

"Not if Opaz wills it," he shouted after me.

So I went out and took myself off. This time I was allowed through. But the looks I took from some of the Chuliks heartened me. They hadn't seen the half of it, yet.

The voller lifted off smartly and I turned in the direction of the Great Northern Cut and Bargom's *Rose of Valka*—and then I clicked the control levers over. No, I did not wish just yet to become embroiled with stikitches. The assassins Melekhi would send must wait. Business before pleasure.

Information was vital, information I needed but that could not have been asked for from any of those in the throne room. Although I have an ugly old figurehead and a pair of shoulders that are somewhat on the wide side, it is possible for me on a world like Kregen to disguise myself adequately. A large hat, perhaps a false beard, a long cloak, the cunning application of makeup and a different walk, these things work wonders.

The voller was dropped at our Delphondian villa, a piece of work rapid in the extreme, for Melekhi would probably send her assassins to all my villas as well as *The Rose of Valka*. With Shadow safely stabled in a public livery, for I might need him in a hurry, I could stroll into *The Savage Woflo*, a riotous tavern where soldiers and guards gathered, and fling a few silver stivers across the table and roar for good Vallian ale.

The sight of my father-in-law's face glinting upon the stivers, a variety of propaganda slogans and pictures on the reverses, did not altogether please me; but the money fetched ale, and company, and I could settle down before the singing began. Here in *The Savage Woflo* information could be come by. Because of the many lords in Vondium the tavern was crowded with their guards. Colors blazed in the mineral-oil lamps. Soon I was being filled in with all the latest gossip.

A few Crimson Bowmen sat drinking, and most looked glum. There were few Pachaks. The Chuliks outnumbered all. This, I owned to myself, was passing strange. Vondium had recovered from the dread spell of impending doom that hung over the city like a pall when the emperor lay dying. Now he was back in his palace, hale and well, Vondium could go back to the usual round of commerce and industry, secure that all was well with Vallia. By careful talk, by intimating I knew more than I did, I got out the story.

Briefly: all the Crimson Bowmen and the Chuliks who had guarded the emperor's door that night had been discharged. I was amazed they had not been slaughtered out of hand. But that would have entailed stringent inquiries. Melekhi stood in a position of great power, that was undeniable. She was being used by an even more shadowy figure of greater power; and for an instant I trembled, thinking it might be Phu-si-Yantong. There was nothing to link him with this plot against the emperor personally; this was a palace intrigue, and Yantong had worked through his Black Feathers of the Great Chyyan against the whole of Vallia.

Her mentor might be this Kov Layco. He was an astute man, holding the empire together for the emperor, guiding with ruthless and clever hands the destinies of all, trusted. Yes, he might cherish ambitions; it could be him. I tended to doubt it would be any Racter, for they attempted, for all their evil, to work through legal means. And for the Panvals the same held. There were many parties and factions ready to strike if the emperor died; now they were muzzled, but any one of them could own and instruct Ashti Melekhi in her evil designs.

The emperor insisted these days on guards hired from the Chulik mercenaries. The Crimson Bowmen, like the Archer Guard of Valka assigned to duty around the emperor, had been sent off on distant expeditions into the country.

Naghan Vanki, who, I knew, or thought I knew, was the emperor's spymaster, had recently, after his good work with the Chyyanists, been rewarded by being made Vad of Nav-Sorfall. The province was lush, rich with ponsho pastures, situated just east of Vomansoir. Because of this addition to his estates Naghan Vanki, the new vad, was off in Nav-Sorfall busily at work consolidating his position. I could not turn to him for immediate information on the plots and intrigues surrounding the emperor.

To think, the woman who had bribed a doctor to poison the emperor was now held in great esteem by her intended victim! She would strike again, and soon. I stirred myself. The singing would begin soon; but because there were so-many Chuliks, the singing promised to be half-hearted and short if the yellow-tuskers did not remove themselves, as they usually did when there were not many of them.

The last piece of information amused me. Queen Lushfymi, the Queen of Lome, whom men still called Queen Lush, despite the emperor's strict injunctions against the loss of dignity, was rumored to be hot on her way to the emperor's side.

If the old devil married her, I'd heave a sigh of relief. That would take a deal of weight off Delia's and my shoulders.

The Maiden with the Many Smiles shone down brilliantly as I wrapped my cloak about myself, pulling it up to my eyes, and set off for the palace. The first moon of Kregen showed those mysterious markings that had so often tantalized the astronomers of Kregen. Up there, on that world floating in space, were continents and islands and seas, and an atmosphere. The ever-changing radiance gave her her name. In that soft and fuzzy roseate moonlight I strode swiftly through the pink-tinged shadows.

Vondium went about the usual pursuits of the great city after the suns had set and the moons ruled the skies. I avoided all entanglements. This time there was another Rapa guard at the Jasmine Tower beyond the Canal of Contentment. He went to sleep peacefully and I opened the plastered niche and, pulling the revolving stone free, passed swiftly down the slimed stairs.

The lantern showed nitered walls, dripping thick with green slime, and the darkly patterned stairs. That first Rapa guard had recovered, all right, and said nothing, greeting his relief with a hearty: "All's well!" So do mortal men's sins find them out and aid hairy old villains like me.

Reaching the secret panel that led onto the emperor's chamber, I paused. He had plenty of bedrooms to choose from. Maybe he wouldn't relish sleeping again in the room in which he had so nearly died. I'd find him, though, if I had to roam all through the palace.

What I really wanted to do was take voller and fly as swiftly as I could after Delia, on toward Ba-Domek and Aphrasöe. But I conceived I had a duty to the emperor; the old devil owed me, and I suppose, really, I owed him. He was Delia's father. I could not let him be killed. I could not abandon him to his fate.

I pushed the panel in soundlessly.

Anyway, I did not want the forces controlling Ashti Melekhi to slay the emperor and gain their coveted powers—I did not want them to win.

Intrigue, dark plots, the shadows of night, the hushed footfall—these were games I would play, I decided, as I padded into the chamber. The room stood empty, a few faintly glimmering lamps reflecting from the old polished furniture. The wide bed lay with its covers turned back. A golden tray rested on a low table at the side. Miscils, palines, purple wine of Wenhartdrin in a golden vessel with two golden cups—the old devil was all set up for the night, then.

A noise at the door, the oiled creak of its opening, light splashing sharply across the rugs of Walfarg weave. I moved back into the shadows of the overhanging draperies. He walked in with a few handmaids and servants, scolding them, full of good humor. Eventually, when he was dressed in a long crimson brocaded gown he shooed them out. As the door closed he shouted out jovially past them to the corridor: "And mind you stand a good watch, my bonny Chuliks."

They were bonny all right, working for anyone who paid them. If someone else had crossed their yellow palms with more gold than the emperor, they'd as lief slit his throat as stand a good guard.

He started up when I stepped out into the lamplight. His face worked with shock. His hand darted to the golden bell.

I put my hand over his and the bell hung mute.

"Ha!" he cried. "Murder, is it?"

"No." I held him gently. "I mean you no harm, as I have told you often enough. I wish to talk to you. For the sake of your daughter and your grandchildren, will you hear me out?"

The bell must be removed from his clutching fingers, for I would not trust him, as I trust no one save a very few on Kregen and Earth.

"Talk? You talk big, son-in-law. But you desert me when danger—"

"You banished me. Forget that. You remember nothing of your illness?"

He shook his head. For a space, so long as I offered him no violence, he would humor me and listen... "No. I remember nothing. I was ill. Ashti cured me."

I let him go but I did not step back. I stared at him. "Listen to me, emperor, and mark me well. You were poisoned." He started up angrily at this, but I went on doggedly. "The name of the poison was solkien concentrate—"

"I know it! Cottmer's work!"

"Aye. And you were fed it, lovingly, spoonful by spoonful."

"I do not believe—how could I? I was cared for, nursed, no one—Ashti would not have allowed it—you lie!"

"I do not lie. I pass over your intemperate words. I tell you the truth."

For a moment he stood there, tall and bluff and robust, filling his crimson gown with the golden cords. His face showed a sudden crafty intelligence. "I know of solkien concentrate. Once it gets a hold on the system its evil results cannot be averted. I was ill, very ill. Ashti told me. If you speak sooth then I could not have been cured."

"Not by normal men. I agree."

He looked bewildered. "But—"

I bore down on him. "You called out in your delirium. You asked your daughter, you begged Delia to take you to those who could cure you, as they had cured her."

His eyes widened.

"Yes—yes—I do not remember—but I would—I did! The Todalpheme of Hamal."

"Your daughter Delia took you there. You were cured. If you do not remember, then that is probably better. Now you are back in your palace, fit and well. Delia did that."

"Solkien concentrate." He wet his lips and took up the golden vessel, poured wine. He did not pour for me. I let him drink. Then I said: "Suppose that wine is poisoned, also?"

He choked and spat and the purple wine sprayed all over the white linen of the bed.

He swung to face me. He was trembling. "If I believed you, your story, if I did—you have not told me who did this thing."

"Ah," I said. I used the old formula out of spite, watching him squirm. "I wondered when you'd come to that."

"Tell me! I can find out if you speak truth. I can seek and find the answers to my questions—"

"Oh, aye. You can have folk tortured to your heart's content."

"Tell me, you insolent cramph!"

"I wonder, sometimes," I told him, "why I suffer myself to bother with you. Only for Delia's sake. Otherwise, I really think I would let you go your own way to damnation."

His face shook with his rage, cunning and powerful, used to absolute obedience. "Tell me!"

"Ashti Melekhi."

He gaped at me.

Then he laughed and sneered, all in one, and sank back in the ornate brocaded chair at the bedside. The golden tassels shook with his sarcastic mirth. He brayed at me.

"You onker! Your sorry story is a pack of lies. The woman cut you down to size and you resent that. Ashti—why, Ashti nursed me devotedly. She found Doctor Charboi. Your story of solkien concentrate must be untrue, this leem's nest of a story about going for the miracle cure—lies, all lies. I shall call the guard instantly—"

"There is no need for that. I have warned you. The woman is deadly. She will try again. What I would like to know is whom she is working for."

"She works for me. She is devoted."

"And Queen Lush?"

He glared, choking with rage, trying to rise from the chair and being held down by my hand. "She is Queen Lushfymi and she has nothing to do with this. Ashti knows she can never become empress. That is not to be thought of."

"I wasn't thinking of that, either. But it would give you a reason to understand. Myself, I believe there are other stronger forces at work here to destroy not only you but the whole of our family."

"Our family?"

"I know how you regard me, a wild clansman; but your grandchildren are Delia's children. You must believe me."

"I cannot. I must think on what you have said and think best how to deal with you."

You see? You see how the powerful of the land think?

I said to him, speaking pretty savagely: "Very well, emperor. You think on. I have warned you and I shall try to protect you. If I leave now I expect no trouble from your Opaz-forsaken Chulik guards. Or you'll have a slew of death bonuses to pay out."

He panted, heaving up as I stepped back into the shadows of the bed. "Sometimes, Dray Prescot, sometimes I think I would gladly pay all my treasury in death bonuses if one of them was yours."

"Oh, aye. You're not the only one."

The door creaked on its oiled hinges and fresh light spurted through the opening gap. No one had knocked. The emperor stood up from the chair, half turned away from where I stood shrouded in the bed hangings. He looked relieved and glad.

"Here is Ashti now. Now we will test the lies you spew!"

So that explained the second cup. The purple wine would be safe, then. I licked my lips, thirstily.

Ashti Melekhi entered the emperor's bed chamber, walking like a neemu, all feline undulation and grace. Her thin mannish figure was clad in the green hunting leathers. At this the emperor's face fell. He took a half-step forward.

"Ashti? You are welcome, welcome—but why this costume?"

She flashed that brilliant scything white smile at him.

"Because there is hunting to do tonight, majister."

"Hunting?" The buffoon was bemused.

Following Melekhi the hulking form of Nath the Iarvin shouldered through the door. With him came six Chuliks. They were officers, Hikdars and Jiktars, and at their head strode the Chulik Chuktar of the guard. Their weapons glittered naked in their fists.

The emperor fell back.

"Ashti!" he screeched.

"Yes, emperor. We cannot wait. Your interfering son-in-law has returned, and he knows the truth. So you must die tonight, now!"

Twenty

Savage Kregen

"Slay him, you fools, and have done!"

Ashti Melekhi pointed scornfully at the emperor, who fell back over his chair, twisting, knocking the golden cups of wine to the priceless carpets.

I stepped out into the light. The long dark cloak covered my face in shadow.

"Whoever he is, slay him also!" cried Melekhi.

The Chuliks advanced with grim purpose.

"You see, emperor," I said. "There's no telling an old onker the truth even if it's staring him in the face."

The emperor choked. He tried to struggle up. "Guards!" he got out in a strangled voice. "Guards! To me! To me!"

"What!" said I. "D'you want more of 'em to do your business for you? This bitch has bought them all."

Ashti Melekhi drew in a sharp breath. Her face glowed with pleasure, her grey-green eyes bright, her pursed red mouth moist.

"The Prince Majister! Two with but a single cast! Now the gods smile on me."

"It depends on which gods," I said as I threw off the swathing cloak. "Some of that fraternity are not too reliable."

"Slay them both," screeched Melekhi. She held her hands pressed to her thin breast. She craned to watch.

The rapier came out smoothly enough, and the left-hand dagger. These Chuliks were past masters at their art, trained from birth. I was in for a strenuous few murs—or however long the fight lasted. The problem would be to keep the emperor from being killed.

I never forgot he was an emperor. Now he struggled up and the look on his face would have quelled an ordinary rabble. He grabbed for the bedhead table. He kept a sword ready to hand there as do all sensible folk on Kregen.

"I am the emperor!" he shouted. "Foresworn traitoress!"

"Now, emperor," I said. "Remember. Remember the fight with the third party outside your very own palace grounds?" As I said this I crossed swords with the first of the Chuliks, who came on with great panache. I twinkled his blade about; but he knew that one, and I had a quick little spot of nimble parry and duck with his left hand companion before the rapier went into his guts and I could withdraw, skip aside and so kick another Chulik betwixt wind and water. He staggered; but I gave him no time to fall, by reason of the dagger that skewered into his eye. Bits of fluid, gristle and blood spurted.

"I remember that fight, Dray Prescot!"

"Aye. Well, I'll pull your hair again if you get in the way."

Two Chuliks were down. The four remaining came on, violently, rapidly, and I had a deal of ducking and parrying to do, using the full of the blade, feeling the solid power of their blows ring and chingle along the steel.

"Get past him, you fools!" screeched Melekhi. "Get at the emperor."

"You stay behind me, emperor!" I yelled, and shoved him back with my shoulder, as cursing and swashing his blade, he struggled to get past the bed and the table.

Because of that wide, ornate, draped bed the Chuliks could not get around me on one side, or leap at my back. They had to come at me from the front and the right. This, I fancy, put them at a disadvantage. There were four of them. Nath the Iarvin stood, blocky, solid, immense, at the side of his mistress, watching it all with those cold piggy eyes.

And I saw, instantly, that the Chuliks would be cut down when they had done their work.

This Nath was good with a blade. Everyone knew that.

A third Chulik staggered back, most surprised. He had thought I would thrust with the rapier, having feinted for that purpose, and he had dropped into line ready for the riposte. But my rapier held down the blades of two of his companions, beating them back. My main gauche whipped across, very fast, horizontal, very nastily.

The Chulik looked surprised because his throat was cut from ear to ear. He grinned at me with a blood-bubbling mouth where his throat should be.

The fourth Chulik, for the moment disengaged, shoved his dying comrade aside to get at me, and as he came on so I dropped and gut-thrust him before he even settled, and sent him toppling over on the last long journey to the Ice Floes of Sicce.

The other two stepped back, their blades snaking up, free of mine, and so for a space we looked at one another.

"What do you wait for!" Melekhi stamped her foot—a futile, stupid gesture. "Slay them both!"

And Nath the Iarvin spoke.

"He is a great swordsman, my lady."

"And so are you—better, by all accounts."

"Then let me—"

"Wait!"

The Chuliks were filled with the blood lust and the purport of this exchange passed them by. They leaped in, still deadly, still ferociously anxious to spill my tripes.

Well aware that this brooding Nath was watching my play I tried to play the next one cleverly and foin a little and a Chulik blade sliced down my face. I cursed and jumped aside and my brand scorched across his face, not where I had intended and I felt the steel jar against a tusk. He screamed.

This was turning from a pleasant little passage at arms into the bloody and squalid fight it truly was.

There was no Jikai here, I surmised.

Blood ran down my chin.

The two were heartened at this and came on. The emperor was still thrashing and swashing about, and he near-nicked me a couple of times.

"Keep you back, you great onker!" I said. "By Zair! I don't want your nose sliced off for my Delia to see!"

"Let me at 'em!" he was yelling, kicking the chair, the table, the bed, foaming.

My blade licked in and out, and the Chuliks, who can handle weapons, played me, one against the other; but I had them in the end, although not as I had expected.

The right hand one stepped back. He stepped away from the struggle of his comrade. Swiftly he thrust his rapier under his left arm and whipped out a throwing knife. It was not a terchick, being altogether heavier and not so finely balanced; but it would do the emperor's business for him.

Fight fire with fire. There was no time. I lifted the left-hand dagger. I hurled it as my Clansmen hurl the terchicks, riding the backs of their voves. Left-handed, right-handed, it makes little difference to a Clansman.

At the same time I slid the point of the last Chulik and presented my point to his throat.

The main gauche flew true. It smashed into the Chulik's face, staggering him, bringing a great splashing spurt of dark blood. And the rapier point slid, cutting through the windpipe and the jugular of the Chulik before me. The distant yellow-tusk screeched, flailing about, spraying gobbets of blood, screaming. The one before me glared madly, trying to wrench the blade from his throat, and that damned fool the emperor came up—well, not between my legs, but close by them—surged up to take a juicy whack with his blade at the wriggling Chulik.

The mercenary flailed over backwards taking my rapier with him.

I stood there, glaring myself, furiously angry.

"Get back out of it, you fambly!" I roared.

And Ashti Melekhi, in a voice like steel, said: "Now, Nath. Now."

Nath the Iarvin drew his rapier and main gauche with the single fluid motion that told of a master fencer. He advanced on me and the look on his dark powerful features meant only one thing in the whole wide world of Kregen.

I stood before him, my hands empty.

"Dray!" screeched the emperor, squirming about between bed and table. "A sword—here—take mine!"

"Too late for that, rast," said this Nath, speaking up, very jovial, very purring-pleased now he had been unleashed.

"True," I said, brightly. "True."

Nath leaped in with that smooth skilful poised motion of the bladesman.

So, with a sigh, I, Dray Prescot, Krozair of Zy, unlimbered the deadly Krozair brand, and with spread fists, met that headlong charge.

His first swift passage aimed at sliding past the long blade was met and repulsed. He dodged back, the main gauche fending. He blinked.

"You'd best put up that old bar of iron, dom. Make it easy on yourself. Just relax and, by the Blade of Kurin, I swear to make it quick and painless."

And, as he spoke, cunning bladesman, he leaped again and so twinkled his blades before my eyes. Cunning, cunning! Oh, yes, he was very good as a bladesman, this Nath the Iarvin. But I have been a bladesman in my time—still am, I suppose. He had not met a Krozair brand before. All that old agony of indecision of mine about a Krozair brand facing a rapier— well, that has been settled. The beautiful blade, perfectly balanced, rotated smoothly, oiled, flaming with power, scorched in past his darting blades, sank in over his silver-studded black belt, sank in and in and burst on through.

I withdrew.

He stood, gaping, bewildered. Even as he began to shake and topple and the weapons fall from his hands, the door opened.

A man stepped through, very alert, intense, filled with an eagerness of spirit I could recognize. My gaze switched back to Nath as the blood bubbled out over his brown tunic. His outspread arms with the brown and green banded sleeves quivered; his hands gripped and relaxed, gripped and relaxed, and they would never more grasp rapier or main gauche. The irony was not lost on me. By the rapier he had lived, and by the longsword he had died.

"What!" I cried. "Another ponsho for the slaughter."

The man who had entered stopped stock still.

He wore Vallian evening clothes, a deep crimson robe, embroidered with silver risslacas, circled by a jeweled belt, very thin, from which swung on gemmed lockets a long dagger. Around his neck a chain formed of gold links and rubies and laybrites caught the samphron oil lamp's gleam and winked and shone magnificently, the red and yellow gems blinding.

"Layco!" cried Ashti Melekhi, and she lifted her arms imploringly.

"Majister!" said this newcomer, this man I now knew to be Kov Layco Jhansi. "You are unharmed?"

"Never better," growled the emperor. "And these rasts are dead, and that she-leem is the blackest traitor this side of Cottmer's Caverns."

"Layco!" shrieked Melekhi again. Her white scornful face caught up all the agony in her, and she screamed. She ripped the dagger from her belt and crouched, ready to spring.

Layco Jhansi appeared to be in the prime of life, short, with closely cropped brown hair. His face was regular, unmarked by suffering, his eyes large and luminous. He carried within himself a shining spirit that marked him out as a man who would adorn any walk of life he chose to inhabit.

Ashti Melekhi poised, the slim dagger held high. In a heartbeat she would hurl it straight at the emperor—it was written clearly on that white and twisted face.

No one there could know the Krozair brand would flick the flying dagger away. The moment hung with menace. Then Jhansi stepped in close to Ashti Melekhi. He whipped his own needle-slim dagger out. She saw him from the corner of her eye.

She screamed and fell back as the dagger plunged into her bosom. The green leathers punctured and as Kov Layco withdrew the blade blood welled.

"No! No—Layco!" she screamed. "Please—please—" The dagger in the Chief Pallan's hand lifted again. This time it would finish her. "Please, Layco! I could not help it!"

"You could not, Ashti," said Jhansi. "But you are a traitoress. Foresworn. The life of the emperor is not to be taken lightly or without punishment."

And his dagger flashed down and buried itself in her heart.

Thus died Ashti Melekhi, the Vadnicha of Venga.

"A just retribution for a foul traitoress, majister," said Jhansi. He calmly left his blade where it jutted from the bosom of the corpse. He walked across to the emperor and bowed.

"You are unharmed, majister?"

"I'm perfectly all right. This great hairy graint of a Clansman stopped me from having any fun again—it's always the same."

I held down my disgust. What did he know of the actual hurly-burly of battle? What fun was there in that? He did not even inhabit the same kind of world my Djangs or my Clansmen did when they spoke of fun.

"I shall have everything seen to, majister." He eyed me with a lively glance. He hesitated, which I fancied was an odd thing for him to do. He glanced toward the door, and opened his mouth; then he closed that firm-lipped mouth and nodded. "By morning the culprits, if there are any left, will have been rooted out. And I shall start with the guards at your door. They must have heard the commotion, and yet they did nothing."

"Bought," I said. "Bought and paid for."

"Aye, prince," he said. Even without the pappattu and the Lahals, he knew who I was. "But who?"

"We'll find out."

"And the quicker the better," said the emperor. "I must give you thanks, Layco, for saving my life. That she-leem would have skewered me with that dagger. But it means she cannot testify."

"I shall do all I can, majister."

"Yes, Layco. On you I rely. You never fail me."

I remained silent.

"You honor me, as always, majister."

"I shall never forget your loyalty for as long as I live." The emperor looked around on the shambles, on the dead, the six Chuliks, the bladesman, the vadnicha. He shook his head. "Indeed, it is a terrible thing to be an emperor."

And I felt the stupid giggle starting deep within me.

The emperor's enemies had attempted to poison him and get him out of the way of their schemes, remove him at the first from the palace revolution. My wonderful Delia and our friends had foiled that plot and cured the emperor. The guilty had been punished. The traitors would be paid off, and the loyal guards return. Layco Jhansi would see to that.

But—but! We had given the emperor a thousand years of life.

Never before had he been seated so thoroughly upon the throne. It was a joke. His enemies would fade away and vanish like Drig's Lanterns. The emperor of Vallia would remain the emperor of Vallia for a thousand years.

I felt the relief like wine bubbles rising and bursting.

It was marvelous!

And my Delia—how we would laugh, together, back with our family in Esser Rarioch.

The emperor was staring at me. Layco Jhansi was staring at me. The stench of blood rose dizzyingly in the room. I glared back at them. I could feel the unleashing of emotions bursting in me, rising like the wine bubbles, forcing their way out.

A thousand years and not a care in the whole wild world of Savage Kregen beneath the Suns of Scorpio!

And I laughed. I, Dray Prescot, Lord of Strombor and Krozair of Zy, I laughed and laughed and laughed.

CAPTIVE SCORPIO

A note on Dray Prescot

Dray Prescot is an enigmatic figure. Reared in the inhumanly harsh conditions of Nelson's navy, he has been transported many times through the agencies of the Star Lords and the Savanti nal Aphrasöe to the beautiful and brutal world of Kregen, four hundred light years from Earth. A coherent design underlies all his headlong adventures; but so far the pattern remains indecipherable.

His appearance as described by one who has seen him is of a man above middle height, with brown hair and level brown eyes, brooding and dominating, with enormously broad shoulders and powerful physique. There is about him an abrasive honesty and an indomitable courage. He moves like a savage hunting cat, quiet and deadly. On the exotic and perilous world of Kregen he has fought his way to become Vovedeer and Zorcander of his wild Clansmen of Segesthes, Lord of Strombor, Strom of Valka, King of Djanduin, Prince Majister of Vallia—and a member of the Order of Krozairs of Zy. To this plethora of titles he confesses with a wryness and an irony I am sure masks much deeper feelings at which we can only guess.

Prescot's happiness with Delia, the Princess Majestrix of Vallia, is threatened as the notorious Wizard of Loh, Phu-si-Yantong, seeks to destroy Delia's father, the emperor. Together with their friends, Delia and Prescot save the emperor from a poison attempt by other factions and return him to power in Vondium, the capital. But their comrades are scattered over the face of Kregen. Now, blood-splashed from the last fight in the palace, Prescot is determined to seek the whereabouts of his daughters, alienated from him during a forced absence on Earth. But the brilliant world of Kregen under Antares will always challenge Prescot with new problems and adventures. Dray Prescot knows only too well that he must continue to struggle against himself as well as the malignant fates that pursue him in the mingled streaming lights of the Suns of Scorpio.

Alan Burt Akers

One

Before the Dawn

"Oh, yes, it is common knowledge," said Travok Ott expansively, leaning back, sipping his light white wine with a most delicate air. "Delia, the Princess Majestrix, is continually indulging in affairs. Why, her latest inamorato is this muscular wrestler, Turko. Oh, yes, a lovely man. Who can blame her?"

The perfumed currents of warmed air moved caressingly about the group of men sitting in the ord chamber of the Baths of the Nine. The chamber presented a comfortable, modish, relaxing atmosphere. Young girl slaves carried wine and parclear in glazed ceramic flagons, and bronze trays of sweetmeats and tempting cakes. No lady bathers were allowed here, their establishment was separated off by a stout masonry wall. The scented air cloyed.

"Surely, this is just rumor, Travok?" said Urban the Gloves, popping a paline into his mouth.

"Hardly." Travok Ott, a slender man with the brown hair of Vallia cut into a curled bang, sipped his wine with a knowing smile. He, like them all, was naked, covered only by a small yellow towel. "Have you seen this Turko? A Khamorro, so I am told, from somewhere outlandish deep in southwestern Havilfar. But a lovely man. Oh, yes, beautiful—"

"I hold no brief for the emperor," cut in the overfed man with the three chins and swag belly, all quivering as he shook his head warningly. "But he'd have your head if—"

"Of a certainty, Ortyg—perhaps!" Travok cast a sliding glance at the shadowed alcove where a yellow towel draped down from the arm of a bronze faun, prancing, abandoned, garlanded with loomins. "But I mean him no disrespect. He understands business, and that is good enough for me."

They were all businessmen here, traders, merchants, shopkeepers to whom war and country-wide distress could bring profit, for they were shrewd in the mysteries of bargaining and gaining a corner and of stocks and the human frailties of supply and demand. This particular establishment of the Baths of the Nine stood at a crossroads in the southern part of the great city of Vondium, the capital of the Empire of Vallia. It was not one of the enormously luxurious first-rank establishments; but its entrance fees were high and it catered to a certain clientele of the middle rank, merchants and traders who could afford to pay for a night's comfort.

These men were habitués of the place, they knew one another, had been coming here for years to relax and gossip. The fellow who sat somewhat removed from them along a marble bench on pink and yellow towels smiled and nodded and joined in the conversation and listened with due respect; but he was a stranger. So the talk was more circumspect than normally the case in these secluded, sybaritic and seductive surroundings.

A beautifully formed Fristle fifi glided forward to refill Travok Ott's glass, for he found the flagons tiresomely too heavy. The Fristle's fur was of that deep plum color that limned her lissom form, made of her a sprite of beauty in that place. Travok grunted as the wine reached a whisker below the rim, and trembled, and stilled. Had the Fristle spilled any it would have gone hard for her.

"I've always stood by the emperor," Travok went on. "Did I not give thanks to Opaz when he recovered from his illness? Did I not put up the shutters on my shops when those Opaz-forsaken Chyyanists went on the rampage with their Black Feathers? Have I not a son at sea?" The wine gleamed on his lips. "Vallia is built of men like me."

"You say this Turko is the princess's inamorato," said Ortyg. "But is she his inamorata? That is a conundrum."

A low, fruity chuckle ran around the circle of men lounging in their chairs or on the benches, warmed and caressed by the scented air.

"The princess owns men's hearts—but I wager Turko has his own little inamorata tucked away somewhere safe in Valka."

Ortyg leaned a little forward, his belly bulging. "The princess does not own my heart."

The shrimp of a fellow in the corner where the warmest breezes blew puckered up his lips, his little tuft of goat's beard blowing. His brown Vallian eyes were deeply sunken under sandpapery brows. He hitched up his yellow towel and said: "Of a certainty, Travok, Vallia is built of men like you—and of Kov Layco."

The words might mean what the listener cared to put into them. This Travok Ott construed them as a compliment.

"Kov Layco Jhansi is the emperor's right-hand man, Vandrop, true. It is said he slew Ashti Melekhi with his own hand. The guards—"

Ortyg laughed, waggling his chins. "Those guards will not be seen in Vondium again."

"All the same, he, too, is aware of the Princess Majestrix's infidelity. She is becoming notorious—"

"And this shaggy clansman, her husband. He knows nothing?"

"He knows nothing of Vallia, that is sooth, by Vox!"

They appeared to be in general agreement about this.

Vandrop put a hand to his shaggy tuft of goat's beard. He stroked reflectively. "This shaggy clansman is shaggy. It is said he has a beard to his navel."

A young fellow on the other side of Travok shouted: "And that's quite long enough for a barbarian."

Travok nodded. "By Vox! A great hairy clansman from far Segesthes has the impudence to barge in and carry off our princess like a graint or a cramph or a leem—"

"But," persisted Vandrop, "was he not there, in the palace, last night? The stories are confused, garbled, but—"

"He was there, Vandrop," Ortyg told him. "I had the news red hot from my freedman who got it from the palace—a shishi there who saw much—and this Dray Prescot was in the palace. How he got there no one knows. But Kov Layco saved the emperor from Ashti Melekhi—"

A babble of voices broke in, and so Ortyg was persuaded to tell them the story as he had heard it. He made the most of it, how the Vadnicha Ashti Melekhi sought to poison the emperor and of how Layco Jhansi had slain her with his dagger. There were dead guards and blood everywhere; but Ortyg's information offered no explanation for them, even though, it was whispered, they were Jiktars of the Chulik mercenary guard—aye—and their Chuktar, also.

The talk wended on in the scented air. With the long night to get through men and women sought rest and relaxation before bed at the Baths of the Nine. Soon these men would rise and then, each to his whim, either dress and go home or partake of the Ninth Chamber. Strangers might elect to sleep in the establishment in the tastefully appointed hostelry. The stranger, a well-built young man with hair darker than the normal Vallian brown, would probably sleep in. Vandrop yawned.

"By Vox!" he said, his goat's-beard tuft quivering. "What you say about Delia, the Princess Majestrix, is hard to believe. I think I shall not believe it."

"You always were a credulous old fool, Vandrop," bellowed Ortyg, slapping his gut, reaching for his towel.

"Anyway," said Travok. "When Queen Lushfymi gets here she will soon find out—"

"—Aye, a sharp queen, that," said Urban the Gloves.

"—And she'll have this Turko's head off and the princess packed off back to Valka, or Delphond."

"D'you think Queen Lushfymi will marry the emperor?"

"If she has any sense, Urban."

They spoke of the Queen of Lome as Queen Lushfymi. The emperor had intemperately threatened to have off the heads of all those who blasphemously called her Queen Lush.

With two strangers present in the ord chamber these men spoke with more restraint than usual. Without clothes their allegiances were not at once apparent, and their words hid what they did not wish revealed. As middling tradesmen and merchants they were probably of the Racter party, some perhaps of the Vondium Khanders, those who looked to the business community for combined strength. The Racters were the most powerful party in Vallia, formed of aristocrats and nobles, and the merchants looked to them for the continuance of the status quo and a stable economy. But without the colored sleeves, without symbols and favors, they were simply men, naked in the flesh, so much alike and each one different in his own personal ways.

They spoke with a caution. But they had said a great deal, also. They were of the general opinion that it was high time the emperor married again and got himself a son to carry on the line, if the prince could hold in his hands what would come to him, and dispatched his daughter Delia and her grizzly graint of a clansman husband back to the Great Plains of Segesthes. One or two even said the Prince and Princess Majestrix could even go to the Ice Floes of Sicce for all they cared.

In these last moments before they left they talked again of the interests most pressing to them, as businessmen do: the prices and sources of supply, trading prospects, the cost of money, the laziness of slaves, the prospects of renewed war with the Empire of Hamal, the hedging against future disasters.

They even spoke of Income Tax; but obscenities found little favor in the Baths of the Nine—at least, of that kind.

Travok Ott, genial, yawning, looked across at the stranger.

"You put up here tonight, Koter? You have not told us your name."

"Yes, I think I shall. And my name is Nath Delity."

The others nodded. Their thoughts were transparent. A provincial, seeing the sights of Vondium, the greatest city of Paz.

Nath Delity half smiled. "I am from Evir, and I find Vondium a trifle warm."

They laughed at this, proud of their city, half-contemptuous of any provincial place and particularly of Evir, the northernmost province of Vallia.

"You should have been here when the emperor lay dying, or the Chyyanists were rampaging or the Third Party was active, Koter Delity. You would have been more than warm then."

Vandrop tweaked his goat's-beard tuft and looked across at the alcove where the yellow towel lay draped across the bronze statue of the faun. "And you, Koter," he spoke civilly, smiling. "You have said not a word. We would not wish you to think we are unsociable here. It is just that we know one another so well. Your name, Koter—if you wish to tell us."

Some of the others had already risen to leave and now while some pushed on, laughing and shouting, others hung back to listen. No doubt they wanted reassurance. Perhaps, their thoughts probably went, perhaps they might have said something less than wise. Spies from anywhere and serving any cause could cause troubles...

"My name is Jak Jakhan," I said, speaking smoothly and just quickly enough so that they would not know I lied. "From Zamra. And I have enjoyed your conversation, Koters."

"Zamra?" said Travok Ott.

"Zamra?" said Ortyg. His three chins wobbled.

"Zamra is, I believe," said Vandrop, "a Kovnate of the Prince Majister's?"

"Oh," I said. "I have not been there since I was a child—"

They visibly relaxed at this. I ought to have said I was from some damned Racter province, or, better still, have said nothing of my origins. Anyway, I am fond of Zamra.

As we went out through the different doors, some to debauchery, some to a night's sleep, others to the many amusements afforded to the night owls of Vondium, I fell into step beside Vandrop. We entered the robing room together and I hung back, for I did not wish Vandrop—just yet—to see my clothes.

"Is it true, Koter Vandrop—about the Princess Majestrix, I mean?"

He squinted up at me.

"I have never seen this Dray Prescot—well, few of us here would have, although Travok claims he was within spitting distance of him at the wedding—still, that is like Travok. But as to the Princess Delia, the Princess Majestrix—I do not know. There are rumors—"

"And who would have told Travok Ott?"

Vandrop edged along to his locker with the key handed to him by the robing slave in attendance on him.

"By Opaz, I do not know. He likes to keep abreast of things."

The slave unlocked the cabinet and began to fuss around Vandrop, whereat he pushed him away and dressed himself in his evening clothes. Typical of Vallia, a lounging robe in a dark rich hue of plum color, with silver embroidery, the clothes at once gave him a dignity, a measure of command, more in keeping with his character. It is said that clothes make the man. I looked at the favor pinned to his left breast. It was not black and white, the colors of the Racters, nor white and green, the colors of the Panvals. Shaped like an opened book, with an ancient abacus and a writing pen, it was stitched in white, green and yellow. The favor was that of the Vondium Khanders.

He saw my glance.

"I believe we businessmen must stand together. You may be a Racter, for all I know, Koter Jakhan; but the Racters will hold for themselves, for the nobles, I think."

"And the emperor and his family?"

He frowned.

At once I said: "I have overstepped the bounds of common usage, Koter Vandrop. Put it down to a stranger's uncouthness."

His frown remained and he sighed, "No, no, Koter Jakhan. Rather, put it down to the evil days that have fallen on Vallia and Vondium. Once, we would all have shouted for the emperor. And for his daughter. But there are forces at work—you may know of some, and there are others I know nothing of, but can sense, can feel. I am almost a hundred and seventy-five. So I know about these things. Put it down to this strange and unpleasant new world in which we live."

The slave handed him a belt with a few tasteful jewels studding its length, and with lockets from which swung the long thin dagger of Vallia. He buckled up the belt, sighed again, and said: "If you are not staying the night, here in the Bower of the Scented Lotus, perhaps—?"

About to say I would walk with him for a space, I checked.

I had things to do. The blood had been washed away. But I still had things—urgent things—to do before I could rest.

And, could I ever rest?

In Zair's truth, could I ever rest?

I said: "Could you direct me to the house of Travok Ott?"

His goat's-beard tuft quivered. But he said: "He is a good man, Koter, do not forget that. He has labored hard for what he has, here in Vondium. He is an ivory merchant, and may be found in the Souk of Chem."

"I give you thanks." I turned to go and, as Vandrop moved away, said: "Remberee, Koter Vandrop."

"Remberee, Koter Jakhan."

I caught a quick glimpse of the stranger, Nath Delity, going past as Vandrop went away to his respectable bed.

The robing slave—he was a little Och and his middle left limb was withered—fussed over me as I reached the cabinet assigned to me and unlocked it. My suit of decent Vallian buff looked the worse for wear. It had come from the wardrobe I kept up in the Palazzo of the Four Winds in Djanguraj. But I shrugged it on, philosophically, and drew on the tall black Vallian boots. The weaponry was rolled in the cloak. I held the cloak and did not unroll it, standing ready to leave as I had entered here, after the fracas at the emperor's palace.

When the Och saw I gave him a silver stiver he babbled his thanks; but I merely nodded and stepped out along the marble floor, over the geometric tessellations, to the doors. Outside, the night of Vondium pressed down, and wayfarers were only too pleased to hear the link men's calls of: "Loxo! Loxo!" and see them come hurrying up with their torches and lanterns.

One of the lesser moons of Kregen went hurtling past, low, casting down a thin scattering of light. Shadows lay heavy and dark, pierced by lanterns at corners and the winking sparks of the link men's torches as they guided their customers home—or, given the nature of a Kregan's desires and expectancies of the good life—to the gaming halls, the theatres, the dancing places, that would carry on right through to what on Earth would be called the small hours.

The palace of the emperor dominated its island between the canals and the River—She of the Fecundity. I passed along, not caring to employ a link man, moving fast. The emperor was safe now. Kov Layco Jhansi, the chief minister, had slain Ashti Melekhi who had sought to kill the emperor, and that particular plot had misfired.

Of course, there would be other plots against the emperor.

That was natural.

But the old devil was now possessed of a thousand years of life, because he had bathed in the sorcerous waters of the Sacred Pool of Baptism. I did not think he knew that fact. Not yet. But the thought had made me laugh, which is a rare occurrence, Zair knows.

A little wind flickered awnings half-seen in the erratic light. Leaves scuttered across the pavings. Vondium is indeed a magical city, fit to be the capital of an empire. The palace reared ahead, a monstrous pile, and I was comfortably aware that I would now be able to enter freely, instead of either having to creep in by a secret stair or bash my way in by brute force, as I had been constrained to do up until the events of this very night.

The guards let me pass. I noticed that the numbers of Chuliks had materially reduced. Just how Jhansi had contrived that I did not then know; but the guards were still alert, and halted me, and then, obsequiously, let me through.

It is a strange and observable fact that most wizards prefer to have their chambers in a tower. One would think they would prefer the deepest cellars, since most of them appear to have truck with the powers who are alleged to lie in that direction, rather than those in the other. But it is so.

High up the winding stair of the Tower of Incense lay the bronze-studded door. No guards were posted here. Some folk say a Wizard of Loh needs no human guards; but although that is a popular belief, it is not so. The Wizards of Loh are famed, feared, formidable; but they remain still mortal men.

A coldness appeared to cling about that door. I say appeared to cling; this was an irrational feeling and I brushed it off testily and bashed the door open with my boot.

Dimly lit, hung with macabre artifacts, the chambers of the Wizard of Loh lowered down. A lamp burned in the corner beside the skull of a risslaca. The skeleton of a chavonth had been wired in a leaping posture facing the doorway. Solemn black drapes swathed the walls. The arrow-slit windows were swathed in long blood-red curtains. A sturm-wood table supported weird objects—human heads, animal bones, bottles of blood, fetuses, jars of colored powder, strangely shaped instruments.

This whole mish-mash was designed to impress the credulous.

This anteroom resembled the working chamber of a common sorcerer. I had never met a Wizard of Loh who put much store by this kind of rubbish.

The Wizard of Loh at the court of the Emperor of Vallia had been Deb-so-Parang; but he had died some seasons ago. The Wizard of Loh who had taken his place was, so I was led to understand, some kind of sibling, and was called Deb-sa-Chiu.

He looked up from a table in the inner room. A thing writhed and screamed on the table, and Deb-sa-Chiu's hands were green.

He frowned.

The shadows threw my face into darkness, and so my form bulked in the doorway, startling him.

"You come hard upon your fate, rast!" he said. He spoke with that harsh Lohvian hiss that some of the redheaded folk of Loh cannot control. His hands flew up. Whether or not he could fashion a spell to blast me, turn me into a toad, do anything particularly unpleasant, I was not prepared to find out. Men credit the Wizards of Loh with supernatural powers and, by Vox, I have seen a few weird happenings in my time on Kregen.

So, quickly, I said: "Lahal, Deb-sa-Chiu. I have come to talk privily with you, San, and to seek your assistance."

He dropped the green-oozing thing onto the worktable.

"You try my patience—"

"Then let me try to untry your patience, San."

I gave him the honored title of San—dominie, sage, master—for although already I had my doubts of this one, I did not wish to prejudice my chances of finding out what I must know. Time was wasting. Perhaps I ought to have come here directly instead of going to the Bower of the Scented Lotus to wash away the blood.

He peered under his hand at me, and then motioned me to stand to the side so that the samphron oil lamp's gleam might fall upon my face. His own face was smooth, unmarked, crowned with that red Lohvian hair. His eyes were wary. He affected the black moustache arranged in two long drooping tails down the sides of his mouth, a fashion I find ludicrous and offensive, for all the chill menace it invariably creates.

Moving to stand where he might see me plain, I said in a voice I knew grated out harshly: "You would do me a favor, San, if you will tell me the whereabouts of the Princess Majestrix."

His smooth and knowing face lifted at my tone.

"And who are you who seeks this knowledge? I have warned you that you try my patience at your peril. I shall see you cast down to the dungeons. Naghan the Pinch will show you the error of your ways—"

He stopped speaking abruptly.

The light fell upon my face.

For a moment he stood, unmoving, his eyes black buttons revealing his thoughts. Then: "I have seen the court portrait of you, hung in the Gallery of Princes. What you ask—"

"I have beforetime asked a Wizard of Loh to go into lupu for me and to discover the whereabouts of Delia, the Princess Majestrix." My regard held him transfixed. "I have not asked them to go unrequited for the service."

If I admit to a guilty twinge of conscience here over the Wizard of Loh Que-si-Rening of Ruathytu in distant and hostile Hamal, it was surely merited, for I had done precious little for him in recompense for his assistance in tracking down Saffi the golden lion-maid. I brushed the thought away and glared at this Deb-sa-Chiu, prepared to be extremely nasty to him if necessary, although heartily wishing that unpleasant necessity would not arise.

"It is said that the Princess Majestrix and a great crowd of her friends left Vondium secretly and in a great hurry."

"It is said?" I forced myself not to mock him. "Surely a mighty Wizard of Loh has sources of more precise information?"

"We have, we have. But information is not cheap."

So ho, I said to myself. A greedy one. Well, we know how they may be manipulated.

I could not smile; but I tried to make myself relax. This would take a little time, for when a Wizard of Loh goes into lupu it seems the very forces of nature are distorted, denied, turned aside from their normal courses to the ends of wizardry.

"You must know I have means of recompensing you."

He inclined his head—a fraction, by a fraction only, for they are haughty and proud in their wisdom—and said: "Then let us come to an arrangement." He gestured with a finger and thumb touching, his other fingers stiffly outspread. "For there have been apparitions within the palace, appearances, specters—"

"Tell me."

"You have the honor to receive the assistance of Khe-Hi-Bjanching. He has made himself a power among the Wizards of Loh who render assistance to princes. The emperor, who is honored to be favored by my assistance, speaks highly of him. You are indeed fortunate."

I said nothing but simply glared.

He went on a little hurriedly.

"Khe-Hi-Bjanching has discussed with me a certain Wizard of Loh who seeks to maintain an observation upon you—"

"Phu-si-Yantong."

He swallowed and moved away toward a side table of sturm wood upon which stood glistening flagons and linen-covered trays. He busied himself pouring wine. I shook my head when he lifted an eyebrow at me. If he wanted to go through this flummery and play-acting, all very well; but my patience was running out.

"Phu-si-Yantong. A most powerful, most puissant Wizard of Loh. His appearances have been observed in the palace. I myself have seen them. Khe-Hi-Bjanching, also. We are concerned."

"So am I. What has this to do with the whereabouts of the Princess Majestrix?"

"She returned alone from wherever she had been." As he said this, Chiu's face shadowed and he took a quick gulp of wine. I knew the fellow knew where Delia had gone with our friends. Aphrasöe, the city of the Savanti, the Swinging City—that was where Delia had taken the emperor to be cured of the poison administered by the bitch Ashti Melekhi—who was now dead—and I knew, further, that the Savanti nal Aphrasöe threw a most dread horror into the hearts of even the greatest of the Wizards of Loh.

So I said: "She returned. I wish to know where she is *now!*"

He smoothed down his silk robe, liberally embroidered with symbols and runes, archaic signs that would daunt the credulous who sought his help. He paced across the chamber, careful to place his curled brown slippers upon the rugs and carpets and not upon the harsh stone. He carried the wine in one claw-like hand. At last he stopped and eyed me.

"I will go into lupu for you, prince, and seek the whereabouts of the Princess Majestrix. The price—"

Almost, I smiled. That was a crude word for so haughty a fellow.

"Name it."

As must be clearly evident to you who listen to my story as the tapes spin through your heads, I reasoned that after all my friends had been flung by magical power back to their points of origin about Kregen, Delia would have been hurled back to Vondium. Knowing her, I knew she would instantly take flier and hare off back to Aphrasöe to find me. But, I had the sense to realize she might have gone to Valka, to the east, first. I did not wish to fly all the way to the island of Ba-Domek, in which stands Aphrasöe, and miss her. And I did not wish to waste time flying to Valka if she had not gone there. I wanted—I hungered—to know where she was at this precise moment.

"Gold," said Chiu, and allowed a smile to crimp that thin mouth of his. "Wizards of Loh are always in need of gold, for we have not so far unraveled the secret of its manufacture." He waved airily. "But gold is only a small part of the price."

He was telling me nothing that was not generally known over Kregen. I looked at him, and he went on quickly.

"The Vadnicha Ashti Melekhi has been foiled in her plans to slay the emperor—"

Here I cut in brutally, rapidly growing tired of his procrastinations. "And no thanks to you. Your duty was to warn him. Why should he clothe and feed you if you fail him?"

He drew himself up at this, a flush creeping under the smooth skin of his cheeks. He looked savage. "You should speak with more care to a Wizard of Loh, prince. Do you forget—"

"I will forget that you failed in your duty to the emperor if you instantly tell me where the Princess Majestrix is. As to payment—gold, you may have gold." I let the swaddling cloak unroll, letting the covered weapons glint suddenly in the samphron oil lamps' gleam as they came free. "And as for further payment I fancy that can be arranged."

His face looked murderous. But he nodded, as though coming to a decision. He squatted down on the floor. There was no need to acquaint him with the person whom he sought; he had met Delia in the palace. He put his hands to his eyes and began to rock backwards and forwards, keening a note that rose and rose until it shrilled into an unheard vibration.

Clearly, Chiu was a very powerful wizard, or he knew more than he had said. He had started on the third phase of going into lupu, bypassing that first long silent struggling with the bonds of the spirit—the ib—when the constraints are loosened and reality and the forces beyond reality strain and merge.

He stood up. His hands dragged away from before his face. He began to rotate, slowly at first, his arms outflung, then faster and faster. There are different disciplines within the Wizards of Loh, and adepts go into lupu in different ways. But the results are very similar. I knew that the ib of Chiu had broken free from his corporeal body, was drifting, was seeking the whereabouts of Delia.

Abruptly, he dropped to the ground, crouched, his hands pressed flat against the rugs. He threw his head back. His eyes slowly opened, and once again I saw that drugged, eerie, *knowing* look.

I waited.

"Yes, prince," he breathed. He spoke chokingly. "Yes. The Princess Majestrix rides an airboat. The wind blows. She flies west."

"Across the Sunset Sea?"

"No."

"Across Vallia?"

"Yes."

So she *had* gone to Valka first, then...

"Tell me more."

"The Princess Majestrix flies to Vondium. I feel the wind. The air cuts. She is alone."

I jumped at this. I didn't like the sound of this at all.

Then this great San, this puissant Wizard of Loh, this Deb-sa-Chiu said: "She is in great distress. And there is a shadow—I see a shadow, dark, hovering—" His drugged eyes opened wide and he clasped his hands together, lifting up from the rug. He glared at me and the knowingness on his face sickened me. "Phu-si-Yantong! He it is... It is he... But the powers fail, the ib grows fragile and must return—Phu-si-Yantong's kharrna overbears all—"

The wizard clutched abruptly at his throat, choking. His eyes rolled up and this time they did not show white half-moon crescents as he went into lupu, rather they showed the awful terror of a man being strangled. I took a step forward and grasped his shoulder, roughly, and shook him.

"Chiu! Chiu! Wake up, man!"

He shuddered and writhed away; but I held him, and shook him again, shaking a potent and devilish Wizard of Loh as one might shake an angry willful child.

Then, seeing this was doing no good I hooked my fingers inside his and dragged his clutching hands away from his throat. So stiffly did his arms move, so much like sere winter branches, I thought they would snap off. But I forced his hands apart and wrenched away those lethal fingers. He choked and blubbered and whooped in great draughts of air. Tears ran down his smooth cheeks. He closed his eyes and a shudder wracked his whole body. He shook in those fine silken clothes with the runes of power embroidered in gold thread.

Presently he had recovered sufficiently to take a glass of wine. He gulped. Then he looked at me over the crystal rim, shaking still; but gathering command of himself.

"Phu-Si-Yantong," he whispered. "The power! The power!"

"All right, San. Tell me."

"The strength of his kharrna overpowered all my lore, my arts, my own devices. I would have choked myself to death—at his command."

"I saw that."

Truth to tell, the notion was eerie and mind-wrenchingly scary; the idea that a man a great distance away could so control another that he would take his own life. It was frightening. I still clung to that scrap of knowledge I had gathered, overheard as I felt by the command of the Star Lords, that Phu-si-Yantong would not order my assassination. He would have no need of paid assassins, stikitches out to earn their gold by stealthy murder. Ashti Melekhi had set her assassins on me and I was not free of them yet. But Phu-si-Yantong—then the thought occurred to me that perhaps one had to be in lupu to be thus attacked at a distance. I sincerely hoped so.

"And you can tell me no more?"

"You have saved my life, prince. But I wonder how long I shall retain it, if—"

"Yantong has no quarrel with you."

He gave me a long pitying look, recovering his composure, getting back to the serious business of being a Wizard of Loh. It is strange but true that these famous Wizards are seldom called merely wizards; usually they are given their full name of Wizards of Loh. The other wizards of Kregen, also, favor those from Loh with the full name. It is a measure of their importance in the eyes of other sorcerers.

"The Princess Majestrix will arrive in Vondium when the suns rise." He puffed out his cheeks, getting his color back. "Now, prince, we must talk about the balance of your payment to me."

I glared at him. I should have listened. I should have waited for him to say what he wanted. It might have saved a few thousand lives, saved a torrent of blood, saved a few burning, looted towns. But, onker that I am, I said bluffly: "As to payment, San, you may have your gold. But I think if you believe I have saved your life you are fully requited and I no longer stand in your debt."

Anyway, at the time it struck me as fair.

But fairness and justice do not go hand in hand with expediency and cleverness and the saving of pride. So, onker of onkers that I am, I nodded to him, scooped up the weapons in their cloak, and stomped out.

Get onker!

I can say that, now, looking back. I was, indeed, still very much of an idiot in those days.

But, of course, as you will perceive I was in a turmoil of fear for Delia. If that bastard Phu-si-Yantong was up to more mischief, and my Delia flying all alone—I sweated and shook and went off running toward the high aerial landing platform where her airboat would touch down.

Any sensible fellow would have waited. I had been up and about for a long spell. I had fought a combat in the emperor's bedroom that some would put down as a Jikai, although I did not vaunt myself that far. The Chuliks who had come to slay the emperor had been dealt with by me, and their employer, Ashti Melekhi, had been stabbed to death by Kov Layco Jhansi. I was tired. But tiredness is a mortal sin.

So I rousted out the guard and yelled and bellowed and acted like a high and mighty prince and secured an airboat and went leaping away into the star-studded night.

Due east I headed, on course for Valka, trusting that Delia's flier would be on the reciprocal of my course, and I would see her airboat in the bright star glitter. She of the Veils, Kregen's fourth moon, was hidden by cloud, but as I flew on eastward of the great circle of the city, so the clouds dissipated and cleared and pink and golden moonshine flooded down. I could see better then. The land fled past below. The wind buffeted my face and roared in my ears. On and on I flew, searching the heavens for the first glimpse of the airboat.

As I flew on searching the sky for that flitting sharp-prowed form, Deb-sa-Chiu's words recurred to me. I puzzled over one word. He had said: "kharrna." I did not know what that was. I would have to ask my own Wizard, Khe-Hi-Bjanching.

Then I checked.

After my friends had dipped the emperor and themselves in the Sacred Pool of Baptism on the River Zelph in far Aphrasöe, the Guardian of the Pool, Vanti, had dispatched them all willy-nilly to their places of origin. That meant that Bjanching was somewhere in Loh, that veiled and mysterious continent to the southwest of Vallia. It meant that Seg Segutorio was back home in Erthyrdrin, the mountainous promontory at the northern tip of Loh. It meant that Inch was home in Ng'groga, in the southeast of Loh. Odd how they all came from Loh, a fact I had been barely conscious of. And my other friends, all my comrades on the expedition, were back home. Gloag was in Mehzta. Hap Loder was back on the Great Plains of Segesthes. Turko the Shield in Herrelldrin in distant Havilfar. Tilly, Oby, Naghan the Gnat, back in Hyrklana. And Balass the Hawk in Xuntal.

There was no help from them in the coming struggle.

Many of these friends had made a new home for themselves with Delia and me in Valka. I made up my mind I would make the most strenuous efforts to assist them if they wished to return, as I felt they would—as, indeed, knowing the comradeship between us, I was absolutely certain they would.

But, first things first.

By the wheeling movements of the stars and the onward progression of She of the Veils I counted the passing hours. Each bur is roughly forty terrestrial minutes, and as another of the little catapulting lesser moons of Kregen vaulted across the sky I knew the burs were rattling away. The good graces of Five-handed Eos-Bakchi, that chuckling Vallian spirit of luck and good fortune, were passing me by, too.

When I reached the point at which it was fruitless to hurry on farther I slowed the voller in its headlong rush. If Deb-sa-Chiu spoke the truth and Delia was due to reach Vondium at dawn, then she must have passed a circumferential line around the capital city by now. So I had missed her.

She was vectoring in on a different approach line.

Instantly, I swung the voller about and slammed the speed lever over full. It jarred against the stop. Well, as you know, that was a bad habit I'd been getting into more and more of late. As to whether or not driving a voller at top speed all the time through thin air materially affected its performance, I did not at the time know. I cared. Airboats still broke down at distressingly frequent intervals in Vallia. We bought our fliers from Hamal, and they continued to sell us inferior models, that broke down, despite the drubbing we'd given them at the Battle of Jholaix. I brooded as the night wind whipped at my face, hurtling back to Vondium under the Moons of Kregen, brooded on the mighty and proud Empire of Hamal and what must be done about that place and its mad and cruel Empress Thyllis.

So many schemes and mischiefs needed attention on Kregen. Four hundred light years from Earth, the planet of my birth, Kregen is a marvelous world, peopled by wonderful beings, filled with light and clamor and furor of life lived to the hilt. But Kregen has its darker side, where horror and terror batten on innocent people, where sorceries rend reason, where injustice denies light.

Yes, there was much still to be done on Kregen.

I am but a simple, ordinary, mortal man—despite that I have been vouchsafed a thousand years of life—and although my shoulders are accounted broad, they can only seek to bear the load I can carry. I was despairingly conscious of all those things I had left undone. But, by Zim-Zair! I would do them. Aye, by the Black Chunkrah, all of them!

The hurtling headlong pace of the voller faltered.

The wind-swept spaces of the sky extended all about. The star glitter above, the pink wash of moonlight, the drifting shadow clouds, all coalesced.

The flier was falling.

Screaming with wind-bluster the flier fell toward the dark earth below.

Many philosophies and religions of Kregen seek to give guidance and reassurance to those at the last extremity. I have spoken little of these things. Each to his own. If I turn to Zair—because I am on Kregen—and, also, to Opaz, this is only natural. Djan, too, holds importance in my scheme of things. If I was to be denied a last long lingering look at my Delia before I died I would curse and rave and then, at the end, perhaps accept that harsh decree. Certainly, I'd do my damnedest to claw back up out of my coffin to bash the skulls of those rasts in Hamal who sold us faulty vollers.

The wind blustered at me, screaming past the fragile wood and canvas of the little two-place flier. She twisted and turned, toppling through the air. Down and down we went, headlong, screeching for the final impact.

The controls appeared to be useless. I juggled the levers and then, intoxicatingly, fancied I caught a spark of response. The cover ripped away over the silver boxes that upheld and powered the voller in flight, I probed in, trying to figure out what the damage might be. If the silver boxes had turned black then that would be the end, for their power would all have leached away. They gleamed dully silver back at me. I began frantically to search back along the linkages of bronze and balass, the orbits that controlled the movements of the two silver boxes, the vaol and paol boxes.

The flier lifted a little, flew straight. I stood up with the wind in my face, gasping, and the flier lurched and slid sideways.

In the pinkly golden rays of the moon I saw another flier, below me, heading west. She was a largish craft, with an upflung poop, and so I knew she was not Delia's voller.

The moonlight ran glittering along her coaming, sparkling from ornamentation there. Flags flew, mere featureless tufts of cloth in that erratic light. My flier lurched again, and slid sideways, and then, recovering, skewed the other way. We wallowed through the air like a reveler reeling from a tavern in Sanurkazz, celebrating the capture of a Magdaggian swifter.

More frenzied bashing of the controls brought me up level again. But it was a mere matter of time before my voller gave up completely and down to the hard earth we plunged, to make a pretty hole in the ground of Kregen.

The flier below flew parallel, surging on surely. By her lines she was a first-class Hamalian-built vessel. I could see no sign of life aboard her; doubtless her passengers were asleep in the cabin aft and her crew snugged down along the bulwarks.

There was a chance.

A slender chance—true; but it was all I had.

I let my voller down as gently as I could, gentling the controls now, handling her like a fractious zorca, light on the bit.

Sink me! I said. Was I not an old sailorman? Did I or did I not have the skill?

Putting my trust in myself is no new sensation for me; but always I do so with a trembling uncertainty. I can never be sure. With a muttered prayer to Zair—and to Opaz and Djan—I let the voller drift down, fighting the controls, feeling the rush of wind, feeling the sinking bottomless sensation of the gulfs of emptiness under me.

Down we plunged, down to a chance in a thousand.

In a thousand?

In a million...

Two

An Aerial Reception

That chance in a million came off, of course, otherwise I would not be here to tell you of it.

The crippled voller responded lurchingly to the controls. There was little time left as I brought her in over the flier's foredeck. Judging distance was tricky. I was for a crazy moment reminded of the time when I swung from a long rope slung to a corth whose wide wings beat the air above me, swinging down to land clawingly on the tower of Umgar Stro. So, now, I swung the airboat down and hit the deck and bounced. We nearly went over the rail. The wind tried to lift us off, and then was miraculously stilled, so that I knew this large flier was of that kind that creates its own little biosphere in which the wind has no power to force an entrance.

The stillness settled and I took a deep breath and put a leg over the wooden coaming of my airboat.

Now, I own my sudden arrival was unceremonious. Out of the night sky a voller had come swooping in to land on this airboat's foredeck. Kregen is a world where abrupt actions of that sort almost invariably herald mischief. So as I jumped down to the deck I called out in a most pleasant voice.

"Llahal!" I called, using the double L of the familiar greeting for those one does not yet know. "Llahal. I crave your indulgence for my flier—"

I was allowed to go no farther.

The airboat was not deserted, as the stray thought had crossed my mind. As though conjured magically from the sleeping decks men sprang up, hard and dark against the last of the moonlight. The bright wink of weapons ringed me in.

Those weapons drove forward with purpose, unhesitating, sword and spear points aimed at my heart.

As I say, my arrival had been unceremonious.

But even so, even on Kregen, a little of pappattu might have been made, a little time taken to sort out the situation, to understand why I had dropped out of the night sky.

But no.

The spears lanced toward me, the swords flashed down. With the instinct a fighting man must needs have or perish very quickly, I was leaping away, my rapier whipping out, the main gauche flicking up out of its scabbard.

These sudden devils trying to degut me were Chuliks. Their oiled yellow skin glistened in the radiance of She of the Veils. Their upthrust tusks glinted. They bore in, silently, ferociously, and I had to skip and jump and beat away those murderous brands.

"Listen, you bunch of onkers!" I yelled, prancing away, scrambling across the deck, around my voller, flicking and flashing swords and spears away. "I'm no stikitche! I haven't come to assassinate anyone!"

But they bore on silently. I own their very silence gave me pause; even a Chulik will give vent to a war cry every now and then, when he fights.

The rapier and left-hand dagger flamed under the moon and I had to exert myself smartly. So far I had not spitted any of them or slit anyone's throat; but they pressed and the cramped conditions hampered free movement. Pretty soon now someone was going to get his fool self killed, and I did not intend that someone to be me. And then, when the explanations followed, there would be a pretty pickle.

"Listen, you stupid onkers!" I bellowed, and slid a blow and my rapier winked out of its own accord, or so it seemed, and I had the devil of a time merely slicing down the Chulik's cheek instead of his throat. He staggered back, and I kicked his companion betwixt wind and water, and bellowed again. I was beginning to become annoyed.

One of them rushed in headlong, attempting to overbear me by sheer bulk and speed. I bent. He went over me, his arms flailing, letting out no sound, no surprised whoofle, simply somersaulting on to fetch up with a rib-cracking thunk against the bulwarks.

These fellows wore dark harnesses, black belts and leathers, and I could see no signs of favors or insignia, no colors. Their swords and spears were the badges of their trade.

A light bloomed from the poop rail. The radiance fell on the man holding up the lamp. He was a Fristle and his cat's face showed hard and angular in the light. At his side stood a bulky figure clad in a black cloak, with a bronze helmet jammed on his head, a bronze helmet with a tall cockscomb of gold and white feathers. Only the deep-set eyes of this person glittered out over a fold of cloth, drawn up over the face.

"Do not kill him!" The words were harsh, fierce, with a rattling, hissing viciousness. They commanded immediate respect from the Chulik mercenaries. I saw the way the swords twitched in the yellow hands. They would use the flats, now...

"Take him alive! The rast who kills him will be flung overboard."

Again the words battered the mercenaries. The man in the concealing black cloak and face cloth clearly handled these Chuliks with the proverbial rod of iron.

Two Och bowmen on the deck of the poop lowered their bows. They might have done for me had they loosed on me unawares. Now they would not chance a shot, under the interdiction of their lord, even though the bows were mere small flat short-bows. I leaped away from the coming attack and bellowed up at the black-cloaked figure.

"Tell these nurdling rasts of yours I come as a friend! I am not—"

"What you are and what you are not are of no concern of mine," came the hoarse, hissing, rattling voice. I fancied I heard a distant resemblance in that voice to a scoundrel I had known on the inner sea, the Eye of the World; but I could not be sure. And what with keeping the swords away from me and skipping about and bellowing at them to desist, I thought no more about it at the time.

How that little scene would have ended I do not care to dwell on—or, rather, how it should have ended with the lot of them pitched overboard— but in the event the black-cloaked figure turned abruptly half-about. He stood in a strained, attentive, silent pose for a moment and I surmised he was listening to someone whom I could not see. After a moment or two in which I came perilously close to sinking the rapier between the ribs of a Chulik who wanted to finish matters, the man turned back.

His hard outline bulked against the last of the moonglow, for She of the Veils sank into the west and flooded the flier with a roseate light. So we had turned in mid air and were heading east. Why, I did not know. He flung up a commanding hand, and something about the gesture, some awkwardness, tugged at my memory.

"Hold!" he bellowed. Then: "Take the flier down. Let that man stand free, do not harm him."

The swords glittered as they lowered.

"Well," I said. "By Vox! You took your time."

The flier slanted toward the shadowed earth. The tableau held. The eeriness of it was not lost on me. If anyone of those Chulik mercenaries made a wrong move, this time he might not be so lucky, and might, indeed, take six inches of good Vallian steel through his guts.

The airboat touched down. A tiny pre-dawn wind sang in the trees. The shadows loomed. The land spread, dotted with tree clumps, with not a light in evidence anywhere.

"Over with you!" shouted the man in the cloak. He pointed with his sword at my voller. "Throw that after him."

The Chuliks stood back, for they were fighting men and the volmen of the flier would handle details like casting a voller over the side. These sailors of the skies were men like me, apim, some of them; others were Brokelsh and Womoxes, diffs whose racial animosities were not too blatant. There were no Fristles that I could see apart from the one on the poop with the lantern, for as a rule, although not always, Chuliks and Fristles do not get along too easily, one race with the other.

My voller was incontinently heaved up and chucked over the side. I heard the breaking and splintering of wood, the ripping of canvas.

"By Vox!" I yelled. "Who's going to pay for that?"

That harsh hissing voice carried not the slightest trace of amusement. "You are a man with much gold. The trifle of a smashed voller will not trouble you."

He said voller, which is the word for an airboat most often heard in Havilfar, where they are manufactured.

I said: "And do you then know me?"

"Aye."

I pondered. He was very sure of himself, then...

He turned his head again, and listened, and when he swung back to face me he held the cloth even higher so that only those dark, narrow, widely set eyes glittered out upon me.

"Now go. Take yourself off. And give thanks to your gods that you still live."

Pondering, I walked to the rail. Of course, I could have bounced up the ladder onto the poop, taken him by the throat, choked a little politeness into him. I might have cowed the crew and done something along similar lines with the mercenaries. But my first concern was Delia, and as these thoughts sprang into my head I saw a light go on half an ulm away. That would be a farm awakening to the daily labors. There I could find transport.

It would take more time than I wished to spare to deal with these rasts and commandeer their flier. All the same, I was conscious of the indignity—no, that is not true. Dignity and I share little in the harsh realities of life. Pride had nothing to do with it. The cardinal rule for me upon Kregen has been and remains always the concern for Delia. Only she concerned me.

At the rail I started to jump over, then turned. A Chulik stood near, lowering down on me. Many apims say, with a casual laugh, that they cannot tell one Chulik from another. They say this about Fristles, and about many other of the wonderful races of people, called diffs, upon the world of Kregen. I saw this big bulky fellow and I would know him again. I saw his sword. It was a rapier, for he was in Vallia, and the hilt and pommel were fashioned into the likeness of a mortil, very fancy. I nodded to him as I went over the side.

He did not speak.

None of the confounded Chulik mercenaries had spoken or cried out.

I had taken a bare half-dozen steps away from the flier before it lifted up, quickly, going low over the ground toward the east. It vanished past a copse of trees. Wherever that cramph in his concealing black cloak and the person from whom he had taken his orders were going, they were going there in the devil of a hurry.

I set off for the farm.

That mysterious lot had been flying west when I'd first seen them and managed to land on their deck. Then, during the fight, they'd changed course a hundred and eighty degrees. Now they had taken off, going low, heading east. I fancied that they had kept low so that once out of my sight they could turn again and head back onto their original course.

They were flying to Vondium. And they had not wished me to know that.

Then I banished them from my thoughts and walked up to the farm and thundered on the door.

Half a dozen stavrers started barking.

"Quiet you famblys," I said, making my voice as soothing as possible.

The stavrer with his fierce wolf-head, his eight legs, the rear six all articulated the same way, with his stumpy tail, is an enormously loyal watchdog of Kregen. He can put in a sudden charge that will leave a chavonth standing for sheer acceleration; but the loyal stavrer has no long-distance legs to him. In a dash to take the seat of the pants off importunate strangers at the door he is hard to fault; but if they get a head start they can usually get away scot-free. I just hoped the stavrers at this farm were all securely chained up for the night.

Lights showed at the windows and the door was cautiously opened. There had been troubles in Vallia of late. I saw the gleam of weapons beyond the edge of the door so, quickly, I sang out: "Llahal and Llahal. My airboat has broken down and I would crave your help, Koters."

After that it was relatively easy. I was in the Vadvarate of Valhotra, of which Genal Arclay was Vad. The province lay immediately to the east of Vondium and, most sensibly, was always held by a family loyal to the emperor. It was rich farming land, filled with fat cattle and good, fruitful earth, bringing forth abundance. I knew Vad Genal as an easy-going likable fellow, with a weakness for riding sleeths in fast races on which he would bet far more than he should. But these people made me welcome, offering refreshment and the use of their best airboat—indeed, their only airboat. She was an ancient craft, much used, and very much a symbol of the farm's prosperity in the surrounding district. The farmer, Larghos Nilner, and his wife and family were clearly loyal to their Vad and through him to the emperor.

I reflected that not all of Kregen is vicious and hostile, and not all of Vallia made furtive and strenuous attempts to get rid of the emperor. He had his friends.

Making proper arrangements for the use of the flier, I bid them Remberee and took off, heading back to Vondium.

The colors of Valhotra are red, brown and green, with a diagonal slash of white. They were painted up on the airboat in the private style, to indicate that the airboat's owner was a Valhotran but not of the retainers of the Vad.

Before the ancient airboat reached Vondium the suns rose.

I took deep breaths of air, the sweet, limpid air of Kregen. Bursting over the horizon, filling the world with light and glory, the Suns of Scorpio drove away the shadows and drenched all the marvelous world of Kregen in light and color. Zim, the great red sun, and Genodras, the small green sun, poured down their floods of radiance. I basked in the warmth and brightness. Over in Havilfar they call Zim Far and Genodras Havil. The suns have many and many names over Kregen. But they remain the Suns of Scorpio, Antares, blazing, superb.

So, if Deb-sa-Chiu had spoken the truth, Delia would be settling down to a landing on the high platforms of the palace at this moment. I fancied she would quickly learn I had returned. But I did not relish the idea that, further learning I had taken a voller, she would at once start the long journey to Ba-Domek and Aphrasöe. I drove the flier on mercilessly; but she was a slow old tub at best and we made poor progress. So I raved and cursed, as is my wont, and attempted to calm myself, as always, and, as nearly always, lamentably failing.

Below the trundling flier the ground passed in a swirl of greens and browns and blues, with the silver-glittering canals of Vallia cutting their lordly way across the landscape. Magnificent are the canals of Vallia. True, their water is a nasty poison to anyone not of the canalfolk. In Vondium there are many canals fed by the waters of the Great River, and these canals are safe for ordinary folk, not of the canals.

The canalfolk of Vallia are a people apart. As far as I knew up to that time they had kept themselves strictly separate from the intrigues and struggles for power within the Empire. Now that the emperor was assured of a thousand years of life, vouchsafed him because his daughter Delia possessed the courage and fire to take him to the Sacred Pool of Baptism, he was most firmly seated on his throne. He could outlast his enemies, and guide and control those who followed after. Oh, yes, there were still plots against him, and factions seeking to topple him. But he had only to last out the current crop of troubles, and then, by Vox, he was safe.

So I thought.

As for myself, after my own problems, I was concerned to discover who it was who had been controlling Ashti Melekhi.

Some shadowy figure of great power had been giving her orders. She had attempted to poison the emperor and been foiled. Then she had brought Chulik guards to slay him, and been foiled.

Now that she was dead the menacing shadow at her back would have to find fresh tools for his nefarious purposes.

I knew, as I winged back to Vondium the Splendid in the mingled streaming radiance of the Suns of Scorpio, that I was in for a few hectic bouts of action. And, so I was. As you shall hear.

Poison is not often a favored instrument of murder on Kregen and the abhorrence of just about everyone concerned at the imminent death by poison of the emperor gave a true indication of that kind of morality. But death by hired assassin—well, now... In that department of murder the stikitches of Kregen have few peers. Which, I suppose, reflects badly upon the morality of those who employ them. My friends and I had been set upon by stikitches, and we had tumbled them into a handy canal; I recalled the promise Ashti Melekhi had made and knew her promise would be kept. Her stikitches would be after me, still.

In that, thinking that her malignance persisted from the grave, I misjudged the niceties of protocol and honor of the stikitches of Kregen.

In the growing light the land spread bountifully. Truly, Vallia is a rich and rosy island. Away on my right hand the lofting twin pinnacles of rock spearing up from the land showed me Vondium was very close. That curious double formation of rock and crag is called Drak's Seat. From its slopes ice is brought down to the city.

The Great River—Mother of Waters, She of the Fecundity—glimmered ahead. And Vondium—ah! Vondium, the proud city. I have spoken but little of that splendid city, and to think of it now brings a pang. The slanting mingled rays of the suns smote full upon the serried array of domes and towers, of spires and roofs, caught gleams from the gilt, struck sparks from the ranked windows. The long granite walls ringed the city, and the buildings spilled out beyond their ancient circumference. Here and there the dots of early fliers spun up into the morning brightness. Across the long-reaching arms of the aqueducts the clear, clean water flowed down from the hills. Smoke from breakfast fires coiled into the limpid air. The boulevards already thronged with people and carriages, a steady traffic that would continue all day. Narrow boats and barges glided silently along the canals. Movement, color, life—all were spread below me as I slanted in over the seeming metropolis of Vondium the Proud, heading for the palace of the emperor.

A number of tributaries of varying size and importance empty into the Great River at or near Vondium. Combined with the meanderings of the River at that point a couple of tributaries contrive to isolate a section of the city, with the adjacent canal forming an aloof enclave. This is the Old City, called Drak's City. A warren, festering in places, sumptuous in others, it attracts both disreputable elements and free spirits, artists, poets, thinkers, students, and provides them with a kind of security. I say a kind of security, for Vondium herself offers that kind of security a man of the cities can understand.

As I sped toward the palace I gave but scant thought to Drak's City, for I then knew little of Vondium. In Ruathytu, which I knew much better, the Sacred Quarter in its way served for the purposes of Drak's City in Vondium. But the two were not the same—very far from the same.

Old and ancient and steeped in the mysteries of its past is Drak's City. Here men first built their camp when they came to the Great River, gradually enlarging their buildings and walls, until what is now the Old City dominated the surrounding countryside. The light picked out the colors along the tall walls of the higher palace. Each fluttering from its own flagstaff, every province flag of the empire flew. The long rows of flagstaffs and their gorgeously colored treshes passed below as I turned to slide in for a landing.

Drak's City sank from sight as I lowered in the air. The Old City completely surrounded by the modern metropolis carried on its own life, had its own mores, gave scant attention to what went on in Greater Vondium. The flier touched down.

The guards were duly obsequious. The Vallian Air Service patrols above had let me through because the Valhotran colors marked me as a friend. Unmarked boats would be challenged.

Because she understands me passing well, Delia had waited for me. The moment she learned I had returned to the palace and of the collapse of the latest plot against her father, she had said something—which I will not repeat—and had gone up to the landing platforms with a picnic basket and a good book. How she does these things amazes me still.

So, clad in my worn and travel-stained old buff, I stomped across the platform.

She looked up and marked her place in the book with a slim finger—I know that gesture well. Then she saw who it was. The book went up in the air. The picnic basket flew the other way spilling palines and delicious fruits and sandwiches and bottles of wine. She flew at me.

Time after time I have come home to my Delia. It is always the same and it is always different. Close, we held each other, close. My Delia—my Delia of Delphond, my Delia of the Blue Mountains!

Three

Barty Vessler, Strom of Calimbrev

I hitched up the huge brown beard on its silver wires over my ears, and smoothed down the golden plates of the helmet. I turned to let Delia see me.

She lay on an elbow, her white gown voluptuous in its curves and lines, and started to laugh so that the little gilt sofa shook.

"Dray! Dray! You look—"

"I look like a shaggy graint of a clansman. If that is the way the good folk of Vondium imagine me—then that is the way they can see me."

Much had happened since yesterday, when Delia had met me on the high landing platform. Now we prepared in our own private apartments for the great thanksgiving ceremony. Much of what had happened was talk. There were other things; but they remain between Delia and me. Now we put on fine fancy clothes, readying ourselves for the dismal prospect of a state function.

"But you can't go out looking like that."

"Why not?"

"Well—for one thing, you're hardly recognizable and absolutely not respectable."

I laughed. "True. And two more admirable qualities I have yet to find. I do not wish to be recognized, and if ever I was respectable, I fancy I'd—"

"I know you, Dray Prescot. If you were respectable you'd die of boredom."

"True."

She sat up. Those soft red lips pouted at me.

"Very well. Wear the beard. But at least have Tilly trim—oh!"

"Yes. Our friends are scattered all over Kregen. Tilly will be back in Hyrklana."

"We must help them—I'm sure Tilly would wish to come home. Valka is her home now."

"We will. As soon as the emperor has given thanks to the Invisible Twins through Opaz the All-Glorious, we can start."

A shadow passed across that face, that face that is the most beautiful in two worlds.

"What is it, my heart?"

"Dayra—"

Now I frowned.

"We have lost our daughter Velia—" The pang this caused both of us had to be endured; neither of us could forget Velia. I went doggedly on. "Our three sons are making their ways in the world. But our daughters, Lela and Dayra—do you know, since I returned from—" Here I checked, and stammered.

"Yes?"

I had been about to say "from Earth." But that would mean nothing to Delia, and I had not yet nerved myself to explain to her that I was born on a world that had only one sun, only one moon, and had only apims as people. So I fished around and then said: "Since I had to leave you on the island of Lower Kairfowen—"

"In the village of Panashti—"

"Yes. I've spent most of the time in the Eye of the World. We have managed to save your father. But in all this time I have not seen my two daughters."

Delia made a small, not so much helpless as resigned, gesture. "It is a matter for the Sisters of the Rose. I have told you much. Lela is very much the grand lady now. She goes her own way. She stubbornly refuses all offers of marriage."

I nodded. "If she gets married and I'm not there, I'll—"

"You no doubt would, you great grizzly graint. But Lela is like Drak. They are twins. Drak can run affairs while you are—away—"

"I know. They call him the Younger Strom and me the Old Strom, in Valka."

"He does not want Valka. You know what he has said. He is a fine man now, my heart. As for Zeg, you did well when you made him the King of Zandikar, and Queen Miam will be good for him."

"I didn't make him. Miam did that."

"That may be. And our third son, Jaidur—"

"Jaidur." Jaidur, sometimes called Vax, Vax Neemusjid, was Dayra's twin. "He hasn't made up his mind about me, yet. But Dayra—"

"Jaidur and Dayra. They were born when you were away. It was a hard time for me."

I could not look at her. The Star Lords who had callously hurled me back to rot on Earth for twenty-one years had a great deal to answer for. I ploughed on.

"Jaidur still doesn't believe I can possibly be his real father—yet, I think, he does know and will not acknowledge it. If I were a true Vallian father I'd take a whip to him if he continued on that tack."

"But as you are a savage and barbarian clansman, you will not."

"So Dayra hates my guts. Well, that is fair. I deserve that. But I shall find a way of making her see—I have to—as I owe it to you and the children."

"She ran away from the Sisters of the Rose. I saw the—I saw the necessary people there and smoothed things over. But she joined up with a rascally gang. Seg and Inch found out about them, or as much as they could. Seg's daughter, Silda, was also mixed up with them at one time. But Seg was there and he sorted that out."

I had turned to look at her and as she spoke a flush mantled up onto her cheeks, and she looked away, and went on speaking very quickly, very quickly indeed.

"And as Inch couldn't wed his lady Sasha from Ng'groga for some reason connected with their taboos he was making further investigations but it was all very difficult and kept most secret and I can say that Dayra fancied herself in love with this man who calls himself by any name that takes his fancy and as the whim strikes him and no one knows who he is although I expect Dayra does." She finished a little bitterly, on a sigh.

I felt the fury mounting.

Calmly, I said: "And this was the problem you had to go away to attend to? You and Lela?"

"Oh, no." She looked up. "That was settled. Well, more or less. Dayra has been led astray. That is what I meant when I spoke of her when you talked of going to Hyrklana to fetch Tilly and Oby and Naghan the Gnat."

"Aye, and we'll bring the others. But I see." I took off the ridiculous golden helmet and scratched the false beard. "We must find Dayra first—and this fellow, what's-his-name—and then we can see about our friends."

"I think—Dray—I think—yes."

"Well then, Delia my lovely, we must dress ourselves up and attend the emperor and see your father right. Have you any idea where we should start looking for Dayra?"

"They used to go around smashing up the taverns."

"Right."

"And Barty Vessler is here in Vondium and desperately unhappy, wanting to help."

"Who," I said, "in Zair's name, is Barty Vessler?"

Delia shook her head so that those gorgeous chestnut tints in her rich brown hair caught the light, dancing, enchanting.

"You knew the old strom, Naghan Vessler? Strom of Calimbrev?"

"Oh. Oh, yes. So this Barty Vessler is the Strom of Calimbrev. How does he come to be so desperately unhappy?"

But I could guess. Calimbrev is an island of about the same size as Valka situated off the southeast coast of Vallia, just to the southwest of Veliadrin. If this Vessler was unhappy and wanted to help it could only mean he and Dayra had been friends. Probably the loon wanted to marry her. I cocked an eyebrow at Delia, and she smiled, and confirmed the suspicion.

"He is a charming young man. Very well thought of. You mind you are nice to him."

"And he has nothing to do with Dayra's running off? Her running with this wild bunch? He's just a good friend?"

"Yes. I am sure. He had a struggle to hold onto the Stromnate when his father died. But he did."

"Well, good for him."

All my hackles had risen at the thought of a man sniffing around my daughter. I thought of Gafard, Sea Zhantil, the King's Striker, who had wed Velia, and I sighed...

"If he's half the man Gafard was then he'll do, I suppose, providing you approve."

"For the sweet sake of Opaz, my heart! It is not as definite as that yet. Not by a long way."

So, bristling more than a trifle, I set about putting on all the ridiculous fancy clothes a state occasion warranted. As was often my custom I deliberately loaded myself down with bright gewgaws, lengths of cloth-of-gold, brilliant silks, tasseled scarves, bracelets, necklaces, and under all a shirt of that marvelously supple mesh-steel they manufacture down in the Dawn Lands of Havilfar.

The mazilla was a thing of wondrous beauty or downright irritation, depending on your point of view. Truth to tell, as it jutted up at the back of my head, gaudy with feathers and sensil and gold, it was both. Only the noblest may wear an aristo-sized mazilla. So, adding this to my calculated insult in the whole stupid finery I wore, my mazilla towered, flaunting, arrogant, insolent.

I stroked the luxurious brown beard and felt that, at the very least, it should upset more than a few of the best-born of Vallia.

Which seemed to me a delicious and highly desirable achievement.

Delia—well, Delia was simply superb.

Dressed in white, with discreet jewels, with feathers and sensils, she floated like a—well, I will say it and be damned to all and sundry—she floated like a goddess as we sallied out to take our place in the procession.

A long Vallian dagger with the hilt fashioned from rosy jewels swung from golden lockets at her side.

As for me, I belted on a veritable armory, well-knowing the frowns such wanton display would provoke. How Delia put up with my contempt for the nobles of Vallia escaped me.

Besides a rapier and dagger I belted on a clanxer, a djangir and a small double-bitted axe. Over my back and hidden by the crimson trimmed cloak and the feathers of the mazilla, went my Krozair longsword. I drew the line at a Lohvian longbow. After all, there are limits, and to push beyond them would have been counter-productive.

The procession was gorgeous and immense. Everyone was there. The nobles lined out in order of precedence and a splendid array they made. The whole sumptuous proceeding went off well. Due thanks were offered up at various temples for the safety of the emperor. He, the old devil, strode through it all with a face like a granite block, hard and yet haughty, lapping up the plaudits of the crowds, conscious of the looks and feelings of those who fawned on him, sorting them out in his shrewd old head, those for, those against, those who might be bought by gold.

The stinks of incense blew everywhere. Perfumes covered the smells that might have proved intrusive. The noise blossomed as the crowds huzzahed and screeched. It was all a terrible ordeal, yet an ordeal that had to be gone through so that Vondium might witness that the emperor was safe and in full health.

Those of my few friends among the nobility—like the Lord Farris—knew that on these occasions I was like a graint with a thorn in his foot, and so they merely acknowledged my presence and smiled and went on with the business. As for my enemies, they ignored me, which suited me.

Kov Layco Jhansi, the emperor's chief minister, was there and looking mighty pleased with himself. High in favor, now, Layco Jhansi, after his valiant defense of the sacred person of the emperor. I nodded to him, and then turned away, and the proceedings ground on.

When they were over and I headed off at once for the palace to strip off the ridiculous outfit, Delia held me back.

A young man, slender, supple, his brown Vallian hair stylishly though decently cut, wearing ornate robes—as we all did—approached. His face looked freshly scrubbed, bright, cheerful, yet with an anxious dint between the eyebrows he manfully tried to conceal.

He wore the colors of gray, red and green, with a black bar, and his emblem was a leaping swordfish. By these I knew he was of Calimbrev. So this must be Barty Vessler, the Strom of Calimbrev.

He made a deep obeisance. Delia gripped my arm. She knows how I dislike this crawling and bowing; but we were still in public and were watched.

"Majestrix, Majister," said Strom Barty.

"Strom, how nice to see you," said Delia.

We stood on a marble platform with the crowds yelling below and the pillars and statues of the Temple of Lio am Donarb at our backs. Lio am Donarb, although a minor religious figure attracting a relatively small following, was considered worthy of a visit of thanks. To one side a group of nobles prepared, like us, to take to their palanquins or zorca chariots to return to their villas set upon the Hills. Among all their blazing heraldry of color the black and white favors showed starkly, proud, defiant, arrogant.

I nodded at the group who watched us avidly.

"You do yourself no good with the Racters by talking to me, young Barty. But you are welcome."

He looked up, quickly, taken aback. He must have heard what a crude clansman I was; he had not expected this. And I piled on the agony, despite Delia's fierce grip.

"The black and whites would like to tear down the emperor and his family. And whatever I may feel about the emperor, he is my father-in-law. You would run a similar risk?"

The flush along his cheeks betrayed him; but he spoke up civilly enough—aye, and stoutly.

"I am prepared for much worse than that, prince. My concern is only for the princess Dayra."

I did not say: "Well spoken, lad," as I might have done in the old days.

He would have to perform deeds, and not just prate about them, if he aspired to the hand of my daughter.

When Delia invited him back to the palace I had no objection. On the journey—and we took a zorca chariot with Sarfi the Whip as coachman— Barty indulged in polite conversation, inquiring after all the members of the family. Drak must be in Valka still, for Delia had seen him there when she'd raced there to find me. Her distress, which Deb-sa-Chiu had so graphically described, had been all for me. She had by now become a little used to my disappearances and was prepared to search across to Segesthes, aware that in the past she had found me against what must have seemed to her all odds. Barty inquired after Jaidur, and Delia told him that that young rip had decided to return to a place he knew well and where he would visit his brother Zeg. So Jaidur had gone back to the inner sea and a few casual questions elicited the unsurprising fact that Barty had heard of the place but that was about all.

Our youngest daughter, Velia, was well and thriving, looked after by Aunt Katri, who was also caring for little Didi, the daughter of Velia and

Gafard. Lela, well, she was about her own life in Vallia. And Dayra... ?

"I have had some news, princess," said Barty, hesitantly, as the zorca chariot rounded the corner past the Kyro of Spendthrifts.

Delia leaned forward. I frowned. Barty sat opposite us and he shifted about, nerving himself. At last he got it out.

"She was seen traveling through Thengelsax. A party left the Great River and hired zorcas. She was recognized by a groom who once served in the palace and had returned home to a posting station in the town."

I held down the instant leap of anxiety—an anxiety akin to fear. The whole northeast of Vallia resented being a part of the empire, still, although their animosity was being fanned by agitators. They raided down, real border raids, and one of the towns around which their activities had centered was Thengelsax. Its lord had complained bitterly. Was my Dayra mixed up with these border reivers?

That did not seem likely; but it was a possibility and I could not discount it, much though I would have liked to.

"Nothing else, Barty?"

"Nothing, prince. The troubles of the northeast are well known. The lords up there do not like us down here."

"It is more likely," said Delia, with calm firmness, as when she demanded one take a foul medicine, "far more likely that Dayra has gone up there with her—friends—to stir up trouble. It pains me to say that; but it is sooth."

Barty threw her a reproachful look; but he knew enough of Dayra to understand the truth of the remark.

"Listen, Barty." I paused and looked at him, whereat he grew red in the face and his eyes widened. It is odd how a simple calculating look from me will change a person's appearance. Most odd. "I've had dealings with the Trylon of Thengelsax. He was there today, as squat and bluff and foul as ever. Ered Imlien—he nurses a grudge against me because I broke his riding crop. He had told me what you are telling me now—only he was less tactful."

Delia was looking at me. Barty swallowed.

"If Dayra is mixed up with this Liberty for the Northeast rot, then, all right, so be it. We will hoick her out of it and if I have to tan her bottom for her, that I will do." I took a breath and saw the streets passing, the wink of sunlight from a canal, the bunting and flowers and brilliant shawls. "Do you know I have never even seen my daughter Dayra?"

"You are being rather—hard—on her, prince." Barty spoke slowly, softly; but he did not stammer and he came right out with it. I warmed to him.

"Of course I am. That is natural. It does not mean—"

I stopped speaking and threw my arms around Delia, hurling her to the floor between the seats.

"Get down, Barty!"

The long Lohvian arrow quivered in the lenken wood pillar where it had split the crimson curtains and severed a golden tasseled cord. The feathers were all shivering with the violence of the cast. Those feathers were dyed a deep and somber purple.

"Keep down! Sarfi the Whip!" I bellowed out at full lung-stretch. "Give the zorcas their heads! *Gallop!*"

The chariot lurched and bounced on the leather straps of the springing. The sharp, hard clitter-clatter of the zorcas' polished hooves on the flags of the street beat into a staccato rhythm. With Delia safely on the floor and Barty off the opposite seat, I could peer up. People were leaping left and right as we careered along. Sarfi was wailing away with his whip, sharp cracking flecks of sound through the uproar. We hurtled past a shandishalah booth and the stink whipped past to be swallowed by the fishy smells from the next stall.

"Where the hell are you taking us, Sarfi?"

He didn't answer; but plied his whip. I looked back. A train of destruction lay wasted in our wake for Sarfi had belted the chariot left-handed off the main street and taken us hell for leather down a narrow souk. Overturned stalls, spilled amphorae, crates and boxes splintered and strewing their silver-glinting fish across the flags, torn awnings and smashed awning-posts, and people—people crawling away, people staggering about like Sanurkazzian drunks, people dancing with rage and shaking their fists after us.

The smells, the sounds, the colors were wonderfully zestful to a man who has just had an arrow past his ear.

Whoever had loosed at us had had no chance of a second shot—and then I checked my foolish thoughts. This was a Lohvian arrow. Before I'd yelled, before Sarfi had ever laid a single strand of his whip to the zorcas—a practice I abhor and will not tolerate—a Bowman of Loh could have loosed three shafts—Seg Segutorio could have loosed four and possibly five.

So the one arrow had been enough.

Delia said: "I will resume my seat now, and then we can look at the message."

Barty and I helped her up—a quite unnecessary act for she is as lithe as an earthly puma or a Kregan chavonth—and we pulled out the arrow and unrolled the scrap of paper wrapped around the shaft.

Sarfi slowed down. The uproar subsided and we turned right-handed into the Boulevard of Yellow Risslacas and so sat staring at the message written on the paper. The writing was in that beautiful flowing Kregish script. A cultured hand had penned those lines. But the paper was ordinary Vallian paper, of good quality, yes—but it was not that superb and mysterious paper made by the Savanti nal Aphrasöe.

The message was addressed: "Dray Prescot, Prince Majister of Vallia, Hyr Kov of Veliadrin, Kov of Zamra, Strom of Valka."

I give all this gaudy nonsense of titles because they at once afforded two clues to the identities of those who had had a bowman deliver the message.

One: the island of Veliadrin was called that and not Can-Thirda, which had been its name until Delia and I changed it in memory of our beloved daughter.

Two: only Vallian titles were listed. Not one of the razzmatazz of titles in the rest of Kregen I had acquired appeared.

The salutation read: "Llahal-pattu. Prince Majister."

Llahal with the double L is the usual greeting for a stranger—the usual friendly greeting, that is—and when written the pattu is appended because Kregish grammatical and polite conventional usage demand it.

The message went on: "You, as the kitchew in a properly drawn-up and witnessed contract, the bokkertu being ably written and attested, are appraised of an irregularity. It is needful that you, Prince Majister, have an audience of Nath Trerhagen, the Aleygyn, Hyr Stikitche, Pallan of the Stikitche Khand of Vondium."

"By Vox!" exploded Barty. "The nerve of the rast. I have heard of him. Nath the Knife. Quoting his spurious and stupid titles at us!"

"Stupid they may be, as most titles are," I said mildly. "But spurious? I doubt it. Is he not the most renowned assassin in Vallia?"

A Pallan is a minister or secretary of state, and this assassin—a high and mighty assassin—was the chief man of his khand, or guild, brotherhood or caste. I guessed he had some fugitive lawyer drafting out this rhetoric for him.

I was to meet him at a tavern called The Ball and Chain (as I have said, Kregans have a warped sense of humor which can greatly infuriate those not attuned to its niceties) and this unsavory hostelry was situated a stone's throw from the Gate of Skulls.

"The Gate of Skulls," said Delia. "Well, you aren't going there. That is inside Drak's City."

"I've never been there. It might prove instructive."

"But, majister!" said Barty. "You can't just go walking in on a bunch of rascally assassins just because they send an invitation! It—" He spluttered a little, his cheeks red. "It just isn't done!"

Delia was looking at me with that look upon her face that gets right inside my craggy old skin, coiling in my thick vosk-skull of a head, itching me all along my limbs, making the blood pump around fast and faster. But she knew.

"I think, Barty... No—I know—that there is nothing you can say. The prince is going and that is all there is to it."

That was not all, and well she knew it. If Delia said to me you are not going, I would not have gone. But, all fooling aside, we both knew that there were weighty reasons for acceptance of the summons from the assassins. Had they wished to slay me the arrow would have driven straight.

"Well, prince," said young Barty, and his fist gripped around the hilt of his rapier. "In that case, I shall go with you!"

So ho, I said to myself—maybe Dayra has found herself a man here. Well, the proof of that would not be long delayed.

Four

Knavery in Drak's City

There are many Naths on Kregen, partly because of the affection felt for the myth hero Nath, who bears to Kregen much the same kind of physical prowess as the terrestrial Hercules does to us here on Earth, and among that number are good men and rogues, heroes and cowards, ordinary folk and men with the charisma about them that transcends goodness and evil. Also, among the many Naths there are many called Nath the Knife.

This particular Nath the Knife bore a reputation at once unsavory and yet respected, a blemished fruit, feared, of course, and yet still remaining very much the man of mystery.

As, indeed, he must. No assassins are going to put on fancy uniforms with favors proclaiming their trade and go off about their business. The community into which one such came with the avowed intent of committing stealthy murder would get together to deal with him. If anyone of the community refused, then it would surely be reasonable to suppose he had hired the damned stikitche in the first place. So, once that was established, the community could dispose of them both. I say reasonable. Of course, it might be the case that the community would not be sensible, or be frightened, or for some reason or another not collaborate. But that would scarcely happen on Kregen, where folk are hardier than most despite the weaker ones and the revolting aspects of slavery and all that that entails, no matter what pundits speculate may occur on other less-favored planets.

In the event I managed to persuade Barty to remain at the Gate of Skulls. I put it to him that he was on watch. He fingered his rapier and shuffled restlessly. We were both dressed roughly, with old brown blanket-coats, our weapons hidden. Around us swirled the never-ending stream of humanity going and coming, busy, screeching, quarreling, thieving, living.

"But I said—"

"And I thank you for it, Barty. But I truly think I will fare better on my own."

As you can see, I was very tender with this young man.

"Well…"

"So that is settled. You stay here and keep watch." With that I marched off through the bedlam at the gate without risking another word. For—what was he watching for?

If I did not reappear within a few burs what could he do? The soldiers and mercenaries would eventually venture into the Old City; but they would do so by mounting a proper battle-group. It was not that they were over-hated by the denizens of Drak's City or that they, in their turn, ever created wanton destruction. It was just that the law of Vondium did not run within the Old City and people preferred to let that lie, and not to disturb the sleeping leem.

The fly in this ointment was that Barty might take it into his head to go in after me if I did not return after a seemly interval.

The bedlam assumed a more bedlamish proportion within the Old City. People still jostled and pushed and shoved, yelling their wares, trying to thieve from the stalls and booths, trying to buy or sell at a profit. The stinks increased. People lived here jammed together. The ancient buildings tottered. Lath and plaster and moldering brick were far more in evidence than honest stone. The noise, the shoving, the stinks, all blended, as they so often do, into a picture that—seen and heard and smelled at a distance—presented a scene of great romantic attraction. This, one would think, was how a glittering barbaric city would carry on, heedless, drinking, wenching, laughing, uncaring, filled with cutpurses and daring cat-burglars and fences and shrill-voiced women and avaricious thief-takers on the prowl and grimy naked-limbed urchins learning all the tricks to take over when their elders went a-sailing down to the Ice Floes of Sicce.

Pushing through the throngs along the Kyro of Lost Souls, which extends within the Gate of Skulls, I kept myself out of mischief and out of trouble and headed for the tavern called The Ball and Chain.

If you wish to call the place a Thieves' Kitchen, I shall not prevent that description.

A straggle of ponshos wandered about, bunching, baaing, getting in everyone's way. Their fleeces were white. It is a fact that Vallians are a cleanly people, and even here in this run-down, brawling, odoriferous stewpot of a wen, and despite the spilled cabbages and rotting fruits and discarded skins, the place and people were surprisingly clean. There are towns on Kregen where even the aristocracy are clean, as there are towns where everyone is filthy. But Vallians take a pride in themselves and their country.

The Ball and Chain looked as though if the loafers moved away from the pillars of the front porch the whole lot would tumble down onto the heads of the throngs in the street.

I stopped under the awning of a man selling second-hand sandals and fingered a pair of curly-toed foofray slippers. They must have been stolen from some luxury-loving lord. The proprietor eyed me and prepared to sidle up to extol his wares. So, looking at the tavern, I became aware of two things.

A thin and incredibly dexterous hand was fingering delicately along my belt seeking the strings of the leather purse. And Barty heaved up, red faced, panting, shoving through, opening his mouth to yell over the hubbub. First things first.

I took the thin and sinewy hand in my fist and pulled. An urchin flew out before me, swinging around the elbow socket, starting to yell, rags and tatters of clothes fluttering. It was a young girl, scrawny, with a mass of brown hair, with grimy streaks down her cheeks. I eyed her with some severity.

"Diproo the Nimble-Fingered abandoned you, it seems, shishi."

"Let me go! Let me go!"

"Oh, aye. I'll let you go. And I will not even box your ears."

"Get away! Get away you hulu!" screeched the owner of the sandal stall.

I felt the second hand stealing around the leather purse strings, and I stepped back, dragging the girl, and took the lad—who was probably her younger brother—with my other hand.

I surveyed the pair of them, and shook my head. Products of a city, living by thieving of any description, free and not slave, well—what were their futures to be? What the futures of a thousand or more like them in the Old City? A thousand—there must be thousand upon thousand of half-naked urchins like this running wild in Drak's City.

"Let us go," panted the girl, her brown hair falling across her thin face. She'd be about twelve or thirteen. "We'll be thrashed."

The lad tried to kick my shins.

Then Barty arrived, almost losing his brown blanket which he was totally unaccustomed to wearing. He wanted to hand over the cutpurses to the authorities.

"The only authorities in Drak's City are the people who employ the fellow who employs these two," I told him.

He was a Vallian and so would know that; but it was not a fact easily digestible. The Laws of Hamal are notorious. The law runs differently, more quietly, in Vallia. Here in the Old City of Vondium the law ran as a mere trickle, the greater torrent passing outside the walls.

I managed to get the girl's raggedy collar jammed up under her ear, and with the lad picked up and stuffed under my other arm I had a hand free.

I pulled out a silver sinver. Awkwardly, for the little devil was kicking and squawking—and no one was taking the blind bit of notice of all this—I gave the sinver to the girl. I released the collar of her tunic and let her go. I looked steadily into her face. She did not run away. Then I dumped the lad on his feet, and gave him another sinver. The two coins, here, were like spitting twice into the middle of a vast and burning desert—but it seemed to me there was little else in truth to be done. I had once fought a duel over seven copper obs.

"Now be off with you, you scamps, and next time Diproo may smile upon you."

The girl looked back at me. Her brown Vallian hair, her brown Vallian eyes—her gauntness could not conceal the beauty she would one day become.

"I give you thanks, dom. And would you be telling your name to any who inquire?"

"I am Jak Jakhan. It is not important."

Barty, wheezing alongside me, tried not to think. He eased closer and whispered. "Should we not ask them about The Ball and Chain—about Nath the Knife? They could give us useful information."

As I say, Barty was trying to think.

"I think not." I glared with great sorrow on the girl and her brother, doomed urchins of Drak's City. The silver had vanished from sight somewhere inside their raggedy clothes. "Be off. Get a decent meal. And may Opaz shine upon you."

The girl said: "My name is Ashti and my brother is Naghan and—and we give thanks. May Corg bring you fair winds."

They ran off and in a twinkling were lost among the crowds past the ponsho flock.

Barty was a Strom, which is, I suppose, as near an earthly count as anything, and a noble and he felt like a stranded whale in these rumbustious surroundings. He gawked about at the spectacle and kept his right hand down inside his blanket coat. That particular gesture was so common as to be unremarked.

"Come on," I said. "You can't just stand around here. Half the urchins will be queuing up for their silver sinvers and the other half of the varmints will be out to pinch the lot."

We kept to the wall and walked along toward the tavern. Once we left the Kyro of Lost Souls the press became less thick. What to do about Barty puzzled me.

He said: "I wanted to ask what I was supposed to keep watch for, prince—"

"Jak Jakhan."

"What?"

I did not laugh. "You have not done this sort of thing before? Not even when you succeeded to your father's stromnate?"

"No, pri—Oh. No, Jak."

"It is sometimes necessary. It amuses me. At the least, it is vastly different from those popinjays at court."

"I do not believe there is any need to remind me of that."

A sway-backed cart stood outside the tavern. Cages of ducks were being unloaded. The racket squawked away and there was no need to inquire what the specialty of the house was going to be this day.

"Look," I said. "Do go into that tavern across the way and buy yourself some good ale and sit in a window seat. And, for the sweet sake of Opaz, don't get into trouble. Keep yourself to yourself. And if you are invited to dice—remember you will lose everything you stake."

"Everything?"

"They can make dice sit up and beg here, that's certain."

"You said you had never been into Drak's City before."

"No more I have. But these places have a character. There are many in the countries of Paz."

The tavern across the way was called The Yellow Rose. Barty took a hitch to his length of rope that held in his blanket coat and started across. He was almost run down by a Quoffa cart which lumbered along, lurching from side to side, scattering chickens every which way. A thin and pimply youth had a go at his purse as he reached the tavern porch but he must have felt the feather-touch, for he swung about, shouting, and pimple-face ran off. I let out a breath. I should never have brought him. But—he was here. I put that old imbecilic look on my face, hunched over, let my body sag, and so went into The Ball and Chain.

There is a keen and, I suppose, a vindictive delight in me whenever I adopt that particular disguise. I can make myself look a right stupid cretin. There are those who say the task is not too difficult. With the old brown blanket coat clutched about me, the frayed rope threatening to burst at any moment, I shuffled across the sawdusted floor.

The room was low-ceiled, not over-filled with patrons as yet. Tables and benches stood about. A balcony ran around two sides, the doors opening off at regular intervals to the back premises. A few slave girls moved about replenishing the ale tankards. It was too early for wine. I sat near the door, with my back to the wall, and contrived to hitch myself about so the long-sword at my side did not make itself too obtrusive.

Outside in the street rain started to drift down, a fine drizzle that quickly spread a shining patina across everything.

A girl brought across a jug of ale and filled a tankard for me. I gave her a copper ob. I stretched my feet out and prepared to relax and then jerked my boots back quickly. They were first-quality leather boots and someone would have them off me sharply, with or without my consent, if I advertised them so blatantly. I was a stranger. Therefore I was ripe game. I fretted about Barty. I should have run him back to the Gate of Skulls first.

This Nath the Knife, the chief assassin, had arranged to meet me here, so close to the walls of the Old City, clearly as a gesture of trust. His bolt-holes would all be deeper in Drak's City. He ventured within a stone's throw of the walls and this gate so as to show me he meant to talk. That, I understood. If they were going to try to assassinate me, they would not have requested this meeting.

My plan, a usual one in the circumstances, misfired.

Before I could get into conversation and so ease my way in and then seek a back entrance to the upper floor, the serving wench pattered across. Already, this early in the day, she looked tired.

"Koter Laygon the Strigicaw is waiting for you upstairs, master." She looked nervous. "The third door."

My imbecilic expression altered. I had put on a medium-sized beard. Now I stroked it and looked at her owlishly.

"Koter Laygon is waiting, master."

"Then he can wait until I have finished the tankard."

"He is—he will have your skin off, master—"

"You are sure it is me he is waiting for?"

"Oh, yes. He was sure."

"Who is he? What is he like? Tell me about him?"

I started to pull out a silver sinver. Her face went white. She drew back, trembling, terrified.

"No, no, master! No money! They are watching—they know what you are asking—"

She backed off, her hands wide, and then she ran away, her naked feet making soft shushing sounds on the sawdust. I glanced up under my eyebrows at the balcony. Up there any one of a hundred knot holes could hold a spying eyeball.

I shifted on the settle against the wall. A tiny sound, no more than the furtive sounds a woflo makes scratching in the wainscoting, made me look down.

A small slot had opened in the wall. A pair of scissors on extending tongs probed from the slot. They moved gently sideways toward me. Had I not moved, the fellow operating the tongs would have snipped away to get at my purse. As I had now vanished from his gaze the tongs drew back, the scissors vanished and the slot closed. I waited, intrigued.

Presently another slot opened close to me. The scissors probed out again, silently, ready to snip most patiently.

I picked up the half-full ale tankard.

No doubt the cramph had a whole array of tools he could fix to the tongs. A curved knife would slice away leather clothing. With all the noise of the taproom that usually created such a massive sound barrier, he could probably even use a drill to get through armor, and not be heard.

With a smooth motion I swiveled and slung the ale clean through the slot.

A splash, a yell of surprise, a series of choked squishing gulpings gave me a more general feeling of well-being. Petty—of course. But it was all a part of the rich tapestry of life—or, as this was Kregen, of death.

I bent to the slot and said in that fierce old biting way: "Thank Opaz it was only ale and not a length of steel."

With that I stood up, hitched the blanket coat around me, and stalked off to the blackwood stairway.

Over my left shoulder I had arranged snugly a quiver of six terchicks. The terchick, the little throwing knife of the clansmen, is often called the Deldar, and a clansman can hurl them right or left-handed from the back of a galloping zorca and hit the chunkrah's eye. Of course, the women of the Great Plains of Segesthes use the terchick with unsurpassed skill.

The drinkers in the area below watched with some curiosity as I climbed up. This Ball and Chain might be situated close to the walls of the Old City and the Gate of Skulls; I fancied the Aleygyn of the Stikitches, Nath Trerhagen, had packed the place with his men. Deep rivalries no doubt split the people of Drak's City, as they do in most places, unfortunately, and Nath the Knife would have chosen the meeting place carefully. I went up and I was ready to leap aside, to draw and to go into action, or to fashion a smile and a Llahal and listen.

The third door opened onto a narrow corridor that led via a rain-swept open walkway to the next-door building.

I had not envisioned this.

Barty could watch The Ball and Chain to no avail.

I pressed on. I remained firmly convinced that the stikitches did not mean to kill me. All this rigmarole would not then have been necessary—I had dealt with assassins before.

Two men in tatty finery met me at the far door and I was able to duck in out of the rain. They wore three purple feathers, all curved the same way, ostentatiously pinned to the breasts of their tunics. They carried their rapiers loose in the scabbards. Their faces, dark and lowering, with strips of dark chin beard, were entirely unprepossessing; but they greeted me cheerfully enough, evidently assigned merely as guides.

"Laygon the Strigicaw?" I said.

"He is waiting, dom. This way."

We went into the building and along dusty and unused passages to the far side. We descended a flight of stairs. The slope of the land here meant we were still one story above the street; but all the windows were covered with torn sacking.

Mineral oil lamps illuminated the dusty, half-wrecked room into which I was ushered. Houses were often left to fall down in the Old City, or knocked down. Rebuilding was on an entirely casual basis.

The air smelled musty. Dust hung in the beams of the lamps.

A table had been pulled across a corner and a tall-backed chair positioned before it. At the table sat three men and one woman. All wore steel masks. Their clothes were unremarkable, save for the badge of the three purple feathers.

My two guides indicated the chair and I sat down.

For a moment a silence ensued.

Then the woman said: "Llahal, Dray Prescot."

I said: "I do not like stikitches. You have asked me here. I am to meet Nath the Knife. Is he here, hiding behind a mask?"

The man on the extreme left said in a voice like breaking iron: "I am here. But you will talk with Laygon the Strigicaw."

"Which one is he?"

The man on the right said: "Here." His voice sounded mellow, full of the rotundity of roast beef and old crusty port.

"Well, Laygon, speak up."

"You are the Prince Majister of Vallia. The writ of Vondium and Vallia does not run in Drak's City."

"I have never cared much for laws that cannot be enforced. Spit out what you want. I am due at the Temple of Opaz the Nantifer two burs after midday."

"We do not much go in for temples, here in the Old City," said the woman. Her voice gasped just a little, as though she had difficulty in breathing. Maybe it was just the stale air. "And you had best keep a seemly tongue in your mouth—"

'Tell me what you want, now, and stop this shilly-shallying."

Nath the Knife nodded his head, and the steel mask caught the lamplight. All the masks were perfectly plain, and covered the whole face. I looked at the other parts of the bodies of these four, studying their hands, the way they held themselves, the angles of their heads.

'Tell him, Koter Laygon."

"The position is, Dray Prescot, the bokkertu has been signed and sealed upon you. You are accredited a dead man and due for the Ice Floes of Sicce."

"I think twelve of you tried, and there were twelve holes in the canal. I, too, can write a fine bokkertu." The word bokkertu, as you know, can mean any number of legal arrangements.

Laygon plunged on, and if he grew warm, I, for one, felt pleasure.

"I have taken out the assignment upon you. You are my kitchew. But—" He paused.

The chill menace of the situation was inescapable.

These men were assassins, dangerous, feral as leems. They would unhesitatingly kill—but they liked to get paid for their work.

Now Laygon the Strigicaw said heavily: "Half the money was paid to me. So far I have not completed the assignment." He paused again, as though expecting me to comment. Again I remained silent. "The irregularity is that the person hiring us is dead. We will not be paid the balance of our fee."

I shifted back in my chair and leaned to the side a little, so I could get the exact position of the two guides fixed.

"That is nothing to me. Stikitches can be killed like anyone else."

He went on, and again I detected the note of suppressed anger. "The Aleygyn is not pleased with the situation. The Stikitches of Vondium possess the highest possible reputation. Our honor is in question."

"I will not ask you with whom this precious reputation is held in such great esteem." I waved a casual hand. "Probably the rasts of the dunghills."

They did not react. I give them credit for that, at least.

"You are a dead man, Prince Majister—"

I interrupted. "Ashti Melekhi is dead. Would you work for nothing?"

Nath the Knife, clearly a most important man here, letting Laygon do the talking because it was Laygon who had taken the contract but prepared to step in with all his authority, said harshly, bending the mask toward me: "We do not mention names."

"You may not. But the fact remains. You are working for nothing."

"Precisely. The offer is this: Pay us the balance of the fee and the contract is then closed. If you do not pay, we shall fulfill it ourselves."

The instant intemperate indignation that flooded me had to be squashed. I took a breath. I said: "You have not mentioned the amount."

"Ten thousand gold talens."

I didn't know whether to be impressed by the value put on my life or insulted.

"My life is worth more than ten thousand."

"We abide by the legal contract. Pay us five thousand in gold and the contract is fulfilled and you live. Otherwise—"

I shifted on the chair again. It seemed to have a spongy feel to the legs, as though it was not firmly anchored to the floor. Probably it was a trick chair, with a trapdoor below. I'd have to be quick.

"I am not in the habit of paying gold to cramphs to save my life."

"You can always start."

This Nath the Knife was an intriguing fellow. He spoke evenly enough. He took no offense from my crude remarks. He wanted his money, or he would kill me.

"When do I pay?"

"At once."

"I am due at the Temple of Opaz the Nantifer, as I told you—"

"Then immediately your kow-towing is done."

With genuine curiosity, I said: "It is clear you know who I am, for your bowman delivered the message correctly. Yet I think perhaps you do not know me."

This trembled on the brink of boasting; but I am who I am, Zair forgive me, and I was intrigued.

"We know your reputation is very high in certain quarters," said the woman. She leaned forward and I caught the lamplight's sparkle from her eyes in the eye-slots of the mask. "But we have certain information that this great reputation is a sham, a bolstered creation because you are the Prince Majister. Of course, the most puissant prince of Vallia must be a great warrior, a High Jikai, for anything less would demean the empire."

"It's a theory," I said.

"So you will pay five thousand gold talens and you may live. It is settled."

I pondered. It seemed clear they believed the story. They would never have taken out the contract to kill me if they did not. I have amassed a certain unsavory reputation, as you know, and there were places on Kregen where no one—not even a raving idiot—would even contemplate trying to kill me. But, here in Vondium, the capital of the Vallian Empire, I was not in one of those places.

The four people at the table believed this business was settled. They began to stir, ready to take their leave. The two guides shuffled their feet and stepped back. I put my feet under me, ready for the leap, and looked across the table.

"Settled? Why, you onkers, I wouldn't pay you a single clipped toc!"

The four figures stiffened as though I'd jammed a polearm up each one of them. These four formed the High Council of the Assassins of Vondium. Their powers were frighteningly great. For that single betraying heartbeat they could not believe they had heard aright.

The woman let out a gasp and leaned forward on her forearm and her hand splayed against me. Jewels flashed. Nath the Knife put a hand to her hand, and restrained her. Laygon the Strigicaw started to curse, his hand reaching to his belt. The fourth man, who had not spoken, yet remained silent.

It struck me then that these assassins couldn't see the funny side of all this. They didn't think it was funny. To me, Dray Prescot, Lord of Strombor and Krozair of Zy, it was hilarious.

What my ferocious Djangs would say of it—their King of Djanduin solemnly being asked to pay someone for being kind enough not to kill him! They would bellow their mirth!

In the instant of the ensuing silence, when everyone in the musty room remained fixed, static, enwrapped with their own personal turmoil of emotions, the heavy beating of rain pelted against the closed windows.

The mineral oil lamps nickered.

Then, and only then, speaking in that iron voice, Nath the Knife said: "You will pay. You will pay—or you are dead."

"Not," I said, "a single clipped toc."

As the instant action followed I commented to myself that my rhetoric was entirely false. A toc is a tiny coin, one sixth of an ob, and who was going to bother to clip that?

Then the chair groaned and grated and flapped back into a black and cavernous hole and I spring-heeled up and onto the floor, and naked steel flashed in the lamplights.

This, then, was more like it...

Five

I Drop in on a Great Lady

The trick chair vanished with an almighty crash into the black maw gaping in the floor like the mouth of a chank. The two guides, flustered by my non-disappearance, flicked out their rapiers. They were stikitches and therefore expert with weapons. They rushed on me, silently, determined to cut themselves a little of Laygon's fee.

My feet hit the wooden floor and dust puffed up. The whole floor groaned; the place was as rotten as the worm-eaten hull of the Swordship Gull-i-mo.

"Cut him down!" grated that iron voice. "He refuses an accommodation in honor, now he must pay the penalty."

My own rapier ripped out—a nice blade but not a top-quality brand in its decorations, serviceable, well-used, the kind of rapier a fellow might wear in Drak's City—and the steel jangled and slid as the blades crossed.

The two assassins brought their four blades into play at once. I ducked and weaved and fended them off with the rapier alone. I did not draw the matching main gauche.

Before Barty and I had ventured in here I had insisted that he wear one of the superb mesh-steel shirts Delia and I owned. We kept them particularly well-cared for, on formers, well-oiled, safe in the armory of our Valkan villa in Vondium. One of those shirts cost more than even a relatively well-paid working man could earn in his entire lifetime.

The blades clashed and the lamplight glinted from the steel.

I vaulted back, slashed away, foined, and kept one eye on the four chief assassins at the table. They were the real danger.

One of the guides thought to play it clever and slid in below his fellow. His dark face glared up at me. He tried to hold his left-hand dagger up so as to parry any downward cut I might make, and thrust me through with his rapier. At the same time his companion pressed in strongly, seeking to pin me.

I leaped, thrust, landing a high hit along a shoulder above any armor they might be wearing under their drab tunics, brought a yell of agony, withdrew, and so kicked the clever one in the nose as I went by. His blade hissed past. He sprawled back, his nose a crimson flower, spraying blood.

I hit them both with the hilt—left and right, one two—and sprang away from the spot. A dagger whistled through the air where I had been standing.

The two guides sprawled on the floor. The woman still stood in the pose of throwing as I whirled to face the table in the corner.

One of the stikitches had gone. A door was just closing in the left-hand angle of the walls.

He was the silent one. Laygon and Nath had drawn their blades. They stood, clearly expecting the woman's dagger cast to finish me. Now I waggled my rapier at them admonishingly.

"I do not wish to kill any of you. Though, Opaz knows why not, for you are all ripe to die. But I am willing to spare you and so save future trouble."

I know. I know. That was weak. But I had work to do in Vallia and I didn't want a pack of rascally stikitches on my neck, interfering. If they could be convinced they had no future trying to assassinate me, then I would have achieved a great deal.

That was the new Dray Prescot talking, of course...

"You will die, here and now." The iron voice of Nath the Knife held not a single note of hesitation. Inflexible, he could not understand why what he wished had not already occurred.

A mocking thought occurred to me.

The two men, Nath and Laygon, rounded each end of the table to get at me. They were quite clearly hyr stikitches, top men, superb with weapons. Killing was their trade and they would have made of it an art.

"If I have to slay you, I will," I said. "But think. If you kill me, here and now, you will never have the chance of another client. No one else will offer you gold for my death."

As I say, I mocked them.

They did not reply but bore on.

The woman was the danger, now. She'd have another dagger or three stuffed down her bodice. I'd have to skip and leap and against these two my attention was likely to be fully engaged. Time for Remberee...

The window, probably...

It would be nonproductive to attempt to return across the rain-swept walkway to The Ball and Chain. The door through which Silent Sam or Tongueless Tom had disappeared would open to a trick lock, and there wouldn't be time. So it would have to be the window.

The woman came back to life. Her hand raked out. Steel glinted.

My left hand flicked up to my neck, the fingers gripped, twisted, withdrew and the terchick flew.

Like a homing bee it buzzed clean into the woman's upper right arm. She let out a hoarse gasp, never a scream, and staggered. The dagger fell from her nerveless fingers.

"I would crave your pardon, lady," I said. "If you were not a stikitche. As you are, you may rot in a Herrelldrin Hell for my talens."

Then the two men were on me and I ripped out the left-hand dagger and we set to.

Even as the blades crossed a thought so shocking occurred to me that I faltered, and stamped back, and then backpedaled most rapidly around the room aiming for the window.

What an onker I was!

These men believed I was a warrior of the imagination, a figment of the Vallian Empire's publicity machine. They had seen me enter the tavern, no doubt of that, and they took me at face value. The woman had been devastatingly contemptuous. And here I was, at last beginning to warm up, freed from talk and intrigue and into the business of bashing skulls, and taking that evil joy from it that sometimes overcomes me—to my shame. But—but! If they realized I could handle a sword that would make life far more hazardous in the future. And it was to the future that all my efforts had been directed.

All this talk, and inanity, and inaction—all had been designed to give me breathing space in Vallia. I did not wish to take on the work I had to do with a gang of cutthroat stikitches dogging my heels all the time.

If I slew all these, there would be more...

The very correctness of my estimation of the situation was borne out as Nath and Laygon charged on.

"It is true!" bellowed Laygon in his rich voice. "We had a report from our spies. The twelve who were slain and of whom you boast, you rast, were killed by your friends. You did not even draw your blade."

That was true.

"Stand and die like a man," grated Nath the Knife, and started to work his way around to my back.

"I have had luck with the knife," I said. I ran backwards, casting a single quick look to see where I was going, aiming for the sacking-covered window. "But you are hyr stikitches—good at your foul work. But, you cramphs, you will not get my gold."

I was at the window.

I spun about, bracing myself.

"Nor my hide!"

And with a single leem-leap I went head-first through the window.

All this idle chatter as I fought—I was really lapsing into some fairy-tale layabout, all silks and graces, quite unlike the hard and vicious and totally practical fighting man I am...

Rain lashed at me as I fell. I went head over heels. I had thought to land on my feet, and back, rolling, and so come up ready to fight.

Instead as I sailed from the window I turned over and fell splat into the back of an overfilled dung cart.

Muck pulsed up around me. The stink sizzled. I scrabbled around in heaving nausea, sloshing about in the odoriferous and sticky collections of a hundred cesspits and stables. Shades of Seg and his dungy straw!

I flailed my arms and heard the squishings and squelchings.

The man on the cart yelled as the brown spray hit him.

I got a knee onto the rotten wood of the cart and heaved up.

Above my head three faces peered out of the shredded sacking. The woman's face was, like them all, hidden by the steel mask; but I fancied she was whiter than usual. I hoped so. The cart lurched and I managed to slide off the back.

Nath let out a yell.

"Seize him up! Tally ho! Stikitches! *Slay him!*"

The rain slicked across the cobbles. The smell rose despite the rain. The cart lumbered off. Men and women appeared in the shadowed doorways of the street. I was around the corner from the front entrance of The Ball and Chain, and if I went that way Barty would come prancing out of the door of The Yellow Rose ready to fight and ready to be chopped.

So I ran the other way and, by all the confounded imps of Sicce, here came Barty, red-faced, bellowing, running after me with his rapier naked in his fist. By Zim-Zair! I groaned. Now we're in for it!

"I am with you pri—Jak!"

"Well, stay with me!"

The three steel masks vanished from the window. A few men pushed out into the rain. In a few murs we'd be surrounded. Once the hue and cry was up we'd have all kinds of rascals out for a bit of fun and bashing running after us besides the assassins.

"This way, Barty. And put that damned sword away! Run!"

We pelted off through the rain heading away from the Gate of Skulls, along the side street parallel to the walls. The walls of the Old City of

Vondium are mostly noticeable by their great age and their state of disrepair. But, for all that, they demarcate a very real line, a barrier between the Old and the New.

People stared after us. The rain was a blessing in one way, in that it had driven a considerable number of idlers into shelter and so we had a pretty clear run. But, in the other way, and a worse way, too, it meant there were far fewer crowds in which to become lost. So—we ran.

I, Dray Prescot, ran.

I told myself that I ran because of Barty. I did not want him killed. I had never yet met my daughter Dayra to talk to her and I did not want our first meeting to be shadowed by the death of her fine young man who ran puffing and red-faced at my side. But Barty was young and tough and filled with ideas of chivalry and valor.

"Let us turn on them and rend them!" he panted out.

"Run."

We cut along the first cross street aiming to get back to the walls and find a loophole out. I had no real idea of the geography of Drak's City—I doubt if anyone had much idea of that crawling maze of streets and alleys and hidden courts as an entirety—and so could do no more than run and follow my nose.

It would be nice if Ashti and her brother Naghan turned up and out of gratitude for the silver sinvers guided us to safety. But, again, that was out of fairy books.

The reality came as a dozen men sprang from an alleyway and brandishing long-knives and cudgels and a sword or two came blustering down on us.

Very carefully I gave my palms a good wipe down the old blanket coat—on the inside. The muck fouled me abominably. But I needed fists that would not slip on hilts for the work that promised. As though Five-handed Eos-Bakchi decided it was time to smile—just a little—upon me, I spotted an abandoned orange-like fruit called a rosha lying in the water-streaming gutter. A single twist ripped it into half and I smeared the tacky juice over my palms and fingers. That would help to give a good grip.

It smelled a little better than I did, too.

"We cut through them in one go and keep running," I told Barty.

When they hit us I did just that. I used the hilt a good deal, for I had no wish to kill these fellows. One or two blades flickered around my ears; but with a bash and a whump or two I was through. I poised to run on. I was through—but not so Barty.

He pranced. He took up the stance. His rapier leaned into a perfect line. He foined. He was thoroughly enjoying himself. Like a student fresh from the salle he handled himself with all the perfection of a star pupil. I sighed.

Many a time have I seen these fine young men fresh from sword-training go into rough and brutal action. If they live they learn and then stand a better chance. But all the universities in two worlds don't teach what a man must know to keep a knife from his guts, a knee out of his groin, a flung chain from around his neck.

They'd have had Barty—had him for breakfast and spat out the pips.

Perfect in poise and lunge and parry, holding himself in the correct rapier-fighting position, he would have been easy meat for them. He was lucky—that I own—when a flung cudgel merely brushed past his brown hair. But he couldn't last.

So I went bashing back most evilly, with a knee here, and a clutch at a raggedy coat here and a jerk and a chunk of the hilt, and a bending-forward so that the attacker went sailing up over me, to be kicked heartily as he hit the ground.

No, if you want to stay alive on many spots of Kregen you do no good trying to fence by the book.

A stout-armed fellow with a kutcherer tried to stab the spiked back of the knife into my eye, and I weaved and kicked him between wind and water, and ducked a cudgel from his mate and elbowed his Adam's apple. My own rapier and main gauche flew this way and that parrying blows and thrusts. I jumped about a fair bit. I got up to Barty and put my foot into the rear end of the man who was going to slip a long knife into Barty's exposed back and kicked him end-over-end. I had to beat away another kutcherer, careful of that wicked tooth of metal.

Barty had allowed a ruffian to get inside his guard, and with his rapier pointing at the rain-filled skies was dancing around as though the two of them waltzed, neither able to step back to take a slash at the other.

"Barty," I said, in what I considered a most understanding voice. But Barty jumped, anyway. "Let us get on."

I stuck the main gauche back into my belt, ignoring the scabbard, took the fellow clasping Barty by the ear, ducked a cudgel blow from somewhere, and ran him across the street. He tried to emulate a swifter and rammed head-on into a moldy wall.

I grabbed Barty.

"And this time, young man, do not stop running!"

We took off. They followed for a bit; but I caught a hurtling cudgel out of the air and threw it back. The man who had flung it dropped as though poleaxed. After that the rest of them more or less gave up the pursuit.

But there were others, far more ruthless, who took it up as we reached the walls.

And, as I saw, two thin, furtive, weasel-like fellows remained dogging our footsteps as we ran up to the wall and looked about for the nearest way through or over or under.

The assassins had gathered their strength. Now the mob of men who flowed around a buttress meant to do for us finally.

I took a single look at them and hauled Barty off. We ran fleetly along the wall, dodging refuse, leaping covered stalls, almost treading on a family sheltering under an old tarpaulin. The rain washed away a deal of the muck and stinks; but enough remained for me with my odoriferous clothes to feel at home.

A splendidly orchestrated hullabaloo now racketed away at our heels. Barty kept on laughing. I own the situation amused me; but I am notorious for that kind of perverse behavior and I felt some surprise—pleased surprise, I hasten to add—that Dayra seemed to have found herself a young man of exceptional promise. So we ran along the wall and a gang of kids pelted us with rotten cabbages, green shredding bundles falling through the rain. We ducked into a house built into the wall and leaped over an old fellow who snored in a wicker hooded chair and so rollicked up the blackwood stairs. The upper rooms were filled with all kinds of trash and bric-a-brac indicating the storage places for the junk merchants who thrived on human stupidity and cupidity. Their ruffianly agents scoured around picking up antiques which were then sold at inflated prices to the wealthy of Vondium. Well, it takes all kinds to make a world.

We hared through the piles of old furniture and pictures and tatty curtains, past boxes and bales and bundles, heading for the windows. These were all barred. Barty put his foot against a wooden bar and the old wood puffed and shredded—I hardly care to describe that tired sagging away as a splintering of wood.

We bundled through and then tottered back, clutching each other, poised dizzyingly over nothing.

I grabbed the lintel. It held, thank Zair, and we hauled in. We stood perhaps fifty feet up the sheer outside wall, in a window embrasured out over the cobbled road below. And at our backs the pursuit bayed up those dark blackwood stairs.

One window along a beam jutted out with a rope and pulley. The junk would be collected here and then hoisted out and lowered onto Quoffa carts below.

"Next window, Jak," said Barty, cheerfully.

"I had hoped there would be stairs—at the least a rope ladder." These drikingers of the Old City have their entrances and their exits. Drikingers—bandits of a particular bent—is not too strong a word to apply to some of the fellows in Drak's City. So we bashed along to the next window and kicked it open and seized the rope.

Loud footfalls echoed up from the room at our backs. Men fell over bundles, and a giant glass-fronted wardrobe toppled to smash to ruination.

'Time to go, Barty. Come on."

So, grasping the rope, we let ourselves down as the windlass held against the pawl. We were almost at street level when the first furious faces poked out of the window alongside the pulley-crowned beam.

"Jump!" I yelped. "They'll start reeling us in any mur!"

So we jumped, and hit the rain-slicked cobbles, and staggered and a flung knife caromed past my ear.

Barty staggered up and shook his fist. Men were sliding down the rope. I smiled. Oh, yes, this was a smiling situation.

"They mean to do for us, then... More running is indicated."

"Why can't we stand and blatter them, Jak? By Opaz—I do not care much for all this running. I can't get my wind."

"They'll open up your body quick enough, my lad. Then you'll have wind and to spare. Run!"

Running off I was aware Barty was not with me and swung about ready to damn and blast him.

He was hopping about with his old blanket coat twisted around his legs, trying to disentangle himself, first on one foot then on the other. His face was a wonder to behold.

"By Vox!" he bellowed. "This confounded blanket is alive!"

"Not as alive as most of 'em in there." I dodged back and grabbed for the coat; but he kept toppling away and almost falling and staggering about. In the end I whipped a horizontal slash from the rapier at him and shredded the rope. The blanket coat fell away. He kicked it wrathfully.

"Opaz-forsaken garment! I nearly knocked my brains out on the cobbles."

"Run," I said. There was no need to draw any parallels between his outraged remarks and what would happen. So we ran.

Now we were outside Drak's City and, in theory, back where the writ of Vondium ran.

Whether Vondium's writ ran or not, we did.

I owe that the sheer zest of this running pleased me. The idea that I ran away from enemies had long since passed. The game now was to stay ahead. That became the object, the running was the thing, the escaping the prize. If we fought that would come as an anticlimax.

The stikitches pelting after us were still yelling. Near the Old Walls, some remnant of their own powers clung.

"By Jhalak!" one of them sang out. "Stand and meet your doom like men!"

"I'm all for standing," puffed Barty. He gave me a most reproachful look.

"Run," was all I said.

Pressing on we came into more respectable streets and Barty, with a comment to the effect that if I intended to run I had best run with him, and that we'd best go *this* way and through *that* alley and so out onto *this* square, at last brought us into a part of the city I recognized. Although we were now in company with many other people all about their business, the assassins stayed with us. They kept a distance. But they dogged our footsteps.

I think most of them had removed their masks; but they all kept a fold of cloth over their faces, and this would be taken as a natural precaution against the rain. Their large floppy Vallian hats with the broad brims hanging down and shedding the water also afforded them a measure of concealment.

When the rain, after the Kregan fashion, started to ease up and the splendor of the suns began to shine through, I wondered how far the stikitches would press their pursuit.

Our mutual progress had now degenerated into a fast walk and we threaded our way between the people venturing out after the rain. No one took any notice of us. There were others running—slaves, mostly, about their masters' business—and our bedraggled appearance bespoke us for slaves or free men with unpleasant work to perform. We came to the broad arrow through either side of the building that is called the Lane of the Twins. This leads to the broad kyro before the imperial palace.

Barty started up it at once and so I followed. Although I say I recognized where we were this does not mean I was well acquainted with the area. Opening off the Lane of the Twins many side streets and roadways gave entrances to the streets and roads pent within two curving canals. A number of broad boulevards cross the Lane. We passed over canals bridged in a variety of the pleasing ways of Vondium. Just under the stalking feet of an aqueduct we were held up by a crowd who jostled and pushed along slowly, mingled with carts and chariots and carrying-chairs. And all these streets and alleys and canals and boulevards and aqueducts are blessed with names... No—I knew only that if I went on along the Lane of the Twins eventually I'd reach the palace.

The crowds grew thicker and more solid. On the right-hand side a string of carts had come to a standstill. Each cart was piled with hay. They were filled to abundance with hay, and they were jammed tightly together, so that the pair of krahniks who pulled each cart were eagerly reaching forward to chew contentedly away at the hay dribbling from the tailgate of the cart in front. The carters sat slumped, hats over their eyes, phlegmatically waiting for whatever obstruction ahead was halting all progress to clear.

I looked back.

The two thin weasely fellows were padding on apace, and with them a dozen or so of the most determined stikitches.

For a moment we stood halfway between two side streets. The doors of the buildings flanking the Lane were closed.

"Now," said Barty, and he started to draw his rapier. "Now we cannot run any farther, thank Opaz. Now we can teach these rasts a lesson."

The backs of the crowd ahead appeared to be a solid wall; but we could worm our way through. I frowned. I did not relish the idea of Barty being chopped to pieces, and I knew he would unfailingly be chopped if those master craftsmen at murder caught up with him. I could not risk his life.

"Up, Barty," I said, and took his arm and fairly hurled him up onto the hay of the rearmost wagon.

He started to protest at once and took a mouthful of hay, and spluttered and then I was up on the high cart with him and urging him along. Reluctantly, he allowed me to help him over the somnolent form of the driver, with a couple of steps along the broad backs of the krahniks, to reach the next cart along. So, prancing like a couple of high-wire artists, we darted along the line of hay-filled wagons.

The massed crowds below showed little interest in our antics; a few people looked up, and laughed, and some cursed us; but most of them were content merely to push on in the wake of whatever was holding up progress.

The rain stopped and the twin suns shone with a growing warmth. The clouds fanned away, dissipating, letting that glorious blue sky of Kregen extend refulgently above.

We hopped along from wain to wain, leaping the drivers and the krahniks. The animals were hardly aware of the footsteps on their backs before we had leaped off and so on.

The assassins followed us.

Ahead the sense of a mass moving ponderously along the Lane turned out to be a large body of soldiery, all marching with a swing. The glint of their weapons showed they were ready for an emergency, which surprised me, although it should not have, seeing the troubles through which Vallia had just come—and was still going through, by Vox. Everybody followed the troops, either unable or unwilling to push past. A number of loaded and covered carts were visible within the ranks of the formed body, and there were palanquins there, too, with brightly colored awnings against the rain or the suns.

Barty missed his footing and I had to haul him up off the head of a sleepy driver, whose brown hand reached for his bolstered whip, and whose hoarse voice blasted out, outraged, puzzled, alarmed at this visitation from heaven. I shouted.

"On with you, Barty. The rasts gain on us."

Ahead along the line of hay wains the purple shadow of an aqueduct cast a bar of blackness. That could cause us problems. We leaped the next two carts and Barty again slipped. He turned on me, then, thoroughly put out by my inexplicable insistence on running away. He held onto the high rail of a hay wain and spoke furiously.

"In my island they used to speak with hushed breath of the Strom of Valka—Strom Drak na Valka. But I have heard stories, rumors, that the great reputation is all a sham, a pretense, something to color the marriage with the Princess Majestrix. By Vox! I do not believe it—but your conduct strains my belief, prince, strains it damnably!"

The hay wains were lumbering forward again, slowly, rolling, and the purple shadows of the aqueduct fell about us.

"Believe what you will, Strom Barty. But you will go on to the next wagon and then jump down. You will mingle in the crowds. You will do this as you love my daughter Dayra."

"And? And what will you do?"

"I will go up." The aqueduct's brick walls presented many handholds. "They will follow me. That is certain. I will meet you—"

"I shall go up, also!"

I lowered my eyebrows at him. He put a hand to his mouth.

"You go on under the aqueduct and jump down, young Barty. Dernun?"

Yes, cracking out "dernun?" like that at him was not particularly polite. Dernun carries the connotation of punishment if you do not understand, meaning savvy, *capish*—but he took the intensity of my manner in good part, only going a little more red. He turned and jumped for the next cart without a word and vanished in those concealing purple shadows.

The bricks were old and here and there irregular patches of new brickwork had been inserted. The emperor liked to keep his aqueducts efficient. Even so, sprays of water spat in fine arcs out across the heads of passersby. I climbed up to the first row of brick arches and clung on and looked back. The assassins were almost up with the aqueduct, leaping like fleas over the backs of the hay wains. I waved my arm at them and then made a most insulting gesture.

The slant of the brickwork ran the water channel out over the Lane at an angle. I climbed through the lower tier of arches into a dark cavernous space, lit by the semi-circles of brilliance in serried rows, feeling the looseness of old mortar and brick chipping below, the glimmer of random puddles showing up like unwinking eyes. Water splashed down from the leaded channel above my head. The stikitches clambered up after me.

The plan was to run diagonally along the first tier of arches all the way across the Lane and so free myself of the encumbrance of Barty. I had ideas on the mores and honor of the stikitches, and if Laygon the Strigicaw was among those pursuing me—as he must almost inevitably be—then I could finish this thing cleanly.

That time-consuming altercation with Barty had afforded the pursuers the chance to catch up. They ran fleetly across the strewn ground at me, spraying water from puddles, yelling, incensed, confident they had me now and uncaring of what noise they made in this arched space, knowing it would be lost in the greater noise from the procession which passed by below.

"*Kitchew!*" they bellowed, and closed in.

They were good. Well, of course, to be employed as an assassin on Kregen you have to be good. Quite apart from the fact that if you are not good you won't last, you will also starve.

The shadowy effect of the brick buttresses and the shafts of brilliant light through the arched openings lent a macabre air of theatre to that fight. The blades rang and scraped and the first two went down. The others pressed in confidently enough and at the first pass with a large fellow wearing a ring in his ear, my rapier blade snapped.

Do not think it odd if I say I felt relief that the rapier snapped. Only eight of the rogues had clambered up the arches and followed me. So I was in a hurry, and with the rapier useless I could hurl the hilt in the face of the earring fellow, and then rip out the longsword.

"By Jhalak," one of the stikitches ground out. "That bar of iron will not serve you."

It served him through the guts, and the next fellow spun away with his steel mask shattered and blood spouting through. Two tried to run and two terchicks finished them. I was left facing the man who by his clothes and mannerisms I knew to be Laygon the Strigicaw. Time was running out. I had to be quick.

"When you are dead, Laygon," I said cheerfully, "no stikitche will pick up your contracts without payment. But Ashti Melekhi is dead, also. So that business will be settled, with full steel-bokkertu and in all honor."

He knew what I meant. Steel-bokkertu is a euphemism for rights gained by the sword and retrospectively legalized. So he leaped for me, snarling, and he died, like the others, and I ran to the edge of the arched space and looked down.

I might have guessed.

The procession was in an uproar.

The two weasely fellows had chosen to go after Barty because they were not stikitches and fancied he, as a Koter of Vallia, would carry a goodly sum on his person. After the assassins had finished with me, the rasts calculated, there would be no pickings for them. The rest of the stikitches must have decided to chance the ranked soldiery. Barty had spitted one of them, clearing a space among the onlookers as the procession passed, and was tinkering away with two more.

It was a long way down.

People broke away from the fight, screaming. In those first few moments of action when all was confusion, no one turned instantly to assist Barty. But he did look a sight, clad in his old clothes, bedraggled, red-faced, swearing away, thoroughly worked up. One might almost be forgiven for believing he was the murderer and the soberly-attired assassins his victims. They had removed their steel masks and now wore only the polite public half-mask often seen on Kregen, a useful adjunct to gracious living, as it is said with some irony.

Whatever might be said, in a mur or two he'd be dead.

The angle of the aqueduct had taken me out farther into the center of the Lane. Directly below passed a cart loaded with sharp-looking objects under a tarpaulin, the edges creased and unfriendly looking. To jump down on that would invite a punctured hide and a snapped backbone. Further along swayed the palanquins with their colored awnings. I eyed them savagely. The largest one—of course. It had to be the biggest and best to take the weight and the velocity of my fall.

I ran along the edge of the brickwork, ducked out of the archway right over the palanquin below, and launched myself into space. As I jumped I saw the soldiers at last break ranks and advance on Barty and the assassins. Just before I revolved in the air, falling, I glimpsed the assassins running off, and Barty twisting in the grip of a Deldar.

Then, rotating, I came down with an ear-splitting crash on the striped awning. It ripped. I went on through trailing tatters of cloth. The blue and green striped material had broken my fall and I landed with a thump on the wooden bed of the palanquin. I spat out a chunk of the blue and green banded cloth, and a strip of the white striping between the colors caught in my teeth. I ripped it out furiously and dived for the cloth-of-gold curtains.

The three women in the palanquin stared at me, petrified.

I took in their appearance at a glance—two handmaidens and a great lady. She was half-veiled, and she looked lushly beautiful, and dominating, and her color was rising and she was getting all set to spit out a mouthful of invective. You couldn't really blame her. Here she was, sitting quietly in her palanquin being taken along with all her people, and some hairy odoriferous blanket-coated oaf falls in from the sky.

I became aware of my obnoxious pong as the stink cut through the scents of the palanquin.

The Womoxes carrying the poles had yielded to the sudden extra weight; but one pole broke and the whole lot came to a shuddering crash, tip-tilted on a corner. The great lady was flung across the cloth-of-gold canopied space. She fell into my arms. I couldn't move. Her dark, intense face wrinkled up, the whiteness of the skin emphasized by the kohled eyes and the artful patch of color in the cheeks. Her flared nostrils widened. Her mouth, hidden by the veil but its outline visible as the silver gauze pressed back, curved down.

"You stink!"

"Get off, lady, I am in a hurry—"

"You dare—"

Somehow the longsword had not done any damage to the occupants of the palanquin—yet. I tried to twist it around to make it safe. She was screaming invective at me now and I half-turned to shove her off, so that she saw me. Only then I realized the medium-sized brown beard had been ripped off somewhere along the way.

She saw my face.

"Oh," she said.

"I am in a hurry, lady. Men are trying to kill me and I must—"

"Yes, you must run away. Well, let me sit up and you may run away—run to the Ice Floes of Sicce, and you will."

"Mayhap I will," I said.

She struggled to sit up against the slope of the palanquin. Her two hand-maidens went on screaming. A soldier stuck his head in the opening of the cloth-of-gold curtains and saw me.

Instantly his rapier whipped in.

The longsword was still stuck somewhere down in among the cushions, the point jammed in the woodwork. I just hoped this great lady wouldn't sit back too heavily.

"Keep your damned rapier out of my face!" I yelled. The guard swept the curtains aside and started to reach for me.

"Do not kill him, Rogor!" snapped the lady.

"Yes—" began this guard Hikdar, and I twisted my foot around and kicked him in the guts through the curtains. I got the sword free. The lady stared at me with those fine dark eyes filled with a blaze of contempt.

"Run—go on, run! That is all you are good for!"

The Hikdar was whooping in great draughts of air. I stood up and hit my head on the awning post and cursed and started to climb out. The lady suddenly laughed. She trilled silver malicious laughter. She pointed.

"Is that what you run from?"

Her guards had caught one of the weasely fellows and they dragged him, all a-yelling and a-squawking, up to the canted palanquin. He was in a frightful state. He screamed as they twisted his arm up his back and the knife dropped with a clatter unheard in the din. His thin face contorted with his terror, and spittle slobbered. He looked thin and frail and ridiculous as a would-be murderer, all the weasely deviltry washed away in his fear.

"That was one of them," I said.

She laughed at me, hard, hating, hurtful laughter.

She did not hurt me, mind; but she would hurt Barty and wound him deeply, if he heard her.

"You carry a monstrous great sword and you run so hard you fall into my chair and ruin it—and *that* is what you run from, what so frightens you."

"If you like," I said. Barty? What had happened to him? I fretted, not giving this great lady much attention and, to be truthful, not much respect, either.

"Get out!" she screamed, suddenly letting her anger boil over. "You stink! You are an abomination! Get out! Get out!"

"I'm going as soon as I—" I started.

Then I saw Barty, bawling into the ears of a guard Hikdar and gesticulating, and so I knew he was safe. I own, I felt a great flood of relief, and let out a breath.

"Go on running," spat the great lady. "There are a lot more rasts like this one for you to run from. Take your stupid great sword and clear off. You are not a real man. You are just a fake, an apology for a Jikai, a puffed up bag of vomit! *Run!*"

Six

The Black and Whites Make a Promise

The separate wing of the imperial palace in Vondium given over to the private apartments of the Prince and Princess, Majister and Majestrix, have been decorated with Delia's faultless taste, and yet, as she would exclaim, flinging up her hands in mock despair, you could never get any life into the place. Still, this austere, frowning pile with all its fantastic traceries of balconies and colonnades, of spire and tower, of concealed grottoes and secret gardens, was where, for the moment, we were living. The villas belonging to the various estates in Vallia kept up in Vondium—those of Delphond and the Blue Mountains, and of Valka, Zamra and Veliadrin— were preferred by us. So I took a bath—a quick, scalding hot bath and not the Baths of the Nine—in the imperial bathroom and changed into the flummery of grand clothes demanded for the ceremony at the Temple of Opaz the Nantifer.

Truth to tell, I was heartily sick of all these endless ceremonies. Perhaps I have not stressed them enough in my narrative. Certainly, they bored me out of my skull. But I was the Prince Majister and the emperor my father-in-law still reigned and I was constrained to attend whenever I was in Vondium.

That seemed to me one perfectly good explanation for my frequent absences from the capital, quite apart from the periods spent in our estates.

"And she spat at you?"

"Well, my heart," I said as I struggled into the swathing bands of a ghastly pink robe. "Almost. She was uncouth, if that is the word. Crude in a gentlelady."

"And who was she?"

Delia smiled as one of her handmaids pulled up the long laypom-colored dress. We were never sticklers for the protocol that demanded a husband and wife dress in their own rooms miles apart. Mind you, I had always to keep my mind on my own clothes when Delia was thus engaged.

"Some great lady or other. She was not, I think, of Vallia, for she had violet eyes."

Delia gave me a quick duck of the head, a fast look and then that graceful turn as she looked away and said: "Not of Vallia, as you say, my heart."

Well, I imagine I know my Delia and so at the time I fancied she had more than an inkling who this bitchy great lady might be. Being Delia, and therefore a tease as well as the most gracious lady of two worlds, she forbore to tell me. And me, being me, I forbore to inquire.

"Hurry, my love," said Delia, hauling her jeweled belt tight around that slender waist and buckling up the gold clasp. "We shall be late in two flicks of a leem's tail."

"Grab that mazilla," I said to the palace servant loaned to us to take care of our garments. "The very largest, most ornate and ludicrous one in the whole wide world of Kregen, I do truly think."

Each rank of nobility of Vallia has its corresponding rank of mazilla it may wear; the tallest and widest and grandest by the emperor, the next size by any kings of Vallia who might happen to be living at the time, then the princes, the kovs, the vads and trylons, and so on through the Stroms down to the ordinary haughty private koter. The koter—gentleman is only an approximation to the ramifications of meaning to koter—wears a neat curved mazilla, rather like a tall collar, of a dark color, usually a distinguished black, relieved only by braiding of his allegiance. The Koters of Vallia are proud of their neat trim mazillas. As I squirmed into the enormous magnificence of the monstrosity I had chosen to wear, I wondered if the game was worth the candle. Might the insult not better be conveyed by wearing a koter's mazilla in lustrous black velvet?

No time to worry over that now. We buckled on our weapons, slung our scarlet and golden cloaks on the zhantil-bosses, gave a last quick look in the mirrors, and then hared off down the marble staircases and along the rug-strewn corridors to the zorcas we would ride to the Temple of Opaz the Nantifer.

Shadow gave a curve of his head and a whinny to show he was pleased to see me. He was truly a magnificent animal and I was glad afresh each time I bestrode his back that I'd been able to bring him with me all the way from Ba-Domek.

Delia's zorca, a fine chestnut, had a somewhat small spiral horn in the center of her forehead; but she was a fine mare and Delia was fond of her Firerose.

The service of propitiation to Opaz, the spirit manifest in the Invisible Twins, passed. I will not dull your senses with a detailed description, for all that, of the many religions and creeds of Kregen, that of Opaz shines the truest. I swear allegiance to Zair, as you know, and to Djan; but these two lack something of the essential spiritual transcendence of Opaz; Zair and Djan—particularly Djan—are Warrior Gods. In Opaz lies a very great part of the future well-being of Kregen.

So I will pass on to the moment when Delia and I walked back to our zorcas where they had been tethered with many others and looked after by hostlers employed by the Temple. My usual traffic with the Racters was so minimal as to be nonexistent; public functions provided them with an opportunity to speak with me. I turned as Strom Luthien approached, very seemly to all outward appearances, his hat being in his hand and his head slightly inclined.

Yet I knew he, at least one Racter, would be only too ready to slip a blade between my ribs and then call for assistance too late. Luthien was one of those nobles without an estate, his Stromnate being gambled away, probably, lost at the Jikaida board. Now he worked for the Racters as a messenger and agent.

He smiled at me under his moustache, a sleek, knowing, and yet faintly patronizing smile. My monstrosity of a brown beard bristled up, almost as though it had been grown by me instead of being hooked on my ears. I looked at him as he relayed his information. Those Racters with whom I had done business in Natyzha Famphreon's hothouse pleasure gardens wished to converse with me again.

"For, prince," said Strom Luthien, "much was agreed and yet little accomplished."

I did not make a scathing remark to the effect that I did not discuss details with errand boys. I said: "The Black Feathers were routed. Where?"

"The same place—"

"No. I remember the chavonths. And, and you will, convey my regards to Kov Nath Famphreon."

He kept his smile going famously. "Then where?"

"The Sea Barynth Hooked. There is an upper room. Hire it from the landlord. In five burs time."

I turned away almost before I'd finished speaking, and the springy feathers of the mazilla swished. What Strom Luthien made of my hauteur and my bad manners I didn't give a damn. I had to lay the foundations here for subsequent action. Delia, though, favored me with a look that was so old-fashioned as to be positively antediluvian.

We mounted up and shook the reins. Of course we drew disapproving glances from the nobles. The Prince and Princess of Vallia, riding alone, without a proper escort—it was shocking. It was also liberating.

"And what have those infamous Racters to talk to you about, husband?"

"More intrigues to kill your father, wife."

Her face—gorgeous, radiant—drew down, and I felt a pain at her look of sudden apprehension. She spoke quickly.

"You jest, my heart—but take care! There are spies everywhere—and the Racters are powerful. We all know they but bide their time. When they strike—"

"I firmly believe they will attempt to remain true to their own beliefs. They will obey the letter of the law when they chance their collective arms and try to oust your father. They will not order his assassination—not directly. What we have to fear is some lesser light—like Strom Luthien, for instance—taking the law into his own hands. We have come through great perils and your father still lives." I scratched my nose. "Anyway, where was he in the Temple? It is not like him to miss a religious ceremony that brings political acclaim with it."

Delia shook back her hair and the lustrous brown ripples flowed with those glorious chestnut tints glinting in the mingled rays of the suns.

"His Grand Chamberlain excused him. An affair of state that could not wait upon even this ceremony. You did not, I may add, stand in very well for him."

"I would not have done so had he asked. Not when he is in the city. By Zair! All this flummery is his job as the emperor."

She looked sidelong at me as the zorcas paced along the stone-flagged way, past the fronts of other temples, and buildings housing the University of Vondium Ghat, with the passersby jostling along and some turning to stare at us. All the time as we rode and talked I kept that old sailorman's weather eye open. I fancied the Stikitches of Vondium would accept as closed the contract Ashti Melekhi had put out on me; but if they had not done so then I would have to convince them all over again.

During this time in Vondium the sense of great release that had come with the return of the emperor to full health, and the consequent liberation of bottled-up trade that followed, warred with that ordained sense of impending doom. It was as though one half of the citizens laughed and drank and sang while the other half sharpened up their weapons and bolted their doors and shutters.

I guessed what lay in Delia's mind.

"The moment I have settled up with these Opaz-forsaken Racters, I shall ride for the Northeast. Dayra—"

"We shall ride."

I cocked an eye at her.

"And the Sisters of the Rose?"

She looked annoyed. "I have certain duties—that I would tell you if I could—that may prevent an immediate start. But do not think you can go galloping off alone, Dray Prescot, and leave me out of it. Dayra has been going through a tumultuous period in her life. She worries me. And that is sooth."

"She is our daughter. That worries me."

"I agree. She is your daughter, and that is what worries me."

We both laughed, then, for laughing comes easily to me when I am with Delia of Delphond. So we rode back to the palace and to one of those slap-up superb Kregan meals that keeps a fellow and a girl going through the long day.

The Sea Barynth Hooked was situated down on the Kamist Quay—I say was, for it was burned down a few seasons later after a pot-house brawl— and catered for the skippers of the Vallian ships who frequented the Kamist wharves. It was a place where you might, if you wished, sup from superb eel pies. I usually stuck to roast vosk and momolams there. Sea food has never appealed to me.

The upper room was lit by four square windows. The long sturmwood table was covered by a decent yellow cloth and as I entered with a crash of polished boots, the people in the room stopped talking. They surveyed me with the alert interest of a man abruptly discovering a rattler under a rock.

"Let us proceed," I said. "Lahal one and all. I have little time for I have business that presses elsewhere."

Wearing simple Vallian buff, with a red and white favor, with the wide-brimmed Vallian hat in my hand, with a fresh rapier buckled on, with the left-hand dagger to match—the old one was being cleaned now with brick-dust and spittle in the palace armory—and with the longsword a-dangling at my left side, I suppose I looked to them my usual intemperate, boorish, hateful self. The false beards had gone. I was myself, and they knew me.

Strom Luthien motioned to the chair they had reserved for me. I sat down without hesitation. No trick chairs here.

Natyzha Famphreon sat like a parody created out of a nightmare, with her nutcracker old face, lined and shrewish and incredibly vicious with that sharp upthrust lower lip, and her pampered, beautiful, voluptuous body. She nodded to me. She had not forgotten the chavonths in her conservatory.

Her son, Nath na Falkerdrin, was not here.

Ered Imlien, just as boastful, just as bristling, short and squat, shook a fist at me wrathfully.

"Again my estates have been despoiled! And your daughter has been seen—"

He stopped himself. He was shaking. His face looked as red as a scarron. The last time he'd accused Dayra of raiding down onto his estates around Thengelsax from the northeast areas I'd half choked him, and scared him. Now he was harking back to the old sore, and so it was clear that more trouble had blown up—trouble of a serious kind—when I'd been away in Ba-Domek.

I said: "Look at that little fly, Ered Imlien, Trylon of Thengelsax."

The fly buzzed to a swooping landing along the windowsill. A long, slender, incredibly agile green tendril shot through the air and the suckered tip fastened upon the hapless fly. The flick-flick plant on the windowsill started to reel in his next meal. This object lesson, I thought, should not be lost on Imlien. Then an event occurred that always occasions amusement among Kregans—aye, and wagers, too—for a second flick-flick plant entered the struggle.

The flick-flick plant is found in most Kregan homes and it serves admirably to catch annoying flies. With its better than six-feet long tendrils it gobbles flies like luscious currants.

Irvil the Flagon, landlord of The Sea Barynth Hooked, had positioned the two flick-flick plants in their brightly colored ceramic pots too closely together. He'd been over-anxious to please his unexpected and distinguished guests. The two green tendrils writhed and fought over the fly.

Immediately Nalgre Sultant, an objectionable sort of fellow with whom I'd had trouble before, said: "I'll lay a gold talen piece on the left-hand plant."

Imlien did not answer, staring and licking his lips, and so Natyzha Famphreon said: "I'll take that, and make it two on the right-hand flick-flick."

The trapped fly struggled weakly. The tendrils writhed and pulled. In the event they tore the fly in pieces and each suckered tip retreated, curving gracefully, ready to pop the pieces of the fly into the orange cone-shaped flowers.

"Mine, I think, Nalgre," snapped Old Natyzha, triumphantly.

"I think not, Kovneva. My plant took the larger portion."

They appealed to Ered Imlien, who shrugged and would not give a verdict. The evidence was now being digested within the orange flowers. So they looked at me.

"It matters not who wins. The fly was Vallia. The flick-flick plants were, one, you Racters, and, two—"

"Two—this bitch queen!" flared Natyzha. She dismissed the matter of the wager with a wave of the hand. Thus important was the matter to her and the others, that a disputed wager which could be the subject of long and enjoyable wrangling should be summarily dismissed. "This Queen Lush of Lome. The emperor did not attend at the Temple of Opaz the Nantifer today, because he was meeting her. Once she gets her hooks into him—"

"He, then, is also the fly."

"Aye! And we will pull the stronger, if you will honor your promise and assist us."

"Do not think I forget your insolence, Trylon Ered." I said this just to keep him on his toes. He slapped his riding crop against his boots, and glowered; but had the sense to remain silent. "And, Kovneva, I made you no promises."

"We know you have been released from your banishment. But you and the emperor still hate each other. His death—"

"I will have none of that. I have told you. You seek to work in legal ways, or so I believe. But if you forget that and hire assassins to do away with the emperor, you will be brought to ruin. This I promise."

I do not make promises lightly, and this, I think, they knew. At the least, they were not to be sucked in by any pretense I might make at being an ineffective, a puffed-up Jikai of the imagination, a publicity warrior. They knew better.

Again I found myself considering just what position and just how powerful these people were within the Racter Party of Vallia. Nath Ulverswan, Kov of The Singing Forests, was not here this day—not that you'd notice much for he seldom spoke in meetings. Natyzha was, indeed, a very powerful woman, the Dowager Kovneva of Falkerdrin. But the black and whites extended their tentacles of authority into every part of Vallia. They were owners of vast expanses of rich land, they were shipowners, they were slavemasters. I did not like them overmuch. But—were the people here just a front for the inner cabal of Racters, their High Council, their private Presidio?

One fact remained; through them I was dealing with the racters. I wanted to press on to the Northeast but thought I would try a little ploy with them here first.

"If the emperor marries this Queen Lush I, for one, will be heartily glad." I spoke harshly, emphasizing my words. "That will relieve me of an unwanted burden."

Natyzha sneered at me, her lower lip upthrust like the beak of a swifter of The Eye of the World.

"And if they have brats? More Vallian princes and princesses? That will deprive you and your precious princess of the succession."

"As I say, it will be a relief."

"I do not believe you!" flared Ered Imlien, bluff, red-faced, and he bashed his riding crop down with a crack.

It would have been easy to have made some fierce declaration about men who spoke like that ending up with their guts hanging out; but I refrained. He was an onker who ran headlong on his own destruction. How he had lasted as long as he had remained a mystery. And, truly, he was gnawed by fears for his estates.

"So you stand against the Queen of Lome?"

"Aye!"

"And, prince," pointed out Nalgre Sultant in his best offensive manner, "so should you be, too. We stood once before together against the Great Chyyan. I have no love for you. But even though you are merely a wild clansman, you are now of Vallia. When Vallia is threatened we must all stand together."

And, of course, they believe this and it goes some way toward redeeming them, whatever their evil and however you may regard that devalued ideal of patriotism. They considered—no! They *knew* that they could rule Vallia better than anyone else. That being the case, anyone who opposed them stood against Vallia.

I stood up. "The deal we made still stands. I will assist you against the enemies of Vallia. I will make no move against the emperor and I will personally exterminate any of you who try to kill him or any of his family." With a small dismissive gesture I finished: "As for this Queen Lush—let her take her chances with the emperor. The old devil hasn't had much fun lately. And an alliance with a country of Pandahem is a good beginning—"

"That is traitorous talk!" burst out Imlien. "Pandahem, every country in the island, is our mortal enemy."

"You're a fool, Imlien. Hamal is our enemy. We must make allies of all the countries of Pandahem. And, one day, we will conclude a real treaty of friendship with Hamal, too."

They stared at me as though I had taken leave of my senses. What did they know of my greater plans for Paz? They would not understand, could not grasp the idea of all Paz as a single united grouping, standing against the savage Chanks from around the curve of the world. For these racters, Vallia must always stand supreme, ruling other countries, or warring with them.

Because Delia and I had bathed in the Sacred Pool of Baptism in far Aphrasöe, we were possessed of a thousand years of life, quite apart from being blessed with miraculous powers of self-healing. And the emperor had been bathed, also. He would outlive these schemers, he would remain emperor for a thousand years, he could afford to laugh at them and their plans.

All the same, he must take precautions. And knowledge of those plans, information of the intrigues against him, would be essential.

I rubbed my chin, and turned back to face them, saying: "If you can speak plainly and without anger, Ered Imlien, tell me of the troubles you have around Thengelsax."

The gist of what he said, shorn of the expletives and the anger and the spluttering indignation, gave a picture of sudden and devastating raids by bands of riders from over the borders of the Northeast. This was crazy. All Vallia was part of the empire, ruled by the emperor, policed by his orders. But the movement for self-determination had flowered in the northeastern sections which were inhabited by peoples traditionally resentful of the authority imposed by the center and the south. That I could understand. What bothered me was the crass folly of people who wished to break the empire down into small units that could never, alone, stand against the hideous dangers of the future.

"Kovneva," I said, speaking in a deliberately thoughtful tone of voice. "In your opinion, does this threat from the Northeast constitute a real menace to the throne? Could they topple the emperor?"

She screwed up that clever, wizened, vicious old face.

"Yes and no. I do not think they could field an army that could break through to Vondium. But the troubles they cause can lead to such disorder that a strong and better-placed faction could seize the power. Up there they have great faith in their necromancers—"

"Necromancers? Of wizards and sorcerers, yes; but—"

"Necromancers I said, and devilish Opaz-forsaken corpse-revivers I mean!"

I digested that. Then: "And the strong and better-placed faction would be the racters?"

No one answered. The answer was writ plain on all their faces.

"Well, that is where we part company. I will stand against you for the emperor if needs must—"

"You fool! You destroy yourself! He hates you and will do nothing for you. Think again, Dray Prescot. Think of yourself and your family."

I did not answer that directly. I fancied it would too directly put a weapon into their hands.

"And the Panvals? The white and greens? Will they not strike for the power?"

They laughed their contempt. "The Panvals will fade away as salt dissolves in water when the racters strike."

"And the other factions? The Vondium Khanders? The Fegters who grow daily in strength? The Lornrod Caucus—"

"Them!" broke in Natyzha. "They are contemptible. Their only wish is to destroy everything, to pull down what has been painfully built over the centuries. No, we shall have no truck with them."

"As to the others," Nalgre Sultant amplified the kovneva's thoughts. "It is natural that accommodations and alliances will be formed. There are many small parties, formed for a particular reason, with whom we can work when the day to strike comes."

"And in that day you'll try to put your puppet on the throne of Vallia? You'll attempt to make some onker the emperor and then work him with your strings?"

They damn well knew I'd never be their puppet.

I was still smarting under the notion that I was the puppet of the Star Lords. I had been working on that, as you shall hear; but the idea aroused blind fury in me.

They did not say that since my interference they had lost a great deal of their power over the emperor and it rankled. They still held frightening powers; but these days the emperor could act with a greater freedom than ever he had before.

"If you directly oppose us, Dray Prescot, then you must take the consequences." Natyzha looked at me and then away, in that typical slanting look that so largely summed up the racters' way of influencing affairs of state. "You will probably find yourself dead and on the way to the Ice Floes of Sicce when we strike."

"But all legally, of course?"

"Oh, yes, prince. All legally."

So I bid them Rembaree in an air of chilly hostility, tempered only by the understanding between us, and took myself off. I observed the fantamyrrh of The Sea Barynth Hooked as I went out, for the sake of Irvil the Flagon, the landlord. Then I went off to perform an errand and to uncover some more of the information I sought before leaving for the Northeast— and for an uncomfortable ride into the bargain.

Seven

News of Dayra

The place to which I took myself brought back vivid and happy memories, memories of a time that was, in truth, a happy one even though it was shot through with a deep anxiety for my Delia, and for others of my friends. Here we had roared out the old songs and planned what best to do about the dying emperor.

I went down to the Great Northern Cut and there, on the eastern bank, found that comfortable inn and posting house, The Rose of Valka. The landlord, the same Young Bargom, greeted me with genuine warmth and his delighted yells brought the household running. He wanted to know all the news and how we had fared in our voyage to save the emperor. Bargom, who was now grown a trifle grave with the years and his responsibilities, remained still the locus of feeling for exiled Valkans. Exiled no longer, of course; but Valkans who had business in the capital gravitated to The Rose of Valka like bees to honey.

If I dwell too long on my friends, and places that I am fond of, I think that natural. I'd far sooner think of and tell you of The Rose of Valka, and the good times we had there than speak of some of those places of horror into which I plunged on Kregen. But life being what it is, and Kregen being the splendid and terrible world it is, the dark and phantasmagoric times seem always to outweigh the lighter and carefree times. More's the pity.

They brought me through into that wide spacious room with the lights of Zim and Genodras flooding resplendently through the windows, where the flowers bloomed in their pots along the windowsill, and around me the happy sounds of a busy inn life tinkled merrily, and the superb smells of that divine Valkan cooking brought the saliva to my mouth. So I quaffed a few cups of unsurpassed Kregan tea and ate miscils and talked. No—I lie. I did not drink a few cups. I drank many cups.

At last, when my inquiries became more particular and pressing, Bargom put his hands flat on his knees and stared directly at me. This subject had been glossed before. Now he pursed up his lips and looked judicial.

"Well, strom, it is like this, d'ye see. Yes, we have heard stories of the Princess Dayra. Nath ti Javvansmot, who runs The Speckled Gyp, told me what they did to his place. The fight they started smashed most of his windows, the best part of his crockery and a dozen amphorae, and the devils stove in two barrels of the best Gremivoh—begging your pardon, strom, but facts is facts."

"They started a fight and they laughed and left?"

"They laughed all right, strom. But they didn't leave until they'd had their bellyful o' watching the fun. Fun!"

"Was Nath ti Javvansmot recompensed?"

"Oh, aye. Aye. The Princess Delia, may Opaz bless her and smile on her, paid up in full. Although—" And here Bargom scowled his heavy Valkan scowl. "Although 'twasn't entirely the Princess Dayra's doing, not her fault altogether, for she was egged on. I'm sure of that."

"And since then?"

"Nary a sight nor sound of her, strom. Nothing."

Well, no need for me to feel disappointment. If the reports were true, Dayra was up in the Northeast, somewhere to the north of Tarkwa-fash.

"And the name of the man she was with?"

Here Bargom looked at the floor, and twiddled the strings of his red and white apron, which bore the bright stains of wine here and there, and then he looked at the flick-flick plant on the windowsill which was just in the act of transferring a half-starved fly from one suckered and sticky tendril down its orange gullet. Flies found little dirt to feed on in The Rose of Valka.

"Come, Bargom. You and I are old comrades. Have no fear of offending me. I know Dayra is mixed up with a scoundrel."

"He's a scoundrel, well and true. And there is a gang of 'em—a dozen, at the least. But who is this scoundrel? Now there you may as well ask Poperlin the Wise! He calls himself any number of names, and not one of them his. Some say he's the illegitimate son of a high noble, others that he's a fisherman from the islands who stole a purse and bought himself an education beyond his real capacity. Others say he's a paktun, probably a hyr-paktun who may wear the pakzhan, who is living high on the vosk of his ill-gotten gains. Others—"

"Aye. Aye, I hear. You have not seen him? You can give me no description? No name, one name at the least, with which I may begin inquiries?"

Bargom frowned and scratched his ear. "I did hear Nath say that his cronies called him Zankov*."

"Zankov. Now that is a strange name, indeed. Who are the other nine?"

"Why, strom! There aren't any, to be sure."

"Yes. It is only a use name. But it is a handle to begin with."

Now there was little time for more of the pleasant talk about the old days and of the beauty of Valka, and so I patted the heads of his smaller sons and daughters and gave them a gold talen each, and then I stood up and stretched and said: "I must be off, good Bargom. I thank you for your hospitality and your news. Zankov. I shall remember that."

They were disappointed that I would leave so soon; but the whole household waved and many were the shouted "Remberees!"

Bargom yelled after me: "And, strom, I wouldn't put too much store by Zankov. It's probably Naghan na Sicce by now!"

This was a great joke, if a standard one, as you who have followed my story will understand. Naghan is almost as common a name on Kregen as Nath, and Sicce; well, we all get shipped out to the Ice Floes of Sicce when our time is up on this mortal coil.

As my steps took me out of the gateway of the yard where a team had just been unhitched from a posting carriage and the passengers were alighting, ready to resume their journey on the Great Northern Cut, rejoicing that they would have a far easier passage on the canals, I reflected that Bargom had throughout called me strom. We had been in private. With other high nobles in attendance he would have sprinkled in at least a few princes and majisters. I would not call his attention to this, nor even think of venturing to correct him. Plenty of Valkans call me strom to this day. There is far more to it than simple forgetfulness. Often, I think—and thought then with greater cause—they were jealous that their strom was some prince of

---

* Zan: Ten. Kov: Duke. Zankov: the Tenth Duke.

Vallia, as though that removed him a trifle from their loyal protection and special relationship.

A quick, a very quick, trip to speak to Nath ti Javvansmot at The Speckled Gyp yielded no new information save the man who dubbed himself Zankov was a right slender spark, with dark hair, and merry eyes— "Brown Vallian eyes, prince. But, I swear, when he laughed, they went so dark as to be black. Odd." Thus Nath ti Javvansmot.

Thanking him, I mounted up again on Shadow and trotted smartly back to the palace. As ever, my weather eye rolled leeward and windward; but I fancied my dealings with the stikitches had borne fruit.

Although Kregans can tell the time to remarkable limits of accuracy by the positions of the suns or the moons, and many kinds of mensuration devices are known and used, truth to tell, I fancy, most Kregans tell the time by the state of their insides. Good square meals dominate the time-structure of Kregen. And, provided all get enough, who is to say this is not an admirable system? The trouble is, there are many who do not have enough, many who starve, many slaves who subsist miserably. These evils Delia and I had vowed to remove from the fair land of Paz, and, if the gods smiled, to eradicate entirely from all of Kregen.

But that objective—that dream—lay decades in the future.

Decades! Well, I was still, despite the length of time I had lived, still a comparatively young man then, and I was naive, hurtfully naive...

So I knew the twin suns were telling me that my interior clock was true; I went roaring into the palace and toward the stairway that led to our private wing. The palace is enormous and convoluted, as I have said, and to save time I slid through a cross corridor that would chop off a whole section of the ornate courtyards. The Crimson Bowmen of Loh stood guard, where they were accustomed to stand, and of the Chulik mercenaries only a few were left. Their proud dark eyes looked alertly about, their sharp fox-like faces with the bristling whiskers reminding me that they were a race of diffs well-thought of as mercenaries. Their Hikdar was a paktun, the silver mortil head, the pakmort, looped on its silken cord over the shoulder of his corselet.

These were newly hired mercenaries. Kov Layco Jhansi, the emperor's Chief Pallan, had been busy.

A Crimson Bowman standing beside a tall balass door with silver chavonth heads adorning the bosses recognized me and stamped to rigid attention, his three-grained staff flashing into the salute. He was Log Logashtorio.

Seeing the old professional salute me, the Khibil paktun bellowed an "eyes right" and brought his sword into the salute.

I was hungry. But these niceties of military protocol are overlooked at one's peril. But it was no venal thought of that kind that made me return the salute with all punctilio.

I called out to the Hikdar as we passed: "A smart turnout, Hikdar. Congratulate your men for me, please. I welcome you to Vondium."

He was a waso-Hikdar, that is, he had climbed five rungs up the rank structure within the rank of Hikdar, which is, I suppose, nearly an equivalent to an Earthly captain, in that he commands a pastang, or company, usually of eighty or so men.

Going rapidly on I gave a half-turn to look back and saw the Hikdar speaking to Log Logashtorio. So he was finding out who I was. That was all a part of the duties he and his men must perform here. Being hired by the Emperor of Vallia to serve in the imperial palace was a plum job.

A parcel of slaves, all wearing the gray slave breechclout with red and yellow armbands, went past carrying an Azdon which they treated with all the care and frightened anxiety such a precious object always demanded. Past them I hurried, with a respectful salute from the Chulik matoc in charge of them. His tusks thrust up from the corner of his mouth, and he'd savage any poor damned slave who caused the slightest trouble.

A Relt stylor hurried past, his scrip bulging with ink and pens, his robe stained with blobs and spatters of ink. Everyone hurried in the palace. There was always a toing and a froing. I made my way along past the Chemzite doors and saw one of the emperor's Lesser Chamberlains scurrying toward me.

He looked puffed and immensely relieved, and he shook with the release of some pressing fear.

"Majister! The emperor has been calling for you these last two burs! He awaits you in the Sapphire Reception Room. Majister! We must hurry."

I try to be polite to these fussy, pompous little fellows; for they have been made as they are. His red and yellow robes with the silver embroidery fluttered as he waved his arms, his balass, silver-banded rod of office almost hitting me on the nose.

Having studied a deal of the palace architecture when I'd first taken up residence here, I had a fair idea where the Sapphire Reception Room was. I glowered at the little chamberlain whereat his knees knocked. It was in my mind to tell him to say he hadn't found me—him or his fellows who would be out looking—and bash on to my apartments, for I was sharp set. But that would only prolong whatever lay in store.

"I am hungry," I said. "Is there any food there?"

"Yes, Majister. A spread buffet—and the Princess Majestrix, upon whom Opaz shine the light of his countenance, also awaits you there, Majister."

That settled it.

So I followed the gaudily-clad Lesser Chamberlain to the Sapphire Reception Room, more interested in the spread food than in what my father-in-law wanted.

The Reception Room had been decorated out in colors that were predominantly green. Well, I have no need to elaborate my ambivalent attitude to that color. Long tables were spread with food. I barged in through the door. People stood about in groups, talking, eating and drinking, laughing. It was a proper reception. The air smelled sweet with perfumes and, best of all, with the appetizing aromas of exquisite food.

Four clowns in gaudy uniforms at the door slapped long silver trumpets to their mouths and blew blasts that nearly took my ears off. The major domo in his fantastical rig of red and yellow, silver and gold, burnished, awash with feathers and lace, bellowed in a voice that would have stood a trick on the quarterdeck of a seventy-four off Biscay.

"The Hyr Jikai, Dray Prescot, Prince Majister of Vallia."

He knew everyone and bellowed their styles as they came in. I gave him a dirty look, and rubbed my ear, and then headed straight for the food. Bargom's cook's tea and cakes had merely sharpened up my appetite.

This scene presented the refined, polite, society face of Kregen. Men and women in their early-evening attire stood about, daintily sipping and nibbling. The conversation was light and frivolous, and yet, here and there, serious talking went on as people disposed of Vallia's wealth and slaves and mines and ships. Politics was never a taboo subject here, either. A knot of people, somewhat larger than the others, contained the emperor. His leonine head towered, massive, purposeful, and he threw that powerful head back, laughing.

Well, let the old devil have a good time. He'd been at death's door until Delia had carried him into the Sacred Pool. He did not see me and, as I could not spot Delia, and the food beckoned, I strode across to the tables.

He must have heard the trumpets and the majordomo's bellow. He must have thought I'd go straight up to him and be introduced. Well, maybe I would have done had I known the purpose of the reception.

There was no time for shilly-shallying around with a tiny plate and a few miscils, a few thin sandwiches, canapés, a spot of yasticum on the superb Kregan bread; I went for the real stuff. I piled the largest plate I could find with food. I stacked the biggest cup of tea available on the plate. Slaves hopped here and there trying to help people with silver trays of goodies; I brushed them away and got on with the job of loading the plate. Truth to tell; it was all light frothy stuff with not a solid mouthful all along the long table. The slaves wore white instead of slave gray, for they were privileged to wait on their masters here. I had to ignore them. The idea of slavery could always put me off my food, and I was sharp set. Come the day, I said to myself, and not the day which those damned racters dreamed, either...

So, wearing still the buff suit in which I had traipsed over Vondium, my hat hanging by its string down my back, girded with weapons, a monstrous plate of food in my hand, and a cup—it was a basin, really—of tea to hand, I sauntered across.

The crowd around the emperor saw me and they eased back, moving away to let me through. The crowd was not so much congregated around the emperor as around the woman with whom he was having a delightful conversation, that kept making him roar with laughter and brought his color up brilliantly.

She saw me as I saw her.

Well.

The emperor half-turned to glare at me.

The woman started to laugh, a low malicious, velvety laugh that put my teeth on edge.

Delia was suddenly at my side.

The woman laughed her malicious laugh. "At least you are not still running, prince. And the air smells quite sweet."

I said nothing, half choking on a piece of squish pie.

"You are late, son-in-law!" boomed the emperor. "You have been asked here to have the high honor of being introduced to the Hyr Serenity, Queen Lushfymi, the Queen of Lome."

I got the piece of pie down. I gulped.

I swung a fishy eye on Delia.

"You knew."

"I knew."

By Zim-Zair, but they breed princesses that are princesses in Vallia!

Eight

Queen Lushfymi of Lome

For my own part I would have liked to have taken myself off to our own apartments in the palace and indulged in a long wallow in the Baths of the Nine. Then I could do justice to a six or seven course meal—a light meal, that, by Kregan standards—and see about preparing for the coming journey.

But protocol demanded otherwise.

The scene hung sparks for a moment, as Delia's smile ravished me, and the violet-eyed woman, Queen Lushfymi—whom I would not call Queen Lush just for the moment—sipped daintily at her Yellow Unction and eyed me mockingly over the crystal rim of the goblet.

In some traditions it would be in order for me to say to you words after the fashion of: "And now I draw a veil over what followed," and then go on to tell you of what befell me on that Opaz-forsaken trip to the Northeast.

There are many events of my life upon Kregen I have not related, for one reason or another, many people I knew who have not figured in my narrative, and much, very much, of the customs and mores, the color and pageantry, the religions and the metaphysical aspects of that marvelous world I have omitted. But things were said here that proved of some importance later on.

The emperor wanted to know, by Vox, what the hell I meant by not being on time and why was I late.

I indicated my clothes and said that if he'd told me the Queen was to be met in this unofficial reception I would have been pleased to attend in proper style. For these kind of early evening functions, that are styled unofficial—as, indeed, in comparison with the stiff formality of public functions they truly are—people wear clothes that are relaxed and yet formal. Long gowns of bright dark hues, much gold lace, a modicum of decorated collar, the nikmazilla, and a dress sword or dagger complete a costume that is half-formal, half-lounging, relaxed and proper, really quite charming.

The emperor looked pointedly at my rapier and at the longsword.

"You are trusted by the guards now, and Kov Layco has vouched for you. I do not forget Ashti Melekhi."

A white-clad slave girl wearing a tall yellow and red mitered headdress—so she could easily be seen in a crowd—went past with a silver tray and I used my free hand to liberate a glass of Wenhart Purple, the emperor's favorite wine. I sipped. After I had taken just enough time to get the old devil in a mood, I said cheerfully: "The Melekhi is dead, slain by Kov Layco here." The Chief Pallan stood watchfully at the emperor's side, fingering his golden chain of office. "I leave you to remember how her friends died."

"All this talk of death," broke in Queen Lushfymi. She turned her violet eyes to the emperor in a long, languishing look. "Let us talk of happier things."

"Yet is death always with us," said Kolo York, the Vad of Larravur, a powerful, spare man with a lined wedge of a face. He wore a tastefully executed diamond brooch in the form of a krahnik. He was, so I understood, loyal to the emperor.

"The queen's commands are to be obeyed instantly!" exclaimed the emperor. He beamed. He was beside himself with pleasure in the company of this woman.

Well, I was forced to admit then, and see no reason to change that opinion, she was indeed splendid. Her full creamy throat, the brightness of her lips, her mass of dark hair and those great violet eyes, all were calculated to dizzy a man. Her deep-blue gown, relieved by green and white embroidery, stood out sharply in that Vallian gathering where blue is a rare color. She wore, I thought, rather too much jewelry. But she radiated charm and a dominating sense of womanliness, a mystery of perfectly controlled sexual allure. And, at the same time, I, for one, sensed in her a hidden and deviously repressed spirit, as though her outward form and the brilliance of her person and character concealed depths of feelings and emotions she would reveal reluctantly and at peril to those who inquired too diligently.

She took every opportunity to mock me with our first meeting, privately, between ourselves, malicious and bright and derisive.

She took pains not to stand too close to Delia.

She kept close to the emperor, laughing up at him, sipping her wine, nibbling miscils and daintily chewing palines. Why she did this was perfectly plain to me.

This Queen Lushfymi carried the reputation of being the most beautiful of women, mysterious, almost witchlike in the best sense, ruling her country and bringing fantastic wealth and prosperity. She was fabulously wealthy.

But beside my Delia she glowed as a candle glows in the radiance of the suns.

Delia wore one of her long laypom colored gowns, a pale yellow so delicate as almost to be platinum, and her brown hair with those rebellious chestnut tints shone magnificently. Her only jewelry, two small brooches, one in the form of a red rose and the other the spoked hubless wheel I had given her, eloquently destroyed the jeweled opulence of Queen Lush.

But, of course, Delia merely dressed naturally; it was through no fault of hers that other women faded into insignificance beside her. And, to be fair, Queen Lush was a beauty.

The talk wended on. There were even a few tentative feelers about the pact to be drawn up between Vallia and Lome. I spoke in favor. There was resistance to the idea from many of the nobles there. Of the racters I knew, only Nath Ulverswan, Kov of the Singing Forests, was present, and his black and white favor looked lonely and forlorn.

Queen Lush would get no real grasp of the true feelings in Vallia, then...

I fancied she would have her spies busy, and was shrewd enough by all accounts to take the pulse of the empire.

Vad Kolo nal Larravur took the emperor's remark about the commands of the queen as a personal rebuke. He withdrew a little, his face shadowed. I kept the frown off my face. If the emperor could so thoughtlessly upset his own people, he would make himself even more isolated.

Vad Kolo's daughter took his arm and spoke quickly, softly, in his ear. He scowled a bit, and then edged himself back into the group around the queen, forcing a smile.

This daughter—she had some courtesy title, of course—was lithe, well-formed, glowing of face, open of countenance. She wore a dark yellow gown with silver lacing, and a long thin poniard of typical Vallian manufacture swung at her girdle. This was Leona nal Larravur. On the left shoulder of the gown she wore a brooch fashioned from ronil gems into the likeness of a purple bush, with a green emerald stem. By this device I knew Leona nal Larravur was a member of the Order of Sisters of Samphron.

One of the ronils was missing, the one on the extreme tip of the bush-brooch. It was unlikely that the brooch for so meaningful a symbol was of Krasny work—inferior—nor was it likely that the stone would be knocked out by an ordinary accidental dropping of the brooch, even on the hardest of stone.

The gold mounting had been painted over purple.

A small vertical frown kept dinting in between Leona nal Larravur's eyebrows, then she would force a smile, and the skin would smooth out and those two worrying lines disappear.

The conversation became more animated as less tea was drunk and more wine flowed.

The emperor's huge bark of laughter crashed out with more and more frequency. Colors in cheeks heightened. Eyes grew warm. I looked across at Delia. It was time we departed.

Now, I did not then hear the words spoken, nor was I a witness to the entire scene. But voices around the queen were raised. The tones were still polite; but the venom was unmistakable. A hush fell over the rest of the Reception Room. Everyone looked and listened.

The queen's color was up. Her violet eyes were flying danger signals. The emperor was furious. His bulky body towered over the small, slight form of Foke Lyrsmin. Old Foke quivered, staring up, his elegant dark clothes shaking. A small, cheerful, wiry fellow, Foke Lyrsmin, the Kov of Vyborg. We had had a right old time of it at the uncompleted wedding ceremony he'd planned with Merle, the daughter of Trylon Jefan Werden.* The Lady of Vallia he had subsequently married was enchanting; she stood at his side, her face scarlet, her lips trembling. Their two strapping sons and two delightful daughters hesitated, as it were, on the edges of this ghastly scene.

"...and I don't care what it is you meant to say, Kov Foke! You call yourself my friend." The emperor's voice boomed, rich and heavy, and everyone heard. "I do not account those as friends who insult Queen Lushfymi."

"Majister—I did not insult—"

"I heard, Lyrsmin! I am not deaf! Be thankful I do not order your head off this instant."

At this the Kovneva of Vyborg let out a little squeak of pure agony.

Her two stalwart sons held her arms, supporting her. How Old Foke had managed to get them was a mystery.

"But, majister—"

"Begone, Foke Lyrsmin!"

"But—"

---

* See: *Wizard of Scorpio.*

"Shastum!* Not another word. Go! Leave my presence."

Poor Old Foke looked shattered. His thin body writhed in the elegant gown. He turned about, and his teeth chattered.

"And, Foke na Vyborg—I shall expect a written apology to be transmitted to the Queen of Lome, together with a gift of quality sufficient to show your sorrow and regrets and your wholehearted desire to make amends for your disgusting behavior."

Foke couldn't say another word. The emperor had commanded that. He trailed away. His delightful wife followed, helped out by the twin sons, and the twin daughters tripped along afterward, like naughty schoolchildren chastised and sent to bed. The colors of Vyborg, maroon and silver, looked pathetic as they left.

The Reception Room filled again with conversation as people started talking away. Scenes like this were no longer as common as they once had been. Delia caught my eye. I nodded sideways. We started to make for the doors.

If there can be said, at that time, to have been a party in a political sense around the emperor, then Foke was certainly a member. I suppose the people near him might be called the Imperial Party. They had nothing like the organization or the power of the racters. But they were men loyal to the throne.

"Poor Foke," said Delia.

"He looked shattered. Did you see what it was?"

"No. But Queen Lush was most put out."

"Oh no, my heart." We had reached the doors and the gaudily uniformed flunkeys were opening up again after the doors had been closed after the Vyborgs. "Oh, no. Old Foke was the one who was put out."

Nine

Into Hawkwa Country

"Now," I said to Delia when all the preparations were complete. "This water bottle."

"I see it, my love."

We had gone up to our Valkan villa, which was still not fully brought back to habitability, despite the length of time that had elapsed since I'd acquired it by virtue of being made the Strom of Valka behind my back. But there were apartments enough beautifully furnished to make it a real home.

---

* Shastum! Silence.

Nalgre the Staff was the current Chamberlain, a stout fellow and one I would trust. We kept no slaves. The villa was set somewhat back from the road, bowered in greenery, presenting an outward appearance of decay and neglect. I did not object to that. Further along on the Hill—the Valkan villa was situated on the Hill of Vel'alar—the villas of the nobles presented all the munificence of aspect expected of the rich and mighty of the empire.

"This water bottle." I hefted it. Plain leather, scuffed, worn, it was a scruffy-looking object. "We must keep it safely locked away in the stoutest iron chest."

Delia nodded understandingly. After I had mended my hurts in the Sacred Pool of Baptism I had filled this water bottle with the milky fluid that conferred life. My return from the island of Ba-Domek on which stands the Swinging City of Aphrasöe had been rushed with the help of my Djangs; but I had managed to bring back my weapons, that superb zorca Shadow, and this water bottle.

"It will be safe here." Delia placed the bottle in humespack, wrapping the cloth over it, and then wadding down household linen so that the iron chest almost overflowed. We closed the lid and sat companionably upon it and did up the locks. They can make fine chests in Vallia, for they have much gold and silver, jewels and precious objects to preserve.

The four keys and the master key were secreted away in a brick hole concealed within the wall of our bedroom. No picture covered that lenken paneling there; the wood had been carpentered to a close fit by men long since dead. I had found that small hiding place only by chance, and regretted it was not large enough to accommodate the water bottle itself.

As we went up to the landing platform I said to Delia: "We keep up five villas here besides the quarters in the palace. It might be a good idea to sell one or two."

She cocked her head at me. The night air breathed sweet about us. She of the Veils rode through a tracery of clouds. The landing platform was dusty, and dead leaves blew with brittle rustlings into the corners. We had slept enough to feel refreshed. I was sorry that Delia could not fly with me; but she was adamant. The Sisters of the Rose had to be attended to first.

"You may, my great grizzly graint. But I do not think I shall sell the Delphondian villa—"

"Of course not!" That was a superb, a delightful, a magical home.

"And the Blue Mountains—"

"No."

"So, as you have an affection for this place, that leaves the villas of Zamra and Veliadrin."

"Um," I said, throwing off the restraining chains on the flier I was using. "You are thinking of the children? They will need villas?"

"Perhaps."

I climbed in and Delia climbed in after. She looked at me gravely. The flier was a small two-place craft, trim, reasonably fast, and one I hoped would sustain me in the air. We must think about buying some more vollers for the villas we kept up at different places; one never knew when a fleet air-boat would be required in a hurry. As you know, I had been in that kind of need before and was like to be again, Zair knows.

She kissed me good-bye. I said "Remberee" with a deal of anger; but this was a case of having to accept the needle.

When Delia stood once more on the dusty, refuse-blowing landing platform I looked down and waved, and shouted: "Remberee, my heart!" and took the voller up in a savage lunge of power.

The Twins broke through a carpet of clouds and the two second moons of Kregen, eternally orbiting each other, cast down their fuzzy pink light. She of the Veils, the fourth moon, rolled along before them.

So, once more, I, Dray Prescot, Lord of Strombor and Krozair of Zy, raced through the nighted skies of Kregen, under the hurtling moons, driving headlong forward to action and adventure.

The thought of seeing Barty again cheered me up. He was to meet me in Thengelsax. Sax means fort, and many of the towns and cities along the arc of the old frontiers of central northeast Vallia grew up from the ancient fortifications raised against the barbarian reivers. There are plenty of other words for castle, fortress, fort, Kregish being a rich language; but one thing they all share in common: they refer to serious concerns, matters of building pride and cunning military fortification. The sprawling cities that festoon the old walls would give heart palpitations to those ancient builders. And this, as you will perceive, was the nub of the affair. For Vallia was a great and puissant empire. There should not be, under the law, conflict within the boundaries of the empire between province and province.

The emperor would be better advised seeking ways of settling these troubles instead of running after beautiful bitch-queens.

But then, he was a man. And Queen Lush was a woman—that was blatantly obvious. If she occupied his attention perhaps I could get on with my own affairs. At least, he had not made too particular inquiries about his grandchildren. I had to hoick Dayra out of the mess she was in and straighten her out before the emperor decided to take a hand.

And, again, that implied that I knew best for my daughter. That I was totally unsure must be obvious. But I thought, at the least, that smashing up taverns and raiding with a bunch of hairy reivers against innocent citizens of Vallia were not occupations she could in all honesty claim as morally defensible. Mind you, by Krun! She could easily have some explanation that would make me change my mind.

The Suns of Scorpio flooded down their mingled streaming lights of jade and ruby as I circled once over Thengelsax and slanted in for a landing outside the designated inn. The city presented the expected appearance of a well-ordered city of Vallia. Clean, neat, prosperous, situated where the River Emerade flows into the Great River, the city looked justly proud of itself.

As an interesting light upon the importance of those old fortifications, the Trylon took the name of Thengelsax, from the city, and not that of Thengel, from the trylonate.

Barty met me as the airboat touched down and the hostlers ran out to see to her. He looked excited and I felt a welling of hope that he had discovered some vital clue to the whereabouts of Dayra.

My hopes were dashed. As we went into the inn and posting house, The Hanged Leemshead, Barty started on cussing about the Strom of Vilandeul. He windmilled his arms and when we had pots of ale before us he sloshed suds about, scarlet-faced, almost incoherent, and yet, in the end, making lucid sense and betraying the very real depths of his affection for Dayra.

"That Nath Typhohan!" he raved. "I know him! I've wrestled him, and thrown him, and fenced with him and pinked him. Now he's the Strom of Vilandeul he has the effrontery to lay claim to the most beautiful land of my island! He wants the Shadow Forests of Calimbrev! I ask you!"

I nodded. "I had trouble with his father. Well—" I said, uncomfortably, "not me. My son Drak and Tom Tomor. I was away at the time. The Strom of Vilandeul laid claim to parts of Veliadrin, west of the Varamin Mountains."

"The trouble is Nath's Stromnate of Vilandeul is small and is penned in by powerful kovnates. He is land hungry."

"You can understand that."

"We must stick together, pri—Jak. If it comes to it, we'll have to hire mercenaries and go up against him. No damned Typhohan is going to steal my land from me, by Vox!"

Mildly, I said: "In Valka we have our own army. And I would heartily dislike having to fight Vallians. We threw the aragorn and the slavers out. Don't they trouble you?"

"A little. They take a few slaves from me. Nothing I can't live with."

My mildness vanished. "If you entertain any notions of marrying Dayra, I fancy you will have to manumit your slaves. The whole lot. And I will help you deal with the slavers."

He blinked.

Even so good-hearted a fellow as Barty could not really understand my attitude about slaves. Had not Opaz made slaves for other men to use? Of course he had. Therefore a good citizen of Vallia must employ what Opaz had put into his hands.

This must be pursued later. I said in my harsh old voice: "What have you discovered about Dayra?"

"I have spoken to the landlord. She was seen with a rascally gang of Hawkwas hiring zorcas and riding northeast."

Hawkwa was the contemptuous name given in hatred and fear by the civilized people of Vallia in the old days to the reivers from the North-east, and in turn used by the barbarians in boastful pride and reciprocal contempt.

"Also, I have hired a guide."

Well, I could not complain. Barty had done well. In the time I had been making inquiries in Vondium and hobnobbing with the emperor he had been hard at work here. I warmed to him. He must cherish genuine feelings for my daughter, for he had not gone rushing back to his island to fend off the predatory demands of Nath Typhohan, the Strom of Vilandeul. Well, I would help him there, for his island lay close to Veliadrin. And the Elten of Avanar, Tom Tomor, had given the old Strom of Vilandeul a salutary lesson over land-grabbing.

"We will not ride," I said with a snap. "We will take your flier, seeing she has space for a dozen or more and the zorcas. My two-seat craft will be useless. The guide you have found—"

"Uthnior Chavonthjid. A hunter with a fine reputation. And expensive, by Vox."

"Well, this Uthnior will have to get used to airboats if he is not already familiar with them. We have no time to lose."

Transferring the gear I had brought to Barty's flier did not take long, despite the mountains of stuff Delia always insisted I take along with me on these expeditions. More often than not I lost most of it, and returned draggle-tailed and almost empty-handed. Weapons, food and—well, little else, really, on Kregen, apart from necessary clothing against the weather— are all that are required.

Of food we had wicker hampers piled up. Of weapons we took the usual Kregen arsenal.

Uthnior Chavonthjid turned out to be the picture of a leem hunter, lean, rangy, broad-shouldered, with that weather-beaten face that conveys an ample sense of experience and wide horizons.

His history contained nothing out of the usual, save for the incident that claimed for him the coveted jid appended to the animal he had slain bare-handed, or the danger he had overcome. The chavonth is a feral big cat, savage and tirelessly vindictive. Uthnior had met and bested one, breaking its back. The word jid is seldom used alone, which is why I always use bane—as, for instance, in the Bane of Grodno. I felt confident that Uthnior Chavonthjid would prove a fine, tough guide for us. As to his reliability, that remained to be weighed in the balance.

As we flew at the sedate speed of Barty's capacious flier toward the Kwan Hills, in which rises the River Emerade, some forty dwaburs or so from

Thengelsax, I was once more forcibly struck by the incongruity of having to hire a guide to any part of Vallia. But the truth remained—and, alas, still remains—that some parts of Vallia are barbaric and untamed still.

You may recall the Ochre Limits. There nature set the obstacles in the path. Here, the Kwan Hills, densely forested, alive with game, untracked and mysterious, were the haunts of the drikingers, the reivers, the Hawk-was, who set the limits to strangers.

Uthnior, to my surprise, had refused to take zorcas.

"Koter Jakhan," he said in his grave manner. "Where we are going the totrix is the mount for us."

Only a half-mur's pondering convinced me I must heed the specialist knowledge of the man on the spot. Nath Dangorn, called Totrix, would have chuckled. But he along with the rest of the newly created Order of Kroveres of Iztar, was far away. This was a family matter, and Barty had his rights in it, also. So we took six totrixes in the rigged-up stalls in the rear of Barty's flier, and the awkward, stubborn, six-legged riding animals did not take kindly to being thus hurled helplessly through thin air.

We touched down at the edge of a wood well clear of the outskirts of the town of Tarkwa-fash. From here, with the blue haze of the Kwan Hills beckoning us on, we would ride. The voller was hidden in the trees with cut branches piled upon her. Uthnior eyed the mass of weapons and gear. Then he looked at Barty and me with a wary, reflective glance that was instantly appreciated by me, at least, although Barty soon understood.

Uthnior himself slung his personal gear on his baggage totrix. All six were provided with the riding saddle of this part of Kregen, a tall, broad, comfortable seat. Uthnior buckled on his crossbow with care, strapping the quivers of bolts alongside, checking the swing of the three swords and the variety of polearms he carried. His provision bags went the other side. Barty pulled his lower lip.

"You have brought a mighty fine array of weaponry, Jak. Tell me, Uthnior, what is it best for us to take?"

I did not fail to notice that the guide carried a short but powerful bow, a compound reflex weapon of considerable beauty and precision, over his shoulder. The quiverful of arrows to match were fletched with a neutral greeny-browny set of feathers. But the steel heads were all wide, keen, wedge-shaped flesh-cutters, with vicious barbs. This bow, it was clear, was his personal close-range missile weapon. The crossbow was for the fancy shooting.

Uthnior looked at my Lohvian longbow. The quiverful of arrows were fletched with the brilliant blue plumage of the crested korf of the Blue Mountains. As to the piles, they were my usual mix, different heads for different tasks. "That is a bow from Loh, I think," he said. "A longbow?"

"Aye. You have seen one before?"

His reply astonished me although it should not have.

"No. Never."

This showed yet again the sheer size of the island of Vallia. Away up here the hunters used crossbows or the reflex bow. The longbow was virtually unknown. And yet, the weird thing was, if I took a flier and flew due east for eighty or so dwaburs I would arrive in the island of Zamra. Most odd. Of course, the heartlands of the Northeast lay farther to the north, mainly around the Stackwamors, which was why the reivers had full rein down here.

"We must shoot a match, Chavonthjid, when opportunity offers."

"I would welcome that. Although I fancy this longbow of yours clumsy to handle."

Not prepared to get into an argument over that—what he said was true for one unskilled in the use of the supreme Lohvian longbow—I urged us to complete our preparations and to mount up and ride. We wanted to get into the foothills before nightfall.

In the end I stuck to my usual custom and took my accustomed arsenal. Barty hewed to the middle path and selected a mix of weapons that made Uthnior merely smile, rather than frown, and we set off. Uthnior, it turned out, had a grandmother from the Northeast. He was at home here. If I give the impression that for a Southern Vallian to venture into these parts was like trespassing into enemy territory, then I give a false impression. We were still in Vallia and the emperor's writ still ran here, albeit very often evaded or downright ignored. These people paid taxes to the Presidio and emperor in Vondium. They were Vallians and proud of it—if they could be Northeastern Vallians. It was the agitators who fomented unrest, hanging their banditry on the respectable peg of self-determination—or so I was led to believe. I thought them wrong. But, equally, I know that big does not equal best, and small can, indeed, be charmingly beautiful.

There is an old saying that has its echo on Kregen—A good big 'un will beat a good little 'un.

I looked always to the future, past the time when Vallia would have come to an arrangement with the countries of Pandahem, and achieved peace with Hamal—and I hoped without having to thrash them in a long and costly war—and brought in the whole fantastic continent of Havilfar. When the groupings of islands and continents called Paz were truly one— then we could deal with the Chanks.

We would have to deal with the devils from over the curve of the world before then, of course, dolefully so, as best we could.

We broke in among the foothills of the Kwan Range and we made camp in a secluded gulley with water and fodder to hand. We had seen not a soul. The game abounded, and regarded us rather in the light of trespassers, evidence of the infrequency of human intrusion.

In the course of a regular season Uthnior would guide just the one hunting party, and there were other hunters each with his own patch; he had been free to take employment with Barty because his hunting party had called it off over the recrudescence of the border troubles. He'd never married, seemingly preferring the open freedom of the hunter's life. His home was where he happened to be. He appeared to me a competent, grave, inwardly content man, with a deep understanding and love for the strange ways of nature upon Kregen.

As was becoming increasingly my habit these days when I met fresh acquaintances, I studied this hunter with the Kroveres of Iztar in mind. Would he or would he not be found worthy to be admitted to the Order? Already I had been impressed by his manner. As for Barty, that young man for all his virtues had some way to go yet before the Order would consider him.

We pressed on again while the golden and pink moonlight gave us illumination, She of the Veils and the Twins lighting the way through the broken country. Ever upward we trended. The six-legged totrixes were an uncomfortable ride; but I am used to their waywardnesses and, deprived of a zorca, made the best of them.

We traveled for the rest of the night and as the last small hurtling moon vanished in the haze off to our left Uthnior indicated we should make camp again.

The fire we built was small, compact, shielded by a rocky overhang. When full daylight came we doused it and sat, resting, looking about as the light brightened. Barty could not rest for long.

"Can we not push on, Uthnior?"

The guide pulled a grass stem from the corner of his mouth.

"You hired me to guide you to the camp of the Hawkwas. I know the area they frequent—and avoid it. In general terms I can take you straight there. You will be observed closely over the last dwabur or so."

Listening quietly to him I made no comment; but I guessed accurately what he would say next.

"Complete directions can be given you. I will be happy to do that. But you must go on by yourselves at the end. I shall wait three days for you. No more."

Ten

Of the Pride of a Rapa Paktun

The mizzle of rain eased and a wan grayish daylight seeped through the massed clouds. Hillsides, woods, bushes, open swards dripped water. Barty swung off his hooded cape and the water sprayed. The totrixes ambled along in that skewed six-legged gait. Uthnior slid his cape off expertly and let the water drain off into the grass.

Gray clouds hung about the mountains. The pass ahead glinted with a waterfall's sudden silver.

"Five burs ride beyond the pass," said the guide, pointing. "Then I leave you to go on. There is a cave. Three days I shall wait. After that—"

"You needn't go on!" exclaimed Barty. "If we don't come back in three days we'll be dead. I know."

Uthnior had little experience of airboats, for his hunter clients liked to get into the saddle as soon as possible, and at the time I took at face value his assertion that fliers would be useless in the maze of valleys and gullies and hilly peaks around us. The Kwan Hills were no place to crash in, that was certain. Our six-legged mounts ambled along and the twin suns struggled to pierce the thick cloud layer above.

That pass ahead, with its thread of silver, the dark sodden slopes on either hand, the cavernous bellies of the low-lying clouds above—my fingers began to twitch. *Fingerspitzengefuhl.* Yes, the Germans had the word for it, the twitch in the finger tips. The old breeze up the spine. I rolled my eyes about, looking up the slopes, seeing clumps of vegetation dripping with moisture, vague pale blurs of wan sunshine trying to strike glints from the drops and producing glimmering pearls.

"Here they come!" I bellowed and ripped out the longbow.

They bounded down the slopes screeching like demons, leaping from tussock to tussock, waving their weapons, ragged bands of men and women, their armor and harness dun-earth in color and wet, wet with the wet ground on which they had lain in ambush.

"Hawkwas!" yelled Uthnior, and his bow was in his hand.

Reflex compound bow and Lohvian longbow spat as one.

Barty's bow slapped out a little later, as the hunter and I loosed again.

In this kind of sudden fierce attack as fighting men and women roar at you, screeching, aiming to top you, you have to assume that, have to understand they are hostile and react to that, and not hang about wondering if this is merely a too-enthusiastic welcome. We shot to stop the attack. Men screamed with shafts feathered through them. They tumbled down the wet hill-slopes, tattered bundles, arms and legs flopping.

The arrows we loosed took their toll, and then it was handstrokes.

All the old clichés about letting the mind divorce itself from the corporeal body, the sword being held and not held, the mysteries of the Disciplines, all these things chunked into place.

Because I was mounted and because I was in a hurry to get through these Hawkwas I used the Krozair longsword. The brand flamed in the weak sunlight. Hawkwas shrieked and fell away. Blood splattered. Barty was slashing about with the clanxer I had insisted he bring, the straight cut and thruster more use in this kind of work than a rapier. Uthnior struck mighty sweeping blows with a polearm, a scythe-like blade mounted on a staff, an overgrown version of the glaive my people of Valka know so well how to use. We urged our totrixes on, the baggage animals tethered to the saddles following willy-nilly, and we broke through the screeching mob. The Hawkwas fought us, for they saw we were but three and there were nineteen or twenty of them. But the deadly arrows had cut them down and the swords completed the task.

A last remnant, three men, turned to run back, casting aside their weapons. Uthnior slapped his polearm away and took out his bow. He shot cleanly into the back of the nearest fugitive.

He must have sensed my thoughts, for he bellowed savagely at me.

"They will bring their Opaz-forsaken friends, koter!"

As he dispatched the penultimate wretch, I, with some compunction and self-disgust, loosed at the last.

Practical matters despite all other concepts had to reign here. I valued my daughter Dayra above these bandits of the hills. It was horrible and messy; it was, as I took it, inevitable.

There was no point in gathering up the scattered weapons.

We rode from that accursed spot as quickly as we could move the totrixes along, after I had recovered my arrows.

And the rain came drifting back.

"You have, I think, fought before," observed Uthnior as we jogged along.

"Yes."

"Did you see that one—" began Barty.

"Not now, Barty," I said.

We drew our cape hoods up and slouched in the saddles and rode through the valley and past the feathery glinting waterfall and so came out to the saddle beyond, where the land lifted away from us, misty, clouded by rain veils, gray and wet.

Barty said, with an oath: "What I would give for a piping hot cup of tea—right now—vydra tea, for that is what I like best."

"I, too, am fond of vydra tea," said Uthnior.

I hauled out a wine bottle and passed it across. "You will have to make do with wine, Barty. For now."

"I suppose so."

When we reached the cave of which the guide had spoken, we reined in. The rocky face of the cliff closed down, and the uneven track wound down toward thickly wooded and much cut up land beyond. The veils of rain blew across like vertical sweeps from gigantic sword blades.

Uthnior hesitated.

"To wait here, now, will not be advisable."

"Our tracks will be washed out," I said tentatively.

"Assuredly, koter. But the bodies of the Hawkwas will be found. Their friends will search. It will not be difficult to find a lone man hiding in a cave."

"So you—" began Barty.

"Ride with us until you find a secure hide," I said.

Barty swung to face me, annoyed; but he saw my face and did not pursue the argument. We rode on.

The sense of desolation that depressed me here in these Kwan Hills lightened a little as the rain eased. I knew the atmospheric feelings were mine, that in other circumstances I would have joyed to explore here. Barty relapsed into a hurt silence, unable to comprehend why my companionship had so sadly fallen away. Uthnior led on, alert, sniffing the wind, his eyes forever scanning the distant prospects that opened up with each turn in our winding progress through the hills.

We had decided to approach the areas where the Hawkwas camped from a different direction. That, at least, was all we could do to divorce ourselves from the fight. If we were connected to that massacre at a later date, that was in the lap of the gods. So the way took longer, and we spent the next day jogging across cross-grained country and feeling the spirits of the land invading our ibs. Barty was now most unhappy.

We fell in with a wandering man, wild of aspect, half mad, whose shriveled face and white hair told eloquently that he suffered from that dread disease I have spoken of. A normal Kregan looks forward to better than two hundred years of happy, vigorous life. This disease, this chivrel, shortens a lifespan by a handful of years only, depriving people of that lovely golden autumn of life; but it destroys their strength and their appearance, aging them obscenely, shattering their powers.

Kregans hold in their hearts a deep horror of this particular disease; yet as far as anyone knows it is not transferable and people live in close contact with sufferers without ill effects. The disease strikes at random, it seems.

The camp we made beside a brook with crags above and trees massed about cheered me a little. Uthnior's desires I respected. Barty would come round once I got this black dog off my back. Dayra would be found. As for the wider problems of the empire, these weighed most deeply on my mind, fretting at me, worrying me in that I was traipsing about in some damned back hills instead of acting my part in Vondium and trying to thwart evil schemes against the emperor and keeping him safely on his throne.

Who knew what was going on in Vondium now?

A single dagger thrust can change the destiny of nations.

The old fellow waved his arms about, his lank white hair flying, his wrinkled face parchment brittle. His coarse sacking garment was hitched up by a rope girdle; but he carried beside the usual stout pipewood bamboo stick, a sword blade mounted into a pole, the steel broken and resharpened into a foot-long blade. He said his name was Yanpa the Fran—a suitable name given the pallor of that shriveled face and the whiteness of his hair.

In answer to our questions he said he searched for the fabled Cher-ree. At this, Barty was all set to burst out laughing; but he caught my eye and subsided at my quick shake of the head. In this, Barty was prepared to accept my admonishment. After all, it was patent that Yanpa the Fran was makib, insane, and therefore entitled to pursue a will-o'-the-wisp search.

As my Djangs would say, Yanpa chased after Drig's Lanterns.

"But there are too many Junka-forsaken warriors bashing about the Hills," Yanpa complained. His hands shook. "They march everywhere, spoiling. They drive the spirits away."

"Warriors?"

"Aye! Hundreds—thousands. They gather to the war drums and the trumpets. The banners fly. A band chased me yesterday—"

"Hawkwas?" demanded Uthnior. His lean face jutted aggressively forward.

"Also. Many mercenaries, many warriors, many paktuns."

"Where is their camp?"

"Camp? Camp?" His withered old arms windmilled. "There are many camps. The leathers fill the valleys."

"The chief camp?"

His eyeballs rolled. If this moment of lucidity passed before he answered we would be no better off. But he licked his cracked lips, the spittle shining, and laughed and hugged himself. "They meet at Hockwafernes. I saw the temple. I saw and they did not know." He hugged himself in glee.

Uthnior pulled an earlobe. "Hockwafernes. I know it. Some would call it a place blessed and others a place damned. It is certain devils reside there."

"Devils!" tittered Yanpa the Fran. "Aye! Junka has taken them all up into his hand and some spilled through his fingers and scuttled away and hide and tremble in Hockwafernes."

"And others say, old man, that the devils wait there for the tombstones to be lifted, for the funeral pyres to suck in the smoke and flame, for the Ice Floes of Sicce to melt—"

"May Opaz the Light of Days protect us all!" exclaimed Barty, on a breath. He shivered, and looked across the fire into the enveloping trees.

A clatter of stones along the bank of the brook brought us about, instantly. Barty stared toward the source of the noise, hidden beyond a bend in the stream and a stand of trees. Uthnior looked about. I nodded, grim-faced, to the trees and we eased back into their cover. Yanpa came with us, casting a nervous glance back at his riding preysany and his pack calsany. The animals cropped grass alongside our totrixes.

The Rapa who trudged into view, walking sullenly along the river bank, was a fighting man, a warrior, clad in war harness and carrying a monstrous blanket-wrapped bundle on his shoulder. He muttered to himself as he walked, casting dark savage looks from side to side. The instant he saw the camp and the animals he threw the bundle down and the sword appeared in his fist in a twinkling glitter of light. He glared about, uncertain.

I called: "Llahal, dom. We mean you no mischief."

He was confident enough. Where he stood he commanded our approach and before we could get to him he could make the decision to fight or run. I caught the silver glint at his throat, above the armor, and guessed he would not run.

How he would withstand a cloth-yard shaft driven straight at him was another matter entirely.

I did not test him. I stepped out and held up my empty hand.

"Llahal, dom," he said in his surly way. People say all Rapas stink. This is not so. He turned his massively beaked face to regard me. He was of that family of Rapas with brilliant red feathers around the beak, and bands of red and black feathers running aft, and white feathers circling the eyes. His fierce vulturine face leered at me. I went forward.

After we made pappattu and learned he was Rojashin the Kaktu, a paktun, on his way to join Trylon Udo na Gelkwa who was raising an army and employing many mercenaries, Rojashin said with a surly curse: "And my confounded zorca fell and smashed two legs. I have walked two dwaburs like a common slave." His predatory eye fastened on our animals.

Uthnior's hand tightened on his sword hilt.

"You are mercenaries, also? I see you are not full paktuns."

He spoke with some contempt, this Rojashin the Rapa. The little silver mortilhead gleamed at his throat, the pakmort, proud symbol of mercenaries who have achieved the coveted status of paktun. Of course, the word paktun is used loosely these days for almost any mercenary, and usage is changing. Kregen is a world that is not static, that is not stamped into an unchanging mold. Customs, habits, traditions evolve. It was becoming the fashion to call all high-quality mercenary warriors paktuns, and those with the pakmort consequently were called mortpaktuns. Hyr-paktuns, who wore the pakzhan, would then be dubbed zhanpaktuns. But it would be foolish to call a youngster newly left the farm and run off to be a mercenary a paktun. So new hands, green fighting-men, coys, tended to be called a variety of unflattering names, of which paktunik is perhaps the least offensive.

We were like to have trouble with this one. Rojashin went on grumbling, fleering derogatory remarks about a bunch of thieving masichieri masquerading as soldiers he had seen. He kept on looking at our animals, and fingering his sword, while he ate the food we gave him.

He answered our questions readily enough. Trylon Udo was gathering a great army in the Northeast. Men were coming from all over. Many traveled from across the seas. He, himself, had been lured by gold from North Segesthes. But for the mischance of the fallen zorca he would have been at Hockwafernes, having the directions written down safely. Then, he had been promised by the recruiting agent, the army would march south through Vallia and storm and take Vondium. The plunder would be enormous. The sack of the greatest city in this part of the world must yield fantastic wealth to anyone lucky enough to be alive after the assault.

"And, by the Ib Reiver himself, I am like to be cheated of the opportunity."

I decided I would offer this braggart Rojashin the Kaktu the use of my pack totrix and we would ride into Trylon Udo's camp together. That way I would discover at first hand the details of the threat to Vondium. Also, I had the shrewdest of suspicions that Dayra would be found there, too.

But fate has a nasty habit of knocking my schemes askew.

To call this Rapa a braggart may seem harsh; but I saw the newness of his pakmort, the sharpness of the silver edges, and guessed he was still in the grip of the elation that comes with the achievement. He stood up and drew out his sword with his right hand, wiping his left hand across that damned great beak.

"I will take a totrix now. If you resist, I shall slay you all."

I sighed.

He had summed up Uthnior as a guide, and us as his clients, and he disregarded Yanpa the Fran as a diseased madman.

"You may ride with us—" I began.

The Rapa bellowed. "By Rhapaporgolam the Reiver of Souls! You cowardly rasts! I shall cut you all down and then take all."

With that he charged full tilt at Barty.

Barty had been sitting cross-legged munching on a handful of palines. As the Rapa bore down, the sword flaming lethally, Barty let out a yell and rolled sideways in a tangle, berries spurting up like pips from a squeezed fruit. Yanpa let out a pure screech of terror and dived for his preysany. Uthnior held back, glancing at me. I gave no sign.

Barty, all in a tangle, rolled desperately as the sword thwacked down. Uthnior let out a growl. His fist closed on his sword hilt and the blade slid halfway out.

Then, and only then, I said: "Shaft the cramph, if you have to, Uthnior. He will have only himself to blame."

Barty yelled again and flopped about like a stranded whale. He got a knee under him and shoved up, dragging his rapier out.

I sighed again. One day, I supposed, he would learn.

By my right side a usefully sized rock lay to hand. I picked it up, weighed it, tossed it up and down a couple of times, and then hurled it full at the Rapa's head.

The rock clanged off his neck guard. He staggered forward, arms flailing, tripped over Barty and sprawled onto the ground. His beak cut a swath through the mud.

But the helmet had prevented a knock-out blow. The Rapa was up on his feet, moving with ferocious speed, slashing the rapier away in a grating twinkle of steel. In the next second he would have had Barty's head off.

Uthnior loosed.

The shaft passed cleanly through the Rapa's wattled neck, bursting past the wrapped scarf, scything on to break free in a gouting smother of blood. Rojashin the Kaktu stood up, very tall. His fingers relaxed on the sword and it flew into the trees. He stood. Then he fell. His legs kicked. He lay still.

I felt most disgruntled.

"Why these idiots have to bulge their muscles and strut about like con-quering heroes beats me," I said. "By Vox! He misjudged us, the onker. And a paktun, too."

"A very new paktun," observed Uthnior.

We went across and looked down on the body. The Rapa did not die well. Barty stood up, untangling himself, and, looking most mean, said: "You cut that damned fine."

Gesturing to his rapier, I said: "Rapiers are city weapons, my lad. There is a different knack to using them out here."

"Yes, that may be true, but, well and all—"

"He could have had a free and pleasant ride to the camp. But no—he had to prove himself a great and mighty warrior." I noticed his smell, then, and turned away. Yet I have known Rapas with whom a great comradeship was possible. It takes all kinds to make a world.

Later on, when Barty's color had gone down and he had his breath back, I told them I would have to leave them at this point. They looked blankly at me.

"You," I said to Barty. "You will get back to Vondium as fast as the air-boat will take you. Report on what we have learned. See Naghan Vanki. I expect Kov Layco Jhansi will be interested, also, and will arrange an interview with the emperor. The threat from the Northeast is more serious than they imagine."

"And you?"

I picked up the pieces of armor we had stripped from the Rapa. I would make them fit me. "Oh, I think I will join up with Trylon Udo's new army. Dayra is likely to be there—"

"Then I shall go with you!"

Uthnior wrinkled up those huntsman's eyes. "Yanpa the Fran has gone. I think my employment with you is terminated."

"Yes, and I give you thanks, Chavonthjid. Go with Opaz."

"And I," quoth Barty, "shall go with you, Jak, to the camp and—"

"And do you think you can carry off the part of a paktun?"

"We-ell—"

In the end I convinced him. It was not easy. But I bore down.

He would only be a hindrance. The life of a Strom at court and on his estates is far removed from the life of a mercenary. And that despite they may both meet on the field of battle.

We buried the Rapa, Rojashin the Kaktu, paktun, with decent observances, and then struck camp. I stood to watch Uthnior and Barty ride off, back-tracking, trusting they would get through safely to the secreted airboat. I gave them a cheerful Remberee, and then mounted up on the totrix and turned his head toward Hockwafernes and the rebel army of Trylon Udo na Gelkwa.

It was very good once more to be my own lone self, that old Dray Prescot who roared and bashed his way about the brutal and beautiful world of Kregen.

Eleven

Zankov

The valley was indeed, as Yanpa had said, filled with the leather tents of an army. The glitter of weapons and armor, the rustle of brilliant flags, the curveting of saddle animals colored the scene, and the sounds and scents of an army in camp brought back pungent memories as I rode down the trail.

A gang of masichieri—mercenaries who for one reason or another are not regarded as highly as really professional mercenaries, the paktuns, and who consequently are not paid as well, are not usually armed and accoutred as well, and thieve to make up the difference—had fallen in with me. A few cracked skulls and broken noses convinced them I was not to be trifled with, and we rode into the camp together.

This, although giving me good cover, also raised questions. No paktun would consort with masichieri on a social basis. They would stand in the line in battle together; that was as far as they would go.

Down at the far end of the valley where a river emptied into a lake, gleaming with silvery-green reflections in the lights of the suns, a township had been built. It surrounded with its wooden houses and stockade an edifice of considerable architectural splendor.

This was the Temple of Hockwafernes.

Truth to tell, I then paid the place scant attention. One glance convinced me the temple was of remarkable workmanship and outstanding beauty to be found tucked away here. Then I had to ease my way through the protocol demanded. Pappattu had to be made. The curvettings of social and military positions had to be observed. Rojashin the Kaktu had been traveling alone—to have donned his gear would not have been worth the trouble had he had companions—and I had to pick and choose most carefully among the various commanders recruiting their regiments.

The camp was large and was only one of many. Many races of diffs thronged the alleyways between the tents and crowded the open spaces. The usual camp followers plied their varying trades. I downed a long drink of parclear to ease the dust, for the rains had stopped and the twin suns shone clear, and looked about. The sheer size of all this could defeat my purpose.

Where, among this host, was my daughter Dayra to be found?

The hundreds of professional free lances were outnumbered by the thousands of irregulars. I was halted half a dozen times with offers of instant rank within this regiment or that, for the glitter of the pakmort at my throat attracted the regimental recruiting Deldars like flies.

It seemed a good idea to take the thing off. As you know I had been elected a paktun by a duly constituted court of honor, and was entitled to wear the pakmort. My own mortilhead lay somewhere in one of the drawers in the bedroom in Esser Rarioch in Valkanium in Valka. At that time I was not a hyr-paktun—at least, not officially so. I dodged behind a tent and unlooped the silver symbol and the silken cords. The name on the back read simply: KAKTU—presumably they had not felt there was room enough for Rojashin also. I stowed the pakmort away in my pouch. After that, clad in the Rapa's armor, let out around the shoulders, I was able to progress more easily, although still importuned to join up—though now as a simple swod.

The uproar and the noise and the rising clouds of dust and the stinks were all familiar. Fights broke out. Bets were shrieked. Some kind of drilling was going on, and a couple of parcels of totrix cavalry were attempting evolutions. Some of my first fears eased. This army was not ready for battle yet.

As to finding Dayra—well, if all I had heard was correct then it was not sheer stupid pride that led me to the commander's area. Dayra was running with the big boys of this outfit.

No one of this raffish mob being fashioned into an army was allowed through the gateways into the wooden-built town around the temple. The Hawkwas maintained their own integrity. I did not blame them. Chuliks stood guard. There were not a lot of them; but they had clearly been selected for the important positions as was sensible. I did not see many Pachaks, and for this was glad.

A Chulik ob-Deldar chased me away from the gateway where the men of his squad stood guard. I allowed myself to be chased off, not without a casually ripe insult or two. One had to maintain a camouflage in situations like these.

To occupy myself during the time until the suns went down I found stabling for the totrixes, paid good money to attempt to ensure some security for them and my gear, ate a huge meal, talked to the swods, sang a few ditties in the ale tents, and, in general, kept my eyes open and ears fully extended.

The talk was all of the plunder of Vondium and the south.

There were also darker rumors—and that shows just how murky they were—of a great enlightenment, a marvelous intervention of supernatural powers, that would be revealed before the army marched, giving the signal for the great adventure. The Trylon Udo had command of wonderful forces, and these would be summoned to aid the army.

The swods in the ale tent with whom I was drinking and singing were just finishing up that rollicking song well known under its euphemistic name of "Bear Up Your Arms" when the last cadences faltered and died, and the men broke out into cheers and jeers and lewd remarks. A company of women warriors swung past in the gathering shadows. They looked purposeful and businesslike, their spears all a-slanting in line, their helmets gleaming in the last light of the suns.

Intrigued, I threw down my reckoning and wandered out and so followed the martial ladies. Straight to the Chulik-guarded gate they marched. The Chuliks sprang back, at attention, and the Hikdar at their head led the Amazons through. I shook my head. No matter how matter-of-fact the custom is on Kregen, still I suffer from hidden phobias, deeply-driven ideas of womenkind, that make me view with unease the idea of girls taking their part in battle. That they do so—and have done for more years on this Earth than they have not, and will do so again in the future—has no power to move me. But I accept what is, as a fellow must. I was about to turn away with that dark feeling of unease strong upon me, when I saw the Chulik guard had been changed. I saw the Chulik who stood by the gateway, the fading light glistening on his tusks; I saw him clear.

There was little need for a flashing glimpse of the rapier swinging alongside the thraxter at his side to remind me. That rapier hilt was fashioned ornately into the likeness of a mortil.

At once I knew him, and at once I turned away, forcing myself to move with the casual lecherous movements of a swod watching the women warriors. That Chulik was the one who had seen me over the side of the mysterious flier when I'd gone chasing from Vondium after Delia.

A blaze of speculation burst inside my old vosk skull of a head.

The man who commanded the flier had known me, so he had said. I moved into the shadows, smoothly, and breathed more easily when I was out of sight of the gateway and no alarm went up.

The fellow with the gratingly harsh voice commanding the flier had attempted to conceal the fact he was flying to Vondium. He had mischief planned there, and now he was here. At least, it was a fair assumption he was here. There were few fliers parked in this camp; I had heard the aerial wings of the army were quartered to the north, south of the Stackwamors.

In the eternal circle of vaol-paol all events may happen many times. In the tiny moment of darkness between the setting of the suns and the rising of She of the Veils I was up and over the wooden stockade and dropping lightly down inside the town.

I avoided the guards in preference to putting them to sleep, for many of the soldiers guarding the walls were these same warrior women I had watched marching so smartly in.

The wooden buildings surrounding the opulent temple revealed the types to be expected and I aimed for the largest, which must be the Kregan equivalent to the Town Hall. I will pass quickly over that episode, for although I wormed my way in and looked about I learned absolutely nothing. The trylon was away. Guards lounged about, and nothing was afoot. So I withdrew and waited in the shadows under the wooden eaves.

A great deal of noise spilled out with the yellow lamplight from a tavern across the dusty street; but I did not venture in. The troops in the city would be the trylon's own men, Hawkwas and well-trusted paktuns like the Chuliks who would be known. I would face instant exposure as an interloper.

Over there they were singing "King Harulf's Red Zorca" and then they started on "Sogandar the Upright and the Sylvie." A group of Chuliks staggered out, half drunk and disgusted with all this decadent singing. The swods were bellowing out the refrain and killing themselves laughing as they warbled: "No idea at all, at all, no idea at all," when a fresh group of men emerged, their cloaks about their faces, and their swords drawn. Instantly I merged with the shadows and followed them.

There was little chance that the Star Lords or the Savanti sent the chance my way, even though Maspero, my tutor in Aphrasöe the Swinging City, had personally aided me recently. The credit was most probably due to Opaz, although I would not exclude Zair or Djan from the reckoning. Whoever it was guided me to those men, and I heard one of them whisper in a cutting voice: "If we are late because of your drinking and singing, Naghan the Neemu, Zankov is like to have your tripes out. You know what kind of maniac he is if crossed."

"Aye, Nundi, I know! You should have hauled me away before."

"Let us hurry, famblys," growled another. Wrapped in their cloaks, their swords bright in the rising moon, they bustled swiftly along the rutted street between the overhanging houses. I followed.

Zankov!

At last. At last I could feel myself closing with the heart of this mystery.

They led me to a shuttered house in darkness. The door opened and shafted yellow lamplight and then closed tightly again. I eyed the roof. To climb up was simple enough for an old sailorman and I gained the ridge and prised open a skylight. No matter how many times I stealthily clamber into a house to spy nefariously, it always sets the old blood a-thumping. Softly I padded down the blackwood stairs and so came to a tall curtain from which spilled the lamplight in a long beckoning finger from the central parting. Cautiously I applied my eye, saw what I needed, and then set my ear to the narrow opening.

The curtains covered a high window, a kind of mezzanine floor above the main hall. Below, a group of men and women sat around a table on which stood flagons of wine and dishes of fruit. To describe them all now would weary; suffice to say I recognized none of them. I could not see those directly below me. Had I done so—well, that is for later.

The man called Naghan the Neemu was being properly contrite and being cut to pieces by a slender, dapper, sharp-faced fellow clad all in black leather. I looked at this one. There was about his taut nervous manner, the sharp gestures of his narrow hands, the quick stutter of his voice, a sense of burning frustration, the smell of hidden fires, the idea of resentment spilling over and barely contained. He flayed Naghan the Neemu. And, as he spoke vicious, cutting words, I saw his eyes, and saw the Vallian brown change and darken and so remembered Nath ti Javvansmot's words at The Speckled Gyp.

For Zankov laughed as he verbally flayed Naghan the Neemu. He reveled in inflicting his own power on others, that was plain. He laughed hurtfully, and told Naghan what his punishment was to be, and his eyes darkened in that narrow feline face.

"Lucky it is for you, Naghan, our guest is delayed. Had he been constrained to wait for the likes of you—"

"I serve loyally!" spoke up Naghan. "I believe in the Cause. I care for the zorcas—"

"And you will personally sweep out the stalls! Personally! With bucket and broom. Our guest brooks no delays from your kind. Remember and do not forget. You are a mere tool and I shall use you as a tool—so keep to your zorcas and do not be late in future."

And Naghan the Neemu—and a man does not obtain that sobriquet upon Kregen lightly—meekly bowed his head.

The women gathered here looked as ruthless as the men. Probably they were far more vicious, I thought then. I had the macabre idea I would recognize Dayra. I had not recognized Velia. But I thought—then—that I must know my own daughter after the harrowing experiences through which I had gone with Velia, my Lady of the Stars.

She must be sitting directly below me, if she were here.

Gently I drew forth the longsword.

The longbow remained cased, for I had deemed it prudent to conceal that weapon in the camp. There was general talk among the swods about facing the Crimson Bowmen of the emperor, and tales that the bodyguard had been bought, which eased many an uneasy thought for the future in the army.

I would leap down among this unsavory little lot and hoick Dayra out of it and if anyone of them tried to prevent me he would feel what good Krozair steel might do.

These, of course, were the maundering and chauvinistic thoughts of a fond parent who failed to comprehend the working of his daughter's mind. But I would learn—bitterly.

Easing up ready to get a good purchase and so leap down with a skirling yell to throw a startlement into them, I heard Zankov saying: "He is here now. You will all stand."

Amid a scraping of sturmwood chairs they all stood up. A door opened and a bulky figure appeared below me, going toward the table where Zankov stood, smiling, holding out his hand.

I saw the dark cloak of the newcomer, saw the low round helmet without feather or ornamentation. I saw a furtive flicker of steel and a whiplike tail bladed with a glittering dagger slice up in the long slit in the center of the cloak's back.

A Kataki.

And Zankov was saying: "You are heartily welcome. I bid you Lahal and Lahal, Ranjal Yasi, Stromich of Morcray."

Silently I resheathed the longsword and sank back into the shadows.

Twelve

Concerning the Throne of Vallia

They were all laughing and cheerful down there now, chattering away, handing out wine, quaffing, exchanging toasts, all very merry as nits in a ponsho fleece. I sat back in the shadows and glowered, my fists white on the hilts of my swords, my thoughts black as the cloak of Notor Zan.

"Your pass brought me safely through the gates, Zankov. But only, I think, because my men were on duty. There was a Deldar there also, a Khibil, most insulting. I would like him flogged tomorrow, flogged jikaider."

"It shall be done, Stromich."

"Are we all here?"

"All save for the Princess Dayra. She is expected the day after tomorrow."

At this I roused myself. My savage thoughts refused to come to order. So Dayra *was* mixed up with this evil bunch—and she was not here. The day after tomorrow. Almost, then, I withdrew. But the knowledge that with the arrival of this Kataki, the twin brother to the Kataki Strom, an old enemy, the stakes in the affair had been raised to an entirely new plane, I remained.

The Stromich Ranjal turned to shake the hands of those below me I could not see. But I could see his face.

Low-browed, the squat face of a Kataki, fringed with thick black hair, oiled and curled. Flaring nostrils and gape-jawed mouth with snaggly teeth has a Kataki. Wide set his eyes, brilliant and yet narrow and cold. Slavemasters, Katakis, aragorn, evil men to all they enslave. Their bladed whiptails curve arrogantly above their heads. Yes, Katakis are diffs who give to Kregen much of the evil in its brilliant reputation.

Many thoughts rushed through my head. Strom Rosil Yasi and I had clashed before. I had heard of his twin brother, this Stromich Ranjal who strutted below me now. The pair of them were prime candidates for the Ice Floes of Sicce. Down south in Hamal, the enemy of Vallia, these two Katakis held high office. They were here to injure Vallia. More—they were the tools of the Wizard of Loh, Phu-si-Yantong. That devil had been balked in his attempt to control Vallia through the false creed of the Black Chyyan, and now, here he was again making a fresh attempt through these Katakis.

The man who had stood on the poop of the airboat upon which I had so incontinently landed, who had given his hoarse-voiced orders to throw my flier over and to spare me—that man was this same Stromich Ranjal na Morcray. There was no mistaking that voice, now I heard it again and had a face and form to put to it. I marked him. I marked him well.

Who had been giving Ranjal his orders in the flier?

Could that have been Yantong himself?

Could it?

I did not know; but somehow, even then, I doubted it. From what I knew of Phu-si-Yantong, and that was precious little, I fancied he operated whenever he could at long distance through tools like these Katakis and like Vad Garnath ham Hestan. An old chapter of my life was being re-opened here. Yantong sought to employ me as a tool for his insane ambitions. That was why he had ordered that I should not be assassinated. I began to think again, around about then, and thought that just perhaps Yantong had grown weary of waiting, and with the Black Feathers of the Great Chyyan, and now this plot to arouse the Northeast of Vallia, he was committed to moving on an entirely new front in his aggression against Vallia.

As to myself, maybe I no longer figured in his computations.

As I listened to the conversation below some of the outlines came clearer.

"I look forward to meeting this Princess Dayra," Ranjal was saying in that hoarse croak. "My masters have great plans for her. You, Zankov, can answer for her?"

"Assuredly." All the nervous energy of Zankov showed in his nervous twitching, the spread of his hands, the wriggle of his shoulders, the fleer of nostrils. "She believes in the Cause. She is devoted. She has proved that."

"Good. When the army moves we shall strike swiftly. The Trylon Udo is a fool and will be put down. But he is a figurehead and lends color to the endeavor. But the throne and crown of Vallia will not go to him."

Everyone in the room—and I, aloft—knew who hungered for the throne.

Zankov fluttered his fingers against his ears, and cheeks, and then snapped his forefingers and thumbs together.

"No. Not to Udo. To him who deserves it—who will lay unqualified claim to the crown by virtue of marriage to the Princess Dayra."

Stromich Ranjal nodded matter-of-factly. "You will see to disposing of the rest of the family? There must be no other claimant."

"I shall joy in the task! I have a right to the throne—my ancestors demand it of me, in blood. But Stromich, your orders have been to spare the life of the Prince Majister. What—"

"Those orders stand, as of now. I think my masters will shortly issue new directives."

This was fascinating, listening to these schemers dispose of my life. I own I felt a little sorry for them...

Now it is important to know that when a paktun is elected by those who thus become his peers, and receives the silver pakmort, he receives also a little silver ring by which the pakmort is attached to the silken cords. In the case of a hyr-paktun the ring is of gold. When a paktun slays another in battle or in the ritual of the Jikordur—the strictly controlled duel to the death—he does not take among the consequent loot the dead man's pakmort. That goes to the stocks for reissue with a new name, generally, although there are other uses to which it is put. But the victorious paktun claims the silver ring. This he strings upon a silken cord and wears about his person as a badge of prowess. If the slain paktun has a string of rings, the victor will take them all and string them with those he has.

These savage customs of Kregen echo down the long seasons and the ages reverberate with the clash of arms and glow with the brilliance of shed blood.

The dead Rapa, Rojashin the Kaktu, had owned a silken string of seven rings, one of them gold. These were attached to the left shoulder of his harness. This symbol, usually, is referred to as the pakai. The pakai I now wore hung down by my left shoulder.

"You will remember, Zankov, when you seat yourself upon the throne in the palace of Vondium, and are duly crowned and given the Jikai as emperor, to whom you owe all your fortune? You will remember to whom you owe your loyalty and to whom you will dedicate your service and your life?"

Zankov twitched his fingers and nodded. He was so suffused with anticipatory glory he could not speak—an unusual condition for him, I judged.

The door opened again—I could not see it; but it creaked upon a hinge—and a sharp hard voice said: "Jens! Koters! Koteras! Trylon Udo has returned unexpectedly and is calling for—"

The speaker got no further. At once the people at the meeting started to rise and to gather their cloaks and weapons and, at that moment, I shifted incautiously, and the pakai struck its string of rings against my armor.

The sound rang like a carillon.

No wonder, I said to myself fiercely, no wonder I abhor dangling adornments. Flying tassels and trailing scarves and whirling belts are no fit gear for a fighting man.

Zankov glared up at the curtained mezzanine window.

"Up there!" he shouted. "Quick, you cramphs! Someone spies on us!"

He was quick enough on the uptake, I'll give him that.

"Right, you nidge," I said under my breath. "By the Black Chunkrah! I'll sort you out and damned quick!"

I freed the longsword and prepared to leap down and slice them up a trifle. The thought of settling affairs with Zankov and with Stromich Ranjal pleased me mightily.

Then—and then, by Zair, I hesitated. I, Dray Prescot that wild leem of a fellow, took thought for events beyond the immediate prospect of a brisk bashing of skulls. My daughter Dayra was expected the day after tomorrow.

Who knew what other villainy these fellows had planned? Far better to wait. Far better to be the calculating, cool, cunning Dray Prescot who took thought for the future and bided his time to strike.

So—as Zair is my witness—the Krozair longsword went snap back into the scabbard and I turned and ran back the way I had come so stealthily.

Even then it was nip and tuck. But I eluded them and I did not have to essay a single handstroke, which, I might add, displeased me at the time, for all my good resolutions.

Back over the town stockade I went and avoided all trouble. I found my billet, all paid for, and bedded down. One day I had to live through without trouble, and then I would see Dayra and bring her out of this rasts' nest.

The last thing I did before I slept was to rip off that damned jangling pakai and stuff it away in my gear. Confounded unwarrior-like trinket—it had nearly botched the whole affair.

Thirteen

The Battle Maidens Squabble

I sat next morning in the early radiance of the Suns of Scorpio polishing up the armor. I had bought a choice breakfast of vosk rashers and loloo's eggs, swilled down an inordinate amount of good Kregan tea, chewed a handful of palines, and now, stripped down to a breechclout—which was, incidentally, a normal sober yellow—sat companionably with a couple of other mercenaries hard at the task that would keep us alive on the day of battle.

We spoke in that rapid shorthand of warriors, at ease, knowing our own worth—or, at least, they did—and bending diligently to our tasks.

The Rapa paktun's armor had been fashioned from good quality iron with bronze fittings. The breast and back were molded, and so formed a quality kax, a corselet that covered the trunk and extended in a graceful curve below the belt and yet afforded free movement to the legs. I retained my own weapons. The longbow and longsword I kept covered; the other of my weapons excited no untoward comment, being a Vallian clanxer and a Valkan shortsword, and a rapier and main gauche. The Rapa's spear was not a quality weapon; but I kept it for the color it afforded.

Nalgre the Shebov worked on his armor on the other side of the blanket. He was the seventh son of his family and had taken up the mercenary life as a release from farm work. Now he carefully buckled up his armor, a kax tralkish—what on Earth is called a *lorica segmentata*—and whistled cheerfully as he worked.

Dolan the Sling methodically oiled his scaled kax, seeing that each bronze scale was firmly affixed to the leather. At his right side his sling lay ready to hand. With a leaden lozenge-shaped bullet Dolan fancied his luck against any archer. But then, as he said, he had not faced a Bowman of Loh.

"Although, Jak the Kaktu," he said, "we routed a bunch of Undurkers three, four seasons ago when we were working for the King of Sanderdrin. Quite a dust up, that was."

"We're likely to square up to Bowmen of Loh if they don't win over the emperor's guard," said Nalgre. "And damned quick."

"Undurkers," I said, rubbing the oiled rag methodically. "I had a dust-up with them a while back. Some Bowmen of Loh did for them, skewered 'em right through well beyond their range."

"Which side were you on?"

"Well, by Vox, I'm here, aren't I?"

"So you were on the right side."

They laughed. The paktuns of Kregen can see the humor in the situation, when from day to day they may be victors or slain. It gives them the old zest to life.

A whole day to get through. Forty-eight burs to the day. Fifty murs to the bur. And a Kregan bur is roughly equal to forty terrestrial minutes. A long time to keep out of mischief for a wild leem of a fellow.

Not that, recently, I'd felt much like a leem. Like a calsany, perhaps. And everyone knows what calsanys do when they get excited. Nalgre and Dolan talked on about the female warriors—Battle Maidens they called them, Jikai Vuvushis—and we sent a camp slave for a couple of bottles of parclear to ease our throats. The suns rolled across the heavens and everything was going splendidly, for these two like myself were tazll mercenaries, unemployed, determining to enlist with the trylon's regiments or none. I did not tell them Udo had returned overnight; the information had not yet percolated through. Even when the dust of a squabble rose beyond the next row of tents I felt no inclination to become involved.

But when Nalgre and Dolan stood up and peered across and said: "That looks interesting," I realized I would have to go, for to do otherwise would be most odd in a paktun.

So we yelled at the camp slave—he was shared by the two comrades and for a fee I could join in the syndicate—to guard our gear. We strapped on a sword or two and ambled across to see the fun.

The dust billowed up from a cleared space and rose over the heads of the gathered swods. I call them swods, P.B.I., soldiers; in truth they were much more of a hastily gathered rabble, with a leavening of hardened professionals among them. No doubt, given time, Trylon Udo would smarten them up. By the time they'd marched all the long way to Vondium they'd either be an army or they'd be long since dispersed. We had little difficulty in shoving our way to the front of the ring. Bets were being wagered all around, and the excitement fizzed.

The sharp smell of the dust peppered nostrils and stung eyes. I was pleased Nalgre had thought to bring a bottle of parclear, that sherbet drink that so refreshes. The noise blattered skywards. The Suns of Scorpio shone down. On the morrow I would see my daughter Dayra. I knew the house. This time I would not wear a stupid dangling clanging object and the Krozair longsword would find business.

Two girls fought in the dust.

I grimaced my distaste.

So that was why the swods were so wrought up.

Inquiries elicited the fact they were not fighting over a man but over the ownership of a fine string of amber beads. So they remained girls despite their martial kit, and the daggers, and their spitting snarling invective. The blonde girl was having the worst of it, the redhead being altogether quicker and deadlier. I wondered, with a shiver of disgust, if they would fight to the death, for, as we quickly learned, this was not a Jikordur but merely a common brawl.

A knot of Battle Maidens on the far side of the ring screamed advice and insults and encouragement. There were two sides here. The two girls fighting were not naked; but they might just as well have been. For an agonizing instant I wondered what Delia, if she were so unfortunate as to be here, would make of this spectacle. Then I brought myself up with a shock. Why should not girls fight and brawl in camp like men? Just because I viewed the scene with reservations meant nothing. If girls could tend wounded men and see the ghastly sights of the battlefield at, as it were, second hand, and if they could don boots and armor and wield weapons, as they did, who was I to say they could not act completely as warriors? Did I not demean them by suggesting otherwise?

Each person must act out his own nature, as the scorpion said to the frog, always—and this proviso is one I hew to for it is so often overlooked and disregarded, always provided that the free-doer does not harm his or her fellows in the liberated exercise of his or her own psyche.

And by harm I do not mean the harm one of these girls was going to sustain in this free-for-all.

Blonde hair, damped with sweat and slicked with dust, bent to the ground. The redheaded girl, who was screamed at as Firn in wild excitement, had the upper hand. She had fought cleanly. All saw that. And now she was on the point of victory.

Already coins were jingling, changing hands as the bets were paid out.

With a wild scream a third girl bounded into the informal arena. Clad in green leathers, she wielded a rapier and main gauche. Her dark hair flowed loosely. Her face was brilliant with malice and vicious determination.

She raced toward the two girls, the blonde submitting and Firn, the redhead, triumphant. With a shriek the girl in green leathers kicked the dagger from Firn's hand. The rapier twitched down. Its point hovered at the redhead's throat.

A hullabaloo broke out in red riot. Girls yelled, men cursed. Through it all no one took a single eye away from that central tableau as the dust fell.

"Firn! I challenge you! Prepare to die, here and now!"

"Karina the Quick!"

The noise lessened as we all struggled to hear.

Someone threw a rapier and dagger onto the settling dust.

A ferocious-looking apim at my side said: "Karina the Quick is notorious. Firn is as good as dead if she does not submit."

"Firn! Firn!" came the screeches and yells.

"Karina! Karina the Quick!" flew from the other group of Battle Maidens.

I felt the sorrow for redheaded Firn. To submit would bring life and to fight might bring death; but in these circumstances she had no choice.

Firn threw back her heavy head of red hair and picked up the weapons. She held them in a practiced grip. But at the first handstrokes those who knew about these things saw that Firn faced a swordmaster—or, in this case, a swordmistress. Karina played with her, pinking that bright skin, bringing forth the ugly spottings of blood and all the time she taunted, foul-mouthing Firn, taunted her with torture and death.

This was a case for the Krozairs to decide. Could I, a man, step forward and stop the fight? No—this was not a case for the Krozairs, or for me. This was Savage Kregen, alive, vibrant, pulsing with blood—and ending with a life and a death.

If I attempted to intervene I'd probably be torn limb from limb by everyone present who could get a hand on me.

Now Firn's superb body was splashed with her own blood. Her scanty clothes hung in bloodied ribbons. Her hair swirled. The green leathers of Karina the Quick glimmered in the suns' light, unspotted, unfouled.

Very soon if Firn did not yield she would be dead.

The Battle Maidens had now clearly separated into two groups. If there was a preponderance of green about one group and of red about the other, I put that down to coincidence and my own views on those two sky colors. Looking across the swirling dust that billowed up as the girls stamped and retreated and stamped and advanced, I saw, abruptly, clearly, as though focused in a telescope, the face of one of the Jikai Vuvushis. The face swam clear through all the confusion and tumult.

Open of countenance, glowing with the excitement of the moment, her brown Vallian eyes wide, Vad Kolo's daughter, Leona nal Larravur, stood and stared hungrily upon the fight.

She wore the green leathers, with a profusion of purple feathers. Now I understood why the topmost purple ronil gem had snapped away from her jeweled badge of the samphron bush. Rejecting the Sisterhood, she must have hurled the brooch from her in negation and disgust, and then, calculatingly, have picked it up to wear to the emperor's reception for Queen Lushfymi. The missing gem not being found by her cowed slaves, perforce the missing socket had to be painted over. Yes, Leona nal Larravur was a real right scheming miss.

Dust puffed across as the struggling girls grappled and swung about. Firn was clearly weakening. Her blood glistered darkly upon her body, and dust patched her like camouflage.

The group of Jikai Vuvushis who wore russet leathers began to shout. "Ros the Claw," they called. "Ros the Claw."

In all the confusion others took up the yell. Money which had changed hands twice now returned. The issue was, then, still in doubt. A girl in black leathers was thrust into the ring by the Battle Maidens, who chanted her name. Slowly, she walked to the center. Firn, panting, shrieked out: "She will slay you, Ros!"

The girl in the black leathers moved forward. The fighting girls staggered apart. Karina the Quick looked as lithe, as ferocious, as deadly as ever. She stood back, her blood-smeared rapier and dagger slanting up, smiling lopsidedly as Ros the Claw moved in. Firn collapsed, panting, disheveled, done for.

"Do you challenge me, Ros the Claw?"

"If you will it. Either way—you cease and desist from tormenting Firn."

"Then you must make me."

"It is the Jikordur, then."

A gasp swept the assembly. The bets hovered, uncertain, for both girls possessed reputations. I knew the one in black leathers. I had seen her before, in those abominable caverns beneath Vondium where my Delia had been offered up on a basalt slab under the obscene idol of a giant toad to the fangs and claws of a real chyyan. I had seen her then, this Ros the Claw, as she released a mangled wight from a prison cell.

Two more girls in black leathers stepped forward. They looked grim. They were addressed as Zillah and Jodi, and they bore marks of authority. Ros flung out at them.

"This is overdue."

"Maybe. But we cannot allow the Jikordur. The Trylon has forbidden duels to the death."

"This began as a squabble over a bead necklace. What—"

"The Trylon Udo has commanded."

"To the Ice Floes of Sicce with Udo! This bitch leem has tortured enough. She must be—"

"You may be called a tiger-girl, Ros. You may stand high. But in this you cannot go against the orders of the trylon."

Now it was the turn of Karina the Quick to laugh.

The sightseers swayed this way and that to get a better view. All recognized this as a woman's affair; but with rapiers and daggers in play, a universal sympathy was involved.

I wondered what, if Dayra was here, she would do. She must have witnessed sights like this before. And that struck me as a most deucedly odd thought, I can tell you, I who had never to my knowledge seen my daughter. I wondered to which side she would hew. I did not think, with some assurance, that having a brother like Jaidur, Dayra could possibly have any truck with the green.

That, here in Vallia, was a stupid concept, where green was merely another heraldic color, where blue, if any, was the color of contempt. And that was a pity.

The streaming opaline radiance of the suns brought out the colors of the soldiers and the irregulars, glittered from armor and weapons, struck glinting metallic highlights in the hanging dust.

"Desist, Ros the Claw, or we will take you into custody."

This girl with her lithe feline form, the blood suffusing her cheeks, the sparkle in her eyes that told of venom and intelligence, hauled Firn to her feet. The redhead swayed.

"Look! Very well. As Dee-Sheon is my witness, not the Jikordur—a common brawl, then, a gutter fight."

At the words Dee-Sheon many of the women made tiny reflexive gestures with their fingers. Did they convey worship or did they ward off evil? Gods and goddesses and spirits throng the pantheons of Kregen. A New York City directory would contain not a half of them.

This was the moment I decided I could stand and watch no longer. I half turned to move away. The girls would not be constrained by the ritualistic trappings of the Jikordur and they would not fight to the death. This Ros had her way. But Karina laughed, derisively, showing her white teeth, her lips very red. Her body arched magnificently as she stretched, her rapier licking out in swift cunning passes. She vibrated confidence.

Slowly, Ros pulled from her waist pouch a thing of shining steel, an artifact shaped like an articulated metal glove, clawed with razor steel, sharp and cruel. She pulled it onto her left hand. The talons glinted. Metal splines extended up her wrist. She turned the tiger-talons this way and that. To call them tiger-talons is correct, for they shared much of the cruel curved beauty of a killer bird's claws.

The massed crowd fell silent.

The girls faced each other, Karina the Quick flicking her rapier and dagger about expertly; Ros the Claw poised with rapier ready and left hand glittering with clawed steel.

So, I, Dray Prescot, sentimental onker, turned away and pushed through the crowd. I had no wish to witness what might follow. But, if I had to lay down any bets, my money would be on Ros, every last copper ob.

I had gone barely a dozen paces when a bubbling scream burst up into the bright air. I continued walking. I did not look back.

A vast sigh oozed from the crowd.

That was woman's business. They were welcome to it.

Fourteen

"You May Choose the Manner of Your Death."

"You are sure, Nalgre? Certain sure?" The seething anger and violence in me had to be held down. I could not show too much interest in the politics of Vallia here.

"Certain, Jak. I spoke to a flier pilot who returned with the trylon. The Lord Farris has been arrested and charged with treason. And others of like kidney, too."

"It will make our task easier," put in Dolan, idly swinging his sling around his legs. "Farris was loyal to the emperor."

"Yes," I said. "He was."

"And as Udo is back in camp we will go and enlist today."

"Very well," I said, to keep up my cover.

This news was bad. It indicated quite clearly that scheming people were burrowing from within. The Lord Farris was devoted to Delia and the emperor. How could he possibly be accused of so outrageous a crime? Accused, yes; that would be all too easy. But the accusation must be false. I was convinced of that.

Before we went to enlist the three of us ambled across to an ale tent, for the suns progressed across the sky, to spend some of Nalgre's winnings. Dolan had bet on Karina the Quick. And, as Nalgre said, with a guffaw: "That cat-girl cut her up a real treat."

I was not interested. The day passed too slowly for me. On the morrow Dayra would arrive and I knew I would have to be quick to fetch her out of it before Zankov moved. I'd summed up that villain, as I thought, and how I kept moving and speaking and acting normally I do not know.

The problem of this acting as a paktun and hiring out to Trylon Udo also worried me. If I gave my sworn oath to serve, as any mercenary would do, I would not wish lightly to break my word. That the whole thing was a sham, a facade, would not count. My word would have been given, and here, in the camp of Hockwafernes, I *was* Jak the Kaktu, paktun.

Well, it is the same with problems as with plans. Men sow for Zair to sickle.

Coming out of the ale tent after a goodly interval—a goodly interval—Nalgre wiped his lips and belched.

"By Beng Dikkane," he said, comfortably. "I am in the mood now."

A pang for old days and for Nath and Zolta swept me. We turned along the line of booths and tents where the trafficking went on all the live-long day. A party of warrior women marched along, all in step, all spears ranked, their helmets gleaming.

Dolan nodded.

"I warrant they'd not be so regimented when the moons are in the sky, eh?"

"They wouldn't give you a calsany's offering," quoth Nalgre, and he laughed.

The Jikai Vuvushis marched with a swing. There were equal numbers of those in green leathers under their armor as those in russets. On duty animosities were forgotten. At the head marched Zillah and Jodi, and Ros the Claw was there, with Firn. They approached and we three together with other swods casually sauntering nearby moved out of the way.

Leona nal Larravur pointed at me.

"There he is!" she shouted. Her voice rose, cracking with strain and excitement. "There he is! The Prince Majister! Seize him!"

It was damned quick.

I was ringed by spear points. My comrades fell back, gaping. Many of the irregulars ran off in terror. Zillah, tall, buxom, high of color, fronted me. Her rapier glittered at my throat.

"You are the Prince Majister of Vallia?"

I stared about the hostile ring. Damned quick, by Krun!

To go drinking in camp we had merely donned rapier and dagger. My fighting equipment lay buckled up in its leather coverings along with the gear of the others, guarded by the camp slave. Even then I could have broken free, skewered a few of the guards, slashed a few more, and so broken to liberty.

But I hesitated.

These were women. Mind you, they were women dressed up as warriors, carrying arms, armored. All the same, they remained girls. At that time I couldn't bring myself to stick a length of sharp steel into any one of those delightful forms. It was a weakness.

"No!" I bellowed, for everyone to hear. "You are mistaken! For the sweet sake of Opaz—take that rapier out of my Adam's apple."

"You are the Prince—"

"No! No—do I look like a prince! I am Jak the Kaktu. A paktun, ready to fight for you—you make a mistake—"

Some of the girls believed me. But this Zillah and this Jodi, and this Ros the Claw and Firn did not. And, with her fine frank face glowing with passion, this tricky Leona nal Larravur knew absolutely I lied.

"Take him to the trylon!" she brayed, swirling her rapier. "I shall soon convince him. Oh, what a prize we have here."

"Yes," spat Ros. "A contemptible rast of a man! A cramph ready to be unmanned and chopped and flung down unmourned to the Ice Floes of Sicce."

I shook my head. "You are mistaken—"

"March him off!" shouted Zillah. Her nostrils widened. "How the sight of him offends me."

Amid a scathing torrent of abuse they led me off. I went. A few sharp spear points up my stern convinced me they hadn't heard Phu-si-Yantong's orders not to kill me. Anyway, maybe that schemer had changed his mind. I'd soon find out.

Trylon Udo na Gelkwa turned out to be a square-set man with a sharp brown beard and thin harsh lips, with eyes that were darker than the normal Vallian brown. This is common in the Northeast of Vallia. He did not rise as I was prodded into his room in the town hall. The place was bare and sparsely furnished, with furs hanging on the walls and a large table smothered with maps and lists. He looked up narrowly.

"So you are the Prince Majister."

"No—"

The girls at my back all took their chances of giving me a crafty prod or two with their spears. I jumped. They'd taken my rapier and dagger away. I had let them. Every time I tried to speak I was poked by a spear.

"Larravur says you are. She frequents the court of the imperial buffoon and decadent drunkard in Vondium. She is our eyes. You are the Prince Majister. You will receive scant courtesy from anyone here in the Northeast. But, one boon I will grant." Here Udo leaned back in his chair and pulled his beard. He smiled. "You may choose the manner of your death."

I opened my mouth and Udo lifted a ringed hand.

"Let him speak, Zillah."

The girls glowered at me. Even Karina the Quick had come in to see the fun. Not a one of them showed a single spark of mercy; now all believed I was that miserable rast I was accused of being. Karina sported a large bandage over the right side of her face. But she had not lost an eye. She did not stand near Ros. Jodi and Firn separated them. The animosity I felt from these girls puzzled me. It seemed to me overdone, abnormal, almost unreal and certainly damned unhealthy.

Leona pointed a rigid forefinger at me.

"He does not speak. He admits his guilt. His terror contaminates us all. Thrust a sword through him and have done."

Ros whipped out her steel claw. "Let me take him apart!"

The others voiced their own highly unpleasant ideas on the way I should go.

The whole episode smacked of a dream sequence. It was not even a nightmare. It just seemed unreal. Had I been hemmed in by foul-mouthed guardsmen then a flick of a leem's tail would have seen a few of them down, spitting blood, and a sword in my fist, and a corpse-strewn trail of blood to the door, if one of them did not try to shaft me as I went. But these were girls. As I say, I was weak in these matters in those days.

By Makki-Grodno's disgusting diseased dripping left eyeball, I can tell you! I felt the hugest of huge idiots, a nurdling onker, a get onker—a ripe charley, the complete fool. And yet—and yet, at that stage in my development on Kregen, what else could I have done?

A stir at the back of the room and a swaying aside of the Jikai Vuvushis heralded the intemperate arrival of Zankov. He stood twitching before Udo, shaking, controlling himself with an effort of will I found amusing. He wore a fancy uniform which included a gilt cuirass all carved and engraved into the likeness of a writhing devil face, fangs and staring eyeballs and wild hair—I think it was intended to be one of the devils of Cottmer's Caverns—and he kept running a finger around the collar and hitching himself about. I judged he was not much used to wearing armor.

"This man is not to be harmed, trylon," he said without as much as a Lahal.

"Oh?" shouted Udo. "And who says so?"

At this Zankov checked. He managed to get his finger from the cuirass to spread his arms and shrug. "It would be unwise. He is a bargaining counter, a hostage—"

"I run things here, Zankov—or whatever your name is. Remember that. But—" And here Udo pulled his beard again. "It is so simple as to be moronic. But it might be useful."

Ros pushed forward. "He deserves to die, here and now." The claw glittered ominously.

"Oh, aye, he deserves to die."

"Well, let me scratch him a little.'"

During all this I stood silently, watching the byplay, wondering just how much of his gloating feelings of superiority Zankov could not stop from showing through. He was making a good job of appearing the zealous subordinate to the trylon. They argy-bargyed, discussing my life like a rotten sack of moldy gregarines. Finally Udo waved his hands and gave his judgment.

"Take him away and bind him and set a watch over him. If he dies or if he lives is my decision. I will take it myself. You will be told when necessary."

A couple of girls grabbed my arms to drag me off.

I remained where I was, with the girls tugging away. I stared hard at Leona. She tossed her head back, her eyes bright.

"If I was this confounded prince, girl—why would you hate me so?"

"You are, and you know."

"Take the rast away!" bellowed Trylon Udo.

The two girls were joined by two more who tugged at me. I remained firm. "Hold on a mur," I said. "I want to know what this fellow, this Prince Majister, has done to you to arouse such heated emotions."

"Get him out of here!" The words slashed from Zankov.

Ros pushed forward. She was breathing heavily, and patches of color mantled her cheeks. The claw looked highly unpleasant, for she had donned it over her left hand and wrist. "I should rip your eyes out, here and now! You betrayer! You deceiver! You lecher! You heartless wretch! You—you—"

"Now easy on," I said, for she broke down from the violence of her emotions. Firn took a swipe at me with her rapier and I had to sway aside. This was getting out of hand. Leona kept on shrieking at me. Zillah and Jodi, who were clearly in command of the Jikai Vuvushis, added their yells and orders. I shook the girls free and took a step toward Trylon Udo. Instantly a shortsword flicked up into his hand.

"All right, all right, trylon," I told him. "I'm not going to hurt you."

"Get him out! Drag him by the heels!" foamed Zankov.

One, two, three strides took me to Zankov. He tried to rip his rapier out and I took him by the throat and lifted him up off his heels. He dangled in the air, choking, his face turning that old interesting purply-green rotten gregarine color.

"Hear me!" I bellowed.

The walls of the room did not shake to that foretop-hailing voice; but a silence dropped.

I shook Zankov, who was bubbling like a punctured boiler.

"Just suppose I were this Prince Majister—" Here I swung my left arm across and swept away a flung spear. Another was caught and reversed in a twinkling. I looked at the girl who had hurled, and smiled, and shook my head. Her face went as white as the underside of a chank.

"Can't you hulus tell me what is going on?"

Strangely, no one wished to speak. I glanced up at Zankov and, regretfully, plunked him down on his feet. I let him go. He fell to pitch forward into Karina's arms. She glared at me venomously; but a flicker in her eyes, a swift betraying gleam of sympathy? I was not sure.

But she said: "Zankov may overrate himself. But he is one of us. You are a southerner—a clansman—prince."

"If I were. And is that all? That the Prince Majister is a stranger?"

"Aye!" said Firn, looking at me with scathing contempt. Her red hair looked marvelous. She breathed deeply and unsteadily. "A stranger. A stranger to Vallia for all of the time. A no-good calsany, a rast who betrays those who love him."

The bewilderment would not leave me. I looked around them, at those lovely faces, all flushed and bright-eyed, all staring accusingly at me. Contempt, hatred, disgust—all were written clear on those fair faces ringing me.

I shook my head.

Zankov held his throat, croaking, trying to speak and unable to force out a sound. The marks of my fingers glowed in livid weals.

"I'll go," I said. "And I will go peacefully. By Vox! But if I really were this Prince Majister then I truly think I'd begin to feel a little sorry for myself."

I did not. But I wanted to test still further the way the wind blew. But no one responded.

Trylon Udo had summoned male guards. He did not know it; but that was a mistake. Had he done so before, I might be away from here now, cleaning up a blood-splattered sword. As it was, I had said I would go peacefully, and so I went. Spear points ringed me as I started off. It was left to Udo to have the last word.

"The reports are true; and yet I harbor a doubt." He was speaking to Zillah and Jodi. "Prescot is a Hyr Jikai only through the proclamations; he is a puffed-up image, we all know that. And yet—"

"He took the spear smartly enough, Udo."

"Yes, well, that is a common trick. Guard him well. You have a great prize there, for the Princess Majestrix will pay an emperor's ransom for him. That is well known."

I heard a gasp at my back, and I turned. The girls tautened up instantly; but I raised a hand to calm them. I decided not to let the trylon have the last word, after all.

"It is well known, Udo. Do you know also that she will have your head and your tripes into the bargain?"

And with that I, Dray Prescot, Prince Majister of Vallia, did my best to stalk out.

Fifteen

Of San Guiskwain the Witherer

They tied me up as they would tie up any common criminal and chucked me into a narrow wooden stockade by the town wall. Captive—I was a captive once more. Well, by Zair, I've been captive before on Kregen and plenty of times since that occasion in Hockwafernes. Being a Captive of Kregen is an occupational hazard to a wild leem of a fellow like me. Or so I am led to believe.

The guards were prattling on about the great news the trylon had brought and how on the morrow the tremendous ceremony would be performed and all the promised and looked-for supernatural powers would come to the assistance of the Hawkwas.

Male and female guards took turn and turn about to stand watch outside the wooden cell.

The thongs broke free after a bur or so. I stretched and felt the blood tingling. They didn't know me, then...

So far I have spared you the innumerable aphorisms widely current upon Kregen attributed to San Blarnoi. He was either a real person of wide learning or a consortium of misty figures of the dim past. Either way, many sayings are attributed to San Blarnoi. He is a fount of wisdom, both superficial and of deeper significance, and among the many maxims are to be found one or two to fit almost any situation.

Some are merely of the order of: "San Blarnoi he say..." Others are Christmas Cracker mottoes in scope. Some give a little comfort or insight.

It was Filbarrka na Filbarrka who first told me of the saying that I used now. Filbarrka, as you know, is that wide and marvelous area south and east of the Blue Mountains that is zorca country supreme. I think there are few finer zorcas bred on Kregen anywhere else. Filbarrka ran the area. He was not a Blue Mountain boy. His name and that of the land were as one.

Anyway, in his bluff, red-faced, cheerful way he'd once cautioned me: "As San Blarnoi says, waiting is shortened by preparation."

I had the remainder of the day to wait through. It was clearly useful to be able to spend that waiting time in this prison cell as a captive, out of mischief. If this sounds paradoxical, it is; but it was, nonetheless for that, true.

So, unwilling to break out at once, I perforce followed San Blarnoi's dictum and prepared myself in the only way left. I thought. I pondered the problem.

Dayra would arrive on the morrow. And on the morrow the trylon would produce his miracle that would make his army invincible. He was well known in the occult areas, and had a wizard in his employ, not a Wizard of Loh, who was one of these renowned Northeast Vallian sorcerers, a Hawkwa necromancer.

Natyzha Famphreon had spoken of them, calling the ghastly practitioners Opaz-forsaken corpse-revivers.

Brooding in my cell it occurred to me I might wisely pay a visit to the ceremony on the morrow. Dayra must come first. But from the guards' conversation I learned further disquieting information as the day wore on. The rumor of the arrest of the Lord Farris on treason charges was confirmed. And, with him, other men I would have sworn loyal to the emperor had been imprisoned. I had distinguished company as I languished in prison. Also, an army had landed in the south, west of Ovvend, and was marching on Vondium. This news caused me grave concern. That the army had come from Pandahem seemed reliable information. The emperor had marched out to destroy them. Everyone awaited the outcome. There had been only a slight panic in Vondium. I chafed. But, this close, I had set my thoughts and desires on Dayra, and I was not prepared to change my direction now.

My careful preparation of hard thinking led me to the unpalatable conclusion that this Opaz-forsaken ceremony might include me as a sacrifice. It would be in keeping with all those dark and horrific forces of the occult side of Kregen. If that were so, I'd best be about my business a little ahead of the time I had set myself.

The time to make the break came, I felt, when the guards were a mix of Fristles, Rapas, Khibils and apims. No women stood outside my cell door. The guards talked among themselves in desultory fashion. But they'd be alert enough.

A Rapa was saying in his vicious hissing way: "And the rast knows nothing of all this?"

The voice of the apim talking, which had been a mere mumble before, strengthened and grew clearer as he approached. He laughed.

"Know? He is a fambly, that one. I know it to be so."

"His fearsome reputation is all a make-believe—yes, that is known. He is no true Hyr-Jikai. But, this other—?"

"I had it from my second cousin twice removed. He was in Vondium at the time. Oh, yes, this precious Delia, Princess Majestrix, is notorious. Her lovers are legion."

I listened, flexing my muscles, waiting until they positioned themselves just so.

"Before she took up with this Turko fellow it was a Bowman of Loh—a Jiktar, I believe. And there was a visiting diplomat from Tolindrin—and where that is, Vox knows."

"In Balintol. And?"

The apim started asking about Tolindrin; but the Rapa, who was joined by a Fristle, although they were stiffly polite one with the other, wanted to know more about the amatory exploits of the Princess Majestrix. This gossip was all over Vallia.

"She has a secret room furnished erotically in all her villas. She spends money like water. Her lovers—mind you, dom, they don't last."

"No?"

"No. It is a sack and a leaden weight and the Great River for them."

"Bitch."

"Aye. Leave well alone there, if ever her eye falls on you."

"I am a Rapa." The surprise was genuine.

"It makes no difference to her. You're a man, aren't you?"

The Rapa courts of women are notorious. I had once gone chasing madly through Zenicce at the mere threat. The guards changed their positions casually, leaning on their spears. I watched them through the wooden bars. The Khibil was likely to be the most dangerous. When he moved in, half-interested in what was being said about the amatory adventures of the Princess of Vallia, his alert fox-like face bright with all the intelligence of his race, I fancied my time had come.

With a surging shoulder charge I burst through the wooden bars, shattering three of them in a welter of flying splinters. The hands and arms they thought so securely bound whipped up from behind my back and two throats clamped into my grasp. Two savage shakes, and then two clouting blows, and the four guards lay stretched senseless upon the packed-dirt floor. The Rapa, the Fristle, the Khibil and the apim slumbered. I had killed not a one of them.

The cramphs had not fed me, and I found a crust and an onion in a scrip and wolfed them down. I took a clanxer, a dagger and a spear, and set off.

The dawn would soon be here in a washing radiance of jade and ruby light—and with the dawn, Dayra.

Pretty soon the hunt was up. But I sat tight in a space under the roof of the house where the conspirators met, and I, Dray Prescot, chuckled as they searched for me in vain.

Again it was a question of waiting. But to this house they would come to plan the final schemes, and to this house would come my daughter Dayra, to be duped and betrayed by them. I was wrong.

Wrong—completely wrong.

The day wore on. The heat began to build up in that tiny cramped space under the roof. And the house below me remained ominously still and silent. Outside, the sounds of many people moving convinced me the time for the ceremony grew near.

What form that ceremony would take I had no idea. This dark wizard of the trylon's, this San Uzhiro, would officiate. After all the mumbo jumbo, the poor swods of the army and the irregulars would believe they were invincible. This is a trick that has been tried on armies before, and, oft-times, it boomerangs. So I sweated and waited and then, as the murs ran away through the glass eye of time, I jerked up as though in that confined stinking sweaty-hot place someone had flung a bucket of ice water over me.

Fool!

Of course—the house was empty. Dayra was flying in to attend the ceremony. That was where I would find her—not here.

Chagrined at my own stupidity—more than chagrined—raging with a vicious intemperate self-scorn, I swung down from the roof and dropped into the street. The town was practically deserted. Everyone had gone to mass in the wide space surrounding the temple. In that temple, that blasphemous Temple of Hockwafernes, that was where I should be.

A passing Och halted as I called to him. His six limbs trembled under the weight of a sack, and he wore the gray breechclout.

"What time does the ceremony begin, slave?"

"Master—a bur after mid—"

I jerked a thumb and he staggered off. My face must have scared him clean through.

Time, then, for an errand...

That errand took me over the town wall contemptuous of the guards. One saw me and shouted, and I bellowed back a rigmarole about a message for Jiktar Haslam, and blast your eyes, you rast, and so ran fleetly across the dirt toward the leather tents. The quietness everywhere lay a strangeness over the camp. Not all the army by any means had been invited to attend the ceremony, even to stand outside the temple, for that would have been an impossibility given the numbers; but enough had gone to leave the rest feeling lackluster and out of it. They would partake of the good news to be bought by occult means, and so did not complain more than soldiers ordinarily do. Which is to say they grumbled and cursed most fearsomely.

Nalgre and Dolan were not at their tent. The camp slave cringed back as I ripped out my gear. It was all there. I strapped on my weapons. I did not have a rapier and main gauche; all the rest I had and intended to use if need be. Then I hared off back to the town, having to dodge down a side avenue of tents as a search party ran past, no doubt alerted by the sentry on the walls I had shouted at.

Gigantic gong notes began to reverberate from the temple.

I had to hurry.

The cape I swathed about myself attracted no attention, being similar to a thousand worn by the swods, and the cased bowstave easily passed for a spear. The crowds outside the temple moved like a cornfield in the breeze.

The suns shone. A wind blew the dust. The noise susurrated like waves on pebbles. I pushed through, gently, gradually working my way toward the front. If this Opaz-forsaken temple was like most there would be a side way in. It would be guarded, of course.

There was a small side door, and there was a guard.

The door opened easily enough after the guard lay scattered about, and the door slammed harshly in the faces of the shocked men who had witnessed the fury of sudden destruction that had fallen on the guard detail.

As I sprang four at a time up the spiral tower steps it occurred to me, wryly, that all my careful planning might as well have never taken place. So much for the good San Blarnoi.

The stairs led onto a balcony and I peered between carved stones onto the scene below. This was not planned at all.

The vibrant gong strokes rang still in the air. But the gong hung silent. Men moved below on the dais, men in garish costumes. I checked them all, swiftly, judging them to be priests or sorcerers engaged about their diabolical pastime, and raked my eyes over the gathered mass of people.

Where was Dayra?

Then, the destructive thought hit me, would I, could I, recognize her? A girl I'd never seen? Born when I was four hundred light years away from Kregen? I cursed the Star Lords then, and went on looking intently at the gathered people.

The temple was, truly, a marvel of architecture. The people filled it tightly, so that not a speck of floor was visible. The dais stood high at the center, and incense rose, stinking. Grotesque carvings entwined obscene forms. A crystal ovoid lifted at the center of the dais, draped in black and purple hangings, with golden tassels. Bells were ringing now, bells twirling and clanging in the hands of girls, half naked, dancing and twirling around the catafalque.

Like Bacchantes, with swirling hair and naked rosy limbs they danced and pranced, gyrating, ringing their bells, arousing everyone to a feverish anticipation.

Trylon Udo stepped forward. His costume was a sumptuous blaze of jewels. He lifted his arms high into the air and the bells ceased their clanging and the nymphs ceased their gyrations, although as they stood they swayed rhythmically like fronds of seaweed.

He began to speak in a high chanting voice.

Someone would be doing something about the guard detail now; the locked door would be forced, more guards would pile up the spiral stairs. Other guards would block all the exits. I moved around the high balcony, and found half a dozen more sentries who died quickly and cleanly. Now I could see down onto the catafalque more clearly. Beside the trylon stood the Hawkwa necromancer, San Uzhiro. Clad all in purple with golden tassels, he presented a grave, chilling picture of absolute dedication to the occult forces beyond the bounds of normal human knowledge.

Udo's words formed merely the prelude, in which he promised much and, chiefly, that his army would be invincible.

Then San Uzhiro stepped forward upon the dais below the catafalque.

With shocked gasps of surprise from the congregation, abrupt and brilliant bursts of flame and colored smoke shot up from the crystal ovoid. It glowed with an uncanny inner light, like torches seen through rain-spattered windows.

"Behold!" thundered Uzhiro. Every word rang and vaulted in echoing clarity around the wide temple. "Behold the corpse of San Guiskwain! San Guiskwain the Witherer, San Guiskwain na Stackwamor. Behold and marvel. Behold and tremble."

The people trembled in all truth. This Guiskwain, a most highly remarked sorcerer of Vallia, had lived and died no man knew how long ago, but it was certainly more than two and a half thousand seasons. And here he was, perfectly preserved in his crystal ovoid, his form and features showing clear and clearer as the lights spurted up. Here was sorcery at its most dire.

For Uzhiro waved his arms, sweating, chanting cadences of power, sprinkling dust, sending ripples of fear through the throng. We all knew what he was doing. The guards chasing me would have left off doing that; they would be transfixed by the awful powers being unleashed in this place. Everyone craned to see, barely breathing, as Uzhiro chanted on and the corpse within the crystal coffin upon the catafalque grew in clarity and all might see the thunderous expression on that lowering face.

That was a mystery, how plainly the face was visible, even to me, high on the balcony. At that distance the other people's faces were mere blurs. But the ancient sorcerer's face glowed with supernatural tyranny.

The foul stench of the incense puffed high into the interior of the temple. The dome opened, it seemed, onto infinity itself, although common sense said that the myriad specks of light were merely painted spots of mineral-glittering pigments. The long low moaning chants of the acolytes, the rooted swaying rhythms of the temple maidens, the cloying stinks of incense, all were calculated to tear away the senses from the brain, to impose false images, to induce a phantasmagoria of hallucinations.

Did San Guiskwain the Witherer really open his eyes? Did he reach out a skeletal hand? Did a man dead two thousand five hundred seasons really return to life?

San Uzhiro chanted and he had no doubts. His commands imposed themselves on the multitude, so that they saw with his eyes and heard with his ears.

Guiskwain, dead yet alive, sat up in the crystal coffin and looked about, that skeletal arm raised admonishingly.

No one fainted, no one passed out. All were transfixed, held scarcely breathing by the sheer occult power. And a sense of darkness gathered and coalesced under the dome. A brooding sense of power beyond the grave, of a stubborn life that two and half millennia could not quench, of perverse defiance of the natural order of life and death pervaded the temple and puffed upward in the rotting miasma of swamps and the fetid air of tombs sealed against the light.

"He lives!" screamed Uzhiro. "San Guiskwain lives!"

The cry was taken up in a tumultuous swelling cacophony of voices raised in rapture.

"He lives!"

Here was the miracle. Here the proof of the necromancer's power.

"Through Guiskwain the Witherer shall the army become invincible!" screeched Uzhiro, flailing his arms. "Through the greatest sorcerer dead yet living shall the Hawkwas gain all! Guiskwain lives!"

The long moment of triumph hung fire. The darkest pits of a Kregan hell had been opened. Now all, everyone present, turned to gaze with rapt adoration upon the lowering, vindictive, ashen face of Guiskwain the Witherer.

Transcendental, sublime, blasphemous—call it what you will. It was certain sure that all gathered here and held in this hallucinated trance believed with all their hearts.

But—was this hallucination? Was this trickery? Or was a long-dead necromancer really revived, brought back to life, dragged once again into the light so as to destroy all I cared for in Vallia? Could the trick be no trick at all?

Did Guiskwain the Witherer, dead two and a half millennia, live?

Sixteen

The Fight Below the Voller

Whether he lived or was dead made no real difference.

Whether he still moldered away in his crystal coffin or whether he had been blasphemously raised by necromantic power into a semblance of full-blooded life did not matter.

What mattered was the belief, the impression, the effect.

These people believed.

The long low moaning shudder passed over them like a rashoon of the Eye of the World. They bowed. In a giant sighing rustle and the jangle of weapons and accoutrements they bowed their heads, crouched, extending their arms in swath after swath of ranked submission.

Was my daughter down there now, one of that hypnotized host? Did Dayra bow her head and tremble with all the others at the sight and stink of a long-dead wizard raised from the grave?

How in the name of Makki-Grodno's disgusting diseased tripes could I know?

I was shaking. Sweat ran down my forehead and stung into my eyes. I blinked, swallowed, cursed—all the actions of an idiot without a thought in his thick vosk skull of a head.

A girl in the russets and armor of a Battle Maiden ran lightly up past the half-naked temple girls. She spoke rapidly to Udo. His head went up; he gestured to Uzhiro. They conferred. Then Uzhiro swung back and called for everyone to rise and stare upon the sublime face and form of Guiskwain.

Trylon Udo stepped forward. He held up a hand. He spoke with tremendous emotion, forcefully, jolting these people.

"Now are we invincible in battle. Now the potent force of San Guiskwain the Witherer is with us. He will waste away our enemies. Long and long have the Hawkwas waited for this time. And now it is here." His lifted hand gripped into a fist. "There is more. The army from Hamal landed in the south of Vallia has gained a great victory. The hosts of the emperor are withered away, his warriors strew the ground in windrows, their blood waters the dirt. This is a further sign! Guiskwain is with us and nothing can stand in our path."

I had to stand peering through the stone bars of the balcony and listen, grinding down my nature that sought to burst out in bestial ferocity.

So the cramphs had come from Hamal, the bitter foe of Vallia, and not from Pandahem. An armada of skyships had brought them; that was a safe conclusion. And the emperor, Delia's father, had been worsted. Had his bodyguard, the Crimson Bowmen, bought and paid for in red gold, betrayed him?

What of the men loyal to the emperor? What of the Blue Mountains, of Delphond, of my own Archers of Valka who had been sent for from Evir? What had happened down south?

And Delia?

Dayra... Dayra...

I had selfishly sought out my daughter here, and in that space of time I had been away from Vondium the empire might have fallen. Udo was shouting again, flushed, triumphant, overweening.

"Our own fleet of airboats will fly us south. We will join with our friends from Hamal. We will march upon Vondium and take that great city and utterly destroy all who stand in our path. All hail to San Guiskwain! All hail to the Hawkwas!"

Here once again was the hand of Phu-si-Yantong. I was convinced of that. He had extended the tentacles of his authority through Hamal, manipulating the pallans around the Empress Thyllis. He had provided the money and the weapons and now a fleet of vollers for Trylon Udo to take and sack Vondium. And, when the time was ripe, Phu-si-Yantong's tools, in the guise of Stromich Ranjal and Zankov, would strike down Udo and take all for the greatest puissance of Phu-si-Yantong.

It must be so.

"Sink me!" I burst out. "If you are alive, you necromantic kleesh, you'll soon be dead again!"

The bowstave hissed from the cover, it seemed to string itself of its own will. The blue-fletched arrow nocked and the bow bent in a long sinuous flow of motion. The steel pile glittered. I loosed. The shaft flew sweetly. Clear across that wide space under the dome the arrow sped, piercing through the winding veils of incense smoke, drove hard and savagely full into San Guiskwain's breast.

I saw it. I saw the arrow curve upward. It ricocheted up with a high singing note of steel against crystal. It curved to fall away and be lost among the gathered host.

And San Guiskwain remained upright, unmoved, unharmed.

"By Krun!" I shouted. "Sorcery and more sorcery. I'll have you yet, you cramph."

Twice more I loosed and twice the sharp steel-tipped shafts caromed with that high crystal ringing from the unholy form of the dead wizard who yet lived.

Guards boiled along the balcony toward me. They were men. If I had to fight I had to fight. But, for the last time, and even as I loosed knowing the gesture was futile and useless, I cast a last shaft at the blasphemous form of Guiskwain.

Had I used the few brains I boast I should have shot at Uzhiro. Trylon Udo was a mere pawn. But my incensed fury was all directed at that towering, impregnable, loweringly obscene form of a living dead man.

Then, after a handful of shafts into the first of the charging guards it was handstrokes along the high balcony.

The shortsword, built by Naghan the Gnat to specifications drawn up from careful measurement of the deadly shortsword of my Clansmen of Segesthes, chunked in gleaming silver and ripped out gleaming red. I put my shoulder down and bashed into the guards, anxious to carve a way through them and reach the outside air. The notion of finding Dayra in all this hullabaloo had still not left me, although I was having to face the fact that with all my plans gone wrong I was hardly likely to find her now.

Four Rapas tried to work as a team and do for me. No doubt they were accustomed to quick victory utilizing their intricate teamwork on the battlefield or in camp brawls. But a fighting man must tailor his work to circumstances. The balcony was narrow. Even as the first Rapa prepared to open the gambit and feint away I slashed his beak off, burst past him, sank the blade into the next one—just far enough—ducked a wild clanxer swipe and so chunked left, right, and felled the other two.

They couldn't know, of course—but anyone who did would understand why the shortsword gleamed in my fist and the deadly Krozair longsword snugged still in its scabbard.

The guards expected me to go one way, and so I went the other. A narrow slot opened in the wall, one of the many runnels all these huge old buildings possess, crevices between facing walls, cavities under domes, tunnels left for the maintenance that must unceasingly go on to stop the whole fabric from toppling to destruction. With a last flicker of the short-sword I ducked down the slot.

The first fall was some ten feet and I hit with a thump. On my feet in an instant I padded between rough brick courses, a thread of light wanly illuminating the patches of damp and the mold. The way led via wooden ladders and dusty passages downward. The sounds of pursuit followed me. I stepped past a skeleton—it had been a plump wallpitix, poisoned by the temple caretakers, and crept away here to die—and pushed on boldly. Wherever the way led I was sure to meet guards.

Brittle bones crunched underfoot. A whole nest of wallpitixes, those furry, bright-eyed household scavengers, had died here. Beyond them and around a harsh masonry corner where the dirt had been cobbled over, a lenken door, banded with bronze, barred the way. I gave the door a look and put my shoulder to it.

With a creak like some poor soul being crushed between millstones, it grated open. Red and green light flooded in. Cautiously, I poked my head out, the blade raised, ready to defend myself. Around me stretched the ranked arcades of stone coffins. Some had toppled over and a detritus of bones and skulls littered the stone-flagged floor. I had penetrated below the temple and entered the crypt. That seemed apt at the time. Thought-fully, I closed the door and shot the massive iron bolts, turning the heads over with a succession of sharp and satisfactory snaps. That took care of the bloodthirsty soldiers at my back. Now for the no-less bloodthirsty war-riors in front.

The light streamed from tinted fireglass crystals set in niches along the coves. I guessed San Uzhiro had been down here earlier, needing light, to fetch out the crystal coffin of Guiskwain the Witherer. There were telltale marks in the dust. A skull rolled away as I marched across the flags.

The eerie effects of witnessing a corpse brought back to life began to wear off. I found I was thinking again.

I have always said that if you can't join them, beat them. As a principle of life on Kregen, I think that well-exemplified in the account of what befell Dray Prescot there. But, now, it would be convenient to join them for a space.

The fusty smell in the crypt led by way of the almost imperceptible wash of fresher air to the outer door. By its configuration I judged it stood at the bottom of a flight of steps cut into the earth leading up to ground level. Carefully, easing the door open a whisker at a time, I peered out.

No matter how many times I tangle with guards, I am forced to fight sentries, hide from or dispatch watchmen, I can never think of them as mere lay figures. Guards on duty face a thankless task. At times it seems they are there merely to be slain by the princes and captains who seek to go where they should not. But a guard is a man, doing a rotten job, and glad when his duty is over and he can traipse off to the guardroom and take off at least a little of his equipment and put his feet up for a time, until he is due to roust out again.

Guards stand in gaudy uniforms with ornate spears and are ripe targets. No—I do not devalue guards, no matter that I have been forced to deal harshly with them in my time.

The guards at the top of the steps were Chuliks. This complicated matters from the point of view of joining them, and made the physical exertion of dealing with them that much more hazardous. Chuliks are not apims. They are diffs. They are powerful, ferocious warriors, trained from the earliest age in the manipulation of weapons, lacking in the lighter side of humanity, abhorred except as mercenary warriors. This, at the time and, I admit, to my shame, made the moral side of the problem that much easier of resolution.

I could not join this little lot—so I was forced to beat them.

The fight boiled up along the steps and out onto a grassy sward between upflung buttresses. The courtyard closed in with gray stone walls. It formed one of the many surrounding enclosures penned by the cyclopean walls that uplifted and supported the bulk of the temple. Roughly wiped, the shortsword slapped back into its scabbard.

The Krozair longsword twinkled out, and flamed silver for only a heartbeat, and then turned into the bloody brand of destruction that shears through all opposition.

"Cut the cramph down!" And: "By Likshu the Treacherous! The man is a devil!" And: "In the name of Father Chalkush of the Iron Brand do not let him pass."

Blades clashed and slithered, blood flew, we leaped and contorted across the grass, Chuliks spun away, pierced, slashed, degutted, the longsword flamed a circle of savage destruction. The very size of those towering walls deadened sound. We trampled across the grass and I had to skip and jump right smartly, for Chuliks are rightly renowned as superb fighting men.

But for the dead Rapa paktun's armor I would have been nicked a couple of times. But, in the end, I had them all, and so could plunk the dripping point of the Krozair brand into the turf and spell a moment or two, breathing deeply, gulping the air which stank now with the tang of freshly spilled blood.

The Chuliks wore the colors of Gelkwa. The colors were green, silver, black and yellow, arranged in the Hawkwa fashion as a regular pattern of circles, silver, black and yellow, upon their green sleeves. Finding a tunic that was not too bloody I stripped my own tunic off—or, rather, the tunic that had been Rojashin's—and donned the garment of Gelkwa. All the same, the kax that had served me well went back on. The letting out of the shoulder straps and pauldrons had not affected the harness's efficacy. The longbow could be unstrung and slid back into its sleeve. How long that would pass as a spear remained to be seen; it had deceived before. Settling a fresh helmet on my head—gaudy with colors, heavy with feathers—and curling the long cape about me I surveyed the scene.

A grassy sward filled with dead Chuliks. Blood. Stink. Flies. And me, Dray Prescot, helplessly and hopelessly looking for a wayward daughter, and all Vallia in flames.

Through the far gateway I came out onto the temple precincts and was able to mingle casually with the departing throngs. The talk centered on one subject only. I walked with bowed head, as though profoundly affected by the awesome occurrences within the Temple of Hockwafernes.

I felt that all Vallia was alight. Once the emperor was seen to falter, once a blow was struck against his authority, many people would stand forth from the shadows and openly challenge him. You know of many of the parties and factions; there were more, people determined to have their own way with the Empire of Vallia and to the Ice Floes of Sicce with anyone who opposed them. There had been a battle and the emperor had been defeated. I wondered if he had been there in person or had sent a general to deal with the invasion. I wondered if the old devil was still alive.

My course was now clear cut. Despite all my ineffective attempts to see Dayra and to rescue her, I had achieved nothing. Even this corpse revived to blasphemous life lived and I had been unable to send him decently back to the grave. Between Dayra and Delia I was being forced to choose, and the alternatives were odious, agonizing. But—Delia. Yes I must assure myself she was safe first. If her father went down in ruin, Delia would become the prey of the leems prowling and scenting blood.

Somehow, I sensed that Dayra had survived with the wild bunch with whom she ran because she knew how to handle both herself and them. She would not be suddenly in dire peril now, just because I had not seen her. Why should my arrival make any difference to her? After all, I had not affected her life up until now. She had lived and grown to womanhood without me. So, feeling the deep hurtful wounds pressing in on my spirit, I set off to see about stealing a flier.

The careful watch of the guards lay all at my rear now. The temple was still the focal point. How long I would have before that dreadful court-yard was discovered I did not know. But a flier I needed and a flier I would have.

At the least, I have some skill in stealing vollers.

The Chulik guard had included a Hikdar among their number and I assumed he had been checking up on his posts. That was the last item of military procedure he would ever perform. A Hikdar—nearly enough to an Earthly captain in that he commands a pastang, a company of around eighty men—is the first of the more important ranks, and it is possible for wealthy young men, well-connected and with military aptitude, to enter the army directly as ob-Hikdars. What the Deldars say about that may be imagined. So I had hung the Hikdar's rank insigne on my harness and was prepared to be somewhat blunt to any swod who offered to halt me.

Everywhere a transformation had swept over Trylon Udo's army. Where they had been a collection of irregulars, leavened with a few profession-als, and aware of that and apprehensive of their own capacities and of the emperor's Crimson Bowmen, now they were a united force, filled with a surging confidence that would carry them on despite casualties to ulti-mate victory.

With sufficient spear carriers to hurl forward, and with the hard-core elite troops to follow swiftly on, even well-disciplined enemies may be overcome. It is all zeal, morale, burning conviction, the sense of invulner-ability through belief.

And the emperor had already been once defeated in the field.

My duty, clearly, lay in Vondium and the rapid creation of forces to withstand the two-pronged attack Phu-si-Yantong had thrown against Vallia.

As I walked steadily on, avoiding the areas near the leather tent of Nal-gre and Dolan, fliers cruised into view, high, then circling and descending. The transports were gathering. I watched, counting, estimating, storing away information. To amass an aerial fleet of this size, and with vollers of this capacity, was a task beyond the resources of a trylon of the North-eastern part of Vallia. Once again the hand of the Wizard of Loh showed itself.

One of the tragedies of the situation was that Udo desired self-deter-mination for the Northeast and his Hawkwas. Yantong's ambitions ranged further, for through his tools he would rule Vallia himself. Udo was expendable, and where men and women are concerned that is a concept that always fills me with disgust. And yet—and yet it is a tactic used more than once. But, always I think, with volunteers. Not a pleasant business...

The fliers were parked neatly and I strolled along marking out the small flier I would take, judging from her lines whether she was a swift craft. She would have to serve me well and not break down. And then I smiled—just a little. If Yantong had provided these vollers from the arsenals of Hamal then they would be first-class, they would function, they would not break down. Capital!

Now I have indicated that very many folk of Vallia believed their Prince Majister was a blown-up paper tiger, a fake Hyr-Jikai, holding a reputation he had not earned and did not deserve. This belief had been fostered by my long absence. And my enemies had no doubt put these rumors about. Phu-si-Yantong would know differently, Rosil Yasi, the Kataki Strom, knew differently from personal experience. His twin brother, the Stromich Ranjal, would therefore presumably know better, too.

I overlooked that fact, and as a consequence prepared to stroll up to the little voller and send her racing into the sky without any fuss.

There were guards about, as was natural, and volmen working on the craft preparing them for the triumphant expedition south. These people I ignored and walked steadily toward my flier.

A group of guards and volmen and Jikai Vuvushis stood gaping upward as a large flier circled preparatory to landing. Others looked aloft. This was my time. I advanced toward the craft I had selected more rapidly. Unfortunately she was not at the end of a row; half a dozen other craft surrounded her.

The Fristles jumped me when I had but a score of paces to go.

Scimitars upraised, their cat-faces distorted, shrilling spitting war cries, they flung themselves at me.

"The rast! The Prince Majister!" They screeched their rage and triumph. "He is here! Ho! Guards! The Prince Majister!"

In an instant I was surrounded by a glittering hedge of steel.

This was inopportune. The longsword flamed out, striking away scimitars, slashing cat-faces, carving a path toward the voller. More guards were running up. The whole place came astir like an ants' nest. I started running and slashing in real earnest. So near the voller I was not going to be denied.

That particular pack of Fristles went down. I reached the voller. Before putting a hand to the coaming and leaping aboard I swung about. The old Krozair Disciplines snapped into place. Four Undurker archers were lifting their laminated bows, were letting fly. The Krozair longsword swatted this way and that and the short brightly-tufted arrows slapped away harmlessly.

Heading the group coming up from the side ran Zankov. I wouldn't mind spitting him; but beside him raced the dark and sinister form of Stromich Ranjal. That wicked tailblade lifted high. The Battle Maidens were there also—I saw Leona nal Larravur, and Ros, and Firn, and Karina the Quick, the bandage awry, pelting along. I had no wish to slay them.

This group fouled the range for the Undurkers. Those diffs with their supercilious canine-faces ran up, trying to spot me and shaft me properly this time.

Zankov was yelling: "He is a coward. A no-account! A nulsh. Take him alive."

"I'll stick him through!" screeched Leona.

"I'll take his eyes out first!" screeched Ros. The left-hand claw glittered menacingly.

I leaped up into the voller and slammed the levers over to full forward and full lift.

The airboat lifted two feet and then halted with a shuddering surge, a violent constriction of effort, hung swinging. I stuck my head over the side.

"By Vox!" I yelled, baffled.

The cramphs had affixed thick chains to the keel and locked them firmly into stakes driven deeply into the ground.

I was anchored fast.

Then they were on me.

Even as Zankov hurled himself forward, his rapier a glinting bar of light, Ranjal yelled: "Beware, Zankov! He is a warrior—"

"A bag of vomit!" shouted Zankov and slashed wildly at me.

I slid the blow and put my left fist into his face. He fell backward from the voller with a scream.

Ranjal flicked his tail at me and then hauled it back just in time. The longsword hissed through air.

"Let me get at him!" Ros was screeching.

"Let me!" screamed Leona. She knew how to use a rapier and the thin blade snickered past my ribs. Mind you, that was a waste, for the rapier would never puncture through the kax.

I clouted her over the head—very gently.

An Undurker arrow whistled at my head and I ducked and flicked its fellow away with the longsword. A Rapa tried to climb onboard and I cleft his head down. There was nothing else for it. I would have to go overboard and release the chains.

With a wild whoop—a deliberately theatrical war cry which was not, in those circumstances, an entire waste of breath—I jumped from the flier.

A short and violent scuffle ensued in which various guards staggered away holding bloody fingers to various portions of their anatomy, or who slumped to the blood-soaked grass, and then I was familiar with the chains hooked into the stakes. One came free and the longsword bit around in a flailing slash that left a grotesque wake of lopped limbs. This was not fancy any more, this was sheer savagery in the attempt to remain alive. Zankov came at me again—he had courage, that one—and I hit him again with the hilt and the blade shocked on to skewer through the neck of a Rapa following him. Zankov dropped and I put a foot on his wrist, grinding fist and sword hilt into the dirt.

Firn tried to spit me and I had to knock her away.

In the next split second I had my hand on the last remaining chain.

A blow thunked down on my helmet and I whirled, the longsword slicing, and a Chulik—who should have known better—staggered away looking surprised. He collapsed. And then—somehow, somehow—with devastating speed, the lithe feline form of Ros appeared before me. She disdained her rapier. Her left hand whipped for my face.

My own left hand leaped from the longsword hilt and caught her wrist. I felt the harsh steel splines. Her face—that glorious, glowing, superbly beautiful face—bore down on me with hateful virulence.

Under my foot Zankov thrust himself wildly sideways. He squirmed. With a vicious grinding twist I tramped down on his arm and he screamed.

And then—and then I felt a spiteful cutting agony pierce through the fingers of my left hand. With an oath I let Ros go. Along the metal splines sharp teeth stood out, and gleamed wetly with my blood.

I could have thrust her through then with the longsword.

I did not.

I staggered as Zankov writhed around, yelling.

The cruel curved talons slashed toward me. I warded them off and Ros whipped her hand back in a cunning backhand blow that revolved at the last minute and so brought the claw in a long razoring slash down my face. The slicing blow stung.

A Chulik tried to degut me from the side and the longsword twitched and he fell away a dying man.

"You devil!" gasped Ros.

Zankov was screaming now, screaming all the bile and viciousness out, screeching words—impossible words.

"Kill the rast! Slash his eyes out!"

Again the claw razored toward my face.

"Kill him!" screamed Zankov. "Dayra! Kill him. Slay him for good and all, Dayra! *Dayra!*"

Seventeen

The Gathering of Shadows

I looked down into lustrous brown Vallian eyes. I saw that glowing face. I saw and I could not understand.

Almost, almost, then, I was a dead man.

But the longsword, of itself, sliced and slashed and the two Chuliks screamed and spun away, bloody wrecks.

The blood dripped down my face from the razor slashings of the steel claw.

"Dayra?"

Zankov screamed again: "Now is your chance, Dayra! Slay the rast and have done."

I stepped back, out of the lethal swing of the claw and kicked Zankov in the side of the head. He slumped. My left hand reached for the last hooked chain.

"So mother was right, after all, and these fools wrong," she said, this girl, this Ros the Claw who was my little daughter Dayra. "For no other man could do what you have done and lived." She lifted the steel tiger talons on which my blood glimmered darkly. "You are a Hyr-Jikai."

"Only a fool would do what I have done," I said.

"That is sooth."

"You have fallen among evil company—Dayra. Come with me. I must go and see if Delia your mother is safe."

"She will be. I have given orders—"

I broke in, exasperated, still dizzy with the shock. "Don't you know what kind of villain this rast is? He means to kill all of us—all the family—"

She shook her head. "Not true."

"If only I had known... They said you were arriving today."

"How do you know that? I do as I please. I take orders from no one—from no man—least of all from a father I have never known."

This could be resolved later, for now soldiers pressed on and time was on a short fuse. I gripped the harsh steel hook ready to slip it over the ring. "Come with me, Dayra. Your mother—"

"You are not fit to speak her name! Leave her out of it."

An arrow pitched into the blood-soaked ground. Another punched through the fabric of the airboat by my head.

"You must hurry, Dayra, or they will shaft you, too."

"Go, go away! Run! You have been running all your life so go on running. You betrayed us all and you will continue to betray us, no matter what you say. Go before I slash your eyes out."

But since she had understood that I, at last, knew who she was, she had made not a single move to attack me as she had been so savagely doing before.

A quick glimpse of booted feet and the glint of a bladed tail past the keel of the flier warned me I could dally no longer. If this wayward sprite of mine would not come home with me, she would not. And if I tarried here arguing I would be dead. I gripped the hooked chain fiercely in my left hand and flicked the longsword about and so deflected an Undurker arrow.

"Then I bid you Remberee, Dayra. I shall tell your mother I have seen you." The metal hook lifted. Around me now the guards were closing in, confident I was at last done for. There were very many of them. I could not slay them all. But not a one of them showed anxiety to be first.

With the incongruity of the situation strong upon me, I said: "Take care of yourself—daughter."

She spat at me, and slashed the claw and I wondered as I lifted the hook if she would, finally, have tried to do for me at last.

The flier jerked away as the last chain came free. Gripping the hook I was wrenched aloft, dangling and swinging under the keel of the voller, hurtling away and up into the air.

A few arrows winged after me; but the voller leaped away so fast and gained height so rapidly the arrows fell away uselessly. Like a parcel of laundry at the end of a rope I was whisked up. Climbing the chain proved tricky; but without sheathing the longsword I managed that maneuver and tumbled over the leather-wrapped coaming. Presently I took the flier under command and set the controls for full speed for Vondium. Udo and Ranjal and Zankov—if his headache improved—would send the pursuit after me; but I had chosen exceeding well and the voller outran all pursuit.

When I considered what I had just discovered I was aghast. I was beset by confusion, unable to believe it had really happened, and yet knowing that what Dayra said was true, true, damn the black Star Lords to hell and beyond.

The only sane course for me to follow was to do what I could for Vallia. I could not put out of my mind that terrible experience—how her claws had slashed—but I could attempt to comfort myself with the reflection that she had lived this long without me and so could live a while longer until I managed to persuade her I was not entirely the rogue, the cheat, the liar, the deceiver she dubbed me. I was those things; but not in the way she meant.

That was a dark and dismal flight back to Vondium. The claw cuts in my face could be cleaned up and in time they would heal without a scar; but the real scars on me they would leave might never heal. My own daughter! But—at the end, she had stood back. She had made no further effort to stop me. She had bid me go.

Better, I suppose, to be thrown out than to be killed, to a pragmatic kind of fellow, although the more sensitive might well dramatically prefer death. To me, they are the fools, for although one can see their artistic point of view, they do rather show their contempt of the gift of life, which is not to be taken lightly. Perhaps a taste of the Heavenly Mines would cure them...

So I forced myself to look at this unnatural situation with Dayra's eyes. She was perfectly entitled to her view of me. I fancied the company she kept could be revealed to her as the bunch of villains they were and their dark purposes destroy her belief in them. That was one area in which she could be straightened out. That was general. In the private and family quarrel she had with me—that was something else again.

Even then, in those bleak moments of near despair, I once again forced myself to consider the concept that Dayra's companions were honorable people, working for what they truly believed in, and seeing Delia and the emperor and me and the family as villains overripe for the chopping. It was difficult. But, as Zair is my witness, I tried.

And, by Vox, it was not too difficult where the emperor was concerned, either...

All these worries must for the moment be pushed aside. However difficult that might be, I had to realize that all Vallia could be drenched in blood. I had to do what I could to prevent that. Also, it would not hurt to remind myself I had two other daughters, not to mention three sons, to worry over...

All the same, the story of how Dayra had spurned the Sisters of the Rose and taken the name of Ros and learned the trick of using the Claw and become involved with Zankov and that gang would make a fascinating task to unravel and learn. Like me, she used aliases as it suited her. In that, at the least, the very littlest least, she was like me.

It was damn small comfort.

Vondium hove into view and the place was burning in many areas, the fierce orange flames reflecting in the canals, the proud buildings on their hills and islands burning and collapsing. I stared, shocked back to present crises.

The long straggling black fingers of fugitives clogged roads leading away from the capital, the canals lay deserted with all the narrow boats gone, and not a flier sped through the sky apart from my own sole voller I had stolen from Udo.

The palace was not burning and a Pachak guard ringed it to prevent looting. The devoted loyalty of the Pachaks through their honor system of nikobi was never better demonstrated.

I landed in the great kyro before the palace. A guard checked me quickly and efficiently—those guards again, men, just men, doing a job, and faithful, not mere lay figures to be spitted and chopped and cast down all bloody and forgotten—and I was led off to their Chuktar.

A few quick glances told me that all the Pachaks hired by the emperor for duties in various wings of the palace had been collected together. Even the Pachaks from the wing given over to the use of Delia and myself, for with the Chuktar stood our Pachak paktun Jiktar, Laka Pa-Re. He greeted me warmly. The Chuktar, the highest of the military ranks apart from princes and kovs and generals and kings and their like, was Pola Je-Du. He looked more haggard than I liked.

"Lahal, prince. The situation, as you see, is ripe."

"Lahal, Pola Je-Du. Your orders?"

"To guard the palace. Since the defeats the emperor—"

"Defeats? I had heard of one."

"The Hamalese fought well, so I am told. The Vallian army was defeated in detail. The Crimson Bowmen fought brilliantly, those that marched. The others—"

I looked at Laka Pa-Re, remembering how he had warned me that the guards were being bribed. Laka nodded. "The guards who took bribes were weeded out. Naghan Vanki saw to that. But the damage had been done."

"And the various elements disaffected in the capital and the provinces took the chance to rise. There has been much mischief, prince." The Pachak Chuktar pulled his moustache. Smoke billowed up from a dome across the kyro and the distant sounds of shouting and the crashings of masonry reached us, thin and attenuated. "The emperor marched out with all that was left to him. For us, we guard the palace."

Not for the first time I wondered how the emperor had ever remained emperor for so long. With these Pachaks a great deal might be done—and then I reconsidered. There were perhaps five hundred of them. Against the Hamalese army, against the mobs and the irregulars and the mercenaries of the factions, would they have made all that much difference? The Pachaks would fight in their superb fashion when the first looters arrived with whichever army reached Vondium first. As a reserve, as a hard core, they would serve. Maybe the emperor was still the crafty old devil I thought him.

"And the Princess Majestrix?"

The question was followed by a general shaking of heads in the small, round, unadorned Pachak helmets. No one had any news of the Princess Majestrix.

More information was given me—of the arrests of men hitherto considered loyal to the emperor, of the way Queen Lushfymi more and more obsessed him to the exclusion of all else, of the riots, the burnings and lootings and killings, of the exodus from the capital as the various hostile armies closed in, Hamalese, rebels, insurgents. And I knew a fresh and powerful host inspired by a revived corpse could now be added to that number...

It seemed to me that Phu-si-Yantong was drawing ever closer to his insane dream. But he could not control all the foes of Vallia advancing on Vondium. In that, paradoxically, lay a slender hope.

In that wide and grandiose kyro with its surrounding colonnades and superb architecture the slender line of Pachaks ringing the palace and the small knot of officers all looked fragile, alone, gray chalk marks against the brilliance. In the radiance of the suns a chill wind blew dust across the flagstones.

A confused noise drew our attention to the far side of the square. The sound of a multitude, the ragged tramp of feet, the jingle of weapons, the creaking of carts, made the officers walk along the ranks, tautening up their men. The Pachaks moved with the quiet, well-ordered air of men waiting for business. They were ready. They would earn their hire.

Calmly the Chuktar gave a last few orders. I said: "I will stand and fight with you, Chuktar Pola Je-Du, if you will."

"I will it so, prince, and deem it an honor."

No victorious army of irregulars, no raging army of mercenaries broke into the square. A beaten army debouched and began to straggle across the stones. They were wounded, and dusty, wrapped in bloody bandages, exhausted. At their head mounted on a drooping-headed zorca rode the emperor.

This was an army shattered and near-destroyed.

Krahnik-drawn carts brought in the seriously wounded. A few flags drooped here and there, ripped and bloodied standards. A couple of squadrons of totrix cavalry retained their guidons. But for all else these men formed a mere mob.

The emperor rode slowly toward the group of high ranking Pachak officers. At his side, mounted on a pure white zorca, rode Queen Lushfymi. She wore armor. Somehow, it did not look absurd; gilded breastplate, flaunting helmet crowned with the red and yellow of Vallia, a jingling assortment of weapons buckled about her and her mount. I stood, grim-faced, prepared to be exceedingly nasty.

Eighteen

The Hand of Phu-Si-Yantong

In the emperor's private inner sanctum he placed his goblet of wine on the polished table and banged a fist down on his knee.

"I'm not finished yet, son-in-law, so don't take that tone with me. Queen Lushfymi thinks we have as good a chance as any of defeating these rasts from Hamal."

Only a few of us had gathered here after the shattered remnants of the army had been attended to as best we could. The Pachaks still stood guard. Now Queen Lush, half a dozen of the pallans who remained, Chuktar Wang-Nalgre-Bartong and myself conferred with the emperor. The news was as bad as it could be without being total disaster. In detail all the forces arrayed against the foes of the emperor had been defeated.

"Kov Layco Jhansi will yet bring in a victory, son-in-law. Once he disposes of these scheming rasts of Falinur the rest will see they had better toe the line."

"Falinur?" I forced myself to remain calm.

"Aye! The kovnate you made me give to your so-called friend Seg Segutorio. They have risen like flies and march to war—and where is this precious Seg Segutorio, Kov of Falinur? Skulked off as you do—or does he lead his host against me?"

The emperor's hand curled in a claw about the stem of the goblet. I couldn't tell him that Seg had been hurled back to his home in Erthyrdrin after his baptism in the Sacred Pool—banished like all my friends to their homes. So, instead, I said: "And what of Vomanus? His Kovnate of Vindelka marches with Falinur. They quarrel over Vinnur's Garden, so—"

"Vomanus? That great rascal. Where is he you may well ask."

I judged that many a wight had taken himself off from the capital in these troublesome times; but I felt disappointment with Vomanus. He was a careless fellow, true; but he was half-brother to Delia...

All the time we spoke and argued and planned meaningless plans in the face of the catastrophe, Queen Lush sat upright, toying with her wine, looking at the emperor fixedly. When he glanced fondly at her she would smile. She wore a simple robe of a deep yellow, and not a scrap of jewelry. She looked different from the easy, casual, bitchy minx I had left here.

"Layco Jhansi will subdue the central provinces. The southwest awaits events. The southeast—" Here the emperor looked pointedly at Lykon Crimahan, the Kov of Forli. Him you have met before. Now he was the Pallan of the Treasury, the new pallan, for Pallan Rodway had long ago passed away and the last incumbent suffered from a cleavage where his neck should be.

Forli, often called the Blessed Forli, lies up an eastern tributary of the Great River and extends to the east coast opposite northern Veliadrin. Lykon Crimahan had no love for me. Yet, I believed he hewed to his own faith with the emperor, evil though he might be, and had the welfare of Vallia at heart, even though he had tried to obstruct my plans to build a great aerial fleet. So I waited for Crimahan to speak, ready with bitter, mocking words of my own.

"I can vouch for Forli, majister. As for the rest—they attack my lands. I would be there to fight for them; but—"

"Your duty is here, at the emperor's side," said Queen Lush.

Her face was bright, her eyes alive with passion. I looked away from her. Her influence, I felt sure, along with many other fighting men, had weakened the emperor, and yet the old devil was full of fight, firm in his resolve to go on with the struggle.

"And, Lykon Crimahan," I said, "where is the great fleet of skyships I wanted to build? Are your friends in Hamal pleased at your handiwork?"

He would have drawn his rapier and rushed on me; but the emperor put up a hand and bellowed, and protocol saved the fool.

"I am loyal to the emperor and Vallia, prince majister! I sit still under no insults—"

"Still, Kov Lykon. Remember the skyships we do not have when those from Hamal cast down their firepots upon the city."

"Our varters will shoot them down," said the emperor. He believed it, and he had taken part in the Battle of Jholaix.

"The Northeast is solidly against you—" I began.

"That I know."

"They fly an army here." I told them what I had learned. Barty had not reached Vondium. Probably his flier had broken down. In these last dark hours that witnessed the death of an empire Barty Vessler must take his own chances. Maybe he had gone home. I did not speak of my daughter Dayra who was called Ros the Claw.

"Trylon Udo. Very well. I have a high tree ready for him. As for this Zankov, he can be dealt with when they get here. I am the emperor, and I understand these foolish plots. By Vox! My emissaries are already hiring thousands of paktuns for me from overseas."

"By the time they arrive all will be over," said Chuktar Wang-Nalgre-Bartong. He licked his lips. He was a Bowman of Loh and he did not like to say what he had to say. "My men are loyal. They have been selected—"

"Aye," put in a pallan, fierce and intolerant and with a wounded arm in a sling. "The rest of the rasts took bribes."

The Chuktar was the last in a line of commanders of the Crimson Bowmen. He had been vouched for by Naghan Vanki, the emperor's spymaster. Now he roused himself again to say: "We fought. We fought as Bowmen of Loh can fight. But we were ambushed in detail—do not ask me how for it is a mystery. Our plans were divined. We had no chance. So, I repeat and with sorrow, I see no other course for us than honorable capitulation."

The Vallians glared at him. He was a mercenary, a hyr-paktun with the pakzhan glittering golden at his throat.

Softly, the emperor said: "And Chuktar, when you capitulate in all honor and take service with our foes, what becomes of us?"

"That is the way of the fall of empires," said Chuktar Bartong. Again he licked his lips. "It is all one in vaol-paol."

The wrangling went on. These men were like children whistling in the dark to keep their courage up. All except the emperor. There was about him a spirit I had not expected. He was far from cowed, disdaining defeat, eager to resume the struggle. A calm and supreme confidence radiated from him.

In those burs in his private sanctum as we planned against catastrophe, I understood how he could be the father of Delia.

The Chuktar of the Crimson Bowmen would from time to time shake his head and repeat: "We had no chance. All our movements were known in advance. No chance at all."

"And the northwest?" demanded the emperor briskly.

"Racter country," said a pallan with the exhausted and yet vicious air of a rast trapped in a spring cage. "The last reports remain unmodified. The Black Mountains and the Blue Mountains are bathed in blood. What will happen no one knows."

I felt the pang of that. The Black Mountains was Inch's kovnate, and the Blue Mountains—I forced myself to ask for details. All that was known was the northwest had tried to raise a host and the Blue Mountain Boys and the Black Mountain Men had barred the advance. After that, silence.

So the schemes of the Racters had not gone as they planned, then... The black and whites were waiting quietly in other areas, waiting to step in and take up the pieces after the holocaust. Well, the onkers, they did not know that Phu-si-Yantong was there to forestall them.

For, make no mistake, I felt, I sensed—I almost *knew*—that Phu-si-Yantong was this minute employing other agents to wreak his will in Vallia quite apart from the duped tools of his I had so far encountered.

So far there had seemed no good purpose in telling the emperor the truth of this Wizard of Loh. He would be best employed fighting each threat on the ground uncluttered by an overall fear. And, anyway, it was most likely he would not believe me.

"All known Racters have left the city," said Lykon Crimahan. His jaws rat-trapped shut, and his thin fuzz of dark beard below his chin, the prominent cheekbones, the malicious intelligence of his dark eyes, all conveyed the seething frustration and despair in him. At times of troubles before, he had contrived to be away on his estates. This time he was here, in the capital, Pallan of the Treasury; and this time the trouble was likely to be the biggest of the lot and final. That, at the least, was good for a laugh.

Now he opened that rat-trap mouth again to say with some evil satisfaction: "The Fegters rose to loot and burn and many of them were killed." He looked at me. "Your trip to the northeast was fortuitous, prince majister."

"Had I been here," I began. And then stopped. To boast would be criminal and foolish—and also useless; Kov Lykon saw my hesitation, and misconstrued it. I had been about to say something entirely different from what he expected.

But I wouldn't tell this bright malicious rast that concern over my daughter Dayra might have cost an empire. It might have. And, again, it might not have; for could I have done any differently from what the emperor and his advisers and the Presidio had done? The forces arrayed against us were too strong.

As I suspected had been the case with all the war councils the emperor had been holding, we broke up with nothing decided.

Only one thing remained clear. We would go on fighting for as long as we could. But that time was short and was growing shorter with every bur that passed.

Just before we rose to leave, with the emperor already turning to Queen Lush and smiling at her, holding out his hand, I said: "I'd like you to consider certain—speculations—I shall lay before you." I'd been about to say facts; but that would put their backs up too firmly. I stared around the gathering as they paused, some half-risen, some in the act of finishing their wine, others gathering their cloaks and weapons.

"Consider the plight of Vallia. A puissant empire and a strong emperor who yet must manipulate the factions within the empire. Consider the ambition of another, someone of equal or greater stature, someone with—extraordinary powers. Someone who can extend his tentacles of power over vast distances and subvert the good and use the evil for his own ends. Someone who will take Vallia and rule it through his puppets."

"How can there be any such man?" demanded Crimahan.

I went on doggedly, wondering, to tell the truth, just how much to reveal, and knowing they would hardly believe.

"All these risings are connected. There is a master plan. Where, emperor, is your personal Wizard of Loh, Deb-sa-Chiu?"

Queen Lush gasped.

The emperor smiled at her, patting her hand, and turned to me.

"He was ill. He craved leave to return home."

"And you let him go?"

"One does not easily ignore the reasonable requests of a Wizard of Loh. Their powers are—are strange."

"Quite."

I'd bet a first-class zorca against a broken-down calsany that Deb-sa-Chiu, who had sought out Delia for me, had been made ill by the conjurations of Phu-si-Yantong. It was one more carefully arranged part of his plan. Even though no other Wizard of Loh might be as powerful as Yantong—with the possible and hoped for exception of Khe-Hi-Bjanching—that devil would take no chances and had got rid of Deb-sa-Chiu.

"What has a Wizard of Loh to do with—" started Crimahan in his spiteful way.

But the emperor was not Delia's father for nothing. His smile for Queen Lush altered, subtly, as he said: "And, Dray, you think—?"

"Aye. And not think. Know."

Queen Lush put a hand to her breast. She was very pale.

"Rest easy, my queen," said the emperor, and I noted the form of address. "Here, a glass of wine. This news, if true, is very dreadful. But you have been a comfort and a support to me. I could not have gone on without you at my side. Do not fail me now."

"I shall stand with you. I swear it!" She looked distraught and this was no wonderful thing, for the idea of having a Wizard of Loh pitted against you is unnerving, to say the least.

The others in the room looked shaken. Even if, later, they would pooh-pooh what I had said, at the moment they were a badly rattled bunch.

Well, I had told them some of it. Maybe that was a mistake and I certainly would tell them no more. But the black pall over Vallia needed men and women now who would fight to the end even when they knew the end would be evil and filled with sorrow, people who would rend that black pall even though the end was doom-laden horror.

A somberness held them all as they departed to go about the petty business of supply and reorganization we had decided. Not a one knew a whisper of the whereabouts of Delia. As for my inquiries about the islands of Vallia, they were out of it. Nothing from Rahartdrin, Ava, Womox, all the others, not a sound or sign from Veliadrin or Zamra or Valka.

Deciding to make myself useful I took a tour of the sentry posts and found all quiet. There was time for a yarn and to chew a handful of palines with the Pachaks. Then I crawled off to our wing of the palace hoping to get in at least a few burs sleep before the alarums and excursions of the morrow.

Queen Lushfymi waited for me in my bedchamber.

Of slaves there were none here, they had all run off. Even the emperor's apartments were served only by a few slaves left to him. I gaped at her. Magnificent, she looked. Sheerly clad all in white that threw the ebon glory of her hair and the long passionate violet eyes into startling contrast, she sat up on the bed and clasped her hands together over her breast.

"The emperor—?" I said.

"He sleeps. I must talk to you."

"You make that plain."

If I expected another wearisome scene after the fashion of those I had endured at the hands of willful, passionate, lovely women in the past, I was swiftly disabused of the notion. She was no new candidate to be spurned after the style of Queen Lilah, and Queen Fahia, and all the others.

"The Bowmen of Loh were most wroth at their defeat."

I poured her wine and took some myself—in chased silver goblets—and sat beside her on the bed. Her perfume scented with a mysterious power I ignored. She appeared to radiate a light and a warmth in the dim chamber.

"They would be, seeing they are proud fighting men."

She was nerving herself to say something. It hovered on those full voluptuous lips, and would not come forth. So, to ease the situation, I sipped my wine and offered palines, and tried not to be too much amused by the ludicrous affair.

Then, seeing she was having this difficulty, I said: "You and the emperor are very friendly. You have got on like a house on fire—"

"I love him."

She said this simply, unaffectedly. I sipped wine. She was a cunning, devious queen. She had brought her country of Lome to a position of immense wealth and power in Pandahem. She was possessed of witch-like powers—or so it was said. Why did she tell me this? Was it even true?

"It is true, Dray Prescot."

I sat up.

"No, I cannot read your mind. But I can divine much that is in a man's heart. So I would not attempt to seduce you, for I know of your passion for Delia, the Princess Majestrix."

I said nothing.

Then, out of deviltry, I said: "And if that were not so and if you loved the emperor as you claim, would you try to seduce me?"

Frankly, her violet eyes bearing down on me, she said: "Yes. I would. If by doing so I could help the emperor. Believe me."

I rubbed my chin. I needed a shave. I said: "When we met—when I fell through your palanquin awning, you did not much like me and, I confess, I did not much care for you. Why do you seek me out to tell me this?" Then, thinking I understood, I added: "I shall not stand in your way. I should be glad if the emperor wed again and brought forth a whole regiment of princes and princesses—"

"It is not that."

"Perhaps, Queen Lush, you had better tell it all to me."

I used the name without thinking—and she amazed me by smiling. "From you, Dray Prescot, that comes as a declaration of intent."

"There is nothing wrong with the name Queen Lush. Anyway, it suits you. Names are more important on Kregen than most folk care to admit—"

"Yes. Oh, yes!"

That surprised me. So, ignoring a sudden wash of unease, I told her to spit it out and have done.

"It is not easy. Promise me you will remember that I truly love the emperor?"

"If you like."

"I know you, Dray Prescot, know far more of you than you can possibly dream—so that answer will suffice. I know of you—" She held up her hand to stop me asking her how she thought she knew so damn much about me, and she rushed on now, in full spate, getting it all out. "The Crimson Bowmen. Their defeat was horrible. How do you think their enemy from Hamal knew the plans, knew what the Vallian army would do? How was it that the Hamalese lay in wait and slew and slew?" She nodded and I reached over and gripped her wrist. Her flesh was like ice. "Yes, Dray Prescot, yes! I told them. I, the Queen of Lome, through my occult arts, I told the Hamalese all the secrets of the emperor's plans, and the army was destroyed and the blood flowed, and—"

I slapped her face.

When she calmed down—but only a little, for the situation was fraught and she was in a sprung-steel state of nervous excitement and remorse, I told her to tell me the rest.

"The Hamalese conquered Pandahem as you know and Queen Thyllis slew my father. But at the Battle of Jholaix the Vallians conquered and Pandahem once more threw off the yoke of Hamal. But new enemies arose. Far more powerful." She wrenched away and stood up. Her long white gown glimmered in the dim, tapestry-hung room. She began to walk up and down, jerkily, her hands now clasped together, now raised to heaven, her lovely face passionate with remembered terror, a drugged horror that turned her violet eyes into shadowed deeps. "I must tell you, for you are the man to support the emperor now and the southwest will rally to him, and the islands, and we can still win, still win against—" She faltered, and that lissom body drooped.

"Who made you betray the Vallian army?"

"I think—I think, Dray Prescot, you know."

She turned away, half-fainting with her emotions; but I made no move to assist her. A shadow moved in the doorway at my side and I held up my hand to the emperor, a commanding gesture that would ordinarily have sent him flying into a rage; but he looked long at Queen Lush and listened to her, and the old devil remained silent, a shadow among shadows of the bedchamber.

Speaking in as soothing a voice as I could manage, I said: "Lome has become rich and splendid since you took the throne. Is this also the work of he who now owns you?"

Her shoulders trembled. "Yes." The whisper barely reached.

"In return for all he has done for Lome, with you as queen, he demanded you come to Vallia, seduce the emperor, gain his confidence—and then betray him?"

"Yes."

The emperor moved and I reached out my hand and grasped his forearm, and gripped enough so that he understood. Truly, the times had wrought on him. He stood, a bleak dark statue, in the shadows of the bed at my side, and, together, we listened as Queen Lushfymi of Lome choked out her confession.

Phu-si-Yantong.

She had never met him. But his agents and his own lupal projection had convinced her. The terrors she felt were reflected palely in her stammering voice. Yantong had moved into Pandahem in the wake of the dissolution of the Hamalese armies and in his own surreptitious, cunning, devious ways had exerted his own authority. His puppets now occupied the thrones of the kingdoms of Pandahem.

A fleeting twinge of guilt at thought of Tilda and Pando passed across my mind; but that was of and for another time. Here and now the dark and treacherous scheme to destroy Vallia was being revealed to us.

"See!" cried Queen Lush, her laugh too close to hysteria for my liking. She drew from her sleeve a black feather. "See! I was prepared to make the emperor a convert to the Great Chyyan; but you, Dray Prescot, destroyed that scheme. Now my master sends warriors to do his work." She blew the black feather from her. It gyrated and was lost in the shadows. She laughed again, the hysteria hideously near, so near as to be madness. Her glimmering form moved in the shaded lamplight of the bedchamber. Silently, the emperor stood at my side, watching and listening.

Queen Lush drew from the bosom of her dress a dagger, sheathed, ornate, crusted with gems, the style of weapon a queen might carry. She waved it wildly. "Look upon the death of the Emperor of Vallia, the man I love, the man I was forced to betray, the man for whom I would give my life—the man for whom I *will* give my life!"

The stiletto flashed clear of the scabbard. Twin deeply cut grooves marked the shining blade.

"This blade is poisoned. One nick and the emperor is dead. I am to stab him, when my task is done—but I cannot, I cannot."

Moving with a purposeful slowness I reached out across the bedclothes and hooked my hard old fist around the hilt of the rapier that hung by the bedpost, angled so as to be drawn in a twinkling. I had vaulted ahead in my thoughts. Khe-Hi-Bjanching had shown me what gladiomancy could do and although I did not know if a Wizard of Loh could manipulate a sword or dagger over immense distances, I wouldn't put it past that Wizard of Loh who had contrived our downfall.

I said sharply: "And will the death of the emperor make so much difference to the schemes of Phu-si-Yantong?"

"He must die. The master has said so and must be obeyed."

"This evil man is no longer your master, Queen Lush. Do not think of him as your master ever again."

She turned her head, slowly, tilting, peering at me with her head on one side, half over her shoulder. She looked quite mad. "No. He is my master—"

"He is not your master. He is a real right bastard and a kleesh—a damned Wizard of Loh. But he owns you no longer."

The poisoned dagger looked mightily unpleasant.

Now the emperor was an emperor and anyone who forgot that deserved to have their heads off; but, far more important, he was the father of my Delia. That was the fact that gave him character in my eyes, and now he proved himself.

Without faltering, he moved past the bed, stood upright in a patch of light thrown by the shaded lamp. He stared at Queen Lush, who regarded him with a bright, avid look that made my hand jump on the rapier hilt.

"Queen!" declared the emperor. "You say you love me as I love you. We have meant much, one to the other, in these dark times. Will you stab me? Can you slay me? I am here—see, I lift my arms. Stab, Queen Lush—if you can."

As they stood, facing each other, frozen, I wondered if the old devil realized how he had called his queen.

She took a tottering step. Another. The dagger lifted. I eased the rapier out and stood up.

With a shriek of virulent fury or of hysterical triumph—a shriek of such violence that the emperor jumped—Queen Lush hurled the dagger to the floor. It thwacked into the floorboards through a priceless carpet of Walfarg weave, thrummed with the gems glittering in its hilt, the poisoned slots dark and sinister along the blade.

"No, my emperor—" Then they collapsed into each other's arms.

A sharp and chilling tang struck through the close air of the bedchamber. Queen Lush screamed. The emperor, still holding her, swung about. We all stared at the far wall.

In a ghostly swirl of color and shadow, a mist of madness, a shape formed in thin air against the wall. Hunched, that dire form, hunched and malicious, malefic with power as the two dark eye sockets abruptly glittered with twin spots of light. The ghostly form thickened and solidified and yet remained insubstantial, unreal, a projection of the mind.

"Master—" croaked the queen. She would have fallen but for the emperor's arms.

The lupal projection of Phu-si-Yantong writhed in my bedchamber. What forces he was employing to overcome or bypass the sealings placed there by Khe-Hi-Bjanching I could not know; but the lupal projection wavered as sand wavers on a stream bed, as the mirages dance in the burning deserts.

An arm lifted. Clawed finger pointed. The queen screamed as though tormented with red-hot pincers.

The emperor shouted, an agonized bark of pure horror.

I saw the tableau hold for a heartbeat; then the sorcerous image of the wizard shimmered and faded and I thought I heard the distant sound of golden bells, tingling and tinkling in a dream, fading, dying, gone.

"Dray!" gasped the emperor.

His face looked gray in the patch of lamplight, gray and filled with a horror so great he could barely stand.

The woman slumped in his arms, the white dress strangely loose.

He turned her so I could see her face.

Queen Lushfymi—so glorious, so darkly glittering, so regal with beauty and voluptuousness—hung slackly on the emperor's arm. Phu-si-Yantong had smitten her with chivrel. Her white hair straggled in brittle strands, her shrunken face bore a spiderweb of cracks, the wrinkles destroying all the purity of that face. Spittle slobbered from brown and leathery lips.

Hideous, a hag, Queen Lush whimpered feebly and clung with skeleton arms to the Emperor of Vallia.

The decaying smell of her stank in our nostrils.

Nineteen

Vondium Burns

The moment of doom for Vondium the Proud could no longer be delayed.

The day dawned with a particularly brilliant flood of jade and ruby lights, pouring in commingled beauty from the Suns of Scorpio. But this day would see the end of the empire, the death of hundreds, perhaps thousands, of people, the enslavement of hosts, the shedding of blood to stink rawly into the shining benign sky.

We did what we could for Queen Lush. An aged crone, trembling, shaking, her white hair brittle as dried leaves, she gasped with the effort of breathing, her eyes filmed, her mouth slack and drooling. The devil-cast chivrel had not much longer to run for her. Old before her time she was doomed as the Empire of Vallia was doomed.

The emperor was stricken.

"My strong right arm," he said, clasping his head, his strong handsome face ashen. "Stricken down—torn from me when I needed her most."

I was torn, also, at sight of this great and puissant emperor in these straits. I had little cause to care for him save only that through him I had been blessed with Delia. He had ordered my head off—had banished me—I do not to this day know whether he hated me or merely tolerated me. Certainly from time to time, when he recollected, he showed he appreciated a little the services I had rendered him. But now all that was mere tawdry tinsel. The empire was doomed, Vallia was rent asunder and Vondium burned.

The manner of the burning was strange, for we could see the boiling black smoke clouds from one section or another of the city rising into the bright air, and then they would dwindle away and die. Fresh smoke would rise elsewhere and we would hear the distant clamor of mobs, and then the smoke would die away. Chuktar Wang-Nalgre-Bartong had the explanation.

"The mobs burn and loot, led by the Lornrodders, and someone else is putting out the fires to preserve the city. And, I think, seeing we have had no sight of the Hamalian skyships, it must be the Hamalian army."

That made sweet sense. Phu-si-Yantong had no wish to preside through his puppets over a destroyed city. He was methodically taking control. His men were putting their new house in order. Only the imperial palace and the great kyro and the webwork of surrounding canals remained to be taken. It seemed the Hamalese high command was in no hurry.

Two probing attacks were made and were flung back with ease but not without loss to us. We had the remnants of the Crimson Bowmen, a handful of Chuliks and Khibils, a few Rapas and Fristles, mercenaries all, and the Pachaks. Of artillery we were woefully short, having but five pieces, two catapults and three varters. Of cavalry we had the two squadrons of totrixes and they were in sorry case. At the first real attack despite our determination to fight we would be overwhelmed.

Kov Lykon Crimahan told the emperor: "You must flee the city, majister. There is no other way to preserve your life."

"And where should I flee?"

A babble of voices answered this, all proffering different destinations. I felt the ugliness in me. In these circumstances I would not care to chance any of the provinces on the main island and even, dare I say it, even Valka might not offer any sanctuary from the avenging hosts determined to do away with the emperor.

"If only," said that great man now so shrunken, "if only the queen could advise as she used to do."

I turned away in disgust. To go to Lome now would be to go to certain destruction. There seemed but one thing left.

I said, turning back and barging through the excited, gesticulating group: "You had best flee to Zenicce. My enclave of Strombor will welcome you."

"I cannot—"

"Here they come!" bellowed a Deldar, leather-lunged, and we turned to the walls to repel the third attack. This time the Hamalese put in more weight, ready if we did not resist to charge home, but prepared to melt away under opposition and to let us stew a little longer. They played leem and ponsho with us.

"The confident cramphs!" snarled Jiktar Laka Pa-Re. He was wounded, a long glancing slice in his left biceps—his upper left biceps. The Hamalese were shooting crossbow bolts at anything that moved along the battlements of the palace. We had lost the kyro and had been driven back over the first of the canals. "They do not use their catapults—"

"No. Their masters do not wish to deface the palace. The place is beautiful and priceless. They fight for it, just as we do."

The Crimson Bowmen could outshoot the crossbowmen of Hamal; but their numbers were small and dwindling. Of the mercenaries with us I fancied we could rely on the Chuliks and the Khibils. As for the Rapas and Fristles and few oddments of other diff races, most of them would be gone by nightfall, slipped away to loot a little and then either hire out elsewhere or—or what else? Was not that a mercenary's life?

As for the Pachaks, until they released themselves from their nikobi, which they would not do and lose honor, they would fight to the death.

Many voices among the emperor's rump of advisers lifted in favor of flight. The Pachaks could be discharged, their nikobi satisfied, all the others could be let go. The Crimson Bowmen might stay or leave as they willed; their Chuktar kept them screwed tightly down; but...

Of the people I knew in Vondium I fancied few if any would be left. Bargom of The Rose of Valka had friends along the cut and he and his family should be away to safety along the canals. The city lowered under shifting palls of smoke through which the suns struck lurid gleams of crimson and jade. The incessant nibbling attacks continued against us; men fell.

More than once I had to warn the emperor in strong terms not to expose himself too freely on the battlements. By this time we had withdrawn into the palace and taken up our positions along an inner ring of fortifications, for we were too few to man the entire cincture of walls. I remembered the way he had thirsted to get into fights before. This time the outcome might not be so jolly.

"I am fighting for my empire." He said this with a fine fierce air.

"Oh, aye? Your empire is gone, emperor. Vanished, blown away like thistledown. You imprisoned your friends, spurned those who would help you, embraced the bosoms of your enemies—"

He rounded furiously on me, and I relented, and said: "At least you let them go before it was too late. But if they were with us now—Lord Farris, Old Foke, Vad Atherston, all the others who would serve you loyally—"

"I know, I know! They were put away from me through the wiles of the queen. I know. But she repented and has she not paid the price?"

I nodded. I found I felt a great sorrow for Queen Lush.

They say speak of the devil. We looked up as an airboat flew sluggishly toward us from over the city. It staggered in flight and black smoke streamed back, so I knew the voller had been shot at with fire arrows. She made some kind of landing on a high aerial platform and the guards brought down the Lord Farris—and with him—Delia.

She looked gorgeous in her russet leathers, strapped about with rapier and dagger, striding limber and free, her brown hair magnificent under the suns. After she had embraced me she said: "Dayra?"

I touched my scratched face reflectively; but the gesture meant nothing to Delia. She regarded me gravely.

"I have seen her, my love. She is well. But there is a very great deal to tell. Can you not persuade your father, the stubborn old onker, to abandon the palace and fly to safety?"

"I will speak to him. But he never forgets he is the emperor."

"Not any more he isn't."

Greeting the Lord Farris kindly, for he was a great-hearted man, I broke the news of Queen Lush's personal tragedy. Delia touched her lips, lightly, and looked down.

"I felt she was a bad influence—many of us did. But this—will she live long?"

"Not long, I judge. She looks as though she is passed two hundred and fifty years old."

Delia shivered.

The emperor greeted his daughter, and was polite to Farris, which amused me. The old devil tried to make amends.

It was useless to look for relief. We could expect no succor in the shape of an aerial armada. From Valka was only silence. Delia said that Delphond slumbered, which did not surprise me. As for the Blue Mountains—when I told her the news her brows drew down and her eyes took on that dangerous look that indicated someone was in for it in the neck. But nothing could be done there. And Strombor—well, we faced an army of Hamalese, plus the multitudes of irregulars and the factions, all whipped into frenzy by false stories, rumors, bitter animosities fanned by Phu-si-Yantong. We were isolated.

"The Empress Thyllis has prepared long for this," said the emperor. "She takes her revenge upon us Vallians." He rubbed his fingers together, absently, and then gripped his rapier hilt. "If only the queen were in full health, blooming like a rose—if only she were herself."

So, looking at Delia, I said: "She might be—it may be possible."

Delia shook her head; but her father rounded on me.

"Well? What mean you? Spit it out!"

"I promise nothing. But—" I tried to look at Delia; but she would not meet my eye. "I must go to my Valkan villa here in the city. When I return, we will see what may be done."

"Dray—" said Delia.

"I know," I said. "But even though I am an onker of onkers, it was you who made me go down into the pit—and more than once—to bring the famblys out."

"I remember."

"You cannot venture into the city, prince," said Farris. "The place swarms with looters and rioters, and Hamalians putting them down. Anyone out there—*everyone* out there—is a foe."

"I'll fly." I made up my mind. "And I'll use your flier, Jen Farris. The one I stole from Udo is a fine craft and will serve the emperor."

Before I left I took Delia aside. "Look, my heart. Make sure your father does nothing foolish while I am gone. I have warned him, and I think he understands. The flier is a good one and will carry you and him, as well as Farris, if a little cramped—"

"And you!"

"Oh, aye. I'll be back. Count on that."

The flier carried me sluggishly over doomed Vondium. For the most part the place was deserted, with stray bands of looters and rioters thieving and burning and parties of Hamalian soldiery attempting to preserve the city—to preserve it for Yantong. That truly mighty city, once proud and sublime in its confidence, lay now enthralled under the cloak of oppression. No vollers offered to stop my progress and I began to think that the absence of Hamalian skyships indicated they might be engaged somewhere over Vallia in a last supreme struggle with the Vallian Air Service. Farris would rage that he was denied that final proof of his devotion to his Air Service.

The Valkan villa was abandoned but I guessed its unkempt appearance had deterred looters. Going through those dusty halls and corridors gave me a shivery feeling; I remembered the circumstances of my last departure from here. That was prophetic; too late to realize that now. The keys were in the wall niche and the iron-bound chest opened easily and disgorged household linen and the scuffed old water bottle. This I fastened securely to my harness.

The dusty smell of the villa would have depressed me but there was no time for self-indulgence of that sort. Once we'd put Queen Lush to rights I'd make the emperor take the flier and leave Vondium. The little craft would take him and the queen as well as Delia and Farris... As to whether or not I would go I was not decided. To be a wanderer on the face of Kregen, hunted, outlawed, whose destruction was avidly sought by powerful and greedy men, cruel in their strength, this was a fate of the most profound abhorrence. I fancied I knew what Delia would say.

All the animals of the villa had been released and I assumed Shadow had trotted off with them. I felt the strongest presentiment that I had not seen the last of that superb zorca. My thoughts rattled on as I sprinted across the open space for the flier. My splendid enclave of Strombor in the city of Zenicce lay to the eastward on the coast of the continent of Segesthes. There the emperor and the queen might recuperate while Delia and I planned our next steps. We could gather the exiles. There were still men loyal. Lord Farris was one. Even Lykon Crimahan, despite the malice he felt toward me, was loyal. Maybe, now we had lost our estates in Vallia, much of his resentment of me would be finished, for he had his evil eyes on Veliadrin—along with plenty of other nobles of the eastern coast.

The voller took off sweetly enough and carried me perhaps half an ulm toward the palace. Then she went into a steep nose dive and only luck and a thick skull saved me. I went pitching out and into a canal, splashing, spouting water, flailing for the bank. The flier sank with a bubbling gurgle. From now on the journey back would be on foot. Well, on my own two feet I have tramped a fair old bit of Kregen.

I set off, and I loosened the longsword in the scabbard. The way was barred in a couple of places by the detritus of fallen buildings. Naghan the Mask's fine new theatre had been gutted, I was sorry to see. The temples looked unscathed. A party of looters tried to loot my equipment; but half a dozen of them having lost blood and other inward essentials, the rest ran off shrieking.

An arrow past my ear heralded the attempt of the Hamalese army to detain me. But there were only ten of them, a strong audo, a section or so, and after three casts of my Lohvian longbow the others decided in prosaic military formula to retire to reform and seek fresh orders. They were wise—the seven who thus lived.

The going became a trifle tougher as I neared the palace and ran into the rear echelons of the besieging forces. There are usually ten audos in a pastang, ten sections in a company, and the Hamalese, notorious for the severity of their laws, organize tightly. Crouching down by a brick wall I stared out at the backs of the Hamalese. The swods and their officers moved about with the sure confidence of men approaching victory in their own time. They kept busy. I saw the glitter of their helmets and weapons, the panoply of their appearance, the square shapes of their shields. I chose my point with some care.

A pretty little flower-bowered bridge spanned a canal ahead and the Hamalese swod set to guard it hefted his stux, the throwing spear, at the poise. He whistled a cheerful little ditty I had heard many times in Hamal: *When the fluttrell flirts his wing*, and there was no passing him without question.

A fight would alert his comrades. So taking up the refrain at the point where the fluttrell flyer, discovering the buckles of his clerketer have parted and the saddle is sliding down the big bird's back, claps his hands over his eyes—always raises a laugh, does that, among flyers—I marched up with a swing. The swod eyed me and the stux lifted. He could punch a hole in a kax with that, at close enough range.

He shouted: "*Llanitch!* Halt! Stand you still, dom."

His shield bore the painted devices of the Twenty-ninth Regiment of Foot. I waved a friendly arm and bellowed: "Where away are the Fifteenth of Foot, dom? By Krun! This place confuses me even more than Ruathytu. What I'd give to be strolling through the Ghat Gate to the Jikhorkdun of the Swods."

At my familiar mention of places in Ruathytu he eased up. He should not have done so, of course. I reached him, still chattering on about Ruathytu, capital of Hamal, which I then knew better than Vondium, mentioning certain lively and low dopa dens, and smilingly took his throat in my hand and choked—only a little. I held him upright and propped him against the flower-drenched bricks of the bridge. I leaned his stux against his lorica. With a merry quip about the sylvies at The Stux and Mirvol, I saluted him and tromped on, turning down by the canal, and after a scything glance showed none of the swods cared about me, ducking down into a hedgerow of a private garden. The hedge let me through, not without a scrape or two, and I belted across the lawn and so through the house. Using houses and gardens I worked my way up the avenue, having passed into the engaged zone of the enemy.

No one had taken alarm. That swod would recover with a sore throat. His Deldar would scream at him; what his Hikdar would say would flay him; and when the Jiktar commanding his regiment spoke to him—well, I felt sorry for the swod, believe me.

Pressing on toward the palace, darting across side roads, crossing canals and all the time keeping out of sight, I wormed close to the edge of the great kyro. A few murs more...

Three Hamalian reconnaissance vollers flew over the palace in wedge formation. They kept their eyes on us from time to time. From a propped-up varter a couple of bolts were let fly from the battlements. The Hamalians, trailing bright flags, flew on unconcerned.

They disappeared beyond the jumble of rooftops and another voller leaped up from the palace. Crouching down, I looked up and recognized her as the craft I had stolen from Udo. She swung away, going fast. Before she had time to gain height the Hamalians were back. The three closed in. Bolts flew and arrows crisscrossed the wind-streaming gap. The fliers turned and passed above my head. I saw the Hamalians clear—and saw the way the fleeing voller from the palace turned end over end and fell to a smashing destruction on the stones before the palace.

Twenty

Delia of Vallia

In the ensuing confusion as the soldiery boiled across to gape at the wreckage and the blood-soaked refuse within I was able to slip past. Of one thing I was certain. Whoever may have been in the flier, Delia was not one of that company. A Chulik offered to bash my brains out at the rampart until I rapped out the password. "Zamra!" I had chosen that. The confusion without was matched and overmatched by the confusion within.

"Dray! You have it?" Delia ran up to me, eager, alive, ready to let me have an earful for endangering myself. I shook the water bottle.

Together, we went to the small private inner room where Queen Lush lay on a pallet, panting shallowly, withering away. The emperor sat by her side, frightened even to hold her hand in case the brittle bones snapped.

The men in the fleeing voller were three certain pallans. I will not mention their names. They came to an evil end.

But they indicated very clearly the deterioration of morale within the palace. And, the means of flight had been snatched from the emperor. Delia bent over Queen Lush as I thought about the implications. Vondium was decidedly unhealthy right now and was like to get worse.

The fliers we saw did not drop firepots on us. Phu-si-Yantong did not wish to destroy the palace. He coveted its priceless treasures. Of course, he could have razed the lot and built afresh and to a greater scale of grandeur; but that would not have slaked the greed in the man, of that I felt sure.

"Water?" said the emperor. "Is that all—?"

"Hush, father," said Delia, whereat I smiled alarmingly.

The withered brown lips were somehow coaxed into receiving some of the milky fluid from the Sacred Pool of Baptism of the River Zelph in far Aphrasöe. Delia poured a golden cupful, and we helped Queen Lush to lift herself, and Delia coaxed her gently. The crone moaned and slobbered and much of the priceless fluid ran down that withered witch-like chin.

"How much, my heart, do you think?"

"I do not know. But Yantong is a mighty powerful devil of a wizard. Give her plenty. Better more than less."

"You are right." Together we fed the magical fluid, sip by sip.

The emperor rocked back. He was shaking. His eyes opened wide. "By the sweet sake of Opaz!"

"Yes, father," said Delia, impatiently, "and don't jog the cup. You have wasted two mouthfuls."

For Queen Lushfymi changed. The lines and wrinkles sloughed away and her skin took on that smooth peach bloom. Dark tint suffused the stringy white hair; slowly it resumed that lustrous darkness that shone with blue-black light. Her body filled, her shrunken flesh restoring that voluptuous outline, the skeletal claws firming to the shapely hands with which she gestured so gracefully. In not too long a time Queen Lush glowed seductively before us, fully restored to beauty.

"My love—" She turned those limpid violet eyes on the emperor. Delia blinked and smiled. "How can I thank you? You have made me—made me myself again—"

"It was not me, my queen. Rather, thank the wild leem Dray Prescot—and my daughter Delia."

She took Delia's hand in hers. The reconciliation would have been most affecting; but the sound of conflict and shouting and the screams of wounded and dying men burst savagely in. I stood up.

"There is work to be done—but, emperor, we're finished here. You must discharge the mercenaries in honor and then we must leave."

"There is no airboat—"

"I shall arrange that."

He stood up and faced me. We stood looking at each other for a heartbeat. Kov Lykon and the Lord Farris—who was a kov, also—burst in. "The devils are through the Peral Gate! We must pull back—"

"I am coming," I said. "We will hold them at the Wall of Larghos Risslaca." That was dangerously close to the very heart of the palace.

"Hold!" The emperor spoke thunderously. He bore down on them all, imperious. "I may die soon. I do not know. But this I swear as my testament. Long have I held my son-in-law in contempt as a clansman and, also, regarded highly his skill at arms, his boorishness which he calls integrity. He is a Hyr-Jikai—"

"Get on with it," I said. "I'm going out there to bash—"

"Wait! Should I die, then you, Dray Prescot, will be Emperor of Vallia. Witness this testament of my will, all of you. This thing will be—will be, by my decree."

"You won't die yet, emperor," I said. And then, in the heat of the moment, burst out: "Sink me! You've a thousand years of life yet. Now—let us go and bash a few skulls."

Delia ran swiftly out with me and I turned on her and bellowed: "I don't want you fighting on the walls! Stay with your father and keep him company."

"You told him. A thousand years of life—he'll want to—"

"Later, my heart—"

That little fight proved harder than those preceding as we held the Hamalese on the walls, pulling back to the Wall of Larghos Risslaca and shooting down on the rasts as they raced with their scaling ladders. We halted them. It was hard. But the next onslaught would be harder still to halt. I went back to see the emperor. I found him gazing at Queen Lush as though dyspeptic—and realized my ill humor was affecting my judgment. I had to hold up. The emperor would live a thousand years, and with Queen Lush at his side could be kept out of my hair. The future looked promising, if we could escape the here and now.

"Those cramphs of Hamal have fliers out there," I said without preamble. "They build them well for themselves. I'll fetch one. Meantime, arrange to discharge our paktuns and mercenaries. As for the Crimson Bowmen, they are mercenaries, also, and should be discharged. Make the compact that we must leave in safety, all we Vallians. Do this."

Queen Lush said: "And—me—?"

"You're a Vallian now, by intention of marriage. And we'll take Lome back for you. There is little time. And, while I am gone, emperor—stay out of trouble."

"A thousand—what did you mean?"

"Delia may explain, if she will. Just make sure you stay alive to enjoy it. With my blessings." I ran out.

Kissing Delia, I said as I let her go: "Take care of yourself."

In a much lighter frame of mind I took myself off through secret tunnels I had used before. Vondium was a buzzing hive of danger; but there at least I could strike out freely. I felt a keen pleasure that Delia's father was proving himself more human day by day. He wouldn't change, of course, so much as actually come to like me. But that didn't matter. What mattered was Vallia—and the country was in a sorry, blood-soaked state at the moment. Once Phu-si-Yantong got his hooks firmly wedged into the country people would realize they had seen nothing yet.

Outside the palace I dodged like a grundal from bush to bush of some ornamental gardens, got across a canal, insinuated myself past a group of wounded Hamalese and so, in the guise of an irregular mercenary hired to the Empress Thyllis, set off for the fliers. They were easy enough to spot. Only at the last moment, as we lifted into the air, was there any trouble. Some old oily rags in the voller served to wipe the longsword clean.

Skimming low over the ground, taking the voller in racing curves around temples and over villa walls, I avoided detection from the air. Ahead the massive bulk of the palace lifted. I looked up.

Casting down twin shadows onto the white walls, rank after rank of fliers slanted in for the palace. I knew them.

Trylon Udo and his Hawkwas smashed in to strike the final blows.

And then, beyond the armada from the Northeast, another fleet hove into view. They were not as many. They flew the flags of Kov Layco Jhansi. He was the emperor's chief pallan. I did not give a cheer; but I felt like shouting in glee.

Among the fliers with Jhansi were many whose flagstaffs flew treshes of checkerboarded ochre and umber, the colors of Falinur. I frowned, suddenly. Layco Jhansi was supposed to be fighting the rebellious Falinurese. It looked as though he was in alliance with them. I sent the voller hurtling flat out for the palace, treachery stinking in my nostrils.

All was confusion in and around the palace.

That frowning pile had become the centerpiece for all the vindictive hatred, the scheming, the vengeance, the sheer outright deviltry of all those attacking Vondium and seeking to claw down the emperor. The voller leaped across the sky. Quarrels spat toward me. Varter-driven rocks hissed past my head. Now smoke and flames rose from the bewildering maze of domes and towers of the palace. The unceasing shrilling of fighting men beat a diapason to the bright sky. The suns passed across the heavens, and cast down their mingled streaming light, and an empire went down in flames and blood.

Into a niche high along a flower-hung balcony I dropped the voller with a precision of handling that would have pleased Delia, who had taught me my flying. I leaped out. Smoke blew chokingly across from a burning roof. In a courtyard below men fought and struggled and died. I saw the colors. I raced away, leaping down well-remembered stairs, haring for Delia.

Faction against faction—hatreds and jealousies were tearing the heart out of the empire. Those colors down there—Jhansi's men fought them both, and the Hamalese fought all. It was a madness. Blood clotted the bright tapestries and fouled the priceless carpets. I raced along the corridors and so came, at last, to where Laka Pa-Re and his Pachaks fought the last great fight.

The longsword flamed, striking this way and that in the vicious yet fully controlled fighting technique of the Krozairs of Zy. Hamalese fell away. A group of Hawkwas surged up, screeching, and together, the Pachaks and I, we bested them and drove them off, running.

Chuktar Pola Je-Du was wounded, a slashing gash across his shoulder armor, where the plates hung down broken. His face showed only firm resolve.

"Pola—you have not been discharged from your nikobi?"

"No, prince. We fight to the end."

"No—that is madness. You need not be slain—from me, will you take your discharge, in all honor? Will you save your men?"

"If I do, I think you will die here."

"That is as may be, by Zair. The emperor—"

"He is sore wounded."

I felt the shock. "The get onker! I told him—the moment I leave him to his own devices the idiot gets himself wounded." Smoke boiled down the ornate passage and the Pachaks braced themselves for the next attack. I bellowed at the Chuktar. 'Take your nikobi back, in honor, Pola Je-Du.

And you, Laka Pa-Re. Take what you will from the palace in payment for your service—and my thanks to you for your devotion, in the name of Papachak the All-Powerful."

"Let the compact be unraveled," said Pola. And then he said: "And you, prince?"

"By the Black Chunkrah! I'll have a few words to say to the emperor, believe me! Remberee, Pachaks all." And I turned and belted along the corridor toward the inner apartments.

As I ran so I marveled that the Pachaks had consented to be released from the compact by me, who was merely the Prince Majister of Vallia. Their hire had been to the emperor...

At the door of those sumptuous apartments Delia met me. The tears stood brightly in her glorious brown eyes; but she would not weep. Not just yet...

"My father—oh, my heart! My father is dead."

I couldn't believe that.

I pushed through. Lykon Crimahan and the Lord Farris stood with dripping swords within the doorway, their faces ashen. Queen Lushfymi crouched over the body of the emperor. He had been killed by a slashing blow that had near severed his head from his body. Despite the Baptism in the Sacred Pool, he was dead. No man was going to recover in time from that kind of savagely mortal blow.

I stood looking down on him. I did not know what I felt.

Then I took Delia in my arms.

"He said—he said you are the emperor, Dray."

"That is so," shouted Farris, suddenly. He came to life. "Hai Jikai! Dray Prescot. Emperor of Vallia."

"There's no time for that," I said, savage, incensed, sullen, vindictive—anything but pleased. "We must get out of here. And bring the emperor with you. We will give him proper burial."

Delia shook her head.

"We cannot carry him and fight as well. He will lie here, and he will burn in his own palace. What more magnificent funeral pyre could an emperor have than that?"

I bowed to her wishes. He was her father.

"How—?"

"Hawkwas. We fought them off; but one did for him."

I knew.

"A bright, nervous, malicious bastard—?"

She nodded. "Yes, I think so." We hurried along the corridor past the Pachak dead who had fought to the last. "That sounds like him."

A few more words convinced me it had been Zankov. Zankov. He had slain the Emperor of Vallia. I swallowed. Carefully, I said: "Were there women with him? Jikai Vuvushis?"

"Yes—and very dreadful—renegades from the Sisters—"

"Was there one who—who fought with a sharp steel claw?"

"No."

Thank Zair, I said, but to myself.

Delia bore herself like a princess. But I watched her narrowly. The shock of her father's death would prey on her and I felt the agony for her tearing at me. I had watched my father die, with that damned scorpion scuttling, and I had been only a little lad. Delia had known her father for far longer than ever I had known mine, and the wrench, the agony, the shock must affect her far more profoundly—so I thought.

Useless to prate on about how I had warned him to keep himself safe and stay out of trouble. He had pushed to the forefront of the battle, convinced, determined. Now he was dead.

We reached a stairway leading up and a gang of Falinurese sought to stop us and we carved a path through them. Bitterness directed our strokes, anger and vengeance and sorrow. We smashed our way through our foemen and raced up the stairs.

We cut our way through a confused and struggling melee of Layco Jhansi's men fighting Hamalese. So Jhansi had sought the supreme power for himself. Ashti Melekhi... Some veiled acts came clear. And Jhansi was interfering with the plans of Phu-si-Yantong. There would be no easy path to the throne for Zankov, for all he had slain the emperor, when faced with the dark and secret ambitions of Kov Layco Jhansi.

Up onto that high balcony we stumbled and so over and down to the niche where the voller nestled.

Delia stood firmly at the controls. Queen Lush huddled on a bench, wrapping flying silks about her, weeping and weeping. Lykon Crimahan and the Lord Farris stared back and up, viciously, hungering for a head to appear over the balcony and so give them the opportunity to take one more blow at the hated enemies who had ruined all of Vallia for them.

"Jhansi," said Delia. "He is proved foresworn. He must have given Ashti Melekhi her orders to poison my father." She stopped, then, and her mouth trembled. "My father—"

"Take us up and away from this accursed place, my heart."

"Yes, Dray, my heart. We will go. But—one day—we will come back. We must return..."

I put my arm around her waist as she sent the voller slanting up in the declining rays of Zim and Genodras. The Suns of Scorpio flamed along the horizon and bathed the burning city in crimson and emerald fires.

"Oh, aye, we'll return. I don't pretend to be perfect—or even particularly cut out for the job—but all Vallia is captive to Phu-si-Yantong and the other villains now, and that is something I do not like and must, in conscience, try to alter." I held my Delia as we shot away over the doomed city. "Anyway, there are the children to consider. What's to become of them?"

"Outcasts," said Lykon Crimahan, his voice faltering. "We are outcasts, unwanted, fated to wander forever—"

"I do not," said the Lord Farris, "think so."

"But Vondium is fallen. The emperor is dead."

Farris pointed at me. "Not so! The Emperor of Vallia stands before you!"

I warmed to him; but it was nonsense. Crimahan put a trembling hand to his mouth, the realization of what he had seen and heard breaking fully into his consciousness. I saw the expression in his eyes, the shifting of the planes of his face, the dawning of painful emotions.

"That is of no consequence now," I said in my rough old sailorman's voice. "If I am emperor then I am emperor of nothing."

Delia moved in my arm and looked up at me, the last of Zim's glowing light rosy on her face.

"Vondium is doomed—but there are other places of Vallia."

"Aye. We fly to Valka. We will collect Velia and Didi and Aunt Katri, for I am utterly convinced they are still safe. If Valka has been swamped by foemen, we will seek others—"

"Strombor?"

"Aye, my heart. Strombor. My enclave of Strombor will welcome us and will love Velia and Didi as they love you." I looked away from her tear-filled brown eyes. It was in my heart to tell her that I would as lief remain in Strombor. I, Dray Prescot, of Earth and of Kregen, a Lord of Strombor. But—Vallia. That proud and puissant empire was torn and shredded from end to end. Could I, in all honor, turn my back on that agony?

And, so, I looked up. Against the sulphurous masses of smoke coiling from the burning city floated two wide-winged birds.

I knew them both.

Oh, yes, I knew them. That great hunting bird with the scarlet and golden feathers, circling high above me, was the Gdoinye, the messenger and spy of the Star Lords. And the white dove peering watchfully down was from the Savanti. So the two agencies who had directed so much of my life upon Kregen spied on me still in these last cataclysmic moments as a proud city burned and a puissant empire slid down into degradation and ruin.

The birds flicked their wings at me and circled and flew off once they were sure I had seen them. They reminded me of the continued existence of their masters. They did not speak to me.

Delia turned the voller eastward, toward Valka.

The burning city dwindled away below, great and magnificent and reduced. I would have to tell Delia about Dayra, about Ros the Claw. I did not think she knew. One thing piled on another, and the importance of each became distorted with viewpoint and time and emotions. The fate of one wayward daughter set against the death of an empire... Did they balance out?

I, Dray Prescot, Lord of Strombor and Krozair of Zy, held my Delia close, close. Did anything else matter in two worlds?

"Empress—" gasped a soft, breathy voice. For a space no one took any notice. Then we understood. The understanding forced a small but significant change in my intentions. For her, I would dare anything... "Empress," said Queen Lushfymi, pale, weeping, speaking through her sobs. "You will not cast me off?"

"Rest easy, queen," said Delia, Empress of Vallia.

The flier hurtled out of the smoke into the east, and at our backs the Suns of Scorpio threw a last sheeting refulgence of jade and crimson into the nighted sky of Kregen.

GOLDEN SCORPIO

Dray Prescot

Dray Prescot is an enigmatic figure. Reared in the inhumanly harsh conditions of Nelson's Navy, he has been transported many times through the agencies of the Star Lords, the Everoinye, and the Savanti nal Aphrasöe to the terrible yet beautiful world of Kregen under Antares, four hundred light years from Earth. In chronicling his brilliant adventures on that exotic world I have been forced to the conclusion that there is much he does not tell us as he records his story on cassettes. A fresh supply has reached me and will form the subject matter for the next cycle of Dray Prescot's story.

His appearance as described by one who has seen him is of a man above middle height, with brown hair and level brown eyes, brooding and dominating, with enormously broad shoulders and powerful, even brutal, physique. There is about him an abrasive honesty and an indomitable courage. He moves like a savage hunting cat, quiet and deadly. On the marvelous world of Kregen he has fought his way to become Vovedeer and Zorcander of his wild Clansmen of Segesthes, Lord of Strombor, Strom of Valka, King of Djanduin, Prince Majister of Vallia—and a member of the Order of Krozairs of Zy. To this plethora of titles he confesses with a wryness and an irony I am sure mask much deeper feelings at which we can only guess.

Prescot's happiness with Delia, the Princess Majestrix of Vallia, is threatened as the notorious Wizard of Loh, Phu-Si-Yantong, seeks to overwhelm the empire. Many factions rise to seize the supreme power and with the death of the emperor, Delia's father, and the burning of Vondium, the capital, Prescot and Delia are forced to flee Vallia. *Golden Scorpio* tells how Prescot reacted and how he came to terms with himself, if not altogether satisfactorily in his own estimation.

The volumes chronicling his life are arranged to be read as individual books. A clearly-marked change has overtaken the character of Prescot as he relates his story, and, indeed, the story itself reveals this, illuminating him in ways of which he himself is probably unaware. Future volumes can only be awaited with the fascination of the unexpected.

The next cycle of volumes in the Saga of Dray Prescot I have called the *Jikaida Cycle*, carrying the linking word Kregen in their titles. Life is a continuing process and the enigmatic figure Prescot presents of himself might lead us to imagine that he understands only the belief that the effort of life is soldiering on dauntlessly against Fate. There is more to him than that. I feel sure he is fully aware of the many other facets of human belief in understanding our natures and harmonizing them, in the theory of abnegation, in the idea of letting oneself slide into the infinite, of bending with the current to cope with existence, of acceptance. But on the vivid world of Kregen under Antares, in the streaming mingled lights of the Suns of Scorpio, Prescot has had and will continue to have more than his share of setbacks and hurtful adventures. I do not think it is Dray Prescot's nature to allow the destruction of himself or those he loves.

Alan Burt Akers

One

Dragons in the Fire

We flew from burning Vondium.

Sulphurous masses of smoke rolling from the doomed city cast dark palls between the streaming mingled radiances of the fading suns. The spreading fans of jade and crimson light cupped the city below. Vondium burned. Along the wide avenues rivers of fire, across the canal-bordered islands lakes of fire, upon the terraced hills volcanoes of fire—incandescent, lambent, roaring with unchecked power, spurting yellow and orange flames, shooting myriads of sparks like discharges from Hell's furnaces, the fire burned.

Our airboat shook in the windrush.

"This was not planned," said Delia, guiding the airboat out of the last swathing bands of smoke. The suns shafted light behind us and swiftly the emerald and ruby spears drained down across the sky, dwindling and shrinking as the pit of fire that was Vondium blazed up. She shivered. "Not planned—"

"The factions fight it out down there. They all struggle for the supreme power and," I said, looking up, my fist closing on the hilt of the sword, "here come those who would dispute our passage."

Two fliers spun out of the shadows ahead, the light glittering along their sides, glancing from their brazen embellishments. In the weirdly coruscating lights the two airboats looked dark and magical dragons, glinting with fire-jewels.

"Hamalese," said the Lord Farris. He moved forward from the shelter deck aft, and his face lay shrunken in shadow.

At his side Lykon Crimahan spoke in words still slurred by witnessed horror. "They have destroyed all of value in life—I will have my due of them."

"The queen?" said Delia, not glancing back, but guiding our airboat skillfully upwards so that the cramphs of Hamal might not have the advantage of us. The airboats flitted up into the night sky and the smoke dropped away and the clouds were tinged in orange and gold about us.

"The queen sleeps." Farris had already drawn his sword. In the encroaching darkness the bulky firmness of his body as he moved up struck me as mightily comforting. "She is exhausted."

We were all exhausted. But only a fierce continuing, a savage determination to go on, an unyielding struggle against all odds would get us through now and save our necks.

In this airboat I had taken from the Hamalese were ready racked a dozen crossbows. I took one up and spanned it and said to Farris: "Put up your sword. Delia will outfly these rasts."

"Yes," said Farris. "The Princess—I mean, the Empress—has consummate skill."

The three airboats whirled about the night sky, leaves tossed in the maelstrom of the fire and the high winds of the night, darting and swooping, climbing to secure the height advantage. Delia swung us up superbly. I leaned over the wooden coaming and let fly. The bolt skewered into the dark mass of the Hamalian airboat below. In the wind bluster I could not hear a shriek of anguish, I did not know if I had hit; but I respanned the bow and let fly again as we circled in.

Farris and Crimahan joined in. They were unused to crossbows; but every bolt that hit the Hamalians would count.

And then in the way of these wild skirling affrays as fliers spin and grapple at night, one of the Hamalians flew awkwardly across and fell athwart our bows. Delia made a last frantic effort to avoid the onrushing mass. The two airboats came together with a great crushing of wood and ripping of canvas. But the craft I had selected was stoutly built, as one would expect from the damned Hamalese who made the things and denied us Vallians the right to make our own, and she was stouter than the other. Amid a shrieking splintering of wood the foeman's airboat tumbled full into our own.

Men spilled out to stagger and stumble across our deck.

Over our heads through a rent in the clouds the fat blue shine of the first star of the evening suddenly caught me up with a swift and entirely unexpected sense of the beauty of the night. That first star that Kregans call Soothe was not as large or as fat now, as the conjunctions of orbits opened out, for Soothe is a planet of Antares as is Kregen, but that blue lambent luminosity reminded me of the fabled Goddesses of Love of Kregen. And as no Goddess of Love of two worlds has ever been or can ever be as precious as my Delia, my Delia of Delphond, my Delia of the Blue Mountains, I hurled the crossbow down and leaped yelling into action.

Delia was ready for the Hamalese from the wreck of their airboat. Together, we hit them. Like two perfectly-machined parts, we meshed, she taking her man with her rapier, I chunking the Krozair longsword around into his comrade's ribs. Armor crumpled.

"Hanitch! Hanitch!" The Hamalese kept up their battle yells, fierce, predatory and yet highly disciplined fighting men.

"Vallia!" yelled Farris and hurled himself forward along the deck, his sword a glinting blur. "Vallia and Vomansoir!"

These warriors of Hamal did not carry shields, although their Air Service personnel habitually did so, and I guessed the shock of the collision had not so much left them with no time to seize up that article of combat as the demands of scrambling from the wreck of a flier about to plunge over into nothingness had made them concentrate wonderfully on having two hands free. Now, had they been Djangs, or Pachaks...

The little fight raged for a space. I squared off my man and thrust the next one through. Crimahan was bashing away and yelling all manner of frenzied insults and taunts, half off his head with grief for what had befallen Vallia and him.

With every blow he struck, Lykon Crimahan, Kov of Forli, took out a payment for his lost lands on the hides of his enemies.

"Hamal! Hanitch!" screeched the Hamalese, and fought and struggled and died. I feel the very fury of our vengeful attack threw them off balance. They had flown up from their empire to sack and burn and overthrow the Empire of Vallia, acting under the veiled orders of the Wizard of Loh Phu-si-Yantong whose maniacal ambitions knew few bounds, and if they were surprised at our vengeful resistance then they were fools. In that moment I felt the enormous weight pressing in on me that my own plans called for Vallia and Hamal to join hands in amity. To accomplish that with the blood-debt that now soaked the two countries seemed almost impossible.

So we fought.

Toward the end of the fight when but four Hamalese soldiers remained alive, the rest either slumped in death on the deck or pitched with a despairing shriek overboard, Queen Lushfymi tottered out of the aft cabin. She held a poniard. She looked distraught, her dark hair disheveled, her violet eyes wide and drugged.

She would have rushed upon the last soldiers; but I got her right arm in my left fist. I held her very very carefully.

The poniard she brandished with drugged abandon had two dark channels cut into the narrow blade, and in those runnels clung a virulent poison...

"Let me go. I will slay and slay—"

She spoke in a slurred, drugged fashion, her words heavy. Her face showed demoniac devilishness and exhausted despair, struggling to gain the ascendancy.

"They slew the emperor, they murdered my beloved—let me repay the debt."

That she had to be held back was quite obvious, although she was a queen—the Queen of Lome in Pandahem—and therefore might be expected to know how to handle weapons. But the Hamalese soldiers of the air were no amateurs. Their swords flickered in these dying moments of the struggle as they sought to take us and so win all—and, in truth, even now we could lose. I shook Queen Lush.

"Hold still. Do you want to throw your life away after the emperor's?"

That, of course, was a stupid thing to say. I recognized that. I gave her a push back into the cabin, before she could screech out some cataclysmic determination to end it all and die to join the emperor, and slammed the door.

I swung back to the fight, raging.

Delia had taken her man out with that neat precision of effort girls are taught in the military establishments of the Sisters of the Rose. Crimahan missed his stroke and had to duck and dodge back, his left-hand dagger fending off a thraxter blow. Farris was in the act of withdrawing his rapier from the throat of his man. So that left the fourth, the one I should have been attending to if Queen Lush had not staggered out brandishing her poisoned poniard.

"By Vox!" I bellowed as I leaped. "I should have let the silly woman at these rasts with her poisoned dagger."

Then the Krozair brand flamed left, twitched right, sliced and was still, sheened in blood.

Farris looked at me and Crimahan staggered back, shaking with the violence of these last few moments. Delia tut-tutted and caught at a dead Hamalese by his belt.

"They're bleeding all over the deck. What a mess. Give me a hand to push them over."

We did so, with a will. If you imagine this to be strange behavior, insane, then you are not correct. Death is a part of life. Delia fully understood that. But, even so, even so, no girl should have to go through the things Delia had been through, events and horrors that would have destroyed a being of lesser fiber. But Delia was right. We had a way to fly and we already had enough blood to clear up as it was.

Highly practical, highly professional, highly commonsense is Delia of Vallia—just as she is highly romantic. Her father, the Emperor of Vallia, had been slain this night. No—Delia could not act completely normally, not for a space yet.

I made up my mind. You who have listened to my story as the tapes spin through the heads will know how wrought up I must have been to nerve myself, actually to pluck up the courage, to open the talk I had promised Delia for long and long.

Tentatively I spoke to her in one of the aft cabins as Farris took the steering, speed and height levers and Crimahan having indicated he wished to be dropped on his own estates, tried to sleep. Queen Lush slumbered, her demoniac energy temporarily exhausted.

So, Delia and I sat on a ponsho fleece spread on a bench and talked as the airboat slid through the nighted air of Kregen.

"A world with only one sun and only one moon! But you can't expect anyone to take such a silly idea seriously."

"Yes, I know it sounds a silly notion. But I'm asking you to examine the idea. After all, it's not impossible, is it?"

"Impossible—one sun and one moon—we-ell—I suppose not."

"Look, Delia, my heart. Try to imagine a world very much like Kregen—well, something like—but instead of Zim and Genodras shining down in glory there is only one sun, a little yellow sun."

"But Opaz! The Invisible Twins visibly vouchsafed us in the fires of Zim and Genodras, the Eternal Spirit of Opaz—how could that be if the world did not have two suns?"

"That's a poser, all right. But say that the Eternal Spirit is manifest in some other form—that is possible."

"You would run into charges of heresy at many of the religious colleges for that, Dray. People have been burned alive for casting doubts like this. And talking of only one sun in the sky is blasphemy—"

"To some people. But the Todalpheme could discuss this as a proposition. The wise men, the Sans of the world—the Wizards of Loh."

"Oh, yes, as a theory. But it runs dangerously close to blasphemy against Opaz, and that is something no honest person can possibly tolerate."

I wanted to burst out into a roar of laughter, I wanted to shout aloud in frustrated fury, and I wanted to cringe away and have no more stupid talk of planets orbiting solitary stars. But I owed Delia an explanation, and so I ploughed doggedly on. This was one eventuality I hadn't bargained for, that religion would rear its beautiful head to deny the possibility that I came from such a crippled world.

"Instead of the seven moons of Kregen there is just the one—"

"Oh, Dray, Dray—if I didn't know you I'd think you were determined to blaspheme. So—there is only one explanation. You are making fun of me."

"No." I was about to go on by saying I was in deadly serious earnest; but I paused. Tsleetha-tsleethi, as Kregens say, softly, softly. "No, I would not do that. But what I have said merits thought..."

This business about a world possessing just a single sun and a single moon was only the beginning. What would Delia say when I tried to explain to her the concept of a world that had no diffs, no splendid array of peoples, no enormous variety of morphology, no halflings; but only had a single sort of human being, apims, like ourselves? How could she accept such an absurdity?

For a space we were silent as the airboat sped on through the level air and Vallia passed away below. Poor Vallia. That was where our thoughts lay. Poor, proud Vallia, an island empire torn and savaged by implacable foes, by power-hungry maniacs, by coldly ambitious men and women— and we flew in all haste from a shattered city and a burning palace which provided a funeral pyre of somber magnificence for the body of Delia's father the emperor. Yet it was precisely at this point that I chose to begin this my late and lame explanation. I tried to talk to Delia of Earth, of that strange planet distant four hundred light years from Kregen, and hoped these transparent means might provide the anodyne she needed. Mysteries partially revealed, I thought, might exercise her mind. But I miscalculated the power of Opaz, the pure religion that, I felt sure at the time, was one certain way to raise Kregen from its barbarity and savagery. Perhaps I was being selfish. All I know is that I was savaged by grief for Delia, whatever may have been my ambivalent attitude to her father, and I was desperate to ease her suffering.

Up front the Lord Farris, Kov of Vomansoir, piloted the flier and left Delia and me to talk in privacy. He had witnessed the death of the emperor, for I had not been there, and had struggled with blood-stained sword to prevent that deed. Now he, like us, was a hunted fugitive.

Lykon Crimahan, Kov of Forli, had also been there at the emperor's death. He had never liked me, being bitterly opposed to my schemes to create a strong Air Service to withstand the attack from Hamal we knew must one day come across the sea. Well, that day had come and gone. Even if the whole power of Hamal had not been thrown into the battle, as I judged, the maniacal Wizard of Loh, Phu-si-Yantong, who controlled through his puppets all of Pandahem and plenty of other spots besides, had gained enough strength to do the work. And, as well as the Hamalese marching against Vondium, there had been traitors from Vallia herself. Layco Jhansi, Udo, the various factions, they were fighting and gnawing at the bones of empire, seeking to snatch the richest portions for themselves.

The Hamalese army that Phu-si-Yantong had somehow got out of the Empress Thyllis had possessed no aerial cavalry of any strength that I had seen. Maybe the flyers were away in another part of Vallia engaged in the campaigns that Yantong must surely carry out to bring as much of the island empire under his heel as he hungered for.

If there were no aerial cavalry mounted on fluttrells or mirvols flying over the corpse of Vondium, there would certainly be plenty of red meat there for the warvols, those vulture-like carrion-eaters. The thoughts and images rose into my mind, most unprettily, most pungent.

All over Vallia as the days passed there would be slaughter. Vallians are accounted a rich people, and most of their wealth comes from trading. They are great seafarers. Inland they are farmers and stockmen and woodsmen. When Vallia needed an army to fight some war or other she would hire mercenaries, and the mercenaries would be secure in the knowledge that Vallia could transport them safely in her fleets of galleons. But as for indigenous fighting men, warriors, they were few and thin on the ground.

That enormous wealth existed within Vallia herself was undeniable. The forests, the mines, the broad cornlands, as the emperor had once told me, they are the sinews of wealth and the muscles of power.

At Lykon Crimahan's request we dropped him off near his provincial capital of MichelDen. MichelDen lies a hundred dwaburs northeast of Vallia's capital Vondium. The provincial capital of Forli stands on the River of White Reenbays, an eastern tributary of the Great River. The kovnate of Forli extends from the Great River to the eastern coast opposite the Thirda Passage between the islands of Arlton and Meltzer to the north and Veliadrin to the south. We had taken a dog's leg passage to Valka in order to let Crimahan off at MichelDen.

He stood with one hand on the coaming of the flier, looking up at us before he jumped down onto the grass. The stars glittered. She of the Veils cast down a sheening diffused golden light and the night was very still.

"I give you the Remberee, Dray Prescot, Emperor of Vallia. I—" And here Crimahan paused, and swallowed.

I own it, the sound of my name coupled with the emperor's landed with a strange sound in my ears, a leaden sound of doom. But Drig take me if I would let this fellow see all the hesitation and indecision tormenting me. I nodded; with a hard and curt gesture of my hand I hoped he would not mistake, I ground out in the old hateful way: "If I am the emperor, Kov Lykon, then your fealty I take and welcome. Now you will do what you can against these cramphs. I shall contact you." His face bore that pained expression of unwelcome comprehension. I finished, surly and domineering: "And mind you don't get yourself killed. May Opaz go with you. Remberee."

The others called their Remberees as Crimahan dropped from the airboat and vanished into the uncertain shadows.

"Up," I said to Farris. "Valka."

The voller rose into the air as Farris hauled on the levers. "He may be going to his death, majister—"

"Very likely, Farris, very likely. But he wanted to go home and I forbore to prevent him. I know how he felt."

"As do we all. I do not need to be told what has overtaken my kovnate," went on Farris in his dogged way. "Vomansoir, like your estates, like Lykon's, must have been marked down for destruction. All those about the emperor and who gave him their loyalty will find only grief in their homes. Once the structure of empire creaks and bends, once the first blows succeed, the collapse is swift."

"There will be fighting and bloodshed all over the land," said Delia, and her lovely face shadowed with the horrors we had seen and the fresh horrors to come.

"Not always," I said in my intemperate, vicious way. "Sometimes an empire will hold out tenaciously. But, Farris, I hope you are right in your estimation when we return."

I said this, and all the time I was totally unsure if I had the right, the moral right, to return to Vallia. But I went on speaking in that old savage way.

"So," I said, only half-believing my own words. "Before we can do anything we must secure a base and see about men and resources—and that means Valka."

The voller rose against the stars and sped eastward.

"Only," I told Delia, "you will take Didi and Velia and Aunt Katri and fly to Strombor. The continent of Segesthes is far enough away from Vallia and these troubles. There they will be safe."

"But—"

I shook my head. Delia did not like the idea of leaving Vallia at this time, even for a short period and even for so important a mission; but she saw the sense of it and agreed to go.

Below us under the glinting moonlight the coast passed away. We struck out across the sea.

We flew across the Rojica Passage that separates Vallia from Veliadrin. We flew along the Thirda Passage, eastward, to the north of Veliadrin. We did not fly over the land. To the south we could see fires burning in the night.

Delia took my arm and I could guess her thoughts.

"Veliadrin is attacked, like all our lands. No doubt the Qua'voils have stirred their prickly selves again. But there are good men down there, as well as evil. Our duty lies elsewhere this night."

It was hard. No doubt of it. We could only guess at what deviltry was going on down there to the south. But little imagination was required to understand that all of Vallia was in turmoil, with old grudges being paid off and with rapaciousness leading men and women on to blood-soaked excesses.

From MichelDen to Valkanium is about two hundred dwaburs in a straight line, what the Havilfarese call 'as the fluttrell flies'. But we circled around over the sea to the north and so took longer over the aerial journey. The Maiden with the Many Smiles joined She of the Veils and although the night was cloudy the two moons shed their fuzzy golden pink light upon the sea.

In the sheening water sparkle below in the light of the moons the dark shadowed mass of Valka rose before us out of the sea. Valka. Valka, the place I had made my home on Kregen. The place that, along with Strombor and the Great Plains of Segesthes and Djanduin, meant more to me at that time than anywhere else. Valka...

"Dray—"

I held her gently, for I knew what Delia intended to say, what pained her to say, how she had struggled and sought for the right words.

"Dray—Valka. All our lands have been attacked, we know that Phu-si-Yantong would not overlook Valka."

I spoke cheerily, and with a certain confidence, for Valka was not quite as other lands of Vallia, because the island had fought its battles and won. "I would not expect that villain to do so. One day he will be chopped. But Valka is not the same easy prey to mercenaries and aragorn and slavers as the rest of Vallia. We have regiments of strong fighting men—"

"But Phu-si-Yantong is a Wizard of Loh. He will have employed sorcery—"

"Yes."

That was, indeed, an unpalatable thought. This damned Wizard of Loh sought to make himself the supreme lord of Paz. He didn't care what he did to achieve that insane ambition.

"If only Khe-Hi-Bjanching was with us—or had been in Valka." Delia's hand trembled against mine. I did not think she trembled in fear. "But he will have been sent to Loh as all our other friends were sent home from—"

"There are other forces of superhuman help," I said, cutting in briskly, over-riding Delia's words. I did not want Farris—or anyone who need not know, for that matter—being apprised of what had happened to our friends. They had all been incontinently hurled back to their homes from the Sacred Pool of Baptism. So far they had not found their way back. That was a contributory cause to the misfortunes that had overtaken us; but we would have been overwhelmed even if all my friends had surrounded us. That I knew with a somber chill.

The dawn would soon be with us, and I suggested that Delia try to sleep. It was not so stupid a suggestion, for she was exhausted and despite her feelings, despite the grief for her father, she did sleep. I could soldier on for a space yet.

I fancied, in thinking of Yantong, that the cramph no longer cared if I lived or died. I had to examine the notion with great care. He had given orders that I was not to be assassinated. I did not know if he had canceled those instructions. Yantong had contrived the death of an empire. His tools fought in Vondium and over the land against the armies of other men, highly placed nobles and demagogues, who sought the throne for themselves. Of all those ambitious and greedy would-be-emperors, I fancied Phu-si-Yantong would be the eventual victor.

And, among his instruments, numbered in the ranks of those who fought for him, was our own daughter Dayra. Unwittingly, perhaps, she served the Wizard of Loh, thinking in all honor that she fought for the rights of self-determination for the North Eastern section of Vallia and this damned fellow Zankov; but she had served Yantong well. Dayra. I would have to tell Delia about her, tell Delia about Ros the Claw, and of her entanglement with Zankov, that same cramph Zankov whose bloody brand had struck down the emperor, Dayra's grandfather.

This was a tangled web, and there was more, and I could not see a clear path to steer.

"Well," I said to myself, and if I had spoken aloud my voice would have cracked out harsh and ugly under the moons, "we will take Didi and Velia and Aunt Katri out of Valka if the place is closed up as tight as a swod's drum. We will see them safely to Strombor. And then—" And then—what?

If I did what I had said I would do, speaking in the heat of the moment and out of anger and foolish pride, there would lie seasons of campaigning ahead. Vallia would run as red with blood as ever it had. How could I justify this? I had pushed these thoughts away before, but they recurred. What moral right had I, what morality was there in it, if I raised armies, fought the usurpers, destroyed their armies, restored the throne of Vallia to its rightful heirs? Did my honor demand that? Can honor ever justify the deaths of thousands of honest people?

Perhaps, as I had wistfully half-suggested to myself, perhaps I would just stay quietly in Strombor, that beautiful enclave of the city of Zenicce, and live life the way life is intended to be lived and enjoyed.

We had taken all night over this flight. The flier was reasonably fast, having covered three hundred dwaburs, about fifteen hundred miles, and it would be full daylight before we reached Valkanium and the Bay and the high fortress of Esser Rarioch.

Below us Valka fled past. Farris had gone back to sleep and as I cogitated with such melancholy with my tormented thoughts and watched the suns rise off to our larboard, I felt the soft warm hand creep into mine and felt again all the magic of my Delia enfold me.

"Dawn," said Delia.

"Aye. And the Suns are rising on a sorry land this day."

"But it is a new day, my heart. A new beginning. A new chance. In Valka—" She expected me to interrupt; but I did not. "In Valka we must find help. We must."

"If we do not, if we do, it makes no difference. You and the children are for Strombor."

The Suns of Scorpio, Zim and Genodras, rose into the clear air. The day would be fine, with perhaps a little rain after the Hour of Mid. Delia sighed.

"I have been thinking of your blasphemous suggestions of a world with one little yellow sun and one silvery moon. It is possible, I grant you. But where is the sense in it? Why do you raise a philosophical point? Is there anything more?"

"Oh, aye," I said, turning so she could nestle into my free arm. "A lot more." I spoke slowly and carefully, trying to make what I said sound sensible, which, to a Kregen, it did not, could not.

"Only apims?" She stared up at me blankly. I leaned down and kissed her. For a space nothing else mattered. Then—

"Only apims. People like us. No diffs, none at all."

"Now I know you make fun. Such a world would be—would be flat, would be—dull!"

"Well—no," I said, defending this our Earth which is so marvelous a world in its own right. "Not flat or dull. Just that Kregen is so much—so much—more," I finished lamely.

She drew a deep breath.

"Very well, husband. Since you choose to mock all the religion and the learning of the wise men—suppose, just suppose a world could exist like that. Then what?"

It was my turn to swallow.

Below us Valka began to show all those myriad colors of her forests and lakes, the mountains of the Heart Heights, the wide open spaces, the serene areas of ordered cultivation, the thread of rivers and the glint of waterfalls. The air breathed sweet and clean, that glorious air of Kregen. This was my own island of unsurpassed beauty, wild and rugged, tranquil and fertile, rich with the goodness of the earth. I drew another deep breath and the fragrant dawn air of Kregen dizzied my senses. For this I would give much, give very much...

Delia looked up at me, her brown hair catching the radiance of the suns so that those outrageous chestnut tints glinted. The richness of her lips, the clarity of her brown eyes, the perfect purity of her face and form—I swallowed again and opened my mouth.

"From such a world, distant a long long way, my heart, I—"

She broke away from me and her chin firmed and the danger signals flashed from those brown eyes that changed from melting tenderness to hard authority. "Flyers! Hamalese! They see us!" I swiveled about, checking my words, stared out. Flyers lifted toward us, their wide wings spread against the light, the flyers on their backs shaking their weapons.

"Not Hamalese," I said after that first flashing glance. "Flutsmen."

The mercenaries of the skies wheeled their flying mounts up toward us like a gale-driven whirlwind of leaves.

Ahead of us the Bay opened out, and the City of Valkanium spread in beauty up the slopes where vegetation bowered my home in verdant beauty. The massive pile of Esser Rarioch reared above the city and the Bay. The light picked out every detail.

Our own flags of Valka still flew from the battlements of Esser Rarioch. But ugly smears of smoke rose from the city. There were sunken galleons in the Bay. Flames spat spitefully from warehouses and from the villas along the shore and overhanging the water. A confused mass hurled up and forward against the fortress and the wink and glitter of weapons splintered shards of light into the morning.

"Esser Rarioch is attacked," I said, and the bitterness choked me with bile.

"But it still holds out." Delia leaped for a crossbow. "We must break through these flutsmen and reach the fortress."

Feathered wings flickered about us. Feathers streamed back in those clotted clumps from their helmets that give to flutsmen their devilish, reiving, headlong appearance. True mercenaries, Flutsmen of Kregen, hiring out to the highest bidder and ready to betray him for a price. They share nothing of the high honor of nikobi that give Pachaks their unmatched reputation as paktuns. Flutsmen often band together and simply reive on their own account. Now, with Vallia torn by strife, these aerial devils struck out for themselves.

I slammed the control levers over to full and bellowed for Farris. The voller lanced up into the air, spraying flutsmen away. Delia, braced against the coaming, loosed, and bent at once to respan the bow.

Some remnants of honor still cling to some flutsmen. I had no way of knowing of what calibre were these aerial foes; but I knew with everything I held precious that I would never allow Delia to fall into their hands.

Farris lumbered out and belted up the deck to the controls. Flutsmen were urging their flying steeds on. For a space we outclimbed them. I shoved my head over the side and looked down. The dark mass of men attacking Esser Rarioch had broken through the first portals of the long stairway and were forcing their way up. The pavises borne before them bristled with arrows. Esser Rarioch was due to fall soon. And the flutsmen bore in toward us, screeching, their weapons glittering.

"Down, Farris!" I bellowed. "Straight down—straight for Esser Rarioch!"

The Lord Farris flung me a single questioning glance. He saw my face, that ugly, demoniac, headstrong old face of mine with the look of the devil, and he thumped the levers over.

Straight through the whirling cloud of flutsmen we plummeted, down and down, hurtling toward the fight raging on the long stairway leading up to Esser Rarioch.

Two

The Folly of Empire

The brave red and white flags of Valka still flew over the battlements, the treshes bright and defiant in the morning light. Down we plummeted. Flutsmen screeched and drove in and were buffeted away and left, trailing far above us. The wind scorched about our ears.

No flyers attacked Esser Rarioch. I smiled. I, Dray Prescot, smiled at the grim and bloodcurdling thoughts—for my Archers of Valka must have remembered and put to good use the techniques they had been taught of repelling aerial cavalry.

So we roared down toward the fight and I peered about intently. Birds and flying animals used as steeds had been virtually unknown in Vallia until the confrontation with Hamal had forced the unwelcome information upon the Vallians. Down south in the magnificent continent of Havilfar there were many and many a variety of flyer, and of them all, I fancied—aye! and still do!—that the fabulous flutduin of my ferocious four-armed Djangs is the finest. A corps of flutduin mounted flyers had been formed in Valka, trained by Djangs brought to my island for the purpose. Where were they now?

Why was not this assaulting mass of infantry being harassed from the air?

These thoughts had to be banished as with the wind blustering past we dropped headlong into the attack.

Queen Lush staggered out, almost falling down the steeply canted deck.

"Take up a crossbow, queen, and let us see how you shoot!"

"I'll shoot, ma faril, I'll shoot—"

So we had three crossbows to loose and Delia and I spanned a half dozen more as we rocketed down.

White and colored blobs showed as the faces of the men in the ranks below looked up. Their wide pavises were studded with arrows.

Varter-hurled bolts splintered off the rocky sides of the stairway, and chunks of stone ricocheted away. I judged that there were few Valkans left in Esser Rarioch to carry on the defense.

Time, time... There is never enough time...

Up the stairway the infantry struggled in the shelter of their large shields, and down we plunged at them. At intervals in the long flight of steps there are generously proportioned landings, places where a fellow might pause and catch his breath as he climbs to Esser Rarioch. The head of the assaulting column had reached one such landing and now it halted. Bows bent against us and arrows flew. The voller was of good Hamalian construction, built soundly of stout wood, mostly sturm, with lenken bracers. The arrows either failed to penetrate or missed and fell away.

The Lord Farris was a fine flier. He would needs be, seeing he was a Chuktar in the Vallian Air Service. Now he eased the voller out of her headlong downward plunge, aiming to bring us up over the heads of the foremost foemen.

Queen Lush leaned over the coaming and let fly. She loosed far too early and where her bolt went Opaz knew.

"Save your bolts, queen!" I bellowed. She glared madly at me, and seized up another of the crossbows.

Farris was swinging us up now in a sweetly contrived curve that would put us in a good shooting position. Queen Lush's second bolt disappeared into the dark mass below.

Delia began to shoot.

We discharged our crossbows and I saw one of the pavises sway and tilt as men fell, their hands lax in death slipping from the cross-struts. But our combined shooting would not make the decisive difference the desperate situation required.

Now Farris was a fine flier, as I have said. I bellowed at him as I frantically wound a windlass.

"Down, Farris! Drop full on them!"

He glared at me, and all the reluctance of an Air Serviceman to hazard his craft showed in his seamed, wind-lined face. The crow's-feet at the corners of his eyes deepened.

With a curse that apostrophized Makki-Grodno's foul and diseased anatomy I hurled myself at the controls. I thunked the lever down, hard. The voller dropped like a leaden plummet.

"Majister!" yelled Farris, aghast.

The airboat smashed down onto the head of the column, onto the pavises, onto the infantry. If there were squashing sounds they were lost in the uproar. The voller lurched. She stuck her stern down, over the rear of the steps leading onto the lower flight. I juggled the controls, lifting her and letting her fall. We ground down as a pestle grinds in a mortar.

Presently, with only a few arrows flicking about us, I lifted. The voller rose smartly enough and I turned her in the air. We looked over the side.

The column was in full retreat, broken into flying fragments. Men ran and scrambled down the stairs. Many fell to roll in brightly swathed bundles of uniforms and armor down the long stairway. I did not smile. But, for the moment at least, we had gained a respite.

"The chance," breathed Farris. "It was a gamble—"

"And the gamble succeeded," said Queen Lush. She had just spanned a bow, struggling with the cords, and now she took careful aim at a wretch running down the steps and sent the bolt full into his back. He leaped into the air, convulsed, and then collapsed, to fall and tumble headlong down onto the pressing backs of his comrades. In a wild tangle of arms and legs and weapons they all slithered down to the next landing.

"Now," I said. "We will find out what is going on here, by Krun!"

"It won't be good news, that is no gamble," said Farris.

"But," said Delia, her chin lifted, her face bright. "Esser Rarioch still stands. The flags still fly."

As we flew up to the high landing platform I fancied that my fortress palace might still stand; but not for long. Anyone of the villains who wanted the downfall of the Empire of Vallia as a prerequisite to assuming the crown himself—or herself—would not allow any strong place of the Prince Majister's to stand. My plans for starting the counter-revolution from Valka must be re-thought. But, then, I'd half-known that all along.

The folk who met us as we alighted from the voller bore the marks of hard fighting. Yellow bandages bore ugly stains. But the men greeted me with a roar of welcome, the women smiling at Delia. Esser Rarioch is a place dear to me, as you know, a place where no slaves were kept. Everyone in the fortress capable of bearing arms did so. We were engulfed in a human tide of talk and explanations of what had happened here and enquiries of what was taking place elsewhere and a determined defiance of anything those rasts outside could do to us.

Chuktars hold high ranks in any army, the name in its original barbaric connotations meaning commander of ten thousand. Nowadays, a Chuktar commands a grouping of regiments or units each under a Jiktar. The Chuktar who met me as I went up onto the battlements gripped my hand in his own brown fist and beamed. I agreed with his decision not to meet me at the landing platform. He was occupied where he was and he pointed out what deviltry was afoot out there as we talked.

The flutsmen had been employed to bring the fortress to a rapid submission, and they had been seen off with volleys of accurately loosed arrows. Chuktar Nath Fergen ti Vandayha pointed at the gathering masses far below filling the Kyro of the Tridents, and he had no need to say they prepared themselves for the next attack.

As we talked I knew Delia would be seeing about Aunt Katri and the children, that Queen Lush would be exciting sidelong glances from the folk of Esser Rarioch, that our own preparations were being made. The Lord Farris joined us on the high battlements, and the pappattu was made between him and Chuktar Nath Fergen.

Jiktar Exand, the commander of the fortress guard, had been wounded early on, and I would go down and see him and give him words of comfort. Nath Fergen had chanced to be in Valkanium when the attack developed. As he said, with a round oath: "Tom took most of the army off to Veli-adrin, for those Opaz-forsaken cramphs of Qua'voil burst out and burned three towns and started to march north. I came here to pick up the Fourth Archers and was just in time to get myself into the castle."

He sounded most wroth. The Fourth Archers, a fine regiment, had been scattered in billets around the town and only a half pastang had made it up the long stairs. Among that number was Naghan ti Ovoinach, now an ord-Hikdar. Panshi, my Chief Chamberlain, came up and superintended the supply of tea and parclear and fruits. Long before Esser Rarioch could be starved out the attackers would have broken their way in, for there were very many of them, and barely a hundred and fifty souls left in the fortress. As for the Valkan army, that was away in the island of Veliadrin, to the west, fighting those porcupine-like devils of Qua'voil who would rejoice to see the destruction of everything apim within their reach.

So, as I listened to the news tumbling out, there was precious little to cheer me. I remained firm in my decision to send Delia and the children to Strombor. All those incapable of fighting must be crammed into the vol-ler. But, I thought with what I hoped was shrewd cunning and not footling incapacity, suppose the voller was used to take everyone out of the fortress by turn? They could be taken into the Heart Heights. We could resist from there as we had in the old days. Yes, I said to myself, and swung about to tell Chuktar Fergen what I proposed.

"But strom! To abandon Esser Rarioch!"

"Aye, Chuktar Nath. Aye! I would abandon this place that I love so dearly to those devils. What is the importance of stone and sculpture against flesh and blood? I would not lose a single man or woman of Valka to save Esser Rarioch." I thought of the emperor, grimly holding onto his fine palace, and getting the place burned down around his ears and himself slain for the sake of it. "The important strategy now is to save our people."

"Yes, my strom—and then we will rise and kick them out—all these invaders, every last one." His full-fleshed face showed the thick blood-pulse beneath the skin, his beaked Vallian nose outthrust. "As we did in the old days, when we chased the aragorn out of Valka! Hai, Jikai! We will write new stanzas to *The Fetching of Drak na Valka!*"

"Hai, Jikai!" shouted the others from the high battlements. "Hai, Jikai!"

The moment was emotional, no doubt of it, and I responded, thinking that, perhaps, if we did what we said then it might well be a Jikai we did. And then those people of mine had to go on, and bellow it out, as they loved to do.

"Hai Jikai!" they shouted, and the swords whipped up, glittering in the lights of the Suns of Scorpio. "Hai, Jikai! Dray Prescot! Strom of Valka!"

It was all proud and stupid and a folly. Pride, pride—well, I have no truck with pride, having fallen flat so very many dreadful times. But, I own, if we all fought as well as we shouted, we should be home and dry.

On that sour mental note I looked out and saw that our shouting had attracted the attention of some of those miserable cramphs below. They were running about, mere black ants so far below in the kyro, preparing to ascend the stairs again and, I trusted, many of them to ascend not to any of their heavens but to the quickest way to the Ice Floes of Sicce.

Joining our group on the high battlements, Delia looked down. Her face drew down in a frown that always has the power to seize my heart up in a constricting grip.

"Is this to be Vondium, all over again?" she said.

I forced my craggy old face to smile for her.

"No. We will evacuate. Everyone will be taken to safety in the Heart Heights. From there, as we did in the old days, we will resist the invaders."

At once she fired up. For only the most fleeting of fallible moments I thought she would protest. But she saw at once that by abandoning Esser Rarioch, for all that we held the place so dear, we would shed an encumbrance and gain freedom of action. To be mewed up in a fortress with a hundred and fifty souls against an army is no way to fight a war. Memories of the Siege of Zandikar ghosted in, and scarlet memories of other sieges; but I looked away to the distant purple haze of those ferocious central mountains of Valka, and took heart.

We held that attack, shooting sheaves of arrows and bolts upon the attackers, rolling masses of stone down the steps, bounding, crunching into the shield, scattering them in a splintering wash of wicker and blood.

In a pause of the action, Jiktar Exand clambered up onto the ramparts, a yellow bandage over his neck and shoulder already glistening with fresh blood. The enormous arch of his ribcage swelled as I greeted him.

I said: "What in the name of the black lotus flowers of Hodan-Set are you doing up here, Exand? Look at that wound!"

Exand's square face bristled under his helmet and he bashed his red and white banded sleeve across his breastplate. I tensed up for his bellow.

"Strom! I cannot skulk in bed when there is fighting to be done! Strom! We fight to the death!"

He was just the same, massive, bulky, creaking in his armor, bulbous, filled with the fanatical devotion of all my fighting men of Valka.

"Well, Exand, my friend. It is indeed good to see you. Now stand you clear of that varter and get a fresh dressing on that wound. You hear?"

"Quidang!" His bellow vibrated against our eardrums. "I hear, my strom!"

The Lord Farris bustled up and took Exand's arm, leading him off, talking. I saw Exand halt as though shafted. He swung about. His quivering alertness took everyone's attention and the shrieking of the infantry below struggling to climb those murderous stairs faded. Exand's face turned that purple that the best Wenhartdrin wines hold within their bodies.

"Majister!" Exand fairly roared out, purple, immense, consumed with overwhelming joy. "Hai, Emperor of Vallia!"

My first thought was that Farris had to go and open his mouth. He was loyal to the emperor—to the emperor that was—and to Delia. I knew a loyal man, and I valued Farris far too much to fault him in so petty a thing as this.

After that, when we had thrown the attack back and could take a breath, the buzz went around the fortress. The emperor was dead: long live the emperor.

I have mentioned how my folk of Valka continue to call me their strom, somehow or other conveniently overlooking the rather comical thought that I was the Prince Majister of Vallia. Well, now they knew I was the Emperor of Vallia. Although, at that moment, I was the Emperor of Nothing. But they continued to call me strom, with occasionally a lapse into more formal majisters for the sake of propriety.

This somewhat farcical interjection of emperors and majisters into the grim business of staying alive within the besieged fortress served to force upon me the thought that I was more like the fabled Pakkad, the outcast, the pariah, than any emperor. I had not wanted to be emperor, had not sought the throne and crown of Vallia. And, the plain fact was, I did not have them. The corpse of Vallia was being fought over as lurfings fight over a corpse on the great plains.

The desire to dabble my fingers in that stew appeared more and more unattractive, more and more unworthy.

Thrusting these morose broodings aside I joined in the preparations. The voller would take out the people in relays and with them weapons and supplies. Up in the Heart Heights we would find refuge. As an accomplished flier, Farris offered to make the first journeys. For the moment the attackers had drawn off and so I decided to catch up on a little sleep. The first voller load was seen off and then I went into our private apartments and stretched out on the bed. Before I went to sleep two thoughts hovered lazily in my mind and the first of these was cheerful and reassuring.

Among these defenders of Esser Rarioch and all the other fearsome warriors of Valka who would continue the resistance there would be found no place for that robust figure of legend, Vikatu the Dodger, the archetypal Old Sweat of most of the armies of Paz. That mythical old soldier is loved and sworn by with enormous gusto by the swods in the ranks, a paragon of all the military vices, the old hand who looks after Number One and knows every trick in and out of every book and manual of soldiering ever written. The fighting men of Valka might cuss away in Vikatu's best style, but they were not soldiers in the strict regimental sense, not even the swods of the regiments we had formed, disciplined, controlled, trained. In the struggles that lay ahead I thought that not one fighting man of Valka would misunderstand the reality of Vikatu and dodge his duty.

So that, as far as it went, was all right. We would, as Kregans say, blatter them with a will.

But—by all the grey ones of Sicce—but the other thought coiling in my head made me twist and turn uncomfortably on the bed. I was still totally undecided. I had spoken out about returning, had half-promised to regain the throne and crown. But, even with all the strictures laid on me, the ideas of honor, the knowledge of evil that would cover the land unopposed in any meaningful way, even with all this and the high ideals of the Kroveres of Iztar, even then I was not fully committed to a course that would bring further bloodshed. What was Vallia to me? I cherished estates in other parts of the world. Delia's father the emperor was murdered and his empire sundered. Why should I seek to restore all that blaze of pomp and pageantry, resuscitate the power and the glory? Were those ends moral? Could the suffering be tolerated? How could all this maelstrom of future misery be justified?

So, as I slipped into sleep with a million torturing thoughts troubling me, you will see I was in a most foul mood. Only that last thought before sleep of Delia held any power to sooth me.

Three

Delia Looses an Opinion at the Star Lords

The sleep lasted long enough to refresh. The voller made two more trips and the defenders of the fortress were very thin along the battlements indeed. We had to take thought to arrange the best way of the final evacuation.

"The folk are being cared for at friendly farms in the Heart Heights," said Farris. He looked windblown and tired. "But it is wild country up there—wild."

"Aye. Valka will never fall to invaders whilst the Heart Heights stand."

The remainder of the force was split into two. I moved along the sun-splashed battlements to talk privately with Delia. I knew I'd encounter opposition.

"I do not think, husband, that that is a very good plan at all. In fact, if you ask me, I'd say it was a plan suitable for Cottmer's Caverns."

Below us the incredibly beautiful vista of Valkanium and the Bay spread out, dappled in sunshine, the light drifting of rain after the Hour of Mid burnishing everything with a glistening patina of gold. The attackers far below were thinking of forming up for another onslaught. They had lost a great many men, and they could see no other way of getting at us in Esser Rarioch than of climbing up those blood-spattered stairs.

They did not know of the secret entrances and exits far below the rock.

I persisted stubbornly.

"You will fly out with the children and Aunt Katri. I want you with them."

"But Aunt Katri is perfectly capable—she may be getting old, now, true; but the nurses—"

"You. You will take the penultimate trip. We may have to cut and run for it on the last one."

"I know. And don't you think I would be at your side?"

A shadow fleeted between the ruby glory of Zim and the ramparts. I looked up. My fist tightened on my sword hilt.

Up there, planing in its arrogant wide-winged circles, flew the Gdoinye, the spy and messenger of the Star Lords. That gorgeous golden and scarlet raptor circled up there, his head on one side, one beady eye fixed upon us.

Delia said in a voice that almost but not quite trembled: "There is that bird again—"

"Aye... A Bird of Ill Omen. Delia—I have promised to tell you why I am sometimes dragged away from you when all I want is to stay with you. Not like now, when it is sensible for you to go with the children. But, the other times—"

"I remember them, I remember them all. They were horrible."

What was horrible to me in that moment, as well as the enforced absences I made at the orders of the Everoinye, the Star Lords, was that Delia could see the bird. I knew Drak my eldest son had seen it, and I had lied to him and said the bird was not there. But the Star Lords did not reveal their powers to many. I feared and hated the idea of my Delia being caught up in the schemes of superhuman unknown and unknowable beings who demanded so much from me without explanation.

"The bird is connected with your—disappearances."

"Yes. And the Scorpion."

"On the field of the Crimson Missals, when you said you did not want to go to Hyrklana—and I went there—and—"

I tried to make a laugh and failed. "I'd be sorry, now, if I hadn't gone to Hyrklana and fought in the Jikhorkdun of Huringa. Then we would not have Tilly and Oby and Naghan the Gnat and Balass the Hawk as friends."

"And where they are now, Opaz knows."

"We will fetch them back, if they wish to come."

"I think they will make their way back here, to Valka, for they are true Valkans now—"

"And what a sorry mess Valka and Vallia are in!"

The scarlet and golden bird circled, watching us. I shook my fist at it, and it continued on, indifferent.

"And when the shanks attacked that little village of Panashti, on the island of Lower Kairfowen, and you fell from the gate and we carried you to a hut. It was all a confusion. The walls and huts were burning. Those terrible Leem Lovers were breaking in—the walls came down and the smoke blew. We fought. Oh, Dray! You should have seen Drak. He was like a young zhantil. You would have been proud."

Drak had grown up since then, become a man, a prince, a Krozair of Zy. His life had not been easy. Now Delia poured out all the wonder and the hidden-away hurt, the bewilderments she had felt over the years of our life together.

"I had gone to see you in the hut and—and you were not there! Only your armor and your weapons. I feared, then, remembering the other times, Jynaratha, over the Shrouded Sea—and then, even your weapons were gone. We fought as hard as we could and then Tom and Vangar came and we were saved. Drak was suddenly aware. Men looked to him. He and I, between us—and there was Turko and Naghan and Balass and all the others. There was such a lot of shouting and confusion. It was given out that you had gone to punish the shanks. Men believed. We were able to leave Panashti without any suspicion that you had died being voiced. Later, it was suggested—but you know—and, anyway, you have gone before to visit other lands, as all men know."

"Twenty-one years," I said, and I shivered.

The Star Lords had banished me to Earth for twenty-one long and miserable years because I had defied them.

Delia put her hand on my arm.

"And then you disappeared from the voller as we flew to Aphrasöe—that was mysterious and terrible—"

"The Scorpion," I said. "I will tell you why I sometimes have to go away, and why I have decided to resist in different ways that do not mean I go back to—go away for twenty-one years."

She looked at me and a wary look warned me.

"Back to—where?"

I did not reply.

"Back to the Great Plains of Segesthes? To your Clansmen?"

It would have been only a little difficult to lie. I shook my head.

"But where, my heart, where? Tell me—"

"If I do tell you, you will believe, I think, for I love you enough to know that—but it will be hard."

She looked at me, and I knew my stupid remark had not only been unnecessary, it showed her how tangled up I was.

The wind blew the red and white flags of Valka out in a fluttering panoply. We would leave them flying when we deserted this beautiful place. For a time they would convince those rasts below we still resisted them. The red and white of Valka...

Among the treshes fluttering from the flagstaffs someone had hoisted my own old battle flag, the yellow cross on the scarlet field, that battle flag fighting men call Old Superb.

I wondered then if I could bear to leave that behind.

What I did know and with sharp agony, was that if I defied the Star Lords who had brought me to Kregen I would leave more than a flag behind me when I was ejected with contempt from this exotic and cruel world.

The bird volplaned away, turning in a gentle glide, and the suns sheened a brilliance along his feathers. I wondered what Delia would do, what say, if the Gdoinye slanted back to us and spoke to me. The messenger of the Everoinye usually insulted me—well, we understood each other's tempers in that. But I did not want to risk what Delia might say if the bird did speak to us. I wanted to move us along. I wanted—what I wanted was just about anything than having to go through this.

The quick, intuitive empathy between Delia and myself has always given me a trembling feeling of possessing beauty beyond price. Always, I stress that we call each other 'My Delia' and 'My Dray' and the togetherness is complete, unshakeable, unremarked on save as I speak this record, and yet that possession is mutual, not a diseased obsession of property, one or the other. We are two people, two rounded persons, and yet together we are more than a single rounded one, more than merely one and one, more than two; and through all this rapturous spectrum of feeling, the dark hollow secret I carried dragged at me, tearing at me, and I knew that Delia sensed that apartness and grieved.

So, with that empathy between us, I was not surprised when she began to speak in a low, serious voice, as we stood there in the radiance of the Suns of Scorpio. But her voice faltered, hesitated, her face was half-averted, and those brown eyes did not regard me with that same old brave look I knew and loved. All my primeval instincts flared into my thick old skull. Her mouth trembled as she spoke and yet she controlled herself, and I saw the way her hand fingered the brooch upon her breast and fell away and so crept up again. I felt the blood in my head.

"You have watched performances of *Sooten and Her Twelve Suitors*, I know." She would not look at me. "The story is old, as old as Kregen itself. An abandoned wife is prey. There are many men whose minds dwell on their opportunities, whose desires, whose hands—" She stopped speaking, unable to go on.

Sooten, as you know, is a legend of Kregen that parallels in emotional depth the brave Earthly story of Penelope, wife to Odysseus, mother of Telemachus. Like Penelope, Sooten kept her suitors at bay. I sensed that Delia was trying to feel her way to telling me things I had best learn at first hand, if at all, and my mind went back to what I had heard, posing as Jak Jakhan, in the Baths of the Nine called the Bower of the Scented Lotus in Vondium. There those oafs had nudged and winked and repeated tales of the notorious affairs of the Princess Majestrix of Vallia. The rubbish had passed from my mind as the cess pits are emptied and purified with that remarkable concoction made from the little blue fallimy flower. And, chained in a prison cell, I had heard other salacious stories.

In the many rich pantheons of Kregen there stands the archetypal figure of the seducer, suave, groomed, glib-tongued. He knows well how to comfort and feed the vanity of women and this Quergey the Murgey is charmingly versed in the ways of breaking down the defenses of wives who, for whatever reason, are estranged from their husbands. I should add that I give this contemptible figure a name that is not his own, his real name being much contumed over Kregen, and I choose to use this alias. Perhaps, one day, his own name and not his use name will be revealed. Odysseus was gone for twenty years. I had been gone many times, and once for twenty-one whole years. As I looked at Delia I understood that many men had essayed her, and I knew they had failed. Her own inner spirit and strengths would not fail her, and although she knew my opinion of the sin of pride, in this case her own pride would rise and she would draw her virtue from our love. Her strength would not fail no matter that I was absent, gone, removed. What we meant to each other remained steadfast despite my seeming rejection of her, leaving her distraught and abandoned and prey to the scum who batten on unhappy women.

One of Quergey the Murgey's favorite techniques is to practice the sympathy routine, offering help and a firm shoulder on which to lean and cry, and so lead on, subtly, delicately, to the fulfillment of his desires. He feeds the anguished ego with words the woman craves to hear. Delia would see through all that. But she felt she must try to make the oafish, foolish, thoughtless Dray Prescot understand the load she bore. And, understanding, my anguish for her agony almost destroyed me—almost, for my Delia of the Blue Mountains was with me now and no matter what happened we would be together in ways of love far beyond the comprehension of mere mortal flesh and blood.

That belief is not rooted in religion or mysticism of a mundane kind—and that is not a contradiction in terms—is not understood by the seducers of the world. The meretricious creeds that condone the acts of Quergey the Murgey offer cheap substitutes for reality, like the evil creed of Lem the Silver Leem, and claim their reality is of life when it is of death.

The scarlet and golden bird circled, watching us.

My wife must understand that my absences were forced on me and not of my own free will. The idea that she would fail to grasp my ludicrous story of a world with one sun and one moon and only apims for people appeared to do her a most injurious injustice. Was she not Delia? Of course she would understand, and in understanding, gain strength to repel with the contempt they deserved all those moist-mouthed, hypocritical well-wishers, the suitors infected by the poison of Quergey the Murgey. She looked up at me and her chin lifted. She looked marvelous.

"Yes, my heart. There are stories. I beg you—do not un-sheath your Krozair longsword against those little people. They do not merit that worth of attention."

"You are with me, Delia." I spoke most soberly. "That is all I want."

"And all the rest," she whispered, and leaned toward me and the Gdoinye flew down and hawked out a coarse barking cry. She glanced up, and said: "These absences—you will tell me. But there are puzzles, sorely troubling, in the times. Time seems unreal." She spoke in a reflective way now, the storm over, searching for knowledge, remembering our partings.

The messenger and spy of the Star Lords hovered over us.

Delia eyed the Gdoinye with a speculative eye. "You made yourself Strom of Valka when—"

"I was made, my love," I corrected, mildly.

"Yes. You were Fetched to be Drak na Valka. And that happened—it *must* have happened—when you and I, and Seg and Thelda were marching through the hostile territories. I have thought about this. I have thought that I spent but one day apart after we met, whilst you were off in Segesthes and your Clansmen, or at least, so it seems. A person cannot be in two places at once, can they?" Here she moved a little way away, pensive, troubled and struggling with her thoughts. "Also, you are King of Djanduin and when did that happen?" She looked at me, and caught that luscious lower lip between her teeth. "And will you say you were Fetched to be King of Djanduin?"

"No." I spoke with humility and with anger. "No. I own I set out to make myself King of Djanduin. But I changed along the way. It was a long and wearisome wait through the seasons."

"So," she said, and sparked up. "So the sorcerer is very powerful. I do not think even a Wizard of Loh could match what I suspect."

"That is true—if you suspect truth. That, I do not know."

The Gdoinye angled closer, ruffling his feathers, slanting down toward us.

"And does this great bird come to take you away from me again?"

At my troubled look Delia gave me no time to answer. She whipped up the crossbow to hand, one we had taken from the voller. It was ready spanned. She triggered the nut, the bow clanked, the bolt sped.

I gaped.

I felt the chill. What would happen now?

Delia, my Delia of Delphond, had loosed at the Gdoinye!

What thunder would roll from the heavens? What lightnings spit down and split the castle walls? What hailstones might lash us to a bloody froth? I let out a yell and rushed for Delia, swept her up into my arms, pressing her head against my chest. I glared up madly. The bird circled and the bolt whickered up and in my heightened state I followed the cast with raking eyes. Delia had shot true. The bolt would hit...

So fast it all happened, so fast, pelting fleeter than a zorca over the plains. A voice hammered against the brightness of the day.

"Fool! Onker! Have you learned no lessons, Dray Prescot?"

And a stunning flash of blue fire illuminated the sky, washed over the stone walls, burst in thunder about my ears. The bolt burst asunder, limned by blue fire, smashed and broken, falling away, twisting, dropping.

Even then, I knew no other eyes but those of Delia and my own would have seen that coruscating display of power.

For a heartbeat, for a single heartbeat, I thought the blue smash of fire destroyed the crossbow bolt alone. And then I knew differently, knew better—I, Dray Prescot, Lord of Strombor and Krozair of Zy, knew I had another lesson to learn.

Blueness coiled around us.

"Dray!"

The radiance twined grasping tentacles around us—between us. I felt the old hateful sensations of falling. Delia was no longer clasped in my arms. I glared up, my whole body and mind wracked with hatred. Up there, blazing against the sky, drowning out the refulgence of Zim and Genodras, the enormous bloated form of the ghostly Scorpion glowered down on me.

Gropingly, frantically, I reached for Delia. The stones of the ramparts beneath my booted feet scraped harshly. Coldness fell over me like the chill cloak of the grey ones. Delia—she was gone, torn away from me—no! I was being torn away from her as I had so often been dragged away before.

Hateful memories of those other times when I had been wrenched away from Kregen by this ghostly blue representation of a Scorpion battered at me. I tried to shout, and nothing came save a wheeze. The blueness deepened.

And that blueness wavered; the Scorpion trembled as though formed of smoke wafted from a campfire, and being blown this way and that by the evening breeze from the high mountains.

The Scorpion dissolved.

A flush of crimson light spread across the firmament from starboard, and I switched instinctively to search the larboard side for that welcome glow of yellow gold.

But the yellow fascinating gold of Zena Iztar did not appear to cheer me and give me comfort and help.

A vivid acid green jaggled into the sky, hard-edged, sharp, cutting across the blue.

Voices, as though confined in an echoing cavern shielded miles deep in rock, ghosted across, hollow voices, muffled and echoing, yet clear, distinct, so that I heard. And, hearing, I braced myself, prepared to meet the new challenge and attempt with all the will-power in me to resist. Perhaps—I had been told—perhaps a mental force alone would suffice. I did not know. All I knew was that I must resist and summon myself, the inner me that was plain and simple Dray Prescot, to stand against these superhuman forces.

"He is mine. I run him, for you are weak and old..."

The acid voice dripped with power.

"Not so, Ahrinye! Not so. For we are the Everoinye—" The answering voice boomed, muffled, half-choked, yet deep with the reverberations of habitual authority.

"You may be Everoinye, but you have forfeited your rights. I am a Star Lord, also. I—" And then the acrid voice screeched into an incoherency that jumbled the passionate words together like the screech of metal against the grinder's wheel. The bitter green light fluctuated wildly.

This quarrel among the Star Lords affected me and yet I felt a frail confidence that the Everoinye did not know I could hear them. Their own passionate natures were well hidden, repressed, controlled by the flame of their purpose, that I believed. They were superhuman and therefore would not think as a man would think. They wrangled and I listened, and all the time I watched for the yellow golden flush of light that would herald the arrival of Zena Iztar.

What they said contorted thought; I could not then comprehend all and it would not be proper to attribute what little I later learned to the Dray Prescot who was the me who listened in such awed and yet defiant fascination.

The Star Lord called Ahrinye, he of the jagged acid green light and sharp acid voice, showered his youthful contempt upon the elders of the Star Lords. As I braced myself up, ready, hating them all, raging, I yet had time to reflect that the Star Lords in this but followed the same time-consuming course as fragile humanity—except that, I knew, the Everoinye were by thousands of years older than the oldest man who ever lived, on Earth or on Kregen.

They wrangled over me. Ahrinye wanted to use me with a greater force than hitherto and, I realized, a greater harshness, a lack of even the rudimentary concerns for my skin the Star Lords had shown. Mind you, I did not think they cared for me one jot after I had done their dirty work for them. And then the name spurted from the maze of shrouded talk and I snapped into even more alert listening.

"Phu-si-Yantong?" said Ahrinye. "Your lordling suffers from him and I would send a summary Gdoinye to settle that."

"You think you may stand against us, and you know so little. The lordling Prescot has been given a measure of protection against the Wizard—for their puny powers quail even at the thought of the Savanti. And the Shere'affo Iztar meddles—"

I winced. The viridian green light exploded into whorls of jagged lightning. Enormous thunders crashed about my head. The blue light pulsed and, tiny, creeping, but there, real and penetrating, a golden yellow glow grew low on the horizon.

And I understood. At the mention of the name of Zena Iztar these puissant and superhuman beings took notice, took cognizance—I could not believe they feared. But they became wary—yes, wary would be the name for the emotions I sensed coiling there in the sky colors coruscating above my head.

The crimson beat a steady pulse of glowing ruby light through all the other clash of color.

All the time I stood upon the battlements of Esser Rarioch, in my capital city of Valkanium, in my island Stromnate of Valka—and yet I might as well have been on Earth, or Esser Rarioch have been flung to the farthest depths of space.

And although I say I understood, I understood that I had grasped at a tiny fragment of what was going on. Amid all this frightening display of supernal power I gleed at the thought that Zena Iztar did, indeed, possess some vestiges of influence. However she may wish to influence the course of events, Zena Iztar, I felt with a dim sense of prying perhaps beyond the evidence, must perforce direct the current, seek to steer events rather than to originate them. The yellow glow faded.

I tried to scream out for Zena Iztar to remain, to succor me; but I was falling, falling, feeling the chill biting into me, and I heard, faint and far-away, like the echo of a lost child in the darkling woods: "Dray! Dray! Where are you?"

The cords in my throat stood out as I tried to bellow back. "Delia! Delia—" But no sound forced its way from my ashen lips.

Once again I was being hurtled head-over-heels into fresh adventure, being flung halfway across Kregen to succor someone whom the Star Lords wished to remain alive for the sake of their future plans.

Where before I had insanely contumed the Star Lords and sought to fly back at once to Delia, and been banished to Earth for my pains, this time I would do what the Everoinye commanded, do it fast and quick and ruthlessly. Then I would return to Valka. Better, return to Strombor, for I knew Farris would make sure that Delia was taken with the children to refuge in my enclave of Strombor in Zenicce.

The blueness roared in my head like a rashoon of the Eye of the World.

The Scorpion, writhing in blue fire sharded with the crimson glints of Antares, had me in its grip. Wherever on Kregen I was thumped down to get on with the commands of the Star Lords would not be too far for me to claw my way back.

As always I was thumped down stark naked. A ferocious screaming and bellowing lacerated the hot air. Joe Muggins, Dray Prescot, yanked from all he wanted on Kregen and sent to sort out a problem for the Star Lords. Well, this time I'd do it so damned fast even the Everoinye wouldn't have time to blink.

There was no hesitation in my mind over what I was supposed to do.

I had been hurled down into a small wooden cabin which had been ripped and wrecked and thrown into confusion, with odd bits of clothing and kitchen utensils scattered everywhere. A man lay sprawled on the floor, his right hand trapped under his body. He was dead, his head cloven in. I leaped to my feet, feeling a dragging weight pulling at my limbs, launched myself at the man who was trying to strangle the half-naked woman. She clutched a baby to her and screamed and screamed.

As I say, there was no doubt in my mind what I was supposed to do.

The people were all apims, like me, and the fellow whose neck I took into my fists, twisting a trifle, for I wanted to ask him some questions, wore a hide loincloth and a quantity of beadwork. His head was shaved somewhat after the fashion of a Gon or a Chulik. He tried to slash me with his little steel-headed axe and I ground down harder so that he slumped.

I threw him down and heard the betraying shush of a shoe across the floor. The cabin was lit by a cheap glass oil lamp. The light beamed out mellowly. It was a wonder the lamp had not been upset in the struggle before I arrived.

The turn I made and the immediate sideways step were all done without thought, heritage of the Disciplines of the Krozairs of Zy. The fellow who was in the act of leaping at me, his axe upraised, was dressed as his companion. A tangle of ridiculous feathers tufted about the haft of the axe. It was only a small axe; but I knew that kind of weapon and I knew the fellow wielding it would be exceedingly ferocious and swift, no matter what part of Kregen I might be in.

The axe-head sliced down, glittering. I slid the blow and stepped in and he tried to seize me with his free hand. His face looked a flat-nosed shriek of absolute resolve. He was a savage, no doubt of it, in his fighting techniques. But so was I. I gave him no time to grapple or to bring the axe back.

A knee into his vitals, a chopping blow to his neck, and a slashing smash of my forearm as he went down, finishing with a kick to whatever came handiest as he rolled. He flopped. I gave them both a reassuring tap with the little axe-head, not to slay them but to keep them in cold storage for a space.

The woman was still shrieking. She glared at me with wide-eyed horror and she could not speak. The baby was yelling.

I stepped across to a pile of clothes all tangled up and then my head snapped up. My hand fastened on a pair of trousers made from some hard blue material. But, outside, shouts lifted, the sound of men yelling, muffled words and the trample of feet. Hastily pulling on the trousers, which had to be doubled up around my waist and yanked tight with the belt, I snatched up the axe and started for the door.

Men were yelling out there. I heard a sudden shriek which, if I knew anything, was the sound of a friend of these two sleeping beauties in the act of charging. The first one in the door wouldn't be put to sleep—he'd be flattened.

The door burst open. A man towered, on the threshold, the lamp glinting from his sweat-soaked coppery skin. His axe looked identical to the one I grasped, save that I'd taken time to rip away the silly tangling feathers. He saw me and he gave a single incoherent shriek and charged.

His lank black hair was bound by a fillet and he wore a few feathers there. I sidestepped, hit him over the head, smashed him down and so whirled as another appeared. This one tried to be clever, whipping a broad-bladed knife in with his left hand as he struck with the axe. But I'd fought for many and many a year with a sword and a left-hand dagger, the Jiktar and the Hikdar. I foined briefly, desperately anxious to get these idiots off my back and hightail it back to Valka or Strombor. I pitched him down to lie with his comrades, although, as I had bleakly surmised, he did not sleep. I had to slash half his face off before he'd consent to lie down.

The screaming from the woman and the baby went on and on and there was no time to shout at them as a fifth man leaped into the doorway. He took a single look at the scene within, the shrieking woman and the baby, his four comrades sprawled and bloody on the floor, and me, a right tearaway with an axe fronting him, and he half turned.

He stood in the doorway, the light gleaming from his powerful body.

I was perfectly prepared to let him go. I had no idea where I was, but I had no wish to slaughter more than was inescapable if I was to do what I had been commanded to do. If he attacked the woman and the child, he would probably die. If he ran away I might run a greater risk; but that was an equation that honor demanded.

I shook the axe at him, to help him make up his mind.

From outside the approaching beat of hooves heralded the arrival of a hard-riding group of men. The staccato hammer held much of the rhythm of a zorcatroop; certainly they were not totrixes with their awkward six-legged gait or nikvoves with their battering array of eight hooves. The man in the doorway threw me a look of so powerful a hatred I was minded to charge forward and settle his hash there and then. In the linen and beadwork band about his dark hair he wore more feathers than the others. He moved smoothly, like a chavonth, the lamplight running in gleaming shadow-filled highlights across his muscles.

A succession of strange noises broke from outside—noises I did not at once identify. The first impression was of some maniac hammering a dull but noisy drum, or repeatedly slamming a heavy door. The coughing bangs erupted with the violence of a summer storm, bursting thunder about our ears.

Ready to leap forward and make sure the woman and child were safeguarded from this fifth fellow who had tried to kill them, I stopped stock still.

The man jerked. He stiffened. He dropped his axe. He half-turned, shaking with some invisible force. He staggered and then, limply, collapsed.

From his back a gush of blood dropped down.

I stared.

I looked down on him.

And I trembled.

The banging sounds continued. But I knew what they were.

With a roar of rage and agony I hurled forward, reached the door, looked out.

The shack stood near the end of an untidy row of similar shacks, and a raised boardwalk connected them above the road. Other men clad in loincloths and wielding axes and knives, some with bow and arrows, ran this way and that, and many fell. Up the center of the street rode a party of men, wearing clothes I recognized.

And, over all, the silvery flood of light from a single moon lit the scene in hard metallic pewter brilliance.

Again and again the Winchesters and the Colts and the Remingtons flamed.

I felt sick.

Somehow I was back in the cabin, looking at the woman who stared in horror at me, her sobs shaking her, her cheeks wet. She cradled the baby to her. Slowly, I picked up a shirt, a red and white checked shirt, whereat I felt a fresh pang, and put it on. Boots stood nearby. The woman's husband would not require boots for his last journey to Boot Hill.

"You are safe now," I said, and my voice made her flinch back.

I turned to the door and men crowded in. They were apims, like me—well, they would be, wouldn't they? There were no Fristles and Rapas and Chuliks and all the other wonderful assemblage of diffs within four hundred light years.

"You all right, pardner?" The man who spoke wore Levis, a hickory shirt, a tin badge and a wide-awake hat. He held his Army Remington easily one-handed, and the muzzle centered on my midriff. I own he was wise to show caution. Despite my pants and boots and shirt, I must have looked far more like the Red Indians he had been shooting at than any of the White-eyes with him.

"I'm all right. This lady needs help—"

One of the others turned the bodies over with his toe.

"These two ain't dead, Hank."

The leader, the one with the silver star, said: "See to Mrs. Story, Jess." He eyed me meanly. "Reckon I don't know you, mister."

Carefully, I placed the axe down. The men stared into the room, seeing the lax forms of the Indians, the mess, the sobbing woman—and seeing me, scowling, black-browed, looking more mean and savage than any painted Indian busted loose they'd ever run across.

"I'm Dray Prescot," I said, and although I tried to make my harsh voice easy, I knew my words spat out like the slugs from their guns. "This lady appeared in need of help."

"You did fer them injuns?" The men looked perplexed. The woman, Mrs. Story, was assisted to her feet. The men talked about 'gitting her to the doc' and so I felt she was now safe. If the Star Lords had commanded me to rescue her and her baby, then I had done that. But there was no easy way now of my returning to Valka or Strombor. I was once more marooned on Earth, stranded and desolate on the planet of my birth.

My appearance was easily enough explained—I'd been raked out of bed by the fighting and had run to Mrs. Story's assistance. But the posse eyed me askance for a space, until the easy open-handed way of the West, and question and counter-question, plus the convincing results of my handiwork plain to be seen sprawled on the floor, assured them of my bona fides. I managed to keep track of the situation and not betray an almost impossible to explain away ignorance of local conditions. The Indians had broken out, as they were wont to do, for down here the main fighting had been finished up a few years back.

Down around South Fork things erupted only now and then, and the main action had transferred north, where great disasters had shaken the nation. The local people were still jumpy. All the talk was of the frightful events of the 25th June last. The newspapers carried a leaked confidential report severely critical of Custer and his handling of the tactical situation at the Little Big Horn. I remembered the braves who had tried to do for me and was forced to wonder if not only the tactical but the strategical handling was amiss. They were men, like me, even if their skin was a coppery color. They were not Fristles or Rapas or Chuliks, and they also are men, if not like me.

Around that time a considerable amount of English money was being invested in the West. Having to face the catastrophic fact that the Star Lords had not pitched me into another part of Kregen but had dispatched me back to Earth, the world of my birth, I was still in no frame of mind to settle down. I had the opportunity of going partners more than once in a fine ranch; but I turned them all down. I took a swing through the Staked Plains and checked out Charles Goodnight's JA Ranch, a spread he ran with John Adair's money. They were just beginning their fabulous build up. Then I drifted west through El Paso and had me a rip-roaring time in Tombstone.

This was a couple of years before Wyatt Earp showed up with his kinfolk and Doc Holliday. Rather to my surprise I discovered that men would shoot whole magazines of Winchester ammunition away, or the full six shots from their Colts, and still not hit anything. I could draw reasonably fast; but did not make a habit of it. As to accuracy, given a gun I knew, I could hit what I aimed at. So I stayed out of trouble and drifted north. The 2nd August had witnessed the shooting of Hickok, in Carl Mann's Saloon in Deadwood. Already, men wouldn't play a hand of cards consisting of aces and eights.

So I drifted around the frontier, not doing much of anything. As I have said before, it is not my purpose to tell you of my life here on this Earth. Certainly I got myself into a few scrapes and tight corners during this period, and found out enough to know that a great deal of guff was written then about the West, guff that has been continued to the present day.

My bankers in the City of London sent funds promptly as requested, and I had more or less reached the conclusion of going east, at least across the Mississippi and south, and then of repeating my previous swing around the country ending up in New York. From there England tempted me.

The continuing improvement in repeating firearms interested me greatly. The Spencer I had known in Civil War days was now quite outclassed, although remaining a fine weapon, by the new Winchesters. The model '73 with its stronger receiver than the model '66 proved a reliable weapon, although lacking the range and penetration of military firearms. As for the revolvers, a plethora of different patterns and styles vied for attention. I studied everything I could, and this time I had very much in mind that the wise men of Kregen might be brought to a consideration of a repeating varter. The gros varters of Vallia, the best of their kind in my opinion, might work wonders on the Leem Lovers if some kind of repeating mechanism could be provided.

Of one thing I felt reasonably although not one hundred percent certain. It would destroy a great and intangible asset if gunpowder were to be introduced to Kregen.

By the time I'd reached Saint Louis the thought of spending time in England appealed overwhelmingly to me—until I ran across Amos Brown who had a hankering to go to California. Well, he talked me into it. We outfitted ourselves in great style, and Amos, who'd been a mule-skinner up around Laramie and ways west for a number of years, expressed himself as plumb pleased at our rigs. He was a short, spare, wispy-haired little guy with a mean shot-gun trigger finger. Well, we set off full of high spirits to cross Missouri just as fast as we could and then across Kansas. The place was already being domesticated, and Amos couldn't stand the smell of ironing and scrubbing and stoop-sweeping.

Dodge City was just about played out, too—or so it was given out. We got into only one good fight, and from then on to Santa Fe the rest of the folks with us more or less kept us on our best behavior. But I never got to Santa Fe—leastways not on that swing.

The blue radiance descended on me as I rode drag to the remuda—for we had a few wealthy folk with us—and the dust biting into my throat and the shushing of the hooves for a split-second prevented the reality of what was happening from penetrating.

Then I understood and I let fly with a holler and a whoop and felt the pony slipping away from between my knees. I gave a convulsive snatch at the Sharps scabbarded under the saddle—it was a model '77 chambered for the three and a quarter inch, 45-120-550 load, not too hefty, with a beautiful full octagonal barrel of 34 inches, a real Creedmoor beauty with tang sight—and felt that vaporize under my fingers. No good going for the Winchester on its California saddle horn loop or the Improved Army Remington .44 at my waist—that revolver cost me eighteen dollars, plus a premium to get it—or, indeed, the Bowie knife. The Star Lords were calling me and all the gunpowder in the whole of the West wouldn't stop them.

Whirling up, seeing the radiance enfolding me and watching with a choked fascination the enormous shape of the Scorpion glowing against the sky, I had time for what was a remarkably lurid reflection on the reactions of Amos and the rest of the bunch to my disappearance. When my pony trotted in with everything in place and without me—they'd spend a heck of a time rooting around trying to find me or my body.

Maybe, I said, maybe one day I'll mosey back along the trail and find out what happened.

And then all reflection ended as I felt the ground come up and thump me, felt once again the blessed warmth of Zim and Genodras pour heat into every fiber, drew deep breaths of that glorious tangy air—and knew I was once again back on Kregen, where I belonged.

Four

Jak the Drang Encounters the Iron Riders

To be perfectly honest, as I leaped up I felt my nakedness, felt it terribly. My hand went to my waist. My little arsenal had become a part of my daily round, the Sharps to hit 'em as far off as I could, the Winchester to cut 'em down as they charged, the Remington to finish those that wouldn't go down and the Bowie to take out the last, obstinate idiot who insisted on closing to close quarters.

All this was a long way away from the Sea Service pistol of my youth, the cutlass or boarding pike, and a very long way away from the rapier or thraxter, the spear or the longsword I needed on Kregen—and needed right now, by Zair!

I was on Kregen, right enough, there was no mistaking that. All the agony I had experienced as I'd realized just where the Star Lords had flung me last vanished altogether in that moment.

The mingled opaline radiance of the Suns of Scorpio streamed reful-gently about me; but there was no time for anything other than getting on with the work to my hand, presented to me in the old familiar authori-tative way—I had to fight and do what I had to do, or be banished once again. Or, given the circumstances, to die messily.

It was, I thought then, all one to the Everoinye.

Judging by the frightened looks they cast over their shoulders, and the merciless plying of whip and spur, the mob of men lambasting up the draw toward me were fleeing—were running away as fast as they could make their mounts gallop. These were a mix of various saddle animals of Kre-gen—hirvels, totrixes, preysanys, urvivels—with only two or three zorcas mixed up in the stampede. Dust flew up in a long ochre smear.

I ducked in back of a rock out of the way of the fugitives, guessing my task lay at the interface of pursued and pursuers.

Usually I was projected onto Kregen stark naked and headlong into action. Not always—usually. This time the Star Lords had seen fit to give me a little preparatory time. Of course, they did not deign to provide me with a helmet or spear, sword or shield, and we had struck our reactions to that idea. They would guess I would regard them with less estimation—although, truth to tell, I fancy that as I grew older I might come to regret that hot and impassioned surge of pride of my youth. I had not aged a day since the dip in the Sacred Pool of Baptism; but although my body remained young I know my brain had, slowly and painfully, accreted a trifle of wisdom in the intervening years.

Drawn by six piebald nikvoves the coach lumbered into view. Its felloes shrieked as it skated over the rocks. It kicked up one helluva dust and I could see nothing down the back-trail.

Most of the fugitives were apims, but there was a fair sprinkling of diffs, and a Rapa sat up on the box and flogged the nikvoves on. This coach, these six laboring animals, the dust, the racket—well, it caught at my throat, so like and yet so fantastically unlike the scenes I had just left. Had those different alien riding animals and the draught animals all been horses, had there been no diffs—this would still be Kregen. The smell, the feel, the empathy of the world was uniquely Kregen under Antares.

I saw what must be done. Had those crazed fugitives taken a mur to observe for themselves they must have seen it, too. I was just a lone, naked man. But if I did not do what had to be done I knew what would happen. So I got on with it.

The rocks at the lip of the draw scattered away in a detritus to either side. Starting a likely-looking boulder moving started two or three others. Pebbles rattled. Dust smoked. The rocks tumbled down. I cut it fine, and a couple of fist-sized pebbles bounced into the polished varnish of the coach. But the main mass of sliding rock rumbled down, spreading, filling the bed of the draw. So much dust hung about that it was impossible to see beyond and so I still did not know who or what pursued these men and scared them half to death.

Who or whatever—they or it were not going to ride over that still-quivering wall of rock.

The coach slewed and skidded. A wheel flew off, spinning gracefully, the spokes and hub never designed for this kind of hard hacking cross-country work. In a screech the coach bedded down canting onto its for'ard larboard axle. Slowly, I walked down toward the coach, watching the Rapa, who wore a gaudy uniform, watching the painted and varnished door swing open.

No one down there took any notice of me. The distance was too great to make out features. A woman jumped energetically down from the coach and shook her fist at the Rapa. At once he began unhitching the nikvoves. Two other women and a man got out of the coach. They all stood arguing, waving their arms, looking back at the still-smoking mass of rock barring off the pursuit. I stopped walking down, fascinated by this display of human emotion and character behavior.

Presently, the whole group mounted up on the freed nikvoves and took off, hitting their mounts with the flats of their swords, galloping hell-for-leather. I stood and watched them go. I had carried out the commands of the Star Lords. I had no further interest in those people I had saved. I did not recognize any insigne, colors—the whole assemblage had been liberally covered in dust—or, more importantly, the country I was in. The coach looked to be of the kind I had seen in Zenicce, Vallia or Pandahem. I needed to know where I was to set my course for Strombor.

The Rapa coachman had freed only five nikvoves. So there was one left for me. I felt pleased. I walked down to the coach.

There are very few voves in Vallia, for that magnificent russet-coated, eight-legged king of saddle-animals is a native of the Great Plains of Segesthes. Yet Vallians and other people call his smaller cousin a nikvove, which always amuses me. This piebald specimen looked alertly at me as I walked up to him and stroked his neck, speaking soothingly. He and I would get on capitally.

The coach had been stripped of its interior fittings; but in the box at the rear was to be found a mass of clothing, and from its style of buff and shirts with colored sleeves I judged I was in Vallia. I felt dizzy. The Star Lords might have dumped me down anywhere on Kregen—apart from being put down somewhere near Strombor—or, even, Djanduin—Vallia was the next best place for me in my ugly old mood.

I found a piece of russet cloth, for there was no scarlet, and twisted it around my waist and pulled the free end up between my legs and tucked it in. A broad belt—not, unfortunately, of lesten-hide—held the breech-clout in place. The only weapons I could find were two small daggers, half kicked under the seat. They were of reasonable manufacture, with far too much gewgaw imitation jewelry; but they'd serve.

Despite all the cunning expertise of unarmed combat taught in the Disciplines of the Krozairs and of the Khamorros, Kregen is no place to wander around unarmed. Mind you, Turko the Shield would scoff with enormous gusto at these two ridiculous daggers, by Krun!

A number of the white shirts bore banded sleeves of gold and black. There were others in different color combinations; but the gold and black predominated. Thoughtfully I went back to the door and slammed it shut and brushed off the dust coating the varnished panel. The painted and gilded representation of a butterfly upon the gold and black blazon confirmed the view that I was in Aduimbrev. At least, the butterfly on gold and black was the insignia of Aduimbrev. If I was in the kovnate I knew where I was. Poor old Kov Vektor who had aspired with the emperor's blessings to the hand of Delia was long since dead, having got himself foolishly killed in the Battle at the Dragon's Bones. The memory of that famous old conflict heartened me.

A collateral line of the family had inherited, with the very necessary emperor's confirmation of their claim, and the present kov incumbent was Marto Renberg, whom I knew only to nod to politely. The Aduimbrevs had reckoned on being emperor's men; I had no way of knowing how their allegiances had fallen in the recent struggles for power.

I was pretty well near the dead center of Vallia. Across the Great River to the south lay Ogier. Across a tributary of the Great River to the west lay Eganbrev. And, eastward, the Trylonate of Gelkwa barred my path. Trylon Udo had led the uprising of the whole North East, or so I believed, and the mischief they had caused me with their damned revived corpse and the damage they had done to Vondium would long be remembered in the land. It had been that cramph Zankov from the North East who had slain the emperor. I thought of Dayra, Ros the Claw, and a great deal of my good mood vanished.

It was necessary for me to travel east. The best plan would be to swing across to Thengelsax and in that city discover what had transpired during my absence. From there I'd have to find faster transport and take myself off to Zamra, or Valka, and from thence fly east across the sea to Zenicce and Strombor. Yes. I decided, then, spitting dust, that that was what I would have to do.

Well, as they say, man reaps for Zair to sickle.

To the north spread the emperor's province of Thermin, and in its chief city of Therminsax I might find what I needed. But the obsession was on me to take the shortest route. East, then...

The rout of fugitives had headed south down the draw. I fashioned a saddle cloth from the clothes and cinched it tight with ropes. I took what clothing I thought necessary and then, being a canny old paktun, a soldier of fortune, I broke a long length of hefty timbering from the coach. That would serve as a lance, and a shorter length as a wooden sword. Once or twice before a length of lumber had served me as a weapon, and on Kregen a man needs weapons as he needs food and water.

The piebald nikvove rumbled off with that special smooth elongated rhythm of the eight-footed. I cocked an eye back at the freshly created wall of rock. Nalgre ti Liancesmot, the long-dead playwright whose work is known over many areas of Kregen, is often quoted. "Better to know the smile of the friend who stabs you in the back than the scowl of the enemy who assails you in front," which comes from his cycle "The Vicissitudes of Panadian the Ibreiver" and contains a thought with which I do not always agree, allowing it to have a cogent point. It struck me I ought to find out just what that crazed mob had been fleeing from.

There was every chance now, that, their dirty work done, for them, the Star Lords would let me alone. I was coming to the conclusion, not as clear-cut as I may have made it appear, that there was strife among the

Everoinye. If this Ahrinye really wanted to run me, as he so elegantly phrased it, with so much more force, I might find myself being run pretty sharpish in the future, and without recourse to any of the fragile obstructions I had erected to resist the Everoinye.

So, feeling pretty mulish and bloody-minded, I guided the nikvove up out of the draw. The land spread away in an opening panorama, superb under the suns, lightening from the dusty ochre near me to a fresher green along the horizon. And, in the middle distance, sparkling in the mingled radiance, the waters of a canal ran dead straight, northwest, southeast. I fancied this might well be a direct link through to Thengelsax. Certainly, the Ogier Cut ran east-west some way south of my present position. So, I turned the nikvove to follow the canal.

When I reached the towpath I frowned. So this was one of the results of the chaos destroying Vallia. For the cut was in vile condition, half-choked with weeds, the banks fallen away here and there, the water, although sparkling as the light of the suns glinted from it, sullen and barely moving.

A thin strip of vegetation grew along both banks, trees and bushes breaking the flatness of the land. From the shadows of a missal tree I looked back and saw the dun-colored dust clouds rising. I stared closely. A body of riders broke into view, rising up like a succession of trap-door devils. They appeared in no hurry. They trotted on. Probably the rock-fall had caught a few of them and time had been spent assisting the injured. For whatever reason, only now were they resuming their pursuit. Or, and what was far more probably the correct explanation, the fugitives had been in such terror they were fleeing from these riders when the pursuit was a long way off. Only now had the pursuit caught up with them.

At this unpalatable thought I frowned.

But the people of Aduimbrev ought to be clear away by now. Should I follow them and make sure? They were headed south. Damn those blasted Star Lords! So, undecided, I stood there and heard the splash of water at my back.

Without thought, without looking back, I rolled off the nikvove, hit on a shoulder, rolled under a bush and came up, quivering, ready to defend myself against—against a slender slip of a girl who climbed out onto the bank, half-naked, dripping, shining—and laughing at me with a rosy face beaming rapturous amusement at my antics.

"You don't have to be afraid of me, ven. I won't hurt you—" she started to say. Then she stopped and all the amused enjoyment fled from her face. She saw the dust cloud, she saw the riders, and she seemed to shrivel there in the streaming light of the suns. "Radvakkas." She spoke the word with so much fear and loathing it was instantly clear these riders were a real and terrible threat. "The Iron Riders."

Standing up I put a hand on the piebald's neck, soothing, and looked again at the men out there trotting along with the dust spuming and the light striking sparks from their armor and weapons.

"The Iron Riders?"

"Yes—and keep you still and silent until they are gone. I pray to Vaosh they do not see us."

"We can swim across the canal—they are not of the canalfolk—"

I chanced my arm there; but I was right. She nodded, swiftly, her brown hair gleaming, her water-drenched tunic plastered to her. Her face was small and elfin, and her eyes were very frightened.

"That is true. But their benhoffs would swim the cut with the radvakkas safely clear of the water."

So we kept silent and watched and I digested what this girl had said. For I knew about benhoffs. The benhoff is a shaggy, powerful, six-legged riding animal from North Segesthes. The barbarians up there use them as my clansmen use the vove. And from short and ferocious wars the various tribes and confederations of the North Segesthan Barbarians had long learned never to tangle with a Clansman. They kept themselves well to the north of Segesthes and the continent is large enough for barbarian and clansman to live separately. Although, mind you, it is a truism to say that any honest Clansman is far more savage and bloodthirsty than any barbarian...

But, here, in Vallia—benhoffs? To the best of my knowledge the benhoff was as little known or used as the vove in Vallia. I swallowed down what I was about to say, and instead, said: "You know these Iron Riders?"

"Aye, may Gurush of the Bottomless Marsh take them and suck them down and never spit out their diseased bones!"

"I am a stranger here, just riding through—tell me of these radvakkas."

She lifted one brown eyebrow at this; but let it pass.

She told me her name was Feri of the Therduim Cut. This canal connected Therminsax and Thengelsax. Before I could urge her to tell me of the Iron Riders, other canalfolk appeared. They had no narrow boat; they walked along the towpath, and I prepared for unpleasantness even though I was well aware of the hospitality of the canalfolk. In the event Llahals were exchanged and the pappattu made in a proper civilized way. We all waited quietly until the radvakkas had ridden out of sight.

Then a load was lifted from these people, and they began to smile and chatter again. Very briefly, I learned that trade had been thoroughly disrupted by the troubles, and these people had lost their two boats and, perforce were compelled to walk carrying what belongings they could, until they could reach one of the towns along the cut where they had friends. The Iron Riders had come sweeping in from the northeast and terrorized the whole countryside. They roamed in bands, ravaging and looting and burning, and no one was safe.

Despite the smiles and the warm comradeliness, the impression I gained was that these canalfolk were mightily scared not only of the Iron Riders but of life in general. Vallia was no longer the empire it once had been. The country was split into warring factions. Vengeful townsfolk had sunk the two narrow boats. The town had been sacked by the radvakkas three nights previously; and the townspeople had vented their spite. No—I did not at all care for the truths I was finding out about Vallia.

This Feri had spirit. She had been out ahead scouting and had taken to the water to come up on me unseen. I suppose I'd satisfied her I was not an Iron Rider. But the rest of them were anxious to push on and after I had learned a little more of conditions—much of which I will relate when the telling is needful—I told them I must push on also.

"But the radvakkas went that way, ven." And: "But you are a lone rider, Ven Jak." And: "Come with us, ven." And so on, for I had given them the name of Jak the Drang, conceiving Dray Prescot would be a name with much gravity attaching to it.

"I thank you, vens and venas. But mayhap we will meet again in more happy times."

Amid the calling of Remberees, I mounted up and turned the piebald's head. I waved to them, and guided the nikvove angling away from the Therduim Cut.

Deliberately, for I fancied I had not fully completed the task the Star Lords had set to my hands, I set off southwards, following in the tracks of the Iron Riders.

Five

Of a Rout After Breakfast

Night would soon bring the brilliance of the Moons of Kregen to brighten the sky and I could feel the first tendrils of tiredness. After all, I had begun the day astride a pony riding drag to a remuda heading for Santa Fe, and was now riding a nikvove in pursuit of a bunch of rogues more ferocious than anything the West had witnessed—and had, into the bargain, been pitchforked four hundred light years through space. Not, I hasten to add, that I was then aware of the real distance involved. But I could soldier on for a spell yet and decided to take a swing around the band of radvakkas ahead and catch up with the fugitives.

The level ground began to roll into a series of long tawny-grass-covered dunes as I went on, and presently stands of trees showed throwing long twinned shadows. I kept the Iron Riders under observation and was somewhat surprised to see them pitch camp for the night and settle down. Anxious to press on I skirted their camp and rode on into the darkness as She of the Veils rose luminously over my left shoulder.

If I was on the right track then the fugitives had galloped fast and without let-up. Just before midnight the lights of a town showed ahead. I had only a hazy idea of the detailed geography around here; it seemed likely, if I was right, that the smot ahead was Cansinsax. In a long chain surrounding the North East the forts had been built in the old days against the reivers. The Therduim Cut was a later construction, running mostly along the borders between Aduimbrev to the south and Sakwara to the north. The saxes were not always built directly on the frontier, and, sometimes, the borders had been shifted by imperial decree.

I bedded down outside the town and saw to the nikvove and caught a little sleep, being up well before Zim and Genodras broke over the horizon. My urgency was being channeled into doing what I believed right. If I was wrong, well, I would be the sufferer—for I was still firmly convinced that Delia was safe in Strombor. She had to be.

For breakfast I had a few deep lungfuls of fresh Kregen air. The nikvove chomped the grass and appeared content.

Had I chosen to ride north and cross the border out of Aduimbrev I would have come into the emperor's province of Thermin. The odd thing was, I was in no way reconciled to the idea that I was supposed to be the emperor. Emperor of Vallia. By Vox! How empty could a title get?

Had I done so, I sourly wondered if, even there, I'd have found anyone willing to give me breakfast.

As the twin Suns of Scorpio rose and threw the land into that shimmering opaline radiance I saw a sight that astounded me. I put a hand to the piebald's neck, soothing him. I remained very still in the little stand of timber, peering out under the leaves.

Across the grassy ground a great host approached Cansinsax. Clearly I could see the long extended lines of cavalrymen. They rode benhoffs, shaggy and gray. Their weapons glittered. They wore mail. There were, I judged, something in excess of three thousand of them. So a junction had been made and the forces gathered in and now the Iron Riders rode against Cansinsax.

The evident terror these riders of iron struck into all they encountered was a most potent weapon; but not, I judged, their only or even their chiefest weapon. Just how they would manage the siege of the town I admit intrigued me. But then—well, they say the gods sharpen both edges of a blade—the gates of the town opened. Trumpets pealed brazen notes into the morning air. I watched, spell-bound.

Out from the gates of Cansinsax, a town of Vallia, marched with a swing and a swank the iron legions of Hamal.

Hamal. I saw them. The serried ranks of swods all marching in time, their rectangular shields all in alignment, their banners blazing a rich tapestry of color, the plumes in their helmets whiffling in the dawn breeze. Swods from Hamal. Real soldiers, men trained to fight under the strict laws of Hamal. I marveled. Regiment by regiment they marched out. Squadrons of cavalry surged out and extended into wings on the flanks. A little dust plumed; but the grass here was altogether richer and lusher than the sere tawny-grass along the Therduim Cut.

My vantage position gave me a perfect view.

Following the regulars of Hamal crowded a swarm of mercenaries. Among their ranks were many diffs. Also, as I was quick to observe, there were masichieri there, which was surprising, seeing the masichieri are mercenaries but soldiers of fortune of an altogether different stamp from the paktuns, who more often than not fight with honor and earn their hire.

Two regiments of totrixmen spurred out ahead, and trumpets rang and they hauled back. It was clear this army was anxious to get to grips with the radvakkas. Running an old soldier's eye over the serried array I estimated the Hamalians as putting into the field four or five thousand infantry—ten regiments—and a thousand or so cavalry. The mixed bunch of mercenaries probably added up to another couple of thousand.

Numbers favored the Hamalians. What, I wondered, of the native Vallians of Aduimbrev? Mind you, as I have already explained, Vallia was a powerful trading empire, whose wealth came from her sea power, the superb Galleons of Vallia. If the empire needed soldiers, she would hire them.

The Hamalian army halted. The regiments of foot braced their shields. The regiments of crossbowmen spanned their crossbows. Soon the bolts would fly. I watched, scarcely breathing and, I admit, not a little puzzled as to where my cheering should be directed.

The Iron Riders were clearly a grave menace; but, then, Hamal was the deadly foe of Vallia, temporarily in the ascendant. So, I merely watched and studied, and if my right hand twitched and the fingers curled around the length of lumber—well, they were only simple, stupid reactions of an old fighting man.

Three thousand Iron Riders against around eight thousand Hamalese and paktuns—it seemed to me my services would no longer be required.

The Hamalese cavalry wings overlapped the radvakkas. The totrixmen again almost boiled over into a charge. There was a regiment of zorcamen there, also, whereat I at once thought of Rees and Chido. But the general in command held them in the rear in reserve.

The Iron Riders shook out into three battles or divisions, a thousand cavalrymen each.

I saw no signal given. The distant trumpet notes pealed. The front ranks of benhoffs began to move, lumpy gray beasts surging forward like the gray tide beating against rocks. But the center division rode forward faster and faster. The crossbowmen loosed, pastang by pastang, and the bolts fell like rain, and still the benhoffs came on. A few, only a few, tumbled down to thrash on the trampled ground as their comrades thundered on.

The central division galloped rapidly through the beaten zone and crashed into the Hamalese infantry. The whole front two ranks caved in instantly. Infantrymen were sent bodily flying. The great six-legged beasts rampaged on. Swords rose and fell. Shields were splintered. And now the totrix wings of Hamalese cavalry closed in—and the left and right wedges of radvakkas spurned them. In an instant amid a ghastly racket the whole line was engaged. For only an instant—for the Hamalese army sagged back and back. Totrixes were bounding riderless from the field. The infantry were being cut to pieces. On and on surged that enormous battering wedge of Iron Riders.

The field became a sea of boiling action—I did not see the end of the zorca regiment. It merely ceased to exist. The Hamalese were running. Iron Riders were breaking away from the main divisions now, were hunting and slaying.

Time was being cut so fine I almost did not make it.

My services were, after all, still required.

Piebald roared ahead, his eight hooves battering the grass. A party of Rapas offered to halt me at the gate; but already fugitives were streaming in and the situation was plain. If it was a case of *sauve qui peut* then the *sauvest* would be the *peutest*, that was for sure. I had no trouble entering Cansinsax.

The trouble lay in finding where away was the party I had already once rescued. Just which one in that party was the particular one the Star Lords wished preserved I did not know, which simply meant I had to save the lot.

The town was in the most frightful uproar. Men and women were running every which way—men and women wearing the buff of Vallians. Slaves were being beaten along staggering under loads of household equipment. Everyone was raging toward the western gate in a crazy flood. Just how they expected to get away when the benhoffs of the radvakkas would overhaul them in no time at all did not appear to have occurred to them. The scenes of chaos rang and thumped on and I forced my way through.

A bad time this, when a town falls, a bad time.

In this instance, I think with some degree of certainty, the Star Lords took a direct hand. I remember I shook my fist at the indifferent sky, and hurled a few lusty Makki-Grodno cusses upward—conduct that aroused not one whit of interest from the crazed mobs about me—and so saw a piebald nikvove bolt from the broken-down gateway of a villa. The mobs pushed past and I came up with the nikvove and got a hand into his harness. I hauled back and lay my own steed into him and some of the crowd staggering away managed to turn him. Together, we went racketing back into the villa. Slaves were looting the place, which was a very proper thing to do, considering.

The woman who stood in the doorway of the house yelling furiously, purple of face, wearing riding clothes, slashing about with a thraxter, might have been one of the three women who had descended from the coach. The air was filled with noise, people screaming, the crash of furniture being hurled through windows, the thump of many feet. The smells were interesting, too. I barged across. She looked up.

She saw my face. Her own face, which was filled with that aristocratic fury, venom-filled, that overtakes the high and mighty when they see slaves breaking out or people not obeying them instantly, abruptly hung slack. I vaulted off Piebald.

"Here, lady, a mount for you. Where are the others?"

She was saved a reply as a man rushed at me with his rapier held ready to stick me. I slid the blow, took the rapier away, hit him over the head with it—gently, mind—and caught him as he fell. Even then I felt the old familiar sensations as my fist gripped around the rapier hilt. Two other women, dressed for riding, appeared, screaming. I bellowed them all down.

"Silence, you famblys! The four of you—you will have to share the two nikvoves. Get mounted and get out. The Iron Riders will be here in a mur or two! Ride!"

They were yelling and screaming; but they retained sense enough to mount up. The man held his head, glaring at me with sadistic hostility; but I saw his eyes, and they slid away and would not meet mine.

A preysany stood at the steps ready-loaded. I snapped him across the rump and started him after the nikvoves. We headed out through the gate. Truth to tell, riding through the panic-smitten mobs was not easy and I, afoot, would have been quicker than the riders. But, once they were outside the walls, the story would be different. I knew benhoffs and I knew nikvoves. The half-vove is not a true vove, but he can still outrun a shambling, shaggy, gray-haired benhoff any day of the month.

Now the remnants of the Hamalese army were crowding into the town. The confusion was splendid and awful. I sweated along. The woman who rode like a man and held the man upright as he swayed and cursed weakly, glowered down on me as I led them along the crowded street.

"You, rast. Why do you save us?"

"Just be thankful I do, lady. And no Lahal between us."

She colored again at this, fully aware of the sarcasm.

"Be very careful how you address me. I am the Kovneva of Aduimbrev, Marta Renberg, and your head lies most shakily upon your shoulders."

"Then Llahal, Kovneva. I did not know Marto Renberg; but I once met old Vektor—"

She tried to hit me with her thraxter, and I laughed and ducked away and hauled the nikvove on. Oh, yes, I laughed. It was certainly no time for crying.

She was not very old, I judged, although that is always a tricky business on Kregen where a person changes but little and slowly over two hundred or so years. She had the brown Vallian hair and eyes, a trim figure, a high color, and she was most decidedly a very important person in her own eyes.

Some quality I at first thought indefinable about her—perhaps the way her nostrils curved, the curl of her lower lip, the tensioning lines around her eyes, something—offended me. I felt I would try to like her and fail. We pushed on along the street with the fugitive mobs and I found that, once again, I did not much care for the task the Everoinye had set to my hands.

When a victorious army follows up a victory of this kind and the defeated do not have the nous to run into their town and shut the gates, much may be learned of the character and temperament of the victors by the way they go about consolidating. As we debouched from the western gate in a yelling straggling mass of people and animals, I hauled myself up by the nikvove's mane and took a searching look around.

There was no sign of Iron Riders sweeping in around the city. Then they would be simply bolting in through the eastern gate, charging down the remnants of the Hamalese soldiery and the paktuns, just driving on through the gate into the city. They had not aimed to cut off the fugitives. Not slavers, then...?

Many carts harnessed to the refreshing variety of draught animals of Kregen lumbered away across the plain heading for the forest a dwabur or so off. Mounted people set spurs to their mounts and pelted headlong for safety. Those afoot, wailing and crying, ran and hobbled in a great untidy mass. It was one diabolical scene, I can tell you.

The Kovneva of Aduimbrev leaned down toward me. Her flushed face looked dangerous.

"Take your hand from the rope, tikshim.* There is the forest. We can manage perfectly well now."

She was quite serious. The situation was perfectly plain in her eyes. I had appeared and had helped her to escape from Cansinsax. And this, very

---

* Tikshim. The form of address used by the higher to the lower orders. The higher consider it neutral. As it probably equates with "my man" or even "my good man" the lower orders are almost invariably provoked by its use although quite unable to articulate their reaction or to explain it. Prescot has used the word rarely, but here it fits perfectly. *A.B.A.*

properly, was the duty owed to her as the kovneva by every one of her people. I did not let go of the rope.

"Now, tikshim! We must gallop to the forest before the radvakkas overtake us—"

"Cramph!" bellowed the man, thickly. I had his rapier and so he whipped out his left-hand dagger and tried to slash at me or at the rope. I did not care for the first idea.

I said: "You may ride for the forest, and you will. But if you get yourself killed I shall be most wroth." She could not, of course, understand just why I would be annoyed. "Do not ride with the main bulk of the fugitives—"

"Do you presume to give me orders?" She half-turned and swung the thraxter at me. This time the blade was not turned. She cut at me.

I slid the blow and jumped back, letting go the rope. I held myself under control—but only just. How they conduct themselves, the high and mighty of the land!

"Ride, kovneva. Ride. I shall find you in the forest. Just be very sure you are still alive when I do—and not a bloody corpse."

With that I gave Piebald a slap across the rump and started him off at a run. The other nikvove with the two handmaidens lumbered after. Pretty soon the two angled away from the main mass and lit out for the trees. Nikvoves can run. I let out a gusty breath. This hoity-toity Marta Renberg should be safe now and the Star Lords satisfied. But, all the same, I'd wander across to the forest and make sure.

Amid that swirling mass of terrified folk I had to think about getting myself away; but, I admit, a few nasty thoughts about these mysterious purposes of the Star Lords crossed my mind. I had been given evidence that the people the Everoinye wished preserved did, indeed, affect the destiny of the world. The mad genius king Genod of the Eye of the World proved that. What the Star Lords wanted of Marta Renberg, Kovneva of Aduimbrev, I could not know. But I wished them the evil of it, for I found myself in a black humor with the foolish woman.

Of course, I could not even be sure it was she the Star Lords had their eye on. It might have been the man—she'd called him Larghos and no doubt he served some function or other in her establishment—or one of the handmaidens; pretty, washed out girls whose terror rendered them mute. The preysany, loaded down, I did not doubt, with choice and expensive items, followed the nikvoves. I turned about and looked at the doomed town.

Already smoke drifted over the red roofs, dun, swirling, skull-like in outline, mushroom-headed, vile. Soon the flames would break out and seek to dim the glory of the suns. It was all a ghastly mess, butchery and rapine and pillage—and here, in Vallia. Vallia that had been so puissant an empire.

The cultivated fields swallowed up many of the fugitives who vanished from view in the crops. On the other side the plain was suitable only for those with fast riding animals. Reflectively, I weighed the chances, walking smartly away from the town. The rabble thinned about me, and mostly those who were delayed by excess of baggage, infirmity of limb or care for children, labored on about me now. I gave a hand to people who needed it—hauling a cart out of a rut here, carrying a child for a space there; much though I would have liked to remain and help I could not chain myself down to just one party. In the event, we were all within the first rows of crops before the leading elements of radvakkas debouched from the western gate of Cansinsax and spurred after us.

The appearance of the Iron Riders drove the fugitives into a fresh panic. Shrieking they stumbled on through the crackling fronds. One or two sturdy fellows and I sought to make them move as swiftly as might be along the tracks left for the cultivators. We yelled and waved our arms.

"Go as far as you can before you hide!" bellowed a fellow who sweated away, a leather cap awry over one ear, his apron marked with the burns of his smithy's trade. He carried a blacksmith's hammer. He looked as though he might be useful. His family trudged along, helping a woman smitten with chivrel. I hoped they would make it. So, because I am something of an idiot, I found myself at the tail end of the rout. I could not force myself to run on ahead, as I might easily have done. Somehow—and I cursed myself for it, believe me—I could not run off and leave these people.

The crops swayed about us. Here, where the grass was weeded away, puffs of dust rose. It was hot and sticky work. We pushed on. I kept swiveling about to look down the narrow track between the crops.

Inevitably, out of the mobs hurrying through the cultivated fields, some would be found by the radvakkas, and, equally inevitably, along the row down which I moved after those ahead, an Iron Rider should trot into view. He moved his benhoff with that lumpy power that so deceives. Big ugly brutes, benhoffs, with an immense roll of fat around their chests to store nourishment against the rigors of their northern habitat, with spreading withers, and with loins and croup a trifle too mean for my taste. The Iron Rider saw me and his head went up.

He wore the usual shaggy pelt of furs—no doubt liberally infested—but because the weather was hotter than the thin mizzle to which he was accustomed the furs were thrown back exposing his armor, a simple leather shirt riveted with iron plates, and iron strips riveted down his trousers. His helmet was bulky and square in outline, with a fantastic conglomeration of feathers and benhoff tail plumes. He carried a broadsword scabbarded to his saddle, and a spear; but as was the wont of the Segesthan, he bore no shield. He looked ugly and purposeful, a packed arsenal of power.

From the front rim of the helmet hung down a series of metal plates, jointed and sprung together, with eye-slots, which together formed what was in effect a mask. The sides joined the cheek pieces of the helmet. This Iron Rider had no beaver to his helmet, although the fashion was known.

Oh, yes, I knew these radvakkas well enough. My Clansmen did not often confront them, for, as I have said, the radvakkas had learned the unwisdom of tangling with a Clansman. But, from time to time, they drifted south onto the Great Plains, and if they created a disturbance they had to be dealt with. That meant they had to be dealt with, for if they were good for one thing at all that was creating disturbances. I suppose one should not call them barbarians; but we did, and the appellation fitted well enough.

Dark and ominous, clad in iron, the radvakka urged his mount into a trot and then a gallop. His spear came down. He would spit me as I stood.

My Clansmen learn to stand the charge, to stand alertly, poised, empty hands half-raised, watching the glittering spear point as it hurtles forward. At the last moment they hurl themselves sideways. One hand will rake out and snatch at the spear shaft. It is not an easy trick, it is extremely dangerous; and more than one youngster had his side or thigh cut open or his chest caved in. But with their ferocious abandonment they persist in the sport—for to a clansman this is sport, akin to Rakkle-jik-lora.

So I stood as a Clansman stands, and, withal, as a Krozair would stand awaiting the onslaught of an Overlord of Magdag.

The spear point dipped in at the last moment in the thunder of the hooves. I swayed, not jumping, brushed the spear aside, swung my length of lumber crackingly against the fellow's ribs.

The timber broke across.

How many ribs broke I did not know. The radvakka's yell burst out from him, and he swayed. I threw the rest of the wood at his head, heard it clang on that iron helmet, and then with a leaping spring was up on those narrow hindquarters of his benhoff. One arm went around his neck, and jerked back most cruelly. The other hand pushed his helmet forward and sideways. He slumped.

After that I was able to slow the benhoff down and cast the radvakka into the dirt. I jumped down beside him. His armor he could keep. His weapons and his mount I would take.

So, mounted up on a shaggy grey six-legged beast, with a broadsword, a shortsword, a spear, and the rapier belonging to the kovneva's man Larghos, I trotted along after the fugitives toward the forest.

I admit—to my shame, I suppose—I felt in a much more cheerful frame of mind.

Six

Of the Scorpion and the Ring of Destiny

"And you believe this ring will solve all your problems, kovneva?"

"I am sure it will! I have been assured, personally assured, that the ring will restore all."

We led our mounts along the forest trails. I had ridden in, not without a few quaint comments on the benhoff, and found the kovneva and her party. Larghos had taken his rapier back, and his face was a study. In the dead radvakka's pouch I had found food, crude fare, rough bread and hunks of odoriferous cheese, and had wolfed it all down. Now we walked circumspectly through the forest to Thiurdsmot, a sizable town, larger than Cansinsax.

There we would find other regiments of the Hamalian army—and the kovneva's comments on the conduct of the Hamalese curdled the air. She reviled them bitterly. She had been promised support and aid by the Hamalese and they had sent an army which had been frittered away. I listened. I knew what I knew about the charge of mailed cavalry against sword and shield men, even with crossbow support. One of the handmaidens had told Marta Renberg that she had recognized me as the man who had saved them in the draw. The girl had long eyesight. I passed the incident over; but the kovneva's attitude changed subtly. I was still "my good man" to her; but she used my name now and then, condescendingly, and it was clear she was mightily puzzled why I, a common oaf, should be so tender of the welfare of her skin, when I was not even of Aduimbrev.

"A paktun?" she said. "Well, you earn your hire."

"May I enquire who told you of the powers of the ring?"

"You may not!"

"I am not, my lady, in your employment. You do not pay my hire."

"Are you threatening me, Jak the Drang? Be very careful—I have powerful friends who have dark and sorcerous powers."

"The necromancers of the North East can scarcely be your friends, since Aduimbrev has for many seasons been a buffer against them, against the Hawkwas. All along the area where now the Therduim Cut runs was a March—a bloody battlefield for season after season."

"Once—but not now."

"But they raid—"

"They used to raid, before the empire collapsed."

"So, kovneva, you are all friends with the Hawkwas now?" I chanced my arm. "And Trylon Udo of Gelkwa? Perhaps he—"

"He is vanished, no one knows where. The High Kov of Sakwara has now come forward into the open as the true leader of the Hawkwas."

I pricked up my ears. This was vital news.

And then, even as I opened my foolish mouth to speak, a thought hit me. A horrific thought. If this silly kovneva was mixed up with the Hawkwas, who had the support of the devil Phu-si-Yantong, perhaps it was he to whom she referred when she spoke of great sorcerous powers?

After a space, as though changing the subject, although you will readily perceive I but planned ahead, I said: "And your people, your retainers, your guards? They have not all deserted you, my lady?"

Her face bunched tightly at this, spitting fury and venom. "Those that fled from me are as good as dead. There are others loyal to their kovneva in Aduimbrev! I shall raise a host—paktuns, masichieri, the rasts of Hamal. Together we shall return and sweep the radvakkas away into the sea."

"Caution, Marta," said Larghos, from where he walked on her other side.

I did not fail to notice his mode of address. "Caution, good Larghos? When the Hamalese promised so much for *my* aid, and fail to give me *theirs*?"

Quickly, I said: "And your aid assisted them greatly, I think."

Still shaken by her passion, she burst out: "Assist them? Did I not drive into Thermin and sweep them away, and cross into Eganbrev and drive that insolent numim, Fyrnad Rosselin, from his palace and into hiding, destroying his puny forces? Did I not faithfully adhere to the treaty in every part? Did I not materially contribute to the great victory and the destruction of the emperor? Did I or did I not? And now these cramphs of Hamalese fail me, fail me utterly and leave me to flee through the dismal forest with—with—"

And here she paused in her outburst, and cast me a sidelong look, and clamped her mouth shut. She breathed heavily. The color flushed her face. She was silly, foolish, vindictive; but she was also a kovneva and this she had almost forgotten.

I said nothing but tramped on. I had learned much. So this headstrong woman—girl, really—had sided with the Hawkwas, with the Hamalese, and attacked her neighbors. It was a simple and effective method of taking out of play those people who would have rallied to the emperor. The Third Party had employed the stratagem before, and it would, I guessed, be used again.

And, if this hoity-toity Kovneva of Aduimbrev had sided with and assisted the Hamalese, she had in that helped Phu-si-Yantong.

I still did not know the full commitment of the Empress Thyllis of Hamal to this invasion of Vallia. She would glee in it, of course, hating everything Vallian. But it was Yantong who pulled the strings here, and his the puppets that fought and struggled and died on Vallian soil.

The aisles of the forest passed by. We saw only a few other fugitives. The green dimness about us savored far more of Genodras than of Zim. The day wore on and we walked and rode alternately. The nikvoves were not too happy about this nearness of the benhoff, for the two animals dislike each other's scent; but by judicious management we kept them calmed down.

Marta Renberg maintained much silence after her outburst. She had nothing to fear from me, she would think, of course; but no doubt her own words scored into her mind, making her scratch over the sores of wounded pride, the feeling of being used. It would not have helped to have told her that ten regiments of the Hamalian Army, and a thousand cavalry, were no mean force. The absence of fliers and aerial cavalry puzzled me; but I understood later that the Hamalian aerial forces were very thin in Vallia and the local contingents were all centered on Thiurdsmot. As to fliers in private hands, I soon found out that all the airboats Vallia possessed had been confiscated by the victorious parties. The Hamalese took most; but the Hawkwas took many and many more remained in the hands of Layco Jhansi, who was continuing to fight on, despite crippling losses. All these things I learned, one way and another, and stored them all away and pondered.

Despite her personal anger and humiliation, Marta Renberg remained fully convinced that the new emperor, Seakon, would continue in power and subdue the forces still in arms against him.

Seakon?

"A fine young man," said Larghos, across Marta Renberg. "He has already defeated Layco Jhansi in open battle. But I do not think the Hawkwas and the Hamalese can remain in alliance for very much longer."

From the way he spoke I saw at once that he thoroughly disliked the new emperor.

"What do you understand of these things, Larghos? You are supposed to be a fighting man—you have served as a paktun, have you not? Somewhere in Pandahem? Let me deal with politics." The kovneva's petulant words served to illuminate the depths of her personal frustrations and cares.

I cocked an eye at Larghos. A paktun he might be; he did not look like one. There was not a scar on his body as far as I could see. But he was a spare, limber fellow, with a straight back and a cut about his jaw that showed there was more to him than Marta either allowed or recognized.

He managed a light laugh.

"Oh, I am not a politician. I know that well enough." He glanced across at me, a thing easy enough to do seeing that the kovneva reached up only to our shoulders. "But a paktun—no. No, I was never honored with the pakmort as were you, Jak the Drang." He looked away. "Although I do not see you wearing the silver mortil-head at the moment."

"When I turfed that pile of stones down after your coach I had less than I have now."

The two handmaidens giggled at this.

I had offered no explanations. They would not get any, however much they might ask.

"This ring," I said, harking back to a subject that intrigued me more by its infantilism than anything else.

"The Ring of Destiny, once owned by La-Si-Quenying, a mighty Wizard of Loh of the distant past. Quenying's Ring. Once I have that in my hand no one will stop me."

I did not smile.

"I know the Wizards of Loh hold great and mysterious powers," I said. That was true enough, by Krun! "I have heard of a great Wizard of Loh in these latter days. A most powerful man—"

"Can you call them men?" said Larghos. His face had lost a trifle of its color as he spoke.

We moved forward into a small clearing where two fallen trees had intertwined their branches high above, leaning one against another, and a third lay along the ground, rotting quietly away. Beetles and ants and woodlice were busy about their own businesses. Here we rested for a space and they told me about the Ring of Destiny, Quenying's Ring.

It seemed clear enough to me. Phu-si-Yantong it was whose murky schemes coiled about this possessed woman. She believed that if she could take possession of this so-called magical ring she would miraculously find all her problems solved. She could at a stroke dispose of the perils of the radvakkas, gain everything she coveted. As she spoke I saw more. From the way Larghos glowered, and then smoothed out his face, I saw the way this pretty little scenario was scripted. For the kovneva fancied her luck as empress. She would wed this Seakon, who was without a bride, and become Empress of Vallia. The ring would do this for her, as a mere part of its miraculous properties. And, to cap it all, I was absolutely sure it must be Phu-si-Yantong who had sold her this stinking kettle of fish. But she believed passionately.

She had been on the way to the fortress town of Nikwald in the kovnate of Sakwara when the radvakkas had attacked.

Nikwald was in Sakwara, Hawkwa territory. Now it was over-run by the radvakkas. The Iron Riders would not take kindly to the notion of a Vallian kovneva driving up to their encampments in search of a magical ring. I rubbed my nose.

The thought that occurred to me, to be instantly dispelled, also occurred to Marta Renberg.

She turned from where she sat on a fallen branch and surveyed me, her head on one side. A shafting of the mingled light cast her face for a moment into a softer mold, with all the petulant lines smoothed away. She looked radiant, in that moment, almost beautiful. She was well aware of the impression she created. Larghos shifted and cleared his throat; he did not spit.

"Jak the Drang?"

I sat silent.

"You are a paktun, a renowned soldier of fortune. You could fetch me the ring."

"Perhaps."

"There would be a great reward in it."

"Would not the ring itself—?"

"No!" She flared up, agitated. "No—for Phu—for I have been most solemnly informed that only I have the power to raise the magic within the ring. Only me! I have been told and it is true."

Poor silly stupid girl!

She went on, and now she spoke in a breathless, winsome way she supposed must flatter me, overbear me, favor me with all the forbidden paradises known to Kregen. "Why have you been so good to me, Jak? You saved me from the Iron Riders. Then you saved me again from Cansinsax. You ride with us and are a good companion. Why do you do all these things?" She leaned down from her branch to where I sat with my back shoved against the wood. "Perhaps I can guess, Jak the Drang. Perhaps I know the secret of your heart."

I couldn't laugh; but the statement, the situation, demanded a great gut-bursting bellow of crude and raucous laughter.

What did she know of me? What, indeed!

"The ring is in Hawkwa country, and the Iron Riders—"

"You do not fear them. Do you not carry their weapons, ride their mount?"

About to bellow out some uncouth comment, I was struck dumb.

Among all the scuttering beetles and ants and tumbling woodlice under the rotting wood a bright orange-brown form waddled out. On eight hairy legs he poised, his arrogant tail upflung. I stared, feeling the bile rising. Larghos sat with his booted foot less than six inches from the scorpion, and did not move, did not see. He was not a scorpion. He was The Scorpion.

The forest fell silent. The leaves no longer chirred in the breeze. The very suns' beams lay quiescent, with motes of dust trapped and motionless.

The arrogant stinging tail lifted and dropped. The Scorpion surveyed me very deliberately. So I knew.

After a space of time very sinister to me, The Scorpion ambled to the flaking-barked log and disappeared. The breeze blew, the leaves whispered and the dust motes danced within the radiance of Zim and Genodras.

And not a word had the damned Scorpion spoken!

"Very well, kovneva. I will go to Nikwald and bring back the Ring of Destiny."

Seven

In the Camp of the Iron Riders

Lumpy carried me jogging across Aduimbrev and over the Therduim Cut and so into Sakwara. I'd called this shaggy old gray benhoff Lumpy out of a mixture of disreputable feelings; but, truth to tell, he wasn't all that bad. It is difficult to feel at odds with a faithful saddle-animal for very long.

Seeing the kovneva and her party safely into Thiurdsmot, I had refused the offer of a flying mount from the Hamalian aerial cavalry squadron. They acted under the orders of Marta Renberg. People in Vallia were becoming more and more used to flying cavalry, great birds of the air being used as saddle flyers; but I refused the offer of a fluttrell since I considered that would attract more attention than a benhoff, attention I wished to avoid. I had insisted on going alone. Larghos had offered to accompany me, which made me look at him afresh; but I managed to convince him his duty lay with the kovneva. Truth to tell, he might have attempted to prevent my return with the ring, seeing that if Marta did as she intended then it would be a quick exit for Larghos.

A different route from the one I had followed previously swung me a trifle to the north. The same gradual trending of the land from forest to grassland to the sere plains progressed. On a bright morning I broke camp and set off and just before the Hour of Mid observed a dark mass approaching over the plain. Lumpy and I took ourselves as quickly as might be into a hollow. I watched.

These people were Vallians. They wore Vallian buff and their colors were a mixture of many of the provinces of the North East. But they were no advancing army bent on conquest. Carts were piled high with homely possessions. Women strode along with children clinging to their skirts. The men rode guard on the flanks. They were Hawkwas, well and true; but they were refugees, seeking to escape from the wrath of the Iron Riders. They passed away traveling west. I mounted up again and set off eastwards.

If ever I could say about the island empire, as I often say about other places, my Vallia—then my Vallia was in sorry shape. And I was pattering off on a footling errand for a silly ambitious woman who wanted to be empress, searching for a confounded ring said to be possessed of magical properties. Almost, I drew rein and turned back. But The Scorpion had left me in no doubt. I had to get that damned ring. It was a quest of the most farcical kind; but however ludicrous that side of the quest might be, the reality on the other side was dark and horrifically serious.

Despite all the appearances to the contrary, this was no splendid game of quest in the high tradition I played. I fought and gambled for stakes far greater than those of a simple quest.

I have no desire to go into the full details of all that went on during that search for the Ring of Destiny. Marta had given me all the information she had on its whereabouts, and this proved highly accurate. Phu-si-Yantong would not fail on that. I guessed he used this ploy to distract the poor woman, seeing that his iron legions of Hamal had failed. He, like any other man, had to work through the tools available. In Yantong's case the tools were more often than not other men and women. But the Hamalese had been humiliated in the field. No doubt Yantong in his insane ambitions would assemble other forces; for the moment he kept this woman working for him by means of a transparently dishonest folk tale.

The defeat suffered by the Hamalian Army outside the walls of Cansinsax was not the first time they had been bested by the Iron Riders; but they would not face the humiliating fact that all their expertise, their professionalism, their famous Laws, could not withstand the mailed cavalry charge delivered by the radvakkas astride benhoffs. The talk in Thiurdsmot had been of a fresh battle with flyers and vollers to give aerial support and with batteries of varters to supplement the crossbows. The job could be done, of course; I did not know if I wanted to be there at the time to witness the horror and the splendor of it.

The shrill battle cries of the Hamalese as they clashed with their enemies—the vicious, shrilling, demanding: "Hanitch!" "Hanitch!"—had rung with a desperation, almost an hysteria, over that stricken field outside the walls of Cansinsax.

Nikwald bore the marks of its altered status. Many of the brick buildings and wooden outhouses were mere shells and charred skeletons. But a central section remained around a kyro with pretensions to architectural respectability, and here the radvakkas stabled their benhoffs, set up their cooking arrangements and their armory and generally conducted themselves in the way of bombastic barbarians two worlds over.

Originally there had been four temples in Nikwald, the chiefest being dedicated to Junka, a manifestation of godhood well thought of in the North East. The second, which should rightfully have been the first in view of the real importance of Opaz for all the genuine self-negation that is a small part of that belief, was dedicated to the Invisible Twins. Both had been partially destroyed. Benhoffs and calsanys were tethered within the shattered walls.

Shuffling along leading Lumpy, an old shaggy pelt flung over my shoulders, I passed well enough for a radvakka slave caring for his master's steed. Other slaves went about their businesses, and all wore that hangdog defeated look of the oppressed when in private, and all put on that inane cheerful look of happy subservience when their masters bellowed at them.

All I saw convinced me that the radvakkas had sailed from Segesthes and landed in Vallia in strength. The fate of the eastern islands concerned me profoundly—what had befallen Veliadrin, Zamra and Valka? Had my people managed to hold out against this new threat? The moment the Star Lords were satisfied, I knew where I was going—before, even, I thought, Strombor.

The temple of brick and wood erected to the greater glory of Mellor'An, a local god of agriculture, husbandry and fertility in general, was of altogether lesser proportions and only a part had burned. Men moved about purposefully and I saw they had set up a forge in the outer court where benhoff shoes were repaired and where the iron fittings of gear and equipment might be made good. The armories did not share the same fires and anvils as this blacksmithing work. I meandered along past the outer wall.

In a crumbled corner of brick I took a swift look around. No one watched me. The town hummed with activity. Working with a deceptive smoothness I probed a nail loose in Lumpy's middle offside hoof. I already had a broken chain, and cursed it. I walked Lumpy lumpily back to the smithy.

Inside, the radvakkas in charge bellowed slaves about their work. "Here, slave, hurry!" rumbled one at me as I approached. Then he spat out that vicious, cutting order: *"Grak!"*

So, being sensible in these things, I grakked and handed the broken chain across. Radvakkas, like many barbarians, set no store by money; when it fell into their hands they melted it down for the precious metals to be used in ornamentation. Communal work was done on a communal basis. The radvakka blacksmiths grasped whips instead of hammers, and beat their skilled slaves into the work. The broken chain would be mended as a mere part of maintaining the military equipment of the whole band. Then I led Lumpy around to have his shoe fixed.

For the moment freed of observation I wandered away from the busy activity of the fires, as though seeking a corner where I might eat my bread and cheese and, if I was fortunate, munch on an onion. A hierarchy existed among slaves. Those attending personally to radvakka masters were a cut above the poor devils tending the fires or bashing iron. A group sat on sacks in a corner, and they called out to me to join them in their game of knucklebones, as they waited for repairs to be completed.

"I have had the luck of Ernelltar the Bedevilled lately, doms," I called across. "Give me leave to sit awhile and eat. Mayhap later I will chance a round or two."

They made crude remarks at this, all of them pleased for the moment to be on a duty that gave them a trifle of spare time so rare and precious in their lives. I moved on into the shadows past where the altar to Mellor'An had once lifted and now lay in shards of broken brick and pottery and charred wood.

Without a shred of modesty I can claim that no ordinary Vallian would have escaped detection for a moment. But I was a Clansman—a Clansman of Felschraung and Longuelm and now of Viktrik. If Hap Loder had not been out collecting obi from other clans, also. I knew the ways of the rad-vakkas passing well. Talk of Ernelltar the Bedevilled raised uncouth and sarcastic comments, for all knew that runs of bad luck were attributed to him in North Segesthes.

The space at the rear of the altar was badly broken down. In a cavity within the pediment below the altar, Marta had said. I kicked charred tim-bers aside and swiped at the clouds of dust and ashes. The rumble of voices and the clang of the smithies' hammers resounded comfortingly from the exterior. I poked around. There was a crevice, a slot in the baked bricks. I reached down. A box? Something hard-edged. I got my fingers around it and then took a quick look back. I was still alone.

With a grunt and a heave the box came out. Sturmwood, scuffed, with a brass lock and hinges, it looked nothing special. It went under the shaggy pelt as a warvol devours flesh.

Then I yawned and wandered back to the knuckle-bone players.

For the look of the thing I played a few hands, and lost one of the dag-gers, and felt too amused even to curse.

The slaves laboring at the fires, at the bellows, hammering the iron, would slide liquid envious glances in our direction. Hardly slaves at all, these fellows who so liked to lord it over the less fortunate, cowed before their masters. In a sense they were more like the militarily employed hel-ots of the Spartans. With good and faithful service and the signal proof of courage they might even be given a kind of manumission and join the hard-riding ranks of the radvakkas. The process was continuous, Iron Rid-ers in the making.

Not all the slaves were apim. There was a marked brutality in the treat-ment the radvakkas meted out to the diffs. They would in their rough uncouth ways stand far more from an apim slave than a diff. I saw a Rapa knocked headlong into a fire. A little Och whose job was to bring water for quenching was tripped and his bucket upended over his head and rammed down around his ears. The Iron Riders were intolerant of diffs, that was known.

Many diffs bore the savage marks of barbaric punishments.

"Here, slave!" bellowed a radvakka, and he cracked his whip. "Your work is done. Now schtump. Grak!"

I detest that hateful word grak. As the radvakka yelled so the slaves all jumped, quite automatically, when the vicious cutting word of command bit into the stifling smoke-filled air.

As humbly as might be contrived I took Lumpy and the chain and went out. The air smelled sweet after the singing stink of the smithy.

All this time I had been alert, strung-up, making myself appear relaxed, expecting detection at any moment. Now, as I led Lumpy out along the street, with Nikwald filled with the clamor of the Iron Riders about me, I thought I had done it. I was set. Clear away. I had only to mount up and ride.

That would have been a disastrous mistake.

Since when would a slave, even a master's slave, a helot, dare to ride his master's steed back from the smithy in the barbaric encampments of the Iron Riders?

"By Getranchi's Iron Fist!" bellowed a radvakka as he kicked heartily at a Khibil carrying a sack of flour. "Grak, you useless worm. Or I'll cut your hide to pieces."

They were but a pair acting out the lunacy of their respective social positions, one swaggering, the other staggering. Perforce, I had to look the other way. One day, Opaz willing, we'd have sanity back in Vallia and do away with slavery for good and all. I led Lumpy on and ground down the instinct to whip out the broadsword and lay the flat against the arrogant Iron Rider's skull.

A hullabaloo broke out ahead, with people shouting and running, so I guided Lumpy into the shadows of a tumbledown shack at the side of a ruined house. Men were pointing up. So up I looked, shielding my eyes against the declining rays of the suns. Up there, high, three vollers fleeted across the sky, traveling southwest and going fast. They were mere petal-shaped outlines; but they were Hamalian and they were scouting radvakka Nikwald. Judging from the comments of the Iron Riders, they thirsted for the chance to drive a spear into the marvelous flying craft up there, and were stumped as to how to do it.

An odd sound as of a piece of wood striking the palm of the hand, although heavier, meatier, floated from the ruined building. I ignored it. In this concealment seemed a good time for me to discard the sturmwood, brass-bound box, which was too awkward for easy carriage. I took the ring out. The Ring of Destiny. It looked an ordinary enough ring, with two emeralds, a ronil and an indeterminate whitish stone, not a diamond, all fastened with gold claws. I stuck it down safely into my breechclout.

The slapping noise continued and I pushed further back and looked through where once a window had been and where now a gap stretched from ground to sky. The tamped earth space within was clearly illuminated by the angled rays of the suns. I saw.

The foul bile of disgust rose into my throat.

A circle of radvakkas stood with whips, with pieces of wood, with iron bars. They surrounded a stake. Tethered by his tail to the stake a man stood and was struck and struck again. The game was to make him run round and round the stake, his tail fastened to an iron ring that enabled him to circle, to duck, to dodge and weave. At the side a radvakka was totting up the bets on a wooden slipstick. The Iron Riders sweated over their work; but they did not call out or make any noise. So I guessed there were bets on the shrieks of pain of their victim, also, and they would not wish to miss these.

In a corner lay the corpses of a number of men—all diffs.

The fellow who was now being tortured for sport did not run. He stood there, his four arms bound at their four elbows into his back. His face—his face showed a dark and passionate hatred of these radvakkas, a tawny-haired face, with tawny moustaches and a golden beard, a savage, noble, suffering face. But he did not cry out. He stood there and I marveled at the way he moved himself, shifting on his feet with a litheness that reminded me of the way great unarmed combat men fight in their disciplines—a fluid shifting grace of movements that avoided many of the blows. But many more struck home. His naked body, banded with muscle and yet slender and limber, bore the bloody marks, the weals and cuts, the bruises.

He was a marvel, this man. He was of the Kildoi, a race of diffs not very well known mainly inhabiting Balintol. The immensely powerful physique, the fluid shifting movements, the slide and rope of muscles, all added to the clear and intelligent anticipation of a blow, enabled him to last out in his suffering where lesser men would have been shrieking in shredded agony. But—there was about his anticipation of a blow more than mere intelligence. Much mumbo jumbo is spoken and written about the mystic means whereby a man may judge a blow although blindfolded, and there is great truth in this. Certainly I know what I know of many Disciplines. The Krozairs, chiefest of all, of course, and the Khamster syples of the Khamorros, the Velyan techniques of the Martial Monks of Djanduin, and many more. Much foolishness is written and believed about mysticism in combat; but the kernel of truth remains. In this fellow, this Kildoi, I saw a man who was a High Adept, a True and Proven Master.

This was no business of mine. So why did I stand there?

This was something of a different order from that radvakka who had so thoughtlessly kicked his Khibil slave up the rear. That was of the daily nature of a slave's life and a vileness I and Delia would try to end as soon as we might—a thankless and difficult task, Opaz knew. But this obscenity before me was something else again. Still and all, all the same, without doubt—it was nothing to do with me. So, you see, I prevaricated.

One of the radvakkas slashed his whip and the Kildoi slid the blow easily and instantly swayed the other way and avoided a lashing blow from an iron bar. He was very very good. In the event, before I turned away—for I hewed to my main task and would not imperil that even for so marvelous a fellow as this—one of the Iron Riders threw his wooden bludgeon to the ground in disgust.

"You see?" he bellowed. "By the Iron Helm of Getranchi. Did I not say so?"

"Maybe you were right," said another. "But he affords sport."

"Sport? I have hit him once only. Once! You call that sport?"

"Maybe," put in a third, "you cannot hit straight."

I rather hoped they'd start a brawl at this; but they went on arguing. The Kildoi stood, poised, lithe, his bruises hard and shining upon him, the blood trickling down that plated chest. I felt for him. And, although this was no business of mine, I did not go away.

"Give him another few murs," said the aggrieved radvakka at last. "It was a waste of time exchanging him. He must be kept in chains all day—he's far too dangerous for a good slave. A waste of time."

"A few murs, then. I own, he is worse than a Kataki."

They started it up again, hitting and slashing, and despite all the wonderful alacrity of the Kildoi he took blows. The blood shone upon his tawny skin.

Of course this was no business of mine—a strange diff, a camp of enemies, in a part of Vallia hostile to the center—what possible business was it of mine, who had urgent business with a ring and a willful kovneva and the commands of the Star Lords? And those just for starters—with all the rest of my problems looming and gibbering at me?

Emperor of Vallia. That was just a laugh. But, just suppose I was the emperor. Then the concerns of all Vallia were mine, and the concerns of all the people in the empire. And, anyway, I'd taken a great liking to this tailed, four-armed marvel who stood, shining with blood, yet golden and still defiant. He was a man I fancied I could understand. No business of mine—this situation was the business and concern of all men.

So, not reluctantly, but joyfully, I hauled out the broadsword and stepped silently into the ruined building.

Eight

Korero

This was no time for chivalry. No time for the honored traditions of combat. This was going to be nip and tuck.

I hewed through the necks of the first two radvakkas, just above the iron corselet rims, back-handed a third across his face, chunked the reeking broadsword into the eye of a fourth. But there were ten of them, nine in the circle and the slipstick man taking the bets. The others roared at me, raving, ripping out their swords.

The first two fell smoothly enough, and I leaped across their collapsing bodies to get at the last three. The slipstick man tried to throw a knife. Well, he threw it, but the aim was deflected by my left arm. The broadsword went in and out, swung left-handed, and there was just the one left facing me.

He was mumbling something incoherent about a devil; but I smacked his blade away sharply and chunked him down into the tamped earth floor. The slipstick man was almost at the ruined window-opening, shrieking, getting away.

The broadsword lifted into the air, I caught it at the point of balance. I drew back, let fly. Point first the blade skimmed across that dolorous room, burst into the back of his neck, spouted on out. He stopped shrieking and staggered forward and sideways, collapsing in a quivering heap.

The dagger whipped out and a swift succession of four slicing cuts freed the Kildoi's arms. The rope around his handed tail chained to the ring slashed and fell away. I managed to force a smile for him.

"Llahal and Llahal, dom. Let us get out of here, sharpish."

"Llahal, dom. You are very—welcome—whatever kind of demon you may be."

I padded across to the window and retrieved the broadsword. I looked outside. Someone must have heard the racket and be coming to investigate. I swung back.

"Devil I may be. But we're both consigned to the Ice Floes of Sicce if we don't use our noodles. Here—help me strip this fellow. He looks big enough."

Between us we got the riveted iron from the corpse and I shrugged it on. A helmet from the pile in the corner slammed on my head. The cunning metal plates flapped into place before my face. I slung the shaggy pelt over my shoulder and looked through the eye slits in the metal mask.

The Kildoi had snatched up a shaggy pelt and draped it about himself.

We stepped through the shattered window opening and I leaped up onto Lumpy.

"Take the reins. Lead us along—gently. Keep your head down."

He said nothing but did as I bid. Sitting astride the benhoff, led by a cowed slave, I rode sedately out into the street. A few radvakkas were riding up to find out what the racket was. One of them reined across and started to speak.

"A pestilential fellow," I said, making my gruff old voice harsher and more malignant still. "By the Iron Fist of Getranchi! He took a long time to die."

"Hai!" quoth this Iron Rider. "Did you win?"

"Aye. I won."

We rode on.

As quickly as possible I guided us away from the main street and away from the campfires. Nikwald was only so big and we would never avoid eventual discovery once the hunt was up. We had to get clean away, and the suns would not be gone for a bur yet. I kept listening for sounds that would indicate the massacre had been discovered; but as we approached the broken-down wall of the onetime fortress town nothing sounded apart from the familiar noises of warriors encamped.

We found the second benhoff at the lines under the wall. One radvakka who wanted to know why we took the beast fell down. I did not think he would get up again. The Kildoi mounted up, and I noticed that he fought the stiffness of his cuts and bruises with the phlegmatic calm of one inured to hardship and the injustices of life.

"We must wait until the suns are gone. She of the Veils will give us a bur before she rises. In that time—"

"Aye, dom. We ride."

"Just so. Until then, we keep out of sight."

That was not too difficult in a brawling barbarian camp, even when the racket broke out that told the discovery had been made. Parties of Iron Riders began galloping in all directions. Useless to try to disguise this Kildoi in the time available; I decided we had to try.

Dismounted, we stood in the shadow of the crumbled wall, ready to ride out. A radvakka had the misfortune to approach, without seeing us, to investigate the breach in the wall at this point. The suns were almost gone. Mingled jade and crimson light speared through the gap and threw opaline-bordered shadows across the detritus. I was about to reach out for the Iron Rider when the Kildoi said: "Mine, I think, dom."

"My pleasure."

His tail hand, so much like that of a Pachak, whipped out. It fastened on the throat of the radvakka, choking off his cry, hauled him from the saddle. He crashed to the ground with a savagery that told me much. There was no need to silence him after that. The Kildoi was halfway through trying to fit his artfully articulated shoulders into the riveted iron when the patrol rode up. We two froze. In the shadows, we ought to escape detection; but if one of our benhoffs reacted to the presence of the others...

Our hands fondled the benhoffs, massaging the rolls of fat, giving the benhoffs pleasurable sensations, keeping them quiet.

The riders drew off. I let out a breath.

The suns were nearly gone, drowning in an opaline glory.

"Close," I said. I stared at the shadows that chingled with iron as they rode away.

"Close. I am Korero, dom. Your name?"

My mind was on those damned Iron Riders. I said: "I am Dray—"
And then I caught myself, and said, swiftly: "I am Jak the Drang. Lahal,
Korero."

"Lahal, Jak the Drang."

He passed no comment. But, even then, I fancied he had heard that
confounded stupid word "Dray" and stored it away.

The dying radiance of the Suns of Scorpio stained across the sky of Kregen. In silence we mounted up. He was an old hand, this Korero, a fellow
used to the kind of nefarious business we were about. He made no fuss
about what had to be done but got on with it. An old campaigner, and yet
he was young, I judged, although tall for a Kildoi, being a good four inches
taller than me. He moved with a contained muscular alertness, a springi-
ness, a limber strength. And his reflexes were quicksilver, I had witnessed
that.

We rode away from Nikwald, very quietly, into the shadows before She
of the Veils rose to shed her fuzzy pink and golden light across the land. I
made sure the Ring of Destiny still snugged in my breechclout. We rode. If
pursuit there was we saw nothing of it.

We spoke very little, aware how sound traveled at night over the plains.
I taxed Korero on the absence of any appellation to his name, whereat he
half-smiled, and said: "You are Jak the Drang. I have been Korero this and
Korero that, from time to time. Mayhap, one day, I will tell you."

We rode companionably back the way I had come and in due time
reached Thiurdsmot. Carrying the ring I found the kovneva.

Nine

Bird of Ill Omen

Thiurdsmot girded itself for the fray, everyone engaged in a grim preparation for the coming conflict, and Marta Renberg, Kovneva of Aduimbrev,
was in raptures over the Ring of Destiny.

She turned it this way and that, holding it out at arm's length, admiring
it as it glittered on her finger.

"Splendid!" she declared. "With this ring all my troubles are over."

Larghos looked at me, and away, and said nothing. We stood in the
wide window embrasure of a tower given over to the kovneva's use. The
trappings and furnishing were luxurious, as was to be expected. The handmaidens were flushed of cheek and brighter of eye. All in all, absolute

confidence radiated about the walls and turrets of Thiurdsmot and nerved
the ranks of the Hamalian army and their mercenary allies.

Standing respectfully before the kovneva I looked out through the window. Troops marched in their strict formations in the kyro far below. The
colors of Hamal and Aduimbrev floated everywhere, mingled with the colors of the freelances and the paktuns with their own bands. A fluttrell
formation winged past, the big birds keeping a beautiful precision of formation, the flyers on their backs leaning into the windrush.

Vollers sailed down to land at the vollerpark. These I eyed with a cov-
etousness I trusted did not show on my savage old leem-face. One of
those—one of those airboats I'd have this night and be away, or my name
was not Dray Prescot. Zamra, Valka and Veliadrin, to scout, to discover, to
do what might be done. And then—Strombor and Delia. Yes, my course
was plain.

Marta was transported with pleasure. She had not actually said thank
you or commended me on my action and this did not surprise me. As far
as she was concerned my usefulness to her had finished and one did not
expect civility from a great noble, male or female, in these circumstances.
Had she wished to employ me again no doubt she would have remembered to toss me a crumb of some tawdry kind as a reward. Mind you, this
forgetfulness of favors is not confined to the nobility or the gentry alone.
The poor people, for all there are a great many of them, often share the
same distressing character defect.

To carry out Phu-si-Yantong's demands in this part of Vallia a Chuktar
had been appointed in command. He was an ord-Chuktar, and therefore
an important man in almost any army. He and Marta appeared to get along
together and as she began to tell him just how the ring would discompose
the mailed cavalry of the Iron Riders I was able to ease away out of their
notices. This Chuktar Nath ham Holophar was a strom, the Strom of War-
hurn, and I'd been ready to take action in case he recognized me. But that
was highly unlikely, for the desperado Jak the Drang did not look much
like Hamun ham Farthytu, the Amak of Paline Valley.

Their plan was one of the obvious ones, given the circumstances. Once
the ring had exerted its power, controlled and directed by the kovneva,
the army of Hamal would ride over what was left of the radvakkas. The
aerial might they could bring to bear would finish them off. They saw no
problems.

Scouts brought in details of the radvakka's movements. The battle was
imminent, and I intended to be long gone before that.

The only note that ought to have indicated caution to the Hamalese
sounded in the increased numbers of Iron Riders. Reports estimated at
least three bands had joined, making nine thousand.

Chuktar ham Holophar had thirty regiments of infantry, foot and crossbows, and five thousand totrix and zorca cavalry, together with a strong varter force. With the aerial wings that ought to be enough to see off the Riders—so ham Holophar said, with some grimness—without the magical influence of the ring.

Myself, I owned with a matching grimness that I'd as lief see the paired opponents mutually exhausted, Hamalese and radvakkas alike, so that honest Vallians could claim back their own land.

Filled with her busy plans Marta Renberg saw me as I crossed to the door. Her face clouded and then brightened.

"You will fight in the battle, Jak the Drang?"

Standing with my hand on the door, aware of the guards posted at either side, I felt the need for a little gentle stirring...

"Mayhap, kovneva. I remember a certain promise, made upon a fallen log in a clearing."

She flushed up, as she did so easily, and her lips tightened.

"I have warned you aforetime, eeshim. I do not forget old scores."

"But promises?"

"I do not wrangle in public with a rast like you. Guards! Seize the insolent cramph—"

I went through the doorway before the guards could react and slammed the heavy lenk shut. I was down the stairs of the tower and out into the inner ward, the outer ward, and the kyro swallowed me up in its busy activity long before anyone got a glimpse of my departure. Silly woman! Well, she had her Ring of Destiny. I almost felt sorry I would not be here to see how efficacious it was in action.

Just how serious this petulant kovneva was about having me taken up I was not sure; but it appeared a wise plan to keep myself out of sight until evening. The parallel between this action and the action of hiding in radvakka Nikwald occurred to me, you may be sure, and with an unpleasant reminder of the evil days fallen upon Vallia, a sprightly young Hamalian Air Service man went to sleep in a side alley, perfectly unharmed save for a headache when he awoke and a chilly feeling around his nether regions, because his smart uniform was missing. Wearing that uniform and almost busting the stitching, I sat myself down in a tavern, in a dark corner, to await my chance. Thus placing myself in the jaws of the beast, as it were, seemed the safest course.

These men were off duty, and in the nature of off-duty soldiers or airmen they drank and gambled and chased the girls and sang. They sang the songs of Hamal. Well, I'd sung them, in my time. I listened, not joining in, marking down a weasely little fellow with the insignia of a shiv-Deldar who was trying to sing and could only manage a croak or two because he was so far gone, half-falling off his bench, lolling foolishly near me.

They sang "Anete ham Terhenning," a stupidly tragic song about poor

Anete who for the love of a stalwart cross-bowman of the emperor's guard hurled herself from the Bridge of Sicce. I felt easier when they passed on to the good old favorite: "When the Fluttrell Flirts His Wing." The shiv-Deldar lurched and slopped his ale and I moved smoothly across and caught him, supported him up against the wall. He waggled his head at me, owlishly.

"Whereaway, dom? The old voller's in a real hurricane—"

"Rest easy," I said. "Have another drink."

So we sat and drank companionably and he talked. He was not at all sure he'd been as clever as he'd thought, volunteering for the Army against Vallia. I learned that the Hamalese regiments and aerial wings and cavalry were not regular units of the Hamalian army; they'd been given the chance of volunteering and, as the shiv-Deldar, who was called Naghan the Boxes, said, the Empress Thyllis wasn't paying them. Their regimental cash boxes were filled by prompt and regular payments from the person he called the Hyr Notor. The High Lord. I did not have to be told that was what Phu-si-Yantong had adopted as a cover name for himself in dealing with Thyllis and her people and army.

Vallia was being cut up into different areas, dominated by the forces of different factions and nobles. His lot had been run out of the North East and they did not like it. Come the morrow, said Naghan the Boxes, and drank deeply, come the morrow and they'd chuck their firepots down on these nurdling Iron Riders and crisp 'em in their iron.

You may judge of my joy when, by casual enquiry, I discovered that the Deldar actually knew of Rees and Chido, and could assure me they yet lived and were hale and hearty. This pleased me greatly. Other things I learned, which you shall hear when they are germane to my narrative.

The Deldar blinked at my broadsword. "Naughty," he said. "Where's your thraxter? Your Hikdar will not allow non-squadron equipment." He belched. "He'll mazingle you as the Law allows." By mazingle he meant discipline. The uniform I had acquired was that of a simple aerial soldier, a voswod, so I forced a smile and nodded and offered another drink.

The conversation came around to the vollers of the squadron and I learned what I needed to know. So I excused myself and the suns having set and my appetite for the moment satisfied by the ingestion of a superb vosk pie, I sauntered out into the moonslit darkness. Now, as you know, I have some skill in the art of stealing airboats. It is not a gift of which I am particularly proud; but I console myself with the reflection that I practice the art only to use a voller when the need is dire. It is not a skill used for mere self-gratification.

As I left the tavern with the lights shining from the windows the swods were singing "Black Is the River and Black Was Her Hair," another farcical tragical ditty. They'd roar and roister until the patrols hoicked them out, and they'd maybe have sore heads in the morning; but I knew they were Hamalian swods and they'd fight like demons when the Iron Riders charged.

I hummed a few bars of "The Bowmen of Loh," in a manner to redress the balance, and went up to the vollerpark. I took a voller. I hurt no one. The flier lifted into the moonshot dimness as one of the lesser moons of Kregen hurtled across the sky. The night air breathed sweet about me. I turned the airboat's head eastwards. I was on my way home.

Looking back, I realize the futility of anger. I should have known. That dratted Scorpion had not crawled out from under a rotting log and given me implicit instructions to let me get away so easily now.

The tempest boiled up in a maelstrom of whirling winds that buffeted the craft this way and that, that scythed me with a pelting blast of hail, that drove the voller swooping and skimming to the ground. I hauled at the controls; but the voller flattened out and skidded along the ground, less than two ulms from the town. The noise racketed about my head.

And then—and then the noise and the tempest vanished in a heartbeat, and the Gdoinye flew down, arrogant and bright in his power, and perched on the coaming.

I glared at that gorgeous bird whose plumage sheened with metallic luster in the moonlight as She of the Veils rose.

"Dray Prescot, onker of onkers."

My harsh old lips clamped shut. Confound the bird! The raptor would get no change out of me...

"Do you not understand what the Everoinye demand of you?"

So, my resolution flung to the winds, I burst out: "By Vox, you brainless bird! Do they know themselves?"

"They know, onker, and they know you are the man to fulfill their desires and to obey their commands." The Gdoinye stuck his head on one side and regarded me balefully from one bright avaricious, beady, knowing eye. "A crossbow bolt was loosed at me—"

"I wish to Zair it had pierced your foul heart!"

"You do not. And you know you do not. Now, hearken! You will stop the Iron Riders. The Star Lords command. You will halt the radvakkas and drive them back over the sea to whence they came. This, Dray Prescot, king of onkers, you will do."

I laughed. "Stop them? With what? How am I supposed to halt that mailed cavalry?"

"You saved the Miglas and halted the Canops, I remember."

"Sarcasm, Gdoinye, ill becomes you. And to fight the Canops I brought my Freedom Fighters from Valka and mercenaries from Vallia. You know Vallia never has had a national army—"

"Do not prevaricate, onker! You know the answer. We do not ask you to perform a deed beyond your powers, puerile though they be."

"If they are so puerile, by Makki-Grodno's diseased tripes, then you should be able to do it all yourself!"

The Gdoinye let out a squawking cackle, of amusement, of scorn, I didn't know or care. I glared and shook my fist.

"I'm going back to Strombor—"

"Your empress is safe, Dray Prescot, safe in the Heart Heights of Valka surrounded by your Freedom Fighters. They take a heavy toll of those who invaded Valka."

"She is safe? Delia is safe?"

"Assuredly. Now, emperor of onkers, do as you must and drive back the radvakkas. And then, why you may do as you wish with Vallia. For a space."

I opened my mouth to ask what the damned bird meant by a space; but he ruffled his feathers, struck his wings and soared aloft. In an instant he was a dot against the face of She of the Veils, and then he was gone.

So I, being in truth the onker of onkers the Gdoinye dubbed me, cursed and cursed again. I would have to do as the Star Lords commanded. And, of course, I'd mightily enjoy discomfiting the radvakkas. But I had to admit I would far rather tilt at the Iron Riders on my own account.

Back to Thiurdsmot I flew and replaced the voller. Scowling ferociously, I took myself off. Only one thing pleased me, and that tempered by parting. Delia was safe. I hungered for her and I knew she yearned for me. The quicker I saw the Iron Riders to the Ice Floes of Sicce the quicker I'd see Delia again.

Ten

"Give me your sword, jen, and you would see!"

I, Dray Prescot, Lord of Strombor and Krozair of Zy, hunkered down under a thorn-ivy bush with a crossbow bolt through my thigh and could no longer curse. There was another bolt through my arm; but I was able to break off the leather flights and draw the confounded thing through and wrap a chunk of breechcloth around to check the bleeding.

All about me the yells and screams and moans of wounded and dying men beat fearfully into the lowering sky. The Suns of Scorpio were sinking over the field of carnage, and already the scavengers were out, slinking like gray wolves from body to body—if the body was not dead at first, it soon became dead after.

"You will fight in the battle, will you not, Jak the Drang?" that stupid

Kovneva Marta had said, and so I had, and had fought and this was the result. The Iron Riders had ridden. They had ridden well. They had ridden clear over the ranked regiments of Hamal and the mercenaries, ridden slap bang through the cavalry, gone rampaging on to Thiurdsmot itself, which was the prize they coveted. As for the famed aerial cavalry and the squadron of vollers, they had made no impression, and were long gone. Only the Hamalian varters had put any real impediment in the way of the radvakkas, and that had been for a short space only, the artillery being swept away in the rout.

And the ring? The damned Ring of Destiny?

Opaz knew what the woman had done. She believed fervently in the magical properties of the ring. Well, they hadn't worked. If she knew Phu-si-Yantong as I was beginning to know the devil, she should not have been surprised. Poor old Chuktar ham Holophar—if he still lived he'd not lightly put his trust in a silly woman's belief in a magical talisman again...

The quarrel through my leg was a nuisance. It had to come out and the wound attended to. The crossbows the radvakkas had used had been shot off with a fine abandon, much jollity must have been evinced as the barbarians played with these toys of civilization. Their own bows were puny, mere flat arcs of wood and sinew, and the captured crossbows were, for all the mockery, rather wonderful to them. Anyway, some dratted barbarian idiot had sent a quarrel into me, and his mate had slapped a second to follow the first. Mind you, I must blame only myself. Being hit by a flying arrow or bolt in the midst of a hectic battle is a chance all fighting men must take.

Not wishing to dramatize my predicament unduly, I will only add that here I was, wounded, without transport, abandoned on a stricken field, surrounded by implacable foemen—and with the stricture laid on me to defeat and drive out of Vallia the very enemy who was now so triumphant.

Well. It was a task. It was a challenge. I fancied I would go into the task with a greater zest now.

First things first...

The bolt drew out of my thigh with a deal of unpleasantness. The breechcloth had to be wrapped and pulled tightly. I peered out from under the thorn-ivy. She of the Veils was not yet up but in the last dying wash of light of the suns set the Twins rose in the east, eternally orbiting each other, lurid with a ruddy light. The wind blew soughingly. The yells and screams had mostly died away now and only occasionally a long groan broke that whispering silence.

I crawled out and stood up—very shakily.

The broadsword had snapped across in the melee and the shortsword had been carried off wedged in the breastbone of a radvakka whose iron corselet had been burst through. It had been hot work there, in the press.

Vague ideas of what I was going to do had already formed in my vosk-skull of a head; but I fancied I'd have to walk in on my own two feet—as I have done before, Zair knows. So, grumbling and cursing, I started off, hobbling along. That dip in the Pool of Baptism of the River Zelph in far Aphrasöe would most certainly speed my recuperation and leave me whole and unscarred; but the process of recovery was none the less highly fraught for all that.

Half-under a corpse of an infantryman I found a thraxter.

One of the gray scavengers approached and I showed him the blade, lurid in that ruddy light, and snarled, and he withdrew.

One hell of a racket was breaking up out of Thiurdsmot as I skirted the town. The townspeople would have made good their escape—or I devoutly hoped they had—the moment they had realized the battle was lost. The rout would have been a Cansinsax on a greater and more ghastly scale. Now the barbarians whooped it up in best barbarian style. I flung a few ripe curses at them as I hobbled past in the dappled moons light.

The three water bottles I had picked up were soon emptied and I had to cast about for a stream. I was ragingly thirsty.

The light of a small fire twinkled ahead. Carefully I scouted the little camp. These were Vallians—all of them natives of Vallia, I judged, and not a Hamalese among them. They sat hunched around their fire by the stream and their conversation, low-voiced, made me realize just how low-sunk we Vallians had become.

When I made my presence known the first awkwardness when fists grasped knives was overcome in a quick pappattu. They saw my wounds and one of them, Wando the Squint, helped me bathe them and dress them again. There were about twenty men here, mostly tradesmen of Thiurdsmot of that sturdy class who although employing slaves yet did much of the manual work themselves, being masters at their trades. I gathered their womenfolk had gone back over the Great River a few months ago. And, with them, was the blacksmith with whom I had fled from Cansinsax. When I asked him what had happened, his face clouded over and he beat that thewed arm and iron fist onto his knee.

"The Opaz-forsaken radvakkas! They slew my family—all of them they slew, and I could do nothing." His agony pierced me. "But I shall have them." He spoke quite rationally, this Cleitar the Smith. "I shall wreak my vengeance on them all."

Very carefully, for I had an inkling of what they purposed, I said: "You pitch your camp perilously close to the town."

"Aye," said the fellow who was clearly their elected leader. Tall, darker-complexioned than most Vallians, he lowered down on me, a deep scar furrowing down his left cheek from eye to lip. "Aye. We shall take any stragglers, and send them one by one to the Ice Floes of Sicce. They have conjured up great evil and a greater than they can imagine shall punish them."

"Amen to that," I said. "But—"

This Dorgo the Clis broke in: "We were told the iron men of Hamal were our new friends and allies. The kovneva told us. Well, we did her bidding. And Opaz punished us and sent the Iron Riders to destroy the men of iron. It is just. Now we shall avenge ourselves, as is just."

"Oh, aye," I said. "I'm all for slitting a few radvakka throats. But, as you see, I am in no case for running. And you will have to run—if you can."

They weren't too happy about this. They had a few weapons apart from their knives. One had a bow, a compound arm barely stronger than the bows of the radvakkas. Dorgo the Clis and another hulking fellow had swords, Vallian clanxers. Some of the others had spears, and Cleitar the Smith hefted his hammer. I tried to reason with them—uselessly.

"We may be honest tradesmen and no warriors. I think you are a paktun, Jak the Drang. Well, your paktun comrades ran and were cut down in the battle, as the Hamalese were. Now it is the turn of us to—"

"Listen, Dorgo! What do you know of fighting? I mean real fighting, as a warrior fights, in battle, with edged weapons? You have your town brawls with cudgels and a knife or two. But a real battle is a vastly different affair, by Vox!"

One of the men, a fellow who hefted a spear meanly, said: "My son was always reading the great stories, the legends, tales of the heroes. He ran away to be a mercenary, seeing, as he said, Vallia gave no place for a soldier in his native land. I have heard from him once. He is now a paktun, and fought in a place called Khorundur, wherever in the Light of the Invisible Twins that may be."

I did not tell him that Khorundur was a nation of the Dawn Lands of Havilfar. His son had traveled widely.

"And what is the meaning to your words, Magin?" demanded Dorgo the Clis.

"My son is not here to fight. But I shall. I shall stick my spear into the guts of a radvakka, at the least."

The real meaning behind Magin's words was there, plain as a pikestaff; but he had not yet teased out what he meant himself. He and his comrades, like the great mass of the people of Vallia, had not yet fully understood what they felt, had not yet come to a comprehension of what they must do. And what they must do had ramifications quite beyond the immediate knocking of a few Iron Riders over the head.

Trying to tell them to wait was like trying to melt the Ice Floes of Sicce with a half-ob candle. In the end, when I had told them I intended to raise a proper army to fight the Iron Riders and they were properly incredulous—not to say suspiciously contemptuous of any such grandiose concept—I said: "I am for Therminsax. If you can, join me there."

Dorgo the Clis stroked a broken thumbnail down his scar.

"It is certain you can be of no help to us, Jak the Drang. So we wish you well. But I do not think we shall meet in Therminsax."

"I think perhaps you will," I said. "May the light of Opaz go with you." And so, regretfully, I hobbled off into the night.

That journey recurs now, not, perhaps, with the frightfulness of other journeys I have undertaken on Kregen but, certainly, with a certain frisson. I hobbled. Thoughts of the Hamalese intruded along with all manner of nonsenses as I labored on. Rees and Chido, thank Krun they were safe. Even then I recalled how the Hamalian Army had been suspect against a heavy cavalry charge. Rees being overset by a hersany charge in Pandahem; our own wild charge at Tomor Peak... With an irony I did not relish I had to face the unpalatable fact that in this section of Vallia the only hope for Vallia at the moment was her enemy, Hamal. Nothing stood between the radvakkas and the soft heartlands of Vallia but the Hamalian Army. If I could find someone to listen to me—and I'd do it in the guise of the Amak Hamun nal Paline Valley—we'd strew caltrops, we'd dig ditches, we'd set ambushes, we'd smother the Iron Riders with bolts. It could be done; but at a price. Then I brightened up. That price, by Krun, would be paid by the Hamalese! Capital!

But, no—as I hobbled on through the night to the nearest canal, I knew that was a base thought. Good men would be sacrificed and die and I could take no pleasure from that.

Therminsax lay in a north northwesterly direction and altogether too near the border of Sakwara for comfort. But all reports spoke of the city as holding out so far against the radvakkas. The treacherous attack by the Kovneva of Aduimbrev against her northern neighbor and the subsequent occupation by the Hawkwas and the forces of Hamal had gone through very rapidly. What conditions would be like now I had no idea. So I pushed on and curved around and at last found the Therduim Cut and a little group of canalfolk anxiously pushing on to Thermin. They had seen parties of Iron Riders crossing the cut; but so far had been unmolested.

All the North East must lie under the iron heel of the radvakkas. Layco Jhansi and the provinces he had taken with his own forces and the mercenaries he had hired would be the next on the list. What was going on up in the north, down in the southwest, in the southeast, was anybody's guess. Vondium, the capital and the surrounding provinces, owed allegiance to this new emperor, Seakon, and if the radvakkas or Layco Jhansi did not deal with him, then I would. Vallia was a disturbed ants' nest these days, with every man's hand, it seemed, turned against every other man's.

We glided along the cut and as my wound healed so I helped haul. The canalfolk accepted me as one of themselves, as I was able to drink the canalwater, a true test. The kutven of this group was Rordam na Therduim, a brawny, cheerful fellow much cast down by the evil days and the disreputable state of the cut. Often we had to drop over the side of the lead narrow boat and with spades slice a way through the mud fallen in to make a passage. Once we halted in the shade of a group of missals as a long line of radvakkas passed, and with them wagons hauled by benhoffs, wagons no doubt containing much plunder.

"If only there was some way of getting back at them," said Rordam, wiping his forehead, frowning.

"There will be, kutven. We have to plan and organize."

"Plan what? Organize with what?"

"Once we get to Therminsax we'll be able to see better what to do."

But, I own, my own words sounded hollow even to me. Of the towns and villages along the cut it were best not to speak. This canal, as I have said, ran for much of its course through border-land, march country, and men had not in the old days built anything other than frontier forts. With the establishment of the empire by Delia's ancestors, the need for forts had gone; but the land was barely suitable for anything other than desultory grazing. The few towns were uniformly abandoned, looted and destroyed by the Iron Riders. We did meet other canalfolk and with them hauled on to Therminsax.

Approaching the city the land took on for a space a much wilder aspect, with rocky outcrops and precipitous descents alternating with broader open rides of grassland. The canal scythed through between cutting walls. Then, when Kutven Rordam said Therminsax lay half a day's haul away, the country opened out into the broader fields and pastures I remembered from my previous visits to the city. We hauled on lustily.

It fell to my lot to take the turn at striding out ahead along the towpath, well in front, to scout our safe passage, when we ran into the fight.

Standing immobile in the shade of the trees fringing the towpath I watched the scene on a grassy bank near a tumbledown village. Men fought and struggled there, and yet I saw they struck at one another with wooden cudgels, and fists, and feet, and bellowed and roared their mutual fury. There were two sides to the combat, and one side wore the blue and green of the high kovnate of Sakwara, and the other side wore the colors of Thermin, an emperor's province, colors of crimson and brown. I thought of the Iron Riders and felt my fury rising. This was a nonsense.

The city could only be an ulm or two beyond the next curve in the cut and when I barged out into the fight and grabbed a man wearing the crimson and brown and hoicked him out of it, he confirmed my suspicions of what was happening here. He saw my face and the thraxter, and he was very ready to talk.

"Yes, jen, yes. The devils of Hawkwas tried to cross and we must stop them—"

I shook my head.

"Who is in command of your men here?"

He squirmed around in my fist. The fight raged, with men staggering away holding their heads, and the dust lifting, and the uproar bellowing on. He pointed. "Yonder. Targon the Tapster." Targon, bellowing, struck wildly with his cudgel at a beefy individual who ducked and struck back.

I turned on the fellow I gripped and stuck my face into his. "Just you stand here, dom, peaceably, whilst I sort this out."

He nodded his head frantically, almost choking. I let him go and waded into the fight, got a grip on a Hawkwa. The question to him produced a string of swear words; but he sobered up quickly enough after I spoke to him, and he said: "There. With the black beard. Naghan ti Lodkwara—"

So, for the third time, I plunged into the fight. Men fell as I barged through. I hit Targon on the chin and dragged him along by my left arm, heaving struggling men away, pounding on, took Naghan ti Lodkwara by the neck. I hauled them both back out of the scrum and plunked them down against a ruined wall.

I glared at them as they stared up, quite unable to understand what had hit them.

"Now, you two hulus. Listen and listen well. You may be of Therminsax and you may be a Hawkwa. I can guess why you are fighting. You stupid onkers! Haven't you heard of the Iron Riders?"

"These cramphs of Hawkwas stole six ponshos!"

"They wandered about, lost—we but gave them a home—"

"Aye! In your swag bellies!"

They'd have started up again; but I waggled the thraxter at them.

A couple of men spun out of the fight, saw me and their respective leaders, and came over to lend a hand. I was forced to stretch them upon the ground, where they slumbered. I glared at these two, this Targon the Tapster and this Naghan ti Lodkwara.

"Now, you two, you hulus. Call off your men. Stop this fight. Or, by Vox! I'll go in there and really thump a few heads."

Targon looked pretty sullen. "We are not used to fighting with swords—"

"So tell your men, sharpish. *Bratch!*"

In the event, between us we managed to sort out the confusion. Men sat on the ground, panting, holding their heads. Others leaned on one another, gasping. They were a sorry looking bunch, and no mistake. I stood up and shouted at them. Shouting at people seems to be an occupational disease; but needs must when the devil drives—in this case, far more devils than the immediate deviltry of the Iron Riders.

"The Iron Riders are coming to sack your city—"

"They are way down south," objected Targon sullenly.

"They drove us out," shouted Naghan viciously. "That is why we run and take your skinny ponshos."

"Our ponshos are fine and fat! We do not need nit-stinking Hawkwas to tell us about our ponshos."

"You will all be ponshos in the jaws of the leems," I bellowed at them. I went on in fine style, rhetoric, threats, not blandishments so much as promises of what lay in store for them when the radvakkas had been seen off and peace and prosperity once more enfolded Vallia. I watched their faces. "You are all Vallians. The North East is the northeast of Vallia. The Hamalese—"

At this a chorus of curses and blasphemies and threats of what they'd like to do to the Hamalese broke out. Kovneva Marta had wrought well with her mercenaries in Thermin, and these men were not likely to forget.

"Do the Hamalese hold Therminsax?"

"Aye, dom—" began Targon.

"I am Jak the Drang," I said, and, as though that was a kind of signal allied to what I had done and said, they at once started calling me jen, which is Vallian for lord. I let it pass. If I was to do what I had to do, then any additional slender threads of authority were useful, no matter how ludicrous or despicable in my eyes.

The Hamalian Army was represented in Therminsax chiefly by a regiment of foot and a regiment of crossbowmen. The balance of the forces was made up of paktuns and masichieri, and of men hired by Aduimbrev. That would have to be sorted out. Also, there was a mercenary force of flutsmen.

"If I know flutsmen," I told these men who were stanching their cuts and rubbing their bruises, "they will fly off the moment the going gets tough. After all, Therminsax means nothing to them, nor does Vallia and the North East. They are not Vallians. But, doms, you are."

"Maybe," spat out Naghan ti Lodkwara. "But we have no money to hire mercenaries to fight for us."

I let his words hang. I wanted these men to examine them. I repeated what he had said. Then, putting contempt into my voice, I said: "Gold— you pay gold for other men to fight for you. If you see your wife and child about to be killed and your house burned, you hold out a purse of gold and pray someone will come along and save your family, your home. Is that it?"

"No—no!" shouted some. They were growing warm. "It is not that at all," shouted others. They were all struggling with preconceived notions. Ordinary citizens just didn't go out and fight as common soldiers. Foul-mouthed mercenaries did that, and got paid to do it.

I pointed at Targon. "If you stood in your house and saw your wife and child about to be murdered—" I thought a subtle or not so subtle notion might enhance my argument here, and so I said: "Assuming any girl has been misguided enough to wed you—" which brought a few guffaws out. "And you had that cudgel you've been trying to brain these Hawkwas with—would you not strike down the assassin?"

"Well," flared out Targon, mightily angry. "Of course!"

"So when the Iron Riders get here—will you hit their iron with a wooden club?"

I was surprised to hear a few guffaws at this, and realized I was making headway.

"Give me your sword, jen, and you would see!"

I let out a sigh. About to speak, perhaps to come to the crux, I halted as a man yelled and pointed up.

"There are the flutsmen," he shouted. "What do they want? Have they seen the Iron Riders?"

The mercenaries of the skies, self-centered, wheeled on their wing-fluttering birds, circling the village. Then they descended steeply through the bright air. I saw the way they handled their weapons. I knew flutsmen of old.

"Take cover!" I bellowed, furious, seething. "They are true devils. They will slay us all for mere sport!"

Eleven

Sport for Flutsmen

"No, no, jen," quoth Targon, easy, assuming a superior attitude at my ignorance. "They have not troubled us so far—or, at least, no more than any rasts of mercenaries trouble honest men."

"They'll have you all as slaves—"

The other men of Therminsax made little attempt to conceal their amusement at my agitation. What a fuss I was making, and all over a patrol of flutsmen out scouting. It was clear enough that, detest the Hamalese and the treachery of Aduimbrev though they might, they had adapted and come to terms with the new order.

The flutsmen steepled down through the thin air, seven of them, the clotted clumps of feathers streaming back from their leather flying helmets, their long toonon-like weapons slanting down. They did not intend to shaft us with their crossbows, then. Sport—that was what they were after, sport...

Then I remembered just why I was here. The narrowboats! I was supposed to be scouting for Kutven Rordam and the canalfolk.

Naghan ti Lodkwara pushed up from the wall. He stared up and scratched that black beard. "Flutsmen. They are very devils—"

"Get your Hawkwas into the houses, at least, Naghan. I must back to the cut—"

I started off running, waving my arms, haring along the towpath. The narrowboats were just in view. There were two parties of people and both claimed my attention.

"Get inside and bolt the doors!" I bellowed. "Hurry! *Flutsmen!*"

The haulers eased up and the tows slacked. Kutven Rordam appeared shouting questions. I bellowed over the uproar. "Bolt the doors. If you have weapons, use them," Then I went pounding back up the towpath again past the concealing clumps of bushes toward that stretch of greensward.

On the edge of the village I skidded to a halt. The flutsmen had landed. Naghan must have shuffled his men into the houses, for the colors in badge and favor of the men huddled into an apprehensive and gesticulating ring were all crimson and brown. The flutsmen prodded them with their long polearms, cunningly adapted to aerial work, the narrow blade and curved axe on a shaft that might be anything from seven to fifteen feet in length, the infamous ukra cowed these men of Therminsax.

I had faced the toonons of the Ullars in Turismond and the ukras of flutsmen in Havilfar and I was in no mood to be cowed by these rasts before me now.

Two of the flutsmen carried volstuxes, the aerial throwing spear. They were not all apim, there being a Rapa and a Brokelsh in their number.

Reiving mercenaries of the skies, flutsmen, and they accept any man into their bands, apim, diff, it does not matter providing he swears allegiance to the flutsman band, and obeys their harsh protocol and discipline which, despite their savage ways, control their wild and barbaric way of life. I stepped out into the open and I did not draw my thraxter.

"By Barflut the Razor Feathered!" shouted the nearest flutsman, an apim, with a volstux poised. "Here is one who gapes like an onker! Rast! Get with the others, whilst we decide how you shall die. Bratch!"

"Barflut?" I said, not moving. "A cramph of cramphs, so I am told. A nulsh."

They went mad at this, their enjoyable conversation on just how these onkerish prisoners were to die so rudely interrupted. Some had wanted to tie ropes to the wrists and ankles of a man and then fly aloft with him attached to two fluttrells. How long, the game went, how long would he last before he was torn asunder. Now they heard the name of one of their sacred patron spirits defiled. They foamed with rage.

The apim cast his volstux. I stepped aside. The shaft flew and no doubt stuck somewhere into the ground. I did not turn around to look.

The other one with a volstux, the Rapa, cast also, and again I moved.

Leaving three of their number to guard the prisoners, the other four rushed on me. Two ukras and two thraxters whipped toward me. I drew the thraxter. The swordsmen first, for I slid past the long polearms and crossed steel with the Rapa. He came at me in fine fettle with his sword; but, somehow, his thraxter was not where it should have been, and mine was through his throat above the feather-adorned corselet. Withdrawing, I grabbed an ukra in my left hand and swung its owner around into his comrade. The other swordsman died as he tried to degut me and then I could turn my attention to the last two. One had the sense to drop his ukra and go for his sword; but he was too late and too slow. The other one tried to run and I had to do as I dislike and chop him from the rear. But, then, even as he went down, he would understand that if a fighting man runs then his back becomes the target.

The remaining three shrilled their rage and raced for their fluttrells. They were going for their crossbows; they were not intending to fly away.

And then—and then an arm reached out from the mass of prisoners and fastened on the neck of a flutsman. Targon the Tapster lifted him and shook him and the ukra fell, to be immediately snatched up by another Therminsaxer. The two flutsmen reached their birds. The crossbows came out of their boots with twinkling speed and the next instant they were leveled at me. The two bolts sped.

Because flutsmen habitually shoot from flying birds their crossbow bolts are short and heavy. I had no Krozair longsword. So, not wishing to take any chances, I hurled myself forward and hit the ground. The bolts hissed past overhead. When I sprang to my feet again the two flutsmen were whipping out their thraxters, determined to finish me once and for all.

A chunk of rock flew and hit the Brokelsh in the stomach. He grunted. Quite apart from his armor, his Brokelsh guts were strong enough to withstand a blow twice as hard. With his companion he charged for me, ignoring the rabble who were now throwing rocks with abandon.

I bellowed, high and hard. "Targon the Tapster! Tell your men to capture the fluttrells—the flying birds—before they fly away! Hurry!"

Then the two flutsmen were on me and it was a fine old skip and dance before I thunked them both down. I swirled away to the fluttrells and let out a yell of disappointment. Six great saddle birds winged high into the air, disdainful of the half-scared, ineffectual attempts of the Therminsaxers to arrest them. Only one remained, and he fluttered his wide wings and kicked up an enormous stink, tugging at his clerketer which was held by half a dozen of the men, all hauling as though they dragged a narrow boat up a vertical cut. I laughed.

"By Vox! A single fluttrell, and you act as though you would chain a city down."

"We know nothing of these outlandish beasts!" And, and I swear, one of them, a little squiffy-eyed fellow with a broken nose, snapped out furiously: "If Opaz had meant us to fly he'd have given us wings when we're born."

In the end, more laughing than anything else, I got the fluttrell under control, and then an arrow winged in past my shoulder and buried its steel head in the fluttrell's breast.

Outraged, I swung about. What my face looked like I do not know. But the canalfolk, running up, abruptly fell back. A tall limber lad, a good hauler, lowered his bow. He looked perplexed. Kutven Rordam, wielding an axe, strode up.

"We saved you in time, Jak the Drang! By Vaosh, it was close."

So, I couldn't flare out at them for onkers, for idiots, for hulus—I needed the fluttrell, and now the poor bird was dead, and these canalfolk thought they had saved my life. I shook my head. I would tell them the truth, by Krun, yes! But not right now...

But Targon the Tapster had no such inhibitions. Panting, disheveled, with a raking claw scratch on his arm, he pushed up to Rordam. "You stupid calsany! We risk our lives to capture the bird—and you strut up and kill it! Onker!"

I pass over the next few murs in painful silence.

In the end they were sorted out, and their ruffled feathers soothed. I'd lost the fluttrell. But we had gained a small arsenal. And, more importantly, these people understood a little more of what was asked of them in the future, of what I would demand of them.

Three different cultures were represented here. The canalfolk, fiercely independent, with a way of life peculiarly their own, reserved, withdrawn from the hurly burly of the political life of Vallia, doing their job and proud of that and their heritage and traditions, the canalfolk formed, as it were, the powerful skeleton of Vallia.

The Hawkwas, wilder than the general run of Vallian—if you excepted those howling Blue Mountain Boys of Delia's—driven from their lands just when they believed they had struck a blow for freedom, the Hawkwas harbored a savage sense of repression and injustice.

And the Therminsaxers, townsfolk, for many years accustomed to city ways and an ordered existence, habituated to a way of life centered around their city and its trade, their guilds and societies, the full living of the good life in a wealthy imperial province of Vallia, these citizens were bemused by the catastrophe that had befallen them.

When I had first come to Therminsax, flying in an ice voller, the place had been ranked as a market town. Now it was a city, the dignity conferred by the emperor in recognition of the place's growing size and importance and wealth.

"Gather up all the weapons. You—" and I singled out the man I had first dragged out of the fight, Yulo the Boots—"go and find the volstux that went into the bushes. You—" and I gestured to the Hawkwa I had first questioned, he who swore over-abundantly, Foke the Waso, for he was the fifth child—"go and retrieve the two bolts." They caught the urgency I felt, and all obeyed without question—at least, for the moment. This dominance, this habit of taking command and giving orders, is often hateful; but in the present circumstances a lead had to be given and I am, as you know, blessed or cursed with the yrium, that charismatic power that bedazzles men into total acceptance and loyal following—well, some men and some of the time, as you will have learned.

"Naghan ti Lodkwara," I said. "Targon the Tapster. Stand before me." In the busy bustle of men scouting around finding the fallen weapons and collecting the gear from the dead flutsmen the two leaders did as I bid. "Now," I said. "These ponshos."

They both started in a-yelling and I quieted them and glared at Naghan. He scraped a foot. "We are hungry. My people have marched many dwaburs without provender. Anyway, the ponshos were wandering—"

"That," pointed out Targon, breathing deeply, "is why we are out here looking for them."

"They are safe," said Naghan. He looked up, half-defiant, half-abashed. "In yonder broken-down house."

So we went to look. The ponshos were tied up with cloths around their heads. When we loosened the bindings the poor beasts set up a great baaing and bleating. Targon beamed, pleased to see his ponshos still alive and not eaten.

"Your people?" I said to Naghan.

"Aye, jen. We heard what the radvakkas mischiefed in the south and we came north. Some would have asked the burghers of Therminsax for food and help; but others preferred to take what we could and press on."

By south he meant the southern borders of Hawkwa country. And by some who preferred to take what they wanted, he meant himself, I did not doubt.

"You lead them?"

"Aye, jen. They wait for the ponshos we would have brought a few ulms off—"

There was no doubt in my mind of the correct course. So, in the fullness of time and loaded down with the gear stripped from the flutsmen, we set off for the city. It was not far; and, indeed, Therminsax looked mightily refreshing with its red and white houses sheltered behind the long walls. Those walls were in poor shape now, and suburbs had sprung up outside.

"They will not welcome us, jen," said Naghan.

"Leave that to me," I said.

He and Targon, both, looked at me oddly.

Foke the Waso had been sent off to fetch in the rest of the Hawkwas. The Hawkwas I had run across, down in Gelkwa, had been a tough wild raffish lot. I did not doubt that those living in Sakwara were just as hard-bitten. Their reduced circumstances spoke volumes for the impetuous overawing effect of the Iron Riders.

When Udo, Trylon of Gelkwa, subsidized by Phu-si-Yantong with Hamalese money and arms, had set off to attack Vondium, the High Kov of Sakwara had sat still, biding his time. Now he was the acknowledged leader of the Hawkwas, in fact as well as by rank. So Naghan ti Lodkwara had not been involved in the earlier fighting. That, I admit, afforded me a little pleasure.

In Therminsax I anticipated making the first real opposition to the radvakkas, as I was commanded by the Star Lords. There might only be a handful of Hamalese there; but there were many mercenaries, paid by that damned Wizard of Loh. His wealth would be colossal, seeing he controlled all of Pandahem as well as much of Hamal and what other lands besides Opaz alone knew. So the reality of what had happened hit me shrewdly. I felt the shock. We had all seen the dust clouds to the south and west, and marked their progress as we came into the city, wondering what they portended.

Now I knew.

The Vallian citizens of Therminsax stood about their charming city, wringing their hands, wailing and crying. I did not see any guards of the Hamalian Army, nor did I see any sign of mercenaries. The reason was simple. The Hamalian Army and their mercenary allies had taken every saddle animal, every draught animal and every cart, and had gone. They had marched out, to the safety of the Great River some one hundred and fifty miles due southwest. And long before the citizens could think to abandon everything they could not carry and hurry after the deserting forces, young Wil the Farrow had ridden in on a preysany with the frightful news that the radvakkas had closed in from the south, and had cut off direct escape. Even as we assimilated this information and Naghan's Hawkwas hurried into the city, almost unnoticed, so more dust clouds rose ominously from east and north. The city was ringed. We were cut off.

Abandoned by all the professional fighting men, the citizens of Therminsax faced a future filled with horror, with sack and rapine and death. There seemed to them to be nothing else left to them in the whole wide world of Kregen.

Doomed, they shouted, screaming, distraught, crazed. Doomed.

Twelve

We Shut the Gates

Useless to shout and attempt to calm the frenzied mobs who ran, shrieking and wailing, this way and that. Here and there men stood, alone, in groups, who did not scream but clenched their fists and scowled and knew not what to do. Pushing my way through and being buffeted about and trying not to retaliate unthinkingly, I led the Hawkwas to a central kyro I knew beside the Vomansoir Cut. This joined the Therduim Cut in a sizable basin, with wharves and slips, and here Rordam would bring his people to tie up. I headed for the palatial palace of the Justicar, the emperor's governor of the city.

Damn these Opaz-forsaken radvakkas! The Iron Riders had drifted westward across North Segesthes in comparatively recent seasons, although it seemed we Clansmen had been resisting them for ages. Where they had come from no one could be sure, for most of Eastern Segesthes was completely unknown to us, save for a few coastal free cities and the islands of the east. Once Hap Loder had said to me that I could weld all the clans of the Great Plains together into a single mighty fighting force, and I had chided him, my right-hand man, my good comrade, asking of him who the enemy would be we would fight. Well, in these latter days we knew who that foe was, and rued the knowledge.

The mobs thickened about the streets as I approached the kyro before the imperial Justicar's palace. I pushed through and worked my way toward the front. People were shrieking and tearing their hair, some had fallen onto their knees, their arms lifted imploringly to the facade of the palace. They shrieked to the imperial Justicar to save them, to find some way of salvation, to prevent their destruction at the cruel hands of the Iron Riders.

There were no guards. I guessed the small honor guard maintained here in normal times had been suppressed by the Hamalese. I was able to push through the throngs who surged into the inner courtyards and up the ornate stairways and into every room and chamber. The noise would have been upsetting to a man of stone. And, still, there were these knots of citizens who did not scream out, but clenched their fists emptily, and scowled, and did not know what to do.

Eventually I found the Justicar, standing with his back to a tall window where the crimson drapes shadowed the brilliance of the suns. He looked shriveled. I knew him. He was Nazab Nalgre na Therminsax—an honor title adopted on his appointment. He stood there, created a Nazab by the emperor, trembling, holding his head, surrounded by a few loyal servants and slaves, quite unable to answer the imploring shouts and frantic pleas of the citizenry.

Without ceremony I ripped out the thraxter and angled it so that the light caught the blade and runneled an ominous glitter into the faces of the citizens. I bellowed over their cries.

"Out! Outside! Stop this caterwauling. Let the Nazab have time to think and plan. Out—or I'll crop your ears."

Dazed, abruptly panic-stricken in an altogether more personal way, the people in the chamber hustled to the door, pushing, crying that a madman had arrived, yelling—oh, it was all a bedlam, and not very splendid, either.

I glared at the slaves.

"Out! *Schtump!*"

They scuttled.

I was left alone with the Justicar of Therminsax, Nazab Nalgre. He recognized me. He stopped shaking. His eyes grew round. He put a hand to his lips. I slammed the door and, swiftly, yanked it open and bellowed along the carpeted corridor.

"If anyone hangs about by this door I'll blatter him!"

Slamming the door again I swung back to Nazab Nalgre.

"Lahal, Nalgre. You know me. My name is Jak the Drang. Do you understand?"

"Yes—No, my prince—"

"Jak the Drang, onker!"

"Yes, yes, majister—Jak the Drang."

I lowered my voice. "Not prince, not majister. Jak. Now, Nazab Nalgre, we have work to do."

"Work? We are doomed. The soldiers have all gone. The Iron Riders approach—what work can we do but pray to Opaz?"

"I'll show you," I said, and hustled him to his desk. "Write at my dictation. A proclamation. Have your stylors copy it out, fair, and have it displayed all over the city. By Vox! We're Vallians. We do not run screeching like a pack of witless vosks when cramphs sniff around our city! Write!"

"Yes, majis— pri— Jak."

So I drew a breath and told him what to write. It was all good rousing stuff and I will not repeat it word for word. Briefly, I told the citizenry that the city would not fall, that we would outface these miserable radvakkas, that we'd see them all buried in their damned iron armor, and anyone who skulked would have his ears cropped, if not worse. Then I went on to give orders the import of which will become plain as I go on with my tale. Very quickly, the stylors were summoned and began to copy out the proclamation for distribution.

Then I ran Nazab Nalgre out onto the balcony fronting the kyro and by gesticulations we obtained a quietness in the mobs.

I shouted. I put forth that old fore-top hailing voice and reached out well into the square, and waited between sentences so that they might be repeated to those farther back.

Again I will not repeat all I said. It was perilously near boasting.

"People of Therminsax. Vallians. Hearken. Your Justicar, Nazab Nalgre, has given me the high honor and duty of resisting the Iron Riders, of saving Therminsax, and of burying every radvakka in a plot of soil. Those that are not burned to a crisp, that is. Think how a radvakka would broil in his armor! All the gates will be closed. Now. Those men who wish to shut the gates they know best—shut them. Those men who have iron bars to hand place them in the canals under the gateways so that no skulking radvakka may gain entrance there." I went on bawling, detailing work to be done, seeing groups of men running to obey. I scaled the work so that the most obvious tasks were performed first. Soon I was able to finish with a resounding burst of oratory, rousing stuff, and then go to meet the leaders of the city. The masters of the guilds, the heads of each ward, the magistrates, the Hikdars of the Watch, the chief of the fire service and, most important, the high priests of the various temples. Therminsax is well-served with temples, fine imposing buildings, and the priests held great if tenuous powers.

With this collection of frightened men in the main chamber of the palace I called for quiet and then told them, simply and forcefully, that Therminsax would not fall, that if they obeyed me they would be saved, what unpleasant things would happen to them if they did not obey, and finished off with a direct statement. "You are Vallians. Do not forget that. You have a pride in your city and your land. These rasts of Iron Riders are uncouth barbarians, illiterate. They have no idea how to lay siege to a city. All they know is charging in their mail, brainless. Obey me and you will be saved."

Then it was a matter of giving each group its orders.

All weapons must be gathered up for ordered distribution. If a man possessed a favorite sword—or spear, for they were spearmen of a sort—he might keep that, if he would use it. The weapon most used by the tumultuous townsmen was the stave with the cudgel held ready in the belt. The spears were used in vosk-hunting, and this was not done for a living but as a sport. The wild vosks were vicious beasts, as all men know, and quite unlike the domesticated vosks from which come such succulent rashers. I already had ideas on the old vosks, as you may imagine. Then I took myself off on a circuit of the city. The suburbs built outside the walls were a handicap, no doubt of that.

Barriers were erected across the ends of the streets, from house to house, where we could. In other places I gave orders for awkwardly placed houses to be pulled down. Now that the citizens had a task to do, had been given some hope, and had an intolerant devil to goad them, they saw fresh hope where all hope appeared dead. They worked. City folk are accustomed to working together, in disciplined order, their habits of mind are orderly. They work together, each relying on the next. That is for work. For play they are a wild tearaway bunch, of course, given the opportunity. Both these traits would be used by me in the defense of Therminsax.

The herds of vosks and flocks of ponshos were being driven into the city through the gates specially left ajar for the purpose. Cattle were brought in. The drovers had, perforce, to work afoot, for the only saddle animal in the entire city was young Wil the Farrow's preysany. At my direction stylors were making a count of food. Well and well—for now. If the siege was protracted—and I did not think it would be—then would come the time to search out hidden hoards.

The iron bars under the gates through which the canals flowed were fixed firmly, and I checked them all, ducking down into the water, conduct which brought knowing nods, and whispers that this Jak the Drang was a canalman, then...

A small but cheerfully clear stream ran chuckling through the city, flowing on across the country to swell other streams and eventually to empty into a tributary of The Great River. Along both sides of this little stream, called the Letha Brook, grew tall stands of the letha tree, well mixed with a kind of beech. The letha tree gives a tough, elastic wood, very white, much used for the handles of agricultural implements. The leaves of the letha are light green, frondulous, very pleasant, and afford a pleasing contrast to the red and black buds and flowers. In the bed of the Letha Brook I made sure the iron bars were firmly fixed against the flow of water. The Iron Riders were perfectly capable of pulling off their iron armor and wading up the stream into the city.

These preparations, rushed though they were, filled in the time until the approach of the radvakkas signaled the time for me to go up onto the wall facing their serried ranks. They ringed the city in metal, sitting their benhoffs lumpily, watching us, and an embassy rode forward, under a great banner of benhoff tails, and trumpets blew for a parley.

Chivalric ways of warfare were not for the radvakkas, and a parley to them meant nothing like what it would mean to a professional soldier of more civilized lands. So I did not go outside the gates to parley.

A fellow clad in iron with much gilding and a profusion of feathers and benhoff tail plumes spurred forward. He bellowed.

I heard him well enough.

I was pretty sure they were perplexed that an army had not ridden out to meet them and, in the familiar and highly satisfactory fashion they had established in this new land, be crushed to powder beneath their iron hooves. This fellow wanted us to open the gates pronto, to stand aside as the radvakkas rode in. He made no promises. His absolute confidence was, in truth, somewhat amusing. I guessed this band—an offshoot of the westward horde—had heard of the prowess of their fellows down south and burned to emulate them here. The city lay before them, open and defenseless, for they were well aware that an army had marched out—had run off. Their astonishment that we did not let them in abruptly ceased to amuse me. It affronted me. I leaned over the battlements and bellowed back.

Well—I cannot repeat what I said. It might burn out the machinery of this tape recorder. But I let fly with a choice selection of insults nicely calculated to upset these haughty and brainlessly arrogant barbarians.

I finished: "And any one of you can enter the city any time he likes, horizontally with his guts hanging out."

For a moment a dead silence hung over the assembled host.

Then a deep and passionate diapason of fury burst out from the crowded ranks. A cloud of arrows flew up. Every one fell short. The Iron Riders set spurs to their steeds, put their heads down, and charged. In a thundering roaring mass of iron they hurtled on.

Nazab Nalgre standing next to me took a few paces back across the ramparts. I stood watching the oncoming avalanche and I half-narrowed my eyes, studying them, thinking, scheming, imagining standing on the ground and facing that little lot...

Of course, the radvakkas had to halt as they reached walls and buildings. Some tried to hack through the barricades we had erected across the ends of the outer streets; but the men I had stationed there reported that the defenses held against this passionate, headlong, ill-considered charge...

The riders began to mill, some fell back, others started to gallop around the city seeking an entrance. All the time they were blowing trumpets and horns, yelling, kicking up the devil of a racket. Looking down on them I longed for a great Lohvian longbow and an inexhaustible supply of cloth-yard shafts.

Presently, the band drew off, waving their spears, shouting, reforming their ranks. They had no real organization apart from the war band clustered about a leader, and of discipline their ideas were that anything they did to an inferior was lawful, and if an inferior objected then they'd strapado him or do something equally unpleasant. Sheer brute force was their guiding principle. Everyone in the city was fully aware of the horrors that would ensue if the radvakkas took the place.

For the rest of the day they surged about, like aimless waves, rushing forward, recoiling, riding about, showing off, attempting to awe us. Steadily the citizens improved the barricades. The radvakkas were cavalry—heavy armored cavalry. They had many camp followers and slaves, who walked or rode in the band's wagons. Of infantry they had none. The concept of a man attempting to conduct fighting standing on his own feet was to them not so much ludicrous as insane.

Mind you, in the last idea, my Clansmen shared much. They did fight on foot, for they had experience of the occasional necessity of that on the Great Plains. But any Clansman would regard saddleback fighting as the normal fashion.

When the suns began to decline the radvakkas hauled off and rode back to their camps, which ringed the city, and the fires blazed up. They were finished for the day. The morrow would bring fresh problems, and I would be up nearly all the night organizing.

At meetings with the various civic leaders their questions were all the same and my answers uniformly simple.

"How can we resist them?"

"They cannot break into the city."

"But they will starve us out."

"If we let them. We have food for six or seven months of the Maiden with the Many Smiles. In that time we shall organize. Do as I tell you. Obey me. Have courage. Have confidence."

"But, Jen Jak—"

"Buts are not wanted here, koters. You are citizens of a great city. You have the skills, the discipline, the power. I shall channel that. Believe in me. And, always, remember you are Vallians."

"Vallia is destroyed, the empire fallen—even the emperor is dead."

"So I am told. So we fight for Vallia through the pride you have in your city of Therminsax. Are you not a city of an imperial province?"

"We obey the Justicar through habit, we think, and we tremble for the fearful evils—"

"Enough!"

In one fashion or another the meetings ended on the same note.

"Enough babbling like witless onkers, like wailing women. You are men. Vallians. From Therminsax we will destroy these Iron Riders who camp so uselessly outside our walls. And then we shall march and destroy the remainder. I have spoken. Do as I command—in the name of Vallia!"

Thirteen

The Raid Against the Radvakkas

Clouds sped erratically across the faces of the Twins and the Maiden with the Many Smiles. The land breathed with the quietness of a country night. At our backs the bulk of the city rose against the sky, ill-defined, speckled here and there with lights. The civic leaders were carrying out strict instructions to make sure their people stood an alert watch along the walls and at the barricades. I stole silently across the sleeping land, heading for the nearest radvakka camp. With me came a choice band of desperadoes from Naghan ti Lodkwara's Hawkwas, and a few lively spirits from the city.

The days had been spinning past and I had already set in motion many of the measures needful for the safety of the city and the prosecution of the war against the Iron Riders.

Although it had seemed to me everything lay to my hand, the task was not easy. I had already fashioned a number of armies for specific purposes on Kregen—Fetching the young people of Valka out of the Heart Heights to defeat the slavers and aragorn; creating an army for the Miglas to defeat the Canops; forming the phalanx of my old vosk-skulls from the slaves and workers of the warrens in Magdag; and others I have not mentioned. But now when I thought the task would be relatively simple I was finding odd, stupid, little impediments.

Naghan whispered. "There is a camp, jen." We approached cautiously upwind so as not to alarm the benhoffs, tethered out in long lines. We carried flint and steel and armfuls of combustible. We were a grim and deadly bunch and were not a party to be met with lightly on an overcast night.

Stealing on we passed the first rows of leather tents. We left them strictly alone. A sentry, riding his benhoff, for no self-respecting radvakka would walk when he could ride, was dealt with, silently. A leap onto those skinny hindquarters—hind-sixths—and a grip around his mouth, a heave and a thump. We pressed on. And all the time I was only half there in this raid to create mayhem, for my thoughts kept going to the preparations to be made.

The rapier and left-hand dagger were the arms of the gentlefolk of Vallia at that time, and the clanxer—the common clanxer, as it was called—was coming more and more into favor as the people witnessed the execution of the Hamalese thraxter, which the clanxer resembled. I had with Naghan the Gnat designed new styles of weapons in the armories of Valka, and the new sword we had developed from the thraxter, the clanxer and the shortsword, now equipped the regiments of Valka. Those regiments had been dispersed through the orders of the emperor and the wiles of Ashti Melekhi and Layco Jhansi. Well, much good it had done them...

But Therminsax was not plentifully supplied with iron and steel. We must husband all we had. The women and girls were busily making arrows, and we were using flint heads, for flint is often sharper than steel and is never scorned by even the famed Bowmen of Loh. The bows themselves were compound, fashioned from horn and wood and sinew; but even then our numbers of men who could use a bow were limited. We were fortunate in having Larghos the Bow with us, for his family had been making bows for generations for the city and the districts around.

Now we approached the compound where the slaves were quartered. The meanest of the slaves would be chained up for the night. Those more privileged, those whom I, probably erroneously, call helots, would sleep nearer their masters.

Cautiously, we stole into the compound and started our work.

Slaves—well, there were many slaves in Therminsax, and they were going to prove a problem.

Because of the ease with which the Iron Riders had ridden over and through the legions of Hamal, it was clear to all that a relatively thin line of sword and shield men would never stop a radvakka charge. We had no aerial cavalry and no fliers. We did have one preysany, though... At that comical thought I came back to the present and heard Naghan whispering fiercely to the freed slaves. I did not think they would wait until we had fired the tents before they broke out; but we had to try.

Just as Foke the Waso struck a light and blew on the tinder the Maiden with the Many Smiles broke free of cloud wrack and cast her fuzzy pinkish light over the sleeping camp. We froze. The freed slaves, taking this sudden appearance of the Moon as a sign, broke out. Yelling and screaming and whirling their chains, they surged in a tide of vengeance against the leather tents. I cursed.

"Time to go, Naghan. Pull your men back. Chuck the fire pots and let us get out of here."

"Quidang, jen!" The firepots flew, setting the nearer tents afire. The dried leather burned clammily, belching smoke. But fire shot up satisfactorily from piled stores. We ran from tent to tent, hurling firepots, which contained combustibles and were surer for this work than simple firebrands. We reached the benhoff lines. The animals were restless, stamping their hooves, tossing their heads, letting rip with that raucous whinnying belching sound they have.

"Up with you, Hawkwas all!"

There was only fractional hesitation.

"If you can ride totrixes and hirvels in Sakwara, you can ride benhoffs in Thermin. Mount! Ride!"

There is a fellow in North Yorkshire in England who has trained bulls to be saddled and ridden and jumped. To a Kregen the idea of riding any sort of suitable animal is natural. The Hawkwas mounted up and, bareback, we belted out of the camp.

Uproar rose behind us. Flames leaping, slaves shrilling, radvakkas roaring in rage and tumbling out, women screaming.

We left them to it and racketed back across the land toward the gate of the city where a guard waited to open for us.

I twisted around to look back. By Krun! Following the lead we gave a whole bunch of benhoffs charged out of their lines, pelting along in our wake. Their hooves thundered. We sped along. Clouds obscured the Moon for a space and then shifted across, intermittent shafts of pinkish light flooding down as the Twins rode free. In that hallucinatory light I saw a group of riders bearing in from the side, aiming to join us.

Naghan shrilled a warning, and then the newcomers were yelling: "Vallia! Vallia!"

Well, that is an old trick. I hefted my thraxter, ready to fend them off. My only object this night was to cause confusion to the radvakkas, as much damage as we could, but, mainly to let them know they fought warriors and their task ahead was going to be difficult and unpleasant.

The riders raced along on our flanks. There were totrixes, hirvels, a couple of nikvoves, and a few zorcas. Fleetly, the riding animals closed with us. I saw the fierce dark faces, the flash of eye and teeth, the glitter of weapons.

Now the radvakkas were swarming out of their camp, like a swarm of enraged bees, racketing over the plain after us. In a bunch, we raced ahead of them.

"Vallia!" yelled a man on a zorca, riding with that long-legged, loose style. "Let us into the city!"

As to that, I said to myself, we will see... I didn't like the way he said Vallia, the way his tongue twisted around the word. I kept a wary eye on the newcomers as we fleeted toward the walls. Riding the benhoffs bareback my people jerked and swayed, gripping on, grasping their mounts convulsively. The zorcas moved ahead with their superb speed, and their riders eased them back to pace the slower totrixes. To pace the slower anything, I should say, for, indeed, the four-legged, close-coupled zorca with his single central spiral horn is an animal of fire and spirit and enormous heart and gusto, superb, superb... We crashed on and the radvakkas shrilled in pursuit.

By the time we neared the gate and saw the busy figures of Therminsaxers swinging the lenken portals wide I had more or less convinced myself that the riders who had so unexpectedly joined us were in truth Vallians. Riding as we were without saddles, we would have been easy meat for these men settled firmly in their saddles, booted feet thrust deeply into stirrups.

In a mob we avalanched through the gate. Nodgen the Potter was in charge of the gate detail, and he had sense enough to allow the following benhoffs through as I yelled to him. The three Moons now chose to shine forth at last free of the clinging clouds. We saw the mass of Iron Riders pelting along, the pink light gleaming and sheening on their armor, their shaggy pelts flaring in the wind of their passage.

The last free benhoff lumbered through and Nodgen the Potter yelled to his men to slam the gates and set the bolts and bars. He was a potter, a master of his khand, his guild, and violently resentful of being called

Nodgen the Pots. The gates slammed in the furious faces of the Iron Riders. Some of the citizens on the walls above called down taunts and insults, catcalls that infuriated the radvakkas even more, and gave me heart. We'd do it, yet, despite the difficulties. If we did not, we'd all be miserably dead or even more miserably slave.

Half a dozen dark desperate figures dropped off the last free benhoffs. Before my men could start in prodding with their spears I yelled.

"Do not harm them! They are escaped slaves—welcome them."

Well, we sorted out that little problem. These men had chosen what was, in truth for them, a sensible course, and clambered onto benhoffs to ride after us rather than wander about outside, in the almost certainty of being taken up. I spoke a few heartening words to them and then turned my attention to the group of riders who had joined us.

They were a mixed bunch of apims and diffs—and one diff I recognized at once, now I could see them by the light of a torch bracketed to the wall of the guard tower. I knew him. He was unmistakable.

"Hai, Korero," I said, walking across. "Lahal and Lahal. You are most welcome."

The Kildoi flexed his four arms and his wicked tail shipped over his head. His golden beard bristled. "If I am welcome, Jak the Drang, I would welcome an overflowing tankard of good Thermin ale. Lahal and Lahal. I joy to see you still alive, for I do not forget what passed in Nikwald."

"As to that, the joy was to me. How came you here? These others—" And I looked at them. Well.

Of course I had immediately noticed Korero. But the others—I had told them I was going to Therminsax, and they had shuffled that off, down by that stream outside Thiurdsmot with a crossbow bolt hole in my thigh. Cleitar the Smith still held his hammer, and the head was darkly stained. Dorgo the Clis, his scar livid, spoke for them all.

"We came to Therminsax, because you said so, Jak the Drang." He shook his head, puzzled. "Although why we should do so is a mystery. "But you are in poor case, it seems. We bided our time out there, wondering how best to chop off a few radvakka heads, when you sallied. So—"

"And right welcome you are, Dorgo, all of you. We need fighting men here. And we have ale and wine—the city fathers will bless you and see you have full cups for tonight."

Two men rather in the background, holding zorcas with a bunch of diffs, now moved forward. Dorgo looked and said: "We met these paktuns on the way here. They tell us they are all that is left of an army sent against the radvakkas." He shook his head again and I guessed he was wondering why on Kregen he had come to Therminsax instead of hightailing it for South Vallia.

Among the diffs were Khibils, Pachaks, Brokelsh, a Rapa and a Fristle. They were all hard-bitten professional fighting men, paktuns, mercenaries.

One of them, one of the four Chuliks, stepped forward. He looked mightily impressive in his armor and military insignia, his tusks thrusting arrogantly up from his cruel curved mouth. He surveyed me.

"I am Shudor Maklechuan, called Shudor the Mak. I command here. If you wish us to fight for you, I will draw out a contract. Our fees are high, for we are mighty men."

"I might have expected it, by Vox," I said. I'd been having trouble with the city fathers and the khands over similar monetary arrangements. "No doubt you are capable of bearing arms. As to payment, I am prepared to give you a trial period. I see you wear the mortilhead, so you are a paktun. How many other of your men wear the pakmort?"

"Me!" and "Me!" rose from his men. There were thirty or forty of them, and of that number no fewer than ten were real paktuns. There was not a hyr-paktun, however.

The two men I had noticed gentling the zorcas, caring for them, seemed to be arguing away over some private matter. Their fierce whispers were intended for their own ears; but the heat of the matter made them speak louder and louder. Shudor the Mak turned his head and bellowed: "You two arguing again? May Likshu the Treacherous be my witness! Zarado—cease mewling and leave well alone."

The two men withdrew and they did not stop arguing. They were shadows in the angle of a buttress and so I could not distinguish the details of their accoutrements or weapons. The Chulik paktun swung back to me, very grim, very fierce.

"As to a trial period, dom, that remains—"

"I am called Jak the Drang and you call me jen," I butted in, very sharpish, very prickly. "I hold the commission of command from the emperor's Justicar here. I do not doubt you are lusty fighting rogues; but in these evil days one may be forgiven for suspecting masichieri calling themselves paktuns." Before he could get another word in I went on forcefully: "Now take your men and the city fathers will find you quarters. We are in bad case here; but the radvakkas cannot break in. Soon we will sally out and defeat them utterly. In that day I expect you, Shudor the Mak, and your men, to earn your hire."

He took a good look at me, sizing up my mettle. Then he nodded. If I thought this confrontation was over I was mistaken. One of the Pachaks stepped forward. He wore the pakmort. He spoke in that precise, elegant and yet firm manner of the Pachaks.

"We may take nikobi, jen Jak, if the contract is drawn out properly. Our last nikobi was shattered on the field of battle."

"I welcome you, paktun. Your name?"

"I am Logu Na-Pe, paktun, at present tazll but willing to take employment in a good cause—if the cash is right."

"The cash will be right, and the nikobi, Logu Na-Pe."

So I saw them off to their quarters in a comfortable inn and felt a little cheered. They were hard fighting men, all of them, professionals. They were a valuable addition to our forces. But they were few, very few...

There was a great deal to be seen to; well, there always is, by Vox, but particularly so when you not only conduct the defense of a city but also seek to create an army from nothing. So I was kept busy. The saddle animals we had acquired would be useful in a sally; and if the time for the great offensive was long delayed and the fodder ran out, then we'd most likely end up eating these fine steeds. That would be a great pity. But it would be done, that was true, by Zair!

The great advantage of a citizen army is the habit of working together, of order and discipline, ingrained into city folk, as distinct from the wilder and more independent mind of countrymen. We were citizens arrayed against barbarians. Well, if we couldn't beat that illiterate mob outside we had no right to call ourselves citizens, or to inhabit so fine a place as Therminsax. Numbers, solidity, strength; these were our tools for the job, our weapons of war.

Toward morning, wandering back to the imperial Justicar's palace where I had set up headquarters, I passed the inn where the paktuns had been quartered. This was *The Golden Ponsho*. I thought a little quench would do me good before I turned in, and I might find some of the paktuns about to talk to and find out a little more of their history. So I went in, ducking my head under the old blackwood beams.

Two men in white tunics sat at a table, their slippered feet stuck out, arguing away. One, I knew, was Zarado. I helped myself to a flagon of wine and sat down near them. A few other paktuns were still drinking; most had turned in.

"Oh, yes," this Zarado was saying. "The Iron Riders are a fierce-looking bunch, Zunder. I know, I know. But I wonder how they would fare, say, against the overlords—"

"I'd like to see it!" burst out this Zunder, a man with dark moustaches, fiercely-brushed up. "By Zim-Zair! I'd relish the sight of these Grodno-Gastas charging the Overlords of Magdag!"

Fourteen

News of Pur Zeg, Krzy and Pur Jaidur, Krzy

The flagon halted before my lips. I did not move—could not move.

"May Zantristar the Merciful smile on us! The city is filled with hulus—fambly ready for the reaping. We should never have left the ship in the first place—"

"And whose idea, by Zair, was that? If you'd listened to me we'd be snugly supping in The Fleeced Ponsho again, instead of in some outlandish place at the end of nowhere."

"Me! You were the one who said there was gold flowing out of the rocks in this place! I was for returning to Donengil!"

"And who said we should sign on with those rasts of Maybers? We're a damned long way from home, by Zim-Zair!"

I moved again. I drank. I spilled wine. They looked across and Zarado, his dark curled hair sheening under the lamps, said, "I do not wonder that you are frightened, by the disgusting diseased liver and lights of Makki-Grodno, dom. How came you people to be mewed up here?"

Zunder nudged him. "You great onker! That is the jernu, here, the lord. He was the one telling Shudor the Mak—"

"Oh! Well, I didn't see him—you were nattering away in my ear like two nits dancing in a ponsho fleece."

"Do you call me a nit, Zarado, the sweepings of a Magdaggian gutter? I'll—"

I think they might have wrestled a space then, for it was clear they were good comrades, and continually at odds, one with the other, over everything. And, if no real excuse for an argument could be found, then they'd fabricate one, and joy in the ensuing combat. But I stopped them. I stood up and taking my flagon moved across to their table.

"Lahal, koters," I said. "How came you here?"

I saw their swords now, jutting under the table. Krozair longswords—by their words and their swords I knew they were Krozairs, and not ordinary warriors of Zairia.

By Zair! How I thought of my roistering days on the inner sea, the Eye of the World! My sons were there now; Pur Zeg and Pur Jaidur, both Krozairs of Zy, as was I. I wanted to know of these two—and yet to enquire, to ask the ritual words and forms, to shake hands, would betray me as a Krozair and that would lead to far too many complications.

But I had to know.

"I think," I said, speaking companionably, "that you are from Turismond—"

"Yes, jernu," said Zarado. "But you would not know of our homes, seeing this place is so far removed—"

Here Zunder nudged him again. A right tearaway, this Zarado, bellowing his head off without thought.

"You forget, the galleons of Vallia sail the oceans. They have sailed even so far as a place called Magdag."

They both reacted at this, swearing that they'd like to do certain unmentionable things to the Grodnims of Magdag—and then Zunder said, sharply: "And, jernu, you have been there?"

"Aye."

"And to Sanurkazz?"

"Aye."

They sat back. "Well," said Zarado. "You are the first person we have met since leaving the Dam of Days who knows a little, who shows some knowledge of the world."

This was typical, this regard for the Eye of the World as the center of existence, and the greater outer oceans as being merely the frame. I well understood that. But I pressed on: "I met a man there who said he was a—" I paused, as though searching my memory. "He was a Krossur—no, a Krozair. Yes. Do you know of these Krozairs?"

They exchanged swift looks. I did not think they were Krozairs of Zy; there was something about them, small signs by which a member of the Order of Zy can tell.

Then Zarado laughed in his bluff Zairian way. Disorderly, harebrained, indisciplined, the Zairians. I suppose that very face has produced the mystic Disciplines that make of the Krozair Orders the fanatically disciplined institutions they are. And, I was attempting to bring some of the best qualities of the Krozairs to my Krovere Brotherhood of Iztar.

"What harm is there, Zunder? We will be fighting alongside him before long, and likely all to go down to the Ice Floes of Sicce."

"Or go to sit on the right hand side of Zair in the glory of Zim," I said.

Zunder pursed his lips, let out a sigh, and drank deeply. Zarado merely looked at me. Presently, Zunder said: "So it seems you kept your ears open in Sanurkazz. I, myself, am of Zimuzz."

So that placed him. I turned to Zarado enquiringly.

"Me? Of Zamu."

I know I have a habit of letting rip with a few choice phrases every now and then, in the heat of the moment, and so I said: "I kept my ears open. Also, I may, from time to time, call upon Zair. I mean no disrespect by that."

"If I thought you did," said Zunder, conversationally, "your tripes would be all over the floor before you could spit."

"Aye," said Zarado, quite calmly.

I approved...

We talked a little more, and I intimated gently that I was interested only in their prowess as fighting men for Therminsax. I managed to progress no further in enquiries about my sons, until a chance remark threw up the name of Zy, at which I came quiveringly alert. But to ask outright would be foolhardy, for it was much like a man of Manhattan asking a Borneo head-hunter similar questions, and not expecting to be credited with specialist and, probably, partial knowledge.

I had a happy inspiration, at last, for obvious reasons not even think-ing of the ploy until Zarado, yawning, said: "By Mother Zinzu the Blessed! I needed that—but now I am for bed. I am not your Pur Dray Prescot, jernu."

The door was opened.

"He," I said. "Is the prince majister of Vallia."

"So they say, so they say. But he is a Krozair of Zy and that is much more important. His sons carry on in fine style—" Here Zunder made a face. "I would not admit this if I was a flagon more sober. I would as lief have joined the Order of Zy—but fate decreed otherwise."

"Ha," said Zarado.

"The welfare of the sons of the prince majister is of very great impor-tance," I said. I saw the quick way they looked at me, and knew my carved figurehead of a face was giving away more than I wanted. Neither of these two had ever seen Pur Dray, Krzy, obviously. "Are they well? Are they great Krozairs?"

"They do well, as you would expect—"

You may imagine how I listened as Zarado and Zunder between them gave me a rundown on the exploits and rogueries of my two sons on the Eye of the World. They lived. They fought the devils of Grodno, they pros-pered, and their swifters brought back prizes season by season. Zeg, as King of Zandikar, was growing to be a great power on the inner sea. His fleet was becoming a powerful instrument in the eternal struggle of Zair-ian against Grodnim. So I listened, and eventually, yawning again, Zarado said he was going to bed, or, by Zogo the Hyr-whip, his eyeballs would fall out.

I heard the shrilling of the trumpets from the walls, and so I said: "I think not, Pur Zarado. I think not. The Iron Riders attack. You and your sword may be needed on the walls or at the barricades."

Cursing most fearfully they snatched up their weapons and, clad only in their tunics and slippers, ran out. I was before them. The Iron Riders circled the city, screeching. They swung long weighted ropes, and as they swung them and released, the fiery brands tied to the ends brightened, and sparked, and sprouting flames fell rushing onto the roofs and walls of the city of Therminsax.

Fifteen

Firebrands

"Water! Water!" The yells bounced into the sky, which, luridly lit by the falling firebrands, pressed down darker than it should. Dawn was not too far off. But the habits of order in the citizenry saw to it that the men appointed by the city fathers to stand their watch at the dawn hour should be awake. Trumpets blew. Men ran with buckets of water. The pandemonium racketed on. People were tumbling out of bed and, half-dressed, rushing to join in the long human chains of bucket-passers and precariously leaning over the parapets to haul that sweet and treacherous water from the canals.

The firechiefs swiftly had the situation under control, for many of the barbarians' brands puffed out in their swift passage, many merely spluttered and died on tiled roofs. Some burned up venomously and caught in combustible materials; and these were attacked with gusto, drenched with water, hammered into black-smoking quiescence.

The attack had come in from the west side of the city where the Letha Brook ran out through a battlemented gate and then, odoriferously, past the vosk-crushing mills and the waste-disposal plants. Downstream all the muck could be washed away from the city. Naturally, the radvakkas had established their main camp to the east, upstream. Their muck floated down to us. In addition, as we discovered with increasing frequency, they threw carcasses and offal and filth into the stream to poison us. Therminsax was provided with wells that produced crystal water, so we cursed the radvakkas, and drank deeply in safety. But with the extinction of the last fires, which took a bit of a hold on the water-mill outside the wall, protected by lesser outer walls and barricades, and a watch being set afresh, I figured that we would have to take steps to unblock the upstream end.

Sleep, then, would have to wait a little longer.

The excitement of the fires had brought the city to life early. As the suns rose with the promise of a fine day, with perhaps a little rain drifting across in the afternoon, perhaps not if the clouds were burned off by then, I paused to watch a group of men attempting to form up in lines. At this early stage I had weeded out all the men of Therminsax who had had military experience of some kind. In the city, to my disappointment, although common sense insisted I was lucky to find so many, there were just forty-three men who had once served in an army. There were ten men who had served in galleons, and these lived near and frequented the inn called *The Swordship and Barynth*. There were, also, over a hundred men who had served in the Vallian Air Service. This, being an imperial service, naturally would take many recruits from the imperial provinces. With these men, then, in the first instance, I had begun.

I had said, speaking forcefully: "I want you to become drill instructors of the most abominable kind. Get the men to march in ranks and files and keep together. If any man complains that you overtax him, or mutters in any way, and you are not able to discipline him yourself, send him to me. I will talk to him."

No one was sent to me.

I really thought, then, that they were under the impression I would personally crop the ears of malcontents. At any rate, the men sweated over their foot drill, learning to keep a dressing and to maintain a steady line. This, as I say, was a beginning.

The men saw me watching them, and a kind of miracle abruptly appeared in their lines. The ranks straightened. They began to march together. The idea of marching in step was well known and practiced; but many of the men with military experience would have no truck with that. They had been paktuns and used to a free and easy life. I had borne down, hard.

Now I stepped across and bellowed: "Halt!"

The ranks ground to a shaky halt, with men bumping the backs of the ranks in front. I started in to harangue them. Briefly, for it was a speech I repeated over and over, I told them they must learn to march in step, to keep their dressing and their distance, and to maintain the different paces as ordered, with an even and regular step, which I had specified out at twenty-eight inches. The figure was not lightly arrived at.

You will recall I had served at Waterloo, where the foundations of my Earthly fortunes had been laid, and I had watched the army, spoken to men and commanders, learned much of the land-side of the Peninsular. The British Army marched with a pace of thirty inches. The French Army with one of twenty-five and a half. While the British marched seventy-five paces to the minute in ordinary time, the French marched at seventy-six. But—the French marched faster than the British. The reason for this lay, therefore, not in statistics.

It was not so much a question of marching faster as of marching better. For what I had in mind for these citizens of Therminsax, accurate and regular marching, all in line, all in step, and all as one body, was vital.

Spending a bur with this body and being properly courteous to the drill instructor with them, one Hargon the Arm, a bluff old fellow with a pot belly and a fund of stories of his youth when he had been a mercenary and failed—only just missed it by a hair's breadth, by Vox!—to achieve the pakmort, I did feel that they improved. They marched with more of a swing and they kept together. Chalk lines had been marked out on the flags of the kyro to give them their paces and dressing. I bellowed and ran and pushed and hectored, and we all sweated. At the end of the bur I halted them and told them they were coming along nicely and to keep up the good work, and that if they didn't keep together as a strong and ordered formation they wouldn't have to worry so much about the certain fact that the radvakkas would chop them as that I would crop their ears, and that would be far, far worse.

The citizens took turn and turn about to stand watch along the walls and to drill in the open spaces. If any of them thought to wonder how this intensive drilling would help them to fight from the walls, not one ventured to voice the question.

A pungent whiff floated from the warehouses containing hoffiburs and we would have to see them all used up quickly before they went rotten on us. The people were regaining a little of their cheerfulness, and the Vallians, normally a phlegmatic and stubborn but highly independent people when the mood takes them, were of the stuff from which I could fashion a winning instrument of war.

The idea of that could not be allowed to depress me. What I did I did for Vallia, for Delia and, of course, for my family and myself. I made no bones about that. I was a bright devil in the eyes of many people; but I was crass enough to think that I, Dray Prescot, was a lesser evil than the radvakkas of Phu-si-Yantong. I hope I was right.

Resuming my walk to the upstream end I found myself, as always, feverishly calculating. Odds and gambles, the certainty of defeat if we sat on our hands and did nothing, the trust I must place in others, the agonizing decisions about delegation of duties and responsibilities... I could not do it all myself. This was an entirely larger operation than that in the warrens of Magdag. I needed men who understood what I wanted, had been trained by me, and who could then train their own men.

And yet—and yet this was altogether on a lesser scale than the warrens. There I had had the services of hundreds of skilled slaves and workers who could fabricate what I needed. Therminsax was well-provided with smiths and with leather-workers and carpenters and trades of that ilk; but, for a start, we were desperately short of iron and steel. Of copper and tin we had bulging warehouses. So, bronze it would be.

The stink wafted toward me as I neared the upstream bridge and gate of the Letha Brook. Rotting carcasses washed downstream now cluttered the iron bars. The filth stank.

"Volunteers," I said. "Volunteers to clear the mess. And bowmen to cover them in case the radvakkas disapprove of our efforts to stay clean."

The job was done. The paktuns who had ridden in brought their bows and crossbows up and we shot off a few radvakkas from their saddles when they ventured too close. The volunteers sweated away in the slime and emerged, panting and odoriferous, with the stream cleared and running sweetly. That would be a daily chore until the Iron Riders saw the uselessness of their efforts to poison us and desisted.

I called a meeting. I did not allow it to be called a Council of War. The city fathers and the civic leaders now well understood that I acted by commission of the Justicar and through him for the emperor. That the emperor was dead was not allowed to confuse the issue. I based the argument on the continuation of Therminsax as a city, and of Vallians as Vallians.

So I outlined what we must do to be saved.

Much of what I told them was very similar to what I had told the slaves and workers of the warrens of Magdag of the Megaliths. We faced a heavily armored cavalry host. We had no cavalry of our own, apart from the almost a hundred benhoffs we'd brought in quite inadvertently and the paktuns. Our missile force was limited to around five hundred men who could use the compound bows. Of crossbows we had a small number; but they would have to be discounted, at least from the battle to come although of great use along the walls. And for artillery, although the carpenters and smiths were busy building varters and the wheelwrights making them mobile, our standards of proficiency in that arm were almost inevitably bound to fall far below what would be absolutely essential for any traditional use of the artillery arm. So we were thrust back on the mass of the citizens themselves.

In Magdag I had thought we would be fighting from behind walls and in confined spaces of the warrens. In the event we had successfully bested the Overlords of Magdag in the open—and then in a tragedy I still looked back on with fury and regret, had been forced back to the holes and the stinking labyrinth. I'd been hoicked out of it by then, flung by the Star Lords across the Eye of the World, to meet Seg Segutorio. If only Seg was here now! And Inch and Turko and Balass—ah, each one of them would be worth a regiment!

The long room buzzed with talk as, my thoughts for the moment making me fall silent, the chiefs of the city broke into eager, naive, angry, puzzled conversation. One of them said: "We have few swords, jen. We know a little of using spears, by reason of vosk-hunting. But the soldiers of Hamal were beaten by the radvakkas, this you have told us, and they were profoundly impressive warriors—"

"Not warriors," I said. "Profoundly professional, yes. Swods. Soldiers. But they were sword and shield men. We shall beat the radvakkas, as I say, by using a weapon with which they are unfamiliar. It will not work against the Hamalese, and do not forget that in the hour of victory."

Lists had been prepared by the stylors detailing the state of the city's stores. We would have enough, I estimated, just enough; but it would be very tight indeed.

The iron bars in the canals and the Letha Brook were replaced by bronze grilles. All the iron and steel we could discover in the city was meticulously collected up. I showed the smiths a template whittled from wood. The master of the smith's khand, Varo the Hammer, brought up the subject in his turn at the meeting.

"We are making these spearheads, Jen Jak. They consume only a small amount of steel each; but you require a vast number. Yet—" and here he scratched his bristly side-whiskers— "they are main different from any spearheads I have known."

"Before I answer you, Varo, let me ask Rivate the Chisel how he is coming along with the hafts."

Rivate, a dapper little fellow with an eye that could true up a line or an angle to a hair, nodded quickly. "We have produced many hafts to the incredible lengths you ask for, Jen Jak. The letha wood is of the best quality, as you specified—the trees are being cut down—"

He would have gone on; but I waved a hand.

"These long shafts of springy white letha wood, and these small sharp steel heads, will make the weapon with which we will beat the radvakkas. The name of the weapon is pike. The shafts at the moment are eighteen feet in length; later they may increase to twenty-two, or be decreased to eleven or twelve. Just at the moment we must produce them, and train the men in their use." I stared challengingly at the master of the carpenter's and smith's khands. "I need sixteen thousand of them."

When the uproar of protestations subsided, I said: "Sixteen thousand. And the quicker substantial numbers begin to be produced the quicker we can make a start on thrashing the radvakkas. The men are already tired of drilling with broomsticks."

The question of payment as always came up. I met this in the same way. "The Justicar is empowered to sign assignats. The bokkertu is perfectly legal."

They shuffled at this. Each man who signed up in the army was given an assignat which we all hoped would be collectible. The death of the emperor proved a knotty point; but the assignats were secured also in the name of Nazab Nalgre and on lands available in Thermin. More than once I was tempted to tell them that I had been the fellow to take over the crown and throne of Vallia—I'd not had my hands on either!—and that I was the emperor and Therminsax the extent of my empire. I think you will readily see why I did not, and why I persuaded myself that Jak the Drang could be of more use than Dray Prescot. Maybe I was wrong; there are those who say so, but at the time I considered I was pursuing the correct course.

And that course demanded that I create an impenetrable phalanx of pikemen upon which the Iron Riders should dash themselves to destruction.

Plans are usually bedeviled by someone who thinks only half-logically. I knew I took a terrible risk in thus throwing all our hopes on this one chance. The Phalanx—well, it had served me before and, by Zair, it would serve again. But the chief priest of the temple of Florania—a prissy little man who devoutly believed in his point of view—had no doubts at all that my plans would fail. He gathered his robes about him and stood up, pointing the forefinger of his free hand at me.

"There sits the man who wishes to cast all our sons down into the bowels of Cottmer's Caverns. The Iron Riders desire plunder. Then let us open our gates and satisfy the greed of the radvakkas, for we are a rich city. We shall, of course, previously hide all our most valuable treasures. When the radvakkas have taken their plunder, they will ride away. Our city will be spared and in a few seasons we will have recouped all our losses." He stared around at the chief priest of Opaz, a spare, ascetic man with feverish eyes and a bad skin that kept erupting in spots and boils. "What say you, brother in Opaz? Are not my words the words of wisdom? Why do we bow the neck so meekly to this wild paktun, Jak the Drang? The emperor is dead and the assignats are worthless. Let us preserve our city."

No one spoke; but all looked at me. I gave a swift glance to the chief priest of Opaz, and saw with what I confess was great relief that he half-turned his shoulder on the priest of Florania. I stood up. I put my hands flat on the table and my old vosk-skull of a head thrust forward, and I do not doubt that my chin stuck out like the ram of a swifter.

"I will tell you, priest of Florania, why we will not open our gates except to march out to fight. I do not like fighting and battles and warfare. I detest and abhor the deaths of fine young men and the wails and agonies of the young girls and of the mothers. You want to open the gates and offer the radvakkas gold and silver, corn and oil and flour, all the good things of Therminsax. And when they have taken what you offer they will laugh. They are illiterate barbarians. But they are not fools. Some of you they will kill at once, as an object lesson. Some, the less fortunate, they will torment until the city rings with their cries of agony, until they are only too thankful to reveal where you have hidden the rest of your wealth. And then they will slay you all, after they have had their sport with you and your women folk. If you want that, priest of Florania, open the gates and welcome the Iron Riders."

He tried to bluster. "You do not know that! They were resisted by the Hamalese at Cansinsax and Thiurdsmot and Meersakden. There are many millers and master bakers in my congregation, devout men, and my power—"

"We shall have scant need for millers and bakers before long," I interrupted, uncouthly. "And if you have had information you should tell us. I know of Cansinsax and Thiurdsmot—what of Meersakden?"

This was a fine city of Sakwara, of which I had heard, containing better than seventy thousand souls.

"The Hamalese were routed by two bands of radvakkas. There are two bands outside our walls. You cannot hope to beat them—"

"I do not hope, priest of Florania. I *know!* They will be destroyed, they will be utterly discomfited by the Phalanx of Therminsax. And," and here I put a great venom and a horrible evil into my voice and face. "And if you try to play the traitor or speak against the honest burghers of the city, you will be restrained, placed in irons, and cast down the dungeons beneath the Justicar's deren. Is that clear?"

We sat in the council chamber of the deren—the palace—and we all knew that there were noxious dungeons below. He flushed up. I felt quite sorry for him; but he was wrong, so wrong that if he had his way he would open the city to death and torment in forms so hideous he could never comprehend them. But, then, he had had no dealings with the Iron Riders.

The chief priest of Opaz, scratching his cheek, said in a gentle voice: "Sit down, brother, and keep your peace."

With that out of the way we could go on to plan just how we would fashion the killing instrument of victory we planned to hurl against the mailed cavalry of the Iron Riders.

Sixteen

In Crimson and Bronze the Brumbytes Form

The days passed. The men sweated and marched and drilled. We had them learning how to march in file, for the organization would be based on the file. I prefer the line; but in this instance the file seemed to be the correct procedure.

The pikes were produced from the manufactories. Also the superb springy white wood of the letha tree, somewhat like ash, was mated to steel heads fashioned with spike, hook and axe, hefty, vicious cutting weapons, halberds. Leather jerkins were wired and sewn with bronze plates to form corselets, and shoulder pieces were artfully fixed at the back to be drawn over and fastened on the chest. The same old arguments went on over shields; but the citizens were not warriors and they were far more pragmatical about the thorny question of shield and no-shield. They had seen the Hamalese and their shields, and although the regiments of Hamal had been defeated, still, it struck the citizens as eminently sensible to have something behind which to stand. The shields, in a very real sense, were to them a continuation of the city walls and barricades. From chin to thigh, the shields were designed to protect a man. Also, springy bronze greaves were made for the lower legs. Now, helmets—the manufacturing capability of the city was fully stretched.

Well, the old vosk-skulls had surged forward under a rain of arrows before; they would do so again.

Vosk-skulls are notoriously hard. Piles and piles of them may be found outside most habitations of men on Kregen. The Vallians had built water mills and by harnessing the power of rushing streams had built trip-hammers that, with difficulty, could smash and crush the skulls to form a fine fertilizer. The vosk-crushing mill had almost burned. Around it were heaped and piled the skulls, hard as iron, waiting to be processed. We took these skulls, removed the jaws, scoured them out, affixed leather and quilted linings, riveted straps, added high brims to protect the eyes and grilled or barred face-coverings. For the nape of the neck overlapping and sliding bronze plates formed the well-known lobster-tail.

I rather liked the look of the resultant helmets. Grim, rounded, well-fashioned and offering high protection, they looked business-like.

Then I ran into a little example of the power of legend and story.

"But we must have plumes!" exclaimed the Justicar. We were watching men being issued with the helmets and relishing the looks of pleasure as the men felt the protection as well as the weight come on their heads. Foreheads must be well-padded. The helmets must sit firmly and yet not too tightly, not too loosely. The brim must give protection from falling arrows.

"Plumes?"

"Aye, Jen. Feathers and Plumes."

Then the Justicar and his council produced the old stories and showed the old books. All heroes had tall and imposing plumes in their helmets.

"We are not heroes," I said. "We are sober citizens doing a job of work."

But they wouldn't have it. So plumes were affixed to the helmets by thin bronze strips, and, of course, the majority clamored for that fashion of plume that rises like a giant question mark from the crown of the helmet. I had to give way.

I did say: "If a sword or axe strikes that plume-holder it'll knock your helmet off—if it doesn't break your neck."

So the Justicar's people, with enormous glee, arranged the tall nodding plumes with holders of stiffened leather which would be cut off or bent when struck. I left them to it, mindful of the thought that in this they showed themselves to be their own men, and increased their importance in their own eyes.

We were distressingly short on swords, and so I could not contemplate, with the scarcity of steel, the mass manufacture of two-handed swords, which would have worked wonders on the iron armor of the radvakkas. Stabbing spears had to be substituted and long knives. Anyway, for hand-strokes the halberds and axes would do a fine job—or so I hoped.

While these preparations continued and increased in tempo day by day as the people saw the results of their work, and the men drilled in their files, and the files joined together in ranks and grew daily more solid and regular, I worried over the tactical aspects I must decide.

It was clear to us all in the ringed city that the radvakkas, having plundered the surrounding countryside and being awash with food and wine and good things, were content to sit down and starve us out. They tried their fire-throwing a couple of times further; but our fire service quenched the flames with ease.

We kept an alert watch at all times. The radvakkas made not a single attempt to scale the walls. If they couldn't ride their benhoffs, then they weren't interested. All day they rode about and we watched them in mock combats, in sports, in drunken orgies. All in all, the time passed, and still the tactical questions remained unanswered.

The men in the files would be armored as best we could manage. They would carry pikes and shields. If the Macedonian and Successor phalanxes could contrive that, then so could we. The Renaissance and pike and shot man did not carry a shield—or not very often—but the cavalry charge had dwindled away a trifle by his time from the mailed charge of chivalry, resplendent in the panoply of plate. I worried over our serious lack of missile power. Our five hundred archers practiced religiously each day and the stock of arrows grew. Once the Phalanx had come to grips with the foe then I was completely convinced we would succeed. It was getting them there, and protecting their flanks, that exercised my mind.

Because Europe pushed out into the world, the military institutions and titles familiar to us came into very wide being. On Kregen the Empire of Loh had given the impetus to the terminology with which, so far, I have acquainted you in these tapes. As the Landsknechts handed down administrative ideas and organizations to succeeding armies, so the army of Walfarg that carved out the Empire of Loh left its methods to Havilfar and Pandahem and to Vallia, also.

With the eager help of the Justicar, who delved deeply into the history of Kregen, we reached past the time of Chuktars and Jiktars, of Hikdars and Deldars, back to a time when the organization of warriors was based on the figure six—one of the twin calculating systems of Kregen.

"Twelve men to a file," I said. "With the file leader, the Faxul, in front where he belongs. A half-file leader, the Nik-Faxul, and two quarter-file leaders, the Laik-Faxuls, each in their allotted stations. And, in the rear, the file-closer, the Bratchlin. He should be a steady man, hardy and stubborn, and, I may add, ready to thump a comrade in front who lags too tardily."

The Justicar pored over his dusty tomes, bashing the stiff pages open in his enthusiasm. The pages were filled with colored illustrations of the pageantry of old, filled with the legends and heroic stories of Kregen—the Quest of Tyr Nath, King Naghan, the Canticles of the Rose City, Prince Nalgre, and many many more.

"I have the utmost confidence in you, Jak the Drang. Where you came from, Opaz knows; but, also, thanks be to Opaz you came to our city. We would have been lost without you."

"Vallia," I said, foolishly touched by his words. "I am concerned for the people of Vallia." I would have to break the news to him about the slaves, and then he and his wealthy friends might not be so kindly disposed toward me.

"Each file of twelve joined with two others, the whole commanded by a Danmork, the center file by a Terfaxul, just so that there is no confusion who gives the orders when they suffer casualties, or form close order."

The Justicar nodded, no doubt thinking of the pageantry of the men marching shoulder to shoulder, their bright plumes nodding proudly over the serried ranks.

"Twelve files to form a Relianch," I went on, roughing out the diagrams with paper and ink. "The whole one hundred and forty-four commanded by the Relianchun, marching at front and right, and assisted in command of the second half of six files by the Paltork. Yes, it is a plan almost like others I know of, and yet adapted to our needs. Each Relianch of a hundred and forty-four men will have its own flankers of medium men, halberdiers and axemen, the Hakkodin, twenty-four of them, with their own file leaders and half and quarter file leaders." I did not smile, but I felt my lips rick. "I shall choose these Hakkodin, these men to guard the flanks, carefully. They will not have a file closer, a Bratchlin, with them."

Slaves pattered into the airy room in a brightly lit tower of the Justicar's deren bringing trays loaded with the superb Kregan tea and miscils and palines. We were not hungry yet, in the beleaguered city. But I had to get my phalanx organized and trained, disciplined, able to march in step and line, perfectly moving as a single gigantic organism. "There will be six Relianches to a Jodhri," I said. "Eight hundred sixty-four pikemen and one hundred forty-four Hakkodin to a Jodhri commanded by a Jodhrivax."

We drank the tea and wiped our lips and then sorted through a list of stores stylors brought in demanding instant attention. Also, a lesser chamberlain reported that a certain butcher was charging ten times his normal prices for meat. I told Nazab Nalgre to send around first of all a deputation from the butcher's khand to reason with the fellow and to bring his prices to levels where the folk might afford meat. If he would not accord with common decency then we'd send around a posse of our volunteer pikemen to make him see sense. The people of Therminsax were one—or ought to be one. I knew enough about sieges to know that those in authority must never be seen to favor any one class over another—save, always, that the fighting men must eat. And, of course, if this damned siege was prolonged, therein lay the rub. Not that this was a siege in the real meaning of the term.

Those illiterate unwashed hairy barbarians outside had no real idea how to prosecute a siege. Had we faced them when we'd been hemmed in in Zandikar, we'd have laughed at them. So we went back to the organization of the phalanx, for, as you will readily perceive, this was my way of obtaining the positions in the phalanx for the men I wanted there.

"Each Jodhri will be one thousand and eight men strong. Six of them, I think, will form a Kerchuri, six thousand and forty-eight men strong." I cocked an eye at the Justicar. Nazab Nalgre was looking pleased that his old legends with their continual references to the six and twelve organization and the names of ranks was once more coming into use. He was a fine antiquary, whatever kind of imperial Justicar he might be. "We may find that unwieldy. But I want two commanders of the Kerchuris appointed, two Kerchurivaxes."

"You have the men in mind, Jen Jak?"

I nodded. "Aye."

He studied my face. I knew that the commanders of the two wings of the phalanx would have to be Therminsaxers. There were many bright sparks anxious to command, although very many of the lesser nobility had already packed up and left long before the radvakkas appeared, and many women and children, also, had left.

"Men of integrity, stubborn, physically strong, courageous," I told Nazab Nalgre, speaking a trifle heavily, I fear. "Men who have a presence, who know they will be obeyed when they give an order. Men who are respected by their fellows."

I merely described the generality of Vallian koters.

"They must be Therminsaxers," I went on. "Otherwise I've half a mind to install that defiant man Cleitar the Smith, for I know him to have discovered he is a bonny fighter when it comes to push of pike. I want Targon the Tapster to handle the Hakkodin." I looked directly at Nazab Nalgre. "Your son, Nalgre, your fine limber young son, Nath. He will command the first Kerchuri."

I brushed away Nazab Nalgre's babble. I was doing him no favor. But Nath na Therminsax, for he was allowed to adopt his father's style for all he had no rank of nobility so far, was a fine young man in truth and, over and above all the qualities I have enumerated, he was quick-witted. "I will make a break with tradition here, Nalgre, and Nath will ride a mount and conduct affairs from outside the Kerchuri. The right hand position—the lynch-pin—will be taken by that pillar of the city, Bondur Darnhan. The second Kerchuri will be commanded by Strom Varga, and the right-hand man will be Jando Quevada." I sighed. "I pray to Opaz they will live through the battle. But the front rank men—well, that is why they are there, why they wear the tapes and the feathers, why they are respected, why they are followed."

Nalgre nodded brightly, seeing only the brilliant nodding plumes over the massed files, the onward surge, the pageantry and honor, seeing his son Nath riding back with the victory. Again I sighed. When honest citizens turn their hands to war they are usually highly practical; Nazab Nalgre, the Justicar of Therminsax, shared the other side of that character, the romantic, the high idealism, the shining honor. He was a man of parts, for the governor of an imperial province, called a Nazab, ranks with a kov. His son Nath might if he wished take the surname Nazabhan. Delia's father had not been altogether a fool in his choice of men to run his affairs, and although he had been sadly led astray in his capital of Vondium, he had appointed sound men in his provinces. Nazab Nalgre was now fully recovered from that mortifying crisis of nerves that had afflicted him after the Hamalese rode out.

Continually, the Justicar moved among the training men, exhorting them to effort, to the acquisition of the skills they must have. The paktuns smiled and quoted the old proverbs about the length of time it takes to make a fighting man; but I put my faith in the innate solidity of the burghers, their strong feelings for their city, their orderly habits of mind, and saw day by day the growing cohesion of the phalanx. Mind you, we carried out most evolutions at this time with the Relianch, the tactical unit. When six Relianches formed and stood shoulder to shoulder in a Jodhri, and we filled the kyros with the Jodhris formed in file, then we could bring them into close order and present a front of four hundred and thirty-two pikes. Drummer boys, four to a Relianch, and trumpeters, sounded the orders, the drums with their solemn and deep blam-blam-berram to keep the step, the trumpets to shrill their commands.

In the manner of these things, just how the name began no one could tell; but folk began to talk of the pikemen in the files as brumbytes. The brumby was—I say 'was' for the animal was thought to be extinct or legendary—a powerful eight-legged and armored battering ram of whirlwind destruction, armed with a long straight horn in the center of his forehead. Something like an elegant rhinoceros, the brumby symbolized the headlong energy of the pikemen. At once I gave orders that the shields should bear a painted and stylized representation of this formidable beast, along with the formation signs. The ordinary brumbyte carried a clear strip across the top of his shield. The differing ranks in the duodecimal system then carried stripes of color to indicate their status, rising from a single stripe—complemented with a single tape on the buff-sleeved shirt and a single feather alongside the helmet plume—to the four tapes and two stars of a Paltork.

The shields, bronze-rimmed and bronze-bossed, were crimson, the imperial color. The First Kerchuri carried a broad brown chevron and the Second a brown ring upon the crimson.

All main plumes were of crimson. The tails were colored Jodhri by Jodhri. As I said to the officers: "We present a solid mass, a devastating avalanche of crimson and bronze." Then, because these things matter, I added: "But the brumbytes may decorate their kaxes in any way they wish, so long as they do not destroy either their effectiveness or their suppleness."

The brumbytes sang as they marched to the beat of the drum, manipulating their pikes with growing confidence, although you may be sure there were some horrendous tangles at first. When a fellow tried to make a right turn with his pike horizontal—well, the imagination does not boggle, but he became highly unpopular with the brumbytes in the files near him.

Colors, flags, standards, were carried; but these would only be a hindrance after the onslaught, and arrangements were made for them to pass to the rear. Each Relianch had its color, of course, and a grave variety they made, all based on the imperial crimson.

One evening when I was at last beginning to think we were in some cases to march out, Archeli the Sniz reported to me, allowed immediate access as I had ordered. He was a sly, prying little fellow, recommended to me by the Justicar, and I had set him to spy upon the chief priest of Florania.

"Jen!" he said, speaking quickly. The gathered city fathers and officers looked up from their work at the long tables. "The cramph has been in communication with the radvakkas. I did not know what he purported— but now I know he means to open the Gate of Aman Deffler to them. And, Jen, the task was difficult—"

"Yes, Archeli. It was. Go on."

"Tonight, Jen. Tonight he means to open and let them in."

Seventeen

The Battle of Therminsax

The fuzzy pink moonlight washed over the stones of the wall and deeply shadowed the buttresses. Moon blooms opened their petals greedily to drink of the light. The silence drifted with a little breeze, broken only by the occasional sleeping growl of a ponsho-trag. We watched the lenken gates. The Gate of Aman Deffler was the nearest gate to the Temple of Florania. The idiot intended to open up and let the radvakkas in. I had collected the Hakkodins, the halberdiers and axemen, and now we lay in wait.

Presently footsteps sounded pattering along the flags. Dark figures moved on the ramparts, for here the gates fronted an open pasture and no suburbs had been built up against the walls. The watch, alerted just in time, made no resistance but fled. I did not want good men killed. The gates swung open, carefully greased by these deluded followers of Florania.

Crouched in the shadows, tense, I saw the oncoming mass of Iron Riders. I gave the sign.

Up on the walls the watch returned and with them bowmen and the paktuns. Down below my Hakkodin moved forward. We let perhaps a hundred radvakkas in, surging confidently forward in their iron. Then the gates were shut, the way cleared by lethal sweeps from axes and halberds, the opening bolted up.

Then we turned on those Iron Riders who had ridden in.

By Vox! The pent-up fury of the citizens was wonderful to behold—wonderful and horrible in its revelation of the fury honest men feel when their lives, their livelihoods and their loved ones are threatened. The axes cleft mail, the halberds swung with irresistible force. The Iron Riders were swept from their saddles. They stabbed with their spears and swung with their swords; but the devils of my Hakkodin were everywhere, swarming all over them. In a matter of murs the carnage was over, the savage sounds of steel on iron, the shrieking commotion of men in combat stilled.

Panting, his halberd a shining brand of blood, Targon the Tapster confronted me.

"Hai, Jak the Drang. Now you have seen!"

"Aye, Targon. Now you understand the radvakkas are merely mortal men—"

"By Vox! When you leaped on them I almost felt sorry for the benighted devils." He laughed, the reaction setting in. "Although, I swear by the Invisible Twins, you are a greater devil than any of them."

"Clear the mess away," I said, intemperately. "Carry all the iron to the workshops. Take the unhurt benhoffs to the stables and you do not have to be told what to do with the poor animals who have been injured." I looked up at the walls. "Hai! Have they gone?"

"Aye, Jen. We saw them off and emptied a few saddles."

"Shudor the Mak!" I bellowed. "Take your men out and cover the working party. Bring in everything of value the cramphs of Iron Riders have left us."

Shudor, who had signed a contract and accepted good red gold for the services of his paktun band, obeyed. We wasted nothing in besieged Therminsax.

Then I went off to have a few words with the priest of Florania.

The Justicar and the city fathers met in solemn judgment. Everything was done with strict impartiality and adherence to the long-established customs of the bokkertu in Vallia. But the evidence was so strong that the verdict of guilty was the only one possible. So I, being squeamish, left the matter in the hands of the city fathers of Therminsax, whose city would have been betrayed by this misguided man. What they did I will not repeat; but the example, I felt reasonably confident, would deter any other poor deluded wight from plunging so foolishly into an act of treason.

As for his followers, they repented at leisure.

I went to find the two Krozairs, Zarado and Zunder. As always, they were arguing, this time about the relative merits of the halberd and the axe, and so I was able to say: "I have noticed your swords, koters." I called them koters in the Vallian way, for koter, being a word of similar meaning to gentleman, covered our transactions. "I fancy I would like to have the armorer make me one up in like fashion."

They laughed, and showed me their Krozair brands. In Therminsax there were the usual number of smiths any place would need; of armorers there was but one, Ferenc the Edge, for it was said he could hone a blade like no one else in all Thermin. He had been kept busy, grumbling about letting blacksmiths into the high mysteries of his art. I had simply told him that any self-respecting blacksmith could put a good edge onto a scythe or sickle, that I had shown the women how to fashion the scaled bronze kaxes, and to pitch in with a will. Now the two Krozairs showed me their swords, and I took them off to find Ferenc the Edge. With me I took an armful of the radvakka swords.

"Now, Ferenc," I said, in the heat and smoke of the armory. "These two monstrous swords. You see them."

"Aye, Jen," quoth this Ferenc the Edge. "And mighty unhandy they look. The handle length is impossible. And there is a curve, if I mistake me not, in the blade—"

"Good man!" I exclaimed. "The curve is of the most subtle, being more of a rise of the cutting edge to the center point. You will make me a sword like this from these radvakka weapons."

The Krozairs fell about laughing. "It takes skill—" And: "You'll cut your legs off, if not worse!"

But I insisted and left Ferenc to it, with a promise that he must make the blade superb and if it snapped across in battle I'd stalk back and stuff the shattered end up where it would do him no good at all.

But I knew, sadly, that however fine Ferenc's work would be, the blade he would forge would in nowise compare with a true Krozair blade.

More days passed and our preparations drew on. We made thousands of bronzen caltrops, *chevaux de frise* were constructed, and husky youngsters, fleet of foot, were trained to run with them and drop them in position, to pick them up and run again; to the shrill commands of stentors. The benhoffs we had taken were added to our cavalry force, and we could field almost two hundred now. Our five hundred archers were now at the stage where they could loose accurate volleys with an expertise that, while it would provoke Seg to a chuckle or two, would for all that do pleasant mischiefs to the radvakkas.

I was not concerned to choose an auspicious day for the sally, a holy day or a day sacred to some god or other, not even Opaz. I would choose the right day for my brumbytes. As it turned out, the right day dawned on the morning of Opaz Enthroned, which was a good omen. Normally, the long chanting processions singing their eternal "Oolie Opaz" would wind through the streets. I gave the countersign as Oolie Opaz and told the people that that would suffice on this day.

Truth to tell, the sally could not much longer be delayed. Our food was now in sure sight of running out. We had trained to a pitch and now we needed combat to temper our arms. And, as you may well imagine, I was overtaken by the most profound panic of indecision. How could we face the ponderous onrushing might of the Iron Riders? Would not all our careful plans be rendered useless? Our hedge of pikes swept away? Would the burghers change into hardened brumbytes, and stand, and win?

Ferenc the Edge found me, his squat face glowing and smudged with black. He held out the sword.

"Here, Jen Jak. And may Opaz have you in his keeping, for I have tried to swing the blade and took a chunk out of my leg, may Trip the Thwarter take it." He handed me the sword and I felt a rush of nostalgic onkerishness envelop me as I wrapped my horny old fists around the handle. Ferenc eyed me. "Go in good spirit, Jen Jak, and, by the Blade of Kurin, as my clients say, I wish you well."

With the sword in my left hand I took out the assignat I had prepared and handed it to Ferenc. When he saw the sum I had written and which had been countersigned by the Justicar, he whistled.

"You put great store by that monstrous brand."

"Aye. Now go and take your place. Every man must play his part today." And I added: "And may Vox send his aegis to give you comfort."

Whatever happened today, from henceforth it would be known as the Battle of Therminsax. That was inevitable.

The temples crowded with brumbytes and Hakkodins, seeking a last measure of comfort. The women bore up marvelously; but I understood their agonies. I held a last order group with the two Kerchurivaxes, Nath Nazabhan na Therminsax and Strom Varga na Barbitor, and with the Jodhrivaxes. They knew the plan. To dignify what we purported as a plan must be overstating it. We intended to march out, form phalanx, and smash the radvakkas.

Even a well-disciplined phalanx will trend to the right so as instinctively to bring the shields around to face the enemy. To give a little added protection to the right flank we would march out across the open plain with the Letha Brook on our right. The Hakkodins would flank us. If we did go right we'd find our feet getting wet. So I had a private word with Bondur Darnhan and Jando Quevada, the two right-hand men.

Briefly, I told them that the direction of the two wings depended on them—they knew that, anyway; they'd drilled enough times—and that they were to parallel the Letha Brook.

"Put your heads down, your pikes level, your shields up—and go straight in. And tread warily over the clutter on the ground,"

So, dutifully, they smiled at the feeble joke, and went off.

We marched out.

The army of Therminsax marched out.

The two Kerchuris marched. The Hakkodins flanked them. The cavalry and archers took post on the rear flanks, awaiting immediate orders.

And I got the jitters. Were twelve men enough? Was a phalanx twelve pikemen deep thick enough? Ought I to have made it sixteen, like the Macedonians? The pikes projected past the front ranks, forming a multiple hedge of steel; but I could have lengthened the pikes, made five or six project. I looked at that impressive array, superb in bronze and crimson, marching with a swing, with the drums rolling, and I felt the icy shivers of dread.

So much to gamble, so many lives... It is imperative if you are to gain an insight into that formidable and splendid array to grasp something of what it was like to march as a brumbyte in the files. A heavy helmet weighs down your head and the metal visor obstructs vision. You grasp an eighteen-foot long pike, and you hang your shield around on your left shoulder, trying not to let it slide away to the side. You are aware of your bronze-scaled kax pressing on your chest and back. You clump along, in line and file, as you have been trained. The man in front is old Nath, a good fellow if a boaster, the man to your rear is old Naghan, who always wants to tread on your heels. The men on either side you know, have worked and trained with. The dust rises. Your nostrils sting, your eyes want to run with water. The breath clogs in your throat. And you must grip your pike firmly, held aloft until the moment comes when the trumpets shrill and down go the pikes, level, and you increase pace. Then you can hear and see practically nothing as you just press forward until—but then, you have not yet experienced that fraught *until*. All the training and practice in the world, even charging solid wooden fences, cannot really prepare you for the hideous reality that will follow when that *until* becomes fact.

Solid, compact, compressed, shield locked, pikes all slanted, the phalanx moved out.

One of Shudor's paktuns had got himself killed and so I was able to buy his zorca, at an impossibly inflated price, from the band. Gold had to be paid; assignats were of no interest to the mercenaries. So I rode a zorca and was clad in a bronze kax of the same kind as those worn by the brumbytes, wearing a vosk-skull helmet with the bronze fittings, carrying a long spear, a shortsword and a broadsword from the radvakkas—and with the Krozair brand scabbarded over my back. The scabbard had been made by the handmaidens of Nazab Nalgre's wife, the quiet and soft-spoken Lady Felda. From the saddle hung down a steel axe, short-hafted.

Naghan ti Lodkwara and his Hawkwas, riding the benhoffs we had taken, formed a small guard reserve. And I became aware of a monstrous shadow at my back, and turned, and, lo! There rode Korero, bearing an enormous shield. He met my eyes and he looked abruptly shifty.

"Why do you ride there, Korero?"

"You have given me no place in this phalanx, Jak the Drang. I remember what I remember. This shield is large enough for the two of us."

All I could do was say: "You are right welcome, Korero the Shield. But guard yourself, you hear?"

As I swung back to check the progress of the phalanx I found myself muttering darkly: "What in the sweet name of Opaz will Turko the Shield say?"

Cleitar the Smith rode with us and he carried the standard. This was a large banner of crimson with the yellow saltire of Vallia, and, in the hoist, the crimson and brown of Therminsax arranged in their insignia shape. Dorgo the Clis and Magin rode with us. Also, we had a truly enormous brazen trumpet blown by Volodu the Lungs, a barrel-chested, square-faced rogue with a penchant for ale of any quality and in any quantity.

The brumbytes were singing as we advanced out across the open plain by the brook. Where they got the spit from, Opaz knows. They began with refrains like "The Maidens of Vallia" but as we advanced and saw the mailed cavalry riding out and forming to meet us, the songs grew more wild. A couple of times each Kerchuri was singing a different song; but as we drew forward to the place I had marked, everyone was bellowing out "The Sylvie on the Slippery Slope." I did not think the ladies crowding the walls of Therminsax could make out the words, even if they might hear the tune, and that was just as well. It is a marvel how decorous, seemly, orderly townsfolk will transform themselves in moments like these into the wildest spirits imaginable.

The stentors blew their trumpets and the shrill notes halted the phalanx. The radvakkas trotted out, ominous and deadly in their iron. The lads with their caltrops on quick-dispensing rods ran out ahead and strewed the ground. On the flanks the *chevaux de frise* were positioned, ugly trestles armed with spikes, protecting our flanks. The lads assigned to this duty, fleet of foot, collected at the rear of the phalanx, out of the way.

We halted, all the pikes upright, and the banners and standards moved to the rear.

I wanted—how I wanted—to leap off the zorca and grasp a pike and so stand in the front rank. But I had a duty and that duty chained me here, in command, ready to hurl the weight of our attack where it was needed. A phalanx arrayed so deeply and with shields locked can go straight ahead. It is designed to go straight ahead over anything. To wheel, to form, to go sideways, is so difficult that it is barely attempted. We had carried out experiments, and had some success, but usually the phalanx fell into complete disorder. I had chosen to march out with the phalanx facing the main camp of the Iron Riders.

We would go ahead.

But, all the same, despite that, my place was where I was.

And, all the time, I continued to marvel at the way in which the solid citizens of Therminsax had transformed themselves. From a witless bunch of scared loons—with the exceptions of those men I had seen and noted— the burghers now stood calmly in their packed files and ranks awaiting the onslaught of the dreaded Iron Riders. The transformation was exceedingly marvelous, and I felt a warm and choking affection for these brumbytes sweeping over me.

The jitters persisted. Ought I to have provided baldachins, canopies of cloth to hang from the shields to protect the legs? As I lifted in the stirrups and peered ahead at the advancing Iron Riders, I had to make a fierce effort to banish worries like that. The Phalanx of Therminsax had been forged. It existed. It was. In only a few murs it would be in action, in its first action. Everything was going to go splendidly. It was. I had to believe that, believe utterly and with the fanaticism of the doomed.

Dust puffed from under the iron hooves of the benhoffs. The radvakkas had no doubt been astounded to see the gates open and an army march out. I hoped that they would regard us as just another army like those of Hamal they had destroyed in the outright violence of their charge. They had no doubt tumbled out of their tents shouting with glee, arming in all haste, snatching up sword and spear, leaping into their saddles. Being barbarians they would all race to be the first. Their chiefs would, because they were chiefs, be able to control a few of them close at hand. But the mass would dig in spurs and set off.

This they did, and so they came down on us like a spuming unformed mass, bunched as they closed, riding knee to knee. The front ranks tended to draw together, followed by a whole tail of furiously galloping riders.

"What a sight!" said Cleitar. He shook the great banner. In his right hand he grasped his massive hammer, and the head was newly fashioned into a piercing spike at one end and a crushing hammer at the other.

"Very impressive," observed Korero. He sat his benhoff alongside my zorca, but I knew he would haul out to the side and rear when the heat grew. He had no fear of arrows, for the radvakkas were in too impatient a mood. They just clapped in their spurs and charged.

Our own archery rose from the flanks. I had not stationed archers to the front for I did not want bowmen running back through lanes left in the files, with the subsequent movements to fill the gaps and possible dislocations. The phalanx waited like a solid rock against the pounding of the breakers.

The Iron Riders hammered on. At the last moment the bowmen retreated behind the bristling spiked trestles and continued to put in a raking discharge. Any moment now—the noise of the thousands of hooves bellowed to the sky. The dust rose. The twin suns glinted from iron armor and steel weapons. Instinctively I tensed and then relaxed as the forces met.

Bedlam. Sheer awful bedlam. The noise blattered away as if insane imps of hell were beating drums through Cottmer's Caverns. The smashing impact of those superb riders against the steady ranked lines of brumbytes rocked on, rocked in equilibrium, rocked back. I saw a few pikes splinter and sprout skywards. I saw the long level lines of pikes holding, stabbing, transfixing man and beast. The phalanx held. Not a man yielded an inch. The Iron Riders rode into that bristling wall of steel pikeheads and were ripped from their saddles, slashed into the ground, brought to a grinding dusty bloody halt.

We lost men. I sorrowed for that. But only a few, a very few, and particularly in one relianch where the front ranks went down under a collapsing tangle of benhoffs. But the brumbytes in rear moved up, stabbing and thrusting, and the cruel steel pikeheads forced a clearance, and the line held.

The overlap of the radvakka charge lapped around our flanks. This was where danger threatened. But the very vehemence of their charge carried them spurring on. Those who tried to rein inwards were stopped by the *chevaux de frise*, and by the archers who shot lethally into them, and by the Hakkodins who slashed with axe and halberd and dragged the Iron Riders from their tall saddles with spikes and battered them into the ground.

On the right flank a mess of benhoffs floundered into the Letha Brook and were dealt with in water and blood.

I saw the recoiling movement. The Iron Riders following up their first ranks had either crashed headlong into them to add to the confusion, or drawn rein and wheeled away. Groups of radvakkas pirouetted about the plain. They would gather for another charge, of that I was certain. Again uncertainty hit me. Now? Or give them another charge and then? So I waited, confident in the cool heads and high courage of the brumbytes.

The front rank men knelt and thrust the butts of their pikes into the ground, their shields facing front and locked. The second rank men thrust forward under arm, over the shoulders of the front rank. Farther back the two-handed over-arm grip was used. All in all, to face that bristling pike-hedge would take a great deal of nerve and courage.

Of nerve and courage and sheer stubborn pride the radvakkas were plentifully provided. They gathered and charged again. And, again, they were piked to a bloody standstill.

Now!

The rear rank men, the Bratchlins, were yelling and stretching out their empty hands. Men bearing fresh supplies of pikes scrambled forward. As the front rank pikes were broken, so the files passed up fresh ones, levelly, as they had trained. There were no spikes at the butt ends, and no reversing the pikes as though they were mere nine-foot spears. I gave Volodu the Lungs the order.

He blew the "Prepare to advance."

Immediately the front rank men stood up. The pikes came down level. The brumbytes took a grip on their shields, their pikes, on themselves. I nodded to Volodu.

He blew with scarlet and distended cheeks. "Advance."

All the other stentors took up the signal. With ringing trumpets and with the thundering rataplan of the drums bellowing the files on, the whole phalanx advanced.

With helmets bent fiercely forward, with glaring eyes, with clenched teeth, the brumbytes advanced. The level rows of pikeheads glittered. The tramp of bronze-studded boots hammered the ground. Careful of the scattered caltrops that had brought down many a poor animal, of the corpses strewing the ground, treading small, the men advanced. When the phalanx had cleared the cumbered ground, and ahead pirouetted an astounded cavalry, and the main camp of the Iron Riders, Volodu at my nod signaled the "Double, Advance, *Charge!*"

The whole phalanx broke into a double march, a furious yet steady pace, almost a run, that carried them over the ground and, scattering the remnants of the radvakkas to our front, brought us up to the leather tents of the camp.

The "Halt!" brought them up with their pikeheads ripping into leather.

Here the Hakkodins went to work, with the cavalry who now came up. They destroyed the camp. During that enjoyable work the phalanx turned about. This was accomplished with a smartness of drill I admired, for I saw how the taste of action had sharpened the men up. Trumpets shrilled. The Second Kerchuri remained fast. The First moved off. All pikes were vertical. When the First had cleared the Second, the whole Second Kerchuri left-faced. Rank by rank they marched to the rear of the First. When each file was exactly aligned, the trumpets blew again, the Kerchuri halted and faced front. Twenty-four deep, we set off back to the city.

Strom Varga, commanding the Second, cantered over to me.

"Yes, Strom. Nobly done. Be ready instantly to halt your Kerchuri and turn about. Or to face either flank."

"Quidang, Jak the Drang." He cantered off, perfectly composed. The evolution would be tricky if some wight forgot to hoist his pike before he turned. Drill and discipline—resent them though the soldier might, they helped to keep him alive on the day of battle.

So we marched back in triumph. Had we possessed a good cavalry force we would have ridden in a bloody pursuit. As it was and in a way very satisfying to me although regarded askance as less than dignified by the citizenry, we were accompanied back by a whole clamoring host of freed slaves. Radvakkas maneuvered some way off. But we did not march straight back, for the ground was cumbered. That led to a tidy old mix-up in lining up for the gate; but I told Volodu to signal "Relianch." Then the brumbytes sorted themselves out and marched in in good order. The gates were closed. I breathed in deeply. I had struck out one good resounding blow. But the pikes of my men, my sturdy brumbytes, were crowned with the laurel wreaths of victory.

So we celebrated.

The next morning there was not a radvakka to be seen. All the tents unburned had vanished. The cooking fires were cold.

The Iron Riders had gone.

Therminsax had been saved.

Eighteen

Nath Nazabhan

Over the next period of my life upon Kregen I had best tread lightly. Much of what immediately followed stemmed from the facts surrounding the besiegement and Battle of Therminsax. While I had been mewed up there and in the period following when, with a choice band, we traveled from city to city along the old frontiers and pressed on into Hawkwa country, many great events had taken place in Vallia.

My orders from the Star Lords, to be obeyed, necessitated the complete overthrow of the Iron Riders. So I took the matter.

To accomplish this in a short time was patently not possible, lacking a plentiful supply of infantry capable of standing against the armored cavalry charge, and lacking a powerful cavalry of our own. With that choice band—a group that grew together in times of adversity as well as of success—we moved from city to city instructing, exhorting, demanding in the name of Vallia. Where the radvakkas were too strong we bypassed the place. Then, in the fullness of time, we would return and cleanse one more spot of Vallia.

The Iron Riders were slow to counter our measures. We had to make absolutely sure that each province and city we liberated was capable of defending itself against further attacks. With a strong cadre from Therminsax, by expertise that grew with every fresh successful drill no less than encounter, we developed speed in our methods. But, all the same, it was a lengthy business.

To arouse a nation to arms is one thing; to train them to win wars is another.

Our first task, which we successfully completed, was to clear Thermin back westwards to the Great River. On the day we reached The Mother of Waters, I recall, we looked across and saw on the right bank a massed group of totrix cavalry, wearing the checkerboard ochre and umber of Falinur. I suppose, thinking of it, it was fortunate that a bridge was not nearby and the river ran broad and deep here. A smashed and routed band of radvakkas lay in our rear, and we were still more concerned with them than with the rebels over the river. For, make no mistake, rebels they were, Falinurese who had sided with Kov Layco Jhansi and taken up arms in his struggle for the imperium. His kovnate province of Vennar marched with Falinur to the west. Beyond him lay the long range of heights known in their northern sections as the Black Mountains and in that immense amphitheatre to the south, the Blue Mountains.

No good sitting dreaming. We had work to do to the east. Sitting there with the standards and banners about me, I gave the orders, and the cavalry moved out, and the phalanx swung into their dwabur-consuming stride. Oh, yes, these days we marched about the country as a phalanx, made up from men of many tiny villages as well as towns and cities. We trained as we marched, and we picked up fresh recruits every day, it seemed. Mind you, our strength as yet was short of a complete phalanx, and I intended to regularize the numbers out logically. We had almost a full Kerchuri with us, of which four Jodhris were fully trained. Despite my powerful arguments that he should stay with his father and in his city, Nath Nazabhan had elected to march. He was the Kerchurivax. A fine man, a fierce and loyal fighter, he did much to lighten the hearts of the brumbytes, despite his strict adherence to the codes of discipline we enforced.

And, believe you me, the discipline in the phalanx was strong.

We cut south following the river and opened up Eganbrev and then swung sharply east in that broad double-hook of She of the Fecundity and so cleared our way through Aduimbrev. I am making this narrative abbreviated here. We successfully liberated Thiurdsmot and Cansinsax, and, by this time, we had four Kerchuris with us. They amounted to twenty-five thousand men. We had a cavalry arm, also, by this time, mounted on totrixes and nikvoves, and these were organized in the usual system, squadron and regiment. They were all heavily armored cavalry, with kax, spear and sword. In addition we possessed a small scouting force of zorcamen. Gathering men and animals together from everywhere, we at all times observed the proprieties and I signed countless assignats. Well, that is a lie my staunch comrade Enevon Ob-eye would strongly object to.

Enevon—One-Eye Enevon—served as my chief stylor, and he kept scrupulous accounts of every assignment we issued, as well as the army lists. He was from Valka. He had seen me and opened his mouth and I had run him into my tent under the crimson and yellow flag, and cautioned him. He called me Jak the Drang.

He'd been on a trading mission and become caught up with the revolts in their various places and phases and so could give me no late news from Valka.

That reminds me of the day we marched into a ruined town having driven off a wispy attempt by a handful of radvakkas to halt us and found in a tumbledown barn the sad remnants of an airboat. Well, between us, we patched the thing up. So we had ourselves a flier. I called Korero to me. His great shield, and often two shields at once, had interposed between me and the arrows and sword-strokes of the enemy. I looked sternly at him.

"Korero the Shield. You can fly an airboat. You will fly to Valka. You will enter the Heart Heights and there perform a certain function."

He did not want to go. He was from Balintol, a weird, exotic place, if ever Kregen sprouts such mysterious lands, by Vox. But he could fly and he could read a map and he was of great heart and courage. I entrusted a sealed message to Delia into his four capable hands—not forgetting his equally capable tail-hand—and saw him off with many Remberees.

To finish that story anachronistically, as is not my wont, he returned in the fullness of time, finding us easily enough by reason of a burning city and radvakkas lying strewn in their own blood, and reported that he had seen the Princess Majestrix of Vallia, whom men now called the Empress of Vallia, and that she had opened the letter addressed to her by Jak the Drang and had read, and grown pale, and pressed the paper to her heart, and had then treated Korero the Shield with great kindness.

"She was well?"

"Aye, Jak. She commands an army there of the bonniest fighters I have seen in a long time. They are re-taking Valka for the Strom of Valka—wherever he may be, for men did not know."

I read Delia's letter in answer to mine. I cannot repeat its contents; but it was as Korero had reported with his sharp eye. Valka was being won back from the mercenaries who had thought the Prince Majister's Stromnate easy pickings. She understood I could not join her for the moment: she would join me when it was possible, although she sounded a warning note. Her thoughts were with Delphond and the Blue Mountains. As to Zamra and Veliadrin, our people resisted there; but waves of aragorn and mercenaries from all over, drawn by the news that Vallia was in turmoil and there were easy pickings, were flocking in like warvols.

And that reminds me that I had continually to remind my great-hearted brumbytes that they might overtopple mailed cavalry, but that they could not go up against the iron legions of Hamal. The information was not welcome; but I pressed the point and, also, against possible evil, increased our missile force. We were a national army—or almost so. We had a few mercenaries in our ranks and could pick up more as we progressed. We had a detachment of Bowmen of Loh—and none of them had served in the Crimson Bowmen. This corps I did not resuscitate, having strong ideas on the subject of what I intended in that direction.

Time had flown by and we were well into the North East—well into Hawkwa territory. Now the campaigns we waged changed in character. There was no longer the pressing need to recruit and train men to form phalanxes. We marched and we were the phalanxes. As we liberated areas and towns and cities we destroyed the bands of Iron Riders who opposed us, and rolled up in a receding tide those who fled. The operations took on more and more the guise of campaigning warfare. Gelkwa was freed. With the pikeheads of the host slanting against the suns at my back I appointed a Hawkwa noble, Strom Hafkwa, to be the new Trylon of Gelkwa. He accepted; but he did ask: "By what right, Jak the Drang, do you do this thing?"

I relished the moment for its parallels.

I pointed at the phalanx, at the serried files and ranks of pikes.

"There is my mandate."

Of course, I then added that I bore a commission from an imperial Justicar, and was using that to ratify my actions. He was one of those—and there were many of them as there had been many to sing a similar tune in Djanduin—who raised the call, cautiously at first but with growing volume, that we should all march to Vondium and chuck out this traitor Seakon and install me, Jak the Drang, as emperor.

I smiled.

"One day, one day, perhaps. But I seek no personal aggrandizement." That was true, by Krun! "First we must cleanse all Hawkwa country of the radvakkas."

The Hawkwas clustered about in this moment, as a new Trylon of their province was installed, nodded. They said, in effect, and I do not repeat their words: "Much favor is yours, Jak the Drang. All Hawkwas will stand in your debt, for you do not impose alien rulers on us when you might, seeing you have the strength. We accept your rulings." That is more or less it.

I took some pains to make sure I did not come into contact with any who might recognize me from those hectic days I had spent here previously. That was unlikely, really; but it was a chance I was not prepared to take—not just yet.

I think, now, that Korero the Shield put two and two together and came up with the right answer. But he respected my wishes and kept his own council. Also, Nath Nazabhan knew. It popped out one day, and enquiry determined that his father the Justicar had told him, so that he would mind his manners with me. I smiled—again, I smiled.

"Then you have kept silence, Nath, and will continue to do so. But I can tell you that an imperial province lies in your hands once we have this mess sorted out."

And then he surprised me. He said, this tough, limber young fighting man: "I follow you, emperor, for two main reasons. One is to clear Vallia and to flex my arm against her enemies. And the other is because of yourself."

I did not pursue the matter, as we turned to details concerning the new swarm of irregulars who now followed us as we marched. Nath had been promoted to command a phalanx, the other being in the hands of Nev who was a Therminsaxer and who had risen through the ranks being a man of exceptional ability. He had once been known as Nev the Bottle; but now he never touched a drop and my orders said he was now Kyr Nev ti Rendonsmot, a title taken from the town where he had been instrumental in holding his Jodhri firm against almost insupportable numbers, and then of advancing at the double and flinging the Iron Riders back in confusion.

Yes, yes, there were many battles and many campaigns and sometimes the arm grew weary and the brain dizzy; but we persevered, clearing Vallia of the radvakkas.

The irregulars, and I call them that only because they were not as yet integrated into the army, posed problems. Men of Vallia from farm and town, they followed us. They aped our ways, and built themselves shields of wickerwork, and carried long spears, and perched vosk-skull helmets on their heads. On more than one occasion they raced in with a whoop and a yell on the flanks of the radvakkas and materially assisted us in the victory. I had issued orders that the irregulars were to be given the full assistance of our ambulance and medical services, and the doctors with us attended to the irregular wounded in the same way they attended the brumbytes and the Hakkodins. Although we had provided an ambulance and medical service from the very beginning, and little enough they had had to do on that never-to-be-forgotten day of the Battle of Therminsax, the fact remained that once the shields locked and the pikes came down, our men suffered relatively few casualties. This heartened everyone.

So many vivid and burning memories of those days of marching and campaigning and battling rise up before me now as I speak. Would that I had the time and a thousand cassettes to speak of them; but always my thoughts pressed on feverishly to the accomplishment of what I had set my hand to, the liberation of Vallia and then the return to Delia and the surcease from strife.

When men march together and fight on from year to year they change, their characters alter, in subtle and gross ways they become different men from those who set out. The histories of Napoleon and Alexander demonstrate this with stark and pitiful clarity. We were not troubled by desertion. If a man did not wish to march with us, then he was free to leave. We were, after all, not a conscripted army but a national army of liberation, fired by the zeal to cleanse our country. So I deliberately instituted a policy of maintaining a turnover in the files. By this method men would be sent home as others pressed forward, after training, to fill the gaps. I did not wish my little army to become tainted, sour, as happened to other armies of the past.

One bright day after a smart little dustup when a wing, having advanced perhaps a little too far against two strong bands of radvakkas, and having formed a schiltron, pikes out, to resist, was smartly relieved by a cavalry charge in the flank of the Iron Riders, I looked up into the air and saw a flier circle and land nearby. We used our own single flier to recce; I daresay that was the only airboat for a thousand miles or so. And, now, here was another. She bore flags the colors, gray, red and green, with a black bar, and so I knew she was from Calimbrev, that Stromnate island south of Veliadrin, and also I knew who this was who came leaping over the coaming and racing over the torn-up grass toward the group of riders about the crimson and yellow banner of Vallia. I'd have known that slender, smooth-faced, respectable young man anywhere.

If he yelped out my name before my gathered officers...

But in those hectic days we had spent together in the Kwan Hills and Gelkwa, and, as well, in that harum-scarum chase from Drak's City in Vondium, something must have rubbed off on him, for as he came running toward us, waving his arms, almost tripping over his rapier and clanxer—I half-smiled when I saw his armory—he bellowed out: "Jak! Jak! It's me!"

Mind you, young Barty Vessler, the Strom of Calimbrev, still shouldn't have yelled any name. It was lucky for him I was using the same address alias as before, except that I was not Jak Jakhan but Jak the Drang. I urged my zorca out front and center and then hauled up as Barty arrived, red-faced, panting, overjoyed. He was a supple, bright, eager young man, filled with ideas of nobility and chivalry a little rough-hunting with me had not knocked out of his noodle.

"Barty!" I said, speaking warmly, for I felt pleasure at the sight of him. "Strom. You are right welcome. Lahal."

"Lahal and Lahal, Jak. I am here. I will fight. I have heard—Del—that is, a message—" He floundered.

I lowered my voice. "I am Jen Jak the Drang. See me in my tent in a bur. And, Barty, for the sweet sake of Opaz, keep your trap shut."

He nodded, and that wickedly sly grin of the ingenuous at their awed realization they are involved in skullduggery passed over his smooth, polished face, making him look like an apple set out in the front of the greengrocer's stall.

"Quidang, Jen Jak the Drang!"

Names, names... They conceal and reveal all, and can sometimes lead to very messy deaths...

Before I could see Barty the aftermath of the little action had to be tidied up. The Kerchuri that had advanced with somewhat too great precipitancy had done well to form their schiltron, in this case a circle of bristling pikes, and resist successfully until relieved; but I wanted a word with their Kerchurivax, stubborn old Nalgre ti Fomenoir. He would shake his head and agree with what I said and then, the next time, would as lief lead on his Kerchuri in that hard, heavy, pounding advance, the brumbytes all advancing with helmets forward and pikes thrusting. We had become used to charging forward and hurling down all who opposed us. We must not become complacent.

And, after Nalgre ti Fomenoir had been spoken to there was the matter of the Love Story to be attended to.

A certain brumbyte had become enamored of a little lady in one of the towns we had liberated. A fine girl, strong and well-built, she had captivated this pikeman, Nath the Achenor. When the army marched out, Achenor could not bear to part with his ladylove, fair Sarfi. Equally, he conceived that his duty lay with the phalanx and he would not desert. So—so the pair of them stood before my tent and I glowered on them.

They stood to attention with their bronze and vosk-skull helmets gleaming, the barred visors lifted, the crimson plumes lofting. They held their pikes at the regulation position, vertically, the heads stained with blood. Their bronze kaxes shone, and Sarfi's had been cunningly adapted so as to fit her interesting shape. Their shields rested on the ground, leaning against their left legs. I looked at them, this pair of brumbytes, one male and the other female, and I sighed and wondered what on Kregen to do with them.

"So, then, Sarfi, you fancy yourself as a Jikai Vuvushi?"

"No, Jen. I am a brumbyte and I march in the phalanx."

"She carries her pike with the best, Jen," broke out Nath the Achenor. He threw her a swift, fond glance, and then snapped back to glare to his front. "I love her dearly and she loves me and we will not be parted."

"I do not argue with that. I believe she is trained, for your Relianchun would not have tolerated anything less."

"She is well-trained, Jen."

I did not say that I had spoken to Relianchun Anror ti Aventwill, the commander of their Reliance who was due to be promoted to Jodhrivax. I looked on these two lovebirds and I said: "You will return to Sarfi's home. There, no doubt, you will be married and begin to raise fresh brumbytes. That is your concern. I request—request and do not order—that you drill and train the younger men of the town in our methods. You would have made Laik-Faxul very soon, Nath. You have the training. Make sure it is not wasted."

Nath the Achenor started to argue, clasping his pike and shield, saying that he did not wish to leave the phalanx. But I pointed out to him that the phalanx was no place for a girl. Mind you, that was a long time ago and things changed on Kregen, as you shall hear.

So the pair of turtle-doves were sent off, trailing their pikes, unhappy at the moment to leave their comrades. I would not forget the phalanx and what we had achieved. Then I went to find Barty Vessler.

Barty brought news of my daughter Dayra.

He did not know she was Ros the Claw; he had not seen her, brilliant in her black leathers, her lithe feline form very quick, very deadly; he had not witnessed the slashing destruction wrought by that cunning curved metal-taloned glove upon her left hand.

As ever, after he had failed to halt the invasion of his Stromnate by the aragorn, Barty had gone seeking Dayra, for he was passionately enamored of her in his refined, elegant and chivalric way. He had found Delia in Valka, who had no late news on Dayra, and had been told of my doings and whereabouts. So he was here, panting on the trail of Dayra, and with information he had picked up that did, in very truth, give a lead.

"For," he said in his light, quick way, "I ventured up to Vondium and, Jak, you will be interested to know that Drak's City held out for long and long—"

"You did?" I exclaimed very stupidly. Then: "Well, that warren could hold an army at bay. Who took it in the end, Layco Jhansi or Phu-si-Yantong?" Then I had to run over a little of the influence that Wizard of Loh exercised, and of his part in the calamity that had befallen Vallia. It seemed to me that secrecy about the Wizard of Loh was no longer necessary. His acts were plain, carried out by his tools, the chief of whom, as far as I then knew, were the Hamalian Army in his pay and the malevolent Hawkwa party under Zankov.

"The Hamalians control the city with Vallian puppets to make the thing look right. It sickens me. The Hawkwas have fallen out with the Hamalians. Drak's City burned—a good deal of it, like the city—but everything is being rebuilt at a prodigious speed. And Dayra was there; but she was entangled with a bunch of mercenaries—masichieri, most likely. They infest everywhere."

"And?"

"I heard that she had been insulted and had dealt with the masichieri— there was talk of her slicing them up, which puzzled me. Anyway, she left."

It did not puzzle me. The thought of foul-mouthed, sly, treacherous masichieri insulting my daughter did not, thankfully, cause me more pain than it ought, for I was well aware that Ros the Claw would, indeed, slice up any oaf who thought she was easy prey.

"They meet at a place called Olordin's Well. I came to you because—" Here Barty paused, and colored, and looked away.

I had not given him my blessing in so many words; but I had come to an appreciation of him, so I thought. I said: "I am unable to leave the North East until all the Iron Riders are dealt with. Dayra can look after herself. As soon as I am free I shall go to Olordin's Well."

With the courtesy that was also a useful arguing tool, Barty let that lie and we talked of other things. He would return to the subject, that was sure.

With Barty's late information and what we had learned elsewhere, the picture of the present state of Vallia emerged. It was unclear—the condition of the southwest remained obscure. But the North West—not so much a geographical location as a combination of provinces, always staunch Racter country—had combined even more strongly and under the leadership of Natyzha Famphreon, the Kovneva of Falkerdrin, had declared themselves independent of the rule of either Hamal or Layco Jhansi. Now Jhansi fought campaigns along his northern borders. His tilt at the throne had not succeeded; but, at the least, he had taken the pressure off the Blue Mountains. Barty shook his head at my enquiry about the Black Mountains, Inch's kovnate.

"They have been engulfed, Jak. I heard that a strong mercenary army swept through. Some of the Black Mountain Men have moved south to join the Blue Mountain Boys, and they hold out there—or so it is said. But who can believe anything these days?"

The large island of Womox off the west coast had elected itself a king, and severed communications. Womoxes still served other masters in Vallia and elsewhere, as you know; but this was just another indication that the Empire of Vallia was falling to pieces. Certainly, events had not turned out as Phu-si-Yantong would have planned or wished.

As for the many islands fringing the coast of the main island, anything could be going on there and probably was.

Those provinces which had previously been held by nobles who had refused to take up an alignment, and there were plenty of them, like the high kovnate of Bakan to the northwest of Hawkwa country, had been ravaged by greedy neighbors or invaded by hordes of aragorn and mercenaries. Flutsmen roamed the skies of Vallia, these days, and that was good for no one.

As for what was going on north of the massive barrier of the Mountains of the North—that was as remote as the probable carryings on on any of the seven moons of Kregen.

For our part, the officers and men around me, we more and more considered ourselves as representing the true Vallia. As I was told by these choice spirits: "The Empire of Vallia has been destroyed and no one can deny that. Now the island and islands are cut up, fragmented, separate. We are the true Vallia, the continuation of the old, and under our banners march men who are true to you, Jak, and to Vallia."

If this was high-flown stuff, then that was sometimes the way of your bluff Vallian—as of any other of the peoples of Paz on Kregen, so it seems— but they remained for all their quoting of poetry and singing of songs just as slippy at slitting a throat or two.

Phu-si-Yantong was a mere crude conqueror; if he was a sorcerer also, the protections afforded me appeared to be working so far, praise be to Zena Iztar. Layco Jhansi knew very well that his only pretensions to the throne lay in the swords of men he could hire. The Racters had withdrawn and, as so often before, bided their time to strike. Anybody else who sought to become Emperor of Vallia could only be a mere adventurer. This Seakon who now occupied the throne and wore the crown and grasped Drak's Sword was just such a one, a successful one. From what Barty said it appeared the Hamalese sustained Seakon in power. What, then, of the aspirations of Zankov?

Barty seemed to think Zankov led the Hawkwas; but I was not persuaded of that. After the disappearance of Udo, the lead in Hawkwa affairs had been taken by Nankwi Wellon, the High Kov of Sakwara, and we had had a right little flare-up with that prickly personage. He had been downright indignant that the Iron Riders had been swept away by, as he put it, a rabble of southerners. At our interview, when he had put on airs and graces, being the kov and very condescending and mighty with it, I had had to cut him down to size very smartly.

A kov runs a kovnate province; a high kov runs a province which contains a diversity of races each with its own separate organization—the kind of set-up I had had trouble with in Veliadrin with the damned Qua'voils. In Sakwara there were two other powerful groups, one of Brokelsh and the other of Rapas. They were barely tolerated; but they were allowed to live their own lives. The Iron Riders had wrought horrifically upon these communities of diffs, and their numbers had been reduced by better than eighty percent. The carnage had been colossal, obscene, not tolerable.

The Hawkwas with me showed the Hawkwas of Sakwara very clearly where their sympathies and loyalties lay. It crossed my mind, perhaps pettishly, that Sakwara might do better by being divided into a number of smaller provinces, vadvarates and trylonates, perhaps.

In the event, the High Kov Nankwi Wellon had to accept the situation. He remained the high kov. We had cleared the radvakkas from his territory and we left him to rebuild as we pressed on into the Stackwamors, clearing the country out of pockets of Iron Riders. And then, of course, the radvakkas began to coalesce, even to forget inter-band rivalries, and to join together into one mighty horde.

What, you may ask, in all this of that scheming little bitch, Marta Renberg, the Kovneva of Aduimbrev? What, indeed! Well may you ask.

After the fall of her province of Aduimbrev she had gone hot foot to Vondium to berate, to argue and finally to plead—if I read the situation aright—with the Hamalese. She would want them to reinstate her with their iron legions, and they would want to leave well alone and not tangle with the radvakkas. If she returned and claimed Aduimbrev back she would find a very different situation, and one she would not like. I did not particularly look forward to that meeting. To be truthful, I detested the very thought of that coming confrontation, by Vox!

For the talk throughout the army now, in the phalanxes, in the Hakkodins, in the cavalry and archers, was all of marching to Vondium in a mighty host and there proclaiming Jen Jak the Drang Emperor of Vallia. The irregulars, too, were of the same mind. They knew on which side their bread was buttered. I merely made myself smile lazily when the subject came up, saying to them tsleetha-tsleethi, all in good time.

The irony of my devotion in clearing out the Iron Riders from Hawkwa country was not lost on me. The Hawkwas were fully aware that we could have marched on Vondium—no one really believed the Hamalese swods would stand against the phalanx no matter how many times I warned them—and so they regarded me with great favor in that I used the army to clean up their country. I did not mention the Everoinye; but if ever a situation deserved the irony of history, this one did.

The campaign persisted and gradually the great day of the final reckoning approached. We were apprised by our scouts and our two fliers of the positions and strengths of the radvakkas. We marched up, the dusty columns with their slanting forest of pikes trudging over the land, pressing closer and closer.

Having cleared the center of Hawkwa country, the South, East and

West Stackwamors and the other provinces, we marched north through Urn Stackwamor. Ahead, far far ahead, the icy pinnacles of the southern ranges of the Mountains of the North hove into view. We trended eastward, toward the coast, aiming to pin the radvakka horde against the River Sabbator. The river ran down into the sea opposite the island of Vellin and separated Urn Stackwamor from the trylonate of Zaphoret to the north. In this part of the country there were many Peel towers, stark and angular against the sky. The people had resisted stoutly and many of the Peel towers lay in ruins, for the radvakkas had dealt sternly with the people. Food was not too hard to come by; but the host consumed vast quantities, and I knew that we must finish this thing quickly. Assignats might be written but they could not produce food where there was none.

Barty said: "I am no coward, you know that. But I cannot wait any longer. I do not understand your so tender regard for the Hawkwas. By Vox! We suffered enough grief from them. I must be off to seek Dayra."

"Go with my blessings, and may Opaz fly with you. But I must finish what I have set my hand to. I will see you at Olordin's Well. I shall come as soon as I can." I stared at this slender, easy, well-mannered young man. I sighed. "And mind you take good care of yourself, Barty Vessler. My daughter is, I am sure, highly demanding of any man."

He grew red in the face, and stammered, and swore all manner of high-flown sentiments. Barty Vessler. Yes. Well, I stood to see him off as he observed the fantamyrrh boarding his flier, and we shouted the Remberees. He took off.

And I, somewhat savagely, I confess, set my army in order and gave Volodu the Lungs the order to blow the "March" and we set off for the final battle against the mailed might of the Iron Riders.

Nineteen

In the Name of Jak the Drang

That army was superb. There is no doubt of that. They had marched and fought and sung together. Each part knew its duty and did it and more. The Phalanxes, for there were two full phalanxes now, slogged forward in the center, with archers and Hakkodins in the intervals and flanking. The cavalry trotted on the wings. Like an enormous tide of bronze and crimson we advanced. And, too, by now many of the brumbytes had acquired iron armor to replace the bronze. But we continued to use the old vosk-skull helmets, often with iron instead of bronze fittings. We functioned like a cutting machine. We would go through anything.

So the brumbytes said.

The Iron Riders had gathered. They were all here, for they well understood that this was the final reckoning. In one single gigantic horde they would meet us and this time they would crush us utterly, once and for all.

And although the radvakkas were illiterate barbarians, they had learned. They altered their tactics. It was a development long overdue and one against which I had given thought and planned with my officers and men. The army marched forward, singing, confident, ready to sweep away the Iron Riders in this last climactic battle.

We were all chosen men. The word "Legion" carries the connotation of selection. We were the Phalanx, and we were selected from the best. The swarms of itinerants and irregulars hungered to join our ranks. So we marched forward with the crimson banners flying and the bronze and steel gleaming, with the drums blamming their thrilling rataplan.

Ahead the long long line of radvakkas came into view.

At once Nath said: "Hai! The rasts try a new trick."

The Iron Riders did not charge headlong at us the moment they could. Instead, they hung back, pirouetting out there across the plain, with the glinting thread of the River Sabbator at their backs. The wagon leaguers and the camps occupied a vast area of the watermeadows. The twin suns shone.

The banners flew and the trumpets pealed. The Phalanx halted.

I say Phalanx; against this moment we put into practice the plans we had developed. File by file the Relianches moved into open order, the Bratchlins standing fast and the files marching back to turn and come up behind their neighbors, thirty-six men deep. Into the intervals stepped the archers. The evolution was completed smoothly and in good order—and only just in time.

The Iron Riders in clumps and groups swept toward us and retreated and as they curveted so they loosed a rain of arrows.

At this early stage most of the shafts fell short. Our trumpets blew "Shields" and up went the crimson flowers, like a field of roses, ready to resist the falling arrow storm. Our archers loosed careful, aimed shots, from standing or kneeling positions, that took a toll of the galloping radvakkas. For their part, the Iron Riders attempted to press in to the range at which their short bows might reach, but the compound bows of our archers outranged them handsomely. As I have said, one does not fire a bow. Kregans have a word which roughly approximates our terrestrial word firepower. Now Nath half-turned in his saddle, laughing, gleeful, raking me with the demand in his bright eyes, already triumphant.

"See, Jen Jak! Their dustrectium is pitiful! Let us close ranks and lock shields and advance."

"Their attempt to prepare the mass is, indeed, not worthy of our preparations to resist. Mayhap they have another cast hidden from our view. Let our bowmen empty a few more saddles, Nath."

On my other side Nev fidgeted astride his zorca, anxious to bring his phalanx into action. But I made them wait. I needed the radvakkas to appreciate that their new tactics were failing them, and to gather, once again, for the headlong charge that, I fancied, this time they would make with the final fling of desperation.

Well, the story of that old battle is there for all to hear in the song that was made. The "Black Wings over Sabbator," it is called. This is a typical Kregish reference to the incident where a fleeing formation of radvakkas, circling, came across one of our ambulance units tending the wounded of both sides and simply rode across them, slaying friend and foe alike. That was after, at last, I gave the signal, and we closed ranks and locked shields and with helmets fiercely bent forward, plumes nodding, and pikes leveled in a lethal hedge of steel, we advanced at the regulation double pace. The moment was judged nicely. We caught the Iron Riders just as their chiefs had finally collected the scattered bands into that fearsome armored host with which they had so often ridden to victory. We hit them as they formed, before they had even put spur to benhoff. We hit them and the pikes bit and the halberds slashed and we rolled them up and crushed them and destroyed them utterly.

Pinned against the Sabbator they could only stand among the tents and wagons and fight until they died.

Our irregulars swarmed in. Our archers picked off any who sought to flee. Only that one formation which so mercilessly razed the ambulance unit escaped; and subsequently they were pursued and brought to justice. For, believe me, that is how the army viewed the situation.

Relianch by relianch, the brumbytes came back out of the line, pikes tossed, formed, intact, ready to face anything.

As I say, and no doubt will continue to say, by Vox, that was an army.

That it was wildly anachronistic meant merely that it gathered the more honor. Of glory I will not speak. But I had, with the full co-operation of Nazab Nalgre, instituted valor medals, phalerae, and these were worn with pride.

In the history of those skirling days kept by Enevon Ob-Eye the battle was recorded as The Battle of the Sabbator; but men usually refer to it as the Sabbator. It was a famous victory—and, thank Zair, our casualties were less than minimal. On the aftermath of the action I looked up, and there, floating over the Phalanx soared the gold and scarlet Gdoinye.

I put a hand to my helmet and hoisted the barred face-mask, and stared up narrowly. The raptor swung about, and glided down and then, as though satisfied, flirted his wings and soared away.

The very next day I said to Nath: "You are in command of the army now, Kyr Nath. Nev will support you loyally. Appoint whom you wish to command your phalanx in your stead, although I think we both favor Kyr Derson. Conduct the army back to the southern borders ensuring that the whole country is free. Then you may disband and send the men to their homes. The work of rebuilding is pressing."

"But—Jak."

"I have business elsewhere."

"Where, by Vox?"

I looked out of our tent and saw the brumbytes. Four full Kerchuris we had now, and their crimson shields no longer bore the brown of Thermin. They were an imperial host, bearing yellow insignia on their crimson shields. I felt the wrench at parting. As I had said to Barty: "The organization is so simple even the dullest oaf can understand. Twelve pike men to a file, twelve files to a Relianch. Six Relianches to a Jodhri and six Jodhris to a Kerchuri. And each position of command from a Laik-Faxul to the Kerchurivax, is linked in a chain. The rank and function are inseparable." When you spend a part of your life building anything at all, when the time comes for the dismantling, regrets creep in, nostalgia, all the silly unmanning emotions that, I suppose, in some measure indicate the value of what you have wrought.

So I said to Nath: "I shall probably end up in Vondium; but I do not know."

"Then—"

"Command the army well. Make sure we have the whole country cleared. Rebuild. Your father will advance money. As far as the borders are concerned—"

"Layco Jhansi is a traitor!"

"Aye. And he is kept in play by the Racters north of him. Let the brumbytes go home, Nath. And the Hakkodins and archers. As for the irregulars, they will melt away now the fighting is over."

So I took my leave. The island of Vellin to the east ought to be cleared, always assuming radvakkas had fled there; but I doubted that the Gdoinye would have let me go if my work was unfinished. The actual leave-taking turned out to be highly emotional, and my plans to slip away were frustrated. There was a full-scale parade and review, with the trumpets blowing and the drums beating and the banners flying. The army marched in review—and the sight of the solid masses of crimson and bronze, with the pikes all slanted together, affected me profoundly. This farewell was, after all, worth my own embarrassment.

Korero the Shield said, as I saddled up: "You do not seriously think I would let you ride alone?"

The others of that choice band who, even though the country was cleared of radvakkas, still had no homes of their own, said much the same. Cleitar the Smith, who bore the banner of Vallia, may have had a home; but he had no wife and children to go home to. Dorgo the Clis was now so habituated to fighting with me that he was amazed I could even think of sending him away. And this was so of the others, valiant fighting men I had led in battle, who formed a kind of reserve guard cavalry. Mounted on zorcas, we rode south in a bunch, with Calsanys loaded down with provender and weapons and, I confess, with gold. Gold might be very needful, for I had no idea of the kind of situation we were riding into.

It would be useful to point out here that so much plunder was recovered from the radvakkas that, of the raw gold alone, we were able to repay many of the assignats, and I appointed a corps of stylors to catalogue each item of treasure and make our best efforts to return it to its owner. This was justice of a very rough and ready kind; but, at the least, we did not take everything for the army, as—we all know—many would have done.

The depreciation in the value of money which afflicts civilizations from time to time posed a threat which I was concerned to prevent. Armies cost money and the land will provide only so much. With the troubles that had dismembered and disrupted Vallia reducing production drastically, pretty soon the people of the empire would wake up to find themselves poor. The aragorn and the slavers did not help, for their depredations might remove thousands of hungry people; but they created so many terrors that in many areas the land had not been worked properly since the first invasions.

As we rode south we saw evidences of that. More and more I felt the claustrophobic effects closing in on me. We were a band of fugitives where we rode, leemsheads, outlaws, shunned by the people of the villages, with the gates of towns slammed in our faces, with the campfires of armed hosts at night to warn us off. This land was torn with anger and terror and evil. And these were the broad rich central provinces of Vallia! Truly, an emperor would weep to see how sadly fallen away was his patrimony.

The iron legions of Hamal were a different proposition from the Iron Riders. I developed a scheme. The countryside was infested with brigands, drikingers who waylaid any and everyone. In a brief and bloody encounter with one such band my choice spirits discomfited them—rather roughly, I must report. We told the drikingers that if they wished to live they must confine their depredations to waylaying and slaying Hamalese, aragorn, Flutsmen, the mercenaries and masichieri. They were to leave the honest folk of Vallia alone.

"And by what right do you imagine you can make us?" demanded their leader, blood streaming down his reckless face, held by the elbows and forced to stare up at me.

"Do the Hamalese not contume you? You are held in contempt by them. You are nithings. Yet you are Vallians. You were not always drikingers. Very well, then. Men call me Jak the Drang. I tell you that I shall utterly destroy the Hamalese and all the vermin who infest our country. Have faith in Opaz. The evil days will pass."

Such were my words, or roughly what I said, over and over, to the men we encountered in our travels. And, on that occasion and, subsequently, on every occasion no matter that I did not much care for it, one or other of my choice spirits would sing out: "Aye, hulus! Remember, this is Jak the Drang, who is Emperor of Vallia, and will sit on the throne in Vondium and take Drak's Sword into his hand. Remember and tremble at his name."

Well, as we neared the capital, we found the name of Jak the Drang had gone before us, and men were ready to heed my words. The scheme I put into operation demanded that the women and children of these rich lands remove themselves to the North East. Reports reached me regularly from Nazab Nalgre and the other nobles in Hawkwa country, all of whom now called me emperor without affectation. Their borders were secure. Their first harvest of the new season was a bumper one, producing the plenty of the land in abundance. This operated in two ways to help us, for the people who traveled to the North East left their own shrunken fields to enter a land where they could eat their fill, and Nalgre and the others forwarded on food to us as an earnest of our good intentions. And, in a third and altogether more profound way—if anything can be more profound than the state of a man or woman's inward constitution—the news of what had been achieved in Hawkwa country circulated.

At the name of Jak the Drang these miserable cowed people, living in fear of the Hamalese and the mercenaries, took heart. What had been achieved there by Jak the Drang might also be achieved here. The process took time. More than once we were forced to enter the open field and battle bands of masichieri—it was mostly them—in defense of a group of people. But our name and the report of our deeds spread.

When the Hamalese sent a force against us we melted away.

When we ran into real drikingers, bands who had been bandits before the troubles, they were dealt with in a proper and summary fashion. The bands who roamed the countryside now were death on wheels to the invaders of their country, and full of concern for native Vallians. We gathered more people, of course, in our peregrinations until we moved in a tidy little force, daily growing in strength, never halting in one place, but clearing up a spot of trouble and moving on.

The canalfolk were a tower of strength. The vens and venas, the vener, proved themselves fully alive to the peculiar advantages and possibilities of the canals, and long strips of narrow boats carried the refugees into the North East. Of course, occasionally, a caravan was stopped. Sometimes there were tragedies. But gradually, as the season passed over, we cleared the lands of most of the women and children. The task was colossal and, of course, we could never fully complete it. There were just too many people in these lands around the capital.

But we cleared so many that the Hamalese were forced to resort to setting guards on the farm people remaining. The fields were being left unattended, and no crops grew, and the food was going to run out—and soon. The hordes of rasts who had burst into Vallia and eaten of her goodness stored up in barns and warehouses would go hungry—unless they chose to leave.

I suppose—indeed, I know it to be true—that the Dray Prescot who is me was not the person in those days called Jak the Drang. Jak the Drang browbeat bandits, harangued lords and nobles, had no hesitation in dealing with the utmost ferocity with murderers and rapists and those who had battened on the misery of the people of Vallia. The name of Jak the Drang was whispered—in fear by his enemies and in pride and exultation by his friends and comrades.

But—it was hardly me, hardly the new Dray Prescot—although to be truthful, there was a damned lot of the old intemperate Dray Prescot in Jak the Drang.

When we reached Olordin's Well and found the little hamlet a razed wreck, without hair or hide of a soul, I admit I raved and ranted and was like to have done something exceedingly violent—which is against my nature—when Barty, who with a few friends had been waiting nearby, came running up. He had fliers and provisions and friends; and he reported that Dayra must have been at Olordin's Well but had long since departed.

I said: "Bear up, Barty. That young lady can take care of herself exceedingly well." Almost, I told him of Ros the Claw. The tiger-girl, the lissom chavonth-maiden in the black leathers.

"I believe she can, Jak." He eyed me. He was still the same elegant refined young man; but a little of the roughness of life had him. In a lowered tone, he said: "If she is anything like her father, then I feel sorry for anyone foolish enough to offend her."

"There is a task we must do, Barty." I told him of the scheme, and he burbled that, by Vox! he liked the sound of it. "The food has to be grown, say the Hamalese, and the Vallian farmers must grow it. We are seeing them safely away. But some, the rasts from Havilfar mew up, set working in the fields from dawn to dusk, alongside their slaves, put guards to watch and to whip. There is such a farm near here. We have sent out a call and the men will come—"

"I know, Jak," said Barty. "Your name carries much weight in these troublous times. The men will come."

The men did come, stealing by night from their fastnesses in the recesses of the forests or in the hills, for although Vallia is fertile and well-settled, there is still a great deal of it and many wild places remain untenanted save in times of turmoil. The men came and we made a descent on the guarded farm and freed everyone Vallian there, free man and slave alike, and the women and children joined the procession of narrow boats to the North East and the men joined one of the growing number of resistance bands. We laughed and counted it a victory.

It was around this time, when things were going well if slowly for us and I prepared to visit Valka, that an incident occurred whose importance I had no way of knowing at the time, although later on it was to play a vital, a decisive, part in ensuring my hide stayed around my flesh and bones. Our band had freed a group of villagers and we had seen them off and we were in camp. A group of locals—peasants, they might be called in another context—who gave us surly looks and refused help were found to have actively co-operated with the Hamalians. They had sided with the Hamalians against their own kind. When they discovered their error and tried to escape they were arrested.

Now people will always be found who will collaborate; by Zair, it is a matter of weighing evils. Some of my hardened old blade comrades, and Dorgo the Clis vociferous among them, were for stringing up the guilty ones forthwith.

It fell to me to harangue the mob, there in the erratic dramatic sparkle of the campfires. I told them many of the things you have heard me say before. Human life is sacred, diff and apim alike. These were deluded people; yes, they had betrayed good folk to terrible fates; but vengeance for the sake of vengeance destroys him who so callously metes out retribution without thought of the deeper motivations. We would not slay them. They would be set free, and in the shame they would feel they would hew to the path of justice henceforth. Well, even then I was not quite naive enough to believe all of them would never sin again; but for the salvation of a few the many must go pardoned. It was a hard dialectical struggle; but in the end, and because it was Jak the Drang who spoke, my view prevailed.

A small group of people vanished out of the firelight into the shadows as my men, still a little reluctantly, released the prisoners.

That group who vanished so smartly did not belong to my people; but they were gone. They had looked hardy. So we moved on from that area, and I delayed my visit to Valka, until we had established ourselves in another place, where we began at once to cause mischief to the aragorn, the masichieri and the Hamalese.

Then, I borrowed one of Barty's fliers and flew to Valka.

Twenty

Fire Over Vallia

"No. I think the plan to be not a good plan. I do not like it. And, yes, I have been away to—away to where I have promised to speak to you of and will do when this mess is cleared up. But, as to your plan, no, my heart—in this I am not with you."

She looked at me. I braced myself up and returned the look. It is hard to cross my Delia—hard! It is nigh impossible. But, in this, I remained adamant.

"We are safe here in the Heart Heights," she said, and she crossed to the wall of rock and stared out and over into a vast dim blueness separating this mountain fastness from the far peaks. "We resist the aragorn and the mercenaries, the Flutsmen and the masichieri. We drive them back. Soon, we shall retake Valkanium and the war will be won. I am no longer needed here."

"That can never be so—"

"You know what I mean! I shall return with you to Vallia and together will we eject the Hamalians—"

"I do not fight a war like this one. It is not even a proper guerilla struggle—well, more or less. It is dark and unpleasant. I prefer you to stay here and, by Zair! even here you risk yourself every day, for I know—"

"And since when have you, Dray Prescot, ever been prudent?"

I rubbed my chin, abashed. Then, stoutly, I said: "You would hardly recognize me, in these latter days. For Dray Prescot treads mighty small where once he—"

She laughed. The suns sheened in her hair, making those outrageous chestnut tints shimmer and shine. She clapped her hand to her slender waist, and half-drew her rapier.

"Dray Prescot? Aye, he lags well to the rear. All one hears these days is the name of Jak the Drang."

"Oh," I said. "Oh, well, he is a rascal, to be sure."

So we wrangled. I did not intend to stay long, but one thing and another retained me in Valka. Tom Tomor and Vangar fought their wars of liberation in Veliadrin, and my Pachaks were on the verge of clearing Zamra; but the days were hot with the sounds of strife. Drak had gone to Faol to search out the Manhounds, Melow the Supple and her son Kardo, who was the true and trusted heart-comrade to Drak. Shara, Melow's daughter, twin to Kardo, was, I understood, with my daughter Lela. And where she was—

"The Sisters of the Rose, my heart. Lela is much occupied with them in these times. From her I learn much of conditions."

"Lela and Shara did not go with us to Aphrasöe," I said and I know my voice sounded grim. "That must be rectified soon. I do not wish to look forward to what must follow else."

"And Barty Vessler?"

"Dayra is looking after herself. She is well able and—"

"Oh, aye. She learned well with the SoR—so well that she spurns us and goes her own ways." My Delia sounded hurt and more than a little bitter, which struck me with agony.

"So you finish your work in Valka. I will work on in Vallia. I called in on Forli and scouted MichelDen hoping to find Lykon Crimahan and report on his success. But there was no sign of him and the kovnate was still infested."

"He came on here, dejected, and now he is in the north, trusting that when we have cleared Valka and the islands we will march on MichelDen for him. His trust is not misplaced."

"Something may be made of him, yet. But I must play all the time on Vondium. Farris is flying back with me, eager to take over in Vomansoir. The people will welcome him—the fighting bands that remain, for we have made a clearance there."

"You take Farris and you will not take me!"

"No."

Down below in the shelter of the next terraced rocky wall a pastang of Valkan Archers marched out to take up their sentry posts. Delia had worked well in Valka. Those regiments of ours so treacherously sent to the north of the Mountains of the North had not been heard of. I could only trust they continued in existence. Of fliers, all Vallians were pitifully short, and the Flutsmen still roamed, reiving and murdering from the air.

Around the capital, Vondium, I was drawing the net in tighter and tighter. I say I—I mean Jak the Drang. From Vomansoir we had extended to Rifuji and Nav Sorfall immediately to the east. Naghan Vanki, the old emperor's spymaster, had gone to ground and messengers from Jak the Drang sought his active assistance. The capital of Vallia, Vondium the Proud, was surrounded by imperial provinces, as seemed only wise. To the west of the Great River lay Vond, and to the east, Hyrvond. The river ran a long east-west reach here and to the north lay Bryvondrin. In all these imperial provinces the emperor's Justicar had been foully murdered, and men had been in despair. Now the infamous bands of Jak the Drang brought a new resistance and a fresh hope. The net drew in.

We went in presently to sit down to a sumptuous repast, by the reduced standards of the Valka of those days. But there was food and the rations were evenly spread among all.

Delia saw I meant what I said, and contented herself only by saying: "You will take a force of Valkans with you? Some of your Freedom Fighters, old blade comrades—"

"I have but Barty's voller, and that will take a bare fifty."

"Then take fifty fighting men of Valka, for they thirst to battle alongside their strom."

I cocked a cautious eye at her. Her color was up. So I knew what she intended. Slowly, I shook my head.

"You need all the fighting men here, my heart. And I find men who were stylors and farmers and cobblers and a thousand other trades springing up overnight into warriors." She had listened enthralled to my story of the Phalanx. "And, sweet schemer," and that bit of sickly-sweet sarcasm aroused her, by Vox! "I do not want another stowaway as—"

"You knew all the time, then, before we fought at the Crimson Missals!"

"Mayhap I did. But you are essential here. Do you not think the Freedom Fighters of Valka relish battling alongside their Stromni?"

She lowered her eyelids; but she was mightily put out.

"And," I went on remorselessly. "You are not to venture yourself so. Do not go to froward into the battle."

"If I go froward it is because of—" And she stopped, and bit her lip, and so we gazed on each other.

When the time at last arrived when I could tarry no longer and I forced myself to tear myself away, that same Dray Prescot who was Lord of Strombor and Krozair of Zy, besides being Strom of Valka and, now, for his sins, some kind of Emperor of Vallia, she handed me a rolled bundle. It was scarlet. I knew what it was.

"I go back to being Jak the Drang."

"I know. Yet, at the end, methinks you will fly your own battle flag, that famous tresh men sing of, the battle standard Old Superb."

I took the flag. My hands brushed hers. So, for a space, we clung together. Then, with a stony face and a bursting heart, I went out to Barty's voller, and called the Remberees, and took off slanting into the morning blaze from the twin suns, from Zim and Genodras, the Suns of Scorpio fiery and glorious over the face of Kregen.

I did not unroll the flag. I stowed the tresh, Old Superb, away and wondered when, if ever, I would fly that battle banner above the hosts of liberated Vallia.

Looking back now I can see more clearly and understand many things that puzzled me at the time. The very completeness of the clearance of Hawkwa country, the repulse of the Iron Riders, impressed all who heard of it. The Iron Riders had shattered army after army of the Iron Legions of Hamal. And then a new army had arisen from the very people of Vallia themselves, a young, brave, confident army, and had routed the radvakkas utterly. No wonder men talked with bated breath of the accomplishment. All those months of labor had borne mighty fruit. The time had been well spent. No one sought to enquire into the character of that new Vallian army, to wonder how it would perform against the Hamalese. It had won. The laurels of victory crowned its spears.

And—the man who had accomplished this, the notorious Jak the Drang, had aroused the countryside, was gathering a host against Vondium. Then arm, friends! Gather yourselves for the final struggle—once the capital is Vallian once more then the rest of the country must follow.

I did not miss, also, the interesting if ironical fact that this had been made possible by those very people who had once sought so violently to free themselves from Vondium, to become independent within the empire. There were strong forces of Hawkwas who persisted with the old and, in my view, fallacious dream. But the hosts of the North East marched with Jak the Drang for a strong and comradely and united Vallia.

Mind you, I did not share the view that with the repossession of Vondium our problems would be solved. The vaster reaches of the island empire would remain in non-Vallian hands. But, I did admit, if not the end of the affair, then the capture of Vondium would signal the end of the beginning.

Delia had proved herself her usual self in her packing of the flier for the return journey. Among the contents of the many wicker hampers, beside food and weapons, were lengths of scarlet cloth...

Farris, the Lord of Vomansoir, piloted for some of the time. We had much to say, one to the other, yet the words were hard to come by... He welcomed my news of the recent events in his province. He had fought most valiantly in Valka and I in Vomansoir, so we were well quitted.

"Once we march into Vondium, majister," he said. "Once the people can look with renewed hope to a strong central power—"

"Not majister, Farris. Jak the Drang. And a strong central power as you put it may be a mischief in itself."

"You do not believe that!"

"Sometimes I do not. But, sometimes, I wonder. All I want to do is let Vallia alone. To let the people lead their own lives as they wish, happily." Then I was forced to add, to make absolutely sure Farris understood: "And we shall free all the slaves. It will take time and it will be a messy business; but I am resolved."

"There will be much opposition—vigorous and violent opposition. But you know that."

"Aye. I know that."

During his sojourn with my people in Valka Farris had seen much of our ways, and understood much more clearly the way we thought Vallia should go. That we were right was a guiding principle; and we recognized the pitfalls in this kind of blind arrogance and arrogation of superiority. But the sights and smells and sounds of the slave bagnios reinforced our determination to go on, in humility, believing that what we did, in very truth, was the right course.

"The men who were once slaves fight right stoutly in the new forces of Vallia," I told Farris. "They fight because they have been promised their freedom." However despicable a device that may be, I tried to think that in this case it was genuine, that the stalwart brumbytes, those ferocious Hakkodins, the prowling fighters of the bands closing now on Vondium, would not be betrayed. Then I would brighten. Anyway, I would say, who was there who would force them back under the yoke of slavery when they had formed an army, had seen what free men might do, had found themselves as men? There would be farms and workshops and goodly livings for them in the imperial provinces alone.

Taking Farris north to Vomansoir I dropped him off near his own provincial capital, that was, so the rascally leader of the bands of Freedom Fighters outside the city informed us, due to fall on the morrow. I stayed to watch and in the event to fight. The men surged forward to the attack yelling: "Vallia!" and "Jak the Drang!" and we burst in. The people rose. The Hamalese fought and, not always but more often than not, defeated the vicious bands of Freedom Fighters who sought to oppose them directly. But we chivvied and harassed them, and drove them into the fortress, and mewed them up. It would only be a matter of time, and the Lord Farris expressed himself as highly pleased.

As to the men and women who had resisted so stoutly, only to have their erstwhile lord return at the penultimate hour, they welcomed Farris, as I believed, because he was known as a just and enlightened lord, to whom any man might turn in distress in the sure knowledge of sympathy and ready assistance. So I said.

It was left to a one-eared, dog-toothed rogue to say to me, bold with the camaraderie of the Freedom Fighters: "That may be true, Jen Jak. But, also, the Lord Farris is befriended by you and returns with your blessings."

And another, a stout woman carrying a butcher's cleaver, her bare forearms red and shining, said: "We know who has given us back our homes and our shops. No one stands over us but Jak the Drang, who is our lord. And we welcome the Lord Farris because of that. Because he is set back in his place by Jak the Drang."

And the cry went up: "Jak the Drang, Emperor of Vallia. Hai, Jikai! Jak the Drang."

That, as I told the multitudes assembled on the next day, was the rehearsal for Vondium. They cheered. The broad kyro swarmed with people, packing in; the noise reverberated to the skies. Once the organizational details had been finalized here, a great host would march from Vomansoir and descend on Vondium. The timing was crucial. They must arrive when all the other bands congregated. If they were too late their help would be lost. If they were too early they might consume the countryside before we struck. Immense quantities of hoarded food were collected against that eventuality, and fresh weapons were secured from the arsenals, and the people cheered, and I sent the flier aloft heading for the Freedom Fighters ringing Vondium.

During all these periods of trouble an alert eye had been kept on the lookout for people who would serve in the future to create the better land of Vallia these folk deserved. The positions of responsibility must be occupied by men and women with the welfare of the people at heart. Already a strong cadre of people who would take over once the invaders had been driven away existed. And, all the time, doubts assailed me. Was this a dictatorship of the worst kind? Well—no. Vallia would breathe easier once we had cleared the invaders away and could get back to living our own lives in freedom. So we all believed, and worked for, and, many of us died for.

All these high ideals and abstract theories on the best forms of government were swept away when I landed at the rendezvous with Barty. He was there; but he was alone, and the bands were nowhere to be seen. His face looked pinched.

"Prince!" he said, then he swallowed, and got out: "Jak! We must flee this accursed spot at once."

"Tell me."

The trees sighed in the night wind, a few stars pricked the cloud-covered sky, everything shrouded in the mystery of night. Barty shivered.

"The fighting bands have moved away. Hamalese came—a host. They are encamped less than an ulm from here. Let us go."

"Why is the spot accursed, Barty?"

He had waited for me. That had taken courage, seeing the distress he was in. An elegant, refined, very proper young man. Barty Vessler, the Strom of Calimbrev.

"They set up an idol—a weird thing. They adhere to some religion or other—I do not understand it. But they are over in the next valley, a-worshipping and a-chanting—"

"I would see this."

"No! They have guards—they are a host—"

I marched off in the direction he indicated and he pattered along after. The night was dark, although not a night of Notor Zan. We reached the brow of the hill and so looked down onto the heads of Hamalese. In the center of the little valley, a dell in reality, an altar had been set up. An image shone above the basalt slab, an image illuminated in the light of many torches.

I saw.

"And they took a child from the village, and they are going—going to sacrifice it, I think..."

I looked down on the assembled congregation and saw they chanted praises and genuflected to the blasphemous silver statue of a gigantic leem.

Lem, the Silver Leem, flourished most foully in Vallia. I watched and I shivered. This was not in the plans.

Twenty-one

Vision at Voxyri

This I had not planned, had not foreseen. This was not abstract. This was here and now, red, bloody, fiery, utterly demanding everything a man can give, and more which comes from the spirit he does not know he possesses, and I was caught, trapped, held by the mirth of the gods in a vise that could be released in only one way. And that way could undo everything I had fought and struggled for for so long...

"There's only one way to do this, Barty. Come on." I ran back for the flier. Barty, shaking, ran with me.

"What—?"

"It must be quick and sure and certain." I took the voller up savagely, smashed the controls over. If she failed me now, then this was the end of Dray Prescot. Through the night we swooped, low over the wooded crest, skimming above the treetops. The torches burned brightly, illuminating that blasphemous statue. Lem the Silver Leem had no part in civilized men's scheme of life.

"Ready, Barty?"

"Aye, majister—ready!"

I took the voller down steeply aimed at the black basalt slab. The naked, pitiful, tiny form of a child lay there, crying. Priests moved in their cowls and hoods. The sacrificial knife lifted. Abruptly men were yelling. The flier hit the plinth and I was out, ripping the Krozair brand free. Two priests flew in four different directions. Blood drenched down onto the basalt slab, staining darker stains. Men were screaming. Guards charged toward me, their swords lifted. I slashed and swung and the longsword purred through the flesh and bone. The brand may not have been a true Krozair blade; but Ferenc the Edge had forged sweetly and true. Barty was out, a knife slashing the child's bonds. More guards tried to interface and the dripping brand cut them down as weeds are cut down.

A voice lifted among the multitude, for people were yelling and screaming, and moving dizzyingly this way and that.

"*Dray Prescot!*" screamed this voice, high and shocked. "I know that devil! It is Dray Prescot—"

"Aye!" I roared as I whirled the Krozair brand. "Aye! I am that devil Dray Prescot! And there is no place in all of Vallia for Leem Lovers—no! There is no place in all Hamal, in all Havilfar, in all of Paz for kleeshes like you!" And the stained brand bit deeply and chucked on, merciless, as Barty freed the child and leaped back into the voller.

"Dray! Ready!"

"I am with you!"

The longsword twitched this way and that and flying arrows caromed away. This was quite like old times. A last massive figure wearing the brown and silver of Lem attempted to stop me and the Krozair blade hit mercilessly and he screeched and fell away and I was in the voller and Barty was slamming the levers hard over and we lifted and soared away from that cesspit of human depravity. Lem the Silver Leem! No, I shouted down, cursing them all, no, your foul creed shall never sully Vallia.

I was, as you will see, wrought up.

Only speed and audacity had done the trick, of course. Many a Krozair brother, many a Clansman, many a Djang, would have done the same. By Zair! Was there anything else to do?

We flew back to the camp and were able to press the child into the arms of his mother. That, by Opaz, was worth it all.

Then we set about the final preparations for the day of judgment.

The point must be insisted on; this was only the end of the beginning. Many songs were made of the events of the next days. One of the gates of Vondium is called the Gate of Voxyri, and two canals merge here, crossed by a bridge, called the Bridge of Voxyri. Outside the walls, which were tumble-down, extends a wide common land and this is called the Drinnik of Voxyri.

As our forces gathered, fierce, hard, determined men, they brought stories of how the Hamalese were everywhere pulling back to the capital. We could see the long columns winding along the roads and along the canals clumsily using commandeered narrow boats. Something vast was afoot.

These columns were attacked with vicious fury, using the guerillero tactics that struck from ambush and melted away. The provinces around the capital were emptying of Hamalese and their mercenary allies. We watched the capital walls and suburbs and surrounded the city at a distance, and we took prisoners.

These told us enough so that, when we pieced it all together, we understood the magnitude of the event. This was a moment of world history.

The Empress Thyllis in Hamal was recalling her army, was sending for many of the volunteers of her iron legions to return to Hamal. The full details were not known; but a revolution had broken out and there had been reverses in the campaigns in the Dawn Lands around the Shrouded Sea. Men were needed. Taking a calculating look at the situation in hated Vallia, Thyllis must have decided to relinquish those provinces in which organized and determined resistance was costing her too much. Phu-si-Yantong, known as the Hyr Notor, had successfully arranged that those areas still securely under his thumb should remain so. The capital would be held, for its value was obvious and immense. So I looked at Barty and he made a face.

"It is great and glorious news; but it makes the taking of Vondium a thousand times more difficult, by Vox!"

"Maybe. They are short of fliers and must use them to keep open their lines of communication. The Flutsmen are already leaving, as we know, for there are scant pickings for them now. We must redouble our efforts on the columns straggling in. But the plans go ahead."

"It is mortal difficult to infiltrate people into the city now—the mercenaries sew the place up like a spinster's—"

"Given a lead the citizens will rise."

Within Vondium some of our people spread the word. When our Freedom Fighters attacked then Vondium would rise. But I wanted to defeat the Hamalese and their allies and be seen to defeat them—not me, not Dray Prescot, not even Jak the Drang, I hasten to add. But the fighting people of Vallia—they were the ones who must defeat the Hamalese and be seen to defeat them.

Also, it was reported that the Prince Majister, Dray Prescot, had been seen in the vicinity. There had been Vallian witnesses to the events at the shrine of Lem the Silver Leem. It seems to me that in the events of my life I have been recounting there had been precious little of that old skirling helter-skelter hurtling into blood-red action—and yet, the truth is that in these vast confrontations, in these campaigns, in these secret machinations for power, the old blood still does go thumping along the veins, there is still the same old fey passion of combat. The fascination of men and women scheming obsessively for power is undeniable. All I was trying to do was to make sure that power fell into the hands of people with the general good at heart—and that is a trick beset with many pitfalls, by Vox.

My men spoke words that warmed me, and made me want to smile, words that were droll in their context, but words spoken from the heart, with passion.

"Dray Prescot? Aye... Where has this Dray Prescot been in the days of trouble? It is Jak the Drang we follow and fight for. It is Jak the Drang who is rightfully Emperor of Vallia—and will be!" So spoke my men, stoutly.

Couriers spurred into camp with reports of a host advancing from the north and at the same time reports reached us from the city that the last group of infiltrators to go into hiding to await the signal to rise had been taken by mercenaries. We could wait no longer. The city would rise, we would strike from the outside, and the co-ordination would bring us the victory.

Then Nath Nazabhan rode into camp, disguised as a Resistance Fighter. At that, the truth acted as a disguise. I greeted him in my tent very warmly, already half-guessing what he had done.

"Aye majister—Jak the Drang. We owe you. I have brought a phalanx. We marched. We await your orders—"

Telling him how welcome he was did not soften my words.

"You have been warned many times that sword and shield men may not be directly attacked by the phalanx, except in exceptional circumstances—"

"We have many Hakkodins and archers—"

"Thank Vox for that. But this is city fighting, street fighting, dirty work. The brumbytes—"

"I shall bring the phalanx up, majister, and await your orders." He spoke with a persistent stubbornness I found at once infuriating and confoundedly familiar, for I recognized how much of my teachings had rubbed off on him. I nodded.

"Then await the signals. Volodu the Lungs will blow them."

"Quidang!"

So the phalanx of Nath Nazabhan explained the host from the north. We would have to take the city quickly, then...

As he left he said, not off-handedly, but casually: "We have new flags for the Jodhris, now." A fine, dedicated fighting man, Nath Nazabhan, who knew why he fought. "But the great tresh of Vallia flies over all."

The morning of the chosen day dawned fair and bright. The sky shone with a deep lustrous blueness. The Suns of Scorpio cast down their opaline brilliance in a sheening glory, the ruby and emerald mingling and streaming and illuminating everyone and everything as though revealing the inmost spirit and animation of human and object alike.

So I wrapped the old scarlet breechclout about me and drew up the broad lestenhide belt with its dulled silver buckle. An armory of weapons was girded on. Over my shoulder went the great Krozair longsword that had never been forged in the Eye of the World. And, also, because Delia had placed them in the voller I took a great Lohvian longbow and a quiver of shafts all fletched with the rose-colored feathers of the zim korf of Valka.

And so, on the day of Opaz the Deliverer, the signal was sounded.

Vondium rose.

The plan called for small independent groups to attack at selected points around the walls, aiming for particular gates and bridges. These were diversionary attacks, of course, and because there were not too many of them to reveal that fact to the Hamalese we trusted they would draw the swods off. Although the walls were in generally crumbled condition no one seriously anticipated ill-equipped guerillas to be able to storm over in the face of professional opposition. We wanted the swods clear of the main thrust; my commanders were confident we could do it.

The main attack, aimed to get as many fighters as possible into the city in one overwhelming tumultuous mass, would go in over the Voxyri Bridge. The wide expanse of common ground, Voxyri Drinnik, had to be crossed first. The plan called for the civic rising and the diversionary attacks to coincide, and then for the mass to charge into the city across the Drinnik, over the Bridge and through the Gate of Voxyri.

We had chosen the Voxyri complex because the bridge spanned a double canal making it the widest leading into Vondium, and the gate handled the heaviest traffic, and was the widest. These facts occurred in their calculations to the Hamalese high command.

No one ever proved a single thing. It was possible that among our own ranks *Punica fides* existed. The Bridge would have been taken without difficulty against a normal watch.

The Resistance Fighters in the immense mobs waiting for the signal to attack across Voxyri Drinnik were guerillas, Freedom Fighters. They were not line infantry, not even Peltasts or Hypaspists. They had been disciplined on the line of march and in camp and in respect of the proper behavior of fighting men; but they were quite out of hand now, when battle sounded. They would not stand their time in concealment.

Thin spires of smoke rose from the city and we could hear the first clangor from the walls and streets.

"Not long now," said Barty. He sat his zorca erect and his smooth face bore an exalted, shining look that afflicted me sorely. All about us the Freedom Fighters hunkered in cover. We heard trumpets from the city. These undisciplined mobs who fought for what they loved would not wait our signal.

They rose into the open. Screaming their hatred for the defilers of their country they ran out. Half-crazed, brandishing weapons, roaring, they burst all thoughts of discipline.

In a wild shrieking bunch they tore for the Bridge.

The combination of factors collided disastrously. Perhaps there was no treachery. Perhaps the swods merely acted as experienced soldiers. Perhaps in these latter days Catastrophe Theory can indicate on its models the unfolding progression of events, the upward line, the incurve, the downward trend that, curving through a million dimensions, abruptly explodes into catastrophe. Whatever the inner truths may be—here and now, on Voxyri Drinnik, we stared disaster in the face.

This screaming onslaught confirmed our intentions long before the Hamalese had been drawn away by feint attacks. The Bridge and Gate of Voxyri were the widest and quickest way into the city and therefore the best. They were and it was. Except—except that right here and now we saw cogent reasons why they and it were the worst possible ways we could have chosen.

From the Gate moved out long columns of soldiers, swods of Hamal in perfect line and dressing, trotting on with ranked shields, with crossbowmen flanking, with standards unfurled, trotting on to deploy into their long lines of armed and armored men. They were ready. They had not suddenly been called up from barracks or billets, summoned with drumming urgency from their beds. They were ranked and ready—waiting.

And, from the narrower Gate of Rosslyn along the way giving access over the canal trotted squadron after squadron of cavalry.

For whatever reason, the Hamalian army had not been decoyed. Now they deployed, faced front, and advanced.

The roaring ranging mass of people hurtling down on them had no form or order. Archers and spearmen, swordsmen and axemen, all mixed up together in a boiling torrent, they spumed along like the primeval breakers of the sea itself. The long ordered lines of shields would meet them unyieldingly and the swords of the swods, blood-drenched, would be unmerciful.

As the iron legions of Hamal moved into view there was perceptible in the mass of crazed onrushing people the barest check. The noise suffused reason. The regiments of Hamal marched out, deploying, ranking shields. And my people, gathering themselves as men do about to burst into burning buildings, gave a loud vociferous shout, a high shrilling moan of rapture, and flung themselves headlong on.

No rapture, no headlong charge, was going to carry partially armored and casually armed and shieldless mobs over or through that iron wall.

Useless to sound the recall. All there was left to do was to kick in heels and go pelting down after those crazed people of mine and burst through and so lead them, hoping that the inevitable stumbling falls of the zorcas might break a way through the shield wall.

I turned to bellow at my choice band, I lifted out my legs to kick in, and I heard and saw the wonder, the marvel—as, indeed, I had surmised I might, hoping, and condemning my hope as evil.

The brazen trumpets shrilled high demanding notes into the heated air, all together, trilling blood-thumpingly on—sounding the "Advance." I saw—ah! I remember it—I remember it... I saw the long serried lines of vosk-skull helmets, bronze-fitted, glittering, the crimson plumes nodding defiantly above. I saw the level wall of shields, crimson and yellow, gleaming. I saw the thickly-clumped forest of pikes, all slanting as one, rank on rank. I heard the heavy resonant blam-blam-berram of the deep-toned drums, and the trampling onrush of bronze-studded war-boots. Rank on rank, Relianch and Jodhri advancing, the files of the Phalanx pressed on.

A pungent smell of the red flowers of the letha tree wafted to my nostrils—hallucination, memory, evocation of another time and place where this advancing machine of glory, devotion, war and destruction had been born.

I trembled.

I, Dray Prescot, in the evil grip of grandeur, trembled. For Jak the Drang had warned and warned, and the brumbytes had laughed and not cared to listen. And I knew what I knew. My tumultuous mobs of undisciplined Freedom Fighters would be savaged and destroyed by the iron of Hamal. The temptation shook me, terrible visions of what would occur tormented me. The Phalanx advanced, perfect in order, moving as a single gigantic organism.

Could I? Dare I? What right had any man to demand the sacrifice of blood and life from another? Even with the fate of a country, an empire and all its people, at stake?

I knew what Nath Nazabhan would say. I knew what the answering roar from the brumbytes and the Hakkodins would be. And yet—the consequences of selfishness were incalculable.

So, shaking, filled with indecision, hating the fates that had brought me to this, I sat my zorca. What right...?

Because a man is called emperor and sits in the seat of power over multitudes of men and women—does that give him the right? I did not think so. I had been called to be emperor by those crazed mobs who would so soon be destroyed and by those ranked and orderly pikemen who awaited my signal. They had placed the power in my hands, and not because I am blessed or cursed with the yrium. I cupped their fates in my hands. Worthy or not worthy, it was all down to me, and to me, simple sailorman though I am, the fate of empire had been entrusted.

This vision of empire at Voxyri, this fleeting hallucination of power and glory as the Phalanx halted as one, glittering, splintered with sun-glory, waiting my signal—my signal!—overwhelmed me. I saw the flags proudly lofting above the Jodhris. Nath had told me the Jodhris had been given new treshes. Scarlet, those flags, scarlet slashed with the broad yellow cross. So he knew. Nazab Nalgre his father must have confided in him.

Over the brilliant and formidable mass of Phalanx awaiting my orders waved Old Superb, the battle flag of Dray Prescot.

So could I take the granite decision and into my own hands and heart allow the creeping death that such a decision might bring? And in the suns-sprinkled scene I saw a private chamber within some anonymous hotel or high-class tavern, the walls lush with rosy drapes, the samphron oil lamps shining, the wide white-sheeted bed, I saw the room clear as the trumpets pealed and the zorcas tossed their heads and the iron legions of Hamal advanced to meet that headlong, rapturous, pathetic charge of the Freedom Fighters.

And, in that room I saw a woman, standing, half-turned, the samphron-oil lamp's gleam limning her form, supple and sweetly curved, secretly shadowed. The rosy light glimmered on her flesh. I saw her head lift in that old familiar dear way and the heavy fall of her brown hair, rich with those outrageous auburn tints. Standing waiting in that room that was not our own, Delia smiled, and filled all my mind and heart, and I drank her in and slaked my desolation with her goodness. That welcoming smile, that special, secret, intimate smile between ourselves alone enfolded me and I could not feel the zorca between my knees or the helmet pressing my brow, and the dust and stink of armed and armored men shrank and faded away. I looked upon my Delia as I was wont to do in those precious moments of our deepest privacy. And a man moved toward her, taking her into his arms, leading her to the waiting bed. And I saw his face.

Palpitating with love for Delia and ready to cast all the mad desires for empire and power and dominion to the four winds and revel only in her, I saw his face, and saw he wore that tousle-haired, knowing, surely-smiling, handsome face of Quergey the Murgey. I sat the zorca like stone and the suns fell. Pain cleft me. I saw the bitter fighting as my Vallians reached those iron-hard shields and the thraxters struck, in and out, in and out, and scattered their red droplets upon the sundered bodies of my people.

The bodies clung together. The shield wall advanced. The pointed swords thrust in and out, in and out, and the tumbled bodies fell into the dust of the Drinnik. Naked flesh pierced by steel swords bled into the dirt. Together they forced themselves on and together they died.

No anguish touched me for the dead. Not then. The agony within me bit and burned as acid bites, corroding through everything, corrupting, defiling, destroying. My whole body flamed a single blaze of torment.

This obscene insanity was not real. The blood and death all about me was not wanted; but its evil was real. Better, perhaps, the ghostly hallucination than the dreadful reality. Surely better, certainly surely, that neither should be real! A spark I did not know I possessed flared and I saw and I understood. This was the work of Phu-si-Yantong. He had thrown his powers upon me, using his kharrna to infect my mind with this horror. And the horror almost destroyed me. A Wizard of Loh is a bitter and implacable enemy to any man; but ordinary mortals are bitter and implacable, they do not wield the sorcerous and supernatural powers of a Wizard of Loh.

Yantong had determined to crush my will to fight. He infected my mind with diseased pictures. That room, that woman panting with passion for Quergey the Murgey, they were not real, they were hallucinations of the worst kind. But they had almost unmanned me. The crucial time approached as the ram of a swifter slices toward its victim's side. The noise shattered skywards. The stink of raw blood infected the air. Delia—my Delia—would have no truck with a vanity-feeding, suave, seeming-sincere seducer like Quergey the Murgey, no matter how badly I had treated her in leaving her abandoned for so long, for she knew I would come back to her, always.

Phu-si-Yantong's vile trick had failed.

For my Delia knew me as I knew her, and our knowledge encompassed all of pain as well as love. For better or worse, for all the spaces between, in vaol-paol, we were the unity that transcends oneness, we were Dray and Delia.

Shouting like a crazy man—no, shouting as the crazy man I truly was in that anguished moment—I forced the zorca around and sent him haring across Voxyri Drinnik. Straight at the figure at the right flank of the Phalanx I galloped. For there was a Phalanx there, two full Kerchuris. Straight at Kyr Nath Nazabhan I rode, yelling, roaring, screaming at the top of my lungs.

"Jodhris!" I shrieked, whirling my sword above my head. "Jikaida! Jodhris!"

Nath responded instantly and the trumpets pealed. The even-numbered Jodhris from the right moved on; the odd numbers stood fast. The Phalanx formed a checkerboard. Square and trim in their alignments, the Relianches within the Jodhris halted and the glittering mass poised, in Jikaida, ready.

Volodu came crashing up behind me but to one side, for at my back rode Korero the Shield.

"Blow 'Archers to the Intervals', Volodu!"

He blew, the notes ringing out over the screaming racket erupting from the mobs of Freedom Fighters running across the Drinnik to follow their comrades as the bolts fell among them. I had to shut my ears to that frightful sound. The noise spumed on. The stinks drenched us with sweat. The brilliance of the suns splintering from bronze and iron dizzied the senses. The zorca moved under me, bounding on.

"Blow for the Cavalry!"

Now Nath was up with me, beaming, entranced, sitting his mount with the consummate ease of the true zorcaman, his armor a shining splendor.

"Well met, Nath. Your cavalry?"

"Coming up on the flank—there is a canal to cross—"

"You will blow the Charge?"

At once grave, he nodded, aware of the importance of the moment.

"As Varkwa the Open-Handed is my witness, majister, this is a moment that will be remembered in all Vallia." The barred visor half-shadowed his face. He drew a breath. "I will blow the Charge."

Nath called on Varkwa the Open-Handed, the spirit of generosity in Vallia, uniting all Vallians. I knew I had seriously hurt Delia by my enforced absences from her and that the oily minions of Quergey the Murgey would seek to take advantage of her unhappiness and defenselessness and sense of rejection. But I thought she knew me, knew me, plain Dray Prescot, well enough to comprehend that the necessary spaces between married couples were for us illuminated by the mutual light of love.

Life flows on like an ever-running stream and all things are mutable and must change, even to the rocks within that eternal flow no matter how hard their natures, and are sculpted into new and ever-changing never-repeating forms—so it is said. But there are things that never change. We poor mortals must learn to live in harmony with nature and adapt our ways as we progress through life bending with the current, always learning afresh—so it is said. But there are things we learn and know to be true and hold dearly.

The sorcerous trick flung at me by Yantong had failed. But it had jolted me in ways I would understand later. Delia and I should not bear the burden of secrets; between us they would be obscene, as obscene as the advantages taken by Quergey the Murgey in appearing understanding and sympathetic to a distressed wife and offering a fresh focus for affection, feeding vanity and the sense of crippled identity. His offers of help and a ready ear were self-centered. By their dark betrayals they destroyed where they purported to heal.

Phu-si-Yantong had known only too well how to get at me, to cause me the deepest of anguished suffering, to steal from Delia and me, to betray and rob us, to tear me into pieces.

One day, I knew, Yantong and I would meet. On that day I would not forget his use of the despicable Quergey the Murgey against Delia and me.

So, with the name of Varkwa to guide us in generosity, Nath gave his orders. Volodu cast me a reproachful look as the trumpets of the Phalanx sounded; but the moment belonged to Nath and the brumbytes he had brought all the live long way from Therminsax.

The Charge blew. The brumbytes thrust their fierce plumed helmets forward, slanting in the sunshine, the shields locked, crimson and yellow. The pikes came down. The Phalanx advanced. As a checkerboarded mass of bronze and crimson the Phalanx picked up speed, moved with a beauty and power of unison, crashed across the Drinnik of Voxyri—Charged!

Watchful of the flank Jodhris, I saw they would be too far extended as the Drinnik narrowed before the Bridge. Volodu blew "Eleventh and Twelfth Jodhris stand fast," followed moments later by: "Under command Relianches, right, follow on." That would annoy the Eleventh and Twelfth. But what a tribute to their training and discipline! They halted, waited and then, tossing pikes, moved to the right and so followed on in the intervals.

The scene sprawled on that wide expanse of common ground presented an awesome spectacle. The background hemmed in the action. The walls and towers of a great city lofted, badly burned and scarred and now being rebuilt on a grander and vaster scale. Against those lowering walls the extended lines of Hamalese soldiers, smart and brilliant with weapons gleaming, confident in their ability to destroy the ragged hosts who ran upon their deaths, fought with the sureness of confidence. The mobs ran on, shrieking, waving their weapons, racing down to slam into that iron line of shields and those cruel swords. And, beyond all, flowing swiftly on, fired with ardor and passion, the solid masses of the pikemen pressed on with heavy tread and their archers in the intervals showered the foe with darting shafts.

"What a sight!" screamed Barty.

"It is a battle," I shouted back.

But it was not like any battle we had fought before.

The arrows criss-crossed. The Hamalese wheeled up their varters in the intervals between regiments, and the iron bolts loosed. Larghos Cwopin, a good man with a knife and a ready laugh, abruptly vomited from his saddle, the varter bolt piercing him through and through, iron and red with blood. The zorcas galloped on. The arrows fell. Men screamed and fought and died.

Korero the Shield performed prodigies, his four arms and tail hand manipulating his shields with that rhythmic grace of perfect mental and bodily co-ordination, a marvel.

Many feats of heroism passed unremarked. The red mask of horror floated before our eyes. The iron of Hamal remained unbreached. I could feel the armor upon my body, the helmet pressing my head, the grip of the zorca between my knees, I could feel all and know I was alive and yet feel nothing, for death hovered near.

The noise roared on and now the brumbytes broke into a deep-voiced song, almost a paean, a heavy beating song that blended with the solid nerve-tingling blam-blam-berram of their drums. The flags flew. The name of the song does not matter—rather, as the armies clashed at last, the name means so much I cannot repeat it. It has been said that the best position for light troops to stand before the advancing phalanx is two hundred feet out. The guerillas of Vallia were much farther out than that; and so their fight, brief though it was, lasted far longer than I cared for. Then the Hakkodin were up with them and then—and then the savage bristle of pikes crunched into the shields of Hamal.

Even as the guerillas and the Hakkodins passed back in the intervals, the Hakkodins urging the guerillas on, and the archers faded to take up new positions in rear, drills gone through a thousand times, so the second line of Jodhris in the checkerboard smashed awesomely into the swods.

The Hamalian cavalry was caught as it debouched onto the Drinnik and was whiffed away as the Iron Riders had been whiffed away. The Phalanx moved forward, moved on and into and through the lines of Hamalian soldiers. They should not have done, of course. They should not have been able to do that magnificent thing. But the irregulars, the Freedom Fighters, the guerillas, had opened the way, had given the phalanx that little time it needed, and the phalanx swept on.

The thought hit me as I sent our little band hurtling on to enter the city as the Phalanx formed Relianch by Relianch to press on over Voxyri Bridge and through the Voxyri Gate, the marvelous and yet vexatious thought, that there would be no holding the brumbytes now. They would believe themselves perfectly capable of going up as a phalanx against sword and shield men and of winning every time. And I knew that was not on.

Through the Gate and into the city I bellowed for Volodu to sound the "Brumbytes, stand fast." And then: "Archers, Hakkodin—General Chase."

General Chase. Yes, I know. But my old sea-faring days had dictated that, and now, how it fitted!

The city seethed and bubbled with conflict and the noise surf-roared into the heavens. This moment was the moment we had looked forward to, when ragged half-armed people swept crazily upon the army of Hamal and, far more particularly upon the masichieri. Getting these fighters into the city had been the trick and it would never have been done without the timely assistance of the Phalanx. So I believe. I know miracles occur; I can only say that a miracle had occurred there, on Voxyri Drinnik when the brumbytes of the phalanx toppled the sword and shield swods of Hamal.

The conflict rattled and roared and thundered on, surging this way and that. Many a poor devil toppled into a canal. The fight gradually assumed an order, a shape, and centered on the palace. Somehow I was out there in the front, loosing those deadly rose-feathered shafts, whipping out the longsword when the counter-attacks came in, urging on the men, urging them all on, guerilla and Hakkodin alike, cherishing them, giving them by example effective ways of fighting this kind of messy affair.

Every now and then a man or a woman would give a sudden, startled look. I would bellow out in the old intemperate, good-humored way: "On! On for Vallia!"

By the time the kyro before the palace had been reached we all knew that the city was ours. The remnants of the invaders clustered in the palace which reared, lapped in scaffolding, ringed by lumber and stone and all the bush paraphernalia of rebuilding. Phu-si-Yantong had, indeed, sought to beautify his conquest.

The various leaders of the different bands and groups came together and, where necessary, I made the necessary pappattu. We stood, a group of ferocious men in the grip of the victory fever, and stared balefully upon the palace. The wink of weapons and the glitter of helmet and the flutter of plume and flag told us the place was still garrisoned.

"We will not attack," I said. "We do not have to lose any more good men. They will come out, all in due time."

There were arguments, of course. But I would not be swayed.

Many of my men were furious, and Nath Nazabhan and Dorgo the Clis and others of like ilk chief among them.

"How can we proclaim Jak the Drang Emperor of Vallia if we are not in the palace? That would not be right or decent!"

"Perhaps I do not wish to be emperor—"

"But you have the right!"

"The right of the sword."

"The right of leading us all, the right of holding men's hearts, the right of justice—Vallia cries out for an emperor to hold men together in amity— and you are the man!"

Even I, however reluctantly, could see the sense in that last sentiment. Vallia needed to be healed.

With a twinkling and altogether wonderful suddenness, flags of truce equivalent to white flags appeared along the battlements. Trumpets blew the parley. A deputation advanced from the palace across the kyro to where our group of commanders waited. Our people yelled, until our trumpets blew the still. In silence save for a little breeze that whispered with the flags, the men of Hamal, invaders in Vallia, advanced to surrender to the Vallians.

The scene struck brilliance and color, illuminated, stark, vibrating, it seemed to me, with the historical importance of the moment.

And here I must confess that although memory is not faulty, much of the ensuing event, many of the happenings that followed, echo back to me now vaguely, ill-defined, charged with an emotion and a wonder altogether marvelous—and embarrassing, too, to an old sea-salt like me, a simple fighting man.

The commanders formed a semicircle and I found myself standing a little front and center. In that group of loyal men were many to whom you have been introduced; the roll call is profoundly moving. Behind them clustered, seething and yet silent and intent, the victorious forces of Vallia who had retaken their capital city.

The Hamalese made a brave show in their armor and uniforms, but they carried no weapons, and they looked strained and exhausted.

At their head marched a man I knew.

He had been in attendance on Queen Thyllis when that woman had dragged me through the streets of Ruathytu in her triumphal procession when she made herself Empress of Hamal. I had been lapped in chains and dragged at the tail of a calsany. This man, Vad Inrien ham Thofoler, had been a dwa-Chuktar then, a man bucking for power and position. Clearly he had reached both, for now he was a general, a Kapt, in command of the Hamalese forces in this sector of Vallia. He marched up, his heavy face with the bitter lines about the nose and lips held in that rigid look of disdain for what was going on. He halted before me.

The silence held, thin, acute, with only the little breeze to ruffle flags and standards and scurry leaves over the stones of the kyro. He slapped up his arm in salute.

"Hai, Dray Prescot, Prince Majister of Vallia. We cry quarter. We would negotiate—"

The pressing crowd at the back of the group of my commanders sucked in a single gigantic gulp of breath. A few small cries broke out, then more and more, a sudden tempest of yells and shouts.

"Dray Prescot! Dray Prescot! This is Jak the Drang! Our own Jak the Drang, Emperor of Vallia!"

And then—it had to happen, sooner or later—amongst the yelling, Nath Nazabhan and the others brought order. They yelled in their turn, words that were picked up and repeated back through the hosts and along the avenues and boulevards, until the very sky over Vondium rang.

"This man whom you know as Jak the Drang is Dray Prescot, Emperor of Vallia."

The yells—the shouts—the astounded bellows of disbelief.

At last I signaled to Volodu the Lungs, whose mouth hung open foolishly, and he blew the still. Korero wore a tiny sly smile, and that confirmed me in my suspicions that he knew.

"I am Dray Prescot." I roared it out. "And I am Jak the Drang. And we Vallians have gained a great triumph this day of Opaz the Deliverer."

The incredulous uproar would have broken out again. I saw Korero move forward and he took out a certain scarlet bundle. I wondered with dizzied startlement just how much Delia had told him. He hauled out a pike and he tied on that old scarlet flag, to hoist it up. I heard the people yelling again: "Hai Jikai! Hai Jikai, Dray Prescot, Jak the Drang! Hai, Jikai!"

So I looked up, expecting to see Old Superb, that flag with the yellow cross on the scarlet field. And I saw—I saw a flag I had once seen in my mind's eye, seasons and seasons ago as we flew home from the Battle of the Dragon's Bones.

The yellow saltire of Vallia on the red ground flew there, but superimposed upon it gleamed my old yellow cross. The tresh formed a union of colors, a new flag, the new flag of Vallia.

A dark vision crossed my mind. We had Hamal to deal with, we had the vile religion of Lem the Silver Leem to transform into something of worth or suppress utterly, we had problems overseas and at home, and, looming monstrously over all, we had the shanks from over the curve of the world to resist or be finally beaten down. For only a small and precious space could we rest, rejoicing in what we had accomplished, for so much more remained to be done.

In a joyful procession amid a tumultuous host we moved into the palace of

Vondium. The regalia was brought out. Where the false emperor Seakon had gone no one knew or cared. The precious objects, the ceremonial adjuncts, the crown, the throne, Drak's Sword—of which I shall have more to say—were brought out so that all might see. They sat me on the throne and the crown settled on my head and I took the necessary things, hand by hand, and the priests chanted and the trumpets blew and the people yelled.

Through it all a hollowness possessed me, for the rest of Vallia we had not so far liberated remained.

But the moment was sacred and meaningful.

For the fact was indisputable. I was the Emperor of Vallia, chosen by the people, emperor by their will, and seated on the throne because they willed it.

How long I remained there was something I, and I alone, I fancied, would decide.

Men and women passed before me, swearing allegiance. In turn they were promised support, that Vallia would be freed, that life and liberty would be theirs, and happiness too, if they could contrive that profoundly difficult achievement.

I looked up. Of course. The Gdoinye and the white dove of the Savanti floated up there against the blue. They had not forgotten me. I would have more trouble from them in the future.

As I looked a voller fleeted in over the kyro and swooped for the palace. I saw her flags. Valkan flags, and the flags of Delphond and the Blue Mountains, Old Superb—all flew from her masts. But, over all, that new flag of Vallia floated, free, defiant, yellow and scarlet in the blaze of the suns, heralding a new epoch in the history of Kregen.

Surfeited on emotions both transcendental and foreboding and, just for this wonderful moment, blurring into a haze of thankfulness, I walked forward to greet Delia.

The whole of Vondium rang with the exultations.

"Hai Jikai, Delia, Empress of Vallia. Hai Jikai, Dray Prescot, Emperor of Vallia!"

By Zair, I said to myself as Delia and I walked toward each other and the air vibrated with the noise and excitement. I must remember I am a Krozair of Zy and, too, I must not forget the Kroveres of Iztar. The Corruption of Empire must never foul this moment. The Sovereign State must serve every single person, each to each. If ever the corruption of power touched me, if ever megalomania assaulted my sanity, I would remember the good men who had died looking forward to this moment.

The truth was I had not wanted to be Emperor of Vallia; but if I had been chosen for that onerous task by the conjoined will of the people, then—for a space until I talked my son Drak into taking over—I'd be as competent and just and professional an emperor as I knew how, by Zim-Zair!

The uplifted swords glittered blindingly in the streaming mingled lights of Antares, the Suns of Scorpio. "Jikai! Hai Jikai!" roared the multitudes.

It was a moment to treasure, a moment to remember.

"So you are the Emperor of Vallia in your own right, Dray," said Delia. She smiled and the suns glimmered pale in comparison. "Now what will you do?"

"Oh," I said. "Oh, I haven't even started yet."

A Glossary to the Vallian Cycle

References to the four books of the cycle are given as:

SES: Secret Scorpio
SVS: Savage Scorpio
CPS: Captive Scorpio
GOS: Golden Scorpio

NB: Previous glossaries covering entries not included here will be found in *Prince of Scorpio*; *Arena of Antares*; *Armada of Antares*; and *Krozair of Kregen*.

A

Ahrinye: Star Lord of acrid tongue in apparent opposition to other Everoinye.
Aleygyn: Title of chief of stikitches.
"Anete ham Terhenning": A tragic song of Hamal.
Ararsnet, Roybin ti Autonne: Secret agent working for Prescot. (SES)
Arial, Fair of: A fair held for the people of the Czarin Sea on the island of Drayzm after the pirates cleared away.
Arkadon: Pleasant market town in Delphond.
Arlton: Island to the north of Veliadrin. Name means pestle.
atra: Amulet, lucky charm.
audo: Military term for section of eight to ten men.
Autonne: Town on the west coast of Veliadrin.
Avandil, Rafik: A numim assigned by Phu-si-Yantong to observe Prescot. Eventually unmasked as Makfaril.

B

Ba-Domek: Island on which is situated the city of Aphrasöe.
Bakan: High kovnate of Vallia situated to the south of the Mountains of the North.
The Ball and Chain: An unsavory hostelry a stone's throw from the Gate of Skulls in Drak's City in Vondium.
Battle of Sabbator: Final battle in which the Phalanx of the North East of Vallia overthrew the Iron Riders.

Battle of Therminsax: The fight in which the army of Therminsax with the Phalanx as the core gained its first success against the Iron Riders.

Battle of Voxyri: Climactic battle in which the Freedom Fighters and the Phalanx of Vallia defeated the army of Hamal and its mercenary allies across the Drinnik and over the Bridge and through the Gate of Voxyri.

"Bear Up Your Arms": A rollicking song of which this is the euphemistic title.

Beng Dikkane: Patron saint of all the ale drinkers of Paz.

Beng Drangil: Patron saint of Ovvend.

benhoff: Shaggy, powerful, six-legged riding animal of North Segesthes, with lean hind-sixths and a roll of fat across the chest. Used by the radvakkas.

Bet-Aqsa: Island west of Havilfar in the Ocean of Doubt.

"Black Is the River and Black Was Her Hair": A tragical ditty of Hamal which Prescot described as farcical.

"Black Wings over Sabbator": A great song made in remembrance of The Battle of Sabbator.

Blade of Kurin, by the: A swordsman's oath.

Blarnoi, San: Either a real person or a consortium of misty figures of the dim past to whom many aphorisms and sayings current on Kregen are attributed.

blatter: Slang word for quick and successful assault and battery, a headlong attack.

Brassud: Brace up.

Bratch!: Move! Jump! Not as vicious as the infamous Grak! but still a powerful word of command implying move it or you know what will happen.

Bratchlin: The File Closer at the rear of each file of the phalanx.

Bregal: A small town of Ystilbur of the Dawn Lands of Havilfar.

brumby: A powerful eight-legged and armored battering ram of whirlwind destruction armed with a long straight horn in the center of his forehead, the brumby is thought to be either extinct or legendary.

brumbyte: Name for the pikeman in the files of the phalanx.

Bryvondrin: Imperial province of Vallia north of the capital.

C

Calimbrev: Island Stromnate southwest of Veliadrin.

Cansinsax: Town of Aduimbrev where the Iron Riders defeated an army of Hamalese. (GOS)

Charboi, Dr: In the pay of Ashti Melekhi poisoned the Emperor of Vallia. (SVS)

chyyan: A large, heavy-winged bird, all rusty black save for scarlet eyes and claws and beak, with four wings like its distant cousin the zhyan.

Cleitar the Smith: Blacksmith who lost his family in the radvakka and Hamalian troubles and from then on carried Prescot's banner of Vallia.

Czarin Sea: Studded with islands off east coast of Vallia.

D

"The Daisies of Delphond": A charming song celebrating the ladies as well as the daisies of the Garden of Vallia.

Danmork: Leader of the fourth and tenth files in the Relianch of the phalanx.

Deb-sa Chiu: Wizard of Loh at court of the Emperor of Vallia. (CPS)

Delia: Mother Goddess generally associated with Delphond.

Deliasmot: Town of Delphond where a canal trunk system terminates.

deren: Palace.

Djondalar of the Twisted Staff: Spirit or deity of Kregen.

Dorgo the Clis: Tall, dark-complexioned man with facial scar who followed Prescot in fight against radvakkas. (GOS)

Drakanium: Clean, neat, sparkling city of Delphond.

Drak's City: The Old City of Vondium.

Drak's Sword: Part of the regalia of the Emperor of Vallia.

Drayzm: Small island of the Czarin Sea once called Nikzm and named for Dray Prescot.

drikinger: Bandit.

E

Eganbrev: Province to the west of Aduimbrev up to Great River.

Emerade, River: Runs from the Kwan Hills and joins the Great River where stands Thengelsax.

Enevon Ob-Eye: Prescot's chief stylor during the radvakka and Hamalian troubles. (GOS)

"Eregoin's Promise": A drinking song of Paz.

Ernelltar the Bedevilled: Runs of bad luck are attributed to this spirit or deity in North Segesthes.

F

Falanriel: Chief City of Falinur.

"The Fall of the Suns": A menacing song, Prescot dubs this lay, for its cadences and images invite mournfulness. It tells of the Last Days when the twin suns fall from the sky and drench the world of Kregen in fire and blood, in water and death.

Falnagur: The castle fortress dominating the city of Falanriel.

Father Tolki: The All Mighty, chief deity of the religion of Vallia which ousted that of the Mother Goddess and was in turn superseded by the purer religion of Opaz.

Faxul: Leader of a file in the phalanx.

Fegter: Member of the Fegter Party of Vallia against the Emperor and anybody else who stood in the way.

Fist-tail or Hand-tail: Slang term for Pachak or Kildoi.

flamil: A sand-scarf of Ba-Domek.

Fletcher's Tower: Once called the Jade Tower of the fortress of the Falnagur renamed by Seg Segutorio. (SES)

Florania: Deity of a minor religion of Vallia patronized by millers and bakers. The Chief Priest of Therminsax, out of good intentions, attempted treachery against Prescot. (GOS)

G

Gate of Skulls: A gate giving ingress to Drak's City in Vondium.

Gelkwa: A trylonate of Vallia between the Kwan Hills and the Great River. Part of Hawkwa country.

Gengulas: Legendary monsters with the power of Medusae.

Gods sharpen both edges of a blade, the: A saying of Kregen which appears to imply that one evil may destroy another and in turn be destroyed.

Golden Feathers Aegis, by the: A Flutsman's oath.

"Golden Fur": A song shared by numims and Fristles.

Great Chyyan: The black four-winged bird symbol of the evil and synthetic religion fostered by Phu-si-Yantong and destroyed in Vallia by Prescot and the SoR and Naghan Vanki. Adherents called Chyyanists. (SES)

Guiskwain, San: The Witherer, na Stackwamor. A famed necromancer of the North East of Vallia who lived more than two and a half thousand seasons ago. His corpse was revived to inspire the Hawkwa revolt. (CPS)

H

Hakkodin: The axe and halberd men flanking the files of the Phalanx.

Hawkwa: Term for the people of North East Vallia.

Himet the Mak: Rafik Avandil, lion-man, tool of Phu-si-Yantong in preaching the artificial religion of Chyyanism. (SES)

hirvel: A stubby, four-legged riding animal, not unlike a nightmare version of a llama with tall round neck, cup-shaped ears and shaggy body and twitching snout with a performance similar to a good quality waler.

Hjemur-Gebir: a minor religion fallen into desuetude with a grotesque toad-thing as the idol of worship.

Hockwafernes: Temple and township of Gelkwa where San Guiskwain was resurrected. (CPS)

Hyr Notor: Alias used by Phu-si-Yantong in dealing with the Empress Thyllis of Hamal.

Hyrvond: Imperial province immediately to the north of Vondium.

I

Ib Reiver: Soul Stealer—used in oaths.

Imlien, Trylon Ered of Thengelsax: A racter with whom Prescot had a smart run in over his daughter. (SES)

J

Jakhan, Jak: Name used by Prescot during adventures in Hawkwa country. (CPS)

Jak the Drang: Name used by Prescot to rouse Vallians against the Iron Riders and Hamalese. (GOS)

Jhalak, by: A stikitche oath.

Jhansi, Layco, Kov of Vennar: The Emperor of Vallia's Chief Pallan. When his plots against the emperor were frustrated by Prescot and friends, took to the field in the time of the Troubles in Vallia when Hamal and the radvakkas invaded.

jid: Bane.

Jikai Vuvushis: Battle Maidens.

Jikalla: A Kregish game.

Jodhri: A formation of the phalanx containing six Relianches totaling 864 brumbytes and 144 Hakkodin.

Jodhrivax: Commander of Jodhri.

Junka: A deity of the North East of Vallia.

Justicar: The imperial governor of a province.

K

Kadar the Hammer: Alias used by Prescot in Vallia. (SES)

Kamist Quay: Wharves along the Great River in Vondium.

Kapt: General.

kax: Corselet, breast and back, cuirass.

Kerchuri: Formation of the phalanx containing six Jodhris of 5184 brumbytes and 864 Hakkodin.

Kerchurivax: Commander of Kerchuri.

kharrna: Manifestation of power exercised at distance by a Wizard of Loh.

Khibil: Member of race of diffs with fox faces, alert, strong, limber, excellent mercenaries used to outdoor life.

khiganer: Heavy brown tunic, double-breasted, the wide flap caught up over the left side with a row of bronze buttons from belt to shoulder and from point of shoulder to collar which is stiff, hard and high.

Kildoi: Member of race of diffs of Balintol with four arms and handed tail, very strong and courageous with apim-like features and a variety of hair-colorings.

"King Harulf's Red Zorca": Drinking song of Paz.

"King Naghan, His Fall and Rise": Song of Kregen with undercurrents of merriment and discipline and admonishment.

kitchew: Target for assassination on contract by stikitches.

klattar: Parrying stick.

Korero the Shield: A Kildoi rescued by Prescot from torture at the hands of the radvakkas and a good comrade who carries a pair of great shields in combat at Prescot's back.

krahnik: Small form of draught animal of good pulling power.

Kroveres of Iztar: Members of Order of Brotherhood formed by Prescot on model of Krzy to ameliorate conditions in all Paz.

KRVI: Abbreviation for Kroveres of Iztar.

kutcherer: Knife somewhat like a butcher knife with a sharp pronged spike protruding from the heavy back.

Kwan Hills: Range of mountains in Hawkwa Country famed for their plenitude of game, good hunting country.

Kyro of Jaidur Omnipotent: Brilliant plaza or square in Vondium.

Kyro of Lost Souls: Long plaza just within the Gate of Skulls of Drak's City in Vondium.

Kyro of Spendthrifts: One of the squares of Vondium famed for the expensive shops and stalls along the arcades.

L

Laik-Faxul: Quarter-file leader in Relianch.

laybrites: Precious gem of deep yellow color.

Laygon the Strigicaw: Stikitche who to his misfortune took a contract from Ashti Melekhi to assassinate Dray Prescot. (CPS)

letha: Tough, springy, elastic white wood.

Letha Brook: Runs through Therminsax.

Lio am Donarb: A minor religion of Vallia.

Liverspot Bark: Ingredient of the poison solkien concentrate.

Llanitch!: Halt!

Lornrod Caucus: Vallian political faction of whom it is said their only wish is to destroy everything and pull down what has been painfully built over the centuries.

Lushfymi, Queen of Lome: Popularly known as Queen Lush. A dark-haired violet-eyed woman of great poise and beauty sent by Phu-si-Yantong to entrap the Emperor of Vallia. Her allegiance changed and she worked with Prescot to save the emperor.

"Maidens of Vallia, The": A lyrical ballad celebrating the virtuous women of Vallia.

Makfaril: Beloved of the Black, the Chief Priest of the Great Chyyan, the evil and artificial creed of Chyyanism developed by Phu-si-Yantong to destroy Vallia. Rafik Avandil, numim. (SES)

masichieri: Low-class mercenaries, not bandits but almost that, notorious for their rapacity and greed.

Maybers: A race of trading and sea-faring diffs from Donengil.

Mazilla: The high ornate collar much bejeweled and decorated worn by the nobility of Vallia, the simpler dignified high collar of the koters of Vallia. The nikmazilla is the smaller ornate collar worn with evening clothes.

mazingle: Swod's term for discipline.

Melekhi, Ashti, Vadnicha of Venga: A thin, brittle and bright woman, hard-edged like a diamond, mannish, brilliant, with a flame about her that consumed all who were unfortunate enough not to know how to handle her. Came to an untimely end in her machinations with Layco Jhansi. (SVS)

Mellor'An: Local god of North East Vallia concerned with agriculture, husbandry and fertility.

Memph: A tree which yields a part of the deadly poison solkien.

MichelDen: Capital city of the kovnate of Forli in southeast Vallia.

Mustard Gate: A strong battlemented Tower-gate in an angle of the northwest walls of Vondium.

Naghan ti Lodkwara: Hawkwa member of the choice band who followed Prescot in the time of Troubles in Vallia. (GOS)

Nalgre, Nazab na Therminsax: The emperor's Justicar governing Thermin who loyally obeyed Prescot acting as Jak the Drang. (GOS)

Nath the Gnat: Alias adopted by Prescot in the struggle against the Chyyanists. (SES)

Nath the Iarvin: A hard man, ruffler, Bladesman, bought body and soul by Ashti Melekhi, who came to an unexpected end on a Krozair longsword. (SVS)

Nav-Sorfall: Vallian province lush and rich with ponsho pastures to the east of Vomansoir. Naghan Vanki was made vad.

Nazab: Governor of imperial province ranking with kov.

Nazabhan, Nath, na Therminsax: Son of Nazab Nalgre, rose to command phalanx created by Prescot. (GOS)

Nik-Faxul: Half-file leader in Relianch.

Nikwald: Fortress town in the kovnate of Sakwara of Vallia.

Numi-Hyrjiv the Golden Splendor: Great spirit or deity of numims and fristles.

O

Olordin's Well: Insignificant hamlet where Prescot rendezvoused with Barty Vessler in south central Vallia. (GOS)

Opaz Enthroned: Day of festival dedicated to Opaz. The day on which the army of Therminsax sallied against the radvakkas. (GOS)

Opaz the Deliverer: Day of festival dedicated to Opaz on which Vondium rose against the Hamalese and the Freedom Fighters and the Phalanx struck in the Battle of Voxyri. (GOS)

Order of Little Mothers: One of the sororities of Vallia dedicated to good works.

P

"Pachak with the Four Arms, The": A song highly scurrilous of a fine people with an oblique reference to the Kildoi.

pakai: String of silver or gold rings taken from defeated paktuns by paktun victories and worn as badges of prowess.

Paltork: Commander of half Relianch.

Panadian the Ibreiver, the Vicissitudes of: Cycle of plays by the long-dead playwright Nalgre ti Liancesmot from which couplets, aphorisms and character analyses are often quoted.

Peral Gate: Imposing secondary gateway to the imperial deren of Vondium.

Phalanx: Created in Vallia by Prescot to oppose the Iron Riders. A phalanx consists of two Kerchuris totaling 10368 pikes and 1738 Hakkodin. In the field any close-order body of brumbytes called the Phalanx.

Poperlin the Wise: Mythical sage apostrophized by the workers of Vallia.

Prison of the Angels: A gaunt granite prison of Vondium.

Pyvorr, Tarek Dredd: The first martyr of the Kroveres of Iztar. (SVS)

R

radvakkas: The Iron Riders of North Segesthes.

Rakkle-jik-lora: A violent headlong training game played by the Clansmen of the Great Plains of Segesthes.

Relianch: Formation of the phalanx consisting of 144 brumbytes and 24 Hakkodin.

Relianchun: Commander of a Relianch.

Renberg, Marta, Kovneva of Aduimbrev: High-tempered, ambitious lady who assisted schemes of Phu-si-Yantong. (GOS)

Rojashin the Kaktu: A Rapa paktun whose greed and overweening idea of his own importance drove him on to destruction and whose gear and pakai were used by Prescot in Hawkwa country. (CPS)

ronil: Precious jewel of red color.

Rosala and the Eye of Imladrion: An ancient legend of Kregen in its intentions paralleling the story of Pandora.

rosha: Orange-like fruit.

Ros the Claw: Name given to Princess Dayra of Vallia by virtue of the sharp steel gloved set of talons worn on her left hand with which she is very quick and cruel.

Rumil the Point: Tavern swaggerer who insulted Prescot and dealt with by Rafik Avandil, lion-man, in The Savage Woflo. (SES)

S

Sabbator, River: In North East Vallia separates the trylonate of Zaphoret to the north from Urn Stackwamor, running into the sea opposite the island of Vellin.

Sakwara: High Kovnate of Vallia north of Aduimbrev.

Samphron Cut: A canal of Vondium.

Sapphire Reception Room: One of the ornate but less formal chambers of the deren of Vondium.

The Savage Woflo: Famous tavern of Vondium much patronized by the guardsmen and paktuns of the capital.

sax: Fort.

The Sea Barynth Hooked: Pot-house on the Kamist Quay of Vondium catering to skippers of Vallian ships.

Shadow: Magnificent black zorca stallion freed from cruel Kataki owners and ridden by Prescot in Ba-Domek. (SVS)

Shadow Forests of Calimbrev: Beautiful and rich forests in the west of the island coveted by the Strom of Vilandeul.

Shalash the Shining: Fish deity or spirit called on by fisherfolk of Vallia.

shandishalah: Merchandise of booths in the fish souks.

Shastum!: Silence!

Shkanes: Yet another appellation for the Shanks, the Shants, the Shtarkins, Leem-Lovers, reivers from over the curve of the world who ravage the sea coasts of Paz.

Shudor Maklechuan: A Chulik paktun known as Shudor the Mak who was hired by Prescot with his band to fight for Therminsax. (GOS)

signomant: An artifact created by a Wizard of Loh, often in the form of a heavy brass disc covered with hieroglyphs, by which he is able to observe events at a distance without forcing a projection of himself to the required place.

Silversmiths Wharf: Canal side area where silver is traded in Vondium.

Sisters of Patience: A sorority of Vallia.

Sisters of Samphron: A semi-secret sorority of Vallia.

solkien concentrate: A deadly poisonous compound that secretly wastes the flesh, dilutes the blood and destroys subtly.

SoR: Abbreviation for the Sisters of the Rose.

Souk of Chem: Bazaar of the ivory traders in Vondium.

The Speckled Gyp: A tavern of Vondium smashed up by Dayra and her cronies.

Stackwamors, The: Provinces of North East Vallia, the heartlands of Hawkwa Country, north, south, east and west Stackwamor.

stiver: Silver coin of Vallia.

"The Sylvie on the Slippery Slope": A risqué song of Kregen.

T

tapo: Word of abuse with unpleasant connotations.

tarek: A rank of the minor nobility within the gifting of a kov.

Targon the Tapster: A Therminsaxer who became one of the choice band of followers of Prescot in the Time of Troubles. (GOS)

Tarkwa-fash: A town of the North East near the Kwan Hills.

tazll: Applied to an unemployed mercenary.

Temple of Delia: An ancient ruined temple in Delphond dedicated to the Mother Goddess Delia where Prescot had a run-in with the masichieri of the Black Feathers. (SES)

Terfaxul: Leader of a file in the Relianch one rank higher than a Faxul.

Thengelsax: Town situated on Great River at point where River Emerade joins. One of the old line of fortresses against the North East of Vallia.

Therduim Cut: Canal connecting Therminsax and Thengelsax.

Thermin: Imperial province of Central Vallia.

Thiurdsmot: A sizable town of Aduimbrev.

Thofoler, Vad Inrien ham: A Hamalese Kapt who surrendered Vondium to Prescot and the Freedom Forces of Vallia. (GOS)

tikshim: Form of address used by superior to inferiors, equating with "My Man." The superiors consider it polite, the inferiors are infuriated by its use.

Tolindrin: Place in Balintol with diplomatic connections with Vallia.

Tower of Incense: Contains the sorcerous chamber inhabited by the current Wizard of Loh in the deren of Vondium.

Trechinolc: A cactus, constituent of the poison solkien.

Trerhagen, Nath: The Aleygyn, Hyr Stikitche, Pallan of the Stikitche Khand of Vondium.

tresh: Flag or banner.

tsleetha-tsleethi: Softly-softly.

Tunnel of Delight: Leads out to the Kyro of Jaidur Omnipotent in Vondium.

Twitchnose: A chestnut zorca ridden by Prescot in Vondium.

U

Udo, Trylon of Gelkwa: Led rebellion of North East Vallia. (CPS)

ukra: Flutsman's weapon, a polearm from seven to fifteen feet in length with narrow blade and curved axe for aerial work.

Ulbereth the Dark Reiver: Poem fashioned from the legends of olden time on Kregen. The episode of the Black Feathers tells of Ulbereth's disguise to enable him to ravish a fair young virgin with golden hair.

unggar: Beast of burden.

Urn Stackwamor: Vadvarate of Hawkwa country in N.E. Vallia.

urvivel: Saddle animal.

Uthnior Chavonthjid: A leem-hunter and guide with a fine reputation who guided Prescot and Barty Vessler in the Kwan Hills. (CPS)

Uzhiro, San: Necromancer of the Hawkwas who roused corpses from sleep to aid North East Vallian rebellion. (CPS)

V

Valhotra: Vadvarate province of Vallia immediately to the east of the imperial Vend provinces and Vondium.

Vanti: Guardian for the Savanti of the Sacred Pool of Baptism on the River Zelph of far Aphrasöe.

Varkwa the Open-Handed: Spirit of generosity called upon in Vallia.

Vel'alar: One of the Hills of Vondium. The villa of the Stromnate of Valka is situated on this hill.

Veliadrin: Large island high kovnate to the east of Vallia whose name was changed from Can-thirda in remembrance.

Velyan techniques: Mystic martial disciplines of the Martial Monks of Djanduin.

Vend: Imperial province to the west of Vondium.

vener: Collective name for the vens and venas of the Canals.

Vennar: Kovnate province of Vallia between the Black Mountains and Falinur.

ver: Title of pledge of loyalty of Kroveres of Iztar similar to the pur of the Krozairs.

Vessler, Barty, Strom of Calimbrev: Amiable, chivalrous, brave young man befriended by Prescot. Desperately in love with the Princess Dayra. (CPS GOS)

Vetal: Island Stromnate to the east of the Czarin Sea.

Vikatu: The Old Sweat, The Dodger, the archetypal old soldier of Paz on Kregen, paragon of the military vices, legendary figure of myth and romance loved and sworn on by the swods.

Vinnur's Garden: Rich area in loop of Great River between Falinur and Vindelka whose ownership is contested by both.

volmen: Volim, crewmen of fliers.

Volodu the Lungs: Prescot's trumpeter in the choice band who followed him in the Time of Troubles in Vallia. (GOS)

Vondium Khanders: Political party of Vallia who looked to the business community for combined strength.

voswod: Aerial soldier of the vollers.

Voxyri: Complex of Drinnik, Gate and Bridge over two canals providing the easiest entrance to Vondium.

vydra tea: An excellent brew of the famed Kregen tea.

W

wallpitix: Furry, bright-eyed household scavengers living in nests in hidden places of villas and houses.

Walls of Larghos Risslaca: Inner defensive wall of the imperial deren Vondium.

Wellon, Nankwi, High Kov of Sakwara: A prickly kov who took the lead in Hawkwa after the disappearance of Trylon Udo and who was confirmed in his position by Prescot. (GOS)

"When the Fluttrell Flirts His Wing": A song of Hamal detailing the misadventures of an inexperienced fluttrell flyer.

Whiptail: Slang term for a Kataki.

Y

Yasi, Ranjal, Stromich of Morcray: Twin brother of Rosil Yasi, Strom of Morcray, in the pay of Phu-si-Yantong and bitter foe to Prescot.

yasticum: An expensive and rare delicacy spread on the superb Kregan bread.

Yellow-tuskers: Slang term for Chulik.

Ystilbur: An ancient nation of the Dawn Lands of Havilfar.

Z

Zankov: Use-name of Hawkwa determined to overthrow empire, origins secret but subject to many rumors; slender, brittle; the man who slew the Emperor of Vallia. The Princess Dayra's name is coupled with his in unsavory ways. Zankov, the Tenth Duke, is almost a meaningless name.

Zarado: A Krozair of Zy who through some peccadillo wandered from the inner sea and hired out as a Paktun to assist Prescot in the defense of Therminsax. (GOS)

zim-korf: Bird of Valka with rose-red feathers whose quality is equal or superior to the blue fletchings of the king korf of Erthyrdrin.

Zunder: Krzy with the same history as Zarado with whom he is always in arguments.

Kenneth Bulmer

Alan Burt Akers is a pen name of the prolific British author Kenneth Bulmer, who died in December 2005 aged eighty-four.

Bulmer wrote over 160 novels and countless short stories, predominantly science fiction, both under his real name and numerous pseudonyms, including Alan Burt Akers, Frank Brandon, Rupert Clinton, Ernest Corley, Peter Green, Adam Hardy, Philip Kent, Bruno Krauss, Karl Maras, Manning Norvil, Chesman Scot, Nelson Sherwood, Richard Silver, H. Philip Stratford, and Tully Zetford. Kenneth Johns was a collective pseudonym used for a collaboration with author John Newman. Some of Bulmer's works were published along with the works of other authors under "house names" (collective pseudonyms) such as Ken Blake (for a series of tie-ins with the 1970s television programme The Professionals), Arthur Frazier, Neil Langholm, Charles R. Pike, and Andrew Quiller.

Bulmer was also active in science fiction fandom, and in the 1970s he edited nine issues of the New Writings in Science Fiction anthology series in succession to John Carnell, who originated the series.

www.ingramcontent.com/pod-product-compliance
Lightning Source LLC
Chambersburg PA
CBHW031924110726

47902CB00001B/26